ALSO BY JAMES D. MCCALLISTER

NOVELS
King's Highway

Fellow Traveler

Let the Glory Pass Away

Dogs of Parsons Hollow

Dixiana

Down in Dixiana

Reconstruction of the Fables (2020)

Mansion of High Ghosts (2021)

Wando (2023)

STORIES
The Year They Canceled Christmas

Fables of the Reconstruction (2020)

The Night I Prayed to Elvis (2021)

Dixiana
DARLING

Dixiana Darling

OMNIBUS EDITION

PART 1:
THIS INSUBSTANTIAL PAGEANT

PART 2:
HONKYTONK MAN

PART 3:
RETURN ECHO

JAMES D. McCALLISTER

MHP
Mind Harvest Press
COLUMBIA, SC

Mind Harvest Press
COLUMBIA, SC

Mind Harvest Press
PO Box 50552
Columbia SC 29250-0552
www.mindharvestpress.com
www.jamesdmccallister.com

CONTENTS

DIXIANA DARLING PART ONE: THIS INSUBSTANTIAL PAGEANT

DIXIANA DARLING PART TWO: HONKYTONK MAN

DIXIANA DARLING PART THREE: RETURN ECHO

PART ONE

This Insubstantial Pageant

Render thyself, O Goddess, unto pity!
    Open, O lady, the portals of thine eyes,
    And look on me if thou wouldst give me Death!

— GIORDANO BRUNO, EROICI FURORI

Man demonstrates his intellectual superiority over other animals by being the only one that can think himself into a state of profound misery.

— BURKS HAMNER

ANNA DIXON AND DURHAM DOVER

The day my Dover returned to me, a special day. One of the finest, aye.

But no more'n the day I met him first, when he come a-calling from over in Cokesbury, a lengthy traverse to visit anyone, much less my plain old self. One certainly held more call in those days to come to us here in Kennesaw than in the now, in which I await for him to return to a dusty bend in the road and a tumbling of stones in the wide river with the name of Breeley's Crossing.

What remains waiting to which a man might return with vigor and enthusiasm for the near term? The town stands, yea; but what a strapping lad will want to do with himself amidst a desolate and ruined economy, I know not. The war has left us desolate. Destitute. So little left in the Kennesaw District, or anywhere here in Carolina.

And yet... all could have felt as lost as it appeared but didn't, not since I hold in my possession a recent missive, a letter from my sweetheart Durham! In this bitter and terrible time 'tis to this parchment I cling, these few months trapped here, hungry and wondering. Wondering about Durham. Praying how we will go on, all of us. Others will decide. Yankees in blue, our occupiers; carpetbaggers, yea, as we call the men who come to profit. An old man said to me the other day, all war is but profit, except to the losers.

Except to the dead.

Speaking of those profiteers, the townsfolk who remain are forced back to the days of taking a ferry across the Sugeree, at a landing downriver from the pilings of the ruined bridge, and with vile speculators controlling the costs of all necessities like transit. But transit to where, anyway? The bridge, burned, saved the town itself from ultimate ruin, as had occurred in Columbia. The bridge led nowhere except across to Beauchamp District anyway, but with the boys like Durham all gone from this side of the river as well as that, what a gamine lass to do with her bereaved and unrequited self over yonder?

Pine further than she already does?

Eh?

Not I, said she. Not with Durham a-coming back to me. Sooner, or later. Keeping the promise of his letters. Foresworn to do so, says he. In the writing of his own hand. His words and my wishes, this confluence, surely, will make it true.

Would that we had ourselves even a basic bridge rebuilt on top of the old piling, I would wait here no longer—I would strike out to find him, as Agatha of Aberdeen once sailed the mighty blue sea to find her dear captain, or so the story of her failure and self-immolation on our town green is said to go. But no bridge like'n we'd had before the war would be coming soon, the fine covered thoroughfare that'd been set aflame to slow down the blue-boys and keep them from ransacking us like they burned Columbia. The stony river, the falls, a difficult crossing for an army of men, especially as weary as those marauders had been from their terrible march and deathly toil. Too weary to care about Breeley's Crossing. Especially without a bridge.

Oh, how we watched the sky that cold, awful night in February! How the orange sunset stayed aglow all the night through, as though the sun had only just dipped below the trees and remained there, hiding and teasing. If only the glow had been the giver of warmth and life, the assurance of the dawn, rather than the fires set by the hands of the drunken and lascivious and vengeance-minded of General Sherman's men; General Sherman, whom we have heard tell took up arms against his own troops to stop them from destroying the city to cinders. This tale, though, rather in-credible. A monster like him, likely as not cackling with evil glee at the carnage, would not have been well-nigh interested in stopping the hellish fires, no, only in setting more by his own gnarled talons. And then watching as fair and fine Columbia burned to the ground, its ashes sifted and borne upon the cold February winds that only served to stoke the fires further.

With this terrible disaster in mind, one that we ourselves and by only the barest of chances escaped, I have held relief close to my heart by only one fact, and that has been the last letter my Durham sent, when he said the war was waning, my sweet Anna Dixon: The war is waning, yea, and I am weary, but nothing can keep me from returning to your arms.

He had said this, too, before going off to fight; had written it to me in the letters I received, both of which were like miracles in my hands, carried and read anew upon the dawning of each new day until the paper thin as a threadbare gown lying like desiccated crepe against my skin, like all our clothes soon to be. The letters, cradled and clutched until I fear them to fall to pieces.

As I would surely fall, were he not to return.

But at last he comes, my Durham. I heard him first by his voice, and the nickname *he had given his betrothed—Dixie-Anna—echoing and calling to me from across the shimmering water of the river beside which we have made our lives.*

Dixie-Anna. I've come home to you at last.

Would our lives go on here? None of it matters now—none but the moment at hand, with my great love standing by my side. Our people may have lost a war, but I have won my battle, one against time and chance and death itself. My Durham returns, hale and whole. His smiling face, crossing by the ferry. Come back to me, as I had wished with fervency and faith. And here he is, now. Here he is, a manifestation bespeaking the truth that dreams, even in the face of abject horror and strife, can still come true.

[EXCERPTED FROM *THE DIARY OF ANNA DIXON*, A HISTORICAL ROMANCE published in 2015 by Southern novelist and Edgewater County native Cortland Beauchamp. A multiple-award-nominee from a number of prestigious literary groups, the book's success resulted in the sale of film rights to Twin-D Productions, a Los Angeles company belonging to Madeline and Evangeline Durango. In a blog post, Beauchamp related how a 2012 visit to his hometown, and an evening spent at a honkytonk called The Dixiana, helped inspire the novel that resurrected his career.]

ROY

What a cluster-fudge, your latest foray into the mountains.

Following the debacle of Howdy Shull on the green, as well as a less than satisfying pre-holiday attempt at reconciliation with your wife, and in a state of what Button called *saudade*, a Portuguese word meaning a wistful longing for a past that likely could never again be, you drove back up the interstate to try to recapture the fine time you had in North Carolina at the Ponderview estate known as Havenhurst. Not with Button or Heather this time, but on your own.

Button... your pal who, after the horrific circumstances of the quite-literal firing squad before her and your terrified eyes that day two months ago, has withdrawn into herself. Has acted downright squirrelly, more than usual for your little crust-muffin, dreadlocked stoner weirdo.

Oh, how you bent Sheriff Oakley's ear, Mayor Hampton, and the news media who interviewed you. How this has now made you seem like a radical hippie to all of them, and you warily aware of the extreme nature of the heavily armed, trigger-happy police state in your blessed and great and powerful U-nited States of America. Lived it firsthand, twice in one freaking week. You thought you were going nucking futs. A message: give the cops a wide berth, even the ones you have bought off.

ON THIS TRIP YOU CHOSE A LUXURY CABIN, AN AIRB&B RENTAL, IN THE

Virginia Highlands. A different spot, secluded, where you planned to work on the meditation as Button has instructed. To keep visualizing positive outcomes to your life while also attempting to make yourself unattached to outcome. To activate the chakras, all that yadda-yadda your space cadet, Phish-lot dirt surfer has taught you.

From the moment of your arrival, however? A disaster.

Charmed by the small towns through which you passed, one that included a faded, decrepit water tower featuring an ancient ad for Dr. Grabow's Pre-smoked Pipes, you gripped the wheel and navigated challenging roads with nerves still shaken from the scintillating and vivid dramas you've endured of late.

You prepared for this jaunt with a holiday gift that you might have gotten your grandfather: a new set of tires for the F-150, brake work, a tune-up, whole bit, and once accomplished, you sped north for the luxury cabin, one designed to sleep eight to ten people, but in this case only for you. Why that many folks would want to congregate in a house on top of a mountain you've no idea. Any more than why you used to do the group vacations with your Spotted Banana™ Fruitshake Company® partners. Here, though, a cabin for one. All the amenities, of course. Fireplaces and hot tubs and top of the line kitchen and every attention paid to detail, exactly the way you'd pay it. Hell, the place is for sale, and you thought: maybe I'll love it so much I'll come down off the mountain and make an offer.

Four-wheel drive helpful in accessing property.

Helpful. Not required. You got this. The truck, tough enough to take that hill.

But you can't get up the mountain. At all. You had worried about snow and weather, but there wasn't any in the forecast, and hadn't been any precip up here since before Thanksgiving, otherwise you wouldn't have come.

You started out with a spring in your step. Had barreled through the winding roads, untroubled, up scenic and historic Highway 21, through North Carolina above Winston-Salem and then into Virginia, cursing your luck at being stuck behind an eighteen-wheeler, and through a horrendous stretch of road construction. Arriving at the cabin in terrific time, the light fell crystalline in the cold but beautiful air. You would hit the hot tub first, deal with the tension in your neck from the drive. Nothing in the world seemed wrong.

Except the steep angle of the gravel driveway.

Thinking, like the idiot flatlander you are: *I'll get enough speed up to make it.*

But you didn't.

Tires, spinning. Burning rubber against the loose dirt and stone.

Sliding back.

Panic.

Jammed on the brakes. Collected yourself.

Started to reverse down the hill. The tunes, still cranking. A slight curve behind you; a utility pole and guide wire. Turning the wheel, watching the wire, trying not to knock it down and kill power to a whole mountainside of other rich people's summer homes. They'd have your blood.

The tires, slipping off the left side. Spinning on dewy grasses. Into a deep ditch.

The truck.

SLIDING.

Panic anew. Coming to rest against a fallen tree. Pushing the gas. The tires, spinning.

Turning off the truck.

Stuck.

Fudge, dude—fudge a duck!

The iPhone. A tow truck. Experts up here, surely, as everywhere. Services to be offered. Money to pay. Plenty.

No signal. Another warning. No cell reception, or spotty at best; no wi-fi.

Double fudge. With caramel sauce and sprinkles. Two spoons. Napkins. Your stomach, growling. You had planned to eat the second you got settled into the cabin.

Who needed the phone or the internet? You'd be catching up on reading, anyway. Write a short story, your first in thirty years, about your grandfather going off to fight the war against the Nazis. You'd have to imagine it all, of course, since he never bothered to tell you about any of it.

Now, though? You're in trouble.

You jog in your Tevas, slipping on gravel the whole way, back down to the main road, a winding and isolated affair on its own terms. No signal.

You've never felt more alone in your life. Not even your money can fix this. You will be found dead out here.

"God in heaven," you holler, voice echoing up and down the mountainsides surrounding you and nearly blocking out the sky. The fall color, still lingering, but not as bright. Turning to gray. Like your whole world. *"What have I done? I broke my granddaddy's truck! There's no one to help me! FUDGE!"*

A cow mooed from nearby, answering you with bored disdain. And again—a nearby farm. But where? You'd driven back in these mountains for what felt like miles, curves and up and down and far from the town you passed. A fir piece, as they'd say around these parts. Pasture after pasture. One mountain ago, maybe?

Stabbing at the phone. Holding it aloft. No signal.

Fucked.

No; you will simply haul your crap on foot up to the cabin, get settled in, and relax and wait it out.

Wait what out? The bombing of Syria that's going on? Obama, following the PNAC playbook to the letter? You have taken Button's advice and eschewed watching the news anymore, which she says is all lies anyway.

You need to get this truck out of the ditch. You can't relax until you do.

You ain't in control, beau.

A rumbling; a vehicle! You hustle into the middle of the narrow road.

An old man in his own pickup appears, a manifest rescue. He's not like your stalwart grandfather—this man seems slight and stooped and small behind the wheel. Still holding the useless iPhone you want to chuck into the gurgling mountain stream that runs by the road, the one that only moments before you'd found so scenic and beautiful, you dance and jiggle and wave your arms, yelling *stop stop please stop.*

The old dude passes by you, trundling over to the shoulder, albeit with reluctance and caution on his craggy face. It's a dangerous world. You could be a murderer. A thief. One of them meth-heads like they got everywheres.

"I've got a truck in the ditch." Your voice comes high and shrill. "Trying to get to the cabin. The driveway, it's too steep, it's—"

"Another'n in that ditch?" His wariness breaks with a rueful chuckle and a sad shake of his jowly old head. "That boy what owns that cabin, he ought-a pay to pave that drive. But he ain't wanna spend the money to do it."

"Maybe nobody told him."

"Shit, everybody told him. Shoulda cut through on a switchback or two anyway, instead of straight up. But an F-150, son—Lord, but that c'ain't take no hill like that."

"As established."

Looks you up and down, lingering on your sport sandals as though never having seen a grown man's unrestrained toes. "C'mon and hop in. We'll ride over yonder and call Evan. He'll help ya."

The fella said his name was Rex and 'rode' you to his house, and a land-line to call this 'boy' he knows named Evan Tygh. "Evan's got a tractor."

"A tractor? Not a tow truck?"

"Yessir. A tractor."

You picture Eddie Albert in the opening credits of *Green Acres.* "I'm not seeing it."

"Don't worry. Like I said, he done one last week."

"Another nitwit went into that ditch? Remarkable. Now I don't feel so stupid."

"On the other side, down into that ravine toward," *tord*, "the creek. Grill sticking up in the air. A Mercedes, trying to take that driveway." Cackles. "You lucky. They took that feller off in the ambulance."

"Hurt himself bad?"

"Oh, hell no. His wife and kids, they was pitching a hissy fit, though. 'Call a tow truck, call an ambulance, call an ambulance,'" high and mocking. "Even though he was standing there right aside us all. He kept saying, better safe than sorry, and holding up his phone in the air trying to get a signal, so I said for them to sit tight and I'd go and call from up on the landline in the cabin. Me, I sure wouldn't want to pay for no ambulance ride less I was bleeding from the durn ears. Or a tow truck, f'that matter, but Earl yanked them out. That car, she was messed up, boy. Still, coulda been worse. Could've killed hisself. Or one of them squalling kids, I reckon. Coming up here to have 'Christmas in a cabin,' the woman saying all high and mighty like it wasn't no idea of her'n. Personally, I ain't never knowed a woman what could be talked into nothing."

"Well now, male or female, everyone's got a mind of their own."

"You can say that again," spitting and scratching at his nose. "Of course, driving a Mercedes, you know he had money. Wife was younger'n him, too. Hoo, boy. That's how that goes."

Your ears and head glowed with inner fire. A Mercedes. Like yours, sitting in the garage down on Sedge Island. You ought to go get it. A chance to see Creedence again, your own trophy bride—in a sense—now gone astray. Eh. One crisis at a time. "Could've been worse. That's what they should've been saying. Keep a good attitude."

"Yessir. Positive attitude's the building block of a good life. Main one, in fact."

You walk back around the curve to the cabin driveway to wait for Tygh, who shows up in an hour. It's the longest wait of your life, pacing up and down until your calves ache.

Ruddy and red-haired, he's about your age, but seems older and wiser. Capable. Untroubled by your predicament. He indeed has a tractor with giant wheels, and hooks the F-150 with a chain, yanks it from the stony ditch, after which you back with care down the grade, him watching from his perch. Sliding around, peering into the mirrors, you grip the steering wheel with knuckles of alabaster. Sweating bullets.

Like the previous victim of this stupid road, you overcorrect and all but slip off into the opposite ditch, and your asshole clinches. The truck, she ain't driving right. Jam on the brakes. Slide back again. Shit yourself, albeit in a figurative-type fashion. Barely.

Deep breath. Evan, watching your flatlander ass. He shrugs —*well, dude?*

Straighten out the wheel. Ease off the brake. Make it down, finally. Level.

On the flat, grassy area next to the front gate, you see why you had such trouble: a tire emptied of air. A brand new Michelin, flat as hell. Blew it out spinning against a rock. Or whatever happened.

"That's a nice Michelin *tar*. That's a shame. Tree branch musta poked a hole in it. Them *tars* they make now ain't worth a toot. Thin as a gas station rubber."

"Mighty damn expensive to be poke-able with a tree limb."

He nods, grave. "Ain't having a good day, is ya?"

"Now what? I didn't update the spare. Figured these dad-blamed, expensive tires would last a hundred years."

"A *hundred years*?"

"Jesus. You know what I mean. Longer than two weeks, anyway."

His energy moderates and flattens. "Now, I'll fix th*is* for ya. But ain't no call to take the Lord's name in vain."

"Check. No disrespect meant."

"Eh—you hear worse coming out my grandbaby's radio. Pile in and let's get that *tar* squared away."

Another mercy ride, this one to Tygh's place in this tractor of his that sits up high and in which he goes racing around the curves and providing you fresh terror. If you didn't know better, you'd swear you were out of your element.

But in a good way: you were on a journey of discovery. After the tire got fixed, the crisis made the light seem brighter, the colors more vivid, the mountains and meadows and winding road all part of an unfolding adventure in a paperback you might have carried in a back pocket to the pecan orchard, long ago, on a lovely day not unlike this.

❉ ▩ ⊘

SWITCHING TO A MASSIVE FOUR-WHEEL DRIVE GMC, TYGH BARRELS down the main highway into town: Independence, Virginia, not far across the North Carolina line, and through which you earlier passed. You like small towns. Not your own so much, not Tillman Falls, but other such communities with history and Dr. Grabow's Pre-Smoked Pipes adverts painted on water towers, sure. You can dig it.

Tygh chats how he's the go-to guy for road work around here, including building that steep-ass driveway, which he echoes ought to be paved, lord; but the boy don't want to pay for it. He tells you he does all the snow-plowing in the winter, grades roads, lays gravel, while also managing his own farmland with cows. Does this, does that. Calls it "keeping busy."

"Same here. I'm 'retired' from my company, but always fires to be put out. The portfolio to be managed."

Far from put off at your hint about having deep pockets, a fellow ascended money master lets you inside: he discusses stocks and trades and holdings and hedge funds; property is his chief asset, oh, a couple of mountains and a few thousand acres of farmland throughout the valley, but he usually takes an hour a day to look over the numbers over coffee on the back porch.

"My oldest boy's my master mechanic, so he gets the shed here open on most mornings. Allows me a few minutes to myself. Get them trades knocked out, and then don't study on it no more. Do real work with my hands with the rest of my day."

It gives you the chills. "Something real. You got that right. Bet you grew up on one of those farms you still own."

"The farm I still live on, the same house—that's right." Musing, waving at a woman in slippers standing by her mailbox and holding a yapping chihuahua. "A son of these old hills."

"Like me back home. But the trades. It's fun. I don't live or die by it."

"Yeah—I ain't got nothing at stake. Not really."

This hillbilly grease-monkey by appearance has you beat—you don't own any mountains. Not yet. "A hobby. I hear ya."

Leans over, a wink and whisper: "Consider us lucky."

As Tygh drives through town, it becomes clear everybody knows him. They holler from the street or flash high beams from the other lane; he waves. Banners and flags announce cell phone plans and check-cashing schemes. Old Glory, pinkish and faded, hangs outside the post office and needs updating. Could be Tillman Falls. Could be anywhere.

❋◼✐

AT THE TIRE SHOP, DWIGHT, THE MAN FROM WHOM YOU'LL BUY THE NEW rubber, engages your benefactor in a long conversation that from their upcountry dialects and personal familiarity you can scarcely understand.

But in any case, Tygh is You of Independence, VA. Dude owns land left and right, yet still works like a regular guy; and you didn't have to open the CBSI, but you couldn't simply exist down on Sedge as a useless eater and experiencer of the finer comforts life offers those who have prospered. His work, however, speaks of his authenticity—an honest living that no doubt leaves him physically spent. Grading driveways and mountainside construction sites, plus he's got the gig with the state keeping the roads to nearby Grayson National Park plowed, with a Fed contract to keep the interior passable as well. Gracious sakes alive, who knows how much scratch those contracts alone must be worth. A man of the lodge and of boundless resources both within and without, a peer, Gen X like you; but here, upon whom you rely as a helpless child to an elder.

To change a freaking tire. Your grandfather, shaking his head from on high at his durn fool grandbaby.

And you expect fellow stakeholders in Edgewater County to 'rely' on you to lay out their commercial and social future the way Tygh, the town pathfinder, keeps the trails and trade routes open through long, snowy winters? Acting as a literal savior to his people—and to you?

Pathetic. Delusional.

Piling on, you sneer at your noodle-armed weaknesses while Dwight, a sixty-five year man, makes short work of rimming the old tire, he's changed a million truck tires, his broad, burly back flexes as he tosses aside the wounded warrior with nary a grunt.

Asks if you want the letters facing in or out, because it "ain't a Michelin like them other new ones," and as Tygh he keeps saying, damn shame to lose an expensive-ass *tar* so soon; and you reply you could give a crap about anyone seeing the brand name, you need to be mobile.

By the time you pay and get carried back to your wheel-less vehicle, you end up feeling nothing like the Roy E. Pettus who captains his minuscule planetoid, forever rotating, endlessly renewed, the way it happens in your reality bubble at home. Uncomfortable, this impression of yourself, and yet fortifying. Work to be done.

◌▣◌

DRIVING BACK TO THE CABIN WITH THE RIM-MOUNTED AND BALANCED new tire, your buddy and savior points out bits and pieces of local Tygh lore, an array of properties he owns, houses belonging to relatives and other town notables. Outside of town, he notes various fields he had to get 'hayed' before the weather turned, as well a litany of rich folks with second homes

here in the Virginia Highlands who pay him to grade and repair their driveways riven by summer rains before the first snow, which came and went, he
says; and how he will grade those same drives next year, and the year after,
including the one you know so well from your mishap.

"But you can't need that work, not for the money."

"No, lord no. I'm the one who owns the plows," with a hint of irritation
at your flatlander naïveté. "My boy will take it up when I'm done. It's what
this family does here in the valley. Seven generations."

"I get it. You're the man."

"They all sure enough act like it. So, I reckon I am."

After passing one particular house, Tygh speaks with sadness of an aunt
dying of pancreatic cancer therein. Shakes his head about Dwight, whom he
says has more money than he knows what to do with, and how he could've
given you that tire for nothing and probably not missed a dime. Before you
can respond your new friend offers that his 'master mechanic' son, seventeen, has himself a girl 'knocked up,' in his parlance, and due anytime.
Another development, a grandchild, back here in the hollers, which gets
only a shrug from the grandfather who might actually be younger than you.

"So we got a young'un in the house added to our list now, too."

"It don't end, beau."

Slaps his knee. "You got that right. But if I wasn't for work and toil,
what? Sit on the porch with the dog? I do that here and there. Always end
up remembering something I left dangling, else the phone buzzes and it's
someone needing me."

"Damn—that's my life. Or, it was, for the longest time."

"Service is our sacred creed." A truism from the lodge. You can't
disagree, and feel self-conscious at knocking around here in the mountains
instead of chipping at the list back home.

But dang it, you experience a comfortable vibration each time you
venture up here. Maybe it's because your grandfather grew up in hollows
and hillsides not unlike these, only further north. He used to talk about his
childhood in West Virginia, a mining town. They cultivated corn and hunted
and waiting for daddy to come home from graveyard shift below the ground.
No wonder they'd relocated to mill country in South Carolina, where
factory work spinning yarn must have seemed like easy living contrasted
with a daily burial, alive, down in a sooty, choking pit of rough-hewn rock.
"God bless those miners," your Pa-paw would always say, hushed, if the
news talked about a cave-in or other accident underground. It gave him the
chills, like when you would ask him about the war.

You fill Tygh in on the loss of your beloved grandparents, how they raised you, as well as their dog. "I've had a helluva year. I guess running off that driveway, and buying the fifth of five new tires within two weeks, is the least of it."

"Compared to your folks passing away? I should say so." Expresses his genuine sorrow and pity. "Hate to lose them in a cluster like that. Not to mention the dog."

You start to point out how the pet wasn't yours, but remember the miracle of lifting Rico into the truck bed, your heart and mind racing that you had to act, and feel convulsed with grief impossible to hide except for the fact that it's full dark now, and he can't see your constricted face in the truck cab. "Sometimes people have been around so long, you think they'll be with you forever. Pets, too. Time, I guess it snuck up on me."

"Time passes anymore so's I can't hardly keep up. I tell you," hooking a thumb thick and calloused—from doing a real man's type of work—at a local high school that, like everything around here, sits way up on a hill. "Thirty years ago I set yonder in that durn old school, day after day, staring out them windows and feeling like I had so much time I didn't know what I was to do with it all. Bored, with all that time. But almost soon as I got out and started working for my daddy, time took and run faster. Till the kids come. And watching them grow, it went faster still. And ain't quit speeding up on me yet. You can't tell, not usually. Not unless you sit still and really study on it," tapping the temple.

"That's what sitting on the porch is for—making it go slower."

"I think you might be right."

"My hippie friend says time is an illusion, that it's all right now. Maybe so, but by my watch, I can't half believe another year's gone already."

"Ain't it the truth. It was spring, then summer, and it ain't nothing but work all the time for me no way. But that first snow come, and next we was sitting around the Thanksgiving table looking at football and hollering at the TV, and now, here it is January and the Christmas trees is mulched and another planting season's around the corner? Mercy me. You tell your friend that 'right now' we got to put a tar on a truck." Laughing like a big punchline just dropped. "See what their hippie self says to that."

◉ⓜ⊘

AS YOU STAND WATCHING IN YOUR SALMON-COLORED POLO AND FANCY man-dals, he replaces the tire by the light of a brilliant lantern he's produced from his truck, looming in its size and power over your crippled F-150, jacked up and helpless by the turn-in from the county road. You fret about the suspension and the alignment; he says, hell, he don't mess with no align-ment on none of his trucks or tractors unless them durn wheels is a-wobbling where you can see it.

Finishes. Says, wellsir, now you got wheels again.

Tears of gratitude well.

Offers to help you run your stuff up the hill to the cabin, since there's no way you'll get up there with a two-wheel drive on that truck.

No, you tell him. You'll walk it up. You need the exercise. You don't have much stuff. "A suitcase with little rollers and a grocery sack of provisions. It's nothing."

He says, suit yourself. "Long hike with a durn suitcase. But to each his own."

You fish out a crisp C-note for his trouble. Slap it into his workingman's hand, clutch it in a death grip of a formidable handshake. "You saved my idiot, flatlander, city-boy ass," which knowing you'll soon return to Tillman Falls, your own version of podunk, feels like a stupid lie.

"You ain't got to give me no money. Not after that penny-pinching Dwight took you for a hunnerd-fitty. But I surely appreciate the gesture."

"For your new grandson. Now go and get your supper, finally."

"Supper? We still got brakes to fix on one of the dump trucks."

"*Tonight?*"

"Better'n in the morning. That way we can get started."

"Evan, you're my kinda guy. Thank god for your neighbor who came along."

"Yep, my lucky day. Keep them *tars* on the road, now."

"I will. Appreciate it."

Waving and weary, Tygh backs onto the winding mountain road and rumbles away over the narrow bridge spanning Fox Ridge Creek.

You glance up the pitch-dark hill, consider a cabin you haven't even seen hidden away in the towering trees. The seclusion awaiting you. No internet. No cell service. In case you need Evan Tygh again, all you can do is holler down through the holler.

Eff that.

Without spending another moment on this mountain you climb into the truck, crank it, and peel out onto the highway to head back home. You have felt no comfort like you did at Heather Ponderview's estate a hundred miles to the southwest. Maybe you and Button will return together. That's where you felt at home, especially on that tucked-away property Heather showed you. What you thought you'd do up here in Virginia by yourself, you haven't a blessed clue. Meditate? You don't even know what you're doing.

TIME. A MONTH, ONE SPENT IN WINTERTIME LASSITUDE, GONE. MORNING finds you again. For what purpose you've awakened in your Edgewater County bed, you know not.

Thoughts of a woman in your head; sure, Creedence, but in a more immediate and tactile sense, Button Sykes. A long text about a dream she had in which she witnessed a higher-dimension war being waged, she called it a vision of the 'soul-eaters versus the invisible college,' and that you rode at her side on mighty steeds through flaming purple vistas of cosmic energetic conflict, and wondered if you had had any similar dreams.

You texted back *Nah, mainly food dreams.*

What kind of food? she replies.

Dessert this time, a display case full of pies is all I remember.

Sweet, she says with a laughing emoji.

God, how you love her. She probably thinks you're an untrainable idiot at this higher consciousness game. You keep promising, but results are lacking. Not like the bossman at all.

Button hasn't been the same since the death of Howdy Shull. Has seemed physically diminished. Moving slower. Still bright in the mind, full of information and advice and nudging you along, often on the literal path by the river where you walk with her sometimes; as well toward the path of higher consciousness, as she puts it, that has made her spirit soar and her mental habits wholesome. And could yours as well. If you only acquired the discipline. Not that she says it outright. But that word creeps into the conversation so often.

You get it. You receive the message.

Discipline.

And yet, this remains unheeded.

As within as without: Gloomy outside, the gray of lingering winter, at least such as you get in a humid subtropical locale like Edgewater County, SC. You hear a nuthatch, *to-what, what, what, what*, so at least it sounds like spring. A little. Even lacking any snow, damned dreariest season anyone around here can remember. The warmup and reawakening, it's a ways off, still. You're ready for daylight savings time, for shorts, to wear your Keens without the thick hiking socks you bought for the trip you took with Button to see Heather Ponderview.

You believe that it's only weather, sure, but in the long days and nights since your grandmother passed away, and the dog died, the cops executed Howdy Shull before your eyes, Button gave up on her leafletting, and worst of all, you haven't reconciled with your wife, you've devolved back into an internet conspiracy nut. You suspect that, either by necessity or for nefarious and unknown ends, the PTB, as Button would call them, are and have been engaged in a pernicious campaign of jacking with potentially dangerous schemes like geo-engineering. Messing with the jet stream and causing all this weather. Introducing particulate matter into the upper atmosphere to affect the quality of the solar light. Terraformed right the first time, as Button says.

Your peeves? Questions about how WTC 7 fell into its own footprint at the speed of gravity without benefit of an airliner striking it. Mercury in vaccines causing the mysterious, increasing wave of autism sweeping through the childrearing families of America (but Button, she says it could also be all the wi-fi blasting through developing in utero brainpans). Whether the BP disaster and chemical-cleanup in the Gulf of Mexico has caused mutations—last week somebody pulled an eighteen-inch shrimp-like creature out of a Florida tidal creek. If Fukushima radiation was spreading throughout the world, note to self to check on rates of thyroid issues in the Pacific Northwest; and forget salmon and tuna, which is full of mercury anyway, add in radioactive isotopes, sure. A universe of worries and mysteries have come your way. Esoteric knowledge. Or maybe all horseshit. No way to tell.

Not unless you had gotten cancer and needed an explanation, let's say, besides the spiritual ill health of the planet and all its people, which was Button's overarching theory about why modern humanity suffered so many physical and mental illnesses.

Much of this junk came from her pamphlets, which you took day-by-day to be polite, and because so few showed interest during the two months she made her attempt, before the confrontation with the street preachers and Howdy and the cops murdering him to death. An alleged killer, sororicidal, but known as mentally ill and in need of help, not a public execution for no damn good reason. Not simply because a bunch of trigger-happy public servants turned twitchy when an old dude waved a soda pop bottle in their direction.

Yeah. In the aftermath, you had said as much to Sheriff Oakley; had used the words 'cops' and 'scared' to a shocked and frowning TV news reporter from WKNO. You felt deadly force was unnecessary, over the top, uncalled for, and so on. You hoped there'd be an inquest, or whatever the term. Because the police—you'd pulled back from your withering criticism only at calling them outright cowards, and by name—had overreacted. Because they could've killed any, or all, of the bystanders. Bossman, money or not, this riff has made you none too popular with the local gendarmes, and this despite your contributions to their 'foundation.' Oakley, and his Lieutenant, Timmy Truesdale, cool to you ever since. Don't forget who butter y'all's bread, as you keep vibing them.

Shamefaced, is more like it. Guilty at their craven and gutlessly irresponsible behavior. Yeah, right.

The pamphlets; enlightening you, sure. Until your interwebs searches revealed so much more.

That geo-engineering stuff, though. It nags at you.

Jerking around.

With the weather.

Causing this lingering, wet winter.

Just to spite you.

Dude. Get a grip.

Hours spent listening to your Pa-paw's records, selections like 'The Happy Blues,' Gene Ammons, a 1950s bebop saxophonist Manny found in the collection and liked to play while y'all were making dinner, your guest expounding on Ammons's sound and his horn, a Selmer Mark IV; surfing from social media to conspiracy website to Amazon to shop; more hours still streaming Netflix content. Catching up on various TV shows, some you started with Creedence, others you embark upon yourself. Manny got high and watched a few episodes of *Mad Men*; said, *dayum*, Don Draper get an assload of tail, like all consistent and shit, while Manny, though, had to work at it. Laughing, saying he ain't work too hard, come to think of it, falling all quiet and reflective and troubled. For a while. But in general, your tenant in the old house across the way don't got time to lie around and surf BS conspiracy sites and try to decide on another TV series to binge-watch while waiting for the new *House of Cards* season to drop. Boffing Becky L and screwing up his family life or not, Manny, he got a business to run.

Working for a living.

Like you used to.

In private moments, watching old Karen Black movies on the iPad. Discovering one you'd never even heard of, a bleak heroin drama with the ironic title *Born to Win* and featuring a fetching ingenue in Ms. Black, a semi-convincing and serious George Segal as the junkie, and Little Bobby DeNiro as an impossibly youthful, quasi-sympathetic-to-Segal narcotics cop. Right there, streaming for all to see.

Karen Black?

In a dramatic role you've never seen her play?

Hold all my calls for the next ninety-four minutes.

You hadn't been looking for her, but came across this title while finger-scrolling through the offerings, page after page, genre after genre, of New Hollywood-era features. You've already seen it all, or else B-movie crap, direct-to-video as they call them these days. Karen, she's made her later career out of parts like that. Bless her soul. The last 'A' picture you can recall that gave her decent billing had been a Robert Altman, *Come Back to the 5 & Dime, Jimmy Dean, Jimmy Dean*, in which she portrayed a transexual.

The hell you say. What are we saying with this casting, that Karen Black, the sexiest actress who ever moved breath with goddess lungs and filled frames with her pulchritude, appears mannish? Blasphemy. You're still reeling over Button having met the woman. One of those crazy syncs, as she calls them.

Reality—a tapestry, an overlay, a lattice. Add in technology and culture, as your pal likes to say, and you find yourself kicking back with some complex, multi-layered dimensionality unfolding all up in this-here human experience, yours, Button's and Karen Black's energy intertwined in the matrix to produce this beautiful strand of interpersonal narrative. Study on that for a spell, as Evan Tygh might put it.

◌▣⊘

But Christmas, the worst. You drove the truck down to Sedge Island to see Creedence, deal with coffee shop chores and problems, talk about the future, including about your wife's potential sole ownership of the venture. Having your team at Verbrick, Adger and Hagood, Attorneys at Law LLC, draw up many legal documents. Helping Creedence set up her own corporation. No money to change hands, of course. A way to sustain herself. The house, paid and clear. If she wants to stay. The cats, a hard brood to relocate. Loving the Island, she says. A plan in mind, but more and more obvious that it will unfold apart from you.

Ouch.

OUCH.

That visit, yeah. The night before, you streamed a crisp HD transfer of an old Palmetto Grande indelible cinematic experience, 1981's *Body Heat*. The passion on display, you sat up with a start and considered, might offer a harbinger of what was to come on the island and your reunion with Creedence—it could turn into a version of that powerful ham-slapping between lecherous William Hurt and lusty Kathleen Turner, a scene playing out with stylized realism before your engorged adolescent peepers and gonads.

Yes: You envisioned throwing the chair through the garden door and stepping through broken glass to get to your heaving, sweating wife. Making violent love on the floor of the sunroom upon the shards and tinderbox splinters remaining of the shattered doorframe, all thoughts of the unpleasantness of the autumn washing away in a briny Marshside tide of forgiveness and salty-sweet body fluids. Entering her again, at last. The warm glow of connection you can swear you still feel from all your years together.

A fresh consummation. A reset.

Instead? A business meeting. Small talk. The exchange of gifts.

An immediate and telling roadblock? You had gotten her a set of lingerie from Vicky's, and she had flushed red. "These are real pretty."

You could see on her face a boatload of discomfort. "When we talked—the things I said—this is a gesture. A hint, I guess." You had declared how much you loved her. Had not let yourself hear the noncommittal response she'd given.

The payoff?

"That's sweet. But we'll have to save these for another time."

A brief hug like you'd give in the receiving line at a memorial service while saying, I'm sorry for your loss. Surprised it hadn't been a dry handshake over the coffee shop deal. And you had fantasized how you might finalize the details all tangled up in the sheets with her.

And Creedence, shocked to hear of your new plans for The Dixiana, your rebuild of it, detail by detail, instead of forging ahead with the Carolina Beanery brand in Edgewater County. Forget it, you said. Done with coffee. "Done with it all."

In fact, your real gift to her, not the lingerie, a bad joke; rather, your intention to transfer ownership of the CB trademark. Build your empire, you said. Run with it.

"I told Sharolyn one slow afternoon the whole story of watching you build the Spotted Banana from a neighborhood smoothie stand into a brand almost everybody in the South knows. And how much money you made."

"We. Money we made—we were partners in all that."

"If you say so. But then she said, well, why can't we do that?"

"Good question."

"Well?"

"Oh—you want to know what might keep you from succeeding?"

Her beautiful eyes glistening with anticipation, she waited.

"Fear. And not believing y'all can do it. Otherwise—I don't see how you can lose."

"I don't either. Not following in your footsteps."

A compliment. A warmth in the air between you and your estranged wife. It felt like hope. You ran with it. Better than a nostalgia wallow like opening another coffee shop had been. You could never go back. Although Edgewater County seems to have a grip on you, that much for sure.

❂❆⊘

To the Old Market in Columbia, and the scene of your first successes, you returned, however, as a stopover on the forlorn, post-holiday drive back from Sedge.

You swung off the beltway and motored into Columbia, a stop-and-go affair that left you impatient in Rabbit's F-150, which for some stupid reason you keep driving. Having already fixed and upgraded its mechanics, only last week you had the truck detailed, waxed, the pine tar taken off by some meticulous hands and a bottle of Goo Gone. New car smell. Had expert car audio home-slices install the highest-price-point Blaupunkt stereo system, speakers, with Bluetooth to stream tracks from the iPhone. Add in a set of *tars*, one of which you'd be replacing within weeks, and you sat ready to take on the mountains. Oy.

And while maybe not sexy, the appeal of driving Pa-paw's truck remains undeniable. Sitting up all high and mighty. American made. Some stupid crap you can't put a finger on to save your life.

Listening to the rocking tunes all the way back from the island that day had given you an idea. The wall of LPs, your granddaddy's music collection. And nothing to play them on but the old console record player from forty years ago, if not longer. From the goddamn 1960s. You had to find needles for it on eBay.

So you'd upgrade the stereo at home. You mean, in your grandparents' home.

Whatever you bought, it'd be a longterm investment you would take with you, along with all the albums, yeah, one day soon. But for now, you mused, as you continue to prepare the build-out of The Dixiana and to plan your granddaddy's memorial music festival for the coming springtime, you will play his records. With direction from Manny and Jasper you'll grow to know and appreciate the collection, full as it is of old-timey 78s and LPs— jazz, blues, early R&B, plus your own teenage section featuring the Zeppelin and the Floyd and the Who and the Dead and Blue Öyster freaking Cult.

But no online ordering or schlepping out to a big box out in the burbs; you remember well the high-end stereo purveyor plying his trade only steps from the original Spotted Banana™ all those years ago. Much as you love music, however, you bought no gear back then. No money for all that; all your profit, and profit there was almost from the start, either going into the kitty or back into the businesses. Paying off Maxine; and in only five years the duplex up the hill, your first mortgage. Paying down the bank loan. Paying until you owed nothing. A fantasy for most human beings.

Did your young adult-era musical deprivation affect your bottom-line wellbeing?

Proof; pudding.

You are filthy, now.

Because you saved.

Instead of splurged.

Maybe—just maybe—you can allow yourself a new record player.

◌ 🄱 ⊘

CREEDENCE, WHEN YOU MARRIED, SEEMED STUNNED THAT, WITH ALL your resources you chose to live in a crappy college duplex blocks from the Old Market. All you knew is that you could walk to work the way you'd walked to class. She wanted a traditional home, though. Your introduction to pleasing a woman: satisfying her desires for security and comfort.

Memories, ugh; making the back of your shaved neck itch.

The gear. After crawling through downtown traffic and by the State House with its full-size version of the Pitchfork Ben statue gracing the green in Tillman Falls, you cruised over the railroad tracks and down the hill into your old stomping grounds, passing by the beautiful hilltop Charleston-style overlooking a row of townhouses, themselves facing the avenue down to the commercial strip. You always loved that Chuck-town style on the hill, had tried, way back in the early days of the marriage, to talk Creedence into buying it instead of moving south to satisfy her low country fetish; but no, no, no, she had to get away from the home you'd made for yourself, to reside in that fetid mosquito-ridden swamp of a sailor's town of drunks and wastrels on the coast. You could've built your company from anywhere. From inside your little office in the rear of the original Carolina Beanery. From the kitchen table in the duplex you rented out at an enormous profit. Money, turning into more. Your special talent. As though your vibration attracted wealth.

Okay, okay. So moving had had its merits. Still. The Old Market. Home.

As you enter said neighborhood, a warm glow. Until:

You.

Crap.

Your.

Tighty-whities.

Graffiti. Gang-sign. A pair of blood-red Chucks dangling from a power line. Grunge in the nooks and crannies around the once-clean sidewalks. The forest green trash receptacles, filthy. The round, decorative lids hanging off to the side. The matching lampposts, covered by layers of band fliers and peeling, ratty strips and swatches of sun-dried duct tape adhesive. Brick-work framing the fountain, chipped and crumbling at the corners. Sidewalks spotted with gum and stains and grime—where, thy pressure washers, city of Columbia? Ye stout warriors of the trade primed and trained to render these sidewalks refreshed?

Da *fuh*?

If you still owned a business here, these problems would constitute a four-alarm event of phone calls and backroom meetings filled with subtle threats and intimidation. You helped shepherd this place you'd called home into its modern identity as a dining and shopping destination, yes, along with its storied and earned rep as a college ghetto full of beer-bars and dives and holes. In your absence, the neighborhood, itself a fetid basin into which more than storm water flowed, had declined. This shall not stand.

Furious, you whipped into one of the angled spaces along Wateree Avenue near the good-as-gold original Beanery, long sold off to your then-manager. A forgotten endeavor for you, this coffee shop. Not after the fruit-shake money game consumed your life.

By the time you strode with your veneer of anger and confidence masking a wounded soul through the doors of the Carolina Beanery Café— or rather, the Carolina Beanery College Row, as Sean Paul, your old general manager and now owner had, at your behest, renamed the endeavor—you vented free of all steam over the gritty, fading aesthetics of the streets you created, an aborted rocket launch of aggrieved rhetoric which would've only made *you* sound like a nut.

No one to complain to; no one of any consequence, anyway. No owners, no neighborhood association board members, at least none you know by sight. No familiar faces, only hipster kids behind the bar steaming milk and panini-ing some fancy-pants gourmet sandwich like you serve at the CBSI. Two tatted and pierced dudes playing chess. College girlies peering at tablets or phones. Everyone else tapping away on keyboards. Teens with colorful hair out front, new smokers puffing without truly inhaling, looking cool at the coffee shop with the college crowd. Ever thus.

Business; strong.

Good for Sean Paul.

Your eyes, burning with salty water. You said to yourself, for fuck's sake, Pettus, don't cry in front of these strangers. Other than the time it flooded right after you'd taken ownership from Maxine, you wouldn't have walked in and boohooed when you owned the place, and now as a stranger what context you could have for such a display of emotion—they didn't know you, nor Button, Rico and your grandparents, or that your marriage to some redneck girl named Chelsea Colette Rucker had imploded and you couldn't seem to have it back, or how you are lost inside, swimming in grief and fear and uncertainty—</p>

"Welcome to the C-B-C-R." A sweet-faced barista, skinny and freckled and with beautiful piercing eyes like those of your wife, greets with a happy grin. This one's twenty years younger, though, with her hair buzzed off like a punk rocker and tatted, but her youth and sparkle captivate you, make you rue being so old as you've become, and older by the minute—how gray you've gone over the course of the last six months, a shattered Stephen King protagonist after surviving the horrors of a paranormal ordeal. Or maybe you're only noticing, finally, how time goads you from the mirror.

The barista's expression changes to one of shock: "Oh—wait. No way."

"Something I said?"

"Dude, you're the guy. In the pictures. In the office." She holds up her narrow, smooth hand for a high-five. "You're Roy. The original coffee man."

Your ego shines, blazing with the love and light of recognition. But her statement, far from true. You merely rebranded an already successful and legacy business. "From from it. But I owned this place for a dozen years. Yes, I did."

She points a finger-pistol at her temple, goes *ka-pow*. Spins around to turn off a timer on the small oven churning out fragrant scones. Yep—manic pixie dream girl alert. "Mind, officially blown. Are you here, like, checking in?"

"No, a chance drive-by. Sean Paul around?"

She pooched out a lower lip. "Missed him for the day. Message?"

"No message. But, while I'm here, thought I'd sip a cup."

"Well now, that's gonna be on the house."

"Are you kidding?" The money clip, a grand or more, appeared like a magician producing a colorful hankie from within a sleeve. "I prefer to pay."

"I wouldn't have a job if it weren't for you. This one, handsome man, is on *moi*."

Her name, as you find out, is Cassi without an 'e', which she says is short for Cassiopeia, which means both a shimmering constellation as well as a ravishing Greek goddess, heh heh, and flashing those soulful eyes again. You comment on the fact she seems awed by it all, and the gamine youth says, "Hey, man, this is one of the coolest places in the city." She adopts a Bogart-esque hardboiled accent: "Dudes will step over their own mothers to work the CBCR, mister. It's real cut-throat on these wicked streets."

"So I see from all the graffiti." Winking and warmed by her charm, your fingers find a bill, a double sawbuck, and shove it into the tip jar. "I don't remember this gig being so attractive when I owned the place. We had a lot of turnover. But that's what you get in a college neighborhood. People—they come and they go."

Glimpsing your big-ass gratuity, she beamed happy-happy eyes. "Oh, my, are you getting taken care of today, my friend."

"Appreciate it, dear. Your boldest beans, if you please."

As she got your large Sumatran drip-dripping, you noticed two words tattooed on the respective backs of her pale, thin upper arms:

Forgive   *Forget*

Damn if you didn't break out in chicken-skin, and at last a couple of tears pulled the plug on their brief lives and leap over your eyelids, and you fretted she'd notice and think you nothing more than a sentimental oldtimer with misty, past triumphs fading from view.

But: This message on her arms in deep indigo ink, it's what you've been trying to achieve with your estranged wife. The idea you wished to get across when you went down to Sedge—not to exchange holiday gifts. To begin the reconciliation. But it hadn't taken hold.

This, though, is one of Button's synchronicities. That are so all-fired important. You know what it's saying—the words mean you can't give up on her. Not the barista—on Creedence.

When Cassi pours the hot water over the Sumatran grounds, in slow, graceful circles like you trained Sean Paul so many years ago, she catches you wiping the tears. "Oh, sorry, bro—we're roasting onions back there in the oven. Gets me, too."

Terribly relieved, you ground knuckles into eyeballs. "I'm certainly not gonna squirt a few over this old dump. Selling it to your boss? Best move I ever made. Don't even know why I came back today. Whole neighborhood's going downhill."

She froze in mid-swirl for a sec, her face a blank mask... but then you gave her a wink and the patented, warm, slow-spreading sunrise of a just-kiddin' smile, and she got it, right on, right on. "You scared me there for a minute."

"Sometimes I scare myself, kid."

You sat by the front window watching the ebb and flow of the boho college crowd, enjoying the brew and thinking, okay: not giving up on my wife. Now that felt like a plan. Soon as you went around the corner and blew a pile of money on audio gear.

❂ ⚏ ⊘

THE OWNER OF THE UPSCALE STEREO STORE ISN'T CHARLIE, THE GUY YOU knew from before; a younger dude is the current proprietor.

You describe the nature of your pressing exigency. The record collection. How you wish to hear them played to the finest standard money will allow.

Within reason.

Yeah. You remember this persona, now: Moneyman. Thurmond Pike and his Bait & Pawn, on his billboards he calls himself the money man. But you, boy? That's your deal. You have enough that your cheddar ferments its own cheese. That's what a boy wants out of life. Money making more of itself.

Ain't it? So's you can up and buy crunchy audio gear? Or like, whatever you feel like? Shoot, yeah. Bucks to burn.

A hip dude called Kallen Swygert, ginger kinky hair with tiny plugs in his earlobes and one of those ridiculous Van Winkle beards dangling down and obscuring the Audiophile Avenue Hi-Fi logo embroidered on his ice-teal polo, conducts an interview about the collection and your current gear. The sleeves of his shirt aren't long enough for your taste, what with his intricate tattoo-inked forearms. You grew up hearing from your grandfather how only sailors, junkies and assorted miscreants forced ink into their skins.

As the merchant taps on his wireless whisper-quiet desktop keyboard, researching choices for you and your big swinging dick of a request, you asked, "So: Charlie Roquist cashed out and took a house at the lake?"

"You could say that. I worked for him about ten years before taking the reins."

"How long he in the trade here? Already twenty years back when I took over the smoothie shop."

"Hell of a product, those smoothies. I've sucked down quite my share."

"And here I am, giving back. The circle of life."

This strikes him as profound, a glimmer of ah-ha in his eyes. Swygert, chewing on his Uniball Vision Elite, a terrific pen. "But Charlie, I wish it were only retirement. He had—problems."

You leaned forward. "Divorce? Gambling?"

The kid's eyes, clear and bright, drift from the screen, his finger held aloft in mid-click on his mouse-toe. "Health issues. It's really more than I can—should—discuss."

"Not cancer, I hope."

His glistening eyes, betraying a bullseye. "It's going around."

You can't help but note the pack of Marlboros sitting on the corner of the desk. "Epidemic. Must be junk in the water. The air."

Swygert concealed the pack in a drawer, a swift, singular motion. "I'm thinking about trying hypnosis."

"I'm immune."

"To smoking?"

"To hypnosis—you can't put me in a trance." A wink. "And make me spend more than I intend."

"I meant to quit smoking."

"A joke," your way of nudging the conversation back to the matter at hand. "Tough habit to break. Never got started, myself."

"Well look," changing the subject. "Top of the line means different things. I've seen turntables at the CES in Vegas priced out at over a hundred large, as the gangstas would put it. I'm sure you don't mean that price point."

"I want the best I can put my hands on from what you carry."

"It's still gonna be in the range of—"

Enough. You smiled and asked him to put together a package capable of knocking off socks, but below six figures. "Record player, amp, speakers. Whatever else you think I need."

"CD player?"

"Not as important, but yeah. I'm more interested in the old stuff. The 78s."

"What, no wire recordings?" Relaxed and jokey, stars in his eyes over this potential fat sale. "Wax cylinders?" "Keep clicking."

Requesting a few minutes to research, he clicked while you stalked the showroom, low-lit and tasteful to suit the upscale clientele. Thunderous bass from subwoofers rattles glass; another employee demos a home theatre in a glassed-off area set up to resemble a living room. A well-heeled man sits watching The Hulk fight one of the space aliens from the big battle at the end of *The Avengers*. All this crap looks like a cartoon. You had animated Hulk when you were a kid. Why grown human beings need so much of that now, you hadn't a clue.

"Okie-doke." Swygert called you back toward the grinding mechanism of his desktop printer birthing a sheet of letterhead.

Gesturing with the paper, his hand trembling: "Please, sit down."

"Relax. I won't faint."

You snatch the sheet, give it a good squint. A weighty bond, cottony. You're already sold.

- *VPI HR-X* TURNTABLE WITH *(2) JMW 12.7* UNIPIVOT TONEARMS - *15,000*
- GRADO STATEMENT AND GRADO *78E* CARTRIDGES - *3,650*
- AUDIOQUEST WILD BLUE YONDER INTERCONNECTS (TO/FROM AMP) - *5,000*
- AUDIOQUEST OAK SPEAKER CABLES - *2,500*
- ROGUE AUDIO NINETY-NINE SUPER MAGNUM PREAMP - *3,000*
- *(2)* ROGUE AUDIO *M-180* MONOBLOCK AMPLIFIERS - *6,000*
- *(2)* MAGNEPAN *3.71* SPEAKERS - *6,395*
- TOTAL INVESTMENT: *$41,545*

You tossed the paper back to Swygert, pale and anticipatory. "Including tax?"

"Well — no."

"Then it's not the total. Now: nice, even amounts here. Rounding up?"

"With gear like this, the ninety-nine cents retail trick doesn't quite matter."

"Suppose not."

You glimpse Hulk smashing into the glass facade of a skyscraper, a shattering roar of fury, tinkling glass and pulverized concrete and mayhem. "Question."

"Sure."

"How many innocents are killed in these towns obliterated by the superhero fights? You never see the poor National Guard having to bury all the bodies. Or the real meat of the aftermath, when the contracts go out to developers and contractors, and infrastructure reconstruction begins — who has the big ideas on how to rebuild? That's the plot I want to see.

"But, all the collateral deaths? Bodies stacked up down along the docks? Do the heroes take care of that, too? You ever think about the dead? Helluva way to earn a fat FEMA paycheck, though, mass burials. I know a FEMA contractor down on the island who clears a million clams every time a hurricane knocks down a few palmetto trees."

"Never thought about the rebuild. Superman and General Zod really gave Metropolis an ass-kicking. You see that one?"

"As established: I have no need to watch a 9/11-resonating, violent children's cartoon. I'm a mover of worlds—how else could I afford gear like this?"

"Everybody kicks back. Everybody likes movies."

"Movies are none of my business. I'm here about the music."

You can have some fun with this. Inside, you're getting a tingle down your leg, and not like the deadly black blade humming into life. You can get into this. Money, it's meaningless to you now. Because, as Button says, it's all made up crap, an energetic but no less imaginary construct. Of course, it's all imagination, as she also says.

A giggle sneaks out. Looking up to the acoustic-tiled ceiling of the showroom, you note how it has a smell in here, like money and ozone crackling. Or maybe that's the power you wield. Your eyes had teared up so you couldn't even see his numbers.

Swygert, this kid who bought into Charlie Roquist's high-end hi-fi business—a Columbia version of your Uncle Burnie's electronics store in Tillman Falls, which was nothing like this, it sold console TVs with record players like your grandparents used to have, and had hung up the trade long before this audiophile crap came into play, by the time you came of age in the late 70s his shop on its last legs—tries to play it nonchalant about this huge transaction. But you know the truth: this sale will provide the income cornerstone of his whole January.

"What's the cash price?"

Disturbed. "You mean—cash-cash?"

"Yeah. I've got fifty grand in dusty old Southern money stuffed into a leather satchel out in the truck. I received this money for killing a man. You did not hear me say this; I was not here."

Pale. Blinking.

"Relax. A joke. It means I write you a check instead of using the AMEX. Not that I couldn't use another forty-k in reward points." Which was bullshit. You probably have over a million, still. For years you used that AMEX to pay many enormous bills. You and Creedence had been planning to cash a chunk of the points in for airline tickets and hotel stays and occasional merchandise purchases. Back before you opened the Carolina Beanery Sedge Island. And bought the plane, took the flying lessons, and began spending all your time at the hanger with the old guys.

"A—check?"

"You'd prefer literal cash? What kinda business ya running?" Trying to sound like Tony Soprano, you slid his nice letterhead back across the desk.

"I would need to clear it with the bank. Before you left today."

"Of course. Just as I would. No worries, pal."

Oh sure, you could have laid that money of Rabbit's stashed in the old house on him, and blown his mind. Yeah—you know all about that secret mattress-money, have known for years, as did your grandmother. That you have left it alone for now, with two near-strangers camping inside, is only because your ass would draw attention for having so much cash on hand. To a cop that's an automatic indicator of malfeasance or criminality, and license to seize. You'll do something cool with it down the road.

Still, you have the urge and itch to break it out and mess with this kid. Drop it in a big pile on his desk. Be worth running all the way home to get it. Wouldn't it. But no: you plan to blow this money on Rabbit Festival expenses. That's the most suitable and apropos use of the music lover's cash stash, short of donating it to the old bluegrass picker's home. Swygert recovers with a chuckle: "You threw me off. I figured we'd talk financing." Hinting. "Now, we do use a particular company who's offering an unbeatable interest rate, plus six months same as cash."

All right. You produce the iPhone, pull up your balance in the fun-money Crown fund, as the bank calls this rich boy's checking account. Show him the balance—$1,318,727 and change. They forever encourage you to move chunks into $250,000 CDs, so your personal fortune will remain secure under the terms of the government's FDIC guarantees. In case the banks start to fail. You keep meaning to get to it. Your financial guy, Rodney Cowan, doesn't seem concerned. A blur of numbers. Meaningless.

Except in the power it gives you. Over young Mr. Swygert.

Over them all.

Somewhere you can feel Button frowning. Hear her voice whispering, money, it's not only fake, but evil.

The stereo salesman squinted at the figure displayed on your screen. "Damn, dude."

"Shall I get the checkbook?" Breathless: "We don't have all of this in stock. It'll take a couple of days—or, if you want to buy from stock on hand—?"

"I don't rate getting this gear shipped overnight?"

"Of course you do, Mr. Pettus." He snaps out of his bullshit naysaying trance. Assesses the time on his own phone. "Let me shoot off a couple of emails. It's late in the day for overnight—oh, wait. Most'll be coming from Cali."

A thunderous Hulk roar from the demo room makes you lean forward. "*Bali?*"

"As in, California."

"Right right. But you never answered me: what's the cash price? To save you those pesky AMEX discount fees?"

He draws a breath. "What if we said forty even?"

"With sales tax? Or without?"

"I have to collect the sales tax. You know."

You nod. Fair enough. "I do know. I've been in business a long time, m'boy. Forever, it feels like. So send your emails. Get the gear coming this way. And I'll retrieve my fabled checkbook."

"How's this sound? Installation and setup, that's included."

"It's way up north in Edgewater County. Just to let you know."

"Not a problem. We have customers in the lake country."

"I'll bet you do." A handshake. "Back in a jif."

You could feel his eyes watching—he's waiting to see you get in the F-150 and drive away, his amazing sale all a prank. It's a bleak, atonal vibration in the air.

Stop worrying, you try to send to him the way Button Sykes beams you thoughts. This is not a joke; it's not a cock-up. It's capitalism. My largess is your largess.

And you? You won't feel forty grand. A minor tickle. Your portfolio will grow by that much this quarter.

As for Pa-paw's records? They'll sound the best they can. Better than they ever did. Not that it'll bring any dead people back to life, or gain you any spiritual points, or induce excitement in Creedence sufficient for her to come live in the Victorian with you.

From Phil Webhannet's emails, your cop down on Sedge you pay to observe and report, when not at work she's happy enough to spend most of her time alone. How he knows this short of twenty-four-seven surveillance, you don't have a clue.

Back inside, you found Swygert beaming with news: "Immediate response from the distributor. Installation for later this week okay?"

"Damn straight. Now let me borrow one of those Uniball Elites, if I could. Good pen to write checks like these, this heavy bond. And for a reward I've chosen to give myself, such as this system."

Yes, yes, a fine purchase, his voice cracking with awestruck gratitude. What magic money, an imaginary idea, even the satchel full of it back at home, could achieve.

ANOTHER GRAY AND DRIZZLING MORNING, BRACING AND CHILLY — WHAT passes for winter cold in temperate South Carolina — finds you slithering rather than bounding out of bed, and not to listen to records on your forty-grand stereo, nor pursue any meaningful endeavor other than eating and excreting waste.

Hell, admit it: since getting the system installed and tweaked, you've listened to a few old-timey hillbilly songs of your grandfather's, rare discs with haunting, faraway vocals and twanging, stringed instruments; in the early evenings, bebop jazz like the Gene Ammon sides, Coltrane, Miles and Sun Ra; but for the most part, a few cuts from your own scratchy vinyl — thunderous Led Zeppelin or bombastic The Who, tunes to rattle the triple-glass windowpanes and jangle nostalgic nerves. But none of it truly fills you with pleasure, not like one expects from listening to beloved melodies, yodels and power chords.

Manny, still living in the old house, commented on the occasional heavy-rock noise. In his gentle way. Not as though he's paying rent. A favor. Can't work out his family troubles. Besides, he seems to love the wall of records. "Your nigga got Sun Ra all up in here? God-dog."

"Pa-paw seemed like a country boy on the outside, and he was, but his musical taste turned out eclectic."

"Left behind some good shit for us to enjoy."

At this remark, an odd look crosses Manny's face — troubled, no longer getting off on the records. Dude has a hard time setting aside his relation-ship troubles. You can dig it. "I'm pretty lucky."

"Damn right you are."

Motivation: if nothing else, time to wash the sheets. They're stiff and sour like on your single bed in the dorm-suite back in college when you'd lived with Devin and Dobbs, bedclothes fetid with the effluvium of stale beer and burrito farts and dried crusty semen, chicken-choked out of you while listening with nut-busting envy as Devin and his lovely Libby set to moaning and thrashing in the bedroom next to yours. But only months later, Libby, dead and gone, and Devin, lost as well to drink, depression and later, mortal disappearance. Precious memories, you realize, your naughty, aggrieved eavesdropping of love manifesting between your dear, departed friends. Perhaps their souls were reunited, now.

Last night you hadn't been able to stomach binge-watching TV shows, so you turned to reading: the gift your wife got you for Christmas, a thick historical novel by which you've been trying to get hooked, pages that instead lulled you to sleep. Sorry, Cort Beauchamp. Another time, maybe. Sitting in the coffee shop, sucking down strong brew.

A coffee shop.

In the mountains.

Or wherever you end up living.

Wait—was this what they called living?

This?

Maybe you should try meditating rather than lolling about in the depths of empty abandon. It's working, if that's the way you're supposed to think of what Button often reminds is a lifelong practice, not a task awaiting completion and checking-off the list. If you'll only gain more discipline, you're golden.

Never been a problem before. Disciplined enough to get filthy with lucre, eh?

Speaking of filth, you should get Pa-paw's money out of the floor. If anyone found out about a stash like that, it would be gone in an instant.

◎ ⊞ ⊘

HOLD ON, NOW, MAYBE THERE'S HOPE: THE SUN KEEPS TRYING TO PEEK out. Shadows from the windblown, overgrown azaleas outside the window blinds cast a strange and compelling visual dance on the spare, blank wall in front of you, an ephemeral light show that comes and goes over the few moments you continue to lie immobile. Enervated by the prospect both of reading your wife's Christmas gift to you any further, or getting out of bed for any other reason, other than a potential power walk by the river with Button, which hasn't been happening of late, you find no call to get up. Your list of tasks today sits short.

But you need bath soap and bandaids, a mincing, minuscule voice protests, *and the yard looks like world-class crapola.*

No question: You need to get the list whittled.

List-whittler, you—it's a calling, as you once might have put it to a crew of employees awaiting your instructions.

Another action item: One of these days you must clean out your grandmother's lifetime of possessions, and old Rabbit's, too. Y'all had discussed if she wanted to mess with any of that. Mee-maw would sigh and say, oh, lord, not today. I can't think about that today. "Maybe later in the spring. After the festival." Closure, of a different sort. She never got the chance to play her stage one last time.

Gut-punch.

It's not the grass, but the first thistle weeds of the year already poking up that's bugging you. No way would you pay some half-wit to cut the yard, though. This is your place, now. You'll cut your own grass. By god.

For once.

Hell—you haven't done that since you were a kid. Not in Columbia. Not in Charleston. Not on Sedge Island. Certainly not at any of the extended-stay places you lived in with various members of your group of owners, getting a new smoothie store up and running. Sedge had been the end of the transient living. But you sure weren't cutting grass down there. Not in Marshside. Association dues included landscaping. A rubric of consistency and control and conformity.

But still, the yard. It requires mowing, and this despite the pall of winter still hanging over the land. Only two months ago, you sat at the table with Mama Runelle, making a list: cut the yard, a box of baking soda for the fridge. Foil. Tissues. Hand soap for the kitchen sink.

"Not the orange kind—the lavender," she said. "Can't stand the orange."

"You think there's a difference, Mee-maw?"

"Something makes them two different colors."

You said, sure. "Inert dye."

"I don't know 'inert' means, but that orange one makes my hands dry and scaly. Lavender, please."

It annoyed you. Silly old woman. You bickered, barking at her. Like you'd always heard your short-tempered grandfather behave.

You know what? She didn't seem to mind.

You've become your parents-slash-grandparents.

No choice—they're all dead, Jim, as Bones McCoy would say. They have passed into the Oneness, as hippy-dippy Button would put it, leaving only you to make and satisfy the sacred checklists. You need bath soap and band-aids. You must cut the grass and hit the IGA or the new Publix or the Wallyworld.

Oh—and own The Dixiana. That's all. Check.

◌⊞⊘

BUTTON. SHE'D BEEN SO BROKEN UP OVER HER GRANDFATHER'S

depression, ongoing and pernicious since old Rabbit's death. Blamed herself for adding stress to Rabbit's tired heart with her comedy routine protest on his beloved stage, followed by this failure to assist her grandfather in his bereavement. Not because of the Taoist bit about how when one looks to place blame elsewhere, there's no end to finding exterior locations upon which to assign fault, she explained. As she put it, she had wished with such fervor for Burnham Sykes to have peace—not to die, only to acquire serenity—that a vibration of guilt would often twang, out of tune, and screw up her equipoise and the flow of her Q'i and that malarkey of hers, because the only way to have that level of serenity would be to actually die. Dimmed her freaking glowing seven-sister chakras to feel guilt.

"But you didn't make him die from your wishing. He's somewhere cussing and drinking right now."

"True."

"Matter of time, though. I know his clock's ticking. How much more grief can I take?"

"Don't ask that. You have so much ahead of you. Trust me. Levels, and layers to get through."

"Levels. And layers?"

Button had only smiled, a spritely sparkle in her eyes.

You experienced moments when sitting together, high and laughing, where her form and essence shimmered and rippled. As though you could see Button Sykes in the flesh, but also at another vibration. All shifting energies. Vibrations and energies. Coalescing into animated meat skeletons. Stuck to a rock. Spinning around in space.

And yeah. Existing on different levels. Your dear friend thinks like Kramer on *Seinfeld*, that one where he built the platforms in his apartment upon which to lounge rather than having furniture. "It's all about levels," the actor had said, miming surfaces and clean lines with his long, hairy arms. What before seemed an absurdist comedy bit on a television sitcom now holds intellectual multitudes. Good weed, that Button.

◌ ▩ ⊘

OH, HOW YOU AND CREEDENCE, IN THE EARLY DAYS OF YOUR relationship, used to sit close on your couch at the duplex near the Old Market, you and your babygirl, watching *Seinfeld*. By 2004 it'd been a few years since the show went off, but they still ran it around the clock, it seemed, on some of the cable channels. You'd thought, happy, happy, a gorgeous woman at last, and a major iconic adolescent crush come to glorious and explosive fruition; and yet how ordinary and stagnant this life seemed.

More. You had to get more. That was the American Dream. A new century had dawned. The tech would be higher, but the goals remained the same. Cash and toys. The rappers weren't wrong. And so on. But you didn't see how those simple times were golden days in that duplex, a one-business owner, of your favorite coffee shop in which you'd hung as an undergrad; you knew everyone and everyone knew you; you made a difference as a civic leader, a two-time recipient of the Merchant of the Year award from the neighborhood association on whose board you served. Hell, you had loved college so much you stayed in the same ruts, hanging out at the same coffee barn—hell, you bought it! And like the perennial students you served, in between making lattes and cups of fine dark beans you often sat at the bar among them, reading poetry by Yeats and Rilke and Brautigan, novels by the Henrys, Miller and James, the short stories of Cheever, Updike and Chekhov; but taking over the smoothie stand a few years later began to change all that. Not at first.

Creedence had come along, though. A miracle. But: A family.

You had to provide.

To make money.

At about the time this idea became fixed in your mind, the mall in the Northwest suburbs called about the dreaded hole in the food court. And the first of many further SBFC concerns unfolded like one of Button's thousand-petal lotus flowers. What to say of the explosive growth? Right place, right time? The added sugar you sneaked into the 'healthy' product?

On a personal level? After 9/11 you said, *Well now, here's a national imperative to excel in a way I have yet to pursue. I didn't become a writer or a teacher—I became an American businessman and upstanding member of the merchant class. No shame there.*

Am I exceptional, though?

Not yet.

You declared: *I must show them—show her, my wife, and the old honkytonk man—how I can piss so far and so pungent that I mark my territory in multiple markets and states and regions and malls and shopping centers,* and by god if you didn't say it and later see it.

This successful reality, you envisioned it down to the house at the beach which had become the marsh, a discordant wrong note, and in your imagination had changed now to the mountains. Anywhere but back in Edgewater County screwing around with The Dixiana. What a cosmic joke.

You could start over anytime, any place. All you need accomplish here amounted to tidying up. Don't forget that.

How'd all this manifest? Owning the club and the houses, dealing with relatives fighting over the estate like out of a cheesy southern gothic—get me Cort Beauchamp, stat, to write it all up. Plenty of conflict to drive the drama. One of these days you will pay a visit to spooky, crumbling old Hillsborough plantation. Tell them you've stayed in the EC and wish to join the aristocracy, the landed gentry of the county, and need instruction on how such people may be expected to behave.

Soon as you cut the weeds. Buy the items. Run the errands. Whittle. The. List.

❋

THE DIXIANA'S BUILDOUT, PROCEEDING BUT WITH THE TYPICAL contractor delays and rigmarole; all's on schedule with the Rabbit Festival. Fellow merchants like Cecil groused over having fences erected around the neighborhood for the day, but you made it right by pledging to offer grants to businesses affected by the festival activities. You'll write whatever checks you must to get this event on its feet. And over.

You've read how Councilman and Reverend-Doctor Nixon has gotten a special referendum scheduled for April on the name-change issue. Fascinating that he managed to find enough traction to amass the required signatures.

"All come from them mofos over in Easton," you overheard Thurmond Pike complaining as you stood in line behind him at the Publix last week, a throng of consumers buying bread and milk when the TV had called for a dusting of snow flurries in Edgewater County, which hadn't come to pass. "It don't mean nothing. The real referendum won't pass no more'n I'd win Miss America."

Folks are riled up about this name issue, rhetoric like Pike's getting more heated. You fear violence. Jezmund Rembert types worry you the most. He might still pull some retribution over your mural stunt. Eh. That little weasel doesn't scare you. Bring it on. You kinda wish he would.

❋

IN MAKING UP YOUR BED YOU KNOCK A SHEAF OF PAGES ONTO THE hardwood floor, and you say shoot, shoot, shoot because this paper's aged and fragile. Not like papyrus, not turning to dust. But you want to treat your short story with more reverence than that.

Yeah—you've been in bed reading more than Cort Beauchamp's crappy Civil War romance. Last night you'd gone spelunking in your old foot locker into which all the school papers were left behind for your Mee-maw to hold and to keep, including this piece you called 'Five O'clock Somewhere,' a phrase you'd heard batted around in the afternoons when your closest pals amounted to day-drunks holding down the bar at The Dixiana. The English teacher to whom you showed the work thought it accomplished.

See? You were a writer. Once.

Upon contemporary inspection, you found 'Five O'clock' not all that hot —serviceable, as your adult self kept thinking, a charitable assessment of plot and prose. You described a van-load of hippies pulling into a honkytonk not unlike your grandfather's, a dusty dive way out in the desert but on the inside sounding a lot like The Dixiana, because that's what you knew and could imagine and on whose bar top you had worked on the story in question. 'Five O'clock Somewhere' had your hippies, who had embarked upon a quest to find Jim Morrison, whom they believed to still live out in the wilderness—and maybe it was true, to this day, who knew, the thought gave you goose pimples, that and Andy Kaufman coming back finally, holy crap —but alas, they ended up finding no undead rock legends.

Instead? Your hapless hippies get robbed and blown away by rednecks and the old bastard who owned the honkytonk, who also ran a chop shop through which the motorcycle parts, he explained before killing them, will net a tidy profit. A cold-hearted ending. Metaphoric. Political, even. *"Ain't nobody gonna miss them dirty monkeys,"* your chilling final line of dialogue. "Burn 'em out back. And then bury 'em." You had pictured a grizzled William Holden in the part, spitting and sweating like a spaghetti western bad guy. Epic.

The English teacher who graded the story also advised the yearbook and the school paper: Gloria Graymont, late thirties but with deep lines in her face, curly dark hair, tall and cute and from Minnesota, had that accent, and in conversation you always had a hard time not mimicking her. Not to make fun; like you wanted solidarity with this person whom you might as well admit to having loved and desired, but being Roy E. Pettus and smart as hell, you knew it wasn't possible, no matter how you sounded. You weren't a stupid kid like the rest, most especially after the Trudy sex happened that next year, but that, oh boy, forever a scandalous secret.

You'd been old before your time. Something about losing your parents and being raised by codgers. Who knew? Ms. Graymont, though—sexy, smart, quirky and divorced, which only stoked your fires and made you jealous as spades when she dated Mr. Bingham, the history guru. She wafted with a particular spicy-sweet aroma like a warm cinnamon cupcake. Nowadays they'd put her away as a sexual predator for the acts you fantasized about her doing with and to you. Nasty little priapic goat that you were.

Your ardor, dimmed: she only gave you a B on your epic piece of short fiction. Said you employed an evocative style in telling it, and that she could feel being in 'that awful place' as she'd described a bar that looked and acted like the one you walked through on most days of your life, unless you could avoid it. The end of the story reminded her too much of *Easy Rider*, however, which you had never seen, and that drove you nuts because you knew Karen Black was in it.

In those times, however, you couldn't see movies whenever you felt like it. Had to wait for them on TV. By the time you caught up with *Easy Rider*, a most fortunate screening at Southeastern U's theatre programmed by the Cinematic Arts Committee, you'd not only gotten to see Karen Black have a bad or otherwise weird acid trip and take her clothes off in the cemetery, but also the Captain America and Billy getting assaulted by the hateful hicks and shotgunned on the road, and at last understood Gloria Graymont's reservations about the story.

At the time in high school, you'd been terribly disappointed at failing to please this woman in whom you were so invested. The stink of this failure permeated your memories of 'Five O'clock Somewhere,' which wasn't bad, not for a teen who wrote it in a long evening on his blue humming electric typewriter, fixed a few typos with White-Out, and thought himself an author.

What had happened to that?

Making coffee and selling it at a huge profit? Same for the fruitshakes?

Counting money?

Blowing it all on a high-end, highfalutin record player? That cost more than many souls around the world subsist upon throughout an entire lifetime?

Still, the question lingered and nagged: how you ended up living your grandfather's life, only selling coffee and fruit juice instead of booze. Had the dream been to make all that bread, only to end up back here?

In Edgewater freaking County? You must investigate this conclusion.

⚙ ⚅ ☺

PISSING AND STARING AT THE iPHONE FACEBOOK FEED WITH ONE EYE, you peek with the other out the window at the sliver of the old yard. You can see through a hole in trees the power company came and raped that lovely Becky L's sky-blue Prius sits parked with relative discretion on the back side of the original Pettus house, modest and unassuming with its small front porch, low ceilings and tiny communal bathroom.

When are those two gonna get wise, give up this untenable crap? Or else come out and be together?

Perhaps it is but a friendly call, and they've worked it all out. Manny, he doesn't much talk about it. Whenever a hint of the subject comes up, he shuts down. You can't help asking. For the last six months, the science of adultery has held a keen interest. An early morning catch-up to chat and sip coffee? As though anyone would drive this far up River Ridge to visit. Hope it's good pop for them both.

Maybe Jasper Glasscock would come strolling through the pecan orchard with his guitar later. Jasper and Manny, the bluesman and the country crooner—impresarios and tunesmiths alike—often sit on the porch and jam together. That's happened a couple of times on temperate Sunday afternoons, and it reminds you of the musicians who used to pay tribute during the ritual cookouts over behind the other house where Becky L's car sits concealed. Circular, the musical energy around here. That's how Button would explain it. But honestly, you cannot fathom the tension between Neecie and Manny and Rebecca LaFreniere. Has to be crazy dangerous. Eh. None-ya, as they say. Or as Manny would put it, you keeping bossman ass outta that shit.

Pulling off the bedclothes, taking them downstairs and putting in the washer on hot, extra soak, a big scoop of laundry soap—all you need do is remember to put them in the dryer later, and you'll be all set for tonight. Make a habit of this. Hell, start making up the bed the way your grandmother would. Disrespectful to her dear, sweet memory to keep house like this.

Button has told you that at the least you should always smooth over the place where you have slept in the bed, erasing the shape you made in the sheets and mattress overnight. Spirits, she intimated, waited to steal a part of your soul from the impression your body left behind. Your lingering sleep-energy. One of her silly, hippy-dippy truisms.

Horse hockey. In other words.

But you'd started following her instruction. Hadn't you?

Button. You needed to call her. But first? You'd put on a sweater, go and sit on the porch, and meditate for twenty minutes. Your self-chosen mantra —*the weather is here, wish you were beautiful*—had been replaced with a more meaningful one she'd suggested when you were stressed after Howdy's killing:

Soham, a Sanskrit word, as she explained, meaning 'I am that': 'so' on the inhalation, 'ham' which sounded more like '*hahm*,' on the exhalation. A mantra through which to achieve meditation; a mantra to use to center oneself any old time.

So far, it worked much better than the Buffett lyrics. Majorly so. Your prior mantra carried too many syllables, like a poorly conceived haiku that sought to portray cleverness yet lacking in deeper meaning, or even the proper discipline of form. Duh. More words, less content. Far less. Sort of like the national discourse, such as you pay attention to it.

۞⚅⊘

MEDITATION, A SUCCESS; NEAR AS YOU CAN MEASURE IT. BUTTON CALLS it turning the light around. Gave you a book about golden flowers. You have that next on your list since bailing on Cort Beauchamp's antebellum horse-hooey, with prose purple enough to choke Pat Conroy. As the coffee perks with fragrant delight, drip drip drip, much different from your CBSI method, the buzzing of your phone breaks the placid after-trance. The greeting comes warm; it's your homegirl, Button. She must have known you were thinking about her, she who has called instead of texting this morning, as is typical.

You tell her she's catching you right after the best meditation you've attempted in weeks.

"Wait—you broke your meditation? To answer the phone?"

"No, I had finished. I used the new mantra. No breaks to take calls or check the CBSI Facebook or Yelp review pages this time."

"Good. Let the world outside. Continuing turning. On its own." She cleared her throat twice. Sounded froggy. "You must feel good, then."

"Eh—down in the dumps. That's the blunt end of it."

"I understand." And waiting for more info.

You shrug; she can't see you doing so.

Or can she? "A shrug's not much of an answer, dude."

"Wait—you heard that?"

She says she heard the crepitation from your shoulder, the crackling of the scar tissue forming over the break in your clavicle Trudy's monstrous husband Samson caused a few months back. The shoulder, healing, but still stiff, sore, and yeah, noisy. "But it's not. The shoulder. That's got you down."

"It's this eff-all gloomy weather. I think I've contracted SAD."

"You mean, you *are* sad. Oh—wait. That seasonal disorder."

"People get it in rainy places, Seattle, London." Every winter for the last five years you've seen posts and listicles about this syndrome. It was why people moved to the sunbelt. To places like South Carolina. Sedge Island. The snowbirds. "But it could be both kinds of sad. Sure. Either way, these clouds can go screw themselves."

A bolt of electric yellow solar light comes flooding in, illuminating your arm holding the phone. You lean forward, squint out the picture window of the family room into which you've shuffled in sock feet. "Spoke too soon. Looks like it might break up."

"Was gonna say. Sun's coming out. Over on Whaley Way."

A fresh idea hits you. Something to kill multiple birds.

You ask Button if she feels like getting high.

"Did you hear that? Sound of my arm twisting."

"Check; but I mean really, really high."

"Ah—you want to take a ride. In the plane. Is that it?"

"Sharp cookie."

"Not what I had in mind. But—I don't see. Why not."

"We need someone to watch over Uncle Burnie, though."

"Like, who?"

"What about—what about—your friend." You can't remember the black girl's name, the one that Button hangs out with sometimes. A friend; a lover; Jockomora or Jockoramalamadingdong or whatever the fudge the young woman is called.

"Jackie?"

"That's it." Idiot. In your defense, though, you recall that it's short for a more exotic moniker.

"Don't think so. It's a weekday. She has to work."

"Unlike us. What about Letty? You could bring Burnie over this way. They would have crap to reminisce about. I'll call her and see. Sound good?"

As with her sense of shrugging, it's as though you can see Button nodding. "But, to where did you wish to fly?"

You tell your best pal you'll fill her in after you check with Letty.

The secret plan? Time to jet down to Sedge, abandon the Piper Meridian, pay somebody to clean it up and ready the machine for sale. Drive back in the Mercedes, finally, not that you mind the F-150. But it's necessary to ditch the plane, after which you must get back home.

Home, as in: Here.

And also, you want Creedence to meet Button.

As to the disposition of the Piper, you've already assigned Ron

Nawalinski of the Sedge Island airport hanger buddies, to circulate news about the beautiful piece of personal flying machinery now for sale; a hobby for which you no longer have interest.

It's part of what cost you your marriage.

You keep the last bit to yourself, only saying how you'll be glad to get rid of the aircraft, a foolish waste of good mad money. This made Ron chortle and deny, chortle and deny. Dude lives and breathes flying. Thinks you're nuts. Asks if it's cheddar problems, and you're like, do what, beau? Forget it.

Another secret: you had to struggle with learning to pilot. Didn't you. No need to admit this, not halfway out the exit.

Why you wanted to take it up, you'd no idea. Maybe your Uncle Burnie having been a flight engineer in WW2, and the only one of your two male role models to tell you a blessed thing about his experiences. He'd been a hero, saving his comrades in the air. No idea what your grandfather, or your father killed in 'Nam, did during their service. Maybe all heroes, your forebears, but from your grandmother's telling, Pa-paw's time away at war must have been brutal. But you'll never find out now.

◌🄷⊘

Letty's onboard; Button brings Burnie and drops him at the Glasscocks, and while there it's back-slapping from Jasper and a big Southern lunch with chicken and biscuits; with Jasper's habits, you're sure the host will have the decency to let Burnie get into his liquor, else Button's granddad likely to go into the DTs.

On the short drive to the airfield you take the long way around, so as to avoid The Dixiana and all the responsibilities that come with its ownership —or maybe to miss seeing the spot where Howdy Shull burned alive.

Tunes-wise, you blast Button out of the truck. "Ya gotta hear this one. You young cats missed out on all the choice tracks, little sissy."

Button tells you she's heard all this music that your generation, and the one before, can't let go. Play all the songs to death. And the movies? Iconicizing purported classics to the point new work becomes difficult for older viewers to judge with any useful objectivity. Mind-controlled, in other words.

You scoff. The kids, you declaim, are ruining movies by flocking to all the infantile comic book films, none of which you've seen but include no less than forty-five minutes each of animated robots beating on one another, including the excerpt from *The Avengers* you glimpsed in the stereo store: a frenetic sequence of five heroes presiding over citywide destruction that seemed a bombastic, overblown apotheosis of form: too much of everything. Each of these movies now features an entire city undergoing chaotic demolition, even the last reboot-series *Star Trek*, a generic action-movie affair with an incomprehensible plot you detested beyond measure, no more so than when logical and intellectual Spock becomes reduced to a revenge-driven climactic fistfight and foot chase. Obscene. Profane. Ham-fisted and wrong. So wrong. Made by simpletons who would not know *Trek* if it were a snapping turtle from the Sugeree River coming up out of the toilet pipe and biting them on the sack.

But as to the music:

"Get ready to jam." You hit play; *Fire of Unknown Origin* blasts out of the factory speakers, the bass vibrating the screws out of the door frames. The dashboard crackles under the strain. You dial back the intensity of the ringing guitars and synth as Button cringes and holds her ears.

Your discourse: The last decent album; the one that'd come out when you were a senior at Byrnes Hell, as you refer to the high school. A special place in your heart, this 'LP,' as you call it. You crank it up.

"Bad-ass, dude," she hollers over the din. "We'll never stop. Rockin' out. Right?"

"Heck-no we won't."

You wax rhapsodic about the cool BÖC logo. How you went through this period, you and Devin, where y'all drew it on everything including Big Rock, a place out in the woods near Jensen's Pond where kids go to party and screw, and about which Button, as much as local as you, well knows; and on a warped piece of plywood found down in the basement of the Gray-Peele mill, where youngsters would also hang out once it shuttered in the early 80s. You remember an afternoon down there drinking cheap wine like hoboes while Devin, a cigarette hanging out of his mouth and squinting through the smoke, spray-painted a pair of the rock band symbols, one facing up and the other down. The art hadn't looked right to you — the logo held more power on its own rather than being twinned — but you didn't bust his chops. Not Devin. He could turn mean on you — a typical drunk.

"Devin said he liked the Blue Öyster Cult sign because it was both a cross and a question mark. That it symbolized the not-knowing over the knowing."

Button gets that look of hers — wonder, intense curiosity, surprise, all wrapped up in a bare-minimum widening of her eyes, her most Asian feature. "Sounds like a Taoist."

"I liked the sound of his idea because we didn't go to church. My granddaddy said, son, always question the man who claims to have the answers. Because he's only another man. And repeating some 'answers' he received from some other bonehead, and 'all of it about sneaking a hand into your pocket and taking out money they ain't earned'."

"A fountain. Of wisdom. That Rabbit."

"My old dead Pa-paw? I never thought so. But, yeah."

"You better believe it." Gives you that special smile again, a whole face type-deal radiating love.

Seems like you can see her dang cheekbones, though. Losing weight. Too many of her walks and yoga workouts. Time to get some decent food into her.

She's so kind, Button. Humoring you. You admire her sense of duty and service. As you haul ass out of town toward the Edgewater County Airport, such as it is, you give a quick squeeze on the knee as though she's your best gal.

You rock out; BÖC sings about death creeping in through a keyhole, but the possibility of this being one of Button's synchronicities is not apparent to you at this time.

◌◍◌

IN PREPPING THE PIPER MERIDIAN, WHICH SEEMS GLAD TO SEE YOU— kidding—you take a few minutes to tell Button of your long history of riding in trucks like Rabbit's F-150, a make and model of no particular distinction but still solid, and you stop short of talking about how you bought it for your late grandparents; were proud of the act, and how at one time it would have been the most important bit of info—how awesome you were, how all over it, how on top of their material needs. Not so much, now, this need to project awesomeness.

Now?

In their absence?

Your generosity feels more of a fading, futile sense memory, which makes you think about Button's talks on astral projection and past life regressions, and dealing with grief by recognizing the ability for the memory part of the brain to recreate a person you'd loved: a vision but not tactile, or maybe a little, if you learned and concentrated on how to do it right. Remote viewing. Seeing into the future, even. Conjuring them back, your grandparents, and telling them how much they meant in words rather than money-gestures.

Eh. Don't know if you're into all that hooey, nah; but when you try, boy, can you project yourself back onto the bench seat of Pa-paw's truck, cracked and fixed with duct tape you would always fiddle with because it scratched your fat pink little legs. Can hear the tinny high sound of the guitars on the AM country music station, which played classic and old-time country versus the new stuff, as Rabbit called it, with people like Charley Pride and Waylon Jennings playing to packed grandstands and arenas. Can feel his presence. His smell of Old Spice and Winstons. The turmeric-yellow smudges on his fingers from smoking. The way his legs looked when he had them crossed sitting in the old house listening to his records, or out in a lawn chair watching pickers who sometimes came calling on Sundays for the Pettus-Sykes cookouts and played for y'all, a private bluegrass concert, when your granddaddy had looked the happiest. Such obeisance and respect they all showed him—musician after musician, reverent, bowing heads before your grandparents , waving away the bugs and nodding along to the tunes in their folding lawn chairs.

"It's good for their pocketbooks, but it ain't close to the way this started out, anyway. Country music—they called it hillbilly music when I was your age—got played by people who was hurting inside. Who suffered tears and pain and sorrow in their lives, and the music was their way of handling all that mess. Waylon and Willie and the boys sound good, but they don't know nothing about suffering and pain, except maybe a hangover. Them boys do like to put on a good party."

You relate a version of all that to Button, who stands distant as you have your Piper fueled. You tell her about how you'd ride over to Columbia, as Rabbit often did while dealing with tax collectors and liquor licensing and grownup business hooey, or to shop at the Sears or other department stores. "I played in the johnboats for sale, all lined up in the parking lot. Walking in them while Pa-paw watched over me. Remember it like yesterday, but it was decades ago."

"That's so. Sweet."

"One time I darted toward the traffic, and he whipped my ass. I was maybe three; I kinda remember it. Or else recall through their frequent retelling. Part of the family mythology. The time Roy Earl tried to run away."

Button brightens and shields her eyes against what's now full sun. "I recall them telling that story." She takes a sip of water from her Nalgene bottle. "At a holiday dinner? One of the cookouts?"

"That was when they told their stories. The ones they wanted to tell."

Ah. Now it's you who needs to clear your throat. Memory lane this close to their peaceful passing, or 'transit' as Button refers to death, still sits muddy and treacherous with turbid and humiliating puddles you want to step around. "Boy howdy, did he whup me good. Scared the mess outta him, he said."

And you let go a little, a choking, quick sob. She comes closer, comforts you by resting her hand on your forearm.

You swipe the AMEX to pay for your Jet A fuel, much cheaper than on the island, and thank the attendant. As you get settled into the cockpit, going through your checklist and putting on the cans, two pairs of Lightspeed ANR headsets with bluetooth, a thousand bucks apiece, and to which you can listen to tunes and take calls while you fly, you tell Button how once you got a certain age you discovered how cool rock & roll seemed compared to all that awful old people's hillbilly music. How while riding in the truck you'd beg and plead to let you listen to the FM rock station out of Columbia, one you could pick up once y'all got about ten miles outside Tillman Falls. How he'd resist listening to your music.

"Okay. Gimme a sec. Let's cross some Ps and Qs here first on our little list."

"Do what ya gotta do."

"Don't you worry." Superhuman multi-tasker or not, you have two souls for which your flying skills must account, and that high off the ground, a forgotten tidbit could mean the difference between a smooth ride and a panicked you, fumbling around like when you were landing here at this airport six months ago in a fit of pique and grief and confusion. With that incident in mind, you get strapped in and start through the checklist proper.

Actually, it's multiple checklists for each segment of activity: Before Engine Start, Engine Start, Before Taxi, Taxi, Engine Run-Up, Before Takeoff, Takeoff, Climb, and Cruise; on the downslope it's Descent, Approach, Landing Check, but let's not add the one for Go Around/Missed Approach, which you remember all too well. Everything important, and at every level from ensuring that the doors are secured (WARNING: DO NOT INITIATE ANY FLIGHT IF ALL FOUR DOOR PIN INDICATORS ARE NOT GREEN AND/OR THE 'DOOR AJAR' ANNUCIATIOR IS ILLUMINATED) to a balky start-up (IF NO FLAME AFTER 10 SECONDS OF FUEL: CONDITION LEVER to Cutoff/Feather; Push MAN/STOP SWITCH; DRY MOTOR for 30 seconds to Clear Fuel, and then another separate checklist for DRY MOTORING PROCEDURE) to simple but crucial lifesaving attention to common sense details like 'Ensure Taxi Area Clear.' In fact, you find you must refer several times to your laminated pages of the Piper Meridian PA-46-500TP checklist literature, which you hope doesn't give Button too much anxiety. You keep winking at her as you go through the various functions. Smiling.

She smiles back. No worries there. Not Button. She's a rock. The most with-it person you've ever known. Afraid of nothing.

She's *your* rock. A daily checklist outside the aircraft too, one that includes encountering her voice or face.

If only it were possible to love her in all ways. She could be your true partner in life. If only.

Alas; but add to the checklist of crucial tasks to forget your attraction to her. Button not only likes girls but she, like, is totes in love with mysterious and ethereal Heather Ponderview. Outta luck, you are. Not only are you the wrong sex, but compared to Heather's stash, even your fat roll falls short. Not that anyone's counting. Besides you.

✸🄱⊘

NOW, YOU ARE READY TO FLY. YOU FEEL CONFIDENT. THE CHECKLISTS checked off, the cans on your heads, and before long, the Piper rises airborne into clear sky. Smooth air, and much colder up here. Loud. Beautiful, rising into a blue that deepens as you climb.

"So I'm in the truck with him, going to Columbia. Get him to let me listen to Doober Dougie on the rock station. Bitches and moans, granddaddy, but hell, at least I was outgrowing kid stuff already. The year before I had been obsessed with this novelty record called 'Hot Buttered Popcorn,' you know it? No? It's this synthesizer thing. Really silly. I would play it over and over, and he liked to say it drove him up the wall. But anyway, Dougie, he plays this cut by George Harrison, 'Crackerbox Palace.' Wish I could spin it up right now, but I don't think it's in the iTunes on the phone."

Button, with a playful smile, asks that if you're gonna play music again, could it be her pick?

Suspicious. She had forced you to endure a Phish tune called 'You Enjoy Myself,' twenty minutes of frenetic composition and improv followed by an acapella 'vocal jam' that tested the limits of your musical tolerance. "Not Vermont's favorite sons again, I hope."

"Nah. How about good old Grateful Dead?"

You slap your thigh, tell her of-course; that you've a few live shows on your iPhone including your first, the original bootleg cassette recording having been labeled *10/27/89 Collegiate Coliseum, Southeastern University, Columbia, SC.* "Got a hankering for some Jerry? I'm down. But lemme finish that story from earlier, if I could."

"The Dead... they're on my mind. That's all."

"Heard that. Sometimes I gotta hear the fat man rock out."

Why she's looking so mischievous, you don't got a clue. But her impish mirth feels infectious, for which you are indeed grateful.

"It was already memorable, Rabbit finally letting me listen to the rock station all the way to Columbia. I wore him down; he relented. Said, all right boy, lemme hear some of this music of your'n." You rumble your deep-voiced Rabbit impression into the com. *"Bunch of hollering fools, if you ask me."*

"Exciting."

"Doober Dougie, he came on saying, 'And here we go, groovy listeners out in listener-land, with the latest A-side from George Harrison, the shyest Beatle,' or whatever his DJ rap was. And it's this tune called 'Crackerbox Palace.' An A-side, obviously, but not a huge hit. And Rabbit, he immediately bitches about how messy and stupid the song sounds. How they're playing the slide through some piece of hardware that don't even make it sound like a guitar, and the guy don't know what he's doing no way, and what's that noise—some Moog synthesizer, or whatever—but most of all? How old Rabbit can't stand the bass in all them rock songs. *Dum-dum-dum-dum*, he goes, making this face like he'd sucked a sour, green persimmon."

"He tolerated small doses of the Phish. I would sometimes play. Through the PA at work. Only when closed, of course."

"No doubt. But me? Man, I sat there, eight years old, working my leg and digging the tune. I wanted him to shut up his old man's flapping gums so's I could hear it better." Awestruck and aching: "I remember every detail, like I'm still there in that truck cab with him."

"It's like. Somebody talking at a concert."

"Exactly—why'd you pay money, to listen to yourself yapping? I know I didn't. Anyhoo, he kept on about how with music today, or in 1976, I guess, you had all these gizmos and fake sounds and wasn't none of it, steel guitars included, like the music of the old ways. An essential I-don't-know-what had been lost, he said, with electric music. With rock-and-roll. With these enormous concerts folks put on, loud as heck and full of what he called flash-pots lighting up little British ponces strutting around in high heels."

"The world changed fast. For people like him. After the war."

"Especially music. Pa-paw grew up in coal mining country. He heard all kinds of folk music back then, ballads, blues, bluegrass. So that's where his head was at. He didn't much like modern country music, even, but we would see big shows over in Columbia all the time. Conway Twitty and Loretta Lynn at Collegiate Coliseum. I think that was in 1975—I threw up at that one, making them have to leave early, some stomach bug," waving off further explanation. "And more shows than I can remember at the State Fair. And one time we went to Nashville itself, to see Opryland. Lord, but Rabbit and Runelle both cussed up a storm about the Opry moving out of the Ryman and into an amusement park like ought to be in Myrtle Beach, not Nashville, as they said after they saw it all. I wasn't but a little tyke on that trip."

"Memorable."

"Hundred percent. We paid a visit to the late, great Hawg Hickens, who must've played The Dixiana a hundred times on his way to Nashville and minor *Billboard* country chart glory. By then he had had a few hit records, had got himself a big house. Far as I can remember, he just seemed drunk and fat to me. Smelled like cigarettes. Like a full ashtray of butts. Like, more than anyone should. A stink like death, which would come to him a few years later. The Original Outlaw, he called himself. Not enough to cheat death. I never heard any of those guys who came after give him the credit he deserved. I tried not to hold it against Waylon."

"Musician egos — they can be like that."

"But overall, a boring trip for me, except for a blowing snowstorm on the way back through North Carolina. I remember Pa-paw drove through that weather like it wasn't nothing special. Drove along with his finger on the wheel as though we were be-bopping along the river road on a Sunday afternoon. He said as much: 'Grandbaby of mine, this ain't nothing but a flurry.' And Mee-maw agreed, but still told him to slow down, be careful. Rock solid. Car didn't so much as slide once. I guess that seasoning was from when they lived in North Dakota. Brutal winters. Neck-deep snow, he said. Craziest stunt he ever pulled. Another thread of family lore. "Anyway, on the 'Crackerbox Palace' day, we got to Columbia, went to the Sears. I ran right to the records over by the display of TVs. It was Saturday, and they had this show called *American Bandstand*. Dick Clark? The new year's dude?"

Button's like, *yeah, yeah*. "I know about Bandstand and Soul Train, brother."

"Check. So Clark says, hey, we're showing a short film he calls a music video. And I'll be damned if it wasn't — ah." Overwhelmed by emotion.

She already knows: "'Crackerbox Palace.'"

Big smile. "Yeah. Total whoa moment."

"A synchronicity. Very, very important."

You show her your arm — chicken skin. "Shoot yeah, maybe the first time anything like that'd ever happened. And then my granddaddy comes up behind and gooses me, which wasn't like him to be so playful. And I'm all excited, and tell him to come look over on the TV, on all of them, fifteen or twenty all tuned to *American Bandstand*, and damn if it's not the song we were listening to on the radio just now. And he goes, well, I'll be dog. Looky there. He listened to it again with me. 'That don't sound too bad after all,' and he squeezed me on my shoulders. Said, go pick out a couple of records you want, son. That's what I did."

You note Button's eyes shining with moisture as you relate how you ran over to find 'Crackerbox Palace' in the new release singles, the 45s, and after a frantic search discovering only one copy, and stuck in the wrong file. "And yet I found it, like I was meant to. And so he bought it along a few for himself, too. You've seen the collection, which Uncle Burnie helped build — did you know that? At his store he used to order an extra disk just for Pa-paw."

"That's what. Best friends. Do for one another."

"Guess so. But yeah: I played that single over and over all weekend, real low, on my little-kid record player made of plastic."

She says she can visualize that eight-year-old you from pictures in photo albums. "You always had a sweet smile. That's all I remember."

Embarrassing. A chubster. A butterball with Reece's Cups under his nails. "Round as a pumpkin."

"It was forty years ago."

Button has a point.

"A few Christmases later I'd ask for a 'real' stereo, which we picked out at Circuit City. Lord, but you know Pa-paw griped about the price of everything, talking them sales boys down. '*I run a music hall*,' he bellowed. '*Ah know what sound reinforcement s'posed to cost*.' Mercy."

"I'm betting they cut a deal."

Nodding. "Nice set of speakers I came home with that day, plus a receiver, cassette deck, turntable. Separate components. Little blue lights, pulsing and flashing as the output peaked." You mimic the rhythm of the indicator lamps with your index and forefinger, a sideways peace sign. Your voice becomes hushed. Reverent. "Sitting there in the dark. Watching those lights throughout my adolescence. Pink Floyd. The Who. The Beatles. All the greats."

"That's so cool."

"The next year, and at his request, I asked Santa for one more piece of gear," tapping the cans. "A set of choice, mint headphones. They had the long cord, so you could walk around or lie on your bed all the way across the room. And crank it up. That's what I wanted to do most. So my Pa-paw wouldn't have to endure that thumping-ass bass. So that's my riding in trucks and listening to music story."

"That's why. You like to. Crank up the BÖC."

"Right on. But you wanted the Dead. I got just the ticket," and it's one of the remastered Europe 72 shows, the greatest tour, the smoothest sound, Pigpen rave-ups and classic 'China Cat-Rider' and 'Playing in the Band' coming into full flower as a jam vehicle. Garcia's guitar tone, warm and bubbling, makes an apt accompaniment to cruising high in the air.

By the time the big second set 'Dark Star' begins, however, you're already on the approach to the island, and deep space must wait. The trip has gone by fast, as if in a happy Grateful Dead dream. Music, like magic. Wheels down.

◎ ▥ ⊘

CUE THE "THRONE ROOM" FANFARE FROM THE *STAR WARS* ORIGINAL soundtrack album:

In the hanger, Ron Nawalinski and Hodges 'The Colonel' Ringholder greet you with a hero's welcome, all of you standing misty-eyed with fists upon hips, your faces blazing with an admiration more than mutual. The Colonel slaps his big belly with pleasure, crushes your hand. Ron, meanwhile, lean and buff like one of those bullshit pop-up ads you get on your websites with this white-bearded old dude rippling with muscles—*Learn This One Trick to Get and Stay Ripped*, an old guy's face photoshopped onto a cut torso because, somehow, the web crawlers know you're pushing fifty—grabs you in a bear-hug and almost re-breaks your clavicle.

And yet you don't notice the pain. All you hear is another mantra:

Nifty nifty; look who's nearly fifty.

Shudder.

You announce that you've parked the Piper for the last time. They're more interested in Button Sykes, however, a female human they act as though they've never encountered.

Especially when compared to Creedence. Your wife. Like, Button, polar physical opposite. You can't figure out what makes them more uncomfortable, the hanger boys: Button's dreadlocks, bundled and stuffed into a knitted head-wrap, her woven baja pullover and corduroy patchwork hippie pants? The Birkenstocks? The Colonel, he carries a wary expression of near apoplexy, as though Button a re-embodiment of 60s war protesters manifested here before his patriotic, POW eyes.

Or maybe it's the fact she's not your wife.

Nah. The marital troubles, it's not on their radar. And this with the scene that played out the day in September, out on the tarmac and here in the hanger. Couples split up every day. You and Creedence are one more. Next conversation with them will be about setting you up with an age-appropriate former trophy wife widow, an entire sub-species of female found on places like Sedge Island, as a personal investment opportunity.

Introductions; you depict Button as your 'cousin.' Her gentle spirit seems to win them over.

Ron, expressing grudging delight that he's likely got a fish on the hook to buy the Piper, sight unseen, on his word and the mechanic's report. What follows is a negotiation by proxy, and a suggestion from you that the asking price will fall below a million, which Ron says will ensure the quick sale he envisions.

"But I can't believe you're giving her up," in grief. "What a beaut."

"Bigger fish to fry," is all you can respond. "Priced to move."

"Bigger than flying?" The Colonel, rapping his cane with its golden-eagle handle against the concrete floor. "That I'd like to see."

"Guess I'll be keeping my feet on the ground for a while."

"But still reaching?" A big Button smile. "For the stars?"

Everybody but the Colonel chuckles and nods. Casey Kasem has recently died. You get a lump in your throat remembering how you listened to *American Top 40* every week. More music memories. You needed to make some new ones, wistful old man.

Enough of this. You punch up an Uber to take you to the house to get the Mercedes. Instead, however, a brouhaha erupts as Ron asserts with vigor his intention to drive you over the connector in his Lexus SUV, which he says is so new it 'still stinks.'

But this imposition upon him, it cannot stand—he is too important to play chauffeur, as you put it. The debate rages, but you finally acquiesce.

In bidding the Colonel adieu, you all leave him alone in the hanger, tapping his cane and staring into space from the sofa in the lounge, a flat-screen behind his head pixelling the latest from Fox News. You get the sense you won't be passing this way again, not much nor soon, except to transact with the buyer of the Piper. Another chapter, ending. New hobbies, in the works. One day.

For now, though, no plane means more cash in hand. What you'll spend it on, you haven't a blessed clue.

Platinum-plated beer taps for the rebuilt Dixiana?

Tiles of solid gold in the spruced-up restrooms?

Make it into a bar called Heaven?

Maybe you'll give the money to Button. She deserves to live better than she does. Damn that Uncle Burnie, pissing away his businesses. What kind of legacy is this?

And you? You've got nobody to whom to leave squat.

A problem—you could die anytime. What would happen to the money then? You'll have to change the will. Leave a chunk to Button Sykes. Yep yep. Action item for later.

Perhaps you'll bring it up; Button seems eager to talk to you alone. Says, she wanted to hang out today because she has important matters to discuss, and time short in which to do so. She conveys all this to you with a troubled flash of her dark, almond eyes.

Curiosity, piqued.

Hey, maybe she's ready to come around and switch teams. Whatever she's got to say, you experience certitude it's big; that it'll change everything.

Giving one final salute to Colonel Ringholder, who has followed and watches from the doorway to the hanger building in which you once felt so comfortable, you all climb into Ron Nawalinski's stinking Lexus for the ride across to Sedge Island proper, and your awaiting wife. You hope she'll be at least as interested in quirky Button as your hobby aircraft peers seemed, a condition upon which your scheme to sew seeds of jealousy in re-growing marshy reeds of reconciliation now depends.

CHRISTY BEAUDOCK AND NEWBIE HARRELL

Button's house. Christy, inside.

What?!

Yep. A burglary. Another'n in a series of crimes. But unlike the whole Dixiana mess-up, Christy, this time he tinkled first, out in the bushes where they'd been hiding.

The plan.

Waiting for the coast to clear out back in the thick hedges separating the property from the one behind it, even older, a big two-story house with porches up and down; a Southern mansion like so many in this neighborhood, one for sale for a long long time and with a way overgrown yard and who knew when it would sell, now: REDUCED screamed a red vinyl strip stretched across the real estate sign on the front lawn. A single rain-wrinkled brochure in a Lucite box on the realtor sign informed that they was asking $350,000 for it.

No wonder they REDUCED it, Christy thought and Newbie said aloud, which happened a lot. Christy's mind, more powerful than Newbie's. That's what Christy had finally figured out. Made all kinda mess make sense.

As they sneak in from the back kitchen doorway, a warped old screen door locked from the inside by a simple latch Newbie jimmied with ease, Christy, he notes how it reeks of musty oldness inside Button Sykes's house about as much as it does living in the trailer with Newbie, he who will not clean nor pick up after himself to save his life. Floor to ceiling with old junk, especially books and records and video tapes and magazines, scattered and stacked and tucked and shelved.

And upstairs in what he realizes is her bedroom room, books on stuff way beyond any sense of order Christy could put to it, here in Button's house in which they find themselves, him and Newbie:

ESP. Egyptians. Prehistorical civilizations. Who built the pyramids. Nazis. Mayans. Biographies of dudes with names like Edward Bernays and Edgar Cayce. Rudolf Steiner, which made Christy snort because they had messed up spelling Rudolph, which everyone knew. Duh!

And not Steiner but Stirner, Guenon, Madam Blavatsky, *Spiritual and Demonic Magic from Ficino to Campanella*, *Yeats and the Occult*. *Simulacra and Simulation* by Jean Baudrillard—another foreigner! hoping he wouldn't have to pronounce these names!—and Christy, he wonders if Button speaks other languages.

Plus, the subjects are totes bizarre: Astrology. Astral Projection. Alchemy, whatever that is, which sounded too much like algebra, a class Christy hadn't gotten near so he don't know what it means. But like Biology or Chemistry, Christy can look up on teh internets the info he needs. In fact, he needed a phone or a tablet to carry with him, but that took wireless and networks and hardware and money, and while his mind raced with all these durn old desires and needs, cash wasn't why they did this, not far as he's concerned.

Christy, he checks out this book she's got full of colorful little flags: *Psychic Self-Defense*. He opens it to Chapter 8, "The Risks Incidental to Ceremonial Magic." His eye, it falls on this line:

Everything which moves must have the equivalent of a thrust-block against which to push, something under its feet from which to take off.

Every little nubby hair on his body, alert like little soldiers at attention. "From which to take off." A vision of doing so. In a plane. But how to get there? A video game wasn't no real plane.

Newbie, pestering from outside the closed door. Christy had told him to look around everywhere else while Christy checked out Button's room. "What you finding in there, beau?"

"Books."

"*Books*? Do what, now?"

The loud, mean voice, the leave-me-alone voice. "I SAID BOOKS. NOW GO ON AND LET ME MESS AROUND IN BUTTON'S BEDROOM SOME MORE BY MYSELF."

"Dang. You're nuts, dude."

Christy wasn't fooling around anymore. He would show Newbie how nuts he could get, if that little butthole didn't start acting right.

More books: Tarot cards. Herbs. Magic. *In the Morning of the Magicians.* Magicking—protection, nature, a whole book on working spells with trees. A couple of books by Charles Eisenstein, a name Christy knew—the dude with the big hair and mustache, the scientist. Another volume called *Volunteers*, that from the back of it sounded like science fiction, this lady claiming that 'new' souls were incarnating here on earth right now to help with the transition out of the darkness and death of the 3D realm into the coming time of fifth dimensional consciousness, souls called Indigos.

Yeah. Christy felt that way, kinda. That he was here for a reason, a special one.

Another book was called *The Hermetic Order of the Golden Dawn*, which to Christy sounded like fantasy novel, more fairies and hobbits mess like out of *Lord of the Rings*, which to him was BORING—trying to read it all, sitting that long to watch it. Hours and hours longer than normal movies. Too much info all at once, Christy, he didn't get into all that. Little doses.

More books. Like one on her nightstand she'd been reading, about Millard Fillmore being all crazy against the Freemasons, back when dudes had those wicked big sideburns and beards like the fellas who work at the piercing place downtown. Maybe Christy would get tattooed at the Head Trauma. What he would get, he didn't know, sitting on Button's bed and feeling fat and out of sorts and irritated trying to make sense out of the book, and why he and Newbie had broken in today.

He knew what he could get: The symbol out on the plywood at the mill.

The hooked crosses.

Beards. Tattoos. Symbols.

***

SCATTERED, HIS THOUGHTS. HE DIDN'T KNOW WHY. VOICES. NAGGING. Pestering. Bad thoughts.

Being around Newbie all the time, maybe? Enough to make anyone go crazy.

Christy, weird vibes everywhere he goes. He ought to feel weird sneaking around in Button Sykes's house. But he doesn't.

His attention, it's drawn in particular to the stuff she's highlighted in pastel pink in the sideburns book: about how, prior to Fillmore's role in the Whig Party as Zachary Taylor's vice president and beneficiary of Taylor's untimely death, the thirteenth president's political start came as part of a 'single-issue political movement' and the first 'third party' in American politics, one that took its specific charge from a virulent and suspicious dislike of the elitism and secrecy of Freemasonry, whoever the eff they were!

Why Button Sykes sat reading this junk, Christy hasn't the foggiest. But then, she's into all sorta weird crap. Thing was, it made sense, a lot of that she talked about, with all her pamphlets there under the tent on the green. Christy misses seeing her and the little fliers and such. Misses Button fierce. He rubs his peter raw thinking about her.

In her wire trashcan by the computer desk, an outdated CRT monitor and dirty old keyboard and tower that had seen better days, Christy, he sees a discarded paperback, another book on magic—*Spells and Spirit, A Young Witch's Guide to Life.*

Inside the front cover, he's surprised to find an inscription which he reads with curiosity and wonder:

To Allyson B Sykes—

Have fun, but be careful! Magic is serious stuff. Pay attention to the warnings about using the spells designed to inflict pain. Only work with love. And never, ever open your circle without feeling gratitude in your heart.

Yours,
Heather P, Xmas 1997

Christy don't know who Heather is, but Button must have been real angry to throw away a book she give her. Look at all the books, the records, the video tapes and DVDs. Why would somebody throw this one away?

And why was Heather talking about magic like it's real?

Huh?

In any case, Christy, he says, I'm-a take this one with me. If she didn't want it no more. Slipping it into the big pocket of his cargo pants. One day him and Newbie went to the thrift store in Dentsville to got themselves new clothes. The Newb traded pills for cash, got walking-around money. His only talent. Burglarizing, a close second.

Like Christy's Daddy.

Going in a circle. Hanging out with this little turd.

Grrr.

NEWBIE'S ROTTEN FACE TREMBLED. HE HAD ARGUED AGAINST THIS burglary, their first since the day of the Shull house incident only two blocks away. "I don't get you. Maybe they got Crime Watch and we got seen. Maybe they been looking for us."

"Go home, scaredy-cat," lisping.

"What we looking for, beau?"

"Just chill."

Licking his lips, a quivering rat. "And do what?"

"Stay and wait for her."

"You seen the way they acted that night."

"Only because Pettus was there."

"Dude—she's scared of us. Of you."

True, maybe. Didn't stop Christy from wanting to slaughter Newbie for even saying it could be possible, her fear of him. Only his desire to avoid a mess and a problem to sort out in Button's house stopped him from being done with this turd. Had to speak with her alone. Without the bossman. No other way.

Since bashing Howdy's sister, they laid low. How they had skated clean, Christy, marveled that they blamed the death of the chattering old woman on her crazy brother. They shot Howdy over it. Decided without investigating—Christy kept thinking, fingerprints. If it was me, I would've dusted for prints and seen Newbie's all over every drawer in the house.

But, all worked out. Off the hook. Like magic. The verdict was true and permanent enough for Christy to move along and say, oh-well.

Still. Christy, irritated as can be. Newbie giving him fits, talking to Christy all the time through teeth gritted and grinding. Newbie, paranoid as all get-out. And about more than the gabby crone's murder—a favor to the world, not a crime.

Newbie, doing the crank. Skewing his judgment. Worse, Christy means.

He had had to figure out how to proceed with their relationship, and this had been his version of one of Newbie's big idea-rs. Not to knock and say 'Hi.' No. Waiting inside, the door shut, locked, and time to demonstrate his love without her running or freaking, or with the bossman around to cock-block him.

So, the plan, hatched; Newbie along in case Christy could not reckon on how to break in. A slippery little thief, the Newb could get himself into any door or window.

Firsthand info—Christy watched his partner and roommate do it on two burglaries they pulled after the bungled Dixiana affair, one a jimmied trailer in Mayfield Acres where crackheads lived for a while and left only filth like needles and spent rubbers and crusted, shitty diapers in a trash can full of maggots and flies.

A much better haul came when Newbie wriggled in through a dog door at a nice, new house down at the end of a block in Pine Haven, a family observed leaving on vacation, confirmed when newspapers piled up after three days and ransacking away. Inside, the thieves found pills and a few blu-rays they could watch on the game console. Took two bottles of liquor. A bag full of groceries and cleaning supplies Christy took from under the sink in the master bath, a palatial, unbelievable bathroom like ones Christy had only seen on TV. How they paid for this, Christy wanted to know. Now this he wanted to know.

Newbie, saying he would sell the pharmies to pay for living at the trailer, but Christy ain't seen no money out of it. Newbie, trading the drugs for crank.

Newbie—a problem, more than a partner. Took time during the robbery to knock these pictures of old people and babies off the mantle to shit on them, runny, loose stool he said had been cramping his gut all day, and no better place to put it than on these phony faker photos.

Look at the mess he made.

He's holding me back, Anakin griping about Obi-wan; here, a voice in Christy's head. Shrieking like a siren.

What to do.

Ah-ha—do a best friend trade-in. Say, Newbie for Button. As soon as today.

Houses all over the town sat empty. Christy could dump Newbie inside an old shed here at this place, or another like it, and no one would know for ages. Forever. Be done with Newbie and his mess.

Boy. What a relief. That might be.

✵ ▣ ⊘

As to Newbie's question, Christy, he didn't know what he was looking for. Books. Something about all the books—Howdy's books—and Christy, thinking he was meant to take books from Howdy's house. But which ones? Too late now. The yellow police tape still flapped in the wind the few times Christy walked by there, wondering if he might see the ghost of the old woman, if not Howdy himself. But only silence and the rippling plastic Incident tape, dangling and ripped.

But also: Button. Books. Getting smarter. To be close to her.

Dreams; dreaming of her standing a hundred feet tall in front of Christy, beckoning, flying into her loving arms. Button's face, floating and angelic. Waking up with raging erections that hurt. They were for her. No need to say it.

She looked sometimes like an old-fashioned woman, though, in a big billowy dress from long ago. Blazing red eyes, a demon-haunted pilgrim feeding the Indians at Thanksgiving, her dress and hair singed and smoking and with a pinched mean-old expression. But also still Button, somehow. Dreams, dude. Christy's are effed up.

What to do about Button; Christy, he would make sure she understood the importance of their connection. Christy, he had enjoyed her kind and lovely vibration, wanted to give back. That was the only word for it, how he blossomed in her presence on those afternoons back on the green—lovely. Precious and few, those times.

"I feel old inside." Christy had said this to Newbie the other night. "Sad and old."

"You ain't even eighteen yet. You ain't old."

"I just mean inside."

"Try this, you won't feel old." Newbie, raging the meth, still.

But Christy, cussing and turning his nose up at Newbie and saying, if it was me? I'd quit that mess. He's way into the meth, yeah; still no excuse to keep a dirty house.

Christy, watching day-by-day as his friend's face rotted. Getting green around the gills. Sitting on the same couch as his Daddy had.

His whole body, breaking out in a big goosebump: The spirit of his dead Daddy in the river, now come back as Newbie Harrell.

Newbie, he didn't even beat off to porn like they used to, all during Christmas after Howdy got blown up on the green. After Howdy's Sister got chucked but-good across her stupid talking head.

Christy knows he was wrong to've done that. But the murder had happened anyway, his arm swinging and under the control not of himself, but of another him that seemed to watch over and direct matters. The power over her also felt good. Bad, but good. After two times now of shutting someone up forever, not too shabby. A groove. Newbie would be fine.

Christy, feeling outside himself. Like in a dream. Like watching himself. Two of him. Like with his different voices he used on Newbie.

Yea, Lord, my hand, it is moved by thee. None but thee.

Coming into his head outta nowhere. Whose words were these?

Like, Jesus?

Christy, having panic.

Calming down.

Getting an idea. Considering magic, like in the book out of her trash can. Flipping through, reading some spells. One designed to attract love sounded right. Another to get revenge for wrongs seemed appropriate for another person—the bossman.

Right?! Magic to fix all these problems?

Sensing possibilities. Power.

Totally.

If Button had been into it, Christy suspected there must be secrets and wisdom about magic worth knowing.

"Dude, if you wait here for her she's gonna call the law, and they'll shoot you." Newbie, whispering and shaking like it's super cold but it ain't, kinda mild outside. "Sure as they blowed away Howdy Shull."

Furious at Newbie. "You can't remember nothing."

He's all like, "What?"

"Howard. Not Howdy."

"Aw, whatever, dude. His ass dead. It don't matter."

Christy, reckoning that the possibility of execution by cop presented an outcome to consider. He had thought that, with no Daddy no more, and no Grandmama who cared about him except in the way of piddling out dribs and drabs of folding money when Newbie run Christy to Red Mound to whine till she give it up, Christy, he—he might as well—

Wait—till she give it up.

That's what Christy had to have.

To make sex for his first time, and with Button Sykes.

Yo. Trembling at the notion. An urge unlike all others. Christy, he seen the porn and knows what they want: to be held down and done over like a jackhammer, in the butt, in the face after sucking on it for like twenty minutes and rolling eyes all around and choking on it. Amazed what he learned from looking at the videos over Newbie's shoulder.

But he couldn't no more do sex with her than he could with one of them movie stars on the computer. Button—afraid of Christy.

And like, nothing he'd do would change it, type-deal?

Unless: he done it to her whether she wanted to—so she could see how much he cared. You wasn't supposed to force yourself. But this was extreme.

If he did and she said no: then what? Chuck her across the room like that stupid old woman?

Oh, bother—why not, Christy?

No.

Might as well.

NO.

The voice in his head purred like a cat: Burn her up. There on the green. Like Caughman Howard Shull burned. Now there's an idea, dear.

Christy's short hairs went all stiff and he hollered out. Who was in charge of this brain of his?!

Standing in the house, stuffed and cramped with old people's furniture and books and an old TV, Christy holds his nose. No wonder it stinks. It's like a museum. And needs straightening up something fierce.

What is with people—Christy, disgusted. Tired of mess. Tired of the strange voice in his head, exhorting him to act.

◌◉◌

DESPITE THE HOUSEHOLD CLUTTER EVERYWHERE, CHRISTY FINDS Button's bed an oasis which out of all the crap piled everywhere in sight sits in a beam of afternoon sunlight all made up clean and neat, the pillow fluffed and centered. Dang nice bed like that, it made Christy fill up with love and warmth. Queen-size. With all this room, Newbie could pin her down. If she needed further convincing about Christy's love.

All he wanted was to put everything in order—in his mind, in his big jiggling gut, in what people called the 'heart,' but Christy, uncertain of this part of the trinity. Did his heart sit cold in his chest? He felt nothing about having killed the old woman, or his Daddy.

Well—maybe the woman. A doctor. Dang.

Crap. Maybe he had heard her voice in his head. Haunting him. A ghost now deranged as that nitwit gas-huffing brother of hers.

About Button, though, all inside swelled and throbbed, needing and urgent. Like she held ultimate knowledge he had to gain, and could satisfy only by stuffing her empty rollatini with his purple eggplant and making cheese sauce at the end. That's how Newbie had told Christy sex felt like with the girls at Christy's grandmama's place in Red Mound.

Out of the blue: Christy, in the dining room under an old chandelier dusted with cobwebs, hurting with a cramp in his calf. He beat the twisted muscle with an open fist. *Ow ow ow.*

"What the hale, big C?" Newbie lit up a cigarette, leaning unsteady in the kitchen doorway. "Twist your ankle?"

Christy, waving Newbie off and using the ordering voice for his friend to stay back. "IT'S ONLY A CHARLEY HORSE—I'M FINE."

"Dang, thought you got snake-bit."

"No."

"Now let's get on before somebody catches us."

"Ain't leaving yet."

"Beau—ain't nothing worth taking. Same as Howdy's house, junk and crud. Nobody got no iPads laying around. That's what we can move, bro. You can sell them at the GameStop over in Dentsville."

Christy, glaring and rubbing his calf. "Like you ain't told me that a hundred times already. I get it about the iPads and the GameStop."

"These old people on Whaley Way—the houses look like rich folks live here, but they ain't got shit."

"Ain't here to steal anyway."

Newbie, smoking and eyeing Christy. "I been trying to say something."

Christy, asking 'what' and limping across into the living room full of crap.

"You know who got money? Like, cash on hand, sitting there?"

Christy, eyeing Newbie and smelling fish coming off him. Noting his squint-eyes and the way his mouth sets cocked like he's scheming. Saying nuh-uh.

"That sexy old grandmama of yours. Don't you think?"

"I know she does. Last time she give me the twenties, she took it from a stack thick as a brick." Newbie, snapping fingers. "That's who we should-a been knocking over all along."

"We ain't robbing my Granny."

"You ain't gonna find no easier money nowhere, beau. All's I'm saying, yo."

Christy, looming. "But she's my granny."

"Christopher? Lemme spell it out: She won't let you live with her in that chill crib. Don't care what happened to her own son. And won't let you fuck the house-whores—beau, *won't even let you pay and do it*. That's fucked up."

Christy, whining high and mean. Little turd had a point, but still:

Simmering.

This close.

To knocking sense.

Into the boy.

Until he's like: "What kinda fambly she supposed to be? Leaving you to dangle like this."

Christy, his hands could already feel Newbie's neck, but pulling up short from going over and doing it with the cramping calf again. *Ow ow ow.*

A sign. How they wasn't to be here. In Button's place.

Was Newbie right? Should they bolt?

The pain, easing off. Vanishing, in an instant.

Another sign?

Christy, saying, maybe you're right. Getting out of Button's house, accomplishing nothing, not a durn bit except seeing that made bed. The thought of which felt good. So maybe that was all Christy needed. To find this evidence of their kindred spirit.

On the way out Christy, he makes Newbie try and try to get the screen door shut back like it was, but he can't; maybe no one will notice. It ain't nobody but Button and that old drunk of a grandfather of hers.

No—the bossman Pettus would see the damage to the door, Christy wagered. Dude didn't miss a trick.

Christy, concentrating hard on the thought: he was not here, he was never here, the reality of their visit only a dream, and that no one, especially not Roy E. Pettus, will learn of this half-assed burglary netting them next to nothing. At least in terms of folding money.

Christy, however, certain some small development had gone right, here. For once. The weight of the book on magic in his pocket, comforting and real. A score.

◦●◦

GOING TO HIS GRANDMAMA'S TO ASK FOR MONEY, ALONG WITH ONE MORE attempt about fucking the whores, wasn't working too good, especially with Newbie sitting on the couch with his leg bouncing and chewing on his thumb like a junkie.

"Christy, I can't half believe you'd bring this mongrel here and ask your grandmother for what come out of your filthy mouth just now. I'm—I'm mortified," searching hard for the word. "I feel like you done lost your durn mind."

Christy, embarrassed at having said to her what he did. That he thought he might die standing and explaining how to do his business with the girls was only right. For her to let him have one of his own.

What more can he say? "If I'm too big," Christy offers, "I can just squirt onto their faces. I don't mind." She can't half get the words out: "Son, hush —you fixing to give me a heart attack."

"Dang, bro. That's your grandmother."

Newbie, having a point: Christy, he didn't love her like he should a grandmother. He had his inkling like he had gotten with Howdy's sister. To give her what-for and make it stick. Be done with this back and forth. And this time, about more than money or making someone STFU — Christy would inherit the house, and the other with the girls, too.

Right. Who else would there be?! Game changer.

But it was hard. A bewilderment and softness in her eyes. Pitying him his request.

Like she was reading his mind. "Oh, darling. I can't let you do that. Not my grandbaby Christy. Not with them," whispering in shock. "Another girl. One day. Who'll love you like you ought to be loved. Not like this."

All that did was make Christy think of Button. "What's wrong with 'this'?"

She got that look like, well, ain't it obvious. Not to Christy, it ain't.

"Newbie here says it's fat as a double-stuffed sausage, that day he walked in while I was playing." His face now flames red, talking to his grandmother this way. "That's what I mean about too-big."

Her eyes already enormous, she jumps as a knock comes at the door there in his grandmama's formal living room, spotless and immaculate, with Thomas Kinkade paintings on the walls and clean, beige carpet and a glass coffee table with magazines. Sharp and hard and quick, another knock.

"Christy, sit down and hush, now. This is about business."

It's the durn gangster dude, Rembert. And one of his thick-necked thugs, one who rousted Christy and Newbie a few months before. They ain't been back.

Christy's granny tells the crime boss whom she has visiting.

"Wait, is this the 'little one' you always talk about?" Tipping back his hat, Rembert, all smart-ass as hell, says, "Nothing little about you, spud."

Busting a gut along with his thug, the black bro with the shiny head, Rembert smacked Christy on the arm, hard.

Christy, never having seen anyone laugh without smiling. The thug glares and cracks knuckles and gives him a nod that's scary. His stomach hurts at the inappropriateness of it all. Christy's grandmama, fawning all over Rembert and calling him Jezzie and rubbing his face and chest.

Christy, full of hate, also piss. Before coming in here to make his whining and crying request of his grandmother, he had not peed. If he pissed his pants again, like he had when Roy E. Pettus caught him and Newbie breaking and entering, Christy, he might think a problem besides the hard, hurting erections.

"You got off easy cause of your pretty old granny out here. Told me to back off, way the fuck off, her grandbaby." Snickering and icy like a movie villain. "Wish I had a deal like that. Mercy. You can't buy such a warranty, boy. Ain't many Mama Beaudocks what can work that out for a chubby little grandbaby like you."

Christy, saying, "I still ain't heard from Daddy no way."

"I'm starting to suspect," Rembert scratching his chin, "that Christy's Daddy suffered debts owed to folks other'n my organization."

Christy, scoffing. "Wouldn't surprise me."

"Now Christy," all loud and theatrical like the world's most regretful but conscientious-at-heart grandmama while cutting demon-eyes at Rembert, "your Daddy will be back when he runs out of money. You go on back to your trailer and I'll call you tomorrow. We need to talk every day."

"We do?"

"We got to pledge to do better."

Christy finds this a weak-sauce promise and wishes to say so, but he does not have the right words.

"Look here." The gangster, a greasy lizard sucking on a toothpick, rolling eyeballs up and down Christy. "What you boys think about that n-word preacher and him trying to take the name of our town away from us."

Newbie, a dumbass as always. "Ain't heard the first thing about it."

Christy, wheezing through his nose. "Don't make no difference to me."

"Y'all ain't got no durn pride in your history. I'm disappointed in you both. I'm-a tell you what. This generation's gonna run it into the ditch."

Christy's granny sucks her teeth and shakes her head, pats the skinny redneck's forearm. "Jez is right—this is about our heritage."

Christy can't stand his grandmama messing with this nasty man. He wants to bash in both the heads of Jezmund Rembert and his fat henchman who were mean to them. He thinks if he whines in the right manner, his granny will let him get away with killing them both. No doubt she would.

But here, on this fine carpet? Christy, his sneakers looking dirty, already feels shame at tracking in grime.

He wants out; but still needs to get money. He can't whine for it, not in front of those men. They seem to want to be alone with his Granny, and shoo Christy and Newbie on their way.

Whose house is this?

Or ought to be?

Christy should tell them how it is. And will, one of these days. Else the heads get bashed.

Christy, he knows what he's doing. Has been trialed-by-fire and passed on through, twice now.

Yeah—he can kill with a thought. A single decision.

Christy, holding back tears and his piss till his bladder hurts, but still he stands whispering to his granny until she relents and gives money.

Outside, Newbie, already waits in the truck, sits twitching and bug-eyed and hopeful Christy has the scratch, which he does. Christy, pent up. Thinking he should have stayed at Button's and waited. That this pittance of money was the universe's way of saying, you should've gone with your gut and kept on with Plan A, you big fat dummy. This gets you nowhere.

Another method of getting her attention would present itself.

All for later. For now he must hustle Newbie home and into bed, keep him away from the meth by lying about how many folded twenties he has, smelling of cigarettes and perfume and tucked into the pocket of his greasy jeans. Christy, he has Newbie to manage. And light straightening to get knocked out. And books to read and understand.

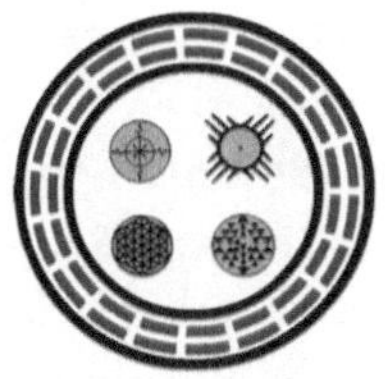

CREEDENCE, ROY, AND BUTTON

Another morning getting the Carolina Beanery up and running. The pillowy gray of first light, the dripping coffee, the fragrant pastries not as overwhelming and appetizing. The scent of toil, and duty.

LaVista Tucker, a friend of Sharolyn's from the off-island and as wide as she was tall, brought in that week's desserts, including a chocolate-peanut butter gluten-free vegan layer cake the health-conscious customers were buying up as fast as LaVista could bake and deliver them, a plant-based-cake-angel ministering to the fine palettes of the CBSI customer base, as Roy might put it. Not that the oldschool fatty and unhealthy cakes she also provided didn't sell, with the baker suffering the figure of a woman who sampled her own wares.

No judgment—Creedence, craving sugar like a candy-fiend. Her face, no longer puffy from drink, but her belly roll, jiggling and making its presence known. She'd get back into exercise. Soon.

Sharolyn had settled into her routine of working two to close, a full-day shift. But even with Creedence covering the early bird hours and the few part-time baristas they employed, they still needed to replace Estes. Despite both boss ladies hitting it seven days a week, Sharolyn, always behind an eight-ball of various and nonspecific financial pressures, and never one to turn down extra money.

Mistrust in the woman's eyes. Resentment. Knowing how much Creedence and Roy had, or at least an inkling. She must be thinking: why his wife here like this? They gonna get rid of my ass.

Not that Creedence was a mind reader. But sometimes she could see in people's faces what was in their heart. Like she did with Roy's boredom and distance. The way she saw the wonder and lust in Estes's dark, deep gaze.

Deep?

No.

More like the greasy perpetual puddle along the curb on the shaded sided of the building from the HVAC units—drop me in the shallow water, before I get too deep. A song she liked as a teenager.

Creedence, not having told Sharolyn yet about Roy's offer of full and legal ownership of the Carolina Beanery Sedge Island. That idea gave Creedence a spark she'd never experienced. Made her want to tumble out of the empty acreage of the king bed each morning and get cracking.

At her business.

Which felt so right.

Saying it that way.

Hers.

In the past, she'd always hated rising early. Something about being not-hungover and soul-sick every sunrise had changed her. Routine crafted her days, safe and familiar, well-trodden paths—the kitty chores, making up the bed, the green or blue smoothie, journaling, affirmations—I will not drink today; best I can promise—all before dawn, the gentle hours when peace seems upon the world. The kitties were still adjusting, but loving their dinner at four in the afternoon, which she served them after work but before taking her walk. Preparing and eating a salad with fruit, hitting up her meeting, and back home to sit sipping herb tea and contemplating the patio's mosaic stonework on which she once lay brushing against death itself.

The sanctity of the routine; little unstructured time. Her sponsor taught her much about discipline, what he called the necessary skill to acquire the three S's:

Sobriety.

Stability.

Serenity.

The recovery honeymoon, approaching half a year and feeling strong; nobody would get a drink of liquor down Chelsea Colette 'Creedence' Ruck-er's throat, not if her life depended on it. And that notion, boy—that this fall from grace couldn't happen—felt like freedom.

Oh, yeah: Rucker. That's how she thought of herself. Not Pettus. She'd kept her hyphenate throughout the marriage, anyway. Not now. Needing to feel her independence.

But poor Roy, holding onto hope. Too hard to decide either way. All too soon.

◌◉◌

With complications: Creedence, enjoying close attention from handsome Officer Phil Webhannet.

But, too young for a romantic partner—how she'd learned her lesson about that, oh boy—and yet, he had fallen for her and thought of getting close to him held a thrill. He hid it pretty well behind a wall of cop-coolness, but a woman picks up on vibrations. His reluctance to hug her, the main one.

They—the men who frequented the Beanery and sniffed around, most of them nasty, monied, liver-spotted retirees with jiggling throat wattles and enormous hairy earlobes—either tried too hard to have contact, or if they were truly trolling for action, not at all. Charismatic eye-twinkles, small gestures she noticed from a few of the handsome and monied, if ancient codgers she served. Rascals and wolves to the end. The thought of medically-enhanced, hours-long erections jutting and bobbing and lunging gave her the willies.

She tried not to bask too much in Phil's attention, his obvious and near constant presence at the CBSI. That's how bad Philly Webhannet wanted to make it with her, as a singer in an old 70s pop tune would have put it. The thought made her sigh, go all gooey inside.

Or, it's only a small island. Residents run across one another with frequency.

Forget it. Aside from the none-hugs, no fooling around, except perhaps in her mind while having a tub-soak. She may be separated from her husband, but until divorced next year—in South Carolina they make you wait that long, some old puritanical crap, she supposed—the girl held no plans for hook-ups with anyone. Another of the essential tenets of sober-success that Russ, her sponsor, had pounded into her head from the first weeks of rehab.

Not that she and Roy discussed divorce.

Yet.

But still, no linkages or fresh complexities on the relationship front. Not until a year of sobriety. And stability. And serenity. Maybe then.

◌◉◌

"ANYTHING YOU THOUGHT YOU HAD TO DO BEFORE—DRINK, DRUG, hookup with a partner, for a night or for a whole life, well, maybe you should consider the definition of 'have to.' If you wanna keep sober. S'all I'm saying."

Russ, craggy faced, bearded and older, advising her in the sandy parking lot outside the VFW where he hosted AA meetings. At first his poise and blunt articulation of the issues at hand attracted her to him, but like he said, in the early days of getting clean, addicts often look to a fellow troubled soul for answers they need to find inside through rigorous self-examination.

"Nobody can take the drink for you; nobody can put it down, either. Only you can decide what sober means for you, and in the end, how to get and keep it. Listening to the stories of others is a good place to data-mine the process. That's why I keep coming—because the process ain't gonna end. Not unless you want it to end, one day, when you find your ass sweating out the decision sitting in the familiar seat at your old favorite connection's crib, or in line at the liquor store, or rattling a glass of ice cubes at the familiar dive." Throat-clearing and indeed, shifting in seats. "Mine sits right around the corner. Pass by it every damn day. Difference now? Easy—I don't go in."

And no answers either in getting it on with a cop-kid, who'd turned out to be (gulp) a year younger than that aging adolescent would-be rock star Estes Patel. But Phil, a much more mature twenty-eight than her other lover, who by now had had his thirtieth birthday, a life-rending event he had been dreading. Maybe dude had gotten some sense. Fat chance.

One should never say never, she scolded herself, and people who wanted to change and growth possessed the ability to do so. Estes was of the generation who seemed to take longer. Longer to move out from the parents' house. To find a career path. To find themselves.

Look how long it'd taken her. Forty, but still searching.

Not Phil Webhannet. A man, mature inside and out.

Unlike Estes, her pal Phil had served, first in the uniform of the U.S. Army, and now in the crisp togs of the Sedge Island police force. Who understood about sacrifice, discipline and order. Not only a grunt; he'd been an MP, a military cop. In freaking Afghanistan. In the shit. And yet so neat, calm and collected, Phil, in his manner and vehicle and his person.

However: Creedence, already thinking, oh-boy. Another neat freak.

How would Phil put up with her and the sloppiness? Any better than Roy?

Why on earth was she debating with herself like this?

How silly. Silly little fantasies, because she hated being alone. Alone-alone. That's all.

Guilt; because no one anywhere could be any more alone than her husband, she figured. That couldn't feel too good for him, yet he kept on insisting it *was* good, it *was* right, and he had his hands full with all his plans to put in a coffee shop up in Tillman Falls anyhoo, now changed to rebuilding The Dixiana instead, some crazy idea.

Boy, she wanted to sit him down and talk to him about that. How, like here on Sedge Island, that coffee shop business was all distraction. A diversion from him not having true happiness and direction, like the alcohol abuse had been her own behavioral indicator.

He didn't want to hear it. She could tell that he still didn't hold much respect for her—that'd been much of the problem.

It was all right; since before Christmas, he had been kind. Kinder, maybe, than she deserved, but then she'd been sick; she'd been in the hospital. And Roy, whatever his faults, had always been mostly a decent man, as she now realized with her newfound clarity. But only because she'd been palling around with Phil, another kind guy, and in whom she saw so many of her husband's good qualities, and understood, now, why a kid—excuse me, a dude—like Phil Webhannet would look up to Roy E. Pettus.

Not so much he didn't fantasize about boinking his role model's wife.

Oh, but the lady, how she hinted hard with Phil that the marriage was over. Even when she hadn't been sure, yet, she'd still let on as though she were. Naughty girl.

He sparkled when with her. Rippled, like a hologram of a perfect and sexy and caring man. So much compatibility, sorta-kinda. Engagement and interest in what she thought and did, the people she hung out with when he wasn't around. With his standard-issue cop shoes, Phil Webhannet stood taller, even when she wore her wedges. Sigh.

❄ ▨ ⊘

ONE DAY BACK BEFORE CHRISTMAS, WITH HER GREEN, ANODIZED aluminum three-month chip sitting snug in her clutch bag, she'd asked Phil to accompany her shopping. While reluctant, being single, off-duty, and hanging around the Beanery left him little wiggle room to tell her no.

Creedence, feeling shaky about being alone down on Sedge Island at Christmas, aloneness that in her newfound sobriety after a bottoming-out seemed fair. Like penance well earned. But lonely. Needing someone to talk to besides Sharolyn, which at best offered a strained work-type relationship with little room yet for friendship.

She had no friends down here. It's why Roy's inattention had been so brutal. A purgatory. At least all this responsibility felt new.

Having seen Roy on a couple of uncomfortable occasions like poor Mama Runelle's funeral, from which Creedence had bolted as though being chased by a mountain lion, she would admit feeling not so much certain but rather a cloud hanging over any future relationship: control issues, lingering aftershocks of the affair, all the communication and respect problems that precipitated this marital crisis.

All of it made her remember all the reasons she'd slithered inside the booze-bottles—listing and counting, an inventory—and thinking, well, how am I supposed to stay sober if it all goes back to the way it was before? Especially now that talking matters through with people, strangers, had lent a different clarity.

"I do have to get my husband a gift." She clomped with Phil through the parking lot of the outlet mall across the connector on the mainland, being sure to remind him of his lower caste while letting him bask in her attention. "Roy's such a reader. At one time he mused on being a writer, or a teacher, before he found out how good he was at business-crap. So, I try to get him a book. Think a book's good? Considering everything? That's—dang it."

At first she couldn't finish and say 'gone on.' Phil might misread her intention and think a romantic hint dropped. But her impulsive streak, still wriggling inside. Wanting her to drink. Goading her to let loose, be naughty, get what her body wanted. "You know. Happened. I don't know what to get, to be honest. He has everything."

"Well, sure, sure. A book." He nodded with vigor and held out his hand, a well-trained traffic cop's gesture, to make sure the lady in the Mercedes rolling up at the crosswalk knew damn well she needed to stop for the pedestrians. "What's he like to read? Dan Brown? Tom Clancy?"

"Roy was an English major. He likes stuff that's over my head."

"Oh—you mean real books. You got me on that. I read for fun. When I was in the 'Stan, there was so much downtime, and everybody else stayed glued to their tablets watching movies. Me, it was a packed Kindle my grandmother sent along."

Creedence, trilling to Phil how thoughtful and sweet a grandmother had he. "I didn't mean to sound all high and mighty. Or make him sound that way. We're just good country people, really. From Edgewater County."

Phil laughed in recognition. "'Good country people.' That much real literature I do know."

"Where'd you go to school?"

He reddened. "I had planned to go after my service. I still might."

She got it—no college. No worries.

What could she say? She'd all-but finished her degree in graphic design, but other than helping Roy with the refinement of his dancing bananas artwork—more influence on the logo, actually, than he ever acknowledged—she'd done squat in her purported field of study. "Dunno why I bothered with college. Didn't learn anything I couldn't on my own."

"That's the way I feel about the army." A Jedi using the Force, he motioned at the automated mall doors, which slid open to receive them. "The officers? All these greenhorns with degrees, but not a lick of combat experience among them."

"So, is it true about the money?" Creedence squinted, looking for the bookstore.

"You're paid well. I was a volunteer. They reward you, but want you to go back."

"No—all that money. Those billions of dollars shrink-wrapped on palettes we dropped over yonder. Dunno why we can't take the money and—fix stuff here."

"That was back in Iraq." Webhannet bristled. "Now listen, that's nothing but Michael Moore talk. If we did spread some cheddar around, though, it'd've been for a good reason. To support the seeds of democracy. It's why I risked my life in Afghanistan. Those people have been craving freedom for longer than any of us can imagine."

"That what the war's for?"

"What else?"

Wondered if she should press ahead. "Thought because of 9/11."

"All connected. If the towel-head mullahs had the decency to give their people freedom, none of it would've happened, ma'am. Surprised you're so interested in geopolitics."

Her husband would have been irritated by Webhannet's anti-Muslim racial epithet. "Roy and I used to go to the war protests down on the corner in the Old Market in Columbia, before we moved down to Charleston. We watched all them war documentaries back then. That money on the palettes, it was for—to pay off—" She stamped her sandal. "Dang it. All that's starting to seem like a long time ago."

Frosty. "That's liberal bull, ma'am."

"I dunno—I think it might be more than just partisan junk."

"Don't believe everything you hear."

"Really?"

"That's correct."

"Phew. I'm relieved." Her arched eyebrow intended to convey mild sarcasm, but the young cop didn't seem to notice.

She asked him what it had been like overseas. He repeated about the loads of downtime, and after deployment—his 'MOS,' he said, whatever that meant, was as a 31B, which meant military police, and involved convoy security and occasional detainee operations—he had been glad to return home, if for no other reason than to smell clean air.

"Clean air? It's all polluted?"

A sense of decorum flitted across that handsome face. "Smells like feces."

"From what? The livestock?"

"Manure would've been an improvement. No, ma'am. It's a third world country. I'm talking untreated sewage. You really don't know how good we have it."

"Oh, my."

"Another reason they need us, and our money. They don't even have the sense to cart away their garbage. They just pile it up outside their stores."

"At least they got stores."

"Not like we have. Little markets."

"What'd you do with all the time you weren't doing MP stuff?"

"MWR." Morale, Welfare, and Rec, he explained, meant going to the gym, watching movies, and wi-fi so that troops could Skype with loved ones back home. "Everybody's got a hard drive full of content. But you could also buy bootleg DVDs from the locals. How they got them, I don't have a clue. I got to see that last *Star Trek* movie, the remake, the same week it opened here back home. Perfect HD picture and all. Damnedest thing, those bootlegs."

"All the way over in Afghanistan?"

"Content piracy, it's a scourge. A problem we ought to stamp out."

She'd read a story on the internet about how more heroin than ever flowed out of that country. She wondered about the opium still being grown. How, if we spent all that national treasure, as Roy would say it, to occupy the country, couldn't we manage that problem? It didn't make sense. If it was bad before we got there, and worse now...

On the verge of asking Phil about that discrepancy in logic, they rounded the corner in the outlet mall where she thought the bookstore to be, and her breath caught in her throat: Creedence grabbed his hand, a brief tug she released after only a hot second of contact. The B&N had a massive, red STORE CLOSING banner draped across the front.

"I'll be shit—going out of business? With all the snowbirds with their beaks in books around the pool, and on the beaches?"

Phil, blasé. "I order from Amazon. Download whatever I want."

"You never have to plug in a book, though. All you need's a candle and cozy couch."

"True that."

In the bookstore, Creedence spied a modest display of the latest from Cort Beauchamp, Edgewater County's own contribution to modern letters, alongside two of his older titles, both of which already rested comfortably on the shelf at home, signed editions Roy's grandmother had gotten when the author had done local signings during the ELMS's annual Springfest. She knew deep inside that the coincidence presented as the easy answer to her question of what title out of the thousands in the big bookstore to buy her husband. Perhaps the continuity with his past would make him more comfortable with the disruption in his present. She took a moment to read the compelling and appreciative blurbs on the back of *The Diary of Anna Dixon*.

When she pointed this out as a gift idea, Phil read the back cover with a wrinkled nose born of clear concentration.

"Sounds good," he finally said. "Kinda like *Gone With the Wind*, though."

"Burning of Columbia instead of Atlanta."

"I don't read too many historical novels."

"Whether he reads it don't much matter. The thought. And the connection. To Edgewater County."

"A meaningful gift idea, Mrs. Pettus."

"Please—call me Creedence."

How he'd smiled at that. Beamed. And she'd tingled.

And said, oh-shit. Here we go.

But if it were to happen? She wanted to make Phil wait, and not only because of the one-year rule, whether it was South Carolina's divorce laws or Russ's rehab advice. Not be so easy—she felt newly protective of her physical body now. Booze had made her stupid. Now she felt smart. Not as much smarts as she needed long-term, but her sponsor had prophesized a rose garden of increasing clarity unfolding for years as she fully detoxed from the alcohol and pills, as well the psychological baggage leading to 'the condition of abuse,' as he liked to put it, always using the air-quotes. Russ had been leading meetings for ages, had his routines down. Twenty-three years clean. Damn.

Years—she didn't want to go that long alone. Maybe Phil Webhannet would wait until she was all better. And free from Roy.

Free from Roy. The phrase filled her with dread. His sweet face and soulful, tender eyes. Creedence, stabbed in the gut by guilt. It came in waves, often unbidden.

Spastic, she grabbed up a copy of the Beauchamp book, in doing so upsetting the stacks of his old paperback titles, including the edition of Keys to the Rain she remembered taking on that godforsaken hiking trip that almost finished their marriage even before the affair. Hurrying along with a sheen of fine dew settling on her skin from an incipient panic attack, she exclaimed how she needed a couple more gifts, shouting and asking whether Phil wanted to buy anything. He shook his head. Seemed a little spaced out, lips parted, eyes drooping.

Until: someone on a nearby aisle dropped what must have been a hefty coffee-table book, a loud boom. It prompted her companion to hunch and flare a stare in that direction, flinty and cold like drawing a bead.

Poor boy—he's got PTSD from being in-country. She wouldn't ask, though. Seemed too personal.

✸▣✦

PURCHASES IN HAND AND HAVING CALMED, CREEDENCE DIRECTED PHIL to the front. "This is fun," gesturing in an arc like, can-you-believe-the-splendor? "Christmas shopping."

Phil, standing on the other side of the roped-off checkout line at the bookstore, moved alongside Creedence as she inched forward and waited to swipe. "Since when was Christmas shopping un-fun?"

"Oh, lord. With mama, rest her soul? An ordeal of drama and arguing."

"Ordeal?"

Creedence arrived at the counter of the B & N Last Chance Remaindered Outlet® to pay, did so with a swipe of her check-card, a new account she'd set up; grabbed her plastic sack full of Cort Beauchamp and little-kid books for Roy's cousin's twins, whom she always tried to remember at holiday and birthdays, even though Roy had never given two poops about the boys.

She speculated he held against the children that their parents had named them Dale and Dale Junior, which she had to admit seemed perverse. She tried not to recall how enraged her husband had been when the elder Earnhardt had crashed his car and died, and all the NASCAR fans were on TV crying, and how he'd ranted and cited the over-the-top displays as an example of the vapid nature of all this fan worship of a redneck who'd learned to drive fast in an oval, and this, too, a reflection on the stupidity of his own blood-kin for naming twin boys after a father and a son. Whenever she called her husband out on his dismissive, nasty view of anyone else's preferences if they didn't suit his particular set of aesthetics, he always justified it by saying, that part of me who's unafraid to call BS has taken us this far. He said, *You think nice guys finish first? They don't.* She didn't miss that side of him. Wondered if he had the capacity for change necessary to avoid the outcome that had so terrified her earlier.

"Mama," Creedence recalled, directing her young beau—no, no, no, a friend—down the holiday-decorated outlet mall breezeway toward the Levi's store, "always had to have a big-old list of things we wanted. Whatever our little hearts desired."

"Wow."

"Within reason. We didn't have that much money. Not like Roy and me do now. But we done all right, the Ruckers. Daddy worked himself hard as a rented mule, so I reckon we ought to've."

He asked what her father did. She described his insurance company, a State Farm affiliate. Her mother, too, one of the powerful and prestigious civil leaders in her role as one of the ELMS. How a mighty tree along the courthouse plaza had been named the Rucker Oak in her parents' honor.

He seemed awed. "Trees around a courthouse square symbolize mighty figures, pillars of any community. That's tremendous."

"Daddy was real good at his job. Had offices in three towns. He'd been coming back from the one in Union the day he—got sick."

"Cancer?"

"Heart." She crossed her eyes and twisted her fist in front of her chest and said *Ack*. "It just come on him all sudden. He didn't suffer—pulled over in a gas station parking lot with his chin resting on his chest. That's how they found him, peaceful as can be. Thank the lord."

"That's good."

"Anyway, me and Devin—that's my brother—when we got to be smartass teenagers? We would sit at Thanksgiving and laugh and make up fake gift lists. After dinner, that's when she pulled out notepads and pens, saying, it's time to write to Santa, little ones." A stab of grief—she reckoned you never quite got over losing your mom. "She was still making us do even after Devin went to college."

"Mothers are sentimental."

Nodding. "But one time? When he was about fourteen? He wrote that he wanted all these different weapons—guns, bazookas, mortar rounds, tanks. And at the bottom, '1 standing army of 500,000 nationalist zealots and a signed first edition of *Mein Kampf*.' Just pure-T silliness."

"*Mein Kampf*? You mean like, Hitler?"

"The same." Trying not to notice how troubled her companion seemed, she draped an arm across Phil's shoulders and leaned on him going *haw-haw-haw*.

She led him over to sit on a bench vacated by an old man in colorful golf clothes, who at her merry outburst had hurried along as though he'd forgotten an appointment.

Children ran screaming up and down the walkways, women pushed strollers, the smell of roasting nuts from a vendor and holiday decorations—business seemed strong. That's what Roy would notice. "What's wrong, suddenly?"

"What's so funny? Hitler was a monster. Evil. Y'all should've taken him to the doctor."

"Mama didn't think it was too amusing, neither. Either, I mean. Poor, messed-up Devin. He had himself one sick sense of humor."

She noted the time, realized she had a meeting starting soon. Meetings—she'd been hitting one a day since getting out of the hospital. And already worried about missing on Christmas Day, or what she might choose to do—her aunt and uncle, who had heard about the breakup and the alcoholism and who lived in the upstate, and called to ask her up there to stay with them. Maybe she was to ride out the holidays by herself in the mansion on the marsh. Creedence didn't know if a suffering phase for all her bad behavior were necessary. Not with the self-punishment she'd already put into the effort.

Not punishment. Temptation—the universe dangling this hunky attentive man like bait.

Like a test.

At her car, she leaned over and kissed Phil Webhannet on the cheek, resting her warm hand on his forearm. She knew she was keeping him stirred up. Couldn't help herself—the beam of his attention made her glow inside.

A year. A year before you try again. She pictured Russ Wetherell shaking his head and saying, girlfriend, don't do it.

Discipline.

Deep breath. "I don't think we'll be able to see each other again. For a while." Her words leapt out, followed by a mild backtrack. "What with the holiday week coming up. Maybe in January."

"I'll be by the house. To check on you. Of course."

"No—please don't."

He stiffened. A cloud of disappointment. "It's part of my job."

"Right. But still—I'll see you after the first of the year."

He turned scarlet. "But Mr. Pettus, he asked me to—"

"I'm separated from my husband. I make my own decisions now."

With that he lingered in silence. Phil leaned in like he wanted another little hug, but at the last second turned on his heel and high-stepped toward his budget sedan, indeed, stiff a conflicted soldier boy marching off into an uncertain skirmish.

Trying to hide his hard-on, she suspected. Sweet boy.

Good. Phil Webhannet was sure to continue pining for her throughout Christmas. And with her thinking about him thinking about her, that would keep assuage the loneliness. Or did that sound crazy? She had no one to ask but herself.

◦▣◦

IN MID-JANUARY, CREEDENCE SUGGESTING HOSTING RUSS'S AA GROUP at the CBSI, closing an hour early to put up a sign reading PRIVATE FUNCTION. Musing that day about doing the meeting regularly, now, which would mean closing at least one night a week.

Sharolyn, scrunching her mouth and looking sidelong like, and I'm supposed to say no to you? "What's Roy think?"

"It's okay—I can decide."

A good meeting. Creedence didn't talk, only listened.

Afterwards, Russ stayed to help her clean up. Every time he came near, she got a little charge. When she looked at his expression, however, none of what she felt could be seen, a stone cold iceman. A man of creeds, codes and discipline. On the satellite radio, the 70s channel, 'When Will I See You Again' by the Three Degrees. Listening to that station made her feel like a kid again, sitting in her mother's kitchen in a state of graceful ignorance about the adult complications and tragedies to come.

Instead of flirting with Russ, she voiced some of what she'd written in her last letter to Devin—about her marriage, Roy's clear generous feelings, his accommodating take on her announcement it might be over for reals, y'all.

"But now that I've said all that, his sweetness, it's the old him again. Like he's sloughed off this skin of evil that came over him the more Spotted Bananas he opened."

"The real guy? As in, the one you fell in love with?"

"You know what? It's true."

"Hear how that sounds? Add in the forgiveness."

Russ knew all the details. That Roy'd read the love letters. Seen the level of intimacy. Had her dead to rights. And yet still forgave and forgot. God, how confusing. Russ, Phil, Roy.

Sweet Roy Earl.

Who'd made all wonders and riches possible.

He hadn't been the only one wrong, selfish and mean. They had made their reality. Which meant, couldn't they fix it together? How strong the team? She'*d* been a partner with him. They weren't OINKs; they'd been DINKs. He'd even said it himself. They got bored—with each other; with themselves. And she ended up drunk. A drunk DINK who oinked and let a boy stick his peterpiper in her and jizz.

Gracious sakes alive. Poor Roy.

"I think I made a decision tonight," Creedence setting the alarm and Russ holding the door and turning the key, the satisfying clunk of the lock tumblers falling into place and another day of business recorded into the books. "For once, I can see my way through all that happened. And where I might-ought to go from here."

"Your husband sounds like he's asking for his rebound shot. I dunno. From what you've told me... it could've been worse."

"And here I'm the one who should be begging. Shouldn't I?"

"We don't judge these personal side-trips." Russ slipped on his leather jacket. "Maybe there's a balance to all this guilt and forgiveness. You won't know, though, until you put them both onto the scale."

He jacked his Harley into life, gave her the raised fist of sober solidarity and roared around the Beanery on its prime out-parcel near the main traffic circle, like a welcome station to the entire resort area of the cypress-shaded, moss-draped island called Sedge.

Home.

All she need do was let Roy finish his business in local-yokel land, get him back here, and they'd see if they could pull themselves a reset. More difficult feats than this had been managed, and all things reconsidered, he deserved as much of a shot at growing and changing as the one she had been granted. A bloom of warm certitude in her gut; a feeling to follow.

❁ ✦ ❃

BACK HOME IN THE KITCHEN, SISSY THE SASSY TORTIE, ROY'S FAVORITE kitty, lead the charge of meowing rascals ready for their overdue nighttime crunchy-munchies—the chubby, short-legged girl had been so sweet since he'd been gone, lingering in the places where his shoes once lay, on his side of the bed.

Creedence took Sissy's crying as a sign to say HI to her husband via text, which she'd do after getting all the fur-babies squared away. Maybe send him a smiling selfie, but only after she freshened up, combed her hair, put on some lipstick.

What was her deal? Dang.

She needed to go back to him. Yes. Settle her ass down. Act like a grownup.

She can hear her mother saying it. Wouldn't Eileen Rucker have been so disappointed, especially over the adultery. And now, for lusting after the cop. A boy.

No—a man. A soldier. Money or not, Roy seemed soft next to Phil.

She prayed, and not for the first time, that heaven was a hoax. That her mother hadn't seen what a mess her daughter had made of her life.

You wait and see, Mama, as she later dreamed herself saying, lying in bed on the cusp of drifting into sleepyhead slumber. Seeing Roy's kindest face, smiling and happy. Beaming love to him, a warm pulsing in the center of her chest, an activation like ET's heart-light. She knew it was silly, but as her thoughts took turns she couldn't expect—faces and people she didn't know streaming through the cascading kaleidoscopic images that tumbled across the optic field of her mind's eye, the coffee shop customers and baristas and folks like that, she reckoned—Creedence hoped her hubby could feel her thinking about him.

BUT HER FLIP KEPT FLOPPING.

I should get back with him.

No, I shouldn't.

I should. Shouldn't I?

No. Wait—I dunno. Maybe.

Or not.

And so on.

Add in handsome, sweet Phil hanging around so much, and a stew of confusion.

Only a few days ago she'd talked to Roy, hinting about seeing him to discuss 'stuff.' He noted, "Gosh—for separated people, we sure are calling each other a lot."

"A marriage being put to bed can't be easy or quick."

He'd fallen silent for so long she thought the call had dropped. "That what we're doing?"

"Maybe."

"I can't thrive on uncertainty. It's either yes, or it's no."

"Don't force me into a corner like that. It's too complicated."

"What's difficult about it?"

"Everything."

"There's no third parties, right?"

A brief pause. "No."

"And you're sober?"

"Yes."

"Well, I don't see what the prob—"

"Two to tango, dude. Don't forget that."

Pissed as hell. She heard him utter a curse word, the sign of extreme emotion on his part. At that he'd hung up, sparing her one of the old angry outbursts.

Only later did she realize her choice of words had been poor, that the tango bit had multiple meanings and layers; culpability in sewing confusion, plentiful. She knew she didn't have good sense.

Knowing wasn't enough. She needed discipline. Structure to her emotional responses. Not just structure to the time spent to keep from wandering off and getting drunk.

Maybe she wanted to piss him off anew. To quit on her for keeps.

But again: the panicky NO feeling. Creedence prayed again, this time that a sign would come, a notion or event that would give her firm direction one way or another.

Speaking of freak, though, when Roy arrived at the CBSI with his little hippy girl-toy, showing off and shoving her right in Creedence's face, at first she became angry; later, more confused than ever. But mostly angry.

Boy, was he gonna get it for this. Whatever this stunt was supposed to prove, no way would Chelsea Colette Rucker—or Pettus—sit back and watch some skank steal her man, especially not another Edgewater County shit-ass. Nuh-uh. Not a freaking chance.

MANNY, NEECIE, LILLYANNE, THE REV. DR. ROOSEVELT NIXON AND THE YUNK-YUNK

Manny keep pondering the worst part of this shit.

He watch the babygirl come stand near the board on Saturday night during Manny set break. The band hot tonight, him ripping off solos like a man half his age, up and down the scales through 'Me and Baby Brother' with the whole band singing backup. Manny got Neecie up, and the place go ape. She do 'Ooh Child,' and wrapping up the set with a bad-ass 'Street Life.' She hot; shout it out loud. People be ordering doubles from that bar, they so excited.

But while Manny dumping spit and mopping up sweat, Lillyanne hit him with big wet eyes glaring right through his ass. Wouldn't even side-eye him since he get kick out the house. Keep asking, what it all about. Got to do with Ahmad, she think, cause he out, too.

She wait and let Manny rap with regulars and solid tippers, an old couple dressed sharp as a tack who drive up from Columbia every weekend. They say it for the barbecue, but he know it because his hot five has been raging it onstage, honking hell out that horn, good wet reed all broke in. He woodshed every day. Been listening to deep spiritual cuts like Pharoah Sanders. Soothe his troubled soul.

Ain't got laid in a month, now. Becky L, done with his ass. Which hurt.

Manny, he ain't know how them two—Becky L and Neecie—sit cross that big table at them ELMS meetings. Women got they way of working it out, he reckon.

"Want you to do something for me." The babygirl and her eyes. Lillyanne. Mercy, but she like grown up as all get-out, all sudden. "Daddy."

Manny, discreet, dumping the spit valve and grinning at tables full of his customers. His fans. Daughter gonna insist his ass come home. Maybe this Neecie way, working through the little one. "Anything for my babygirl."

"I want us to go to church tomorrow."

Manny like to drop his sax. "I ain't getting nowhere near it."

"I want you to go to Reverend Nixon's church to hear the music."

"They put on some old-time gospel. Don't they."

She talk about going to church with one of her little friends. Of opening her heart. And having it filled by Jesus.

"I didn't know you was all about church."

"Maybe if you were home," sounding all sassy like her mama, "you wouldn't get so surprised."

Manny, saying it ain't up to him. Would be back home if he could. "Tonight."

"Mama say you ain't seeing your friend no more."

Manny like to shit. "Yo, now. You watching too many stories on TV. Your daddy don't got no girlfriends, not other'n you and your mama."

Lillyanne smirk. "Get on with yourself, Daddy. For real." Voice breaking, like Manny a teenager, too. "It the truth."

"Might be good you moved out. You ain't no kinda role model for me."

"Don't talk like you no downmarket ho off the street. 'You ain't no?' Your friend Nevaeh talk like that? Do that big-old bear Nixon? Starting to think I need to get my ass back home for sure."

Walking off like women do: cutting her dark eyes back, pissed as hell. His babygirl got that part down already. "Don't rush home on my account."

"Aw, snap." Best Manny can come up with. "Come back to your daddy."

Babygirl flip him off and disappear through the kitchen doors.

Manny, about up to here with it, now—Neecie done turn babygirl sour on him. But he say, aw-ight aw-ight: I'm-a gonna do right. Come and pick up and go to ever-loving church with my women on Sunday.

He hear tell old Nixon's church ain't packing them in no more, not now it's his oldest boy preaching the main sermon. Since Nixon's on council, he say he got a lot riding on trying to seem impartial. That what he doing over getting the name of the town fixed up the way he want can't be for no religious reasons.

Manny, he don't give two squirts bout none of it. Learn his muh-fucken lesson after Dobbs write up what he say in the paper about the change. Damn if old Mauldin Saugus drop in with Nixon one day, both putting the hard press on Manny for his endorsement—a god-durn congressman, eating Manny slop and being all like, now, we got to get on the same page and so on. Manny say, Neecie own the business. I ain't do nothing but cook and honk. What I think and say in the paper don't matter.

Damn the money sitting in the floorboard of the old Pettus house. Damn Roy E. Pettus for being such a good cat. Manny wish his ass was corrupt or irritating or some shit. Anything to deserve losing that bread. But he ain't. Otherwise, not sure his ass wouldn't jet from all this. Go out for a ride and never come back, just like The Boss sing with the Big Man honking in the background to give him the juice to make that shit stick. Word.

ON THE WAY TO CHURCH THE NEXT MORNING, MANNY WITH A HANGOVER after drinking too much gin sitting by hisself out in the house in the woods till five, looking at damn TV till his muh-fucken eyes feel like they dried out. Better for them to dry out with that vape of Roy Pettus, but that routine, it fixing to be over.

One thang fo-sho: ain't got no business drinking liquor. Not being an addict. Deep down, and way back, but still there.

Picking up them ladies of his, he get bitched at for not having clean out the car. Plus, the babygirl still giving the stink-eye. Bad vibes.

"Tell him what you told me." Neecie lean back, big eyeballs bouncing between him and the babygirl. "Go on, Lilly."

Put upon, teenager style: "About what."

"About the Yunk-Yunk."

"Sigh."

Long ass time since Manny heard tell of the Yunk-Yunk. "That old thing come round and bother my girl again?"

"It's stupid. I shouldn't have said anything."

They cross onto the bridge over the Sugeree, thin and brown way below, more rocks than river. He wrench around. "You having them bad dreams again?"

"It's nothing." Lillyanne's eyes fly wide. *"DADDY—!"*

Manny jerk his neck back to the road in time to see his ass drifting across the center line right-smack at one of them chicken trucks, unloaded but still shedding feathers, from the processing plant. He yank the wheel of his Olds, a car they inherited from an old uncle of Neecie's who died last year and that Manny been driving. Horn blows, truck driver shakes a fist, but don't nothing worse happen.

Manny, he like to shit, but don't act none like it. Still steering with one finger on the wheel. Ain't broke a sweat. "Y'all calm ya asses down."

Neecie breathe fire. "No wonder she's having nightmares."

"Don't you worry bout no Yunk-Yunk."

Manny, ignoring the oncoming truck drama and Neecie and her dry-ass accusatory junk. Lillyanne had been having bad dreams even before the storm hit. It take her until, hell, only a couple years ago to get rid of The Yunk-Yunk, who was like Swamp Thing or some shit, coming up outta them rising bayou waters. "Thought we left that nig—that mo-fo behind in N'awlins."

The levees being topped. It affect him, too. Had his own bad dreams. Scare his ass. It's why he didn't mind moving to this po-dunk burg.

His biggest worry back before the storm? Not knowing if he could stay clean. Another reason to bolt the ward and keep gone, and this was even before it got all apocalyptic and flooded, yo.

Truth: Manny had sidemeat issues back in the day, too. Running with the wrong crowd. Drinking too much. Fucking. Wearing rubbers though, yo. Ain't no babies or infections. None Manny know of.

"Maybe you left the Yunk-yunk behind. But I doubt I will ever be able to do so." Now she making fun of Manny, Miss Perfect Diction. "I've suffered fresh trauma."

"You need ya old man home. To help keep that rascal on the run."

"Does *Daddy* need to return? That remains the question." The daughter may have asked, but both women sit girded, waiting on a muh-fucken answer.

Manny get a certain ugly zing inside when the voice go, well, this it, big boy: you saying goodbye to Becky for real with this next move: "Maybe I ought to pray on it today. At church. With my folks at my side."

Both be like, oh, yeah, sure. Like they hear his inner debate; we ain't stupid.

But the joke on them—Manny halfway mean it. He all repentant and shit. The sting from loving Becky'll go away soon enough. "For real, yo. For keeps."

❊▦⊘

THE CALVARY FULL GOSPEL CHURCH OF THE HOLY REDEEMER, A HIGH-peaked roof with clear-as-pin-drop acoustics and custom stained glass that had all sorta kinda shit in it, Egyptian symbols it look like to Manny, and tons of sunlight streaming in, which is what catch his eye. Mercy, but he glad people don't wear coat and tie no more. Everybody here look like they corporate casual, Manny sharp in a black Ralph Lauren polo and shiny Armani flat-front slacks that give his dick good definition down his left thigh, and Ray-bans, which Neecie stick nails in his arm to make him take off.

The music ain't far off what Manny play at his joint: in an alcove next to the choir they got this electric band, guitars and synth, big sound. Diverse — lotta yuppie white people with nice cars in the parking lot, lake country folks. Whole deal feel like money, stuck out here on the county line and cut out of a bunch of scraggly loblolly pine barrens and brown clay, a great square of smooth blacktop and modern building materials, all new, or at least recent.

Only the wooden sanctuary off to the side still a sign of the oldschool past here in the far eastern part of the county. Neecie people come from back yonder, down near where the lake is now. Little towns where people lived, all underwater now. Graveyards and shit. How her granny talk about it and be sad for places nobody ever able to go home to again.

Be that way in N'awlins, if they not careful. Next time, a bigger storm. Who know.

Manny, he don't care if he go back again no way. Even though he keep thinking, he could take that Pettus money and go. Gig; go on the road. Get on with Preservation Hall. Safe paycheck shit. N'awlins tourist-trap music. Bust loose on a fresh crib, play six, seven nights a week.

Start over.

At Manny age. At fifty.

What this muh-fuh saying to himself?

Manny sitting at church in South Carolina with his wife and daughter, that what. The service bout damn near put Manny to sleep, unless the music got going and they was some foot stomping gospel like he hadn't heard in ages, decades.

Nixon's son Eusebius, the head preacher now, and in fine form. Young, but some edge on his sermon, which Manny don't half pay attention to. He thinking about Becky L and her body and never being with her again. Saying, fuck, lord. This shit hurt.

There we go — the Lord. Ask for help with this mess.

Lord? Let me be free of that woman. It was a mistake. I loved every second. Yo. And would tap that again in a skinny-ass minute. But it ain't love. Or I mean, Lord, I want it to be in the worst way? But Manny understand, though, that it ain't copacetic. He got a place in the community. He got a family and the ELMS and Neecie place there and being a town father like Roy E. Pettus say they got to be now. Getting some fine-ass piece of tail, at least with one of the playas in all that other shit, yo—f'real; I know, Lord—ain't gonna cut it. They can't be no 'love affair' with Becky L, not under them conditions. They could only be what it was, Lord. And now it over—pretty much, pretty much for sure this time—one-mo ain't gonna happen no more. With your help, Manny give it up and come home and go on like it was. Side meat ain't love. Don't need love, even it was the best Manny ever feel, being close with that girl. She turn him inside out, and he her. He like a god to her, God. What you want?

Manny get choked up. Neecie, she see this and hold his hand. The baby-girl still look skeptical, but slide over real close. A moment, like they say.

Golden glowing light upon a young black man on the altar, shaking his fist and exhorting his brethren to do better. To give more. To take responsibility. To seize power, by any means necessary, amen, take all this and go out into the weekday workaday world with the wind at your back and God's love fueling your every breath and movement.

Into Manny's heart flood energy, warmth. An aura he can see around the edges of everything blooms before his eyes, and it's like Jake and Elwood in *The Blues Brothers* and the blue light of God. Or some shit.

Outside, Manny talk to the Reverend-Doctor, who stand with his son and the other deacons paying respects to the departing fellowship, everyone buzzy and bubbling and smiling. Big muh-fuh, that one. Roy Pettus say he used to play football. That they was buds in high school. He can't much feature it.

Taking his turn, shaking that hand big as the mitt Manny had back playing streetball and sandlot. "I half figured on you to get up and give a talk about New Jack City."

The Reverend-Doctor, peering down his nose like Manny ripped a ripe one. "We haven't spent enough time together, Manfred."

"You know where to find me."

"Here's hoping you've come around about the referendum."

"Maybe I just ain't worried about no dusty old South Cackalackie mess."

"Me? I'd never discount such an opportunity to wield power. To flex stakeholder muscle. To be makers of history, instead of victims."

"Hey—that one of Roy Pettus's favorite bits. 'We is the stakeholders.' He remind me all the time."

"A good man, Roy Earl. I've heard that you've been living on his property."

Shit. Nixon must know about Becky L. Maybe everybody do. That ain't no good. Manny's face hot like the griddle.

How he supposed to go home again? And get on?

Manny set it aside. He run his women all the way to downtown

Columbia, take them out for a fine-ass Sunday dinner, Indian, Manny tell the waiter he want it hot like them mofos eat at home, but regret that shit cause he c'ain't half eat that curry, like fire, he gonna shit it like that too, later.

Drive back on the country highway, enjoy the afternoon, play smooth jazz. The mood, it lightens. Feels like family again. But let's face it: Manny women, they sassy on a good day anyway, even before all this mess. He got to put up with that. Like he asking them to keep putting up with him. Except, they ain't gonna put with nothing but straight-line-walking and chillin'.

Right on. Tonight he gonna hang with Roy E. Pettus one last time while packing up to move back home. Muh-fucker bound to be tired of Manny ass squatting and laying pipe with his girlfriend, and he know that only remind him — Roy Pettus — of his own woman going and giving it up.

Mercy.

Manny ain't got no sense. Sometimes.

Only other chore? Giving Becky L a shout. Make sure she appreciate it for keeps. For certain their asses done. It gonna go fine.

BUTTON, ROY, AND CREEDENCE

Tension. Gripping the armrest. Roy's aura, changing as they motored over the connector in his friend Ron's luxury vehicle.

Button, not seeing the metallic rusty glow that'd surrounded Roy on the day of Howdy Shull's execution. More like a steel-gray cloud. A rain shower, building in the distance. Thunder, anytime now. Bombarded by tachyons from the near portending energetic signatures of dark times to come, which will soon manifest as Button's revelation of her grim prognosis.

Or: Could be for another reason, one neither she nor Walfredo can foresee.

Yikes.

Why had he wanted to do this? To bring her here?

An ulterior motive.

Like she had had for wanting to see him today: To tell him of her illness. And plans. To pretty much do nothing about it.

Wait—not to tell. Not an order like he'd give. To talk it out. See what he'd advise.

Not that she didn't already know. The control grid in his mind would appear. He said it was like in the *Terminator* movies, or maybe *Robocop*, the POV computer display, a targeting grid. He suffered from the Einstellung Effect: Once people have what they perceive as the best solution in their mind, it's difficult for them to approach problems from any other perspective. Experts, but in the end so inflexible and solipsistic as to manifest ignorance, an effect gone viral in the culture because of 'experts' on TV offering twinned, dialectic fonts of wisdom from the two purported sides to any issue. Well, that wasn't Einstellung Effect, only good-old control propaganda. Bernays, Goering, and others, bowing their heads from way up in heaven, humbled at the ongoing results of their earthbound works.

Heaven.

Right.

Button, on her way. Somewhere. Her game-growth-journey, completed. The time for giving back, now.

That'd been the idea of leafletting; the impetus behind what's to come. A lesson for those remaining here. Those with an open enough mind to receive the download, anyway. Even if only one person...

Even if it were only Roy E. Pettus. His healing and growth and progress, she believed, her final task. Well—besides realizing her most treasured wish, ya know, which involved dying in the enveloping mother-arms of glorious earth-angel Heather Ponderview.

❁❸❁

"Ya know what, Ron? Swing us by the coffee shop."

Roy, who had been gazing at the marshy wetlands as the graceful curve of the four-lane connector brought them back down to sea level and the toll complex that Ron, with his year-round resident sticker, blew through, caught his buddy as they entered the last traffic circle before the upscale plaza featuring the Carolina Beanery out-parcel.

Button, fretting and worried about worrying, but unable to help herself: feeling Roy's arrogance, hubris, whatever, like an additional passenger in the SUV. A mid-range vibration. Not too low, too high. Still troubling.

"You sure? Don't you wanna go by the Ponderosa to get your ride?"

"I feel the need to have a look-see at what's shaking in the realm of third-wave coffee. I'll get the old lady to run us to the house."

"Heard that. Best piece of advice my father gave me? Don't be an absentee owner."

"You're in? Business as well?"

"That's why me and the Royster get along so well. Both of us got the touch." Punching her pal in the shoulder. "Don't we?"

Roy, distracted, staring out at the passing island scenery. "Huh? Oh—damn straight we do."

Owing to curiosity about the placidity she noted in Ron Nawalinski's vibration, Button asked for a smidgen of personal history that Roy's friend seemed gratified to provide:

Yes, he had also been a big success, in his case with a chain of dry cleaners he'd inherited from that same wise 'old man,' presumably. His later prosperity, he continued, came from re-investing profits earned from subsequent ventures he declined to specify.

Before he could continue Ron received a no-miss call, thumbed his earpiece and said, "Gotta take this," embarking upon an arcane, loud one-sided conversation with a guy about a sweet deal.

Meanwhile, Roy whispered in elucidation how Ron's latest business escapades came as real estate speculation, a little developing, this'n that. "Lucky bastard could see hard assets would be where the smart money went to feel safer about itself. Liquidated most of his portfolio except for bonds, got into development."

Gobbledygook. "My goodness."

"Ever tell you how I got out too? Before the poop came down? Got a tip that Bush was gonna loot the treasury on the way out the door."

"Not sure. Maybe."

"Well—I did. And look at me now." He beamed. "I am kinda made of money. Golden goose. Midas touch. Whole bit."

She tilted her head at cell phone-oblivious Ron. "He have? Much as you?"

Roy poked out his lower lip. "Couldn't say. Got a house like the Taj Mahal out at the Point," a top-shelf neighborhood, he said, even by Sedge Island standards. "Dude's filthy."

"Yeah?"

Shook his head, squinted, chartreuse with mild envy. "Rolling in it."

Filth and all, Nawalinski dumped them off at the front entrance to the CBSI, pulling into the handicapped spot for a second or two while continuing his super important phone conversation. Looked pained and shrugging like he couldn't help his pressing call, brief handshakes ensue, hers accompanied by a hushed aside from Ron to have that persistent cough checked out. Waving, he roared across the empty, off-season asphalt of the shopping plaza.

"Get a load of this." Roy, annoyed by a cluster of greasy, visible fingerprints on the glass entrance door at which he pointed with a trembling digit. He guessed he'd get out a rag and wipe it down himself. If his wife couldn't pull herself together long enough to take care of these details. Hissing through teeth gritted.

Uh-oh. Maybe this wasn't the best time to tell Roy about the full extent of her illness. She sensed an unpleasant Drama about to play out. If not worse.

AWKWARD.

From the second he presented her to his ex-wife, perturbed and busy with customers during the entire uncomfortable scene, Button understood the play: Roy's hand, resting on the small of her back, if only briefly. The touching of their elbows, which in the past—before he'd realized the full extent of her love for Heather Ponderview—had been a body language attempt at intimacy and carnal suggestion, here begun anew. Trying to make his estranged special lady a tad jealous.

Really?

Is that why he needed Button today?

Is that all there is?

Duly and sarcastically flattered, Button. Except, um, for her extreme desire to remain free of playing parts in other people's dramas, like this one now unfolding in linear meatspace time; dinner theater, all this human relationship junk. Or perhaps considering the location, only the coffee and dessert course. Tiresome and unexpected.

"Me and Button here have gotten real close, lately. We go on walks. Got a decent trail now by the river down from the old mill. It's like we're the only ones who even know about it."

"Across from the chicken plant?" Creedence, wrinkling her nose and dripping a pair of medium Ethiopians for an elderly couple in tennis whites ahead of Roy and Button in line. "Can you smell it from over there?"

"Nah. The occasional feather drifting around."

"It's not. So bad."

"Sounds horrible compared to our island trail."

Button, ruing the icy demeanor lurking beneath a forced, service industry smile. "It's been rainy. And gloomy all week. So no recent walks."

"Yeah. You ain't wanted to go as much. Since Howdy."

"I get cold easy."

"So anyway." Creedence served the coffees to the customers and turned full attention upon her guests. "Did you want to? Talk about something?"

"Came to drop off the plane. Get the Mercedes." He shifted on his sandaled and sock-footed feet. "Talk about… like what?"

"Business stuff." Cutting her eyes at Button to make clear her unwelcome participation in any such private discussion. "About the plan."

"Not today. Unless you need to ask me something specific."

"Regarding—?"

Roy, shrugging. "You got me."

"Nothing comes to mind." Creedence, chewing her lip. "Or, well—we still need to hire another key-holder."

Panic in his voice. "Sharolyn's quitting?"

"No, but it's a buttload of hours to cover. A couple of good baristas will help." She related the loss of two recent hires already, the CBSI a victim of youthful employment capriciousness common to Gen Z.

"Y'all got to have an assistant GM on salary you can work like a rented mule." Struggling to maintain composure. "To replace the prior position-holder."

Button, foreseeing disaster. She could feel his sudden anger like the yeasty gust of the furnace vent that gushed against her legs underneath her computer desk back home. Diverting the discussion. "Do you guys? Have almond or oat milk?"

"Sure."

She ordered a caramel latte almond milk, warm.

Roy, forcing his banter. "A latte? Throwing me off, here."

"What?"

"You always drink tea."

"I could use the calories and protein. In the milk."

"True; you're skinny as shit. Must be doing extra yoga."

They went to sit in a booth and wait for their coffee drinks, which Creedence said she'd bring over. Button shook her head. "Nah. It's probably. It's more like. Ya know. The fatal cancer diagnosis."

Roy howled with laughter until she put the words into his mind, getting his attention: Hey, beau, I'm not kidding.

"Excuse me?"

"Sorry to have tell you, but, I'm dying."

A long, passing moment as he searched her face, his smile melting into an expression of granite. "All right, now. Cool it with the black humor."

Button, projecting once again: *Roy—it's true.*

A flare of shock in his eyes. The wealthy bossman rose in silence and headed outside in his worn sport sandals and ratty T-shirt and cargo shorts to collect himself, after which it all got weird.

◌🔘⊘

ROY, STIFF, SHAKING, CRIMSON-FACED, SEEMED TO FLOAT WEIGHTLESS back inside the coffee shop, slid silently into the button-tufted Carolina Beanery booth, the leather creaking under his weight. His nostrils flared as a long, pent-up breath plumed out.

Button, sipping her warm beverage served in his absence, could feel the shock in his shattered and stunned silence, the tight lips and eyes straining to appear open and wet, casual and relaxed. How he struggled to maintain a veneer. His aura blazed a color Button lacked the words to describe.

God love him. Heroic.

Due diligence: "I take it you're screwing with me. Creedence's brother Devin, now, going around pretending to be dying all the time, a real comedian with that whole schtick. Not your style. Is it."

"No."

"Totally uncool."

"You know me pretty well now."

"I think so."

"So you know. I wouldn't fuck with you. Like that."

Satisfied. In confidence: "You realize I've been engaged in a battle."

"Really, now."

"Waging a campaign."

"I see. Roy Earl's war?"

"Bingo."

Button, laughing. "On what?"

Leaning in. Whispering. "A war on unforeseen occurrences."

"Guess this one. Snuck up." Ha. Roy and Walfredo, both diviners of future circumstances, each with their own approach. "You've been worrying."

"Shoot-yes I'm worrying."

"About—?"

"Been feeling that something terrible is coming."

Button, certitude like a Walfredo visit. *This ain't that, pal. This is just me dying.*

But what was 'that'? Instilling such dread? In her friend?

No way to know. An unknown-unknown.

Roy fluttered a nonchalant hand as though dismissing an inconsequential, insubordinate employee. He put on his aw-shucks, aphorism-laden air of nonchalance. "This ain't no thang. We got this."

"Me being sick?"

He snorted. "Oh, my, young lady—science. Science will save us. Save you, I mean. We didn't get this far with cancer research and medicines and cures to just lay down and—and—take this crap diagnosis. How many doctors have you seen?"

"A couple."

Looks at her like, Duh. "And the course of treatment?"

Button, rueful and chuckling. "My doctor visits. Were but a formality."

"*Da fuh?*"

"Dude. It's too far gone."

"The fudge it is."

"It's—look. I imagined this. Too many times."

"*Imagined what?*"

"Having cancer."

"And so freaking what?"

"So now it's real."

"No, you look. These last six months I have listened to you, and learned from you. And loved you, Button. Just as friends, I know I know," exhausted and shaking his jowls in exasperation. "But you can't accept this prognosis and do nothing."

"Who said anything about nothing?"

"I did. And I'm saying that nothing is decided. People beat cancer all the time."

"I am. Looking. At this. Particular reality. It's one of an infinite number. Of possibilities. Granted. But this time out, it's the card—that's been—drawn."

"Save the new age crap, *aw-ight*? This is real."

No way for her to respond other than to think, notions of objective reality are but a trap and a hoax.

Roy, nodding, as she feared a hardened position taking hold. "I know why you wanted me here. You need a partner to help fight this thing. Sissy, lemme tell ya: you come to the right millionaire redneck."

"This? It's not a fight. Money can win." She laughed her familiar hah! hah! and projected warmth and assurance. "It's not even. A fight."

Raps his knuckles. Almost looks pleased. Glowing with confidence. "Two words."

Button smiling—a moment of destiny; it must play out. "Let's. Hear them."

"State of mind."

"Now yer talking. Wait." She snickered. "That's three. But, you're on the. Right track. I'm working on that part. To see if. This can be fixed. But I think it's. Well. It is what it is."

"Horsefeathers."

"That's one word."

All right, he almost shouts, telling her to stop joking. Heads, including Creedence's, turn toward them.

Button, in quiet tones, explaining that it's, well, gosh. Maybe it's destiny at work here. That the dream of what we think approximates what the reality we experience feels and seems like. That, in her mind, she had foreseen this end for herself. Had seen it manifest in her paternal forebear. And, presto, here it was in her. Not all tragic. Her work in this realm, perhaps close to done, work including the care-taking of her father, and mother, and grandfather, now mostly squared away. And so, she would have her disease drama. Would stretch out the moments until she dropped her body and got on with it all.

"Besides. Cancer—it's in my genes. It's in my town. It's an idea in the world. Like a meme on the internet. That people won't stop. Forwarding."

"It's a goddamn cottage industry."

"That's my point."

"Button—!" His face, tight like a balloon. Teeth gritted, straining to keep from shouting. Brittle of tone. "This discussion with a doctor is more than a formality; this reality mess of yours is a lie; this thinking your way into cancer represents a delusion of such grandiosity it defies credulity. Newsflash: You will undergo treatment. The chemo will be no big deal—you already have the total hookup," lowering his voice, "with the herb and the vape."

Button, shrugging at all that. Letting him run out of steam.

"Dude. This is all lined up real neat," he thinks aloud. "You've been prepared not for death, but to wage war. A total warrior, you are. And with my resources leading the way—greasing the right palms; let's get real here, you know how it all works, don't you?—this disease is getting its ass kicked right back to Hades from whence it sprung. BOO-yow."

As close as she's ever gotten to angry with him. "I'm not. Your employee."

Smug. "Oh—it's not that sort of attitude. It's that you're in no mental state—*ahem*—to make the biggest decisions. So I'll decide for you, my dear. Easy-peasy."

"Those twisted croakers. Aren't going to. Sink their claws into me."

The spell, breaking. "You sound like you're ready to give up on this life of yours."

Button, sighing; taking a moment to give him the full clinical. That the scans had shown seven major masses throughout her abdomen, from throat to pancreas to kidneys, a constellation of cancer. Had started wherever it'd started. No way to find out now. "Metastasized. Beyond metastasized."

His eyes, filling with tears. Mewling and shaking his head. "No."

Gentle. "The main tumor. It's the size of a softball. Inside me."

"Jesus." She could see his entire body trembling with fear. "Oh, holy crap."

"What ya gonna do, yo?"

"Not much. I guess."

"Ding-ding-ding. We have a winner."

Now the anger slipped out. "This is such—such—*fudging horse-hockey*."

Conversations quieted. Button saw Creedence, frowning and craning her neck over the espresso machine.

The other patrons went back to their discussions. He got up and walked around, first in a circle; next, a figure eight, a pattern going into and around the array of tables in the middle—a pattern symbolizing infinity. Kept pounding the thick white-boy meat of his right thigh, which she expected would bruise. Button, thinking him like an automaton running a routine.

At last, he sank back into the booth. "Fucking goddamn shit."

"Now there's an honest response."

"But treatment—"

"Why put myself? Through chemo side effects? For nothing."

Stunned. "Because—it might save your life."

"Nobody's life is saved. By chemo. Survival rate? Zero."

His epithet this time comes with teeth. "*Bullshit*."

"Not when it's stage IV, bub."

Calmer. "You don't know that. You may know all this hippy-dippy hooey, but girl, you can't make such a generalization. Let me talk it through."

"Nothing to talk through—well, there is. But not right now."

"This is nuts." Now for the metallic aura, rusty and oxidized and rough to the psychic touch. The bossman, one last shot. Voice so low and threatening as to be a whisper, from under a wrinkled brow tilted in her direction, eyes rolling back in his head, his will strong as high tensile steel. "*I'm afraid I must insist*."

"Dude. If I can accept it." A welling of emotion, unexpected. She clasped his hand. "Then you can, too."

Broken; beaten. He took back his hand, hid his face. Heaving once, shaking off all the emotion except for one: disappointment. "All this medicine. The doctors. Shiny buildings. Money—yeah. Throwing money at shit. Charity this. Foundation that. Race for the cure. Little rubber bracelets. Jerry Lewis doing a telethon for forty years, but still with the muscular dystrophy. Science," spat like an epithet. "For what. For what."

A teachable moment. Time for the false gods talk.

Deep breath.

But before she could begin, he asked:

"What do you think Howdy was shouting about? That 'Osiris and Isis' rap?"

Button, intrigued at this possibly intentional and serendipitous conversational feint toward what she wanted to discuss. "A metaphor. For what happened. To his sister? All the stories of gods. Are metaphor."

"Are they, now."

"You bet. We'd do well to pay heed to some. Of those myths. Into which truths. Have been woven. But instead, we worship false gods. This medical crap? It's one. Want to? Hear about? The others?"

A wave dismissive. "Do tell, wise one."

She began by outlining the false gods of modernity—Commerce, Race, Religion, Nation, Entertainment, and indeed, Science. All constructs, all belief systems, all subjective epistemological reality tunnels, none based in any particularly objective shared reality except in the most superficial of manners, though Science coming close with its raison d'être, she explained, being explaining the unexplainable through the Cartesian materialist miracle of measure and number, repeatable results, seeming concretized interpretations of a base reality flowing fungible and slippery.

"Until science embraces. The immaterial. We'll get nowhere. With our particle colliders. And space missions. Radiation. And chemotherapy."

"If you think for a minute you can brush my concerns aside with your gobbledegook, you're wrong, princess."

"I appreciate those concerns."

"*Well act like it*," his voice booming out again. "You little stoner idiot. Don't you want to live?"

Okay. Thinking this through—if it's *his* shining moment of service, she says to herself, to help me decide how I will die, then his life has already acquired meaning from the presence of my illness.

But she knows she can't go into that now. She has to let him feel like he's able to use his powers of foresight and planning and that whole control-grid deal he talked about, but seeing all of it fail is part of the process of growth for him.

All of a piece.

She had to be careful, though, in this growth-gaming phase with her spiritual apprentice. With Roy E. Pettus in conflict, the command feature often manifests itself only to complicate matters, inserting new and worse tensions in place of old.

Such as: Now he has accepted the reality, and a dead-eyed pallor settles onto his features. Button rued this look because she first saw it back on the day when Roy fired Trudy and told them all they were worthless and that The Dixiana needed a carpet-bombing into toothpicks like Button's mother's village in Vietnam.

What she understood, however, was that in this case his grim face wasn't for her but mortality itself, for inserting its inexorable maw into his life yet again.

Death could wait. A little while. She still had work to do—for herself first, to make sure her consciousness remained ascendant and prepared for the coming separation and release from the meat jacket, but also for Roy E. Pettus, whom had come so far in their brief and close friendship.

He mustn't worry about death. No. Nothing but a transit.

They'd discuss it all; plenty of time.

Or not.

He accused her of being a fabulist, of imagining all her fairy tales.

She laughed, which hurt. Said, sure; I thought I was in some psychogenic fugue state. But the CT scans and blood tests didn't lie. "But, like: don't fret. I'm not done. Here yet. It's like Groucho Marx said."

"How's that?"

"Might not be crazy about reality? But it's still. The only place. To get a decent meal."

Laughter. Warm and genuine.

Button, joining in. Trying not to cough. Yesterday, there'd been blood in her sputum, brilliant in the bathroom sink.

"All right, here's the news. When we get back, I'll take you to the oncology center; I will help you choose the treatments. That's why you told me this." His eyes, shining with purpose, but also opaque like two shark-eye marbles, a character in a movie who's fallen under an evil psychic hijack. "Correct?"

Button nodded, kept her small hands folded. Felt no fear. Already had her answers.

But still. Due diligence. A convo with her boy, here. Second opinion. As with the oncologist, she'd let them all feel as though they enjoyed some say in the decision-making. Held some tenuous sense of control in how it would all play out.

Control. How foolish:

Everything that'd be happening had already happened, or rather, was happening now. That was more like it. Nothing to do but wait to receive the manifestation, not only of what already was, but what had been and would be. Her diagnosis, sounding a letter-for-letter match with spiritual informa-tion imparted to her by Walfredo, in a lucid dreaming experience she'd fostered back over the holidays. She couldn't explain this to Roy, not here, not now. Not with him in such a state.

Okay. She'd let him believe that he was here to help her decide how to proceed. Whether to pursue, or forego, the typical treatment. Which had been the path her father had chosen. And look how wonderful he'd ended up.

Never any question in her mind.

How long had she known she was sick, anyway?

Since always.

Ever since she'd embraced the inevitability of the cancer, she had suffered little pain, which seemed impossible considering how much diseased tissue she carried. All mitigated by her coming ascension. Relaxed as she'd ever been. In a way.

Fulfilled.

As if any doubt existed. That she'd get where she needed to be. That anyone didn't eventually achieve Oneness. Maybe not the Agathas of Aberdeen of the etheric plain, causing trouble for still-incarnated souls. Once she got There, Button would do her peeps in Edgewater County a solid, look into that situation.

'Look into.' Hah. By then, all would be revealed with grace, ease and totality.

Heck, it already had, on her last trip to Heather's. Not the visit with Roy back before the holidays; the one she'd made two weeks ago. To take part in a sacred ceremony with her great love—a psychedelic, healing adventure of the mind and spirit, an epic episode almost beyond everyday imagination—even a heady little dirt surfer like Button Sykes.

✸✸⊘

HERE'S HOW SHE DESCRIBED HER EXPERIENCE TAKING THE MEDICINE with the Peruvian shaman to whom Heather Ponderview held a debt of respect and gratitude. Button had written nothing in ages: no stories, no more revisions of her novel called *Miriam Mullins*; no letters-slash-emails to Heather, not now that they talked or chatted online several times a day. Much better.

Preparing and planning for Button's move to the mountainside. To finish her life at Heather's side.

In her arms.

Sitting at home in Edgewater County three days after the ceremony, though, still tasting the callbacks of the sacred vine, a vague hint of licorice at the back of her teeth, and a feeling of assurance that swept away all the pain and fear that threatening to grow inside her along with the cancer, Button, knowing that her trip was short, became compelled to type it all up. If for no other person than for Roy, to whom she'd leave all her papers.

She had meditated in her bedroom, which in preparation for the ceremony she straightened and cleaned, much as she had fasted for a day before going to Havenhurst to be with Heather get mentored into the ayahuasca ceremony.

Once she began writing, words had tumbled out. A glorious experience, the aya, one deserving a modicum of detail and fullness of literary expression.

❂⬚⊘

The Night I Received the Blessing of the Yagé
by Allyson B. Sykes

"A Materialistic consciousness is attempting to preserve itself from Dissolution by restriction & persecution of the Experience of the Transcendental. One day perhaps the Earth will be dominated by the Illusion of Separate consciousness, the Bureaucrats having triumphed in seizing control of all roads of communication with the Divine, & restricting traffic. But Sleep & Death cannot evade the Great Dream of Being, and the victory of the Bureaucrats of Illusion is only an Illusion of their separate world of consciousness."

— ALLEN GINSBERG

The shaman, Manteo, called me by my first name: "Allyson." For some reason, my name did not sound like mine. I chose to present myself under my first Christian name, as they say, rather than the middle one by which I am known, and that most perceive as a sobriquet (and yet is not), because I think I wished to distance myself from the setting of expectations further than I already had, a crucial step in preparing to take into my diseased and broken body the medicine of the vine: the Ayahuasca.

To my right sat a figure, meditating in the lotus position: Heather, my close friend, confidant and spiritual guide who has led me to attending my first, and perhaps only, ceremony with the Grandmother vine. Dear sweet Heather, legs folded and chanting her mantra, the sacred syllable, both of us on padded yoga mats and with coverups in case we became chilled during the long night of working with the medicine, on the floor, in the dark.

The ayahuasca preparation, a potent brew sitting with reverence atop a small altar in front of two chairs, other totems, candles that provided the only light but for that of the fading night sky out the high windows, including a stained glass mandala far above the heads of the shaman and his assistant.

How long have I been preparing for this moment? As it would later be depicted, perhaps several lifetimes. Certainly for the whole of this lifetime, foreshortened as it seems at this point.

At first I thought this seemingly harsh reality only another reason to see my love Heather Ponderview; then, when the extent of my illness became clear, another purpose in coming here: the ceremony. Soul-work, perhaps a final chapter of a lengthy living human novel plotted through with preparation to participate in such transcendent endeavor.

We arrived at the retreat in the North Carolina mountains near Asheville, an hour's drive from Heather's magnificent pyramidal inheritance of Havenhurst. A sunny winter's afternoon, but only mostly sunny: Snow changing to rain had been threatening, had sprinkled us during a brief, chilly hike in the nearby Dupont Forest, trekking as much as my growing fatigue would allow, from High Falls to Covered Bridge to Lake Dense. The woods all around, silent but for the few other hikers and mountain bikers.

A black snake had appeared, slithering across the packed, dusty gravel hiking trail, which as Heather pointed out was very unusual to see this time of year. Snakes, a recurring theme in my life lately, in real life as well as a marvelous and vivid dream I'd had after deciding to take ayahuasca. I had stood alongside my grandfather for whom I am responsible, both of us watching snakes fight in the front yard of my home in South Carolina. The black snake had triumphed over another, nonspecific poisonous snake. Heather had told me she thought this a good dream; that black snakes in real life did exactly that. Were allies.

At the retreat, the sun had broken through in the west and warmed us, but gentle rain still fell through the high green canopy of the old growth mountain firs, pines and upland oaks. Not a storm, only a shower, but a miracle, a waking vision: the sun, heading downward in the sky, blazed shining at me through the falling rain shower, brilliant light illuminating every drop, like Hollywood special effects moviemaking, the kind they now make in a computer, but this scene conjured from the data processor of my own mind. Of all our minds, gathered here for ceremony and communion with the vine.

I felt awed.

"The devil's beating his wife," a ceremony participant noted with a sardonic smile. "That's what they call this."

Artia, a lovely, lithe female assistant to Manteo, the Peruvian shaman who would be 'managing' the ceremony, seemed disturbed by the notion. "Pardon me?" in her accented English.

"It's a Southernism." My explanation, doing little to dispel the negative imagery. "When it's both raining and sunny at the same time. A divided sky."

Artia seemed to accept the phrase's status as a semi-charming colloquialism, but with a small frown. Let's face it: Whether as a metaphor or possibly real entity, the devil, not a nice guy.

I thought: unlike the blacksnake, is this verbalization by the other participant a harbinger of dark spirits? I hoped not. I have been plagued by enough shadow-beings throughout my life, which has been wondrous and fortunate, but also troubled and traumatic. And yet I have persevered and survived. To this moment. Many such difficulties I would overcome, including more than I few I brought on myself. Sometimes we don't even need an external adversary. It is easy enough to become one's own worst enemy.

I went to check into the small, private bedroom where I would spend a few hours afterwards to journal and process the experience, sleep, rest, whatever I needed, with Heather ensconced next door. My name on the first door at the top of the stairs: 'Allyson.' The room number? Eleven.

I began to glow inside—for a couple of years now I have been seeing 11 or 11:11 or 1:11 with great frequency, and being visited by a sense of certitude and purposefulness that feels almost like a second personality, a mirrored one, perhaps, that I call Walfredo. A visit from a future self, a projection of consciousness from another point within the hypercube of expanding and contracting timelessness; whatever it is, this is the feeling. Portent of good energy to come. As though the miracle of the illuminated rain hadn't been enough of an omen, now I knew all would be well.

Lately all the 11s have been replaced, or perhaps merely augmented: I've also begun seeing numbers counting up and down. I will be compelled to look at a clock, or maybe a gas station sign, or the odometer on the car, and see 123 or 456 or 543 or 321. Mostly counting down, though.

I get it.

The ceremony space: A large, carpeted, high-ceilinged room at the mountain retreat now ringed by the dozen or so attendees, many of whom I find have come here any number of previous times, or else to other locations where the shaman holds these ceremonies, a movable spiritual feast. To partake of the brew and embark on their spirit-journey with Grandmother Aya, as she is sometimes called.

I wondered about that—how many times does one need with the vine before the veils are dropped? Near as I could tell, I would only get this chance.

My own preparation had been ongoing for weeks. A detoxing of the body, which wasn't all that toxic to begin with, aside from the aforementioned manifestation of disease: Other than drawing down a longstanding cannabis habit, when it comes to food intake, exercise and meditation I've already been living in a state of carefully considered discernment. The pre-ceremony 'dieta' of veggies, fruits, nuts, and legumes had already become second nature to me, so that posed no particular difficulty. Never one for fasting, however—I'm a grazer—I rued the not-eating rule for five or more hours before ceremony, with the fast continuing until the next day at noon.

At 1:55 I blessed and ate an organic banana smeared with natural peanut butter, one of my favorite meals these days. I hoped I wouldn't suffer any odd consequences from depriving myself of the small snacks I tend to consume throughout the day. I have to make myself eat. It hurts. But I do.

In preparing myself mentally, I recalled the many psychedelic experiences I'd traversed leading up to this night, only a few of which had been truly transformative, I'm sorry to say: a couple of teenage LSD experiences involving listening to Grateful Dead music as well as in person at Phish concerts, and a book-ending, epochal and indelible mushroom visitation I undertook a dozen years later at another Phish show. That trip, like this one, had not been intended as Dionysian revel, rather as a journey of healing, an attempt to reinforce and further define the tenets of the sobriety from both street and prescription drugs I'd embarked upon at the end of Phish 1.0, as that era is known among fans of the band. As it happened, an ignominious end for me, though one that probably came right on time.

In some ways this more recent trip, two dried grams of psilocybin carried in a chocolate like a spiritually-charged Reece's Cup, had felt at the time to be the most liberating, wonderful night of my life. A sense of return, renewal, a cleansing spiritual and entheogenic mental bath. This experience occurred at a Phish show held in an otherwise unremarkable Colorado soccer stadium on 9/1/12, a much better connotation of 9-1-1 than the greater cultural one steeped in fearful mind control and political manipulation, and what I now note as another possible significant occurrence of the 'eleven' phenomenon. Or perhaps the mushroom had so much to say to me simply because I hadn't experienced an heroic trip of such magnitude in a long time. There is no one right answer.

In a moment of ecstasy before the music began (but after the trip had gotten rolling in earnest), a cosmic rope of starlight had dropped down, and I literally held on with both hands; the starlight, filling my spine and lighting up my chakras like a strand of impossibly bright LED Christmas lights. The vaguely mushroom-shaped line of stadium lights across the way, looming over me like the brilliantly back-lit rock-mushroom seen by the academic psychonaut portrayed by William Hurt in Altered States, a movie that began to seem less Hollywood and more real. Much more.

The Phish fans clustered on the field tossed their colorful glow-sticks into the air to greet the music, plastic iridescent squirming coils which in that state of mind appeared to me as strands of self-replicating DNA exploding out of the swirling primal soup, the bouncing heads and dancing bodies of prog-rock fans a roiling, pixillated sea.

Like I said: epochal.

As it happened, that night I had my own hill to climb. A period of struggle with fear followed, a classic psychedelic journey expressing a sort of operatic birth-death-rebirth process endemic to any truly transformative experience with sacraments like the mushroom. A healing fungus.

As the concert went on, one of their best of the modern era, I returned to ordinary consciousness and walked away from the experience drained, refreshed, and most of all, enlightened.

On the flight back home, I wondered: would ever I top my journey?

The moment of death, perhaps, which like the tagline of 2001: A Space Odyssey has been described as 'the ultimate trip?'

From here, where left to go?

Heather Ponderview, as it happened, would suggest that very destination. Having informed me of numerous travels she took in the years since we had been close, including not only the jungles of Peru where she would engage in a plant-medicine ceremony that would open her heart, mind and spirit to new possibilities and realities, as well as additionally exotic travels to places as far afield as a hiking trip to the flooded forest of Lake Kaindy in Kazakhstan, where one of her father's companies, a construction firm, was doing mad contract business in the capitol city of Astana. Heather would explain that the interior journey taken under the watchful and steady spirit of a genuine shaman had been the most profound trip of them all.

I had first heard of ayahuasca through the work of iconic beat writer William S. Burroughs, most directly in the form of The Yagé Letters, an epistolary 'novel' co-written with equally iconic poet Allen Ginsburg, but also from other references sprinkled throughout Burroughs's work. While in the modern age many make the journey to South America, as Burroughs found it necessary, to experience the medicinal vine in action, warnings now come regarding would-be shamans and the practice of 'ayahuasca tourism,' who in certain cases may not in fact be what they claim; may brew the vine with other psychotropic plants to provide a psychedelic or intoxicating experience without the necessary spiritual guidance that goes hand-in-hand with a true medicine ceremony.

And as I found, guidance one needs.

Without a doubt.

The shaman's songs, known as ikaros, are key to the safety and efficacy of the experience—not only are these songs and chants soothing and heart-centered, they involve the calling of spirits, while also providing protection or screening of more malevolent entities who may fixate upon a room of open-spirited individuals in the midst of a visit with Grandmother. She will really be the one watching over you, however, and in her loving arms you will be safe, even if she's stern with you over some issue on which you need to be working.

Luckily for me, as wrenching and harrowing as a portion of this 'trip' happened to seem, between the songs and her protective presence I never felt too terribly frightened. On the edge of an abyss of eternal knowledge perhaps, and somewhat anxious about my return from this precipice, yes; but then, I am well familiar the sort of white-knuckle, large dose psychotropic experiences. Trust me—I've had adequate preparation for a fully introspective, cosmic journey of this type.

Speaking of prep: What one brings to it themselves, or doesn't bring (as it is better to go in with as few expectations as possible), is equally important as the dieta. To drink this brew without the preparation and ceremonial aspect would be a foolish act indeed. Physical, mental, and spiritual preparation. Setting of intention.

Mine?

To find reassurance that the path is the correct one; to reveal the true partners in my life, as if I do not already know.

And then?

To remove all sense of expectation from my mind.

To let the experience occur.

To let Grandmother reveal her secrets as she sees fit.

Luckily, upon arrival at the retreat I felt at ease with Artia and Manteo, who have been doing this work for two decades. I felt no concern that the shaman could be a charlatan. Their eyes, voices and spirits appear to be filled with light and love. One look of greeting, of loving acceptance, and I knew I was in good hands.

Dressed all in white (but for two men who, like Manteo, seemed to be Peruvian or otherwise Hispanic in appearance), the attendees gradually made their way into the ceremonial space and settled into position around the perimeter of the walls. Elaborate personal spaces had been prepared by a number of the participants. Veterans. Later, I would find out that some prefer to spend the rest of the evening there in the gathering area. I would prefer not, though who knows how I would feel should I decide to take this journey again.

Or if I'd even get the chance. Any way you cut it: My trip is short.

As I would discover, people return again and again to this experience. Part of my intention, however, had been to HAVE the experience to its fullest extent this time, in this moment... because who knows when we will pass this way again, if for no other reason than the money-energy exchange with my shaman. Money is limited in my life. I must wield it with care.

Time, even more limited. As we understand and keep it, anyway.

Artia and Manteo sit at the head of the room, the light of the fading sun shining in through the stained glass window near the top of the twenty-five foot ceiling. A small ground-level altar had been set up at the feet of their chairs, several bottles and totems, a silk pillow where the participants kneel and receive the brew. This did not feel as though the shaman had placed himself above the participants. No stage from which to 'preach,' only a collection of sacred objects and candles.

Everyone took their places. A number of veterans had set up their own altars, including, as I noted earlier, bedrolls and pillows for comfort. I meditated and stretched my body, a preparatory process for which I would later be grateful.

We were taken through the steps of the ceremony, which besides this introduction included two phases: the first, lasting seventy-five minutes, involved an initial dose of the medicine and series of ikaros. At the conclusion of that sequence would come the offering of a second dose for those feeling that they required additional medicine to fully explore and extend their aya journey.

Having no practical experience with this, I would need to go on intuition and the way I felt physically to determine the necessity of this additional dose. At the same time, Manteo would use his own intuition to ascertain the strength of the dose(s) participants would receive.

Manteo and Artia, their auras visibly numinous, lit the candles. Called one by one to kneel on the pillow before the altar and receive our gift from Grandmother, my odd-sounding name came to me in the echoing space. Spoken by Manteo, 'Allyson' sounded more mellifluous and beautiful than I've ever considered it. I rose and padded over in my bare feet on the soft carpeting. No fear. Only wonder and a big smile. Kneeling.

The brew, dark and mysterious, poured from a bottle. A blessing, and offered to me across the altar, and the breath of the shaman blown into the shot glass-sized vessel I accepted from him. A full dose.

My breath and intention, also blown into the brew. Guide me, Grandmother. Show me the way.

I drank it down. Not unpalatable, but very unusual. Licorice-like, yet not. Unidentifiable; earthy; strong; new.

"Thank you."

Full of wonder and awe at what lay ahead, I floated barefoot across the carpet and back into my space, eyes closed, a requirement throughout the ceremony. As though from faraway I again heard Manteo's beautiful voice, this time with a certain familiarity to his accented inflection, her third ceremony with these healers:

"Heather."

As the rest are called, the medicine, settling into my stomach. My body, struggling. I anticipated the possibility of purging unhealthy energy—if only I could purge all the ill health contained within my broken vessel of a body! —but here, it feels more like a struggle to keep down something the stomach does not want.

I cannot purge yet, I thought. I have not fully received the medicine.

With this strong quality of determination fixed in my mind, the rejection of the brew is reversed, and as it is received into my system I feel a glow, a spreading warmth I often get, and associate with being touched by my guardian angels. Comforting. Good; this is the primary physical feeling and idea that now fills my body, which otherwise is fairly wracked with pain from the tumors.

The songs begin, at first only whistling accompanied by the swish-swish of a blessing with small bundles of straw. Flowing and chant-like, whispering, repetitive, the singing carries through the first 'segment' of the ceremony, which I will find goes by fast:

Visions.

Flowing vortices.

Snake imagery—as I had anticipated. Indeed, wriggling blacksnakes not unlike the manifested serpent from earlier in the day, shimmering and elegant. Star-scapes, sidereal and synodic, blue beams twirling and dancing like the lighting rig at a Phish concert. Faces—a helmeted snake, a warrior, cold eyes. My father. My mother. My grandmother. My grandfather. My sister. Heather.

And next… a brief but powerful vision of hell: red light. A high shelf of rock over a chasm. Standing beside a powerful figure, but sensing my own sense of immense power as well. A partner to that figure; a king.

A headdress, a staff. Serving in his court.

Serving a master.

The king's magician.

Is this me?

Yes. Presiding over suffering.

The red glow, from a pit of hell.

Human sacrifice.

Bodies, crying out.

Tumbling into the flaming amber void below us.

Thousands of years ago.

No. NO. It cannot be—not me.

And yet… it could. The magic, it flows through me in this life, too.

Perhaps in all the lives.

Resistance—then, and now. Sensed by my master. And punished: Forever cast out from power. The magician's regret.

A tunnel of fractal snakeskin. Feelings of return.

Where have I been?

The ikaros, ending. A feeling of certainty and sobriety, if that's the correct term. By now, I sense I have fully returned.

Was this over? Already?

Did I come here for the full experience? Or what?

Then comes the offering of a second dose.

As several others including my friend Heather decide to take the medicine a second time, my intuition says but one word to me, and it is YES.

I rise, moving across the room, and Manteo whispers my name with satisfaction and certitude: "Allyson." Pleased, now he saw my full commitment. He knows; he knew.

But the dose this time is small. His own intuition had already ensured that I would have the full understanding with the initial dose, and here he knows that I may take this experience too far if not careful.

And so begins the next segment of the aya journey.

The purge comes during the second ikaro of the longer portion. It's not like nausea followed by subsequent vomiting, it's more of a pressure inside that must be released. I'm resistant to the idea, but recall the advice given as part of the ceremony introduction: at our side are gallon-sized Ziploc bags in case of purging, and Artia has cautioned how we should feel free and comfortable to use them. That the purging is a positive aspect of the ceremony, and not necessary indicative of a problem with the participant or the medicine—it's a release of toxins in need of removal from the body, mind and spirit.

"A young woman in a recent ceremony was so self-conscious that she held in her purge rather than use the bag. You mustn't do this—the purging is good. A necessary part of the experience."

I didn't want to be like that person. A bathroom was available nearby, too, because the purging could come from the lower body as well, and this worry had also been with me. Except, whether it's related to setting intention for an aya ceremony or simply getting through the average day, if there's one thing I've learned it's not to set my expectation in a negative direction. After all, setting the intention to that of the concept of solution rather than problem is part of the path to serenity and higher consciousness.

Worrying I was destined to have a problem—cancer—got me into such a reality. You have to be careful about this whole thinking business.

And so, as the purge comes over me I feel resistance, then remembered Artia's words, as well as my own thoughts. I pick up the plastic sack, open it, feel the vomit come out—once, twice, three times a puking lady. A cough; a burning throat, but no water may be had.

What comes after feels so good. My body is well, not sick, and for the first time in a long while I almost forget the cancer that's eating away at my healthy organs. I close the bag carefully, place it beside me on the floor, and recline onto my mat and pillow.

What comes next is a long period, formless and indistinct and not so much full of visions, rather of full-body inner and physical struggle. The ikaros continue, with each song sequence bringing in different energies, some positive, others negative.

A journey; a battle.

More tunnels of fractal-like 'snakeskin'; cold, so cold. I writhe and try to cover my freezing feet with the light sarong I've brought. The cold seems to penetrate and suffuse my body. Not so much shivering as simply a steely, deep-boned chill. My extremities, numb. I get cold so easily now!

The participants are mostly silent, but one woman laughs every so often, or else simply goes 'OH' in an almost sexual manner.

In a moment of weakness, or perhaps fear, I break one of the rules—I open my eyes, if ever so briefly.

What I see overhead is shocking: dark amoeba-like entities floating above. Black, ghostly, undulating. Manteo and Artia's part, I now understand, is to manage these energies, eager to take advantage of the spiritual openness present in the room.

A time of tribulation begins. My body fights with itself. My limbs, restless. Perhaps one of those dark spirits tried to enter me, or else this is merely the battle of ten-thousand years waged within.

In any case, I became concerned. Knowing the potential for telepathy present within my consciousness and perhaps enhanced by presence of the medicine, I called out in my mind:

Manteo, Artia—I am going too far. I have seen too much already. Bring me back. Please help me. Bring me back home.

The next thing I know there is the gentle sound of a flute playing over me, beside me, all around me. Manteo has heard. Has come to me.

A sense of solace. Of comfort. Of return. I am calmed.

I feel hands all over my abdomen, face, head, the back of my neck. Gentle. Female. Soft.

Is this Artia?

No—they are my own. Disembodied and seemingly numb. The hands, mine, but the touch, I finally decide, is neither that of Artia nor the shaman nor my own, but of Grandmother Aya herself.

A sensation of placidity, of gentle floating, comes over me. Later, I will be told that I began snoring. Wait—I fell asleep? Was that possible? Apparently, it is not that unusual.

The songs now change into Artia's voice, gently singing in English, a paean to the wholeness and holiness of nature, of the planet, of Gaia herself.

The river, the river, forever flowing to the sea. The river, the river. The sea, the sea. Forever.

The cold of before now not so much ebbing away as replaced by a suffusion of full-body warmth that recalls the inner glow I get after a long meditation, or else when I call out to the universe—to God—to reassure me I'm on the right path. This warmth, however, goes beyond any such emotion I've ever had, and that I find will persist for many hours.

It is a feeling of joy. Of completion.

Manteo comes around and spritzes each of us with floral-scented water, which makes me bubble with laughter. With eyes still closed, I see the light of a dawn breaking in the distance, in the direction of the altar. A Kubrickian dawn of humanity on the ancient savannah, more ancient than any recorded human history can adequately depict or perhaps conceive. A vast journey backward not of thousands of years, but hundreds of thousands. Millions. Back through the Hindu yugas.

They have lit the candles, I think; the ceremony is ending.

True enough, but when I crack open my eyes for another sneaking glance, I find no burning candles! As I suspected, what I saw represented a vision of light from the past, not of light in the present.

"How is everyone?"

We go around the room to answer. I am so full of gratitude and joy I can barely croak out the words: "I feel wonderful."

Other participants don't sound so certain. A variety of journeys have been undertaken. Purging. A young woman in the back corner voices a thought I have as well: "I've fought a long and arduous battle, and I won... I think?"

In my case, there's no 'thinking', only a feeling: not of victory, but of balance, and as when Manteo played the flute, a sense of return.

Of accomplishment.

Of consummation.

And not a shred of pain throughout the entire ceremony, my disease quiet. Perhaps cowed in the presence of Grandmother. If only cowed enough to withdraw from my body. But this, a wish too far.

"Light and dark," Artia says, translating for Manteo, "is the play on this planet of ours, and has been for time immemorial. This duality is reflected within each of us as well." This is Manteo and Artia's last message to us tonight: As above, so below: the play goes on within each of us, in our own way.

What side will 'win?' To which side will you sew and pledge 'obedience?' These questions are unspoken, yet float in the silent spaces between their words like those dark spirits I glimpsed.

In my case, I felt only the confirmation I sought. My intention, fully realized.

This struggle for balance, however, will go on, as it has for all of time as we understand it; for that is the play. The duality, the balance. No bad or good, nor right or wrong. Lessons I have learned before; lessons I need to absorb and process again.

For there is no destination, only the journey.

A gentle group discussion ensues. One participant describes the decision to come here tonight over issues of personal stress. Looking for answers. Oh, my, but this is much more than a stress-relieving self help session, is all I can think. The cosmic aspects loom so much larger than such mundane concerns as work and home stresses, anxieties, even physical illness as I now suffer. But I must not judge. Our struggles with the 'play' are to be waged within each of us, in our own time and space.

The ultimate message I have heard, however, is that these bodies here in this 3D reality of ours don't much matter. The real action is on the other side, because there we have no end, only eternity within a vast and unimaginable field of perfect love and comfort spent communing with Source, with Love itself. Here, we come to play, and participate in the play; there we exist as pure Being, with perhaps (for some) the choice to come back again to take part in the grand, hair-raising adventure that is the soul dropping into these physicalized vehicles and taking them for a spin. If further lessons are necessary through subsequent and additional incarnations.

In my existence I'm not sure that will be the case, but one must never get too comfortable in how reality seems, or how it ought to be; one must dis-attach from outcomes and endgames, from thoughts of where the path ultimately leads. Again: the journey is the destination.

And this, my friends, is how my evening with Grandmother Ayahuasca unfolded—like all of life itself, it may only have been a happy, scary, wondrous series of hallucinations and waking dreams. You tell me.

◉ ⬛ ⊘

IT HAD ALL POURED OUT OF HER THE NEXT AFTERNOON, BACK AT THE blue pyramid after they had broken their fast. As sunlight streamed in to warm the passive-solar structure to a comfortable temperature, the old friends enjoyed a meal of quinoa salad with garbanzo beans along with fresh fruit and a green smoothie made in Heather's roaring Vitamix, food that Button found difficult to stomach despite not having eaten for an entire day.

Moaning and hunched over the laptop at the conclusion of Button's essay, Heather rushed over to the huge dining table, and the moment came in which Button divulged about the terminal cancer of the pancreas and bile duct and kidney and in her bladder, too, with several blooms of pre-cancerous lesions on her liver, and no hope for cure or remission or a future.

The disease had yet to manifest in lungs nor in her throat nor in the brain, thank goodness. Those organs she knew had been protected by the cannabis, but even that miracle plant, the blessed Godflower, couldn't filter and fight the toxic environment fostered by living in the shadow of a nuclear plant. Of living everyday life in twenty-first century America, as a citizen of a culture gone mad with profit, heedless of pollution, and courting death and destruction of our planet. Our home.

Blah blah. Like one of her pamphlets.

At the news Heather gasped and choked, went into shock. Had known of a problem, she said, but not on this scale. Not this. Not this bad. Anger — not at Button, but at her own failure to have foreseen this particular chapter in the ongoing novel of their lives together.

"But you've found out the secret of secrets, right?" Heather, sniffling and trying to smile. "You've come so far. You had to have by now."

Button, like, no doubt. Time but an illusion, a vibrational response to gravity and chrono-centric in this context to this world and this one only, a malleable and rather finite fourth dimension indeed. Accessing a higher plane, however, gave a psycho-explorer perspective. Of course Button knew. She'd been free of time's constraints for… oh, a good while, now. "Duh."

"I'm relieved."

Holding one another throughout the afternoon and evening, doing Tarot turnings and banishing ceremonies, the lovers again retired to renew their ardor through a program of careful caresses and blistering hot tears of frustration followed by release. Outside, the moon approached its darkest phase, in its twenty-eighth cycle. Button, fully alive.

◌ ▥ ⊘

SHE'D TRY TO GET ACROSS TO ROY THAT STUFF ABOUT TIME. SHE'D already been doing so. But knowing her friend so upset, Button, sitting in the Carolina Beanery Sedge Island, agreed to talk out the idea of treatment, but later, on the drive home to Edgewater County. They'd bat it around between fusillades of amplified classic rock. She owed it to herself, right? They always said get a second opinion.

And no one in her circle did she trust more than Roy, once she'd gotten to know him better, and had helped him through his turmoil and grief. Which, from what he'd been telling her, had looked like it was coming back, but then? Kaput. Poor guy.

How she pitied him. And rued making him go through this with her.

But whom else did she have? Thim? She felt so little kinship with that woman, her selfish sister, who possessed no insight of any use. Pushing Button to embark upon a course of treatment that would surely buy her time. Just like Roy.

Right as he relaxed a bit at being told *yeah-yeah we'll hash it out*, Creedence, appearing over his left shoulder. Chewing her lips. Suspicion. Barely contained fury.

"Y'all better quit this, whatever this fussing's about. Not in my place."

Roy's own ire comes visceral and immediate, like a punch to Button's aching gut. Wrenching his gaze at his wife; Button, knowing you shouldn't twist around that way. "It's not an argument."

"Well, seems mighty durn personal."

"It's TMI. Not your business. She's my friend, not yours. None-ya."

"A pal, eh?" Creedence's face, red as her long hair, pulled back into an attractive French braid and revealing an alabaster neck. "Any benefits?"

"No," way too loud and quick. "Sometimes a spotted banana is just a banana."

Not believing him. "What'd you bring this woman in her for? To parade your little hippie 'friend' in front of me?"

Roy, glowing with pleasure. "You've got the wrong idea. About all this."

"Don't you think I could do the same? Right now?"

"Is that so. Is this a fact." His tone, lowering into an ominous, placid timbre. The shark eyes, returning. "Anybody we know?"

Frightening. Button, knowing this voice meant an abject and absolute shitstorm of ire now building inside him. "Hey, look. It's not what you think."

A forced smile on the coffee shop manager's face, and turning back to her husband. Sounding like Button's fractured syntax: "Let's not. Do this. In here, Roy. Unky-dunky?"

Hands flat on the table. Bowing his head as if in prayer. "How typical. You and your smart-ass little redneck mouth don't got a motherfreaking clue what sort of conversation you're interrupting."

Creedence, an exhalation that sounded like *OOOOOOOh*. A stiff-armed salute toward the door. "Outside. If you don't mind."

"Certainly." Winking and getting up. "Dear."

Button, sipping her tea and watching a furious argument unfold in the parking lot.

How wrong it had all gone. She had been feeling heart centered and oh-so on the right track of revealing her condition to Roy here on the island, on what she perceived as neutral ground, at least when it came to their relationship. How myopic she'd been. How stupidly selfish about admitting her terminal illness.

But as the 29th chapter of the Tao Te Ching teaches:

> *The Master sees things as they are,*
> *without trying to control them.*
> *She lets them go their own way,*
> *and resides at the center of the circle.*

Their voices, Roy and Creedence, so raised and brittle as to rattle the glass in the huge windows. Oy.

An Island cop pulled up in his cruiser. That couldn't be good. Every time Button saw a cop car now she felt a touch of PTSD. Was afraid they were coming to blow her away like they had Howdy Shull. Bullets, whizzing around. But for what had he been executed? The death of his sister?

No.

Control. Tightening the screws. Making sure resisters knew the fate awaiting them.

Button Sykes, in the center of her circle, the eyes of the universe looking back upon itself with remarkable interest and engagement. With Heather's assistance, she'd soon show herself what control really meant.

Speaking of circles, once the drama with Roy and Creedence dissipated and enough got settled for them to part again, he packed up belongings like spring workout clothes and sneakers, cleaned out his Mercedes 450SL and spent time with all the cats, talking to them and promising his return, especially a squat, chubby calico female who scampered after him wherever he went, her tail held high in good cheer at the appearance of the human *pater familias*. Once ready to head back north to Edgewater County, however, Button first asked for a ride to see the ocean; a secluded, sandy spot, if possible. She had a particular image inside a circle to draw, though that aspect of the plan she kept in secret.

❁ 🖪 ✐

ROY AND BUTTON, THE BEACH WINDSWEPT, A COLD FRONT COMING through, and much more pronounced. A county park on the inlet between Sedge and another barrier island, where Roy said he had once taken quite a memorable swim.

"I need to walk alone for a few minutes."

"But it's so brisk."

"How much sicker? Could I get?"

He didn't think her wit at all funny. "I'm scared to death right now. Please."

"That's sweet. But it will be fine."

Button checked the chart on her iPhone, and found the high tide all but finished and ready to withdraw. She chose a spot close to the approaching waterline, the waves near the inlet lapping gentle at the hard-packed gray sand. The wind, like ice through her clothing. Sand being forced into her sneakers.

She knelt and drew a symbol, meditated over its purpose: a spell to give herself the strength to live long enough to do more good, an abstraction representative of the flow of universal energy, a sigil she had found online rather than created herself—her powers, diminished. Still, she infused this adopted sigil with enormous care and intention, the impersonal, mystical circle imbued with the intention of doing the greatest good for the most people, her loved ones and family left alive, the friends and lovers she had known: her real family, her road fam, Heather, Jouquoya, Roy, Trudy, Jasper, Christy and Newbie—the entire world.

She meditated on the altruism inherent in her desire while staring at the symbol, imbuing it with purpose and power and meaning and love; waving her hand over it, she beamed cosmic star-energy into the lines, which began to glow before her eyes. After asking the mighty sea to take the image, to transmute Button's thought and magnify its potential to a point of infinitude —that all should have their fondest wishes come true, into tangible reality— she composed herself, waiting.

"But I can't stand out here forever. I'm cold, and sick, yo. I'm dying."

At first she fretted that she had drawn her sigil too far back in the sand, that the tide would march no further. She reminded herself that such a reality possible only if she first believed it, so she banished the notion and said 'when' the ocean decides to absorb and amplify the sigil. Not if.

A wave, a finger of undulating water, swept over and the markings vanished from sight, the indentions made by her small fingertip disappearing into the foam, sinking into the wet earth, and gone.

Relief. It would work. She had bought time.

A little.

Another, more powerful wave followed, splashing all the way to the tips of Button's shoes, causing her to jump back with a laugh of joy and happiness echoing from a painful throat. Now she knew her plan to make that temporal fourth dimension her bitch by dying on her terms, and in her own time, would work. Winning? You betcha.

ROY, CREEDENCE, AND THE COP

How long had she been sick?

In your head, Button's voice, answering clear as a gall-darn ringtone:

Since always.

Screeching and helpless: "*Who the fudge said that?*"

Your shout echoes across the parking lot of luxury cars resting amidst moss-laden cypress trees, an expanse of lined asphalt bleached into a mute, graying recalcitrance by the seaside sun.

You look over expecting to see her, Button, sitting inside the coffee shop in the booth you've just vacated to escape the news she gave you — cancer? *really*? HORSESHIT — but the reflection allows only a distorted view of Spanish moss hanging from the tree limbs, the luxury vehicles, and coastal sunlight. Button, disappearing before your eyes.

Much quieter. "Who said that? Who's in my head?"

Now, only silence. Birdcalls. Traffic from the circle. Voices, echoing; sure.

But only yours.

Nuts. That's what you are. Fruity as a nutcake. Nucking futs.

But who could blame you? You will lose, lose, lose. Lose everything. Everything but your money, which keeps growing, unnaturally so. Wait till the plane sells. A mad fat stash of cash. Hell, you've got fifty grand of your granddaddy's skimming, in literal bills he stashed away, bit-by-bit through the decades.

Only last week, in fact, you removed it from the hiding spot, before Manny and Ahmad found it. Not a racial bias; who knows about anyone finding a bag of money in the floor. Look at all the movies and books with such a plot device, as though human nature in play, and inevitably leading to ruin.

Eh—so what if they had found it? Skimmed some. Or took it all. Meaningless. Now you will lose your new best friend. Won't you.

It's what you'd said to her on the way home from Heather Ponderview's pyramid, blurting it out, if not in realization, then perhaps hope. Or desperation. "Are we best friends? Or what?"

Button had smiled, so loving. Squeezed your hand.

You gotta go back in. Get over yourself, here. Talk to your pal—this important woman, to you and others—and see what to do about her sitch.

You will nurse this cancer patient through her chemo, that's what. A charge to keep.

A task.

A goal.

A purpose.

At last.

◌▣⊘

BUT IT'S TOO FAR GONE—DUDE, SO MUCH CANCER THERE'S NOTHING FOR it, as she says.

Your response? You can't accept this, shoot no you can't. "We haven't paid for all this science-y medical crap for naught, by God. You know how many—damn 'Race for the Cure' sponsorships I've sported?"

None of that talk washes with her. Chuckling at your shenanigans.

Button goes into this long-ass speech about all the fake stuff to which people hold allegiance, all these ideas about countries and religion and races and every bit being imaginary.

From here on out, you must be careful as crossing mossy rocks in an icy stream. Listen to what she has to say. Her wisdom, it's foolishness. Maybe cancer in the brain. No, not yet, she said. Damn near everywhere else, though.

Creedence, bless her heart, butting in and acting all jealous, and you're back here in the parking lot with her now having it out.

"I'm not screwing Button Sykes." Guilty, your voice shatters. You'd love nothing more, but this is Trudy-guilt. "How dare you—she's sick. She's dying."

Your wife holds her galloping steeds. Looks more horrified than angry. *"Die-ing?* For heaven's sake."

You explain the nature of the conversation she interrupted.

"Oh, fiddlesticks. Cancer?"

Icy adrenaline, coursing into your gut. "Must run in her family."

"They say it does." Sneaking a glance, giving Button a little wave and a forced smile. "What's she gonna do? Chemo?"

"Nothing."

"Pardon *moi*?"

"Meditate her fudging way out, for all I know."

"That's dumb."

"But also: what the freak is going on here?"

Looks caught, like a naughty kid. "With what?"

A rock of fresh grief in your gut. Too much more, and it'll turn into cancer, too. "You're still with him. Or somebody. Aren't ya. Just rip off the band-aid."

Creedence, insisting on her chastity. "What I said earlier? I was —jealous."

Aghast. "Of Button? That's absurd."

"Well. Sorry."

"Listen, I know you had gotten good at spinning tales. After reading what I read? And not having a clue? You had been lying like a rug for however long. So don't think you can start up. The fool-me part. I'll never be that easy."

More anger. "I'm telling you the truth."

Your fists clench. "Go on and let the air out of my balloon, woman."

"Mercy." Creedence, turning red as a ginger can get, which is considerable. Before she can holler at you, a cop car pulls up. Bloops its siren. "Oh —it's Phil."

"*Webhannet*? You're with him?" A surge of adrenaline—the magnitude of the betrayal, unthinkable. "No no no. No way. Not possible."

She punches you in the arm. Calls you a dummy. "Quit it. Now you're being silly. Are y'all *stoned*? *That* girl smells like weed." Realizing the cancer business. "Oh—I'm sorry. It must be medical."

"Check."

Webhannet gives a small wave and speaks into his radio inside the cruiser, sitting in its space you had designated for the Island police to enjoy at all times. With or without a cop parked there, the sign alone— RESERVED FOR LAW ENFORCEMENT USE ONLY—acted as a deterrent to any mischief makers with property crimes on their degenerate, afflicted, anti-social minds.

You wave him out of the vehicle. "My boy. Sight for sore eyes."

His body language, stiff. "Mr. Pettus—didn't expect to see you here on the island today."

"Took a notion."

"Hi, Phil."

"Ma'am."

"*Ma'am*? Now, c'mon."

"Mrs. Creedence."

"You've never called me that."

You watch this exchange as though following a table tennis match. "I still prefer such traditional courtesy. I miss hearing it out of young people today. Pierced, dreadlocked, tatted little crust-muffins, the lot."

Creedence, her countenance brittle. Sighing.

You wonder if she's banging Webhannet.

The dude you're paying a grand a month.

To watch over her.

As established: no way.

But if true? The boys at the lodge, the ring of which both you and Phil Webhannet wear along with all the fellas at the hanger, would censure and berate the young policeman for such a transgression. Again—the police officer, well spoken, a solid service record, an initiate. Too much to lose.

"Everything. All right? These days? Officer? With the goings-on?"

"Squared away. Not too busy."

"That's what we want to hear."

Creedence, watching customers file into the CBSI. "Gotta scoot."

"Be there to help."

"We got it."

"That's my girl."

"'Woman,' if you don't mind." Flashing you with devil eyes. Her braid bouncing, your wife hurries inside.

"See you later. Ma'am."

Leaning against the warm hood of Webhannet's cruiser: "Seems stressed. What's the deal?"

"The coffee shop, it's been busy." His shoulder mic crackles. Pots down the volume, because whatever it is can wait compared to you. Gives you a tingle knowing your check-in carries such energetic heft.

"Good. Proud of her."

"You should be."

"Should I?"

"Yes, sir." An open-palmed gesture you perceive as pleading. "Not a worry. Situation nominal."

You tell him you have multiple balls juggling. A discrete secret hand-shake. "Keep those reports coming. I sent you the latest Paypal this morning."

Relieved by a call from his superior officer, he offers a quick bow and back in his cruiser, speeding around the traffic circle like the Enterprise warping out of orbit.

A realization, heavy on your heart—how will you trust her again? Even if you could get her back. How did folks get over infidelity? Would you suspect every male in her life forever? Seems no way to live.

But for one who *forgives* and *forgets*? The path to serenity. According to Button.

It occurs to you: you and your dream girl have not worked on your relationship the way you must. Haven't tried counseling. Let Edgewater County distract you for half a year.

There you go. Talk out these issues. Meditate on it.

Together.

A plan. You would speak to Creedence about getting on the path. See if she's interested. Take her to classes, to guided meditations. Have Button impart the same hooey she's taught you, which must half-have a smidgen of truth to it. You feel so good after meditation…

And right now…

Your thoughts seem ordered. Not galloping ahead. You quell the roiling dread over Button, and put on a relaxed and happy face. Creedence, she's stressed because you're freaking. That's all that's happening.

Enough already. Time to go grab the Mercedes and get Button back home to Edgewater County. She needs rest. You've got to help her. Priority one. Then? Figuring out your wife and this whole mess. Get it all straight. Put matters in order. No other choice—everybody's counting on you.

YOU GOT THIS.

MANNY AND AHMAD

Caught Ahmad ass fixing to dig into that hole where the money sit. Manny camp in the living room, listening and waiting, until he heard the sound the durn wood panel make when you pull it up. A feeling come over—Ahmad act squirrelly. His ass about to carry out a scheme. Been sour all week in the kitchen. Slamming shit around. His mac and cheese didn't taste as good. Manny think the milk turned, but Old Neecie said it because Ahmad had his butt up on his shoulders. That the food need to be cooked with love, not a piss-pot attitude. She ain't wrong.

That sound, the wood sliding, it haunt Manny. Come to him in dreams. Daydreams, anyway. Him and Becky L, laughing and hauling ass out of Edgewater County like Bonnie and Clyde in an old flivver.

Ahmad standing with his hands on his skinny-ass hips right as Manny bust in. "You cock-knockin', greedy-ass piece of junk, I'm-a gonna—*whoa.*"

Manny's gut drops: the hole in the floor, empty.

Too late.

He go all apocalyptic on Ahmad, lunge and grab and slap: "Where the money at, bitch?"

Ahmad, cussing and slapping back at Manny. "Well, you the one oughta know."

Manny push him off. "I ain't touch shit. *Now where is it.*"

"That's what I'm fixing to beat outta you."

"Champ? You couldn't beat eggs in a measuring cup."

Ahmad, he snort and pace in a circle. "A muh-fuh make up his mind? To lay hands on it? And it gone? *Where that money at?*"

"I ain't know."

"Well, I ain't know, either."

"All right, now."

"I ain't come slinking in from no cotton field. Grew up on the same streets your ass did. Done time—on the needle, on the dime. Done time in Angola, muh-fuh. And you ain't being straight. Who you give it to? The white girl?"

Oh, boy—now they get into it. Hollering, beating on each other.

By the time Ahmad, wiry little shit, clocked Manny a good'un and knocked him on his butt, though, the whole mess blow over. Put a hurt on his eye, though, them bony Ahmad knuckles cracking hard, and a lump already swollen and tender. Manny ass don't deserve no chuck to the head. No sir. "Ain't took dollar one."

"Then who did?"

"Roy E. Pettus must've took possession of that dusty old money. Only explanation." Which don't change nothing—Ahmad was gonna take it. "I knew you was scheming."

Boy like to mess hisself. "I wasn't set on pinching it all, bro."

Manny crack his neck and draw himself up. "Next time you take a poke at me, best make it stick."

"Know what I popped you for? Ain't the money."

"What, little smartass?"

"Running round on my sister."

Shit. "Ain't none of that what y'all think."

Ahmad laugh like Manny doing an old Eddie Murphy routine. "Everybody know you still tapping that stank. Where you think you is, back home in a city? This shit Tillman Falls, man. God-damn."

Manny can't deny none of it—whether the pussy happening or done, his heart conflicted as shit, and okay, he know they all know. "You ain't got no idea what it like, little man. You ain't been married. Hell—I don't know you know what love mean. And I been beat up enough about it all already. So go with with your bad-ass money-robbing self, and see who keep the high ground on this incident."

"Naw. Why don't you go on and keep preaching, preach."

The rancor continue until Ahmad start packing. Say he going back to N'awlins, see what all they done with it since the storm. He tired of this shit with Manny and Neecie, and Manny say, good riddance, till he realize how hard his ass gonna work to make up for Ahmad being gone from the kitchen. Always been that way. They went through a shit-ton of kitchen help back in the city. Manny always starting over.

Manny wait in the living room on an old couch. Heavy. Folks used to make furniture, and everything, to last. This house solid as hell, still.

Manny keep on. "I can't believe you was gonna rob, yo."

"I got me a headstash, motherfucker. Enough to get gone."

"Bullshit."

"Don't you worry bout it. Bet."

Doubt that headstash shit. Ahmad never held onto a nickel, not that Manny seen.

Unlike that old rascal Rabbit.

Dang. Manny wish he had learnt to hold back on Neecie. Put it away in a hole in the durn floor. Woulda got soaked back in Ninth Ward, though. Wouldn't it.

He say okay, okay, and wait for his brother-in-law to get his ass out. Nothing worse than being mixed up with some low-rent sorry ass like a brother-in-law who ain't worth a shit. Blood don't hardly excuse that, much less marriage. Thief. Through Ahmad actions, Manny see how wrong it would-a been to take that money—like getting the moral of a fable. Word.

❋ ⊞ ✐

ONCE HE FO-SHO AHMAD ASS GONE DOWN THAT GRAVEL ROAD FOR GOOD, Manny sit on Ahmad bed. Sheets stink like rotten cabbage, him and his nasty-ass self sweating and jizzing all night long.

Roy Pettus—fuck, bro. Money out the wazoo. Talking about the stock market lately, which seem to keep going on up. Manny ain't got no money in stocks, or socks, or mattresses, or the floorboards.

He ain't got much money period. That small biz ownership for ya.

And in a few years? He looking at babygirl college and shit. She gonna get scholarship-ed out the butt, though. She that smart. Ain't no money worries there.

❋ ⊞ ✐

AFTER AHMAD DRIVE OFF IN HIS BEATER CAMRY GOING KNOCK-KNOCK, IT seem like the last scene in a dumb movie, and it time to fade out and get on with real life. Manny, moving his ass back home. He got to run off that Yunk-Yunk troubling his babygirl.

Moving out the old Pettus house, though, Manny bust into tears like a little bitch. Thinking about that girl. Not getting to do her no more. No-more hang out by the pond, hear the bird-calls and watch the sun rise with her legs alongside his. Her moaning: love me, lover. Love me, honey.

Oh, honey, she would say when she started to get off. *Honey. Oh, honey.*

Manny all decided, though. And yet, he still don't know about blowing up his life again. If he wouldn't pull the trigger, if she said, yo. Can't quite close the door.

Can he.

Manny pull himself together. Wipe his eyes. Quit with this mess over Becky L. That what he gonna do.

❊🐾⊘

LATER THAT NIGHT ROY PETTUS LOOK DOWNRIGHT GREEN WHEN HE come in, from where he don't say, as Manny finish sweeping and cleaning up.

Roy, he spend too much time with that little Asian girl. He don't know, maybe Roy Pettus doing that thang. She kinda cute. Too little for Manny and his thick-old hogleg. He break her mess in half.

"Bossman. I reckon we got to talk about over yonder."

Faraway. Emotionless. He like Dr. Spock on *Star Track.* "Yonder where, Manny."

He tell him about Ahmad taking off, throwing in detail—the argument, him packing up to go home, Manny saying, good riddance. "Think me and the old lady work it out."

That get his attention. "Y'all asses patch it up?"

"Trying."

His eyes search Manny's. "No shit. You lucky sumbitch."

"I don't know bout all that. We'll see."

He sit down heavy in one of the porch rockers. It creak. A cloud come over him. "Gonna be quiet around here now."

"Aw, chill that out. When you get the hunky-tunk back open, we gonna be right across from each other every day again."

Don't seem to help his mood much. Roy Pettus change the subject. "Selling the Piper Meridian."

"Yo, dog. Thought we was gonna go flying one day."

"I did. Today. The last time. With Button."

"Smooth?"

"The flight? Not bad. Always a thrill. I'll never forget it "

Durn if his voice ain't cracking. He all broke up about some kinda mess. His own wife, Manny reckon. He ask his bro if he all right.

Roy Pettus say he is. Thinking about all his people he done lost. The dog too, even.

Manny say, we all lose shit. Common to everybody scratching round on this rock. "But—you best be glad them cops didn't shoot your ass."

"Yeah. Not over all that, either."

Talking don't seem to help him much. But he end up giving Manny a little smile, say his ass happy for them and the babygirl. That he hoped having the house out here was a help—to him, to Ahmad, to them all.

Manny want to say, you lucky you took out that money while you could, yo. Maybe everybody lucky he did. Remain to be seen. Becky L sure ain't leaving town with no sax-man. She mad now. Silent. Ain't no good. He fucked anywhere he decide to drop a deuce. May as well chill in his own crib again.

ROY EARL AND HILL HAMPTON

With you hanging on her every move, Button, stiff, climbs into her Subaru Baja and waves bye.

She's off to pick up Burnie. You withhold the shattering tide of emotion welling inside you. Give her your best grin and thumb's up.

After a long lingering hug and a cry and a pledge to spend tons of time together—with you saying, whatever you need it's covered, anything at all and much appreciated by her, who remains way more calm about the illness than you can fathom; and remind me, she said, to tell you about this mystical experience I had when I went back to Heather's without you—you receive Manny's news from your tenant, who shuffles over and plops down on the front porch, unloading it all without asking what's going on with you. Some only care about themselves.

But you don't give a rip, and wouldn't tell Manny about Button's illness anyway; all you can think is, goody on zipping it up and putting his marriage back together, which makes you call Creedence.

The long drive along multiple interstates, around the Columbia beltway and at last north into Edgewater County, an eternity compared to the plane ride, but not so different when you add in the time taken on fueling and check-listing and futzing around hoe-ing the hay with The Colonel and the other boys at the hanger, had been her sweet freckled face.

Not much said on the drive between you and Button. What was to say? You didn't have the steam to lobby her to try chemo. Her disease, way advanced. You mused on having missed an opportunity with your wife to keep from ruing the truth about your friend's life dangling on a thread. Suddenly-like. Other shoe; dropping.

You aren't an idiot; some puzzles can't be solved, nor all repairs effected, not once the damage is too great. But a part of you vibrates FUCK THAT NOISE and you feel the need to act. Act now; act fast. But how.

No answer.

Through gritted teeth, you shriek: "SIRI: REDIAL CREEDENCE."

This time, you leave a message.

Calm. Measured tones. "Look here, babycakes. I know we were just there together, and why I didn't say it I don't know, but I got some important crap to lay on you. But it ain't crap—it's all good. I love you. *Love* you. Still. Always did. And I want us to figure this out. Finally. And get on with the future. Our future, I mean. Together. The future's coming on, there's no time to waste. I feel like I wasted years already—don't you see? Why I couldn't say it all to your face down there, it was this mess with Button. I got blindsided—she's real sick, hon. Jesus, what a fresh mess that is. But anyway, I don't know if that's good or not, that I couldn't say all this to you. But it's done now. So maybe we could—talk. Talk to someone together. About issues. So, call me. I'm messed up. I'm alone. I wanted to tell you when I was there. And now, Manny and Ahmad, their time living out here is done. It's me. Alone. It's—"

Your voice breaks hard and you get an icy cold shiver. Like your intuition's telling you how 'together' ain't gonna happen.

"You get it, I'm sure. I love you. Call me."

You sound desperate.

Bullcrud. You remember that day at the airfield. How she plead for you not to leave. Begged your forgiveness. All a terrible misunderstanding, mistake. That was desperation.

Ah, wait—all still in play.

Sure it would.

You're golden. Relax, pal.

❁ ᴍ ⊘

WHILE YOU WAIT FOR THE CERTITUDE OF HER POSITIVE REPLY TO manifest, you find yourself unable to sit at home staring at the wall of records and stumbling over the speaker cables snaking their five-grand way across the rug and worse, seeing dust on the gear already.

To escape, you do what any good old boy with a pickup truck in the driveway would, which means driving through the county, taking a big loop-around. The more you drive, the less you think.

You spiral outward until you find yourself in the bump in the road called Red Mound, think about the whorehouse out this way. Also, the few scrubby acres of Red Mound State Park, the long, gentle swell of the mound. Part of county lore that everyone learned as a kid, they said the mound to have once contained giant human skeletons. The far side of the mound, which every Edgewater County schoolchild ended up being taken on a field trip to see, sported the obvious scars of a long-ago excavation and partial, inelegant reconstruction. You always wondered why, if such remains were discovered, wouldn't the rest of the mound have been excavated? Wouldn't that part be in the history books?

Stories. Fables. Still, the thought of giants in the earth, it gives you the chills.

Perhaps when they saw what they found, the crew became convinced to put back the sacred remains of the giants who once roamed and ruled these rolling midlands.

Scary out in the woods. This lonely country highway, hilly but straight, the gloom of dusk a hue of faded denim across the horizon. Not another vehicle coming either way for miles. Moody. Spooky.

Instead of heading further into the Pisgette National Forest you turn north on 231, by the federal prison floodlit gray and hard and imposing as heck behind all the razor wire, more frightening than the mysteries of deep country dark could hope to aspire set way back in a spindly forest of pines. You hook onto a back road you remember and take upcountry highway through Parsons Hollow, which ain't nothing but a literal bend in the road, a post office and a pharmacy and an old general store, which give you a flash of the pre-history of the Dixiana building, its original life as the Dixie-Anna Dry Goods town grocer. You'd apply for Hysterical Society designation, but you don't want to tie your hands re: future development.

Loathe to go home, you hurtle north through even less developed bumps in the highway like Dabney Crossroads, communities but not towns. Next, you flash by Saltcreek's green sign speckled by some kid's shotgun blast, your visit to their fair village of scattered farms and dilapidated mobile homes is over faster than virgin coitus. With nothing but the speed dropping and a farmhouse or two with crumbling, gray barns and other outbuildings, the rotting vine-covered shell of an old filling station, why bother naming this patch of dirt at all, you wonder?

What shall we say—shall we call it by a name? Above-pay-grade alert.

Now that the Reverend Nixon has his referendum scheduled, he'll get his name change and everyone can move on with building a fresh future—god knows you suffer no lack of ideas for moving the town forward, and New Falls City makes all kinds of sense to you. Marketable as hell.

Poor Manny, the dumbass, had stirred the pot by opening his mouth to Dobbs, hadn't he? So much for your nascent merchant's association getting any traction, not with one of your principals having shot his mouth off in the press and made enemies all the way up to Mauldin Saugus.

Christ. You should have known Manny didn't have good sense, not dicking around right under the glare of the streetlights around the town green. Talking about crapping where you eat. Him and Creedence both looking for trouble way too close to home.

You wanted nothing to do with any of it—town politics, soap operas, dramas. After the festival you weren't sure what would be next, but it had to be more than all this farcical nonsense. Edgewater County had felt not like a destination but a way station, rather, as you rode on the existential rails, with next stop Mysteryville. But that's life, isn't it? Who knows what the future holds? That type-deal?

Button would say that the future doesn't matter because it's all right now.

All-right-now. Baby, it's all-right-now.

At least you've gotten your money's worth out of the stereo upgrade in Rabbit's F-150, which you have taken out driving instead of the Mercedes, whose engine still sat ticking into coolness. You crank the tunes. Zep. *Houses of the Holy*.

Righteous.

As the sunset finishes with Western skies blazing scarlet, you drive faster around the bending rural roads here in the northern, hillier part of the county along the ridge, which after the visit Heather Ponderview and your own solo misadventure, seem far from challenging.

A few miles to the west lay the rounded hump of Sugeree Hill, elevation 250 feet. This earthen hump a naturally occurring monadnock rather than another Indian mound, existing as an erosion-worn smidgen of the ancient Appalachian range in South Carolina, a tidbit, a morsel of a mountain. Maybe that's why you feel so drawn to the upcountry: in a sense, you grew up right next door to a little-bitty-baby mountain.

The scar tissue growing around your still-healing cracked collarbone gives you a twinge, and you think, okay, that's a sign I need to slow down.

Button, teaching you to look upon physical reactions as precognitive of coming eventualities.

Ha! There, only seconds after you slow down, a rabbit shoots across the road, proving the point. Jam on the brakes anyway, yeah, but not as hard, and when you do your shoulder flares with pain.

Pay attention to the signs. That's what your girl Button would say.

Or she'd only think it, yet you'd somehow still hear the words. The connection you enjoy could transcend her coming death. Another in a series of who-da-fuh-knows ain't gonna get nobody nowhere, beau.

ENOUGH OF THIS NIGHTTIME CRUISING. ALONE. IN THE WOODS. IT'S LIKE you're playing poor-you, piling on the lonely and hitting yourself over the head with it.

At a stop sign you sit idling like Dreyfuss in CE3K, scrolling through your iTunes looking for something worthy of following up Led Zeppelin. No brilliant white light illuminates your truck, and you end up not picking anything, choosing to drive in silence. In the relative quiet—the F-150, despite being ten years old, purrs smooth at the stop sign—you notice that your ears are ringing, you guess from the noisy flight and all your loud music.

Middle of nowhere. Gives you the creeps.

You put it in gear and turn right, moving on through the deep, thick woods and lonely roads of the northern county. You'd be lost if you weren't so close to home—this is the ground of your people, near the river and heading back south, now, as you come up where River Ridge Road intersects the north highway.

But again, you refuse to return home to the empty house, so you cut over using a dirt road you know through the late J. W. Rembert's land to 79, finally to the bypass around Tillman Falls and zipping over to Chilton. Even at this time of night, knots of traffic form at the few stoplights in the harsh ochre of the light from the commercial corridor, none of which you could have imagined in the 70s, a kid stuck a million miles from everywhere; smack in the middle of no place.

Colorful back-lit signage, the strip anchored on its freeway-end by the Appleby's where, for the half a second you allow yourself to realize it, Creedence saw your worst side all over again and stayed broken up with your bullying ass for keeps.

Ouch.

Out-parcels stand guard before the high walls of the strips behind them, where there ought to be a fudging fruitshake maker minting money from his endeavors, and where's a Starbucks drive-through in this two-bit nightmare corner of bumblefuck? The shimmering, halogen-illuminated acreage of the car dealership. Two, three, four strip centers and eight fast-food and fern bar restaurants lining the roadway on either side; four lanes now, with concrete culverts extending to the rail crossing before town, what had been a two-lane cutting through a pine barren and a few marshy patches which would flood during big boomers and downpours. The road, as it happens, where the car accident killed Devin's girlfriend, crippled Dobbs, and ruined your future brother-in-law's life.

You hated Chilton. Hated driving through to get to Tillman Falls, despised being forced to shop here at the concentration of the goods and commerce. And so, coming tonight was supposed to make you feel better?

What are you doing?

Get away from all this crap. An intonation from on high.

"Working on it."

Back over by Pike's and the big monster truck draped by colorful car lot flags, past the county road leading to dirt turnoff for the fishing bluff, and within a minute or two you're on River Ridge Road, more houses than in your youth, but retaining its lonely, mostly undeveloped status.

But wait. Here, a plan:

You'd talk Letty and Jasper into selling the pecan orchard and working with someone yourself to develop an exclusive—tucked away *and* exclusive—subdivision of premium homes. With this much bedroom community status here in Edgewater County now, it wouldn't take much to attract the monied gentry who'd love to have seclusion and access to the river above the Sugeree Station, away from the clutter of the lake country. You'd cut down trees, make views down the hill to the water's edge, which couldn't see now, but can well imagine. Make some moolah, some real money, yo, off that deserted old lonely patch of useless land, every homeowner a king, with an ocean of pecans under their feet, nuts only they could exploit. And you'd be their Ron Nawalinski. Now, that cat? Suffers nary a care in the world.

Before Button comes down on you all Greenpeace-like, you'd leave the cluster of natural trees down in the Glade. That goes without saying. The rest, you'd remake. In your image. You'd work with the arborist who advised you all in the Old Market when they redid the streets and you planted trees for both eventual shade and brilliant fall color. You'd instill an art to Pecan Orchard Acres (a Pettus Properties® Project) at every perceivable level of reality, with a mind-bending attention to detail designed to ensure both quality of work, appealing aesthetics, and a frugality of construction, finishing and landscaping solutions.

But more: you will name the streets after 1960s and 70s sex symbols who'd given you adolescent sexual titillation and pleasure. Goldie Hawn Crossing. Joey Heatherton Way. Adrienne Barbeau Boulevard. Farrah Fawcett Circle. The biggest and grandest properties, nearest the river? Karen Black Court. A marketing hook on which to hang one's hat. Fat Gen-X dudes like you, with money and who watched too much TV as kids, that's who'd dig this community of yours.

Maybe you could live at the far end of Karen Black. You'd find serenity at such a point of dimensionality, as Button might put it. Feel like it all you surveyed was not only yours, but built in a spirit of benevolence and noblesse oblige. That you made a difference in the life of your hometown.

Invigorated, you consider taking notes. Sounds like a new project. Once the festival's put to bed, won't you need one?

You ask Siri to take a voice memo, which opens up the recorder. By the time it takes for the recording 'dong' to sound in your ear, however, you feel like an idiot.

A subdivision. In your own image.

Christ.

Ego. That's all this is. Trying to get in control.

Still. The vision had come; the warmth in the gut; a tingling along the leg. Worth considering.

◌ 🅱 ⊘

HUNGER, NOW, BUT NOT FOR ENDEAVOR, NOR THE REDEVELOPMENT OF your beloved pecan orchard. Your stomach, empty and growling.

You imagine the cupboard and the fridge. Both sparse.

A mile before the long driveway and the End State Maintenance sign that no one has fixed despite two or three calls from you to the DOT, you cut a three-point turn, burn up more fossil fuels to head back to Chilton and snag yourself some grub. Hit the big shiny new Publix, lay in supplies, stock the larder and such. Skip the drive-throughs like you've been prone to hitting since moving back home. Don't get crap like chicken nuggets. As Manny says, them ain't nothing but beaks and feet.

Beaks and feet. Beaks and feet. A new mantra.

Pink foam. Spumy, fake food foam. Today's special includes FDA certified and guaranteed fifty percent beaks and feet content.

Training yourself to not want that filth. Look at you. Twenty pounds you've put on since coming back here. Still, the emptiness calls for fulfillment, and you press the gas and hurry toward the dusty ochre streetlamp glow on the horizon, an endless false sunset to the South.

YOU GRAB A HUNDRED BUCKS WORTH OF GRUB, INCLUDING FOUR VEGGIE sub sandwiches already made up, one on which to nosh while driving home. You chew through the bread and cold cuts as you catch the last traffic signal at the turnoff to the bridge and the Sugeree Station. You curse a cloud of bread crumbs. If not for another vehicle pulling up beside you on the otherwise deserted highway, you'd have punched it and run the fucker.

Now you have on the Allman Brothers Band, loud. You hear that they've played their final show and retired the band, all one brother left. *Damn!* you said when you news came through the feed. Not like when Jerry Garcia died—that hurt. Still, this one felt like *Damn!*, too. Drawing the curtain. Enough already.

You note it's a truck, another F-150, idling in the turn lane. Black, tinted windows. Rims, spinning backwards. Jacked up. A spoiler on the tailgate. A throaty engine. A beast, a dark dragon—the kinda F-150 that could beat up your granddaddy's aging ride in a schoolyard scuffle. A carload of gang-bangers. Better not make eye contact, not that it's possible through the tint.

The passenger window, rolling down. You tense up.

Not a miscreant—not 'below' the law, so to speak—but instead, that rascal Mayor Hampton. Figures the legacy Ford dealer would have a custom job.

Upon your return to Edgewater County you'd found Hampton's son and grandson running the dealership, while the patriarchal Hampton stuck to his mayoral duties. Who knew how business was in the car trade? Who could afford a new lot-pristine ride besides you, anyway? Somebody, you reckoned.

Hell, Dick Cissel Dodgeland had moved down to the lake country from downtown Columbia, giving the Hampton dealership stiff and direct competition where for many years there had been none. The way of the capitalistic world. Folks were still going into debt for cars. That's all you know.

"I thought that might've been you, Roy Earl."

"Guilty."

"You holding up all right, bubba?"

"Outstanding. Never better."

"That build-out at the honkytonk giving you fits?"

"We're chipping away at it. Yes, we are."

Like everyone, he asks when the sign will be re-hung. "Downtown looks bare without the letters DIXIANA lighting up that corner of the green."

"It's all but done. Sparing no expense, on any of it."

"Seems like a beautiful thing you're doing for this town. And for your granddaddy's memory."

Choking up. All you do is wave him off.

He gets it, changes the subject. "Understand we got another meeting on the festival plans. I hear y'all about got it all squared away."

"Odds and ends. The event planner we hired, she's a pro. I ain't had to do too much sweating. More focused on getting that honkytonk back open again in time. These meetings, though. They gonna wear me out."

"Welcome to my world. I come back from Florida, working on this deal with a developer who wants to—well. Shouldn't yak about it."

"A developer?" This makes your leg tingle. "Sure you should. This is me."

He considers this. "They looking at the old mill and the mill village. Turn it into a retirement community, with condos overlooking the river. Big-ass deal. I'm talking an interstate exchange, new retail and commercial center on one side, industrial park on the other. Them developers already got anchor stores signed on, two or three or four, I can't half remember right now. This is a big freaking deal, son."

Now here's some synchronicity. You think about developing land near the river; news breaks about land near the river teetering upon development. Jungian collective unconscious-nonsense; or, maybe there's meat on the bones of Button's quantum consciousness theories.

"Be good for the county, wouldn't it? But look here—who's gonna live in all these freaking places," a thought whispered to you earlier when you had your divine subdivision vision.

"Columbia's still a-growing this way."

Your balloon pops. How penny-ante, your sexy sirens of 70s cinema street signs idea now seems. "That'll be a real legacy-making deal. Best of luck."

"Speaking of legacies, looking forward to hearing all that music on the green, son. It'll be a good thing. What about an annual shindig?"

A forced smile; an inside-baseball joke to yourself. "Hey—who knows?"

"That pretty niece of mine coming up for it?" Like you to Burnie, Hill Hampton had been Creedence's dad's best friend. His tone darkened. "Somebody told me y'all wasn't getting along that good."

"Oh, naw. Nothing like that. She's running that coffee shop of mine down there, I'm dealing with this mess. We'll get it together again soon."

Satisfied. "Now listen, there's another dangling thread I wanted to talk to you about, a tie-in with the ol' Dix getting back in business. But, too much for here—shoot-fire. I done missed my arrow again."

"Just go through. Nobody here but the two of us."

"And look at who we are."

"That's what I'm saying."

"Hell, the highway commissioner's a friend. I grant thee official permission to run on, Roy Earl."

A wave and you both motor off through the red light, a glimpse of the Mayor in your rearview thumbing his iPhone and making his left turn. Kids today with the texting. Can't it wait?

Not if you were in Button's condition.

Suddenly the festival, the merchant's association, the ELMS, The Dixiana, all of it feels futile and small, and you're so empty you don't even want the good pot Button gets for you.

Wait—from where would you get your doobage? Once she's—gone? The surrealism of her revelation hits you anew.

The weed. A misdirection. That's what you fixated on, a pitiful sleight-of-attention from the hyperemotional aspects of the sitch, like a magician's left hand distracting the audience from the right. If Button Sykes were about to die soon, who'd be your pot connection? Now there was a problem. Yeah.

That fucking Button. Asshole. Leaving you in the lurch.

Sitting in your granddaddy's truck in the yard of the house back in the dark country woods you explode, weeping hard and true. You roar horse-puckey on her crap about not getting treatment. Wipe your nose and eyes, which sting like fire from the vinegar and mustard and pickle brine from the sub sandwich.

But what are you going to do? Force chemo on her? It's Button's life. Hers to lose, hers to win.

Jesus—all starting to sound like a lame-ass Eagles lyric. The Dude had been right.

You pull yourself together. All Button represented was the loss of another great love. You ought to be used to it by now, beau.

So quit whining, slacker. Get these groceries inside. Finish the sandwich. Plot out the rest of your life. Or for once, listen to Button and plan nothing. Wait instead for outcomes to emerge of their own volition, making action arise from non-action. Either way, time's a-wasting.

Try not to forget, however, Button's request that you—or someone—take care of the old Revolutionary War bride grave tucked into an ancient, weedy corner of the cemetery. Why it matters, you haven't a clue. She said your Pa-paw used to do it, a tradition she kept up as long as she still could. Her eyes, so imploring. Like it might be important. You'll add it to the checklist.

GOOCH

By the time Bill Wimmel motored through the intersection that constituted ground zero of the little-populated Red Mound crossroads and into the thick piney woods of the national forest, he'd spaced, as the young ones would put it, his purpose in driving.

Oh—it'd been to take notes. Visit a few historical sites and gather data, yes-sir, for his historical novel. Before, before, before he ended up at some point in which he'd be unable to accomplish the mysterious goal of this peregrination.

He considered reversing course, but by the time he got to deliberating the notion, he'd forgotten why he'd have wanted to turn around, anyway. "Serious question. Not a softball. On the record: What on earth do you want to turn back?"

In a cracker drawl like Mayor Hampton, Gooch answered himself: "No comment. No comment, now. Git on outta here, Gooch."

He cackled, thumbing the simple, digital voice recorder that Dobbs gave him for Christmas, a newfangled solid state job about half the size of a Pez dispenser; one could plug it right into the port on the computer and listen. Yep. You play your interviews and transcribe away and have yourself a good old time, at least compared to the old days of squinting at shorthand. During one brief period Bill tried using one of those micro-cassette deals, but transcribing those tapes, a terrible chore in contrast to stopping and starting a Quicktime file with a foot pedal, a specialized transcriptionist's tool that also plugs into a USB port like the recorder.

No one would accuse Bill of being a Luddite. Sharp and hip and up to the minute. Got himself one of those tablet-phones, too. Too big for a pocket, though. Flimsy. He forgot it back at home, anyway.

"I'm on the way to view the marker commemorating the Colquitt-Gallatin Duel, the final such duel to take place in South Carolina. Fought over a question of business dealings involving the wife of one of the gentlemen, the death of Colonel J. T. W. Colquitt, a decorated war veteran and hero, at the hands of Colonel Nathanial Gallatin, a fellow war hero and attorney before the bar, would prompt the legislature to outlaw the practice forevermore. Until 1954, in fact, public officers in South Carolina were required not only to take an oath of service but also declare that they had never participated in a duel."

Gooch clicked off the recorder. Tossed it into the passenger seat, where it bounced and landed on its face. What he'd just said would be much more than the marker offered about the duel. The marker, a picture of which he had looked up on the internet already.

Terrifying—he'd had another reason for driving into the national forest. One he'd forgotten. Not to see the Colquitt-Gallatin highway marker.

Who knew?

The woods, deep and mysterious, even in the daylight. Bill wondered if he shouldn't stop and eat—he could see it out of the corner of his eye, a brown sack, but one he kept putting off tearing into, but he didn't know why he waited. A perfect spot to have lunch—that was the phrase in his head, or rather that he recalled being in his mind when he'd put that lunch together, which he could remember doing clear as day. Knew that it was peanut butter and fig preserves on whole wheat, a granola bar, and a yellowish Danjou he hoped the sunlight through the windshield would further soften. A sweet, ripe pear—nothing like it.

Out of the mists, there, a shimmering, colorful all-American sign; the interstate. Not the one to Charlotte running through Edgewater County, but the six-lane on the other side of the forest heading northwest into Greenville and the beginning of the Appalachian foothills. Gooch, thinking, *Now there had to be a reason I came all the way through the Pisgette Forest, and so I suppose I'll head north—that part's a feeling he can't shake—and see how long before it comes to me where I was going.*

Up to Asheville for the day?

To find the perfect spot, perhaps on the Blue Ridge Parkway, to eat?

Lunch would taste good. He should have packed one, that much he understood for certain. Hated looking for grub in an unfamiliar town. Never knew what you were gonna get. Didn't matter that cars were parked outside a joint, either. Didn't mean squat. People went where they felt comfortable, even if the fare wasn't all that hot. Especially in a small town. How many choices did one have?

Gooch signaled and merged and picked up the voice recorder, but once he'd gotten it flicked on, the red light stared at him like an evil eye, daring the journalist to remember what in the heck he'd intended to record. Or where he was going. Something about getting lunch. He'd keep driving till he found the right place.

At least he had company to keep him interested — Howard Shull, home from college and riding alongside Gooch in the passenger seat. Oh, that's right — Howard had talked Gooch into taking a run up to Charlotte to hit the Bar-B-Q Drive-In. Flirt and chase girls. Shull said they were faster and easier in the big city than the girls down at Southeastern University in Columbia, where he and Jasper Glasscock were both going to law school one day.

Howard, sitting beside Gooch in the car, smoked a cigarette while cussing up a storm over this'n that. Built up a head of steam over coverage in the paper, he said, about the cops shooting and burning him alive on the green.

Gooch, laughing, thinking how Shull would make for an imaginative attorney. You could be shot to death and burned up and still be riding in a car with Bill Wimmel going to Charlotte to chase girls, which deep down he didn't want. At all. He had loved Howard Shull for some time. But it was 1967, and you couldn't say such yearnings aloud. Not to anybody — in a town the size of Tillman Falls, even a fellow closet queen like him might not be trusted to keep a secret, not under duress. Not unless he wanted his skinny ass beaten — and Gooch's, too.

Bill prayed for release from his desires, but the prayers were only that his predilections remain in confidence. It had cost him his job in Atlanta — it's why he ended up back in Edgewater County. A foolish choice in the newsroom one night, a senior staffer walking in on him and colleague whose name and face escaped him only seconds before, because who would ever forget an unrequited love of one's life caught in the act of consummation?

"You think we're gonna score up here today, Wimmel? I'm hornier than a three-balled tomcat."

"We can't lose. You stink like a fried pork chop, though."

"What do you suppose I'm on about?" Howdy, burned beyond recognition, now that Gooch looked at him, which before was only through a squint. Like Howdy — Howard; he hated that childish nickname — was only half there. "Them cock-knockers lit me up like a campfire, and I wanna know one thing. Who will stand for me? For old Howard Shull? My crazy-ass sister? Those harpies in the ELMS? What I need's a good lawyer. And someone to tell my story."

A statement. "You've heard I'm writing a book."

"A book, you say?"

"Oh, that's right. It will be the ultimate book of Edgewater County lore and mythology and maybe even truth, if I can sneak that in there."

"Well that'd be a feat—the truth part." Howard, musing. "Book-writers, though. They're a dime a dozen these days. In case you hadn't noticed."

Gooch, paging daily through the myriad websites devoted to writing—how to do it, how to get published. He felt like he'd surfed through such articles forever, yet each day dawned as new. A fresh onslaught of advice and information and research to process. "Only so much true work. The rest? Dreck."

"Like in your newspaper."

Gooch snorted. "Well, at least those aren't stories I'm making up."

"Could've fooled me."

"Don't shoot the messenger."

Howard. He didn't seem queer. But maybe he was. Gooch would take anybody. A cripple in a wheelchair. Howard Shull, his flesh hanging from his gesturing arms in thin pink strips. The scent of brisket like they'd find at the Bar-B-Q Drive-In, once they got up there.

Could Gooch reveal himself to Howard?

The guilt and shame of it all. Wasn't supposed to be like this anymore. And yet.

Unless somebody felt the same. A compatriot. Isn't that what we all want in this life? A connection? Someone with whom to take a ride to the cemetery, one day? When everyone got old?

How you got to that place, Bill Wimmel hadn't the first clue, other than to drive there, now underway. He's young. There's time.

Or perhaps his queerness would all go away one day, like the lost memories of an amnesiac, and Gooch would wake up normal. Anything was possible. Howdy Shull, who Gooch had a vague memory of seeing shot and burned to death on the town green, sat riding in the car next to him, smoking not only a cigarette but also from the top of his head and his ears and eyes. A strangeness to it all. But also right as rain. A queer world, indeed.

CHRISTY

Christy, sitting in his trailer all the time, thinking he was going crazy. But he wasn't. Christy figured it out: Roy Pettus took the girl for himself. And hid her away.

After what happened on the green that day, the devil coming down and torching up Howdy Shull like Newbie blazing through one of his little meth-rocks. Howdy, burning up and damn near taking her too; Christy's heart shot into his throat and stayed there beating like crazy for hours. Being near Button Sykes had been the only time he could remember feeling peace in his heart. Before her, he hadn't known such a place existed inside him. And she had done nothing except be. Smile at him; and exist.

But now, Christy, told to stay away.

Unable to see her, did not know how to make contact and talk to her, and this ate at him and was what drove him, yea, oh lord, to go into her house like they done. Since then and the night at his grandmama's he had snakes twisting in his mind, slithering and making a squishy sound like a spoon going through macaroni and cheese.

Newbie worse, too, with his mess. And no money.

Christy, coming to terms: he will never have Aisha, Lillyanne Theodore, or Button, or his grandmother, or any of the girls there—his grandmother thinks he is no good for those girls, either, even though they are down on their luck!

And white trash!

Right?!

Christy's ideas were worth showing them all, and Roy Pettus in particular, about who was smart and who was stupid. He'd learned much since his Daddy and that mess. He found friendship, he thought, but been betrayed. He'd make it all right with a gesture. A big one. That plane of Roy Pettus's, the shiny blood-red Piper Meridian, would get flown for a change instead of sitting unused out at that airfield. Christy hadn't gone to look in a few weeks, now. But he would. The day of that music festival next month. That's when it would be airborne—Christy, he found a hack online for his flight simulator. To make the cockpit appear like a Piper Meridian. Which he'd been flying every day. So when the time came? He'd be ready.

BUTTON AND HEATHER

A few weeks after her flight to Sedge, and after many conversations and flat-out arguments with an angry Roy about treatment, and feeling weaker and in more pain by the day, she had at last returned to Heather. To the mountains.

Had gone back to transition, as she thought of her impending death.

Close. The pain, extreme and worsening. Her resistance to pharmies, crumbling. The sop to modern pharmacological mediation, a prescription the rejected oncologist had given for pain relief, was filled by Jackie, who thought it was for Button's grandfather, until she realized the name on the prescription.

And so that whole scene unfolded later, after Jackie got off work. They cried together. Jackie acted like Roy about the no-treatment thing. But being in professional healthcare, much as being a pharmacist was, Jackie had seen her share of sick people. Took it all hard, real hard.

Button, lying to Jackie about her next trip to the mountains. How she' be back; they'd make time. A white lie. Otherwise, Jackie might want to come along. And Button couldn't have that.

ROY, THROWING HIMSELF INTO THE DIXIANA, OVERSEEING WITH sedulousness every detail of its careful demolition and rebuilding, now well underway. Sniffing around, making a nuisance of himself, but much more even-keeled these days, meditating, keeping his deadly blade sheathed. No longer strong enough to take the walks along the river, instead he would visit and sit with her at home. Paging through the books, shooting the shit with Uncle Burnie, even bringing a twelve pack of PBR tallboys twice a week for the old scalawag, to which Button said nothing. Jasper hanging out one day while Button worked out a few end-of-life paperwork issues. You had made sure she ticked off her boxes. Least one could do for their loved ones.

Roy, doting and attentive and checking on her every five minutes, which you're totally not supposed to do with a cancer patient. He confided in her one afternoon while dropping by several bags of foodstuffs he'd picked up at the new Whole Foods over in Columbia that it felt like further bad news regarding his unsound marriage. That she—his wife Creedence—had chosen for her own reasons to remain apart from him.

And left the rest of the details unspoken, but Button could sense and feel and know them, anyway. A problem with that cop down on the island, the one who had rolled into the parking lot. The body language among the three, the way Mrs. Rucker had come rushing stiff and brittle back into the coffee shop to deal with the customers who had piled up in her absence. Whatever. None of Button's biz. Bigger fish, and all.

Roy, giving her that pie-eyed look of shock he'd had ever since her big reveal. "You just sit there taking all this. I'd be freaking."

"All has led to this. We come through a door. Exit through another. It's a relief."

"You talking about you? Or my situation?"

Both, she'd said. The truth was, not-really—she'd only meant herself. But if he saw in her statement direction and clarification, all the better. "Maybe you're getting. The answer. It may not be what you want. But if it's clear—"

"Right. Clear as mud."

"Then inside, you've some more. Settling. To do. Your mud."

"I reckon so. Sure stays stirred up."

Button, guilty over her illness. "I'm sorry. I haven't helped. Have I."

"You did nothing to cause this."

"Didn't I?"

"What the fudge is that s'posed to mean?"

"We are make our own reality. We all co-create—"

"Oh, enough of your bullshit," he'd shouted, breaking down.

She'd waited until he stopped yelling before asking a favor or two, including taking her to Heather's, and about various documents she'd been giving him for safekeeping. Time, an endless bounty, yet also growing short. She hated to admit it, but no way she'd make it another month until the festival. Bummer.

Roy, sick of feeling helpless, replied he'd do anything she asked; that he loved her; loved her like a sister. The sister he'd never had. "It's trite, but true."

Button, beaming him with love, sizzling inside. "I'm only dropping the body. Remember that. It will be the same when it's your time."

A beaten Roy, quite a sight. Hang-dog didn't half cut it: "Reckon I'll try to keep that in mind."

And with that last gush of loving energy and reassurance to a fellow human in distress, feeling her mind breaking down.

Faced with the pain. And the foreknowledge. And all she'd seen. Thus: ready for Heather's arms.

◌◍◎

COTTONY CLOUDS ROLLED ALONG OVER THE ROUNDED MOUNTAINTOPS, AS so memorably described in her aborted romance novel. Button, reclining in the gravity chair Heather had set up on the grand granite promenade, took in the vista that had drawn her friend's grandfather to this mountaintop.

A flare of pain; a series of conscious breathing exercises. Button, quieting her mind for a deep meditation—Heather had given her a tincture of reishi mushroom to aid in preparation.

She breathed.

She chanted.

Ay-yeem.

Ay-yeem.

The mantra, fading to a vibration in her throat. She visualized healing, white light pouring into her. The light of truth.

Of reality.

But not healing. Much as she wanted to hope and believe. Deep down, she knew.

Chanted *ay-yeem, ay-yeem.*

Oneness called to her, and she believed in her heart that Oneness would see to it that, at the appropriate level of higher consciousness, Button's ordeal here in the physical realm, with her ability to mitigate the pain solely with the force of her mind and spirit fading and finding the only solace in the ceremonial preparation and vaporization of the Godflower, would be over. But the key, as she'd tried to get across, was not to 'do' anything to meditate. That all the mantras and conscious breathing were in themselves acts not of meditation, but concentration. To meditate was to be. That it was a practice. She hoped one day to get better at it. Not that there was time.

Here at the end.

But if the moment were eternal, there could be no end.

Could there? Weren't these meat bodies like transceivers of consciousness? That meant the signal went on after the TV set is broken, as Alan Watts would have put it, smoking and laughing ha-ha-ha at himself and the absurdity of attempting apprehension regarding the disposition of consciousness following physical death.

After the meditation, in which she had traversed the cosmos and the pain had been but a background echo, she returned to a different Now than the miracle-world in which she'd been dwelling for over an hour.

Heather brought out nettle tea and pulled her own matching deck chair over close. The two, sitting side by side on the massive stone deck below the Southern face of the glass pyramid, watching the clouds roll through. Holding hands, a gesture initiated by Heather. And not talking, because it hurt Button to do so. In her throat. Under her ribs. Along her back. Deep in her groin. A deep chasm of mounting, burning pain.

Not that they needed to talk—after Roy left, they'd continued to speak to one another in silence. In many ways.

Ah, poor Roy: his departure, a moment difficult, one in which he'd tried so hard not to weep. To pretend this wasn't real. That he'd be back in two weeks to retrieve her. They'd go for a hike to Max Patch, or Cat Pen. Anywhere Button wanted.

"I'll ride you up there on my shoulders, if that's what it takes." He promised this close to her ear like a lover, his body hot all over with grief, which she absorbed and tried best she could to re-harmonize into positivity.

Button, thinking hard:

Worry not, Roy E. Pettus. When next we meet, we'll be together for keeps.

❂▣◉

THE SUN, WARMING THE MOUNTAINSIDE. SPRING, BURGEONING AND beckoning. Already the sounds of mowing coming up from one of the farms far below in the valley.

"Ah, the music of the mountains." Heather, sardonic. "My summer symphony."

Button could only smile. Hurt to talk.

"That stuff I told you—about the magic? You're not holding it against me. I hope."

Waving this off, furious. Thinking, magic, a dangerous game. "You were young."

"Truthfully... after you left San Diego, I kinda fell apart. Kumari had gone too, and he'd been my rock and my sage and my mentor, more than I probably let on at the time..."

She spoke of the future, which Button had nudged her to do, and her plans to go to herb school, and acquire all the knowledge they'd spoken of learning fifteen years before, when after Phish tour they'd planned to do so much: hike the AT, at least a section hike, and afterwards, homesteading back in here somewhere. Like in the hollow to which they'd taken Roy that day.

Force of will to verbalize: "Quite a. Homestead. You've got now."

"*Shush*. No way am I staying here. M'dad, an OCD whacko with all this."

"No?"

"Like Roy said, it looks like a movie set. Not a home."

Button beamed approval at her old lover and best of best friends.

"But how can I leave the library behind?"

Button, shrugging. They hadn't even gotten to that part of the tour last time she and Roy were here. The library, more of a secret than a showplace. Tens of thousands of volumes, climate controlled, cataloged, no digital back-ups. A repository. Button, remembering how crucial Heather had said books would be again one day. Not that they weren't important now. But real books, on paper. The reasons for this, obvious. To a seer with a long view like Button.

"You're not finished, though."

"No way to finish collecting." Heather, musing on this project of her father's. "He did kinda sorta ask me to—you know. Keep on. Didn't he."

Of course he did. Blinking back the pain. *He could see the necessity, couldn't he?*

Yes. The pyramid, the secret library. He believed an ancient trove of information and scrolls were yet to be discovered beneath Cheops. That going forward, if we wanted to continue the Great Work of the sages and magi and initiates? We'd be wise to have a library, the esoteric through-line, in a form that might not last, but would be accessible still in a world post-electricity. Post technology. Because that is what's coming again. But you know all that.

Button smiled: *Knew it before you thought it.*

You're good, Button. Better at this than me.

But you're the one who taught me this.

I did?

The cancer patient, nodding.

"I only wish you—ah."

Heather, her facade crumbling. Going haw-haw-haw with grief; but then passing, and a deep breath, a return to equipoise. Yogic breathing. Heather had lost weight since they'd visited last fall. Yoga. Button didn't have the strength to do much more than a few t'ai-chi routines. How fast her body deteriorated.

She had wished that if she were to suffer illness like her father, that it would be brief. His suffering had gone on so long. Make hers definitive and immediate, yo.

And there you have it.

A cute frown: *'There I have' what?*

Button, emptying her mind, squeezing Heather's hand harder. Against her now-caretaker's instructions, Button spoke again, quoting a Phish tune they both loved called 'Bug': "It doesn't matter; it doesn't matter." A hand over her heart, which beat on, dogged, despite growing weaker by the day. "Feeling like this work is done. Ready to get on. To the higher levels."

"Do you believe that?" Heather, hushed and speaking from a place of fear, darkness and uncertainty. Grasping her sweater against the coming chill of an early spring night. "Is there truly more? More than this?"

Heather, nodding. "Man—I hope so."

Rather than speaking further, Button opened her channels and imagined her way through all the aspects of physicality we materialize here to encounter; that cannot be grasped while dwelling in our state of Perfect Rest to which we return after departing this physical shell, after our high-vibrational play in this realm is complete, an enormous expenditure of energy to maintain a stable body, the true explanation for entropy and death. Energetic forms like fear offer the contrast and polarity necessary to perceive the emotional experience, sure. Tactile expressions of love important as well.

Eating. Breathing. Smelling. Touching. Hearing.

Being.

Loving.

"We should do some final magic together. You can let me know of its efficacy. Afterwards."

Getting it. Totally onboard. A callback. Confirmation. Can do. Button, giving her great love a big thumb's up.

"I have loved you so." Button, aloud, at which Heather looked pained.

"Unworthy. I forsook you."

"No—our reality. It's a mutual. Creation. Was then. Still is now."

"In any case, I have a deficit. I attracted darkness into my life. It rubbed off on you, the stuff you got into after I dropped off tour." Cautious, quiet: "When I was magicking, I didn't know how to close my circles properly. Played around with the left-hand path—for kicks! Do you believe that? Oh —I let in something, and I'm afraid it attached itself. And when I brushed it off, or tried, it attached to you. Maybe it hasn't left."

Button, shaking her head No. Saying, you were the mage who gave me the banishing ceremony; you took me to the shaman, and I saw those entities, but they are now at a far remove from us here.

All rather tiring. The effort of more words, too much. Her position, uncomfortable. Moaning, involuntary, at a yawning wave of pain emanating from the center of her body. Her spirit, quivering and craving freedom.

Ah, the guilt she carried. At not giving her father all the morphine like he'd asked. Letting him suffer.

"Are you okay, my angel?"

Brushing it off. Getting a second wind. Pretending. "Of course."

Heather, going inside to warm up their tea, to grind more herb for the portable vaporizer that Button gestured toward on the table.

Once alone, a vision, a figure emerging:

"Walfredo?"

No—her father there on the great stone deck, the misty mountains undulating away on the horizon behind him. Young, dressed in the work clothes he wore every day to the plant—his chinos, windbreaker, the steel-toed boots. The pens in his pocket. Ruddy Buddy, young and strong. Not bent and stooped and drooling, a feeding tube and a ventilator pumping, and begging through his puffy eyes and scratchy notes to be released. That he'd experienced enough. The younger man had told his daughter how he felt a calling to pursue his career managing the flow of power and the radiation over at the Sugeree River Station. That as a soldier he had wielded that privilege, godlike, and explicit, to exact a mass killing with every warhead like a sacrifice to bloodthirsty kings seen and unseen, and only God knew what had kept any of those bombs he'd managed from ending the lives of hundreds of thousands—of millions. The benevolence of the flowing power, to him, the other side of that equation. A penance for having participated in the brinksmanship that humanity embarked upon in 1945, the white-hot blooms of earthbound sunfire in the desert and on the Japanese island, a pandora's box, his standard speech when it was only him and Button after a beer or two. One of those fun Sundays out at the Pettuses—the cookouts, listening to the bluegrass music or her father and the other adults talking rather than wanting to run and play. Listening, instead.

How she had not listened to him when it counted.

His scratched notes, instructing her on being careful. On not getting into trouble for giving him the morphine so he could die.

She'd been a coward. Her soul journey had been to learn this lesson. And here was its consequence. The pain. The foreknowledge. The wisdom to get through the exit with dignity and grace and through force of will. All of it had been through force of will. Except when it would've helped her dad. When he asked; when he needed her most. These lessons bore weight, now. Too much.

His smiling youthful form vanished, leaving only the twilit mountain-tops, wispy clouds, always weather moving through, always change and flux. A good perch from which to understand. And accept.

Her throat, closing up on her. Last night, the pain of eating, terrible. The tumors, growing. It even hurt now to chant her mantra. Not a good sign.

"Help me inside," Button asked. "Time for bed."

"Is it time for that?"

Button chuckled, much as she could.

"Okay, angel. Let's get you tucked in."

Button, a hand on Heather's arm as they entered the pyramid, a sliding door. Thinking, *We should do a banishing ceremony. I have a journey ahead. I desire cleanliness before I cast aside this body.*

Heather. Getting it. She had a volume in her hands brought up from the enormous library below, an automated retrieval system allowing members of the household to search a computerized catalog and have volumes delivered by dumbwaiter from the lower level in the base of the pyramid. "Tat gave to Hermes Trismegistus a hymn of regeneration. Shall I recite it?"

"Yes, please."

Deep breath. "Let all nature listen to the hymn. I will sing the Lord of Creation, the All, the One. Open, oh heavens, winds retain your breath, let the immortal circle of God listen to my word. Powers which are in me sing to the One, the All. I give thee thanks, Father, energy of the powers; I give thee thanks, God, power of energies. This is what the Powers cry which are in me; this is what the man who belongs to thee cries through the fire, through the air, through the earth, through the water, through the breath, through all thy creatures."

And inside, to a comfortable room where Heather set up an altar, over though, as she'd told Button, she'd been afraid to do any magicking for so long now she might have forgotten how.

Button would help the love of her life remember. It would involved staying in touch after the transit. They would keep their connection until Heather got there too, after which they'd decide if they wished to incarnate again, play the game one again, or decide they'd gotten far enough this time. It wouldn't matter how long it took. Not to Button Sykes. Not chilling all non-corporeal on the other side.

ROY

All during the drive to the mountains you told yourself:

She's okay, she's okay.

Standing outside the pyramid. "Call me when you're ready. To come home."

"Aw. That's sweet. Heather, she'll just. Ship me. I'm sure."

"Hardy-har."

But then, her shrug and a look like, I ain't kidding.

Nah. What's all this unspoken finality subtext? Sick or not, she's got time.

It's not true.

Oh! This is real. Not an imagined future.

You force yourself to acknowledge that it's goodbye, and you're not going back, you won't see her again, not alive. Heather, you understood, will assist Button's transit. What her special skill set entails besides having a butt-ton of cash, you don't know.

If it's money Button needs… but you already offered.

C'mon, beau. Like this all is a mystery.

Christ, Button had given you letters—to Uncle Burnie, to her girlfriend she called Jackie but spelled 'Jouquoya' on the envelope. A lovely name. Scolded yourself for making fun in the past. Left you a box of papers, including, she said, a novel she'd written about the possibility of finding love in a seemingly loveless world, how maybe you would one day enjoy it, and even share the manuscript if there might be anyone left alive who indulged in reading books.

How many more times would you have to feel bereaved this way?

About someone you loved?

Dude—don't ask crap like that. No worse words ever had been uttered than what-next. You know this. The answer: Again and again.

It occurs to you it's why people have kids, to stave off feeling futile; it comes with passing time and approaching doom. Wise you, coming up with such wisdom you read on a blog post. In any case, you're to never ask, how many more tragedies? Or, what misfortune to come, Lord? What next?

◌☙◯

COFFEE? NOW THERE'S AN IMMEDIATE ANSWER TO ALL LIFE'S WOES AND niggling, unanswerable questions, a boost to get you home from these gorgeous mountains, and to take your mind off the sacred errand you've run, and what's coming, and why you aren't staying with her through to the end.

A wooden placard by the side of the winding, descending road out of the hollows and peaks where Heather's dad's estate lies, and you see you're beside a small river now, and the general store has a lovely rustic vibe—of course. You stopped here the first time you visited.

The girl inside, earthy and natural in a flowing print dress and tie-dyed sweater, makes you a latte with almond milk and an extra shot. You're driving straight through back to the EC, as Button would have called home, and you need the caffeine. Your eyes, swollen with water, don't want to stay open.

"This is the fucking—freaking, sorry—Big Laurel Creek outside."

"That's what it's called."

"So, you're totally saying that that's the trailhead? Right over there?"

The earthy, beautiful young woman, amused by your epiphanies. "Like, totally."

"And how far is it?"

"It's right there, sir. Around the corner."

"No—how long is the trail itself."

About three-four miles, she says. "If you want to go all the way to where the Laurel dumps into the French Broad, anyway."

You know this already, but you say it anyway: "It's an easy hike."

"Compared to most trails around here, it's a cinch—it's flat."

"I've been on a few."

"And you haven't done the Big Laurel Creek? Most people start with that one."

"Sometimes I'm a little slow on the uptake."

⬤▣⬤

BY THE TIME YOU GET TO THE FIRST TURN, BY A QUAINT RENTAL COTTAGE you know Creedence would have loved and would have been so comfortable staying in, you really kick yourself. Stumbling along the damp and often muddy trail through the towering walls of a river canyon, and beside the rocky course of the Laurel you curse and think, if only you had taken her on this hike that day instead of the AT. If only. She'd have been so cozy in that cabin, a couple hundred yards from the highway and five or ten minutes back up the road to an Ingles where you could have gotten beers and wine, and she wouldn't have turned into an alcoholic and it would've been beautiful, a middle age you'd have both eased into like champs. Together.

You stride along. The path gets rocky as shit. Your feet complain—you're wearing these stupid sport sandals, for god's sake, not hiking boots—but you press on. Turning an ankle, almost, a few times; slowing down. Trying to take in the sights, the towering mountains above, the rocky traverse of the river ten or fifteen years wide, tumbles of mini-falls. Foamy, roiling, liquid magic glinting in the sunlight.

Water.

Water seemed to be the key to everything, didn't it? And you meant more than coffee and fruitshakes. Water. Liquid life. The fact of its existence in this form, if you removed your mind from the mundane ordinary every-dayness of its presence in your life, the physical properties of water could easily be seen as manifested magic. What a glorious place, this physicalized realm.

Button, saying all that to you on one of your walks by the river back home. That routine had only gone on a few weeks last year, but now seemed like a precious epoch in your life. An entire chapter of your book. Time seemed malleable. You and Button, seeming to have been together always, and by together you mean as compatriots, but not in the sense of romance or sex.

A pair.

A team.

Partners.

Perhaps you would work together again. Who knows?

You have a team in Burnie, being cared for at the moment by Letty Glasscock. But you were to be his direct caretaker. Mercy, how it had all changed so fast.

Would you go back to the way it was before, say, last summer down on the island? If you could?

Not even if you didn't know what you now knew. Because none of it was right.

Recriminations, flooding in.

Time to meditate.

Emptying your consciousness instead of allowing your mind to race rampant. Sitting on a rock and hearing nothing but the river, the river, the sound of the river flowing, flowing, but trying as she's taught you not to give the sounds a name. None of it may be in your control, it being your life and its attendant circumstances, and not the lives of others like Button, but at least you have the moment. That's what Button said to you before, that the moment was all there was and all that had ever been, one long unfolding instant. The big bang, still banging. You'd been high with her, and it'd blown your mind.

Your consciousness, in this state of expansion for months now, and for many reasons. Another, by having sex with Trudy, and how it felt less like like love than a senseless betrayal of your wife, though you'd let Trudy think the coitus had brought about magical catharsis; and you wonder if you weren't supposed to revisit this peak adolescent sexuality with Chesnee Campobello, with whom you had shared such intense lust, but cheated out of consummation.

But not. Her husband, far too powerful. More powerful that you ever realized with his back room, the back room once hosted by your grandfather, who it seems had not wanted to be a member of this club, one that'd have a schlub like him for membership. You can dig it. Twin poles of power back home, that back room and those ELMS meeting downtown in the old Masonic lodge, as appropriate a spot as any for those puppet masters.

These thoughts creeping in don't make for that grand and transcendent a meditation, but twenty minutes goes by like five and it reminds you that you have a home to get to, that walking along the riverside has a finite timetable. Now? You will hike to where these rivers join. You will take the journey you should have years ago, that would have started your life on a course in which it all didn't go into the crapper.

By the time you're fighting your way through underbrush, you keep deciding that the trail's ending, your feet are killing you, and bugs are biting even though it's not even spring yet, and you're chilled and hungry and thirsty, and you have a long way back. But the end, it has to be close, and you wish you had the pedometer Creedence bought you back when you first walked, trying to lose weight.

"No, no, no, it's by time—you workout by time, not distance," you'd said after opening the gift. "And I already have a watch."

So disappointed you weren't thrilled. "I know, hon, but distance is important. Maybe you'll get so fit you'll want to run a marathon."

"Fat chance."

"Hardy har—Roy, I keep telling you, you're not fat."

"Hell I'm not. I should keep up with the distance. See how far a fat guy can walk."

How sour. And her, how sweet.

How supportive you could've been when she saw this hike on the website, saw it was easy. Said, oh, that sounds nice, let's do that one. But you'd said, no, no, gotta do it up big. You said, screw all that, we ain't doing no pussy-assed easy hike. You had your sense of urgency about heading to the mountains and hiking, having the best experience possible, pushing the limits and what could money buy to make this all happen. None as the case was, because you couldn't buy that million dollar view from Max Patch. Couldn't buy everything. Not your marriage, nor Button Sykes's life back from the edge of ending. Hell no you can't, not even for your millions of dollars in cash and investments and private property and business owner-ship and the airplane, which as you figured had sold fast, and there, another windfall you would need your guy to put somewhere to shield from taxes and fees.

Still not enough.

You knew that much now, didn't you.

Knew how little money could accomplish.

A spectacular stretch of the river. You follow from a high ledge and that reminds you of the sequence in *Deliverance* after Burt Reynolds breaks his leg and Voight has to climb the cliff; you're not worried about murderous rednecks, though, because you haven't seen a blessed soul for the ninety minutes you've been tromping, your legs already shaking and weak, but here you emerge from the grassy reeds and willow trees to discover signs of civi-lization.

You scramble up the high embankment of a railroad trestle, over a wall of cascading gravel that tears up your tender feet even more.

A small metal sign posted reads:

No Trespassing
Highly Dangerous Area.

Hesitation — should you cross the tracks?

Hell yes. Who is this sign to tell the bossman where he oughtn't go.

Clambering over and down the other side, a well-worn path into marshy areas, and you're walking along the Sugeree River at thirteen again with your best buds Devin and Dobbs, that's the way the light is falling and the smell of the river hits you in a certain way and you worry about snakes. Sense memories. Powerful stuff.

You follow a narrow path through the reeds for about twenty yards, and under enormous willow trees you stand at the point where the Laurel joins the flat, placid expanse of the French Broad. Not only had you expected to see falls or some spectacular occurrence of the rivers merging, the wide rivers flows opposite what you anticipated, showing how you don't know which direction you're heading, not in the least, and you're glad there's a trail, and you have a compass app on your iPhone, but it's good you won't need it because the battery's almost dead, and you don't even have the car charger with you, and who gives a fudge? Piece of planned obsolescent supercomputer crap full of heavy metals and all the knowledge of humanity at the tapping of fingertips and the sliding of touchscreen levers, eh? Well. You will do fine without its precious high-tech app.

But a dude-bro like you, not cut out for rough camping in the back country, and unprepared for the coming collapse of our hubristic and destructive civilization Button believes is not only imminent, but necessary and cyclical and normal. You need a compass, all right. One that doesn't need charging. That's what she'd say. If she were here.

Which she is. Only twenty miles back behind you in the higher mountains closer to the Tennessee border. She has gone nowhere, yet. Maybe she's the one putting all these ideas in your head.

You listen there along the river for Button's voice, but don't hear it.

You toy with chucking your pocket supercomputer into the river. But you consider those heavy metals in the device which, like those ridiculous new lightbulbs, must be disposed of responsibly and properly and safely. Not shot-putted into a beautiful mountain river for symbolic, dramatic effect no one else will see.

A better idea:

You pray.

"Lord, I don't know if I should call you 'God,' or Universe, or the Big Kahuna, or how any of this works, and I'm not asking for anything because I don't have to have anything—I've had it all. All you could want. Well, not really. But I could get it, and I mean tonight. I got the money. That ain't the issue.

"God: look here, beau. I've never known where I was going. Or how to get there. Only that I was pushed on. That urgency thing. I only knew I needed to get someplace I wasn't, and that I couldn't even imagine or see in my head. Well, sorta—those dreams about being on top of the mountain, which I keep having. And being able to see forever, it seemed.

"Where is that, though? Forever? Where's there after being atop the high mountain? It doesn't seem like I have anywhere to go from Max Patch, except—back down into the valley?"

Is that it? "Do I need to return to the shore? To Creedence?"

You fall to your knees. You thank the universe for all your blessings. But you still need more, you say. You need an answer. A direction.

A direction home.

Hell—you need a home now. Your grandmother, bless her heart, was wrong. That house you built wasn't for you—it was for your parents, who'd never known their own place, their own house, together, a family. They hadn't had a chance.

"God?" Praying, now, for what only felt like the first or maybe second time in your sorry life, on the beach that night in gratitude for the dolphins having saved you from your own death. "Tell me which way to go. Where I'm supposed to be. Where I'm to build my home and hearth. Who my partners are. And don't let me ever forget all the people who've loved me. And that I loved, and still love. Maybe if I build it in the right place, this time, they will come. Or come back to me. Whichever."

The crickets and cicadas chorus in praise of your one-sided, divine dialog; the rivers merge in their relative stillness, their watery silence. A blue heron calls out as it glides low along the water, flapping enormous wings, gaining height and disappearing over the tree line.

"Where is this place? Here, by the river? In the mountains? Tell me, and I will go. Where?" You plead this to the heavens, otherwise quieting your mind and feeling the stillness inside, and all around you, take hold. "Am I home yet?"

Silence but for the blessed birdsong.

At last a voice comes—the magician's call, the one you'd sworn all along had to be Button, but you realize is the divinity within to which she's so often referred, and gives you an answer. It makes sense and sets you to striding back, high and mighty and over the railroad tracks and through the grasses and the stone gardens, stepping true and confident, with purpose and vigor, and the voice said not one word but two, and it was a call from God and from All, but also Button Sykes, like you'd always thought. Of this you're certain; and here, its wisdom:

Definitely maybe.

REBECCA LAFRENIERE AND THE ELMS

I've faced up to the choices I made—lately, and long ago, and each one in between. All the decisions, not simply the bad ones. I learned to give credit where it is due. I'm a grownup. It's not about me.

But for all the effacement, heartbreak and contrition, humiliation, a humbling yet to come. A conclave was called over my affair with the husband of a fellow Edgewater Lady. The transgression, which I knew well violated not only the rules of ordinary social decorum but a number of tenets laid out in the Ledger of Conduct to which all members were more than signatories. No more serious news to a member than such a meeting, as it is only convened under the gravest of circumstances and transgressions. In short, a rare and extreme occurrence.

I don't know what to tell anyone. I'm forty-two. Despite a number of professional accomplishments, directing community theater shows and constant fundraising and working with the same set of artists year after year to design programs for the arts center, my life had turned out empty. A series of relationships, going from unfulfilling to worse.

Manny's attention filled a void. I mean, sure. But only men measure the happiness of a relationship by the sex. Manny's an amazing musician, has a vision for the town—how many people can say that? My attraction to him isn't that hard to explain. I'd be more apt to question the risks he took than what I did. In fact, if it hadn't been for his obvious encouragement, does anyone think I'd have gone and started an intimate relationship with one of the town stakeholders, or rather, the husband of one?

Another mistake. Who did I think was the boss? And of Manny's life? And, as it happened, my own as well?

⊙🅗⊘

A TRIBUNAL OF THREE ELDER SISTERS OF THE ROSY STAR, THE OFFICIAL society to which the membership of the ELMS show fealty and remuneration, and convened in my honor. Yay for me. Paying spiritual dues through private ritual known only to members and no one else, not family, not lovers, I had crossed several lines.

Again, and perhaps worse? Quite willingly and knowledgable. We clear on that part?

Accordingly, a question-and-answer session takes place between me and the tribunal. DeKalb, quite the crusty old matron, and her cohorts, Alice Faith Westmoreland and Calliope Gilderbloom, sat watching in the small conference room where ordinary lodge business like meetings with outsiders are held; the temple floor proper, too sacred a space to be profaned by the discussion about to be carried on in a Sister's conduct review by a Conclave. Here the room, appointed like a nice but nondescript board room, had been redressed with drapery and the muted lighting, the conference table moved out in favor of the sacred mandala carpet and the ornate, carved ceremonial chairs. Only Westmoreland could be thought of as a peer; the others were true elders, in rank as well as age. I prepared myself for lambasting.

Ruth DeKalb spoke for the Conclave. "Rebecca, Sister of my Sister," referring to my mother and truthfully my grandmother as well, "I do not know where to begin with this process, the shock I feel. The ripple of unrest throughout the Sisterhood. It is remarkable."

Really. "I've sewn seeds of contrition where I could."

Calliope Gilderbloom's tremulous, breathy rush to admonish: "Short of a stay in Thirty Acres," a private residential behavioral rehabilitation hospital across the river in Beauchamp County, "your repentance is for simple poor judgment absent mitigating factors."

"So—I should be an alcoholic or pill-popper? That would negate the effects of the transgression? In the Conclave's eyes?"

"It's a better excuse than, 'I was horny' and didn't stop to consider the ramifications."

"I did, though. It's in the decision-making that followed. I acknowledge this."

Alice Faith lit a slender cheroot here in this private club. Blows my mind they still allow smoking. "Bernice Theodore is a powerful and productive member. It could almost be seen as a vicious and specific attack."

"Wait—how has this error been categorized?" The Ledger contained transgressions and it recorded high crimes, at least when it came to perceived attacks on a fellow Sister, or a Sister's outside business interests. "Is this filed under General, or Personal?"

A settling in the room. "I'm sorry," DeKalb said. "It's that serious."

"Wait—oh. Oh, no."

"I'm afraid so."

I was being kicked out. Of the ELMS. Of the Sisterhood. "I—I invoke —my right to—bring in the aggrieved Other to address—"

"Stop it." Alice Faith shook her head. "You know what you did. And Bernice, she's decided your defamation requires the severest punishment possible. In fact—we all did."

It settles over me. "I won't be able to run the Fine Arts Center. I need to be a part of this—of the town's affairs. Over one bad choice? With a man?"

"Afraid so." Calliope, snorting and impatient. "I have a doctor's appointment."

A sacred copy of the Rosy Ledger appears, passages of reprimand are read and remarked upon with invidious scorn, invocations made and my responses recorded. A key turned in. And the three, watching as I fold my tent to leave the lodge of the Sisterhood for the last time. Pledging to assist with dignity and grace in the search for a new director of the FAC.

❁❁❁

ALONE AT JENSEN'S POND, THE SUPPRESSED EMOTIONS ROIL. DESPAIR, grief, failure—the darkest of days have befallen me.

Whippoorwill calls across the still water at sunset, the croak of frogs, an outtake from *On Golden Pond*. We put on the show at the FAC, once. It was a beautiful, heartfelt production, excellent makeup to age the actors.

How can they take it all away?

I took it from myself. That's the truth. I could've walked away from Manny with more discretion, could've managed my emotions better. Been a grownup. Forever a bridesmaid has left me bitter, though, and it extends to more than relationships with men. The missing of auditions by this-much, or so it felt in my tenure in New York. Opportunities just out of reach. A plan to go to LA, never materializing. And back home, finally, after falling down the steep stairs into the basement of the restaurant where I waited tables, shattering my tibia and ending my ability to either wait tables or go to auditions. My apartment, a third-floor walkup in Brooklyn, rooming with Lucy Latham, another Edgewater County girl gone off to the big city.

And once back home, a number of events conspiring to keep me here — a relationship with a hometown boy. A cancer diagnosis, first in my mother and later in me, necessitating a hysterectomy.

After my recovery, a decision to go to grad school. And to serve my own community, as well to care for the same father into his dotage who had denied me resources and encouragement. Had forced me to leave with next to nothing, when he could have helped. And all because he didn't want me to go far away; to be put at such risk in that horrible hive of humanity at its worst.

What if Edgewater County were the festering hive?

What if I didn't just fade quietly away, the way Reynolds Pettus had insisted the mural be allowed to evaporate into obscurity rather than be either covered or otherwise changed. Inscrutable, all that had been to me. I cannot argue with the procedural natural of the expulsion from the Sisterhood, and I probably can't try to hang onto my job, not inextricably linked to the ELMS covenants I profaned. So what does that leave? This little lake cabin?

Manny; it leaves Manny. Maybe he is the opportunity I mustn't miss. Perhaps my willing separation from all I had before is the sacrifice I must pay to receive the fullness of his love and commitment. I will explain it to him. He will see. And he will respond.

ROY AND HEATHER

A couple of weeks later, time for the funeral of Button Sykes.

Get your head around that, eh?

"She's gone." The call from Heather Ponderview hit you like a thunderclap. As though another outcome possible—denial, it's a mother. Another in a series of unrealities. You shouted invective to the heavens. Ran over and kicked the red granite Ben Tillman pedestal with the toe of your left Keen, almost fracturing a digit.

Manny had come bolting across the green, finding you on the street hanging onto the bright yellow construction dumpster overflowing with the ripped-out guts of The Dixiana. Fury burbled like acrid pitch, like nothing Manny had ever heard *out* of you.

His own voice, shredding with concern, indicated panic and investment. "What, what, bossman?"

And when you told him, his ass couldn't believe it. Said, well I'll be shit. Walked in a circle outside The Dixiana, at his place, shook his head, asked how old she was three times, had hugged it out. Let you cry on his big shoulder the way men are never supposed to, except maybe over fallen comrades in war. He allowed you your tears a good, long time. Until you could again breathe.

It occurs: since getting back to Edgewater County, you've acquired multiple best friends. You'll be fine. You'll just miss her, that's all.

Per Button's explicit wishes and instructions, her service a subdued affair held in Forest Knoll Garden behind The Dixiana. With only a few principals in attendance, including an international celebrity, the whole shebang attracted scant attention. The way she wanted it.

Burnie and Tinky and Thim, all in shock, all in their Sunday best. Your Uncle Burnie, catatonic, holding onto you and smelling like booze, but you? Glad for his presence at your side. A sense of continuity. Of family.

۞۩۞

But yeah, you'd been so startled when Heather called. To tell you the news. Her words, stumbling, less assured than you've come to expect from Heather Ponderview. Coming not unlike Button's own fractured speech.

"So soon." Cold water dumped over your head. More of a statement. "Fuck me."

"Yes, the time came quickly. She was—ready."

"I know. I get it. How—what—"

Silence. You could see Heather shaking her head, no.

No, really—you had your eyes closed. But could still see her. "I get it."

"I know you do. But listen—she wasn't really sick; she didn't die."

"Could've fooled me."

"She dropped the body. That's all."

Heather let that thought hang; you tried to grasp the implications, but foundered and fumbled and instead let it go.

Button had asked to be buried in the Sykes plot where a place awaited her, but instead of the ten-thousand dollar vault and coffin and all that unsustainable jazz, she'd specified in the end-of-life document—one Jasper had helped her draw up in secret some time ago, a secret he kept—a green burial. You had had to get this cleared with many dumbfounded local authorities who'd never heard of such sacrilegious foolishness. So, lowered into the earth was her body encased in a 'mushroom suit' designed to return the physical shell back into the earth, in a fashion that allows the residual energy of the form to reintegrate with that of the earth element. Providing nourishment for the future.

All one more action item on your list; the executor of multiple estates.

As you consider the grounds, the weathered monuments and the plastic flowers in receptacles all sloping down the hillside and pointing to the backside of The Dixiana, you understand her actions now so much better than you did before: Button, trying to lead by example. Whether getting people to think about nuclear power, or Fukushima, or eating healthier, or green burials, she walked her talk.

And, by dying with dignity. On her own terms. Own space and time.

And you claimed to be in control of *your* trip? Amateur. That's all you are. Next to Button Sykes, anyway. Dropping the body at will when it no longer served its function. Helluva way of putting ideas, that gal. You look forward to one day reading the short novel she wrote, and her journals, the Button archive bequeathed to you.

And yeah, her sister and mother and grandfather, dressed and tearful and stunned. You had called Thim upon hearing the news. A complicated conversation, delicate. You didn't want to recount it. She had gone ballistic over your conveyance of Button to the mountains, called for an inquest and authorities, but at last calmed down. Had a reasonable discussion. Said she knew her sister was sick. Not that this sick, but yeah, as you confirmed.

Thim, still ungodly sexy. You wondered if she would cry over her sister and would that be sexy, too, your mind playing a juvenile, lustful game to keep your own grief at bay.

◐⋈⊘

As requested you read a few words from the Mitchell translation of the *Tao Te Ching*, speak what you know about Button's life. You asked her old Foothills State instructor Brenda LaRose to do a reading from a book of poetry that Button admired, an enormous and embarrassing honor, as she says before reading the piece, called 'The Cherokee Path,' an allegorical prose-poem about a young girl's quest for identity in the shadow of her domineering father.

Next, Heather Ponderview billows to the portable funeral home lectern like Stevie Nicks about to rip into 'Landslide.' With a papery countenance of shock, Heather, reciting from memory in a quavering, breathy cadence a passage of what sounds to your English-major ears like Shakespeare:

> *"Our revels now are ended. These our actors,*
> *As I foretold you, were all spirits and*
> *Are melted into air, into thin air.*
> *And like the baseless fabric of this vision,*
> *The cloud-capped towers, the gorgeous palaces,*
> *The solemn temples, the great globe itself —*
> *Yea, all which it inherit — shall dissolve,*
> *And like this insubstantial pageant faded,*

> *Leave not a rack behind. We are such stuff*
> *As dreams are made on, and our little life*
> *Is rounded with a sleep."*

Last, a boombox supplies the song Button requested, one of her oldschool favs: 'I Wear Your Ring,' by Cocteau Twins. Your throat tight as a vice, you introduce the tune by saying, "Our girl said that, of all the music she loved—and there was a bunch—she dug got into 'frequencies' like these, her words, at two important times in her life: when she was young and innocent; and when she was young."

The gathered mourners, they chuckle and shuffle their feet. You note a black girl, heavyset, standing off to the side with water sluicing down her cheeks. Not chuckling, stony and still, suffused with wide-eyed, quiet grief. A friend of Button's, you suppose. *No-duh, Sherlock.*

"But seriously, she said this song reminded her of a time when anything was possible, and the questions seemed like they would answer themselves, and pretty darn sooner rather than later. She said the music and art we love, it's like this: who you are is where you were when. Well, I'm here to tell you all that, whoever and whenever Allyson Button Sykes was, not only are them old questions all answered, but now anything's more than possible— when you're off dancing on a beam of light, I can't imagine how the sky ain't the limit."

"Amen." A male voice, maybe Fridge.

Not eloquent, but what did they want? You're a good-old-boy from Edgewater County, a river rat over on the east side of the county with red clay under your fingernails and staining the cuffs of your jeans. All the stuck-up Old South monied nitwits like those crusty birds on the ELMS, you knew what they thought about you, then as now. And you didn't give the first fudging crap.

A synth intro shimmers atop a thudding drumbeat along the hillside of gravestones, followed by the singer's lilting siren-like call to the cosmos, incomprehensible warbling holding less than no meaning for you. The sun doesn't break out of the clouds with sudden reassurance; it's only another funeral.

Dobbs tugs on your sleeve and bids you to lean down to his level. He whispers, "Liz Fraser? What—no Phish?"

Your frustration leaks out: "A dang tune I don't even know. Sounds like a game show theme."

"What funeral dirge would you choose? If you got the chance to pick?"

"Why? Know something I don't?"

Dobbs shrugs. "A writer keeps his eye on the end."

"Hush, y'all." The crying black girl. "Please."

You face flashes hot. A finger to your lips, a forced smile.

You admit that 80s and 90s music like this conjures a time of innocence and happiness and possibility of your own: Button had been but a teen girl looking at the long throw of her life ahead, while you, fresh out of college and instead of writing poetry or books, to become the bossman. And which you have been, in spades and to the peak of your abilities.

Have you ever been bossman of yourself? Truly?

Button forces you still to ask this, repeatedly, since this sojourn in Edge-water County began with the death of your grandfather. Have you mastered the universe, but missed mastering yourself? A difficult question, but one burning and aching for an answer.

The song ends after a powerful modulation, its opaque lyrics fading into silence. Until, a commotion—Button's crying friend collapses, a bustle, she's on the ground and a circle forms around her. Beating her fists against the grass, the poor girl thrashes and shrieks, "*Oh, lord, no, please, let me wake up—it can't be happening. Aw, God, don't make me keep dreaming this no more. Please, god.*"

You catch your dear Uncle Burnie's eye, a shrunken man inside a funeral suit too big for him. When it was his time, you would pay for a new tailored suit. He would go out in style.

Your most crucial adult mentor notices you looking about the time the girl calms; a squatting and whispering Thim offers comfort. Burnie strides toward you, brandishing his cane and hobbling out of the cemetery. "I'm-a tell you what, Roy. This crazy-ass town beats all I ever seen. Now, I'm gonna drink, and I'd like to see one of you noodle-armed shit-asses try and stop me."

AFTERWARDS, AT A GATHERING INSIDE THE HOLLOWED-OUT DIXIANA, THE walls covered with plastic sheeting and mourners clustered around folding tables where the bar once stood, Trudy and Letty Glasscock have put on a spread of food and fine wine and other goodies.

One treat in particular of which you, Trudy and Dobbs partake back in the office: a glass pipe passes around of a hybrid Button scored called Girl Scout Cookies, and terrific it is, heady cannabis that smells fecund and tastes sweet and being smoked instead of vaped gives you all an immediate brightness, clarity and relief. Like you're cruising barefoot through the fields of heaven. Rabbit would whip our butts for this, Trudy says, but takes a hit and gets all pie-eyed and saucy and flirty, which you enjoy seeing.

The movie star, Maddy Durango, also attended the service, but disguised and only revealing herself to you in the back office at The Dixiana. While she appears disapproving of your pot breath, after you ask if she'll consider coming back to help emcee the now-renamed Rabbit Pettus and Button Sykes Memorial Bluegrass Festival the actress agrees, but only if she can also serve in another capacity: as the voice of Button's continued protest against the nuclear plant, which Maddy seems to blame for the cancer running through both Button and her late father and everyone suffering from the disease. And how she'd see about bringing a few show-biz friends to help.

Coolness. Throughout the conversation you suffered a slight dissociation you've felt every time you meet a celeb like this—in the flesh, instead of made of pixels. As when you shut off the screen and they vanish, after the wake you ponder, was she ever here at all—Button, Maddy, any of us? Good weed. You need a new connection.

❋ ❋ ❋

A THREE-QUARTERS LIT JASPER PLAYS A FEW TUNES, DITTIES HE KNOWS Button loved from the Phish catalog: "Waste" and "Lifeboy," followed by the Merle Haggard weepy "Sing Me Back Home," a familiar Grateful Dead cover which inspires Dobbs, drunk and sad, to raise his bottled beer in unspoken memory not only of Button, but all the others you've lost.

So much emotion running rampant. Bill Wimmel, suffering from dementia, has gone missing, a county-wide search turning up no sign of him or his vehicle. All tragic.

So sad, in fact, that you hoist a few yourself. You and Trudy clink glasses, and you feel love emanating from her like almost never before. Maybe it's because she's standing in the almost-new, still-its-old-self honky-tonk, which you have accomplished with your money for one reason and one reason only: to make her happy.

Sure, you're down with Manny's big Music City scheme, and now your granddaddy's tavern feels and smells fresh inside and will last for many years, maybe, if there's anyone to run it who comes after you and Trudy. But her, your old lover, your first real love, you want to offer her a present only you can give, and that's The Dixiana itself.

❋ ❋ ❋

With Thim's permission you go to visit Tinky at the old folks home, where you find that not only does she not seem to recognize or remember you, or about her daughter's death, you find she's made friends with Dobbs's mother.

"Button said for me to tell you how much she loved you. And sorry for the last few months that you couldn't be together. Ride this thing out, how she put it."

"You married to Button-Button. You take her away?"

Or maybe she remembered you, the cute routine. "If only... I did love her, Mrs. Sykes. Yes, I did."

"You get her. You go and get din-din and bring back. She fix good."

"I know she does."

"I teach her. She fix good."

"Yeah, she did."

Dobbs's mom, Mrs. Vandegrift, gives you a clandestine wave, shakes her head, mouths, *She doesn't know. It's all right. It's all right.*

You leave them in the day room watching *The Price is Right.* And feel okay about Button's mom. Not that you need worry. Button and Thim took care of everything. What a gal. Both of them.

And yeah, Thim, alluring as heck, even in grief. The black dress and stockings she wore to the funeral had driven you nuts. That night you endured a mad and inappropriate rush of funeral horniness. A welling of unbridled emotion, but nowhere to direct it.

The next morning, with nothing pressing other than detail crap about the Rabbit Festival in two weeks, you head down River Ridge Road to go to sit at the fishing bluff, where you find trash: used rubbers, beer cans, cigarette packets and plastic sacks, and all you can do is shake your head. Call these rednecks every name in the book. Pledge to put them all in their place, one day, one way, somehow.

Finding an IGA grocery bag mushed down into the clay—it doesn't take long—you spend the next hour cussing and policing up other people's garbage. For the good of all, you keep reminding yourself. Rising out of love and service, your actions.

As Button taught you.

In everything move with love, her voice whispers, and it's as real in your ear as it needs to be to get its point across.

Now you enjoy your task, and when you finish the bluff looks like it used to when you and granddaddy went there to fish, a million summers ago. When you were a boy. And Button, a girl. Alive.

All of you, still alive.

But only you left to carry the torch, right?

You'd better—they'll kick your chubby pink ass if you arrive 'up there' and announce how you didn't carry on. Were a lazybones. Button, most of all. She'll bludgeon you with love, in her case.

Love, a tonic; love, a suitable punishment for having lived life, you think. For having grieved like a son of a bitch, as your Pa-paw foretold that you would. A wise man, him. Like he could see into the future. Like he knew.

Lord, you hoped you would do him, and the town, proud with this festival in his honor. Tasks and chores nag, but no matter how many lists you check off you feel incomplete; like you keep forgetting an important step.

It will come. You're the bossman—three moves ahead, even when you're stuck dwelling on the truth of a past you can never change; you will never fully know.

PART TWO

Honkytonk Man

Every man has his own reason for living, and his own price for dying.

— JESSE L. LACKY JR AND SAMUEL FULLER, HELL
AND HIGH WATER (SCREENPLAY, 1954)

Country music radiates a love of this nation—patriotism. Country music therefore has those combinations which are so essential to America's character at a time when America needs character.

— PRESIDENT RICHARD M. NIXON, GRAND OL OPRY,
1974

LETTY GLASSCOCK

Flying and fire and fear; sensations more than actual memories.

Letty, the indelible terror of the conflagration sewn into her being, the memories vague but nonetheless threaded throughout the tapestry of her soul. During the school play, a sudden crash and a hum of bewilderment followed by flames and pandemonium; ripped from her mother's arms, the sharp crack of an elbow into her soft skull, choking black smoke and blindness until aloft, dreamlike, as strong hands heaved her out a window to fall twenty feet below.

Not to the ground—her face, slamming into the rough-hewn cloth of the man's coat, he who had caught her. More panic—the man, hollering and running from the heat. Letty, feeling this action more than seeing and hearing.

Voices—yelling, crying, screaming. The smoke. The smell. To this day she abhors cookouts, as well when Gooch Wimmel comes calling for his every-decade fire anniversary articles.

All this came far as Letty remembered, and none too specific. The Sunbury fire, it happened when she was only two. The baby. All older sisters. Her mother. How they had passed the baby from one to the other, all smelling the same. Her family.

Gone.

As time went on she began to doubt what she remembered versus what her mind imagined about the harrowing night at the Sunbury School, for the final official event in the life of the school. Her daddy never talked about how he'd lost most of his clan, the womenfolk but for the one, that night—worst of all, the eldest daughter, Letty's big sister Harriet, had been set to graduate following the school play, a musical production Letty could not remember. The other sisters, June and Irene, dead at eight and twelve. And their mother...

Family lore, that awful fire. the sort of which she and her father, as the only survivors, were rare to speak. But live it did inside her and persisting all through her childhood and adolescence, if fading as adulthood and responsibilities took over her attention. Still, Letty Glasscock's participation in this epic trauma of loss and death remained baked into the crust of her being, and surely haunted all who had witnessed the fiery horror of the Sunbury tragedy.

⊙⊞⊘

FINALLY, IN FIFTH GRADE AT THE SCHOOL THAT REPLACED SUNBURY, ONE of her teachers who had also been at the fire described the circumstances to Letty, but only after being asked what happened.

"What do you mean, darling?" Mrs. Dunwoody, kind and frail. Later, Letty would realize her fragility probably came from traumatic memories. "In what way don't you know?"

Letty, ten, shook her head. Shrugged. Found no words.

As they went outside the schoolhouse to the playground, in a corner far from the other children gathering in their recess games, Mrs. Dunwoody wove the horrendous and vague memories into a narrative. This, a big brick county-run building compared to Sunbury, a schoolhouse paid for by the mill money that gave the area what slight prosperity it enjoyed.

Mrs. Dunwoody, a good person to ask. She was old enough to be a grandmother and looked it, was born in Edgewater County and knew many who died in the fire, including Letty's mother and her sisters, whom she had also taught. She dabbed at her eyes and explained to Letty that the Sunbury School, named for a wealthy businessman who paid for its construction, had also burned two other times in its history. If one could believe it.

"Mr. DeKalb, who owned the mill at the time, he donated land for the third school, which they built about a half-mile from where the other two had burned. They thought that maybe some bad spirits didn't want the school where it was."

"*Was it haunted?*"

"No, darling. Nobody set them on fire, not such that we know. An i-dents, all three—wait. The first time, a lightning strike during a storm caused the fire. Well, I suppose that's an accident."

"I guess so."

Mrs. Dunwoody described how many were in attendance to enjoy graduation, especially since that next year they would open the new brick school closer to the Westside Highway. "People felt sad about the school's closing because it had been there for a long time, thirty years, with this graduation set as the last one. With a big picnic planned for the next day."

The teacher's voice caught and broke, which she tried to cover with a cough, as though it weren't grief stoking her hesitancy. After collecting herself, she continued: "A wonderful feast to celebrate the students and say goodbye to their beloved academy. That's correct—folks loved their school, all those who attended. But we'd have to bid farewell in a different manner, wouldn't we?"

After clearing her throat she added the terrible details, her tone taking on an iciness, matter of fact in cadence until softening at the end: "Eighty souls perished that night, four of them your own family, my precious darling. But you did not. Your mama saved you instead of herself, and her other children. Only a few people lived to see the dawn of another day. And you, Letty, represent the youngest survivor of all. That makes you special. A real-life Edgewater County angel."

Letty nodded. It sunk in—she imagined Daddy losing all his folks. Thinking about it from his perspective, she grasped her father's worrisome ways. His frightening moods. The crying jags. Now, she understood.

She would help him, best a little girl could. The Lord has a plan, keeping him and her alive together but not the rest. This was what she decided, sitting in church that next Sunday—also that she would serve as her Daddy's savior. If this is what the Lord has in mind, I must live up to His will, no matter what He may ask of me.

In exchange, as she bargained, she wished to spend no more time than necessary dwelling on the Sunbury School, and as the years passed far more pressing concerns came to bear on her soul much more than unpleasant half-memories born in her babyhood, in the moment before consciousness is fully aware of itself and such mortal dangers as lurk in the wide world outside the womb.

RENNIE, RUNELLE AND BURNIE

The sooner you got your narrow white ass out of these mountains, the better. This drive south from the high prairie, throughout the night and now getting into Tennessee—you don't want to waste time, not with an infant in the car, not this far from civilization—has taken much longer than you'd have liked.

How long you been saying that, son?

Your whole life?

Like a dummy you thought farming the prairie, the solitude and toil of it, would suit you fine—your pal Eddie'd sworn up and down you'd feel at home there. The farm boy who didn't want to escape, that was him. Who loved the life working with his hands and mind outside on the peaceful land. Like nothing you'd known. And different, yeah; that's all your spirit could tell that you wanted.

A farmer? Why not.

You'd come from miner stock, had turned down the chance to become a millworker like your daddy, who'd left the mines and the dust for the looms and the lint, but at least there were windows through which light could come—unless you worked graveyard. In the army you learned to be a truck mechanic, but couldn't settle on wanting to do that forever.

Ed Schulein had warned you, however, how North Dakota got so cold in the winter that spit would freeze before it hit the ground. That didn't bother you. It was the thought of being stuck in the mountains again, whether as a young'un in West Virginia or a soldier boy in the Rhineland, that raised your hackles. Majestic and pretty, all that scenery, but not being able to see what's coming? Shoot—you're sick of that feeling. Tired of it before your daddy moved y'all to South Carolina, for him to work in the mill instead of the mine. But after the war? Shit—you wouldn't stand for mountains, trees, fir needles and poor sight-lines; nor foxholes, shrapnel, and bleeding bodies and heads without faces.

But settling with your woman in North Dakota, have open space and quiet and peace all around, yet still having them awful dreams start up?

Bumfuzzled. That's how life has left you.

Ain't supposed to be like this—contentment and prosperity, that's what was waiting for you after the war on the Great Plains. Growing food from the ground—flax seed, brown seeds they make oil from, and another kind they use for its stalk to produce fibers. You didn't know from flax, but Ed said, lotta money in it. Little blue-white flowers, he told you. Real pretty to look at but worth a small fortune, if you knew what you was doing: you needed to rotate it in soils along with wheat and barley. Ed's father had been farming flax since before immigrating from Sweden. He would teach you both how to do it, your friend promised.

Coming up in the mining hollers? Folks growed patches of corn and a few scraggly other crops, but life for most men spent working graveyard shifts in the mines, and the women left nursing the babies and sitting up to read and rock by candlelight. These represent your earliest memories: greeting the morning with your Daddy returning home covered in coal dust, as though the night itself left him and his brethren marked ashen and sepulchered from the below-ground confines of their hellish work lives.

Nope; ain't found any peace yet. Not in your head, anyway.

That had been the thought—restless. Restless like your sweet, slender wife. Restlessness, as though snakes living inside your legs. And in hers, too. Which in a woman ain't good. Wasn't worth a durn.

She don't know that you had got concerns about Ed Schulein, and his intentions toward Runelle. That you ain't as dumb as you might seem.

So, all that in mind, a plan to find a new version of that peace. For now, it means back to South Carolina. That's the choice she give you, at least.

It was fine. Even when she was stern and scolding as a mama needed to do sometimes, your Runelle's voice rang out song-like. More when she sang, which gave her the most happiness. Singing, and loving on the towheaded baby y'all made together.

"I'm returning home to South Carolina, and you are welcome to come with us," she'd declared. "Otherwise, we will see you down the road. Or not."

That's what struck you about the necessity of accepting her deal. Three of you now—a contract with reality extending beyond the marriage license, the boy you created. No question about you going with them.

Too much uncertainty with the flax farming, anyway. You had to do everything just so, plant at the right time, harvest in this little narrow window, and if you didn't? You could count on living through a hungry winter waiting to try again. Maybe back in Carolina, you'll get into a regular trade. Grease monkey at a car lot—now that's work you can do in your sleep.

You will choose different from what had come before. You have been to war, and on the other side of the world, and your place in it—reality—looked a damn sight different from it had before you left. You will make up a new life for yourself—you don't have to work in the damn mill. Or the mines. Or with greased and scabby knuckles from digging around in oily, hot engines. Anybody who thinks any of that crap is worth doing has a screw loose. Sorry, but to you it's true. A reality about the world exists for you both below and beyond the machinations and civilization of man, a phrase your grandmother used to use in teaching you about powwow and hex.

Your daddy wouldn't understand a lick of that—she kept her powwow secret from everyone but you—but a year after you enlisted he went toes up anyway, and thus you needn't seek his permission to proceed with life. Knew his death was coming, you did, a feeling after you went in for basic. And it had happened. Not a comfort, your premonition.

Never got to say a proper goodbye, either, other'n when you went off on your Panama posting after basic at Camp Jackson. Last your Daddy said to you? "Live up to that uniform, and that flag."

You tried your best, as much as a teen-age hillbilly set loose out in the wild world was able. Honoring his request was the least you could offer him —your father had only been fifty-one years old. Seemed too young to be dead already.

◉ⓢ⊘

WHY'D YOU GO SO FAR? TO NORTH DAKOTA?

To escape from the unpleasant dream-reality you encountered back home. When you saw German POWs being housed in Edgewater County, one of dozens of camps all over the American South, you had said, whoa-nelly. *Y'all got to be kidding me.* Not more jerries in POW camps for you. Not at home, too. A sick, and sickening, joke.

Your bony ass, ready to be done with German boys. You killed a few. Hard to stomach, though it was right and true in the sense of living up to the mission, and they were set on doing it to y'all. You murdered a teen-age soldier, scared and skinny and screaming as he tried pushing a sidearm into your face. Ran a knife into his guts and twisted.

Another boy. Like you.

Not murder. Your duty at the time as a soldier, though for the most part your MOS involved fixing and driving trucks rather than front-line combat, at least at first. War had the tendency to necessitate killing, however, no matter a soldier's official job. He breathed his last at you; you blessed him, asked forgiveness—both of him, and the Lord.

For all you seen and done, though, and that scene was bad but not the worst, it's that kraut boy's cries what chase you in the dreams. Calling out. Begging, in his guttural tongue, for mercy.

You had to get away from German POWs.

Far as possible; or within reason.

To no avail, though. The dreams, following you to North Dakota, too. God-durn it.

☉✹⊘

IN THE WINTER OF 1944-45, IN RHINELAND, THE REALITY OF THE towering forests and steep mountainside hadn't been a dream, no sir. You were twenty, which in those days wasn't young, not after being in combat. Joined up in late 1940, before the war broke out enough to bring 'the yanks' in, as the British called y'all in England while training for D-Day. God help you, how different from Panama and working the canal zone as a truck driver, where your worst worry had been swatting mosquitos instead of surviving a snowy forest ordeal. After the Japs hit Hawaii, though, no more truck driving for you. Infantry.

Well—truck driving and repair still involved, only overseas in muddy Europe and with hot lead a-flying, but not for long once the war got going good, when soldiers of all types were moved into fighting units fast as the pencil-necks could shuffle the paperwork to effect the physical transfers. Panama? A memory you couldn't hold—once you got to England, the canal days seemed unreal. Wasn't long before you'd pine for Central America, boy. Tequila and women. Had been a day at the beach.

But now, you never dream of that pleasant tropical sojourn. Only the hell of the forest.

Biggest drama you suffered in Panama? Getting the clap from your first lay, a whore with an infected snatch. Can you beat that? You said you'd be damned if you'd make that mistake again, and you hadn't, but then, when home on leave not long after that little adventure in discomfort, you met Runelle Kittery. Your daddy, a late-life interest in religion and God-talk—thanks to your granny, such has always been a part of your worldview—dragged you to a camp meeting and a singing. Everything about women and getting up close to them changed after seeing Runelle sing gospel music. What life meant. Like in a fable, seeing her the first time. Violins, all right, but not the voice of the Lord. It was of earthly attraction and love. But maybe they're the same, the Lord and love. Hard to get your mind around.

Panama to Normandy. What a difference in beaches between your U. S. Army postings. You went from guarding the Canal, standing around and smoking and bull sessions and time on your hands and readiness drills relating to defense of the waterway, since the war bubbled up on the horizon, straight from worrying about your dick leaking pus to putting lead into other young boys like yourself. Like the night and the day, those poles of experience. You reckoned some balance to the whole equation. Didn't make the memories of fighting the Germans any easier. Nor getting the drip from a Panamanian woman with greasepaint on her bored face, and lines around her mouth, and if you hadn't been so excited by the thrill of your actions you might have been disgusted.

Thinking that despite how other fellas act: *I shouldn't be making sex with a stranger without no love in the act. It's why I got sick from that one whore. Now if that ain't a hint, you'd like to know what was.*

With a couple years in uniform and having landed in the third wave on the Normandy beach, you fought through the next months in France, which had its horrors and stresses to be sure, close calls, but nothing like being in the forest to come. Because of attrition, you moved up fast to being a platoon guide, like an assistant staff sergeant, who's next in line to the platoon sergeant who has the real backbone, sees that the officer's orders are carried out. But by the winter, attrition—wave after wave of it—and experience advanced fellas like you in rank. Five stripes.

On the push through the forest you brought up the rear, the squad of a dozen riflemen suspended between your two poles of responsibility, with a corporal hauling a Browning Automatic, a light machine gun, noisy, tended to draw fire. Your ball-sack swung low. You kept what was inside to a slow boil and learned how to look away best you could. Not the same as a sixteen-year-old hillbilly. At nineteen? A different rascal, Reynolds Pettus.

Greenhorns? Now they looked up to you.

As the winter dragged on, you became Rabbit. The boys started calling you that after a barrage from the German 88's, when, scared shitless, you were seen crouching and hopping in desperation across a snowy expanse from one foxhole to the next looking for cover. Probably hadn't moved as fast since that game in school against Andrew Jackson High the year before you quit to join up. You had busted your ankle hustling a ninety-nine yard runback in the second quarter, but kept playing on the injury until it swelled up big as the pigskin. You and your pal Burnham Sykes, himself off in the Army Air Corps in the Pacific, teammates, later reveling in the victory, saw your ankle and helped carry you into the locker room, his face knotted with concern.

Them German 88's was worth fearing, and not possible to run fast enough to get away, not if your number was up—them guns delivered razor sharp shrapnel that would cut through a body like a surgeon's scalpel. You didn't mind the nickname. Reynolds was fruity, Rennie was someone's mutt, and your middle name, Elder, sounded like an unearned royal title, so you welcomed a new one besides the others you'd been called, 'boy' and 'young'un' and whatever rank you attained. By December 1944, in fact, Sarge is what you had not only become, but how you thought of yourself.

❂ ⬛ ⊘

AFTER EVERYONE SQUATTED IN SNOW AND PINE NEEDLES FREEZING THEIR nuts off for a spell, a day of advance came in which your squad tried to flank behind a German pillbox, one you stumbled on after first discovering a minefield, conveniently enough, marked with a sign reading MINEN. A scout shouted "Pillbox!" with throat-screeching terror, followed by machine gunfire streaking across and everybody hitting the frozen fir needles and scrambling for precious cover and digging into the stony earth.

After pulling back and on the second attempt achieving the flank around the embedded jerries, your platoon leader, Lt. Wetherell, not much older than you, came up with the idea that you were going to take that pillbox with a TNT charge right plumb through the back door. As far as ideas went, this happened to be the only workaround to busting into those concrete-reinforced blockhouses from the front. Poured into the mountainside, twenty-five feet across, forty-five feet deep, cement thick in places to five or eight feet, these machine-gun nests were the hardened, glittering jewels of the Siegfried Line. Them smart, disciplined, industrious bastards was playing to win. Wasn't competition like running on the ball field with your old buddy Burnie Sykes, gone off to fly planes in the Pacific theatre. Higher stakes than that. Blood-stakes.

By now, you had advanced by default to platoon sergeant. A status of 'still alive' counted much toward swift advancement in Uncle Sam's Army on the ground in Europe. Experience humping around an M-1 and a bandolier of grenades, unlike the greenhorn officers who came and went, was currency on that battlefield like gold.

Before falling back from the attempt on the pillbox, you lost half the squad on this hair-brained scheme. Had seen silvery moonlight glimmering on a running stream down the hillside from the dug-in Germans running rusty-brown with blood from two men you knew well. What worked on other pillboxes here didn't succeed. You were glad it hadn't been your idea.

❂🅱☉

As if the nightmares to come later weren't bad enough, you had a different sort while still in the forest, the shallow kind where it don't seem like you have slept at all. Coming-to in a foxhole after trying to grab Zs, you might find another GI rubbing your sock-feet to keep off the frostbite. You'd do the same for him as he tried to sleep. None of it was queer: survival mode among brothers, all of you freezing together in a vast forested area the damn jerries called *Hürtgenwald,* for what felt like an eternity of unforgiving winter-time stalemate warfare, thousands of casualties on both sides.

In those dreams, you had to see your Daddy coughing up blood again. Hear his hacking. Going from room to room in a house to escape during his dying months, which you had done by lying and joining the army and leaving at sixteen. Was gonna be a mechanic living in steamy old Edgewater County. Or a linthead. Hearing your father cough till he died, that's what you feared. Might as well go in the army to get away from this death. Which you did. And which was why he haunts you like that, you reckon, and maybe you deserve it.

He had died while you were in Panama, after that furlough home and the camp meeting and Runelle Kittery. Since the war wasn't on yet, they had let you come back again, this time for the funeral. In the coffin, your daddy looked at peace. His suffering and death, though, trailing after you into the fighting, following you in the first round of bad dreams that started before you even returned home.

Wasn't but in his fifties, Daddy. He choked on his own blackened spit; had not left the West Virginia mines soon enough. Death, coming in many forms and with many sufferings to accompany, like the organ player in church on Sunday. Not that you attended services. Maybe if Runelle wished to, upon your return home.

In the European forest, though, you got to see another form of mortality than a goner croaking up his black-bloody lungs. Dying of a disease wasn't nothing compared to being shot into pieces or having your nuts or legs blowed clean off, your guts pulled out and some GI trying to stuff them back in long enough to haul your dead ass down off a burned and ripped-up hillside. Or freezing all night after seeing such scenes, imagining them occurring to you the next day, waiting for fire to rain out of the sky, the trees to explode, and hear grown men hollering for their mamas out of pain and fear. War.

⊛ ▣ ⊘

IN THE HIGH CATHEDRAL THAT HAD BEEN THE FORESTS OF THE EIFEL, defeating armies since time immemorial as you heard somebody say of the Germans you boys would later push back and subdue, the heavy snow-topped branches were like a mighty roof. The spongy, wet earth underneath, stony and backbreaking to dig for the foxholes. Cutting four-inch pine trees to fabricate makeshift stretchers to carry the wounded and the dead down steep, rocky hillsides. Ground fertilized through time by the blood of humanity at war with itself. A living hell amidst what ought to have been the grandeur of nature.

Back in France before your unit moved onto the field of battle that began in Hürtgen, a Catholic chaplain preached how upcoming hardships should be considered not suffering, rather penance for past, or ongoing, sins.

"May that you all come back washed and renewed in Christ's glory. In almighty God's forgiveness."

"Oh, we'll show up washed in blood, all right," the platoon sergeant—at the time, anyway—had said. "Jerry blood."

Despite the grim image, everybody busted a gut as though the unit sat watching a Marx Brothers movie. The priest continued trying to bless you all, but few attempted to engage with the process. As for you, you blessed yourself every day of your life, and this time of war no different.

⊛ ▣ ⊘

AFTER V-E DAY, THE ARMY, FACED WITH A MASS OF MEN, INCLUDING you, to decommission and repatriate in a semi-orderly fashion to civilian-hood, dumped you off in New York with no way home, no transportation. The flood of demobilized troops overwhelmed the mechanisms that under ordinary circumstances might have seen to your disposition, that functioned like clockwork in transporting all of your asses away to war. Typical.

You turned around and out of the throng came Ed Schulein, whom you met in France and also made it out of the war alive. Running into him after coming through processing at the Brooklyn Army Terminal seemed a minor miracle because of the numbers of men shipping back all at once.

After your release, you went gamboling with Ed to find a hot breakfast from a griddle, fresh eggs and warm toast and real butter and syrup on hotcakes, and as you both ate this magnificent meal, he told you of his plans spend the rest of his life in peace farming on the high prairie. How you ought to come, too.

Maybe; if only you didn't have a pretty woman waiting for you back home in Carolina.

"Otherwise, ain't much for me there," sounding like *thar*. Had gone to fight and kill, and later tend to POWs, and haunted forever by what you saw and did and condoned, yet still with a thick-hick West Virginia tongue. "So's I reckon I ought-a go."

"You better get back to her, then." Eddie, his blonde hair slicked back, face unlined and youthful despite fighting overseas. Ruddy. He looked wind-burned all the time, one of those types. Swedish blood. "Good woman's hard to find."

When you asked if she might like it in a town called Oakes, North Dakota he said, Sarge? "Only one way to know—take her there."

In fact, as you both walked around Brooklyn—later on you got hungry again and picked up these oddball snap-case wieners from a street vendor, like no hotdog you'd ever tasted—your mind tried to adjust back to being a regular person, one not prepared to shoot and kill and stab at the slightest provocation.

This had been the long and short of the mission in Europe: if you encounter the enemy, kill him; and, any left alive? Capture, imprison and allow to starve to death. You hoped and prayed no one would ever make you divulge the truth of your actions overseas. God forgive anyone who does, for they know not what they ask.

◌▣⊘

THE WAR BEGAN TO RECEDE FOR YOU, BUT IT TOOK UNTIL EARLIER IN THE spring this year, 1951, when y'all decided to quit North Dakota and come home. Or rather, Runelle declared that's what the future held for the Pettus family.

Going home now didn't make you fret. The German POWs they had working old man Glasscock's fields back in Edgewater County, long gone. Maybe being out on that flat land, with an uninterrupted view for miles in any direction, would give you peace.

Eddie had been right: The immense silence, but for the wind cutting across your ears. The deep winters, bundled up sipping tea and listening with your wife to the radio, the Opry or swing or other popular music, or a small collection of wax you got going on a trip into Fargo, on a stir-crazy winter day when the snow had melted during a rare warm spell of forty degrees; folks went out in shirtsleeves. You had found some old-timey pressings there, Buell Kazee banjo records and stuff like that. Single songs, too, like 'Is You Is or Is You Ain't' by Louis Jordan. That was a favorite of yours, a B-side of a hit song called 'G. I. Jive,' another'n to which you could relate. After what you seen and suffered, life felt like heaven, sitting in your farmhouse with your woman, playing records or the radio and putting another log into the wood stove.

Your spirits settled.

You stood smoking there in the farmhouse's yard, which this year you planned to repaint inside and out, from the second story on down, and trying to not think about going home. Then you remembered it was okay, now. The Germans were gone.

You took to sucking on butts to get the stink of the other smoke out of your throat, because it had not left you, not after five years of trying. A ripe, high, unnatural reek that got into your nose and mind from the few weeks of guarding the camp of German boys overseas—not the one they'd set up to process Jews and gypsies and queers. The barbed wire POW pen the Yanks managed, a makeshift, open-air prison laid out in a barren field to which you and your outfit were assigned at the end of your tour, also carried death. The taste and smell and thought of the cruelty and rot of watching men die, it lingered at the back of your teeth. Another mass of victims penned up, conscripts of a failing army enduring a final insult.

Quite unlike the soldiers stacked in bunks and hammocks would experience on the troopships returning them home. Way different circumstances: the victors bobbing on a boat and perhaps seasick, but nowhere for these defeated jerry wretches to bivouac but the hard, cold ground. And nothing offered them to eat.

Begging. Suffering. Dying day-by-day.

On your watch.

Before your eyes.

Too many.

At the time you still mulled and fretted over what you done—under orders—as well that they'd been the enemy who'd kill you soon as look at you. But their faces were those of hungry and scared boys, or else old men squinting down the barrel of a crappy-ass way to finish up life. As though getting shot by you wouldn't have been bad enough. This, worse.

For you, anyway. And for them.

And for all the horrible stories about their own death camps—the piles of corpses and the smell and shaken at the concept of what folks done to each other—you could not let your mind go back to your own POW camp. Not if you and your'n were to stay safe and sane. Whatever their crimes, to stand and watch men suffer and die before your eyes felt a sin and made you downhearted.

None of those orders set right, neither at the time nor years later on the prairie. But you done your duty. And kept your grunt mouth shut. And would keep it so. Regular folks still thought of fellas like you as heroes. Damned if you would be the one to break their ignorance of the truth. Not anytime soon. Not ever.

⚙ ☒ ⊘

YOU KEPT YOUR TRAP SHUT UNTIL TWO MONTHS AGO, ANYWAY, THE NIGHT came when she gave you the ultimatum about going back to Edgewater County. How again you woke up yelling and hollering the way you do half the time.

This dream? A booger. Enough that you got up, trying to walk quiet through the farmhouse but if every board in the bedroom didn't creak, you'd be a monkey's uncle. This noise got your Runelle out of bed, too, and that's how the talk of return happened.

In the kitchen, with the dawn still only a faraway hint on the low flat endless horizon, she put on coffee in the percolator you got her for Christmas last year, or rather got for both of you. She'd said making coffee on the stove made her feel like a sharecropping field hand, which was her way of acknowledging it was more or less what y'all were, but the coffee pot, modern, shiny and new. Best coffee you ever tasted.

"Time, Rennie. The hour is nigh."

"What—four in the A-M?"

She explained how, with the baby in yonder sleeping and you suffering another one of your spells, it was time to confess how this winter had frozen hard on her soul, and lasted too long. That this Southern girl longed for the warmth and familiarity of home. That your life there, a fine farming adventure for five years. And whatever you thought and felt? The day had arrived for her, and their baby, to get on back to Carolina.

"Now, first," you said. "I ain't mad you want to give up."

"Didn't think you would be," in her small and velvety girl's voice, so delicate and beautiful, like her oval face. "How bad was the nightmare this time?"

"Eh—same as always."

"Figured you was having one of your regular spells."

"T'was indeed."

She asked you if going back home made the dreams worse, because this, not the first you'd heard about leaving the prairie. You told her it might, but not for the reasons she thought.

Wasn't like the POWs in South Carolina, a truck full of them being took over to Mr. Glasscock's farm to work the field, and which you run up on after being back home for all of one blessed day, lay starving to death the way you and the others had allowed them boys overseas to do, but still made you feel like you's caught up in a waking nightmare that wouldn't end. All you wanted was to get away from the war and the pictures it left in your head, and you come thousands of miles home to get your separation papers and after saying goodbye to Eddie, hitchhiking down Highway 1 from New York to your woman, who waited like she said she would, all this only to find more German boys behind wire here, too?

You thought you would go around the bend when you heard.

Imagined the war was following you.

That the guilt wasn't never gonna let you go, no matter how much you prayed, how much powwow you worked on yourself.

But you had an out.

Got on the horn to Ed Schulein remembering how he'd said, if you come to where I live? It'll seem like the war's so far away nothing ever happened.

And for the first time that morning, with dawn starting to break and your second cup filled by her, you began to tell her all that, best you could. To explain the dreams. And coming to the farmland. Told her what you had gone through. If this was a breaking point, and she seemed to feel like it was, you needed to make your reasons known to your wife. For dragging her halfway across the country to a place not hers; a world not of her making.

"You don't got to tell me none of that. What you seen. What you done. It was—war," the word sounding like filth, like she had bit down on a bitter seed. "You did what they made you. That's what a soldier does."

When the truth came, it did so thin, high and scared. "No. Was like nothing you could imagine. The worst part was near the end, and them jerries—we had to stand gawking while they died in a big field like cattle. Watching. And letting them." Your whole body, shaking like you was being zapped by current. "And when they was getting close? Some of us? We—they—would drag them away from the others. Put them in another field, over closer to the woods. Standing around till they was—till they keeled over and—but sometimes, we—oh, Lord. I beseech thee to forgive me."

She covered your mouth and pulled your wet, contorted face into her body. You collapsed in those loving arms, breathing in the linden of the expensive soap she insisted upon from the dry goods in Oakes, but mixed with a certain natural aroma on the back of her neck, girl-spice unlike any parfum made by the hands of humanity; even in mortal distress, her smell made you swoon.

"Hush up. Don't you let yourself remember what happened. Don't—don't think about that. And never feel like you must say anything about it to me. Or anyone."

"But I—I'm burning up inside over it all."

"If you don't think about what happened overseas, you won't dream. It won't be real."

You calmed down. Reasonable and comforting, her words, but common sense told you peace wouldn't come so easy. "Worse when Eddie starts jawboning. I told him to make some new memories other than talking up his catting around with English girls, and all the krauts he—he—well."

At that she pushed away, her cheeks gone ruddy. "Eddie Schulein can kiss my foot. Your family needs you here in the present, not over in Europe, still."

Tears busted loose, sneaking up on you and making you cuss—it took all you had to keep them held in abeyance. Howling and barking like a dog, you cried like your baby boy whimpering for his bottle. Getting the pain out, finally, like you could never do in front of nobody but your lovely lady, who had been true and waited and loved you through all this foolishness of your'n. Scared by your weeping, but still she held onto your rough-hewn hands.

Sniffling like a young'un, you calmed your narrow butt down, said a silent prayer for serenity and peace: "Long as there ain't no German boys back home. That's what it'll take. To get me there. No soldiers behind no wires."

"They're all gone. And you know it."

True. There ain't been any POWs for years, not since the last went home in the summer of '46, undeniable, and in the face of the facts, worrying over them boys sounded silly. Like they was ghosts haunting you, and when you got home, they waited to start up again.

Five years ago. Far enough in the past now.

Them Germans kept in stir in places like South Carolina, as you read, got treated better than they probably ought to've been. Especially when it come out what all they had done over in their own camps.

That, ya see, was why you and your brethren allowed your captives to starve and die of exposure in that big killing field—they had sown the seeds of their own destruction. That was how Lieutenant Wetherell put it after you explained how you couldn't take no more POW guard detail. Couldn't march no more dying boys, nor drag no more of their bodies out of that smaller field over by the woods to watch them put down like dogs. But he said, just keep thinking about what they would've done to you and yours if we hadn't stopped them.

"This ain't right somehow."

"The hell it's not, Pettus. The mission's almost done, and the ocean'll be under our boots soon enough. Don't make waves."

But none of that part come out in the early breaking dawn at the farmhouse supper table in the kitchen. When the tears dried up you were ready to do as she asked—forget it all and hit the road. Until the next dreams worried you to tears.

Dream, you will. For the moment, though, your little baby Ronnie woke up and started hollering, and that become Runelle's focus for the rest of the morning, leaving you to go to Eddie Schulein's spread up the way to tell him y'all were quitting the farm. He seemed upset about the news, but what could a man say to another in your position. You hadn't made much of a farmer. Prosperity loomed for Eddie, maybe, but not you.

And now, driving through the Appalachian nighttime and smoking like a fiend to stay awake, you mulled over all this leading to the present moment. Do so without thinking in so many words, trying not to conjure up the pictures and the faces and the dreams. Messing with the radio, the high ghostly stations hard to hold on to in the dark hollows through which you passed, all the while suspecting y'all would not see these parts again anytime soon.

Or—would you? An idea-r has been itching and brewing.

❋ ▦ ⊘

But now you and your songbird wife are all-but back in good-old South Carolina, which sets with you so far as a decent compromise between the two extremes: West Virginia, where you had lived the first part of your life and swore never to return, and the Great Plains, where you thought you would stay until dead, which felt like it could come on you still at any moment, though the fighting and shooting and ducking and digging and dying lay far behind you.

You didn't put up no fuss. But you coulda stayed. Yeah. Because of that silence. And that view, long, all the way to the forever-horizon. Flat. Could see from four miles away the lights of the town near where their parcel lay. You rented the spread from Eddie's daddy, a full-on Swede so pious in his church of likeminded expatriate Scandinavians in the midwest he gives up a third—a third!—of his income as tithe, and made him eager to rent out farmland to anyone, even a jittery Rabbit settling his nerves and soul back down to earth.

The distance. The flat. You could see everything coming. If anything was to come, that is.

That was the part you don't get at all—the constant worry there's a force like, say, the devil, if one was a God-fearing man—a-coming for you and your'n, or else scheming ahead to it. You lack a word for how this feels, like your skin crawling all the time. With nerves on which you can't pin your farmer-rough finger. Thinking of it makes you crushed with weight surrounded by the darkness and this winding road down through the mountains running like a spinal column down to Carolina. Couldn't wait for the light to come up, like back being in them frozen foxholes and desperate for any kind of warm and comfort, a tiny, white-fuzzy dot of a sun blocked out by tree limbs.

Comfort, too, comes from your grandmother's powwow. Convinced it kept you whole and alive through hellish combat, might have helped others along the way, made possible your continued sanity in the face of true horror served up to you like slop on a chow line. The powwow and prayers. A way of life, but nary a soul knew. Part of its effectiveness, the secrecy of such endeavors.

The farming, in its physical and mental labors harder than you'd imagined, more involved than how that Swedish knucklehead Ed Schulein had sold you on the whole deal; the winters, brutal and claustrophobic, maybe too much like your childhood in West Virginia, only colder. More lonely, bitter and bracing than in the snowy hollows where you ran with your friends while the men worked in the depths of the mines, their women fretting and waiting out the shifts halfway up to their armpits in galvanized drums and scrubbing Borax Twenty-Mule Team into blackened dungarees with red-raw knuckles from the work and the winter. One positive aspect the midlands of South Carolina would offer was no snow. Barely cold, compared to the extremes you've known.

Summers, though? Brutal as heck, would take getting used to again. You had done basic training at Camp Jackson, thirty-odd miles from home and during your prime years of teenagerhood. You sweated through six weeks in sandy hills east of Columbia and every minute drawing breath while in Panama, but life felt adventurous, which was what you wanted. Until in Europe, when the journey became too much excitement for anyone sane to enjoy. Once you enlisted, the world got not only bigger, but more dangerous by the second.

Too big—no wonder sleepy Edgewater County sounded comfortable.

As for Runelle, she said she'd rather roast hotter than Hades than spend another winter freezing her skinny citygirl butt off there on the plains. Yesterday when you finished packing it had been the first of March, a new month, the season of leaving—for her, you, the boy. Get a fresh tenant on the hook to work the spring planting once the damnable snow she couldn't stand melted off. Not time yet, not by any stretch.

In fact, as you had driven away there'd come a morning flurry, flakes fat and wet and sticking on your faces and in your hair.

"Good riddance," she'd mumbled, pulling a shawl tight around her broad shoulders. "Enough."

You told her to snuggle up with that sweet-pea of your'n. The old truck will warm soon, and it did. Not as much as when y'all had gotten a few hundred miles away, though, with the snowmelt underway and the air shimmering crisp and clean rather than with razor-like frigidity in your throat and lungs. They could keep that part of the Dakota episode. You only put up with the cold because of being seasoned in the war.

◉ ▣ ⊘

DRIVING THROUGH THE RISING MOUNTAINS OF TENNESSEE, YOU TAKE A detour out of the way; and lord, but the woman wanted to get home. But you was gonna carry her the way West, see if she didn't want to land elsewhere.

Your big notion? Runelle ought to settle in Nashville, get recorded—you didn't care what that fancy-pants Ralph Peer told her years ago about how her voice was too pretty for hillbilly music. That she had a church-singing alto, and that wasn't near what folks expected from radio and records.

She still wants to sing her songs. Have people hear them, listen to them, like them. It makes her feel special; or so she says. Her precious gift, that dulcet warble.

So if she wishes to sing, y'all ought to pull into Nashville for a spell. That's what had come to you about an hour ago on your nighttime drive, how close you are to where the Grand Ole Opry originates, the show you clung to with full faith and anticipation during some pretty boring times stuck inside all winter. And listening as she sang along with that radio, holding her guitar and trying to guess at what to pluck. She improved over that long winter after you got the radio, and better still the next year with a used Victrola you snagged at a swap meet. Then she could play songs over and again, learn how they went note-by-note. The guitar, a gift to her that first Christmas in North Dakota. She had wept and hugged your neck for dear life.

You nudge her on the other side of the bench seat. "You still dozing, lady girl?"

"No." A dark, blanket-wrapped shape comprising Runelle and Ronnie Ed, fussy and stinking up the cab. "Ain't been for a half-hour. I keep putting off changing him."

"Thought you was sleeping."

"Nope. Where are we, anyway," through a yawn.

"Figured on a side trip."

"What for?"

She wasn't gonna hold no truck with going to Nashville. She was in a righteous hurry to get home. Like South Carolina would dry up and blow away if you didn't find yourselves there by morning light. "Don't you worry —we're almost home."

"Thank the Lord."

After a while you hear her nose whistling, and the baby had settled; they was asleep again. Y'all come up to a turn, and it's a moment like in that poem about taking one fork or'n the other in the forest in the woods, and you reckon that if you was moving for her, because you could've stayed on that lost and lonely prairie forever and a day if she'd-a been okay with it, she deserved the change to choose.

"Here's your detour. See that sign?"

Squinting, covering her eyes—a big logging truck turns out from a side-road and rolls on by your overloaded '41 Ford stake-bed like the vagabond hillbillies you are. You don't dare switch off the engine, not out here in the middle of the night in the sticks; it might not turn back over. You want her— your woman, not the Ford—to decide quick. But still make the right deci-sion. The battery, old.

"What detour?" Sleepy and sweet, leaning over and putting her head on your shoulder, which makes you tingle almost like it did the first time, in Charleston, you in your starchy stiff scratchy uniform jacket, and how it'd made little red streaks against her fine alabaster skin, the girl from the camp meeting in the upstate, and again there in the Holy City, a mad coincidence. "Oh—Nashville? What on earth for?"

"If you're a singer, and I think you are, then that's where'n you ought to go."

She scoffed, saying 'p'shaw' and telling you to drive on toward South Carolina. "I'm no songbird. You must be having some sort of fit."

You dispute her on this—to you, Runelle had been a vocalist by trade from the first you laid eyes on her, singing at that camp meeting you went to only because your mama, concerned about both you and your sick daddy, insisted on having the pastor pray over your souls. Wasn't even at war yet, but mamas, you know how they worry. The important part? Witnessing not the coming of the Lord in your heart—He was already there, thanks to your grandmother's explanations of how the universe operated—Runelle had sung 'Precious Memories' and sounded like an angel fallen to the ground. Into your arms, if she'd have you.

And when later you bumped into her on a crowded porch at one of the downtown Charleston restaurants, the boards and banisters creaking and packed with sailors and soldiers and young women, you told her not only of hearing her voice, but how she was the most willowy and beautiful songbird you ever saw. A pledge followed an evening spent walking and talking along the cobblestones South of Broad and by iron railing along the Battery reeking of harbor-mud, at last holding hands, a crackle of electricity and her face blazing hot from a foot away.

A kiss and a pledge accompanied the dawning of a new day, your last on these shores: you would find her after you got out of the Army in two years and damned if you didn't; kept writing to each other, months between letters a couple times almost bad as getting shot at by jerries; but throughout she made clear she was your girl and waited, chaste and patient of purpose, she wrote, whatever that meant—you ain't never been much of a reader nor a writer, neither.

You also mentioned how you'd find satisfaction in hearing her sing every day for the rest of your wretched goddamn life. Her voice rang to you out of the past, from before you went overseas and conducted the war—it had kept you warm in times of greatest fear and crisis like the call of a Savior, if not the One itself.

And so, you owed her this choice. You bade her again to make it, to follow her heart. "We could set up here, there, anywhere I can get mechanic work. And they ain't no shortage of that, not with all the cars on the road nowadays. Get a house for us three. And you'll sing, write tunes. And maybe somebody important will hear ya, or we'll arrange it like your uncle did that time, and—"

"No, Rennie." Cussing under her breath, you can't half understand. "I shan't, damn you. We can't."

"Says who."

Because, she tells you after a moment of clearing her throat, there's a baby, now. "I'll leave it to the singers on the radio. Long as I can listen to the words and sing along, I'll be happy."

"You sure?"

"If I'm saying so aloud, I'm certain. Now: give me a cigarette and put this vehicle in gear, if you don't mind."

You did all of the above, lighting a smoke for yourself, too.

When you crossed the state line, which you only noticed because of the small beat-up sign alongside the mountain road down from Asheville, you get her awake one more time to announce how y'all are on the downslope into Greenville and all but home. If you keep saying 'home' aloud like you were certain as she seemed, you will arrive in that place and at last enjoy a peaceful night's slumber. You don't act you've had one since you left Panama, and damn if that's not ten years. If Edgewater County feels right this time, perhaps you'll lay a whole mess of worries and trials to rest once and for all. Now that you could live with.

AFTER TWO YEARS OF GREASE-MONKEYING BACK IN EDGEWATER COUNTY, you and Burnie Sykes, who'd forged a way different path while you's off trying to farm as old Schulein said you should, was all talk about the future; what's to come and from where the solid money was gonna flow like 'fine wine.' Besides that high-talk, you both loved music and the radio and watching pickers pick and he and his wife, and you and your'n, got on all famous-like. Would sit together and listen to the Opry and other shows, compare impressions about the tunes and the picking.

Runelle, however, loath to strum her guitar and sing in front of anyone. "If I make a feint toward competence one day, I may then perform for you all," she'd usually say, with everyone, you most of all, sitting in disappointment and anticipation. You always tell them how good she sings, your honey. She needs to back up your claims, beau, lest you get labeled a liar.

Meantime? Burnie, fixated on the money-part, which with a young'un and a woman to feed, you listen with eager ears: "Pettus, I tells ya—there's a world of opportunity. It opens up bigger every day, like a flower that never stops blooming."

With family help he started up an appliance store only blocks from courthouse square and down from the Dixie-Anna Grocery, a business in fast decline now that the IGA opened, with its big parking lot and aisles wide enough to walk two abreast. "We whupped them Nazis and Japs," he says one day, gazing off into a Carolina sky bluer than the ocean, "and we'll beat back them egg-sucking yellow Chinese and the slope-eyed Koreans before that all gets out of hand, too. We gonna make the best of everything, especially TVs, boy. Them's the future. That's what I'm-a get into next." He preaches how the time to make inroads, take advantage of the flow of money and prosperity, is here and now.

You don't know what that means to a wrench head with a squalling, bad-tempered toddler running wild in the little mill house y'all rent. You stayed out of working the mill, but the only affordable housing still lay nearby. Same culture, drawing you back, as though the ghost of your daddy beckoned you into the life he chose rather than your own.

He moved y'all down here to pursue mill-work so's he could get out of the mines before the black lung took him. He'd been told how the linthead life, while not too different in some respects was still like night and day when compared with the ordinary dangers and discomfort of the sunken and forbidding mine shafts. A mill hand could enjoy the sun outside dingy but tall windows, and depending on what side of the building, which line you was working, he could even see the river and the falls, the water powering the building and the whole endeavor. If that didn't sound better than being down in a granite hole breathing coal dust, you didn't know what better was supposed to mean.

You supposed you'd be sucking cotton right now but for the chance from Hiram Hampton, at his garage and used car lot. Lucky you. But still. Maybe you would open your own car yard one day. Not that you'd let Hiram know this thought often swims in your head.

You'll tell Burnie this notion soon enough, though. When you manage the nerve. Burnie, smart. Makes you feel like a hick. You choose your words carefully with most folks, but in particular with him. You don't know why.

◌◍⊘

You'd say that once back in Edgewater County you and Burnie

Sykes had hit it off quick, but how hard is it when someone's already been your best pal?

Yep: You met when y'all Pettuses first moved down to Tillman Falls, and had become running buddies while at Ferry Crossing High while playing football together on the starting JV squad, boys of fourteen and fifteen. Now, back from the war growed up into a farming grease-monkey and, in Burnie's case, business school, a college man at Southeastern University on the GI Bill. Both however suffer deep creases in your faces and foreheads to be such relative young'uns, still. No matter your appearance, you stood, as he'd put it, as men of the town and the county. Y'all will be in charge of all this one day, that's his point. And no time like now to stake out turf.

One afternoon you at last told him of the big thoughts in your pumpkin head, about having yourself a business, your own garage. There's not a motor in the world you can't tinker your way through—German, English, you name it.

"Engines need a lotta care. Pieces-parts moving around, stuff rubbing against itself. I got an eye and an ear for it."

"Boy, I hear you. A good living waiting for a man who builds a business dealing in cars. Ain't no doubt."

Burnie, remaining unconvinced, though, and as y'all went down the street from where his store was Now Open and by the barbershop and through the alleyway and under the movie marquee—*Hell and High Water*, a Samuel Fuller submarine picture in Cinemascope you are eager to see—he spat and shook his head and said mm-mm. Walked you until you ended up in front of the grocery. An old-ass building, facing back across the green and the confederate monument toward the rest of town arrayed out before you both, at the far end the courthouse with its plaza and big magnolias and oaks; a scenic little burg, postcard pretty. "But what if we could try less of a sure thing. What about a restaurant, along with a—"

"A restaurant?" You reeled off the ones already here: Louella's there in sight, the lunch counters down the way, the Walgreen's soda fountain and the Congress Street Grill. "And who's 'we'?"

"More than a restaurant. What if it was—?" Burnie, standing with his arms folded and looking over at the gray columns of the old bank building, what the local AFM was now using. "More of a nightclub. A music club. And a—a—well." His lips worked. He couldn't get the words out.

"What, a high class juke-joint?"

"No," offended. "A club to hear old-time music. Hillbilly music. Like on the Opry. Pickers."

"A juke-joint, in other words."

"Boy, you ain't thinking right. I'm talking first-class country cooking and country music. I'm talking about taking over this corner of the green and making it our own. You and me."

"I don't know what you need me for, exactly."

"You don't think I can run this and become the TV king of Edgewater County all on the same plate? I gotta have a partner I can trust."

"What makes you reckon that's me?"

Sour face, spreading wide to a big lusty grin. "Because I could always trust you on the field. And in other venues."

You ask him to explain why.

"You are as you seem. Unlike most assholes."

"Whatever that means, I always felt that way about you too, buddy."

Burnie, a lingering handshake: "Besides, we're war heroes. They owe us our corner of Tillman Falls. Don't they."

"Bet your ass they do." Thinking, aw. Nobody owes you for that cold sit in them woods over Christmas, 1944. "But a restaurant?"

"Gonna need to scrub the grease from under them nails. All I can tell you." And nudging you in the ribs, continuing your walk around town by popping into Louella's and grabbing lunch before you headed back to work at Mr. Hampton's.

Thing was: did you trust him the way he trusted you?

For the most part. Burnie Sykes, he kept his cards played close. Felt sometimes like he was moving chess pieces. Always deciding how, why and what was to come.

Maybe he had earned this sense of leadership, at least compared to you: Burnie, already a man of the town, living in their big house over on Whaley Way along with the other such classic southern mansions with their porches and porticos and columns and azaleas planted all around, many dating to antebellum times, and still here, your friend told you, because Edgewater County boys had burned the bridge and kept Sherman's marauders, exhausted from their ravaging of Columbia, from destroying the township.

Your family name? No such history. Next to the Sykes's, you ain't much of nothing—all you got is fixing cars at Hiram Hampton's garage over on the west end of Common Street, before it turns into the Pisgette Highway going through the national forest toward Newberry. Word come they gonna build one of Eisenhower's new slabs of roadway, plus another four-lane to the east to boot.

Burnie croons and swoons about the fresh money new roads will bring over the long haul and in the short run, too. Old-timers, he explained, still evoked how much grease flowed come into county coffers when they took and built the hydro dam. Workers needed a place to blow off steam, to eat, to drink, to hear music. His vision on how y'all can both prosper, as you'll see, is right clear and thought-out. More than you could ever muster. That's Burnie Sykes.

BURNIE AND HENNY HAD HAD YOU BOTH OVER FOR SUNDAY DINNER THE week that the Dixie-Anna Grocery closed up. A big article in the *Advocate*. Store had been plying trade since Reconstruction, but time has marched onward. Dry-goods grocers, the stuff of westerns on TV. One over in Blackstock still in business carried a particular fishing lure you liked. One day all such country stores would be gone, you reckoned, replaced by modern markets. Newer, anyway. Burnie says if we ain't got no progress, we ain't got squat.

While the women clear away the dishes, you both sit and talk about all the plans, but in whispers. Runelle, carrying a plate or two at a time, listening with her little frown to Henny, who might not stop chirping even in her sleep. Burnie's little dark-haired beauty, all of five feet and a firecracker behind closed doors, to hear him tell it. With Henny Sykes ongoing ramble, however, you finally understood why the Limeys call them birds.

Burnie's bride, prattling on about this'n that—woman issues, gossip, showing off her lovely home, which puts your ramshackle if clean house in the mill village to shame. Her endless chatter about downtown Tillman Falls goings-on matched up well with her husband's big talk. How one day, both wives would be members of the Edgewater Ladies Munificence Society and they would run this town, they would be the next generation to do so, and the time was coming.

"They'll find out who's running what." Burnie, snickering and winking over it all. "Let's go outside for a spell."

He motions for you to follow onto the wraparound porch, where you plop down and gaze into the well-tended yard, its darkness dotted by a pulsing constellation of green-glowing fireflies. Sticky and moist, late spring in South Carolina felt more like high summer up in the plains. Still getting acclimated, on some days.

"Mascaro's gonna jump if we don't, that's the word." Burnie, capping a couple of beers, hands you one; both fire up smokes. You sip that beer, though, being full of the chicken, biscuits and gravy Henny served. "Like having the theater and the drive-in ain't enough for his eye-tie ass, he must-a heard what we had in mind and has been making big talk. I say, we cut him off at the nuts and get going soon."

"You know what they say about opportunity, I reckon."

"And in that spirit? If you wanted to throw in with me, now's the time to speak."

Your head, feeling light along the crown, a tingling you can't figure out and that makes you uncomfortable as heck.

"Damn, son—how long you need to dwell on this opportunity of a lifetime?"

"Here's the truth: I don't know nothing about running what you're talking about. Work I got lined up is honest enough, and in my wheelhouse. What I ought to do."

Burnie, pissed. How he's unable to understand a man saying no to an offer like what he's got in mind. The money on the table.

All you can say in response is that it ain't all over money. "It's about what a man's fit to do and what he ain't. You can't smear lipstick onto a pig and turn it into your prom date. Not even in Edgewater County no more," which makes you both laugh.

"But Rabbit: you don't think this club—the restaurant—will fly?"

"Couldn't say. Sounds right fancy for Tillman Falls."

Burnie, he swears that's what makes it a top-choice business plan. "Couldn't lose if you tried."

You feel warm inside, a gooey goodness you can't put your finger on, but your head still says no. "Can't feature myself running no nightclub."

"Maybe you ain't trying hard enough to picture Rennie Pettus in such a role, beau."

"Could if I wanted. But it ain't me."

"C'mon."

"Nope. That's that."

❊❚⊘

AND YET NEXT WEEK, HERE YOU SIT, GOING IN ON THE SCHEME WITH HIM.

Here's how it happened: Burnie showed up on Monday at your house and said, you will not work at Hampton's today. You're coming with me. And you had, Runelle fussing with the boy and watching you both walk down the cracked and crooked sidewalk to the street.

He drove you over to see Mr. Durham, the owner of the Dixie-Anna. Durham, stooped and hunched and broken by the deaths of his two boys— one, back in the 50s in a car wreck on the bridge across the river, and the other? Easy—in the war, like a half-million other American troops. With no heir to leave his business, the man grateful, now, for a potential buyer on the listing so soon.

You sure loved that building, y'all both said, and that corner of the green. Coming from that direction, the west, it's a true-blue main entrance to the town proper. A gateway. Not to mention having a bunch of ideas about what this important corner could become.

You only told the old man about the restaurant part, not the juke-joint or 'club,' rather. Burnie, particular about what's said in front of others. A language and truth for us alone, and another for folks doing deals with us. That's how Burnie explains it.

Makes sense to you, probably better than most. You already know how to keep secrets.

❊❊❊

Truth is that you don't love engines and grease and hoses and tires. You love music, and the more time passes, this plan about a music club starts to feel right. You don't play or sing, but, Lord! Do you enjoy listening and tapping your feet along with the musicians, and now that Burnie's put the idea in your head, you burn to live out this crazy dream.

The best memories from your boyhood, you sitting and watching those pickers on Friday and Saturday nights tear it up. Those voices, howling about working in the mines, and the fields, their melodies the sound of life in the hollers. A call to soothe everyone's troubled, poor-assed souls, one that'd starting coming out of radios—songs like magic angel-voices calling out of the early-fallen nighttime there in the mountains, at least for those who could afford a receiver and a high-mounted antenna wire.

If this idea worked, you would love music and live it, but better than that?

So would she.

Your lady girl, your songbird.

You would give her the stage she could not get on herself, thanks to Ralph Peer and his notions about who was or wasn't supposed to be a hill-billy singer on the radio.

Standing on the sidewalk outside the building you and Burnie were about to buy, the Carolina sunshine warming the tops of your heads and making you both squint, you said all this out loud. Your voice, shaky. Scared's what it sounded. Or hick. Like you didn't know your ass from a hole in the ground.

But no. Burnie, getting this shit-eating grin on his face.

"Dang, son. We're gonna make a go of this—the entertainment center of Edgewater County," what he calls a hunky-tunk. "Them boys in Atlanta, and in Nashville, they're printing money, man. We're talking about show business, here. We'll transform this burg into a new Tillman Falls."

You amble over toward Common Street, the rounded façade of the building on that corner, red bricks—old, solid as they came. Running your hands along the wall, you say, "We're gonna make this old girl nice."

"Of course she'll be nice, son. But 'nice' ain't half what this place is gonna be."

"But, not like dives I regret seeing in the service. A family joint—all welcome, not just hell-raising rednecks and soldiers from over at the fort. We'll put up a neon sign." You close your eyes and imagine a colorful sign sticking out from that rounded corner. "One to put the Walgreen's to shame."

"Like 'you' saw? Boy, I could turn your head backwards with all I done in Australia."

In the war Burnie had flown with the 400th Bomb Squadron out of New Guinea, on B-26 Marauders—they called them the Black Pirates. An exotic and wild part of the world, he said. Had seen actual natives, brown women with their teats drooping loose and bones shoved through their noses. And in Queensland, he claimed he drank more than he ever thought he could, as did everyone there, those in the service and otherwise. "In Australia, the lager? It flows like well-water. Breakfast, lunch, dinner. And pissing all day like racehorses."

"I ain't running no speakeasy. That's what I'm saying. Is all."

"Naw, naw. Beer only. We can't get away with liquor by the drink, not in this backward state. But worry not—we'll change it all, at least here in our little world."

You would take Burnie up on his idea about the money. Pay him back in due time.

You weren't sure your debt would matter to him: People bought washers, iceboxes and new television sets almost as fast as trucks could bring them. And Burnie, he's got family money, too—that house over where all the hoity-toities lived on Whaley Way is long paid for, two generations before him. You understood, finally, how much Burnie had not needed to work in mills, mines or garages.

Yet now, he was offering you, a coal-mining linthead, a shot at his kind of life. You had to take it. That afternoon, you quit Mr. Hampton's.

For now you worked for Burnie at the appliance store, but in fact you existed as an unemployed, would-be entrepreneur. You couldn't spell the word to save your life, but that's what Burnie Sykes says you are, so that is what you'll be.

Sitting out front of his business on a Saturday, you watch as cars and trucks putter and trundle around the green, with shoppers and diners strolling with sacks clutched in their hands. You wait until it looks not-so busy inside Sykes Appliance and Electronics to finalize the promissory note with your best friend about the loan to buy the property, which would be in your name.

What a pal, Burnie. He put together a group of folks, he said, who'll front most of the start-up capital. "Angel investors," he calls them. "Why mess with bankers when we ain't got to?"

Fine by you. Like everyone, you come up in the Depression. Banks is hard to trust. Who knew when money will go all cattywampus again?

◌▩⊘

WHEN THE OFFICIAL ANNOUNCEMENT COMES ABOUT THE TOWN MEETING regarding the nuclear plant they're to build at the head of the lake, a body of water itself created by them fellas building the hydro dam back in during the Depression, you can't understand at first why Burnie dances a jig. Why he insists on traipsing over to Town Hall to hang on every niggling detail.

"Son, think of the jobs it'll bring in the short and long term." He shimmy-shakes over toward the courthouse square as though y'all wandered into a real juke-joint on a Saturday night. "How many of them fellas gonna want to buy TVs and electric iceboxes?"

"Goody for you."

"Rabbit, old dog—don't ya get it? Them boys also wanna listen to music and drink liquor. Eat barbecue, burgers and chicken. Hear old-timey music."

"Music." You snap into gear with your smarter beau. "Right, right. But, liquor—?"

Waving you off. "Let's don't worry about that part—money's a-coming our way, my boy. A shitload of fellas bivouacked around the county for the next four years. With good money burning up their durn pockets." Burnie's turn to say *hah*. "Only one person we got to get straight with before we can move forward."

"One?" You speculate how this must be the Baptist preacher sure to pitch a fit about a honkytonk going into the old downtown grocer's.

"Shit, no. Somebody more powerful than any of them pencilnecks and

Baptist crackers. We gonna go talk to Davis Macon. He's the one gives us the go-ahead."

"Davis Macon?"

"And Josiah Rembert, too. Rabbit—you got to know the pecking order of things. Don't ya remember being in the service? When it comes to liquor and honkytonks, you need to know the real bosses. Getting the licenses, that ain't nothing. On all other matters, you work with the operators already here. Be a partner to them, but make a space for yourself. Get it?"

You do, or tell him you do. As for the military, most of your time gets spent hazing away the sorriest details of your long service best you can.

"Now: you want to be an officer? Or a grunt for the rest of your linthead life?"

"Ain't no linthead. No more'n Daddy was a coal miner."

"See—he knew. Knew he was on the wrong path in them mines. And fixed it by coming here. And now, like him, like his boy, doing something about his situation. Finding out who he is and where he ought to be." He claps you on your chambray shoulder.

You stand shuffling your feet and spitting, thinking about the booze part of it all, yeah-sure. You want a new sidewalk poured in front of the old mercantile. You need the town fathers for aspects of Burnie's plan like that.

And you need Davis Macon and Josiah Rembert for that, too. You don't even know them—you spent a day or two memorizing the names of the council members and the busybodies in the ELMS, and that at Burnie's behest, too. Scheming, plotting and preparing. That's Burnie.

But already, and after only a year in business, he's able to buy himself a Cadillac still warm off the car-carrier. And put up money, too, to buy the building that's been the Dixie-Anna Grocer and Dry-Goods.

The shell of the old grocer, anyway. You're gonna make it all fresh for the town. That's worth a new sidewalk, ain't it? The old one, cracked and sunken and beat up by delivery trucks rolling one tire up on the curb. Once they start delivering, you'll explain to the beer-keg boys to keep their tires on the pavement.

Yeah. Your sidewalk, soon.

Listen to you. You need to make money, first. You owe Burnie thousands.

But as for the capital improvements you and Burnie seek, other capital you can offer the town in exchange: Covering that long, blank wall running down that side of Common Street into a pleasing color. Or a picture—a painting. What did they call that?

Yeah. A beautiful picture, of nature and flowers or maybe the Sugeree

River, that shimmering stretch before you get to the falls, which once they built the dam twenty years ago don't so much fall anymore as trickle. A painting of the old falls running hard, the water that'd powered the mill and then the whole town, and now would do what it could to cool down that atomic plant they're set on building—none too shabby an idea.

Damn if Burnie didn't sound right about the looming prosperity—good-old boys, after working like dogs all day building the plant, would blow off steam by spending their wages, sure to be decent. It'd been this way in the mill village where you lived there before signing up, when everyone had been grateful and happy to have any jobs at all; you worked and got your scrip and spent it in the store or at the tavern. And the money stayed in the mill owner's hands. The coal mine had been much the same. Your daddy had said that part of moving to Carolina wasn't much better, but he'd still rather mess with cotton than coal.

"Hell, I'd pick beans by hand alongside the coloreds than put that spike into the rock another time," he always said. Your Daddy ended up sick as a dog anyway, and left you but a pittance other than memories and sayings.

Thank god for Burnie Sykes. He knows so much. Says he learned about the way of life in the war, but hell, you already knew he was smart from back in school, before you got fed up with the teachers and the reading and quit to join the Army.

Everything you learned overseas you wanted to forget. If opening up a honkytonk down from your best friend's appliance store wasn't enough to make a body forget all that'd come before, you didn't know what would. Sure have plenty to do—like go hat-in-hand before old rednecks to have their blessing on how you will next conduct your life.

You don't care for that part. Yeah—like you kinda said to Burnie, you remembered how the order of things played out in the Army. All too well. So you had to salute some other Joe to progress to the next step. Surely you can live with the duties such fealty and deference will entail.

❂❋❂

BURNIE SAYS ONE THING Y'ALL OUGHT TO DO, NOW THAT THE BUILDING'S gutted, they built the stage and the framing for the bar and the kitchen around the existing load-bearing columns, is ride over the hills to Nashville. Take in the Opry, see the famous honkytonks. Get ideas about how to decorate, inside and out.

But, to not carry along the wives; keep it all business. Take the girls back later, when y'all can relax, show them a proper good time.

You fret how y'all are already spending enough without burning up petrol going all the way to Nashville and back to see what the inside of a bar looks like. "I went in my share when I was at Camp Jackson, and elsewhere."

"Expect you did."

You speak of Main Street in Columbia, which once hosted a notorious bar district a half-dozen blocks north of the State House, taverns crawling with brawling soldiers, rapscallions and scoundrels of varied provenances. And, if you learned anything from those experiences occurring at such a tender age, it's that you don't cotton to taking part in any roughneck scenes. Not with your wife getting up on stage and singing. Not on your watch. "I seen mess go in bars that would turn the pastor's hair white."

"You got the wrong idea, pal."

"No—it's the right idea. This ain't gonna turn into no dive, Burnie. Last time I'll say it. I'll take a gander at whatever you got in that big city, but what we do here is what *we* gonna do. If that makes sense."

"It does; and I don't disagree one whit. Sometimes you must go and see where somebody else went wrong before you can do right. How you think I figured out the layout of the showroom in the appliance dealership?"

Dealership—as though the trade were a close cousin to the bustle and business of the new Hampton Motors, the biggest car dealership in three counties and an outfit at which you could have stayed and had a role and a good stable job. Maybe as a car salesman, later, instead of a mechanic. Commission checks. Whole bit.

"I been up to Charlotte, down to Charles-town, and over to Atlanta, too, and seen what the big appliance boys are doing. And I've added my flair to the showroom floor," though you couldn't tell what that was, at least not from looking at the setup. "And so, I hear you, Reynolds, my boy. We'll make The Dixiana our own—all our own. It's gonna be about the singing. I've already assured the town fathers and council that it's all above-board, old-timey music. Ain't nothing untoward—it's country music. It's barbecue. Suitable for families of all ages. We'll even use that loading dock on the back to stage outdoor concerts in that scruffy field. A town festival—that's what we'll put on."

"I can't half imagine such," and you meant it. "Of being in charge of all that."

"We'll get the hang of it. We'll get on the good side with managers of musicians. Their agents. Book some names onto our stage."

It's all Greek to you. Managers—is that like a floor boss at the mill? For people who make music?

Back in the hollers it was always groups of men, and often women, picking on fiddles and guitars, crooning and crying in circles, with bigger circles watching and listening and maybe cutting a rug, if enough jug-juice had gone around. Music just happened—it didn't need any management.

Burnie, a smart one, though. A college man. You've no choice but to listen and go along now.

◌ ◍ ◎

SPEAKING OF THE MUSIC, Y'ALL ARGUED OVER DROPPING WHAT BURNIE wanted to spend on the Wurlitzer for the honkytonk, which seemed an extravagance. But to you, much of the money-spending seems lavish.

Thank god for Burnie's generosity. Says the jukebox will make y'all money. That he's got a man he calls a 'rack-jobber' who comes like clock-work to keep the latest records stocked into Burnie's store, also keeping the jukebox full-up with the freshest 'sides,' as they're called in the business.

"Now that these record players are getting cheap, and TVs'll have record players built in, people are gonna want records. Radio, and jukeboxes too, I guess people ain't gonna need those so much. But we'll always have us one in our club. And the rack-jobber, the same man pays us money to put certain records in there, on top of all the nickels we get to keep. Sound good?"

You reckon that it does. Thank Burnie again for all the records he gave you, a whole box full of old-timey music and some jazz, too, which you didn't quite know what to do with. Darkie music. It had some swing. You had put the stack on a shelf in the living room, and played them on one of those small record players Burnie sold you for a song. Runelle, lord but she loved those old records. She loved swing band music, too. It's a decent collection.

Burnie, he said he was making room for all the new ones. "That rack-jobber, he's gonna give us extras for anything we want for ourselves. Between us, we'll build a helluva record collection. Hell, maybe we'll start a radio station of our own one day."

Your head spins at the thought; suggest getting the honkytonk open.

"I need to introduce you around. Let them know who'll be joining the first rank of businesses in the city."

"Who?"

"Quit playing dumb. *You*, boy." Burnie showed you his ring, the familiar Masonic symbol. "I've told them about you."

You think about the lodge sitting a block off the green in the old bank building, with its tall columns. Farmers First Future Savings & Loan had failed in the Depression, its ornate and considerable facade resting empty until the local AFM had bought the building for its temple.

You want no part of that. Your daddy told you to be careful about joining groups, the Rotary Clubs and whatnot, because it's all about the dues, and taking what little extra money you have so you and a bunch-a yahoos can sit around eating and looking at movies of half-naked women. Wasn't nothing in which you wish to participate.

"Let me get on my feet running this joint of your'n, beau. If you don't mind."

"Rabbit—Reynolds—you got to lose the yokel. Some, anyway. I'm begging ya."

"Just talking like I talk."

"I keep telling you—a rube's gonna get taken advantage of."

"Ain't nobody getting nothing over on this one."

"My point's that if they think you're a mark, they'll play you like one."

"They can try. Ain't no mark."

"We'll find out."

❂❖⊘

Runelle, with Ronnie put down for a nap, finished fixing a big dinner for Burnie and Henny and their boy Buddy, two years older than Ronnie. She called you all into the dining room to eat.

The house, a sloped-roof saltbox y'all rent in the mill village, is so cramped and drafty Runelle is skittish and embarrassed at having Burnham Sykes over for dinner—she don't much care for him, feels beneath him and wishes she had a better kitchen to cook in not only for guests, but all the time. Aching inside, you know it'll be awhile before the money comes in to make a move, except into another of these old rattraps.

You would tell her to hold on. Maybe when Ronnie's in school, you'll have bought a better house.

Burnie kept on about land way up River Ridge Road coming up for sale, beautiful farmland that's gonna go for a song. You'll look into it. An opportunity's an opportunity, as he always says.

It might take time before the honkytonk makes real scratch, though, as you keep advising her.

She don't like that talk one bit. Says it ain't gonna be like Burnie selling stoves and fridgerators. You reply, if it don't pan out, I'll keep working for him at the store. "We got it all planned out, sugar. Don't you fret," one of them phrases you reel off to women to have them settle inside, in times when you're far from settled yourself. A man hides such a coward-assed sense of fear from his wife, or he ought to, anyway.

A man hides his fear, and his tears. If he's weak enough to let them come out at all, even in private. Or so feeble he can't control his dreams, and gets no peace at night, which is hard to hide from her.

You and Burnie put away a good bit of beer while y'all plan all this Dixiana mess, and you have to admit you've been sleeping better. You know how it goes with alcohol, though, and if you're squeamish about any part of owning this club, as Burnie keeps trying to get you to call it, it's for this reason. But selling the beer, that's from where the real money will come. You have a family—you must have a steady income.

Burnie, too, has a family. He knows what's at stake. But he's got your flank covered. To hear him tell it, most of your business—and your pay— will come conducted in cash, with an occasional check issued with various fees deducted and remitted to keep the tax boys from sniffing around. Worrisome, but you have pledged to leave all matters up to him—he's the businessman.

⊙▣⊘

THE GIRLS LAY DOWN MANY STIPULATIONS AND RULES OVER THE TRIP TO Nashville, while Burnie says, yeah yeah; to you, he reports how there ain't no time to waste, so let me make a mess of phone calls and he does, after which you're ready to leave.

Next thing your cracker ass knows you're in Burnie's DeSoto humming up through the North Carolina mountains like when you'd brought Runelle home from the prairie, and when Burnie traveled to check out the big-boy appliance houses in the surrounding cities.

"Now look." Y'all have crossed the Tennessee border, almost to Johnson City. "Them rules the girls laid out. Way I see it? This is like being overseas on leave. And so—"

"Now, I might not be the sharpest hook on the lure, but Nashville ain't like being overseas. We're gonna see the Opry; we going visit ourselves a honkytonk—I mean, a club—or two. Get a look at how they do it in Music City, USA. I ain't interested in nothing else. We got to be serious, remember? To make it work good?"

"When the next time you gonna be out of town for two days, boy? Untethered?"

"Don't matter."

"What a wet blanket."

"Too bad."

He huffs and puffs and says forget it. "I'm not saying you ain't right. I'm just saying," he kept saying. "Waste of an opportunity, is all."

❊❄❀

A HALF-HOUR OUTSIDE NASHVILLE Y'ALL STOP FOR GAS, AND WHILE waiting for the jockey to pump and check oil at the Gulf station, you mention to Burnie an idea you been rolling around in your mind, like one of them sourballs like out of the candy machine at the IGA.

"I wanna see about getting my brother in on this mess."

"Oh, really." Burnie, all bright-eyed. "We got ourselves an investor?"

"Shit, no—but I want to give him a way out of that mill, too. If that rascal won't be so stubborn as to reckon on what I'm trying to do for him." Rut Pettus, a floor boss by now. Spending time in the office, not running a machine at all. A right sweet trade, which you mention.

As well: "We ain't that close. Like brothers ought'n to be."

Burnie, his mouth hanging open, a look like he either can't understand you, or else you just ain't got good sense. "Then what the hell you want to go into business with him for?"

You reckoned it would be obvious. "So's maybe we could—feel like we was brothers? Partners?" You feel put on the spot. Thought it would go over. Thought 'family' said it all. "Can't say I know."

"He know anything about music? Running a joint?"

"No more'n I do."

"Then forget it. Let's get this beast running. Get cash moving through on our own. Then maybe we'll see if we need any help. If *you* need help—forget 'we.' You got this, son. This is gonna be your gig—that's what the pickers call a show. But what *we're* gonna do is own this sorry-ass little town. Eventually."

You ponder how this will happen. Think of the people who seem to run it—the mayor and the cops, the ELMS, Rotarians and Masons. You aren't any of those, don't wish to be one. Too much like back in the platoon. Like being in a unit.

Further, you don't know why anyone would want to own anything 'sorry-assed,' but being Burnie, you back down.

Feel swept along.

You hope you can do this.

That this is all gonna work out.

You wish you could see into the future. But you can't—that's fairy tale shit, like at the movie house.

Now that seemed like a decent and easy trade—take their money, turn on the projector, and sit back just like the joes and janes handing over the dough to look at them flickers on the wall. Burnie says TV's gonna run off all that business, though. "They'll be turning these movie houses back into vaudeville theaters then, boy."

Records, on the other hand, was a product that could also put folks into a place like your honkytonk, and vice versa—folks buying records after hearing pickers picking at The Dixiana, which is what y'all settled on calling the honkytonk as a tribute to Mr. Durham, who had gone on and on about wishing some part of his grocery and dry goods could live on. Important to pay homage to the past. You're young, but you ain't green. You have seen death, and impermanence. You can understand his sentimentality.

And yet, it's also clear as corn liquor you got so much to learn, feel glad in that respect you're on this trip. To see up close what your friend has in mind.

You hated having that itchy feeling about Burnie, though: that there's often a crucial aspect of his schemes left out of the explaining.

Maybe it's one more problem the war done to your noggin—made you suspicious of people you oughtn't to be, like Ed Schulein back in North Dakota. But like Eddie, the way Burnie looked at Runelle when he thought you wasn't watching gives you pause. You'll kick any man's ass who steps out of turn with her, though, even your best friend. But again. All your imagination. Probably.

❋🎵❋

"It's Grand Ole Opry time, another big folk music show starring the Texas Troubadour, Ernest Tubb!"

The broadcast from the Ryman, a real corker. You can't half believe you're there, gaping at that stage with them barn doors lit up bright red and white, the colors and the flashes from the shiny instruments half-blinding you with glory and excitement; but with a pit in your stomach at getting to experience this without Runelle, your wife who'd be over the moon about this foot-stomping and heart-tugging music made before your eyes and going out over the radio to who knew how many ears. Buzzing, you're in a place of concentrated magic, so different from your lonely sojourns in foreign forest and frozen prairie. Like you are seeing and hearing for the first time, in a way. The swell of the crowd's applause strikes a particular vibration inside, an electrical feeling in your bosom and down in your gut.

Now you get the idea—music and people in the room and electricity— but still don't see how you and Burnie Sykes can recreate this on your scale back home. In the moment it doesn't matter, not soon as those pickers get going again following the commercial breaks. This here's the big time. This is Nashville. This is music, unfolding before your staring, rube eyes.

You remember back when you and Burnie built that radio. And how that'd been the first sound you heard, the station you dialed in that night. The Opry. How you had got chicken-skin sitting there. You had done it together.

But you didn't. It was him.

Burnie—out of the two of you, he'd always been the smart one. Could take apart engines and machines, knew how they all worked even if he didn't have the right words for what the parts were, at least not when you first became friends after moving down to Carolina from the hollers. You watched as towheaded Burnie put that crystal radio set together, messing around with the coiled copper wire and the diode, and then hooking the antennae up to the screen on the window as though he'd done it a hundred times. Confident.

And the miracle of the music—faint, but there. The announcer, his voice thin and crackling: "WLW, broadcasting from Cincinnati to Ohio, and the world." Ohio, next to West Virginia, and in an instant you felt close again to your old home in the hollers, not that you wanted that. Hearing that announcer's voice, ghostly all the way there in Edgewater County, had made you dizzy. Like Burnie a magician.

Burnie, he'd go on to bigger machines like airplanes, the Marauder he'd flown on during the war, while you squirmed and froze in the mud and misery of Europe. Burnie, he didn't mind talking about being a flight engineer out of Port Moresby. Not like you, who couldn't let yourself think about your tour in Europe for longer than a second. Burnie, a hero next to you. Saved his whole plane—risked himself to do it. All you had done was get your skinny Southern ass back home in one piece. Not a scratch.

And yet you had handled so much death, once your unit came upon the camp. How the stacks of bodies, you soon realized, included those who weren't gone yet. How they looked lifeless, but would move. Or moan. The incidents you didn't think about. What you hadn't even told Runelle—she thought your dreams were only of the fighting in the forest. Finding the camp was why y'all treated the German POWs so bad, letting them starve and suffer. Until that act of retribution haunted you almost as much.

Almost.

Burnie, though, all he had to do was climb into the bomb bay with a wrench: the doors had jammed, the bomber could not deliver its load, hence could not land carrying the weight and firepower of its deadly cargo. He refused a parachute, he explained, because if he fell out, he didn't want to die bobbing in the ocean—the chute would only save his life so long as he plunged. Once in those waters, the lair of the biggest sharks anyone had ever imagined (or so the New Guinea natives warned the airmen and soldiers and sailors, he always added), death would come bloody and horrible.

Hitting the water? From high up? Painful, if still conscious. But quick.

Burnie Sykes did not plummet. He made his repair to the doors, they ditched the armaments, and he saved his crew. No wonder he didn't mind telling his war stories. Had the hero know-how. Knew what you didn't, even as teenagers. Building a radio, for one.

WHISPERING DURING THE COMMERCIAL BREAK AT THE RYMAN: "YOU remember when we—when you—built that crystal radio? And we listened until the sun come up?"

"Hell yeah I do." Pulling up his jacket sleeve, Burnie shows you how the skin of his forearm is as stippled now as yours was back then. "This here Opry called to us that night."

"And now here we are, right in the thick of it."

Burnie, shaking his head at the spectacle and draping an arm around your neck. "As big a time as there is."

Another unspoken thought between you, a look—can you believe we went through the war? And now we're standing here at a durn hoedown? Maybe that's what Burnie's thinking. Or it's only you. Don't matter either way.

"HOW-DEE!"

Minnie Pearl, price tag a-dangle from that straw hat of hers, doing her folksy but ribald bits. Runelle couldn't stand Pearl's brand of humor. Undignified, silly. "My man's putting everything he has into learning the plumbing trade, but I don't like the way it's affecting him—now every time I hold his hands, one's hot and the other'n's cold!" Haw haw haw.

Grant Turner, the radio announcer, stands at his microphone off to the left and talks about the sponsor, Luzianne Tea, explaining his fascination with the product: "When we find a good thing and like it, and so many of our friends like it, we just like passing it on to you folks out there, and so we like Luzianne, a tea with a big bold flavor. Good teas aren't just made, they're created, and the folks at Luzianne Tea go and find the finest of exotic and aromatic teas to make their popular blend. Luzianne Tea—in bulk or bags, you go on out and get yours tonight, or tomorrow."

Then, for the rest of the show it's foot-stomping energy like you can't believe. Pickers just tearing up their guitars and fiddles; crooners warbling and bringing out tears and laughter. And more commercial breaks.

Burnie, hollering in your ear during a loud bluegrass stomp. "We got a high bar set for ourselves!"

"I know it!"

"We're gonna bring this magic—and the scratch it earns—back home. You'll see."

You allow yourself to imagine only a smidgen of this wild scene happening in Tillman Falls, tucked into that building on the corner of the town green. How interested Burnie was at the box office window, watching them taking dollar bills hand over fist. You have to admit, your blood has begun racing. This honkytonk idea, it could work.

❋ ✚ ✐

BUT THE REAL LESSONS COME ON THE BLOCK BEHIND THE MUSIC HALL, where the first dive y'all hit after the Opry's over is Tootsie's Orchid Lounge. From the glow of the Stroh's beer signs to the pawnshops and nudie theaters all around, doesn't seem much like a store smelling of fragrant flowers.

And Tootsie's don't—like all bars, inside it reeks of smoke and stale beer. But what you find that Tootsie's has, however, is style and atmosphere. A sense like it's been in business a long-old time.

Like the Opry did tonight, too.

As y'all sip your draught beers and take in the bar's bustle with its own country music show going on, your recall how part of the Opry broadcast had been somber, as they'd been in mourning for one of their own:

Earlier that week Uncle Dave Macon, an Opry mainstay, passed on suddenly, and folks onstage and off were broke up about it—he'd been a star. Had been recording for Okeh records and heard on the radio for who knew how long—for always. He played this stage only a month ago, they declared with a hush, hats all doffed. Bless and rest his soul, they sang.

You remember Macon's voice well, not only from listening to the Opry on Friday nights but from that one movie that made called *Grand Ole Opry* that you saw not long before basic training at Camp Jackson. The flicker featured the Weavers playing singers named 'The Weavers,' and scenes with Macon and Roy Acuff and his band. Uncle Dave Macon had been a star for so long no one could imagine the Opry without him, Acuff said earlier, but he reckoned now they'd just have to figure out how.

"All right." Burnie, gazing at the neon Tootsie's sign. "Idea number one, we already had—we'll hang the right come-on outside of that juke-joint of yours back home. Bright and loud and drawing a crowd."

"Hey—juke-joint? It's a concert hall. An auditorium we're putting in. Like the Ryman."

"Yep. Sorta. But like Tootsie's, too."

"I like what you're saying—partner." Burnie Sykes grabs you by the elbow, and you get the notion you won't be calling it The Dixiana Concert Hall, as you suggested to show its legitimacy.

But as the night goes on and you hop into other places not unlike Tootsie's, and the more signs you see outside thriving honkytonks packed with drinkers, musicians on stages yodeling and picking and grinning and stomping and hooting, just calling your 'club' back home 'The Dixiana' will do fine. The way one man's saint could be another man's sinner, maybe The Dixiana would be honkytonk to those who sinned alongside the angels who sang, a music hall first to those like Runelle, who, despite not wanting to do it in front of you or anyone, still wishes to sing more than anything else.

Here, the paradox and the goal you must keep in mind. Whiskey and neon, sure. But singing, and Runelle; that's the important thread and theme of this project. Along with a decent living.

◉ ▩ ⊘

By the time Burnie stumbles out of an anteroom in the final honkytonk on the tour, your head swims from all the beer and shots of whiskey.

Burnie's got that look in his eye. Trouble.

"Helluva setup here," fixing his shirttail and adjusting his tie, face all flushed. "Real hospitable."

You've had enough of your tie, having taken it off long ago and left with your jacket in the car. At this point you only want your jeans and a soft flannel shirt instead of this monkey suit. You ain't Burnie. You care little for strutting in suits and hate being pushy. You despise being pushed around by anyone. By him, too.

As in, over his big idea of getting with the hookers. After a time he had got bent about finding women, and wouldn't quit till y'all found the 'right' place with the 'right' folks who knew what's what, a seedy, nasty-ass joint half-full of colored folks in which you feel in danger.

No girls—you were clear. But Burnie, acting like a teenager—the drinking. The whoring.

"Let's go on to the motel, now."

"Shit no—ain't had enough fun. I'm ready to tank back up. Go for round two."

How to put this—you sure as hell can't accuse nobody of sinning. You ain't been in church since you married the girl.

The girl.

The girls. Here's the angle.

"You and me both got pretty gals back home. Waiting on our redneck asses."

"No shit, Sherlock. What you think the point of having fun here—eh." He broke off, acting tired and PO'd. "What, you can't keep no secrets? For your best buddy?"

"I can keep a secret just fine. No more'n I have to, though. If you don't mind."

You have learned one thing with Burnie, and that's giving in at least part-way. "But look here, let's drink one more. And go get some shuteye. Hell, you know what? I wanna go to that Opry matinee tomorrow. That's what we need to see—how to put on a show, Burnie. How to get feet stomping them like we was tonight."

"Like we 'were'." Burnie says this a certain smarmy way, making you mad. "In show business and running a night club, if you sound like a yokel, you're bound to be treated like one by every slicker that comes through. Work on your grammar. Make people think you're smarter than you are."

"Kiss my ass, son."

Burnie fumes and frets and cusses you back, then orders shots, doubles, and makes a drunken speech about the future, and about living: how y'all had come back whole from the war, heroes all, and owed it to yourselves to live for yourselves while you still can, before the Russians send rockets full of death from across the ocean. To make the most of life by doing the least work, to have the most fun doing it, on and on.

You can't think about the war and what you did in it alongside the idea of heroism without feeling like you're gonna puke. But you raise the glasses anyway, until your head spins. "Fuck that war. That's what I say, boy."

"Now, you can't be like that. Commie sum-bitch."

"Ain't getting into no politics. No religion, neither. No nothing, in fact."

You reiterate how you've had enough which sets him off anew, but you pay up and start heading out the door. He follows, arguing about the patriotic toast you pissed all over, which is what you wanted: distracting him off the girls.

Women—they'll be the end of him, if Burnie don't get more careful: In the service they give you information about how bad a body could find itself impaired from contracting a social disease, and what did you do but make that happen for yourself in Panama. Now? You'd bang a knothole before you'd risk your pecker dripping and dropping off.

But you can tell Burnie only so much. The type needing all to be his idea, or else you could take a hike.

"I wish we could-a got in that back room at Tootsie's." Burnie says this as you both hoof it up Broadway to the car. You're trudging past the clubs you've crawled through and by a barbecue joint, all of it neon and hopping with characters, some of whom give you the willies. Feels like a big town that might turn mean in a heartbeat.

"What back room?"

"You didn't see? Up the steps, into the black door with the peephole. Players coming and going. That's where the big-timers hang out."

"Big-timers how?"

"The songwriters and pickers, son." He gets exasperated with you again. "Anyway—the VIP lounge. I suspect that this, a component we need to incorporate into our plans."

"Where at?"

"We clean up that upstairs storage room—paint, refinish the floors. Could be partitioned into multiple rooms."

"Don't see why it couldn't."

Burnie, working his tongue in the side of his cheek like he does when he's thinking hard on a plan. "You hungry? The whiskey's sloshing."

You and Burnie backtrack and go into the barbecue place, get two plates, eat. It's so good you now insist that The Dixiana's menu had to stand up to fine fare like this.

"We got to do-up every blamed part of this deal. Best food. Coldest beer. Hottest pickers for three counties."

"That sauce Runelle makes from mustard instead of tomato catsup? Good eats."

"Damn straight. They'll come from all over." Burnie, doing his little happy-wiggle in embracing your enthusiasm. "My intuition says we're gonna make all our dreams come true, so keep dreaming. Barbecue? Check. VIP lounge? Double check. A real stage, with real music—"

"—authentic, old-timey music—"

"—that's authentic. Check."

You take a long slug of the sugar-sweet iced tea you're both glugging to cut the liquor. You belch barbecue and think Burnie might be right—you feel good about The Dixiana. About this path you've chosen. Good as you can, anyway, with the reality still in the imagination. When y'all get back home, time to make it real.

Step one: the adornment of the future Dixiana nightclub with a hex of your own design, which came to you in a dream, or rather, the two pieces-parts you would combine into one powerful symbol of protection: a Creator's Star seeking permanent abundance in the middle, and surrounded by the Sign of the Horns, to ward off any evil or blackness threatening to undo your developing vision. To everyone else, Burnie included, the hexes you'd paint and hang were only decoration; a remnant of your childhood, and your grandmother's witchcraft passed down to you, and that you wield only in the silence and security of your private thoughts.

Unless, of course, when called on to serve or to heal, at which point revelation is permitted—with restrictions and judicious caution, as you have always behaved in deference to the powers at play. The more one reveals the matter of the magic, the less effective the ultimate outcome of the working. Overseas, you had used hex to help wounded boys when and where you could; magic was about service.

And with The Dixiana, the protection provided would not be for you so much, but for all the rest in your circle, a key lesson imparted by your grandmother: the key to opening the door to heaven came in service to others, from a foundation of stability providing the inspiration, motivation, and material wherewithal to live a righteous life for you and yours. For this ye ask of the Lord; and thus you, and your magic, will serve.

◌❂⊘

ON THE LONG DRIVE HOME THE NEXT DAY, A LATE START AND WITH Burnie sleeping it off for most of the way through the mountains, you list tasks for yourself upon the return. A major chore only you must undertake—to quell the fire-spirit who stalked the cemetery behind the new honky-tonk. To bargain with Agatha of Aberdeen. Soon as you sensed her presence

—it had been a talent of yours not given by your granny but recognized and cultivated by her, the seeing of auras and nearby spirit-bodies—you knew you would need more than a hex to hang and protect the building.

Out into the garden of stone you go one evening to her grave, among the oldest in the cemetery. Strewn with weeds in a back corner closest to the copse of hardwoods and Sawmill Creek which separates Whaley Way from downtown proper, Agatha's stone is rough and weathered and scarcely readable.

After reciting the Lord's prayer along with a more obscure invocation against ill intent, you call out to her, ask to dialog. And while you can never divulge the details of what happened next, let it be said that your part of the bargain—the keeping of Agatha's grave tidy in a gesture and ritual of veneration—seemed a fair price to pay for her to let you "borrow some of her fire," as you put it, to act as inoculation; to secure that The Dixiana remained untouched by the spiritual acetylene torch of her destructive and otherworldly occasional vengeance upon the township.

May it remain so for the life of your home and business. And so on. You would have asked for the whole town, but you are, after all, only so powerful a secret practitioner of backwoods powwow.

RUNELLE KITTERY PETTUS

I n 1955 it's as though summer, hot and sticky and dreadful, will never
end. Runelle, knowing not to complain. Not after escaping the snow
and endless winters.

Late September, and the Friday Night Hoedown on the Dixiana "backyard stage," the old grocery store loading dock, in full swing, with everybody's pits soaked through and dresses and shirts ruined like the chambray
worn by field hands. But music, and money.

The next day would be slow at the club, what with her husband and
Burnie taking a chartered busload of yahoos to the Hank Snow All-Star
Jamboree Show in Asheville. Rennie, doing the driving himself, which,
knowing how much this group of overgrown boys loved to drink beer,
caused her to admonish her so-called 'Rabbit' to the point of curse words
and low decorum unbefitting a Southern mother and matron.

"I drove boys along roads in Europe with ordnance busting off every
which way. I can carry a load of hillbillies up to a music picking."

"You're the boss of it all, you and Burnie. Get someone else to drive."

"Nope. I'm renting the bus in the Dixiana's name. Ain't taking no
chances."

"I just worry about you. Burnie's done give you so much responsibility,
you look stooped over."

"A man's got responsibilities no matter what. That's the way I see it,
anyway."

Tender, she went to him and draped her arms around his neck. Rennie stiffened like he always did at first, having to relax into her loving embrace. Almost ten years later, her husband was still at war, or so she fretted. She worried over everything, though. What and who they were to the town, their little Ronnie going to kindergarten starting this month, how Burnie kept insisting that she put an 'act' together and become some highfalutin show girl prancing back and forth. Her husband, too, saying how much she loved to sing, and how lovely it was. How they could have her as the house band. They had been discussing it for two years, now.

Using the excuse of the baby, a miniature man stubborn as his daddy, wasn't washing with either of them. Especially her husband's best friend and partner in all things, who, when no one else was around, petitioned for partnership and congress in a manner more intimate than she prayed Rennie would ever suspect.

Handsome Burnie, quick and urbane, but a tomcat at the mercy of his gonads. The times they'd embraced, and it happened twice, the second time allowed by her to persist for too long, he showed no hesitancy at making a connection, lips, tongue, eyes, and rather unlike her more reticent husband. Projected a different vibration. Like Burnie's whole body would go hot all over, and all she could do to cool him off, short of giving in, that is. Disappointment, but not pushing on through to get his way as some—many? —men might.

As she said before, this was foolishness, both of them behaving in her eyes like overgrown boys, still. They said and acted like the war made them into stalwart and mature townsmen, but Runelle saw different. Her Rennie, scared of the dark; and Burnie, horny as a teenager. Henny, often complaining with a rubicund face (and not from the heat under the hairdryers at Ruth Anne's, where such talk often occurred) about how Burnie's proclivities came with urgency and frequency. Which made Runelle feel less flattered by his attention than analytical. Less than attracted to the idea. And for many reasons.

Besides, she understood more about Burnie than Burnie did: how upon their return, her husband divulged the adventures of Rabbit and Burnie in Nashville that time back in '53. His shock at Burnie's behavior felt sincere, which had likely been worse than Rennie described. If she knew men.

Runelle, combing through her red hair and deciding what to do with herself on a Saturday night while the honkytonk crowd took their routine on the road. She understood that this situation with Burnie represented temptation in its most obvious, frequent and prosaic form, and while no theological bibliophile or woman of the church (because what congregation would have her, the wife of a honkytonk owner and purveyor of music and alcohol and sin), also reckoned that if she were being tested, she'd best pass. For herself. For Henny. For Rennie.

No—for Rabbit.

Of all the temptation and attention, Runelle, never weak, always true to her Rennie. In gratitude for the North Dakota misadventure—her going along out of pity for him—for years now he had done all she'd asked, including starting to look for a permanent place to live. Delays dame only from his considered and cautious approach to any endeavor or project, as well his assertions he wanted to live out in the sticks, and build from his own hands. Two ridiculous provisos in her opinion, but again, for having done her bidding and returned to the humid South, he deserved the benefit of the doubt and an opportunity to follow his mind and heart.

How it all had ended up with him owning a juke-joint called The Dixiana was beyond her; how it all seemed to be leading to her parading upon a stage—yes; she would do it, would sing songs in front of people, mainly because he wanted it, both of them, the key men in her life—and making a dang fool of herself.

Or would it entail turning that gasbag Ralph Peer into a big, fat liar?

Burnie dreamed of one day hosting a radio show like the Opry or the Louisiana Hayride, on which they'd been hearing this wild singer, a hillbilly cat they called the Memphis Flash, who had a new sound going: country mixing with spook music, and damn if that's wasn't what they were all going to see at this Hank Snow show. Burnie had been tuning in the radio shows using the big antennae he'd installed on the Sykes house on Whaley Way, where folks would gather for house parties and to listen to that show or the Opry. Burnie, of course, made it no secret that attendees could enjoy the music any time by coming and buying a record player set and records, or maybe a TV, too, at Sykes Electronics, his new highfalutin name for his appliance store. Folks wanted a TV more than just about anything.

Runelle had never seen the like, the way having a set was catching on. She had to admit to being taken with watching the stories instead of only hearing them. Novel. Fresh. Burnie was making a mint selling TVs. Enough to keep The Dixiana on its feet, anyway, through some fallow times. They were doing well enough to close the bar down tonight and take their bus trip, for which they sold tickets and would provide cold beer for the drive. It was all a moneymaking scheme. But there was Hank Snow and the music, too.

And the new boy everyone was talking up. The real draw. Shaking his hips like a woman—a possessed one. No, the bus passengers weren't excited to see Cowboy Copas or the Louvin Brothers, also on the bill, or Hank

Snow himself (well, maybe Hank Snow), but instead all fired-up to get their eyeballs on this boy named Elvis, who couldn't decide if he was white or black. Earlier in the spring on the radio during his regular Louisiana Hayride spot, she heard women screaming like they had the devil inside them.

"Damn," Rabbit said. "The boy's got them riled up."

"Now that's an act I'd like to see," Burnie added. That's when this chartered bus plan came to be.

She sat before her oval makeup mirror, thinking about how Henny could keep Ronnie, who would play with their little Buddy all night. Hell—maybe she *would* go with them, if for no other reason than to keep an eye on the boys. She would take her guitar and sing them up the highway to Asheville. And talk to Burnie and her husband about the kinds of songs, besides the few of her own she had, they'd like her to perform. Whom she'd hire to back her on lead and fiddle.

She held so many reservations. Much happened in and around her husband's honkytonk she wasn't supposed to know about, and did a poor job of pretending. But, Lord, the upstairs income from the gambling that passed through Rennie's hands—cash money.

Secret affluence gave her security, as well Burnie and all his connections with powerful folks who all loved The Dixiana, love 'Rabbit' and his statuesque raven-haired honey. Coming up the pious Kitterys had nothing, a far cry from the days when her people owned land and slaves. Security, a feeling making Runelle think she could put up with quite a lot, if only this serenity would stay.

Difficult, though. Not when the Russians might send missiles from across the ocean. No amount of money, or a roof over one's head, would stave off such a horrifying fate. If it all wa'n't a bunch of hoo-haw designed to keep everybody scared and distracted.

RABBIT AND RONNIE-ED PETTUS

On this fine Carolina morning, with lingering dew on the tips on all the sedge grasses not yet struck by the bright yellow sunlight, you and your son, towheaded and all of nine—no, ten in another month, if you can believe that!—sit fishing at the bluff down River Ridge Road, personal time Mama Runelle says you need to spend with Ronnie-Ed.

You wasn't never much of a fisherman, but that's what fathers and sons do together, or so you figure. You had got hooked, ha ha, and had kept on trying to get your boy in a similar condition.

You don't have all day, though. It's Hawg Hickens tonight at the club, and for probably the last time.

The boy, mumbling like he does. You can't break him of it. Something about Burnie and Runelle.

"Burnie does what, now?"

"He comes around."

"Tell me news I don't know, boy. He's like your uncle."

Ronnie-Ed, curious, squints up at you in silence.

"I'll bite. So what's the big whoop-tee-doo about him coming around?"

"She sings for him."

"She does?"

"Yes sir. On the porch."

"Sings what?"

Ronnie Ed shrugs. "Songs she's been messing with. She don't never finish none of them. Sometimes ones off the radio."

You hack one off the bluff, a rope of spit spiraling into the green river below with a *plunk*. Chuckle to yourself. "Well, if that don't beat all."

Your wife did a couple of years singing onstage at the club—Mama Runelle and the Dixiana Darlings, a marquee act's name if you ever seen one. But that got squelched after she couldn't put up with Burnie's side deals in the Blue Rooms, as y'all call the private upstairs area. Less said about all that, the better. In any case, she had hung up her spurs, so to speak, and wouldn't sing no more at the honkytonk.

Except to Burnie.

In the afternoon.

When you wasn't home.

Huh.

❂⚏⊘

THE HAWG'S ONLY PLAYING ONE MORE SOLD-OUT SHOW AT THE DIX AS A favor to Burnie, in fact, into whom this picker, the one you still know as Harold, seems to have gotten himself. It's from the last time Hawg played the honkytonk—or rather, the last time he lost at cards upstairs after playing his uptempo set, country music that leans more toward Jerry Lee Lewis than Hank Williams. But Hawg Hickens has done got himself a record that's making more than music—it's making noise for the boy. He's off to Nashville, now.

So tonight would be it for Hawg at The Dixiana. Prob'ly. Catch him again on his way down. Of course, y'all said that about Elvis back in '56 and '57. Maybe when he gets done making lousy movies, which is all the boy does anymore, he'll get back out on the chitlin circuit.

Hawg's got that new sound Elvis and the other rockabillies come up with. Didn't know how many more records Hawg would get to cut, though, less he either goes straight rock & roll or gets Chet Atkins to put strings and other mess on the records, like they do with Eddie Arnold and a bunch-a others. Harold Hickens, a good-old boy. Wasn't crazy like some pickers that've come and gone on that stage. Likes his liquor, but always puts on a professional show. Yes he does—for you, and all the folks patronizing your honkytonk.

Lord, you say to yourself. I done aged twenty years in ten. Working that club.

It ain't the work, though. It's dealing with the constant battles like with the ELMS, or Flora Mae Harkin, Edgewater County's version of Carrie Nation, and the Reverend Duson Mire, both railing against the beer-drinking. Oh, how little they understood. How much worse it might be, if they knew what-all went on. But you kept as much in check as you could. Running your business.

Secreted it all upstairs, a concealment that carries its own particular and personal price; its own level of bumfuzzlement and intrigue.

So, fishing with Ronnie-Ed, an innocence, a hobby. Good on that. But he don't act like he much cares for sitting with you. Don't know why you and the boy clash so.

Shit.

Yes, you do.

His mama spoils him . Eh. And he ain't become a teen yet. Hoo, boy. Lord knows what lay in store then.

Even at this tender age the boy don't much care for living back down past the pecan orchard, the land old Glasscock sold you. Always bored, Ronnie Ed says. Bored and boring, because there ain't no other little kids to play with.

Burnie's boy, he's too old for Ronnie Ed. Buddy Sykes is gonna get out and see the world one day. That's the kind of talk you manage out of him. It's the durn TV, filling people's heads up with ideas. You seen enough of the world, and would gladly what experience you had for a life spent on your little parcel in the woods.

⊙▣⊘

YOU LOVE IT HERE, NOW. YOUR LAND, THE PIECE OF THE OLD FARM. Stands of gray, knotty river trees sloping down to the river a half-mile away, nothing but woods and former sheep grazing land. Few pine trees, the smell of which you couldn't stand from having been in the forest overseas. You associate pine tar with exploding shells. With finding a buddy of yours in a foxhole, faceless, a shard of white bone sticking out of a bloody stump that'd been his head, while all around you the sharp menthol stink of Christmas trees burning, like on the day after New Year's. This parcel a long way from that province; and yeah, far enough that the nightmares these days are better.

The dream of your ordinary life; the dreams in your ordinary sleep.

Land.

Land that Glasscock sold to Burnie, you mean.

Yeah. That's right. He give you the green and said like with everything else, it's on the tab. After a decade of doing business together, though, tab's well whittled.

The house, you built that out of your own money—you and the old man Glasscock, as well a few farm boys hired to raise the roof and assorted other tasks, did the literal labor in an almost settler-like spirit of cooperation that made you swell with pride at the sense of community in this place, and your country, its freedoms breeding neighborliness and progress. Glasscock, who had built his own house, said helping not only made up a duty, it having been his land, but he didn't have nothing else on his plate. A sad man, half-bent by grief over the loss of two wives, it sounded like, and him left with a teenage daughter and a young son. You go cold all over in thinking of losing Runelle—you cling to her in the night, when she still lets you sleep in the bed with her.

Over the course of the 1956 springtime five years ago you built your own damn house, and that'd felt like real work versus what you did for a living at The Dixiana. But to get the land, Burnie, who wanted you to buy land so bad, had to pony up and grease various financial wheels. You were getting smarter about the relationship, and Burnie's strategy here: You saw how much he desired keeping Glasscock from selling that rolling Edgewater County river country to some developer planning to plop down little brick houses all in a row. Cut down the trees. That remained a ways off, he theorized, but could still happen, especially now they were clearing for a four-lane highway on the other side of the river running between Columbia and Charlotte. Money, oh, it would flow down that new road, Burnie would chant like a native doing a rain-dance.

But as for Burnie and the ongoing tab, you have in mind a way to one day make it right. Do it as a surprise. Had figured on ways of stashing money, here and there. Well—in one place. In your house, the one you had built. A secret receptacle you planned in the floor's design in the back bedroom—in Ronnie Ed's bedroom. You would let Runelle, or your boy, know one day about the money building up. When there sat enough to matter from this practice you started, a long-game plan at five or ten dollars a week.

But you was doing so well, some weeks stashing a twenty; and one time an extra fifty courtesy of Josiah Rembert, when he took drunk and tore up the Blue Room over losing big to Davis Macon on a dog fight, and you had not deigned to call the law on them both in favor of a settlement involving repairs and restitution. An orderliness kicked in among the men who populated the Blue Rooms, and a remarkable meekness had overcome Rembert among his powerful peers. As for you, loyalty to a cause not your own, nonetheless rewarded. And money, accumulating.

Not that you've counted, but they's already a fat stash all squirreled under that floor. You wouldn't never touch it, not unless trouble came calling that couldn't be fixed except by shoving a mess of folding money in some gangster's hand. That's how the real world worked, or so you have learned.

Eh, no trouble to worry over. You don't owe anybody much besides Burnie, bless his heart. Who need not know about your extra. If you was light in paying him his cut, and sometimes you didn't square him on his taste of the downstairs up-front trade, he never questions it. Burnie has his taste of the poker games upstairs, as well the other bid-nesses underway. Burnie's got bigger worries than money, though. At least if his wife Henny caught him running wild with Gretchen Beaudock, that little firecracker, anyway. "Like a gall-darn snapping turtle, that pixie's little snatch. You crawl away dizzy, my boy."

"Take your word for it, son."

What Burnie didn't know is how often the little Beaudock tart offered it to you, too. Not that the gesture felt flattering, or close to love. With her, it's all for money.

Burnie.

Running around.

A character flaw.

Huh.

◌◙◌

"SON — LOOK HERE."

"*Whut.*" Bored as all get-out, Ronnie Ed, waits for more questioning about Uncle Burnie's late afternoon visits. You suppose these occur during the time after Burnie leaves Sykes Electronics, but before he pops into the honkytonk to run games and drink free liquor. You often wonder if your best friend ever sleeps.

"What'd you rather be doing?"

"Than fishing? Ain't got a clue. Nothing."

"You ain't taking a shine to sitting here with your pappy. That much I can see."

As though he didn't hear you, Ronnie Ed said *do-what-now*, in that nasal, spoilt way he's got. Lord, but she doted and coddled that boy. His birth, it'd been a tough one. Breech. The doctor had said, I don't know if he'll live because they had to get him born real careful, as a breech baby's liable to smother on his way out. Hell of a note that would've been, and Runelle had known this, and ever since had treated him real special.

Did treating a little boy special come natural? Your daddy's version had been to knock you across the room if you so much as looked cockeyed, or said a cross word. You couldn't slam a door, raise your voice. You had your rules like that, but it was more for your wife's sake than your own. Her nerves, and all.

Hell—that wa'n't true. And you know it. You can't stand no loud noises or getting startled; you like to shit yourself every time a truck going along Common Street backfires.

Harder is hiding your fear from folks. You can't conceal it from your woman, though. She lives through every cussed night with your squirming, dreaming old skinny ass, whenever y'all sleep together, that is—about 1958, when the house was built and you had more room, Runelle told you to take all your nocturnal thrashing into the guest bedroom.

"Maybe I just don't like fishing."

"Manly endeavor, to fish. Clean 'em up. Eat 'em. That's the lord's bounty right there. Like the grains in the field, and fruit on the trees."

"Like the pecans in the orchard?"

"Yep." Your land goes right up to the edge of the Glasscock farm and the old pecan orchard set back from the road. Ronnie Ed wanders in them woods and plays army all the time, usually by himself. He has his friends, though. Him and Buddy Sykes get along right good, but Buddy's growing up fast, and Jasper Glasscock's too little, only five. He's like his daddy, now—Buddy wants girls and cars.

You don't want Ronnie Ed getting all wild one day. Boys had started running wild, it seemed, in ways that you and your kind would not have dreamed, not in the days before the war, and not back in the hollers of West Virginia, a ghostly memory of your granny teaching you about the spirits and the mysteries, and watching people resigned to their places in life, doing their work, and praying on Sunday. Folks didn't do as much no more, except going off to work. Including you.

Hell—quit kidding yourself. You don't know what prayer nor work is, not running a honkytonk. Long hours, but it ain't work. Not like your daddy, and your granddaddy, both of them dead from coal dust, and later cotton fibers, all up in their lungs.

"So fishing's a man's job," your boy says. "Sitting here doing nothing."

"Yes sir, that it is."

Your boy winds in his reel. Casts it. Says, he reckons he feels like a man sitting there fishing with his Daddy, and you tell him, fishing ain't the half of it. Fishing's what you get to do for being a good father. And husband. And tradesman—or however a body makes his living. "Unless you're fishing to feed your family cause you ain't got no money, this ain't work, here. This's your reward."

"Sitting out by the river? All alone?"

"Yes sir. A man needs a return on his toil besides money. And this is mine."

You felt an urge to go on about that tradesman angle. You wanted the best for your boy. He would own the bar one day, sure, but that was so far off you didn't much ever think about that. Your best hope was for him to apprentice at a trade at which he could make an honorable living. Running The Dixiana wasn't much of a trade anyone would call 'decent' as you've found out, and you don't want your boy thinking it represents a future for him. A trade, skills, knowledge—a boy can't collect enough of all that, or so you preached.

Besides, if the honkytonk ever falls apart, or Burnie, or somebody else, wants to get rid of you—and don't think it couldn't go that way, not if you started mouthing off and making noise and trouble like you've considered doing—what was the family gonna do?

Watch as you work at the mill?

Shit. Ain't no way. Not now that you've been your own boss. You are on your path.

So you take a deep breath, cough up some gray spit from all your smoking, light a fresh one, and go on with your little tradesman speech: Look at Luca Giuffrida, for example, you tell your boy—like Burnie, Luca'd ridden the wave of commerce from the people moving in to work on the nuclear plant and the interstate highway, folks who had mo-money than the old mill workers, and who, if they decided to live here and once they got a taste of the South Carolina summer, were dead set on putting in air conditioners and keeping them machines running full blast. Folks who had lived other places needed them around here in the summers, but everyone else just liked not having to rely on fans and sleeping porches. Made you a believer, that AC unit, but after the forest in Europe and blizzards of North Dakota, you'd always rather be hot than cold. "Luca's got a solid trade that ain't gonna go away on him. Only get bigger."

Ronnie Ed, bored anew with all your grownup talk, starts whistling and casting his line. "Heat don't bother me."

"It's all you ever knew. Except your first winter, back in North Dakota."

Your boy gets that pinched look. It comes whenever y'all talk about things that went on 'before' him, like North Dakota. It's all beyond a child's imagination, the time of before they existed. All he has known is this—the house, the honkytonk, the pecan orchard, the fishing bluff.

◎⊞⊘

MERCY BUT IF THAT WASN'T THE TRUTH—ABOUT THE HEAT NOT bothering him, or you. In your case it's because of how cold you were growing up and in the war, so you don't care nothing about having ice-boxed air blowing across your sinuses and feet. It's like that inside the trailer at Burnie's used car lot, his latest venture, where you stop and shoot the shit on your way into work, where he's got a window unit going full-blast all the time.

Runelle likes it cool as can be, though. That was the first excuse she gave for wanting to quit singing at The Dixiana—too hot under them stage lights.

Someday you'll build her a better house, won't you? If that's what she wants. Or move onto Whaley Way like the rest of the town set. But if you ain't busy with one crisis or drama at that dive of yours on the green, it's another.

When you talked about the future she'd only say, all good tidings in their proper time, and as long as they's food on the table for the family and the roof overhead not leaking, she's right content to keep on keeping on.

Lord, but you love her, still. And hope she loves you, for all you put her through. You didn't sleep with her no more, because of them dreams. You drank too much to deal with them, but that you kept hid.

◎⊞⊘

"WHY'S UNCLE BURNIE ALWAYS COMING ROUND," RONNIE ED ASKS, finally, after you both sit quiet for a while, "when you ain't there?"

"Well—he's checking on y'all."

"I asked mama."

"And—?"

"She told me to be glad we had somebody looking out for us. I don't know why we need checking on so often. That's all I was asking."

"Every—night?"

"Near about."

"Every night while I'm off at work."

"Yes sir." And casting his line. Boy's got a good stroke. You've taught him well.

Couldn't be right, this business with Burnie and Runelle. Not in the way you thought, all cold and hard like a stone down in your guts.

But you don't show it—not to your boy. Little boys don't have to suffer feelings like you got now.

"That's what men do—looking in on their loved ones. You call him 'Uncle Burnie,' don't ya?"

"I reckon."

"The men take care of everyone." You stick with your prior theme, if nothing else to keep your mind occupied. "It's why you get a good job. Or learn a trade."

"Daddy?

"What, son."

"You ain't fixing to make me quit school and go to work somewheres, are you?"

You bust out howling. Remembering the stories your granddaddy told you about going to work in the mines at twelve, and damn near being dead by the time he had finished growing up, but hadn't had the sense to do anything different. You quit laughing, your busy mind wandering, and wondering, something awful.

But you keep on fishing. You watch the lures bobbing, but nothing bites. Not today. Nothing except worries, nipping at the hairs on the back of your neck. And squirming in your gut like the worms you bought at Pike's Gas and Bait, which had opened at the crossroads and wasn't but five minutes away from your fishing spot. Other than not catching nothing but little bream you and your boy throw back, life's good. Far as you know.

❂🅱⊘

NO WAY YOU WANT TO GO HOME YET, SO AFTER Y'ALL PACK UP, YOU swing by Pike's.

Like one of them, what-cha call it, coincidences, at the gas pump you see Luca Giuffrida's repair truck getting gone over by Pike's boy, Marty Harrell, who's about dumb as a box of rocks. You don't let him near your Ford, and ain't afraid to say so short of outright hurting anyone's feelings.

The other cars interest you, too—they include Burnie's Cadillac.

"There's Uncle Burnie's car now." Ronnie Ed, reading your mind. "You reckon he's on his way to check on us today?"

"This early? Guess not. Wait here."

"Check your oil today, Mr. Rabbit?" Marty calls out while wiping off Luca's windshield.

"Not today, Marty. Another time."

"Yes sir. We aims to please at Pike's. That's our new slogan. What you think?"

You tell him it's right fine and go inside, where you find a gathering of men including your best friend and business associate, along with Josiah Rembert, whom you know all too well, and his rat-faced boy Jezmund, whom you can't stand and is a spoiled teenagers who acts like he's got some secret you don't.

Can't stand smart-ass little shits like him. You hated the thought of yours turning into one. Ronnie Ed went straight to the stack of *Real* and *True* and *Argosy* magazines Thurmond kept around for hangers-around to leaf through.

At least Burnie's boy Buddy, he had a good head on his shoulders—an egghead, Burnie always says. Smarter than any of us. Maybe so. Maybe smarter than his Daddy, regarding what he's got to say for himself regarding all these visits. That your wife ain't said word-one about to you.

Not.

One.

Word.

And walking by yourself, where your boy can't see you, you get steamed, now, and your face flushes hot, and your fists clench, and you wonder if in the next five minutes your life will not change forever, depending on what you do at Thurmond Pike's bait shop and general store. Glad you swore off ever touching a gun again, not once you got back home and didn't have to shoot at other men like yourself.

You wouldn't need a gun anyway—Burnie would have an explanation for his visits, like he did everything. You'd buy it, like you did all his others. If you couldn't trust Burnie Sykes, you didn't know who you could. That wasn't a good feeling, not at all—so much you didn't let yourself feel it. But you got good at that. Hadn't you.

So, you don't let on. You listen, nodding, as Burnie advises Luca Giuffrida to call his business something less busy, easier to remember, more American. "Call it Jiffy's—with a J, not a G. Here that would be 'Giffy's' and that doesn't mean squat. Jiffy, though—that means you'll be there in a split-second, and have the job done even faster. You put that idea in their head from the moment they see your name. Jiffy's Comfort Services."

"Comfort Services?" Luca says in his skeptical, Long Island accent. "That sounds like a burly-q house."

"No, no," Burnie insists. "'Jiffy' and 'comfort'—it's a can't-lose combo."

You chime in, saying how Burnie's right about this stuff. "Never steered me wrong. He's the best businessman I ever did know. My best friend, too."

Burnie gets a look like he swallowed a frog. "Same here, beau."

Thurmond Pike, coming in out of the garage and wiping his greasy hands on a shop rag from where he's been in there rebuilding an Indian motorbike: "Mark that down somewheres."

"Do what, Thurmond?"

"That's the kindest bullcorn anyone'll ever say about a snake like Burnie Sykes."

Everyone busts out laughing. You shake their hands, confirm that all will show up tonight for Hawg Hickens at the honkytonk.

"Wouldn't miss it for nothing." Burnie, clearing his throat. "There with bells on."

The moment hangs, until you nod and break the eye contact and head on home. You don't ask anymore about these Burnie visits, and as the next few weeks and months go on, you hear no more about it. Maybe it's all in Ronnie Ed's head. Whatever 'it' is.

ROOSEVELT NIXON, HIS GRANNY-MOM AND OTILYA DUCKETT

Roosevelt Nixon look up to his granny-mom. He sit there watching her run her store. He too little to do much more.

She don't let him run wild. Them her words. No sir. Granny-mom don't let no one do nothing she ain't first say is all-right by her.

Roosevelt Nixon, his whole world is sitting in that store. Watching folks come and go. He didn't know a time when they wasn't all sorts of men, and women too, coming and going. Granny-mom start out selling beans and corn liquor, she say, before she got spectable and started selling it with the labels on.

Her mammy, he hear her say to some customer in the store, start the business back in the 30s when the men come to build the dam. That's when, for the sake of the power to run things, they had flooded out two whole towns, including the one in which the Nixons had lived before the dam; and despite this, the dam coming had changed everything for the better, except for the couple of hundred colored folk, mostly, who had had to give up the houses and homes they had known.

Roosevelt didn't know nothing about no 30s or no towns under the lake. His Granny-mom always telling stories, though, at night when she'd sit on his bedside, her favorite time to read. Stories from the Bible, stories from books. Stories about the old times before the lake, which Roosevelt thought were only more fairy tales. Stories that made him sleepy. He only three.

ONE EVENING WHEN THE MENS IN THE WORK PANTS AND SHOES WERE coming and going like they do on certain days, it was late and Granny-mom was fixing to close up her store when this one green car pull up. Granny-mom didn't stay open past sundown. "Too many strangers and whatnot coming in through Beauchamp County."

She look all frowning. Go on over yonder and sit, she told Roosevelt.

"Who them men?"

"They ain't nobody. Go on, now."

The men came in looking all down their nose at everything, especially the jars of pickled eggs and pig feets on the counter by the cash register. Roosevelt's Granny-mom, a big woman with a voice loud like a train horn, folded her arms and waited.

The visitor's shoes weren't dirty, only a little dust from outside. Underneath, the leather shined. Roosevelt wouldn't never forget that detail. It was the only thing he would member about them. That and their voices, one of which sounded right and the other'n didn't, like he wasn't even from the county at all. Colored folk talk their way and white folk theirs, but Roosevelt, he ain't heard no one sound like that one man, him and his friend in their shined shoes and hats and ties and shirts like they on the way to church. Roosevelt had seen other men in suits also not buying whiskey or cashing checks from the plant they's now building over next to the river. Them mens made him feel cold in his stomach. So do these two.

Granny-mom mad as a snake. "I done told the other ones who come before how I'm running a straight business here."

"Now see here, Ms. Dixon. About all this check-cashing."

"And the liquor," the other man quick to add.

But the first one say, hold on. Put his hand on the man's arm, who look like he don't want it there. "We're concerned."

"*Nixon*. If y'all gonna shake me down, least you can do is get my name right."

"No one's 'shaking anybody down'—you make us out as criminals. We're not."

Granny-mom, she ain't scared. "Good to know. What you on about, then?"

"If anyone's being taken advantage of, it's our workers. Three dollars to cash a check? That's exorbitant."

"S'cuse me?"

"These men, many of them have families. From elsewhere. Sending wages back home. It almost seems like you're taking—"

"What about all the public meetings in Tillman Falls telling us the ec-onomic benefits?" Granny-mom's arms folded even more, if that was possible. She told them the little history of the store. And her mammy. And the dam. And the men back then.

"You got to understand, this's part of how we've always made our living. It been that way since the dam come in. You the first ones to complain, is all I'm saying." Sounding like she mean, and so that's that.

But they talked more grownup talk. Back and forth. Shaking they heads. Talking about money, and them nu-cu-lar re-ac-tors and the fine nature of the work. And about the whiskey she sell to the men cashing checks.

And asking her for 'a favor'—to put water in the liquor.

As the man with the funny accent explain, "The work these men are doing is too important. We can't have them less than coherent each morning, if not still drunk. This kind of reactor building is more delicate than a bridge or other ordinary structure. No detail, however small, must be left to chance or human error."

Granny-mom, chuckling at his high-talk. "You saying it don't matter if that bridge across the Sugeree fall down?"

"Yes ma'am. Or, no'm, rather. It's that—if one of these buildings were to fall down? Everybody would die. Not just the people in the building. Everybody. For a long way around."

"That some hot stuff y'all messing with."

"Without a doubt."

"I'm wondering which one of us ought to water whose mess down."

All them grownups laughed at that, maybe not haha-funny but like, ha-ha-ha, and then sighing. Roosevelt don't got much idea what they all talking about, but he sure don't laugh. He feel scared.

Roosevelt's Granny-mom gave him a smile that make him feel warm inside. He felt cold when the man said about so many people going to heaven all at once, which was all dying was.

"Oh, sorry, ma'am. I didn't see the boy there in the corner."

"Don't know how you could miss him." The other man, smiling. "That's one big-old punkin head."

"Yes-sir. He gonna be big as a barn."

After a pause all three said 'well' at the same time. Granny-mom, Roosevelt noticed, and the man, who sounded like he was from Beauchamp County or beyond, nodded with tight smiles on their faces. "So I'll pop in once a week, and make you whole. And work with us on the 'quality' of the libations. Only the best for our men."

"And for the Sugeree Nuclear Station. It'll be powering our lights here long after all of us—well." He smile over at Roosevelt, wink. "The plant will last a thousand years, but only if we do our job right."

Roosevelt can't figure on what that mean.

He watch Granny-mom walk out with them. "I hate to be the bearer of bad news, but: Y'all just another version of the other white men coming round telling us what to do. Like it always been."

"Look at it from our perspective." The one with the funny voice, sounding like he feel sour. "We're the ones paying you to play fair, ma'am. So please don't insult my intelligence any further."

Granny-mom cocked her head, and Roosevelt slid off his play stool and come over to the open door to see out at the sunset almost gone from the sky. The air feeling cool like fall already, and next year he go to school, and Granny-mom say they building a new one for all the children of the men constructing the plant and buying the whiskey, plus a new school for the colored children. All he knew, he love the way the white men talk. When he get big, he try and sound like that.

◉⬛⦸

LATER HIS WARM BATH MADE HIM FALL SLEEP FAST AND HE WONDERED about his Granny's store and her liquor business and the men with their building full of fire, which sounded to Roosevelt like straight out of the devil's own kitchen.

"What worry me, sugar, is that with the dam? Nobody batted no eyes at drown-ding colored folks out. Oh, they bought land where people like us owned land, which wasn't many. The white people was the ones made money when they took and said the dam was coming. I wasn't too much older than you, then. Lord have mercy, how the grandfolks cried and wept about having to leave. It didn't end up being but ten miles, here where we are now, from the place where your grand-mammy grew up. But it feel much longer and farther ago, with it all being under the water." Roosevelt's Granny-mom twisted around like she got a chill up her back. "Oh. I can't stand thinking bout them graves down yonder. Makes my skin crawl."

He asked his Granny-mom about that building of fire they was making.

"Whatever it is, it better than getting drown-ded underneath a lake that white people build big houses all round and bob on they boats. Where no one can come and visit nobody's people's graves no more."

She also told him how other white and black men both she had to answer to come from right here in Edgewater County, so ain't much gonna change; and them ones to be more careful about than the fancy suit-men.

But the ones today, they'd do a good job building the plant, she say to Roosevelt. They will keep the fire inside. "I hope they as careful as the penitent raising up a temple," she said gazing off the front porch at the last red of the sunset. "They better, anyway."

ROOSEVELT SAT MESSING WITH HIS LINCOLN LOGS IN THE LIVING ROOM of their house. The women in the kitchen, excited. His Granny-mom, all wanting to hear what the visiting younger woman had to say.

"Are you telling me you waited them suckers out?"

"Like you told me to." She did a little happy dance. "It took all day."

"Otilya Duckett, hush your mouth. I know you wasn't sitting there all day."

"I was, too. The men come out, finally. And let me have my say."

"What else they let you have?"

She smile all proud. "An application. That I already completed."

"They putting you off? Or they gonna put you on."

"We'll see." Otilya, grinning. "I done what you told me, and it worked."

"I sure was hoping and praying that advice of mine would work for somebody one day," laughing her cackling old Granny-laugh like she a witch at Halloween. "Good on you, girl. Everybody get to get they chance to work, now. What you should've said to them was, y'all come down here cause they ain't no unions, and so you's can pay people less. You might as well pay it to people like us. We all poor down here in South Carolina."

"That's the God's truth right there. Maybe you ought to run for city council." Otilya, getting her coat and hugging Roosevelt's Granny-mom. "Making speeches like that."

"Oh, honey, running this business of mine, and dealing with my boy, here. That take all my time."

"He's a cute boy. Big."

"He big as can be. He play football. That's what everybody say. Not if his Granny-mom got anything to say about it. Roosevelt smart as can be. He gonna be a teacher one day."

At the door they hugged. Roosevelt heard Otilya talk about the Congress Street Grille, named off men from the neighborhood along with when 'it' was supposed to happen. Granny-mom look worried, their voices hushed.

"I be there, too," Otilya say all sassy on her way out. "But I have my job interview."

"Don't worry about that lunch counter none. You fighting your own good fight. What happens downtown gonna happen."

◉⏣⊘

THE NEXT DAY, WHILE OLD NEBO KEEP AN EYE ON THE STORE — THE ONLY eye he got; he wear a patch over the other'n — Roosevelt and his Granny-mom took a drive. Nebo got a patch but Granny-mom say he not a pirate — when he young he got beat bad and lost it. Later he used to work at the store, but got old. It what happens to people, far as Roosevelt starting to understand. Not that they all get beat up, but wrinkly and white-headed.

Some do get beat, though. Not that he imagine this happening to him. Not little as he is.

"Oh, lord," shifting gears on the bridge. "Don't let no one get hurt today."

The engine all throaty, she roll slow into town. People be walking around and standing on the sidewalk, here and there. Roosevelt see two police cars, which make him scared. His Granny-mom told him to be scared. That for a little black boy to trust the policemen of Edgewater County was 'a practice unwise' in her grownup talk.

She pull the car onto a side street down from the movie theater. Roosevelt has been there in the balcony to watch the movies. He saw some older black boys get into trouble for dropping pennies down on the white people. It had been a movie with Elvis. Too much singing and not enough action for Roosevelt's taste. He preferred a good Looney Tunes cartoon.

Voices, shouting. Men and women, walking in a circle with words on signs. Roosevelt, he can't read them. Asks his Granny-mom and she points at the man turned to them. "'We must eat same as you.' That what the one man's sign says." She tells him that the Congress Street Grille is a holdout in the fight for civil rights and deserves this sit-in and march.

The phrasing she uses stays with him about a fight for rights. Like one of them songs on the radio — a rhyme. A melody.

White men in suits stand and mill around, and women in Sunday dresses, with other black people like them also watching from afar. Voices get raised. There's a ruckus, and Roosevelt feels himself jerked by the arm and picked up, even though his Granny-mom say he too big to hold, and she run him back to the car. *Pop-pop-pop* go some fireworks. The sun, bright and blinding in his eyes and feeling like he want to pee.

In the car Roosevelt stand up in the seat, strain to see policemen and men in suits shouting and bustling to hold another man down on the ground, kicking his legs. His hat rolled off to show white hair over a red scalp.

"That a white man."

"That's what I was worried about. Lord help us. What was I thinking bringing you down here today?" She crank the car. "I do know why—I wanted you to say we was here for this. To be a part of how things gonna change. Cause they are, baby. Lord have mercy, but first? Out come the guns. Ain't never been no other way."

She almost scream as a policeman knocks against her window. "Clear this block," he shouts, mean as can be. "We got an ambulance coming through!"

"I'm so sorry, sorry, sorry." Roosevelt sees how her hands are shaking. "We going, sir. Did anybody get—?"

"Hush your pie-hole, mammy, and put this heap into gear before I yank you out of there for disorderly conduct!"

"Please sir, I got a baby in here—"

He smash his fist into the hood so hard it dents. "NOW!"

All the way home, Roosevelt can see his Granny-mom shaking and almost crying. "That what I mean about the po-lice," she say all shaky once they parked in the driveway behind the store to the house where they live. Tears coming out the corner of her eyes. "We wasn't doing nothing wrong, but he still mad."

Roosevelt ask why.

She bite her lips first. Grit her teeth. "Cause we colored. Get it through your head. It might be all different one day, when you big. For now, it the same. And you got to be careful, son. I can't say it enough. Careful who you with. Careful what you say to the po-lice mens. You too little to understand. But you will. I'm-a make sure my baby's baby grow up knowing the truth."

Inside, she calls to find out what happened and says, oh, lord, oh, lord; and it's that Mr. Josiah Rembert, one of the 'other men' who came to visit her from time to time, had pulled out his gun to shoot the people at the lunch counter with the words on signs, but those same po-lice Granny-mom warned about had been the ones to stop him. And it was one of them, in fact, who got shot in the leg, not any of the colored folks. And that Rembert already out of jail, and ain't charged with nothing. If that didn't beat all! That what happens when you powerful. You ain't pay no price for nothing, she keep saying over and over. Not for nothing.

That night, Roosevelt go to bed halfway confused. The po-lice, maybe you could make friends with them, if you had to. It seemed they was protecting the black men with the signs from Mr. Rembert, and not the other way around.

He wished he could just look at his books or the Bible instead, the big one his Granny-mom keep in the living room on the table. The one with pictures. That's about all a boy little as Roosevelt Nixon can understand, that picture-Bible and the Jetsons and Flintstones on the TV.

Them Congress Street Grille hamburgers sure smelled good, though. Maybe one day he get to eat himself one.

That night he dream about eating a hamburger, but having a po-liceman take it out of his hands, making him cry. Woke up crying for real and scared from it all, but after the sun come up, none of it seemed real anymore. Later, he ask his Granny-mom to fix them hamburgers on white bread for lunch that day, which she do with a smile while Roosevelt build a little house with his Lincoln Logs.

A RABBIT, A JEW, AND A MEXICAN

You watch as the Chevy Impala, a heavy cruiser of an automobile that you and Burnie admire despite it needing a wash, backs out and speeds away, fast as it can. You set them boys right, or from their perspective wrong, you supposed. Told their California asses they'd best get outta your joint, and not five minutes from now. Man, they went hotfooting out to that clunker then, boy. You were a mean sum-bitch when circumstances called for it, but in this case it would be some of your regulars.

You? You would put up with as much as you could stomach out of commitments; other irritations, not swallowed as easy. Like them damn street preachers, for one, who'd arrive later in the wake of the little beatniks and start their hollering on the corner of the green, waving the Bible and catcalling your Friday night customers and employees, and what did you do but deal with it? Hell, the preachers drew folks to the bar they was protesting, all curious over what colorful invective they was shouting this time.

You hadn't a clue why them crackers couldn't see that part of it — how their attention didn't do nothing but further your own cause, which was commerce, selling beer fast as your barkeeps pulled the taps. But all they knew was that their holy message needed preaching. The way the pickers had to play. The preachers didn't see it that way, of course.

Hours before, you had watched with interest as the Impala rolled up out front, how it disgorged the pair of unfamiliar boys. Burnie nudged you—the plate said California, and you don't see too many of them around here. New York, New Jersey, and Florida, people racing up and down Highway 1 which skirted the county, sure, but not from out west.

California—you can't half understand these boys having come all this way. Summer of 1964, a strange year in the American South, but the green of Tillman Falls, and its couple of lunch counters, ain't had instances of violence or protest, at least none that got out of hand. Trends take their sweet time getting to Edgewater County, if they ever do at all.

"Some of them civil rights fellers. S'what I'd bet."

"You think so?"

"All we need on a Friday night."

Burnie says this sucking his teeth, standing and sweating in his suit and tie and hair slicked back, smoking and taking a break from what he's told you is some slow-ass business over there at his shop and the used car lot, and going on and on about this piece of land he's gonna buy to put trailers on for people to lease, an investment property, one of his many endeavors and schemes. Next he planned to run a mobile home dealership. Burnie, he's always got it all figured out. Probably has a mattress stuffed full of cash.

"Ain't nothing around my honkytonk they need worry themselves about —everybody got the same rights here."

"Yeah, bossman. Sure enough they do. Depending on the pictures on their folding money."

You both grunted at that.

But it was true on another level. You hadn't ever had separate bathrooms or any of that mess. Besides, in a deep-south redneck haven like Edgewater County, the blacks kept to their own juke joints and left The Dixiana to the crackers, and what on earth there could be wrong with that? But if a black boy wanted to come in and drink himself a beer, and had folding money in his pocket, you were the type of barkeep who wouldn't say no.

No more than you'd say it to a Jew and a Mexican, which is what seems the case with the two boys, whose names, they claim, are Jerry and Sandy— Yankees, in other words—and who start in not about civil rights, but how they heard about a Friday night hootenanny here that featured some "really sweet" picking.

You find yourself duly impressed. "Heard right, fellows. Music'll start up about suppertime, and go till it goes."

This seems to excite the boys, who ask if they can bring in their own instruments, and damn if the chubby Mexican boy, Garcia, doesn't have a banjo he hauls out, and the other'n a Martin that he'll pick real good later on, as you find out. Both of them could play, even hold their own, but the Mexican with intense, dark eyes—faraway, concentrating on his picking—had the gift. You seen this in players before. The music flowing out of his playing like water.

Said to you, for this hepcat to learn the songs? He had slowed down records to study the sides note by note.

You snorted, hiding how impressed you were. "Here? The boys just get up and play."

"If something's not done right, no point in doing it."

Whatever the attitude, and you don't much care for it, the beatnik's words strike you as wise. You like that in a musician—music ain't only about being made for its own sake. It's about how it's delivered, and with what's behind it in the heart and mind. Wisdom.

The Mexican and all his practicing he tells you about, it makes you recall Runelle back in North Dakota, running up and down her vocal exercises she got off a record in the department store in Fargo—*Learn to Sing Good* or whatever the LP of scales and practice melodies had been called. Back when she was determined. Now, you can't get her onstage anymore. That gets irritating—what did you open this dump for? To scrape by and not make much money so she couldn't sing after all?

Gives you pause. Makes you wonder. But all of life does. And always has, ever since you went overseas. You don't want to think about that, and neither do these boys. They ain't got no idea about war. No idea at all what you went through, just so's they could pick their guitars and banjos and drive across the whole country in freedom, ending up all the way here in time for the Friday night Dixiana Hootenanny. You didn't have no medals, though, none earned nor requested.

◌▥⊘

JEZMUND REMBERT STARTED THE MESS ABOUT THE TAPE RECORDER. YOU didn't give a shit, and you don't think none of them boys onstage give a rip either, standing outside in the warm spring air having one of the first Hootenannies of the year, and so what if these little beatniks have their reel-to-reel recorder. Nifty is all you reckon. That, and how Burnie ought to sell them portable models over at the appliance shop.

But now that Jezmund's a 'grown man' of eighteen—oh, sorry, he wants to be called 'J. W.'—he's getting too much like his mean ass daddy, and starts in about how they can't record them boys playing music from that loading dock and not pay for it. "I'm telling Mr. Rabbit," you heard him yelling like the pissant little spoiled squirt all these kids are nowadays. "He's gonna whip your asses."

The Jewish boy, a budding lawyer: "If it's a dock and not a stage, it's not playing a union gig. We didn't wander in from one of your cotton fields."

The Mexican's more diplomatic than his friend. "Hey man, we want to hear the music again later. Not sell it. So we can learn."

"Yeah, sure."

"We don't want trouble."

That only makes Jezmund madder. "Boy, y'all fixing to know what trouble is," a manner of threat like his old man would have made, only Josiah Rembert never had to yell in his nasal-headed whine like his boy—Josiah's voice, deep like a man's, as though his nuts is made of granite. Jezmund's hadn't never broken all that resonant. Had to make up for it with bluster.

At this point you stepped in. Said, you boys shouldn't run the tape recorder, which had a microphone on a thin wire that the Jew boy held in a hand that shook.

A regular crowd gathered around them, and the pickers all stopped and eyeballed down from the loading dock at the commotion.

The beatniks, more disappointed than angry, hurried out the side gate onto Common Street, hustling their guitar cases and tape recorder alongside the mural.

"Jesus, Garcia, look at this rebel flag—these are real rednecks around here."

The Mexican, nervous, glanced behind. By now Jezmund and a couple of his daddy's other hombres were following. "Let's split, man."

Before Jezmund could catch up, you hollered for him to come back, which he done, albeit with reluctance. You're one of the few to whom he'd halfway listen. Sometimes.

"They need their asses set straight, Mr. Rabbit."

"Let them hopheads go on. We don't want their Yankee mess here."

"That's what I'm saying. I was gonna make it stick. Wanted to beat that jew-boy's ass for trying to steal our music."

Jezmund's whining made him seem callow. All of them his age did anymore—they ain't had nothing to make them grow up, not like you and Burnie and the rest.

Lord—you wish you could have run around the country with a tape recorder, with your wife and a guitar for her to play, back when you was their age. Instead? Freezing and shooting at German fellas.

"Dollars to doughnuts they gonna cut a record and sell it."

"Not now they ain't."

"Damn straight."

"But still. Anybody who loves our music the way them fellas seemed to? Okay by me."

"See, though?" Burnie, a new scheme. "We ought to record this stuff ourselves. Making records. Whatever happened to our radio station?"

"Dunno."

"Maybe it ain't too late."

You shrug. "Let's get Mama Runelle to resurrect the Dixiana Darlings every Saturday night."

"Don't think I could talk your wife into much of anything. You know that better than me."

"I do."

At least these days your bride will still sing at the house, some. She fell in love with Joan Baez and all that folk mess they got going, which ain't too far off hillbilly. You had Burnie order you every protest record that come out in the last few years for her, which she had started learning and singing at home. Now that Ronnie Ed's older and running around like boys will do, she needs a distraction.

Maybe y'all could start booking folk music. Get college boys from the clubs near Southeastern University in Columbia. Goose big city money to flow into the county. You would talk to Burnie.

Hell, before that tape recorder mess got started up you was fixing to ask the beatniks what they thought about folk tunes. Maybe they'd be back one day, or somebody like them. You never knew who'd show up at The Dixiana's Friday night hoot.

MAMA RUNELLE PETTUS

The three amber stage lights burning bright in her eyes, Runelle stood singing at the Dixiana microphone, the notes coming clear and perfect. Meanwhile, the rednecks and shitkickers sat quiet as mice, some of them with tears running down stubby cheeks. Rabbit, in the back the whole time slinging barbecue and snap-case weenies and hollering at the kitchen help to keep their asses in gear.

But that's what it takes to do this job, to be in charge of this joint of their'n, as her husband would say it. One sees the gape in the eyes of the staff when his dander is up about a slow the prep line in the kitchen or any other problem, and if he raised a hand they would mess themselves. Rennie doesn't always realize how intimidating he can be.

Runelle wants to raise a hand to her own boy sometimes, who with each passing year acts worse, worse and worser. She doesn't know what to do, nor his daddy, either. Caught him drinking already, and with a girl—Emma Jane Harken, not only the town floozy but years older. Ronnie-Ed with his hands inside her shirt, face redder than a summer sunset, hollering for his mama to shut the the door to the shed. Five minutes ago—or was it a decade and a half—he'd been a sweet baby. Mercy.

⊛ 🅱 ⊘

She had gotten over her reticence, as well the loss of Patsy Cline two years before, to again grace the stage once a month. Her sets included simple melodies she could strum and warble, familiar country songs along with current folkie stuff she admired from listening to records of Peter, Paul & Mary and Bob Dylan and Joan Baez; and because of who she was, no matter her song choices there would come only approbation, never catcalling nor hooting—anyone who did would encounter one of any number of men ready to pound them into sand. Miss Runelle, The Lady of the House, they called her—the Darling of the Dixiana. Her absence made her into something of a local legend.

P'shaw. Wasn't nothing but regulars on Thursday nights anyway, old boys who'd been greasing stools with their trouser-seats for as long as the club had operated. Coming up on twelve years already? The time had raced.

Ronnie Ed, sitting out back with his smart-aleck teenage friends sneaking smokes like his mama can't smell it on him, he didn't need her anymore. And Patsy Cline didn't require Runelle Pettus grieving for her to the point of hanging up singing and playing—did that make a lick of sense? Only the latest in a lengthy line of reasons.

What renewed her interest most had been Jasper Glasscock, sweet boy. How he sits listening to her play on the porch while being watched by Runelle until his sister Letty gets out of work at the hosiery mill. The girl can bake like a dream, she should make cakes for a living, that's what everyone who tastes one says. Old man Glasscock, a widower for years and left with the two children. Bt there'd been such a gap in age that Letty, a grown woman in her mid twenties, might as well have been Jasper's mama herself, and had helped to raise him.

Mainly because she was mama.

Lord, such a scandalous secret. But Jasper, he'd never know that part. Not if Letty, his caring big sister, could help it. She'd been sixteen when she birthed Jasper. By her own blood.

Such a little angel, though, born of heinous sin. The family, cursed by the Sunbury fire, left her and her Daddy, together, and culminating in her teen years with a depraved comforting having taken hold in the house. What a sad and sordid tale. Jasper, better off not knowing—some secrets should remain uncovered.

But Runelle suffered worries about her own baby, the burgeoning wildness in Ronnie Ed. She hoped and prayed it would not lead to tragedy, or pregnancy, or both. How he loved girls. She caught him gazing at cutouts from magazines of certain movie stars all the way back when he was only twelve. She hadn't known what to think. Such interests seemed to manifest too soon.

Her mind raced with many possibilities, and on some days she wanted to turn to the bottle or pills to keep from the worries so consuming of her spirit and attention. Had Rennie spread his night terrors to her like a virus, she speculated, only one experienced during wakeful hours?

What poppycock. She tuned her guitar and got ready to sing 'It Wasn't God Who Made Honkytonk Angels.' Ronnie Ed would turn out fine. Boys ran around.

After this it's back to the folk songs, but all they want to hear is still Patsy. Everybody always says she sounds so much like her it's downright eerie.

SHE ALMOST REMEMBERED THE TRIP TO WEST COLUMBIA AND THE TOY store more than the audition for the famous Mr. Peer, who came to the Pickin' Parlor on that side of the river from the state capitol of South Carolina because of his desire, always, to find the newest and best pickers to make famous on the radio—and to put them on records, too. Runelle, even at her young age, eight, well-known at her church and in town for her beautiful, clear, steady voice; an angel singing in perfect key, they said. The road that's now called highway 179 down to Columbia was a rough ride in her father's truck, bumping along between the two men. She remembered her teeth clicking together, and the smell of her uncle's after shave, and the guitar case between his huge feet.

Compared to Edgewater County, West Columbia seemed like the big city. State Street offered many stores and a movie theater, not that Tillman Falls didn't. Best was a toy store, and she begged to go inside. With the view of the granite-walled and copper-domed State House across the river, and downtown Columbia proper laid out on top of the hill, her perspective, she would later understand, had been the same as that of General Sherman before he ravaged the city in 1865, none of which existed in her consciousness.

Inside, though, had been a chaotic swarm of children—a giveaway underway, the prize a magnificent stuffed teddy bear. At the last minute Runelle was allowed make an entry, a slip with her name, which the huffy, sweaty store manager snatched from her and shoved into the fishbowl with brusque irritation.

The bear, on a pedestal, displayed perfect, clean white fur and shimmering crystal blue eyes. As luxurious a toy as any she'd seen. A bear-angel. She could feel its softness and comfort against her cheek already.

Held up beside the counter with the cash register by her uncle, Runelle watched as the fat man rooted and drew out the slip. Stretching and peering from her perch, she saw behind his hand her own scrawled writing, the paper crushed and wrinkled from his rough handling—she'd won.

Her stomach filled with cold instead of happy-warm as he called out a different name in a stilted voice with his eyes rolling around, and Runelle knew he was lying simply from the way he acted. A freckle-faced boy came strutting up to rudely grab the prized bear for his own. Disconsolate and aghast, she had to be dragged outside, all the other children and parents watching with disdain.

Wailing on the sidewalk how she'd actually won the prize, Runelle, calmed by Uncle Wally, a picker who often drove to West Columbia to look at fine instruments and play in hootenannies on Friday nights as would one day happen at The Dixiana. He promised a substitute bear, all the bears she wanted. "But first, let's dry our eyes, warm up our throat the right way and go meet Mr. Peer. And let him hear your beautiful voice." She could still taste the whiskey from his flask at the back of her teeth—he had rubbed some on her gums to help her nerves, he said. He called it 'medicine.'

They drove a few blocks up the main highway to the guitar store. The audition went fine, and Runelle, stuffy from her crying jag, still performed with grace and perfection a rendition of 'How Great Thou Art' for Mr. Peer. But she had been oh-so nervous and scared she near about peed on herself through her knickers and stockings, and never once stopped thinking about the stuffed bear.

Peer, harried and impatient, had a ruddy, jowly face and sweaty like the toy store manager, gave a big sigh. Said how cute; but there wasn't no market for pretty little church singers, even ones with a lilt and tone as true as hers. And he shouted for the NEXT! singer to come into the room at the music store up the hill from the river, its walls filled with banjos and guitars and like no place they had back in Edgewater County. A young woman, painted up like Jezebel in a tight sweater and skirt, sashayed in and every man in the room, her uncle included, started babbling with praise before she sang a single note.

On the ride home, Runelle, spent from the excitement, dozed with her head lolling against her uncle's shirtsleeve. Far too young to comprehend the ramifications of Peer's failure to "discover" her, as her Uncle kept whining, only much later would she understand about Mr. Peer—who he was, how all their lives would have changed if only he'd agreed she ought to be heard on the radio. The harsh truth of this judgment, that people did not want to hear, much less pay, for church singing, would make her squeamish about her vocal talents for the rest of her days. But 'Mama Runelle' could blame poor Patsy Cline's plane for crashing all she wished instead, if it made her feel better.

BUT DEAR RENNIE HAD INSISTED, AND BEING BACK UP THERE, YODELING for the yahoos, as she joked before going into another number—one of Patsy's, 'She's Got You,'—didn't seem so silly.

Except to her son, who thought of it all as humiliating nonsense. Teenagers, glaring from underneath their sloppy Beatle bangs. They couldn't imagine that their parents had loved music and dancing. All so uncouth. All so uncool.

What's 'uncool' was being stuck on a farm in the middle of nowhere. Trapped through a long winter's night, wishing hard for a reality in which she had a stage to sing on, to prove Ralph Peer wrong. Here the truth of her abilities lived and breathed, in her own way, and in its own scale.

When she thought in this manner about being onstage—a wish born in the North Dakota night had come true, and she hadn't done a blessed thing but for the wishing—it kinda 'blew her mind' the way beatniks might term it. Almost like a magic miracle, when she allowed such notions in among the myriad, pernicious worries and fears.

She didn't talk about matters like this with her husband or the pickers and grinners at The Dixiana, high-minded thoughts such as these. They'd think she had been smoking grass. She'd better just sing, the butterfly in her stomach quelled the second she walks onstage amidst the hooting and hollering. The backup band vamps, she strums and sings until her neck aches and takes a bow to the dozen drunks at the tables, and thinks, dang, this is one interesting life you've wished up, Mama Runelle. Isn't it, though?

She sure hopes that nothing terrible's coming, worries welling up almost as hard as she used to wish. The exact feeling, only on the opposite polarity —a powerful one. It took it out of her. Maybe her husband offered wisdom when he said she would worry herself—or somebody—to death before it was done. That whether she liked it or otherwise, Ronnie Ed's wildness was here to stay

To either quit worrying, or else get used to living with fear—these were her choices? According to the men in her life, yes.

She would decide when he was older. Praying he didn't end up in the army. Worrying herself crazy about that one. Not the same as hope. Saying please-God-no, instead of yes.

Or was it all the same? Wishing for no, wishing for yes? What difference? Either way, ruinous, the desire for foreknowledge; a sin to try predicting the future. That's what she told herself to quit worrying.

After another ovation, she thanks the crowd. A voice calls to "sing one more for us, Mama," and so she does, a current song she and her husband like by Buck Owens, and that the band knows, called 'Together Again.' Not that they'd ever been apart. Not in twenty years, her and her man. And maybe part of their success together came from liking most of the same music. And working as partners in making wishes most fanciful, like her prancing around onstage, come as true as they possibly could.

RABBIT, RUNELLE, RONNIE ED AND CLAUDIA PETTUS

You are glad for the company gathered here tonight. Across the table, weighted down as with a holiday meal, is a feed Runelle's put on before sending your boy overseas to fight the good fight. You see Burnie; you see your son, and in the presence of both you feel full up with hope and love. If you and Burnie survived the big war, your boy would return from this Pacific Rim skirmish.

Burnie's boy, for instance, has been overseas for a good while. But he's smart, has himself some top-secret job in a unit that ain't on the front lines, or so he claims in the letters.

"He's a lucky little prick, I tell ya." Burnie, like any veteran, feels relieved as hell his kid don't have to fight like y'all did.

Ronnie Ed, though. He's gonna face up to the shit—infantry.

This scares the mud out of you. And you don't know how to talk to him about it. But then, you ain't never been able to talk to that boy. Have you.

T-R-O-U-B-L-E is his name-O. And sass-mouthed? Mercy.

His mama babied him too much. Wouldn't let you be hard on him like you needed. And him going off, now, to fight in a war, from zero to fifty in two shakes. From what his boy had mumbled, boot camp had been nothing like in your day. Soft as hell, these young'uns.

Of course, they would not fight across a whole continent, only a little yellow fingernail of a country full of jungle and tree-dwellers, as Burnie called the islanders he met in his time in the Navy. Screwed himself a mess of them girls, too, or so he claimed.

Burnie, always full of stories and claims and facts and schemes. You had to watch him. Had to pick apart stuff he tells you. You learned this over the years. Burnie spins stuff to his advantage. That rascal.

❉ ⬛ ◉

Y'ALL, YOU AND YOUR BOY, HAVE BEEN DISCUSSING RONNIE ED'S MOS, which other than as a general infantryman includes the designation for being jump-qualified, making him able, in his mother's private and fearsome words, to hurtle that much faster to his death in the jungle below. Runelle, boy, she don't hold no truck with this Vietnam mess, her and them folk singers she likes, a few of which from Columbia you put onstage, here and there, at the club. But you don't go against your country, not the way some behaved. If we weren't able to stop the communists like y'all stopped the Axis, you didn't know why we bothered having an army—a coach fielded a team to win.

You think about that not because you care so much, but it takes your mind off the parts Runelle's talking about. The death part. Of your boy. You couldn't consider the possibility. Fact that he was going off at all? Felt like one of your bad dreams. Not as bad as one of the real ones. Not yet. But it might turn that way.

Oh, hell—buck up, a voice says in your ear. Look at all they flung at you, and you come home fine to run your honkytonk and love your woman and be left alone. Life's good, and Ronnie Ed would serve, return and live his version of life. Shit yeah, he will.

That's how you made the world your own, Burnie told you, and your boy as well. You believe. You imagine. And you make it real.

In your mind, you were already welcoming him back home. That's how you'd sleep at night.

"Boy, you should have learned a trade before you went in. You could've been a mechanic—they stay back on base. Or done better in school. Been a signalman."

"If I'm-a going, I wanna go and fight."

"What you mean if?"

"There ain't no if—it's happening. Saying, I might as well find out what this war shit's all about."

"Ronald Edward—not at this table." Mama Runelle bores into her baby with them squinty eyes of her'n. "The army's made you into a foul-mouthed young man, I'm chagrined to discover."

You chime in before your boy can respond and make it all worser: "You'd cuss, too, if you had some mean butthole of a CO blaring orders into your left ear. Wouldn't she, son?"

"That she would, Daddy." He leans over and pulls Claudia, his trashy little girlfriend, closer to him. She ain't no bigger than a minute, that girl. Don't look old enough for romancing and marriage. He's not but eighteen himself. "But we glad they don't have to know. We go and do this shit so's our pretty ladies don't got to."

"That's true. But they serve. In their own way."

You all would be there for Claudia. You wouldn't let her wait alone. Especially not with what came next out of your boy's mouth, which caused Runelle to drop the tray of cupcakes she'd made, red white and blue colored frosting, that went every which way.

"She's right far along, Daddy. I'm sorry to spring it like this."

"*We're* sorry," nudging him in the ribs and making your boy's face turn red. Her voice, raspy and little-girlish. You can't stand this girlfriend of his.

My boy has gotten this hillbilly urchin pregnant. Oh, mercy. Ronnie Ed—why, son? Why now?

"At least we got something to talk about besides the war and getting killed in it, right?" Which only makes Mama Runelle howl harder in the kitchen, break a glass, and start cussing up a storm.

◌◉◌

"WHY'D YOU DO IT?" BOTH OF YOU OUTSIDE SMOKING. HAVING A LAST chat before he gets on the bus in the morning.

"Do what, Daddy?"

"Sign up."

"They was gonna draft me."

"They might not have, boy."

"I had me a mighty piss-poor number."

"Still."

"They ain't no debate now, I reckon."

Your son spits off the porch, pulls a smidgen of tobacco from his tongue with two fingertips. Come back from basic having switched to unfiltereds. Damn idiot always wanted to grow up too fast. Being a veteran, you could see how training had already changed him—eighteen going on twenty-five. And to help move matters along, about to be a daddy.

"Not unless you want me to desert."

"Naw. I'd've just as soon you hadn't signed up, though. Son—I got to tell you."

"What?"

"It's—" And you struggle to get the words out. So hard. Shaking inside, even more in trying to hide the difficulty of voicing these concerns standing in the yellow porch light, moths fluttering, smoke drifting vaporous around your faces. "Ain't nothing I ever wanted more than for you than to avoid going through what I did."

"Daddy? If you wanna talk about fighting the Germans, that's cool. I always wondered."

"I know you did."

"But I'm-a tell you what. I'd rather wait, now. Till I get back."

"Until you get back," you echo with a kind of awe at imagining the scene of him back safe and sound, done with that mess overseas and with all his arms and legs, still. "Why?"

"That way, it won't be you telling." Ronnie Ed gets that devil's grin of his. "It'll be us *swapping* stories. We'll be brothers in arms, then."

It seemed mighty poetic, which you reckon is what he intended. Much as your son's ever been a poet. Didn't know what he wanted to do. Too busy out running around, raising cain.

But when he comes back—yeah, when and not if, you couldn't let yourself say if, and yet, that is the notion lingering and gelling—he'll have an idea of how to spend his working life. Boys—men—often will after returning from a stint in the service.

Vietnam, whatever the invasion entailed, would be handled soon anyway. Was nothing like going up against Hitler. If for all the treasure spent on the military these days they couldn't mop up a little pissant peasant country, what good were the forces, or the money? Ronnie Ed, hell, he might never see action. The politicians might talk it out and quit anytime.

You say all this to him; nodding, shrugging in response, typical of the boy. You would recite it again and again to his mother, later. To keep her focused on when he'd come home.

When when when he came home.

Not *if*.

But *if* stuck in your craw. The thought you couldn't shake, until it became more than imaginary. Ronnie Ed, what with his MOS as an infantry rifleman, going right into the shit-storm of combat—now aren't you glad you taught him to shoot?

Aim true and straight, son. That's the only advice you have for him at the bus station, a last handshake, and he's gone. To his retreating back you recite the Lord's Prayer and perform a hex of protection, drawing three crosses with your thumb in his direction and reciting certain phrases. But you didn't hold enough confidence your powwow would carry him so far — not ten-thousand miles into the jungle. But you have to try. It's all you can do for him, now.

TRAVIS LATHAM, A GENERAL, A VIETNAMESE GIRL AND RONNIE ED

At first Travis Latham thought himself in good shape in Vietnam. Better than Ronnie Ed and, far as he knew, Buddy Sykes, the other in-country boys from Edgewater County, anyway. As his tour unfolded, Travis became certain of this good fortune. Buddy, smart, a college boy, but still off in the jungle. All a big secret with Buddy. Classified.

Ronnie Ed, though? Infantry. No doubt he was in it up to his eyeballs. Travis, he felt for Ronnie Ed more than Buddy, a Lieutenant. Officers had it good, or so Travis figured.

Eventually he would understand how lucky he was being stationed at the base: He'd see grunts—muddy, filthy, haggard and stoned—stumbling out of the field and straight into the mess. Travis and his unit, who were more like medics, never looked like that—they could shower multiple times a day, if they wished. Polish their boots. It was expected of them, a discipline and order—Travis and his fellow corpsmen, well, they handled the remains.

Yeah. Hard and horrible in its own way, but not like getting shot or bombed while squatting in a mud-bog with snakes falling out of the trees on your helmet alongside the ordnance. Lots of signing off on forms, and making sure the right copy got where it need to go, and futzing around with carbon paper that leaves smudges on fingers.

Smudges. The worst of Travis's inconveniences. He made sure not to complain too loud.

Other than the details of the job, life at Da Nang Air Base, again, none too shabby: The home of MACV—Military Assistance Command Vietnam, which in its Annex of barracks Travis found himself housed—the post crawled with brass, clean-shaven and scrubbed pink, and whose pressed uniforms hung draped and spotless, with the base grounds expected to appear in similar condition at all times; the big wheels rolled through here.

A different sort of war on this base, almost a hundred miles from the DMZ. Other than handling dead bodies, Travis knew his number had come up in a manner allowing him to survive the war. It took about two weeks of handling remains before he settled down and realized it would continue to be these field soldiers, and not Travis, who would have their bodies torn apart in Vietnam. Only later would the guilt over all this luck on his part settle onto a questioning soul like bitter dew.

❊ ▦ ✐

"YOU LITTLE ASSHOLES GOING INTO THE INFANTRY BETTER STAY SHARP. Get your asses shot off."

Redheaded Buddy Sykes, not much older than them but already a Lieutenant, had warned Travis and Ronnie Ed one afternoon back in Tillman Falls. He'd been on leave and standing in his uniform outside The Dixiana, discoursing to the boys about the dangers of signing up for the Army as they were both intending to do, rather than waiting to be drafted, which might not happen. "This is getting to be a hot war."

"You don't look no worse for wear." Ronnie Ed, always a smart-ass, quick with a line or a retort. "If you ask me."

"I've been to college, have an important job. I don't have to worry about the bullets and flak so much," so secret he couldn't even tell his best buddies. Buddy had studied engineering at Southeastern, so who knew what it was. Blowing up bridges. Travis had seen in movies that those guys got shot at too, so he didn't feature what Buddy Sykes meant. "And I got these bars on my shoulders. But you guys? The poets call it cannon fodder. If you ain't careful."

Neither of them had quite known what this meant. Ronnie Ed had said, if it was good enough for our Daddies, it would be fine for him, too. Buddy had shrugged and said, okay, boy. You'll find out.

❊ ▦ ✐

TRAVIS, AS PART OF WHAT BECAME A DAILY RITUAL, PEERED INTO THE latrine mirror at his face and said, "Meat. That's all," after which he bowed his head in prayer over the horrors he saw daily while assigned to the 1st

Logistic Division, with an MOS designated 57-F20. Still better than getting shot. Once you saw the condition of the remains they processed, you sure as shit knew you wanted to stay far from the field:

Burnt, broken, bombed, often covered in maggots; fished out of rivers and bogs and the rich jungle, each type of remains with its own unique smell. The corpsmen all wore masks with drops of orange oil inside, but it was more Travis's ritual that made the work manageable. Taking a step back from the reality. Remains. Never 'bodies.'

Meat.

It made sense. He got assigned to Quartermaster Corps, he reckoned, because of his duties and experience back home at the IGA, to which he rose from starting as a bag boy right before he quit high school. Graves Registration—GRREG—a service with the Corps, would be his home for the duration of his tour, he said, because of internal logic:

"Typical god-damn Army—I told them I used to work in the grocery store meat department," as he explained to a group of green, glassy-eyed shavetails in the mess and fresh off the boat or plane. "Or maybe it wasn't no screw-up. You ought to see some of them grunts," which nobody wanted to hear. "They sure look like they been through a meat grinder. Better stay sharp out yonder. All I can tell y'all."

Ronnie Ed would've said that to those boys out of meanness, but Travis only wanted them to prepare themselves what they were getting into, not unlike Buddy Sykes on that day back home.

❀ ▣ ✐

BUT TRAVIS COULDN'T KNOW HOW EASY HIS SERVICE WOULD BE UNTIL HE got there, and all during the long flights—first to California and onto a big Boeing jet that landed in Hawaii, made an unscheduled refueling stop on Wake Island, a V of coral in the middle of the vast blue Pacific, and whose runway seemed far from long enough for the big plane, both landing and takeoff an excruciating exercise in fear—he sat stove-up with tension. If he might only get on the ground and stay, Travis Latham didn't give a hoot if anybody shot at him or not.

A bumpy leg to Anderson Air Base on Guam for one last fuel top-off, and at last Cam Ranh Bay Air Base, South Vietnam, followed by several means of transport, from truck to bus to chopper, from briefings and customs and assignments and orders to land, finally, at Da Nang, wearing fresh green togs and black boots that would gain not so much as a scuff except from the rubber wheels of the gurneys Travis would later push.

On the descent to the airbase, the whole horizon to the west blazed deep, bloody red, like a magazine ad for a tropical vacation.

"That the way the sky always look over here?" Travis, pondering in his country boy drawl. "Real pretty."

A Lieutenant across the aisle snorted and said, "Private? That's the war, not a god-damn sunset."

"The war?"

"The jungle—it's burning from an airstrike. And yeah, it looks like that on a regular god-damn basis."

Travis, awed and terrified, squinted at that red band on the horizon now become a vision out of hell. Though that image remained as real as the hot part of the war would get for him, his view from on high, it would at times still land close to home.

The most vivid such instance occurred the day Travis and others watched a plane blow up while trying to land at the airfield next door. An F-4 Phantom, sputtering and wounded, its Marine pilot struggling to make it onto the ground, his engines screaming and smoking black but to no avail. They gazed, gape-mouthed and helpless, as the aircraft nosed up and exploded above the runway, raining down flaming meteors of metal. The pilot's remains, incinerated beyond recognition, had come through the morgue later that night. The dental records chumps earned their keep on that one, because everything else had been flash-fried black as char. Nasty work, gruesome and unnecessary—wasn't as though they didn't know who flew the plane. Bureaucracy. All anybody could talk about was that explosion, unlike anything most expected to see at Da Nang.

The war came home daily, however, in every black bag processed, all different, the many ways in which the deceased acquired the condition. But the remains began to run together too, once he got into the groove, noting only that groups of remains often came in with similar injuries—all with grievous mortar or gunfire wounds, else all burned, or groups missing limbs from unfortunate minefield penetrations. Ten, twelve-hour days, when it got real busy, anyway. The enormous thumping of the Chinooks, loaded down from picking up remains at the collection points. Travis would hear the racket and think, well, that's the afternoon. Word came back that we fought against some real dug-in Commie bastards back in them deep jungles. The look of the remains bore this out, but nobody said so aloud. Not around officers, anyway.

Travis got through these days by thinking of himself as a machine, mechanical arms lifting and depositing the black bags and greased, riveted claspers unzipping the remains, which were not human; he had a robot claw like on Lost in Space scratching down the information onto the smudgy carbon forms.

Travis himself was not human.

And these weren't dead American fellas like him.

Maybe when he returned home again, one day soon, all would be real and true again. For now? A stage-play of handling meat.

AFTER THE WAR HEATED UP IN '67, AS TRAVIS UNDERSTOOD THE HISTORY, the Army had set up an auxiliary processing point at Da Nang to supplement the overwhelmed morgue in Saigon, and now two years later remains arrived mainly on the giant, thumping Chinooks, if occasionally on trucks, like today.

Tet happened over a year ago now, and while business still cooking, the flow of remains experienced interludes of quiet—long stretches, sometimes, followed by beaucoup activity. During such times of rest, corpsmen often play horseshoes along the side of the low concrete building off the airfield next to the cooler, as long as the rest of the building. At capacity it could process about a hundred-fifty sets of remains at a time, and often did.

"Latham—you hear that?"

"Damn, son." Mahoney startled Travis, queering his throw way off to the right. "Choppers?"

Blonde and skinny, Mahoney squinted into the sun. "Truck or two, sounds like."

Trucks equalled a lesser payload. Fewer remains. "Well, we got that going for us."

Travis killed time all morning tossing the horseshoes with another private, Mahoney, a kid from Boston, both smoking and shooting the shit and daydreaming about activities following the wake-up. They both sounded alien to one another, Travis reckoned. He joked with Travis about being from the south, too, which was what his neighborhood in Boston was called, Southie. A rough place, from the sound.

Travis followed Mahoney into the office and put on the smocks and got their masks and gloves ready. Corpsmen unloaded remains while Travis scratched on the clipboard and signed documents, bade the driver to countersign. The tissue-thin manifests got torn off copy by copy and further handled, hands rattling and crinkling the documents, the crucial documents, carbon paper fluttering around like the black wings of the angel of death. Drove Travis up the wall, the Army did—if you weren't processing remains, you better be stacking paperwork into unimpeachably good order.

A jeep came tearing to a stop with two officers in the back, a Major and a bird Colonel, dust and gravel in their wake back-lit by the hot Asian sun. Travis and Mahoney snapped to salute in their heavy rubber gloves they pulled on with their smocks as the brass, barely acknowledging them, bustled past them into the mortuary office.

"Some big wheels there," Travis noted to the driver as they handled the few sets of remains onto gurneys and other corpsmen bore them away. "What's the rumpus?"

"Oh, son—we brung you a General on this run," the driver said, signing the last form and pulling up the tailgate. "What you assholes think about that?"

"That don't happen every day."

Mahoney, sputtering and spooked by the news. "Shit—*them fuckers got one of our generals?*"

"Road accident. Wasn't the gooks."

"Good. There's that, at least."

"That brass, they're keeping tabs on the remains. Stay out of their way."

"Gotcha."

Accident or not, a General getting killed in the field made Travis's own blood run cold. He had gotten jumpy at what he was seeing. The frag wounds were the worst for tearing a body up, but worse still? Remains arriving after starting to putrefy in the humidity and heat of Vietnam. They had enough of those they'd adopted a protocol just for dealing with maggots. Travis decided he could get used to any part of this except for wiggle-worms. A layer of wriggling rice on a recognizable human face had the effect of making the remains seem like bodies again, a profaning, much as he would react this way back home in the meat department at the IGA. *What if the manager walked in and found vermin and insects? We be in trouble, ya'll.* A negative connotation, stomach-turning to boot.

But he didn't know what would put him over the edge, not like he had seen happen to grunts. He didn't have but a few months left by this point, though. To rotate home from this hellhole without a scratch? That was still the goal. Only outcome that mattered. Would be worth another couple of months of maggots and meat and planes exploding overhead.

Meat. This job was just handling meat. Even the General.

Travis noted a Vietnamese name coded as Civilian. "Whoa, wait—who's the dink?"

"Sweet doe-eyed little native girl." The corpsman hung out of the window of the truck. "Probably a VC kamikaze. Wouldn't surprise me."

"Why, she try to blow somebody up?"

"Not this'n. Little shits'll booby-trap you, though, if you aren't careful. Women. Little kids. Some grandmother, even. You don't ever know. She was on the main road on her scooter and ran out in front of a Gamma Goat," a six-wheeled heavy truck with a short trailer. "Ended up twisted around in the axle. Dragged her for half a click. Thought at first she was trying to bomb the convoy, but them fellas didn't find no ordnance on her. Said before it happened, she looked more scared than crazy-brave."

Travis whistled. "Guess the dental boys can skip this one."

"You axing the wrong brother." The driver, sweating running off his dark brow, cranked the truck with twin gusts of black diesel smoke. "You worry about your procedures, and I worry bout mine." They rolled up their windows and the driver ground the gears and the truck went on its way, kicking up dusty from tires covered in dried khaki-colored mud.

◌◍◎

A FEW MONTHS EARLIER, THE FORENSIC DENTAL IDENTIFICATION protocol added a twist to the processing, complicated enough as it was, what with the variety of conditions: this was no normal funeral home. The areas inside the prefab, sheet-metal buildings included space for receiving, embalming, refrigeration storage, shipping, followed by the Central Identification Laboratory and the administration area, which included the Major's office. In addition, pathologists attached to the mortuary stood by to perform autopsies, and a unit tasked with conducting ballistics analysis on remains. Their data, as explained to Travis, got used to evaluate the effectiveness of enemy weapons, crucial information used in developing effective countermeasures.

Wasn't as though they couldn't manage before the new protocols, but after several mixups regarding the identity of remains at the U. S. Army Mortuary at Da Nang, a team of medical examiners had received training and assignment to document and identify every set of remains through dental records, if necessary, along with fingerprints and other available data. Another step, another set of records and documents. That's the Army for you.

You couldn't blame their unit for the screw-ups, though. Travis and the rest of the staff at the mortuary had worked with what they had, like the paperwork, and items like dog tags, all of it fallible. Unless it could talk and tell you its name and rank, dead meat often held onto its secrets.

A few weeks into the new protocols one of the dental assistants had suffered a freak-out, had gone around the bend over the condition of bodies. Mortar wounds to guts and faces had become second nature to Travis, but this poor soul had seen the first one, panicked and puked and the whole bit to the point of reassignment. Hollering about having trained to save teeth, not pry them out of corpses. A draftee, green.

Travis and Mahoney could only shrug. Besides cutting meat at the IGA, Travis worked on a farm as a boy, had gone with the farmer to a slaughter-house and had seen blood and death before he ever got to Nam. And as Travis still said, damn, son: handling these remains still better than facing live fire in the field. They rested at night in the barracks by a damn golf course, of all places, with a foot and a half of concrete poured on one side, on the off-chance of an attack. Weren't any bullets gonna get him at Da Nang. He'd handle some meat if he had to. Suck it up, son.

The native girl on the latest run, though, her death made him feel bad. Her face, perfect and innocent and young; back of her head busted wide open, brains hanging out. So pretty that he knew someone in her village had loved and cherished her, now mourned sure as the families of the boys Travis helped send home soon would.

And indeed, the officers sniffed and poked around regarding the General which made the CO, Major Sonsini, pissed because, what? Were they saying the General's remains weren't safe here with the unit entrusted with handling remains according to the standard procedures and excelled at doing so without further supervision? Shouting and tension but it'd passed, the remains got processed, and the General returned to his place of rest in Arlington, probably. Who knew? Not Travis.

Whether native girls or generals, some days 'standard' went out the window. One time they'd had a mine-sniffing dog come in, poor critter chopped in half. His handler, crying like a baby, standing and watching them process that dog like any other soldier. Which he guessed he was. Travis grew up in the country. Respected animals, worked with them. Had had dogs. Knew what losing one felt like. None of his had got blown up, that much for sure.

The girl, though. A mangled mess, but only half of her. Her upper body, her small perfect breasts and milky skin and round face. Lips parted, eyes the same, a mask of repose that didn't match up with the pain on display in her lower extremities, her guts twisted and hanging and with road trash, straw and dust, all stuck in the viscous running fluids of her ruined body, the missing back of her skull.

"That's a pisser right there." Mahoney, hurrying Travis along. "She would've made someone a sweet little mama-san."

"Don't say that."

"Why not?"

"Because. She wasn't in no war. She made a wrong turn."

"Don't turn pussy on me now, redneck."

Travis felt pissed. This wasn't one of those typical bags of ground beef, some grunt getting his ass shot off. This, a little girl. Tried to find words, but couldn't.

Instead: "Give me that," snatching the clipboard away. With the General's processing completed and his remains removed by the other brass and their own team of corpsmen, the rest of the incoming could be processed. "We don't got all day here."

Travis scanned down the list, squinting at the row of bags, compared list to tags. At one name he froze, blinking and stupid with disbelief.

"The boys in the cooler are waiting, Latham."

Mahoney referred to the others waiting. The General's remains had thrown the schedule off, as had the dink girl. They had a whole crew working there, the corpsmen and doctors and coroners, embalmers, some of whom were civilian contractors. Big industry, the mortuary trade. The army version needed to run as efficient as a business—the processing time had been worked to a clockwork three hours, with another eight-hour period elapsing to check the embalming work. Time waited for no corpse.

"Oh, lord," Travis croaked. The clipboard, fumbled in his hands, dropped with a clatter. "Shit. Shit. Please, no."

One the notations on the manifest read:

    PETTUS, RONALD EDWARD, Cpl.

Shaking, Travis went outside, Mahoney calling after him. He walked in a circle, had to remember to keep breathing.

Maybe it was another boy named that. It could be. Couldn't it? In a country big as the US? The world was full of people with the same damn names. With almost two hundred million Americans fielding a big-ass Army full of freckle-faced Ronnie Ed's, there had to be two with the same name.

But it wasn't a different Ronnie Ed, and he had had to get Mahoney to process these remains. Could not look and see for himself. Would keep on reciting it through the rest of the shift—it ain't my friend Ronnie Ed. That's how Travis got through that day and night, and yet knowing the truth.

That settled it. His ass was putting in for graveyard shift. Fewer remains came in.

"I'm sure now that ain't my boy from back home." Travis, concluding this as they went to clean and stow their heavy aprons and gloves and masks. "Some grunt with the same name. That's all."

Mahoney, lighting up a smoke and nodding. "Yeah. I'm sure that's all it is."

"Stranger shit than that's come round the bend."

"No doubt. Don't sweat it."

"I ain't. Don't you worry."

"Good on that."

And yet that night Travis drank whiskey until he puked. Got into a fight in the barracks. Slept it off without further recrimination. As he was passing out, he heard Mahoney saying, cut him a break. His buddy's remains came through today.

Drunk or not, Travis heard the remark and it brought reality home anew. He hazily recalled weeping himself into blessed unconsciousness over poor Ronnie Ed, and for his folks back home, whom he knew well from the grocery store and The Dixiana.

◌▧◌

THE NEXT DAY AND FROM THEN ON, THE BODIES IN THE BAGS WOULD BE different. They would carry more weight. The months until he got rotated home dragged, and Travis stayed nervous like on his initial flights overseas, seeing the red sky and understanding that the stakes, the war, loomed real and dangerous. Despite handling the remains, he had let himself still believe the war wasn't all that real. When your friend comes in dead, though, no denying the reality.

How he'd face Mr. Rabbit back home, he hadn't a clue. He must never tell him. That's how. Express condolences and get on with it. Try to forget it himself.

Thinking it through every day made him sick, so much so he started spinning out the fantasy of the two Ronald Edwards, because the sickness started coming without taking another drink, and would not leave him until he got home, not until the afternoon in the bathroom of the San Francisco airport during his layover, when he took off that uniform and shoved it into the trash can. Pulled on a pair of jeans and a T-shirt he had bought, put on tennis shoes that still had Edgewater County red clay in the treads, washed his face and his body and went on like nothing had happened. No longer in that old Army anymore, but proud of his service, he reckoned, enough that nobody back home would spit on him.

Not after having to process Ronnie Ed.

Travis Latham, a mean enough redneck already, now possessed real gristle. Would whip some hippie's ass, he would. Boys were dying so them assholes could grow their hair long. Boys like Travis's best friend. Yeah. Travis peeled away the layer of that uniform and gave up pretending about Ronnie Ed. Wasn't no other way. Not once back home.

At least in Edgewater County he could ride over anytime he wished and visit the remains, interred in the Forest Knoll Garden cemetery. As the years went on, him and Buddy Sykes made a ritual out of visiting the marker. Afterwards, Travis always felt better. It was his way of making up to Ronnie Ed for pretending during the processing. For not being tough enough back at Da Nang to look his hometown boy in the eye and handle his god-durn remains the way a man—a soldier and a friend—should have done.

His brother in arms had deserved no less, and the regret would fester for life, not that Travis ever found the courage to confess to another soul, other than Buddy, or course. Having also been in war, only he could possibly understand.

BILL WIMMEL AND NORRIE
SORTWELL

Sitting in Norris Sortwell's office at the Palmetto Grande, Bill felt about as nervous as could be—his first feature article for the school paper.

As many movies as he'd seen there, a certain magic burbled up in going behind the scenes: taking the tour of the popcorn-popping room, watching Sortwell twirl a combination lock on the candy closet as though a sealed bank vault, and last? The mythic and magical projection booth, in reality a dusty, cramped space holding the twinned lamp housings from which the images flowed like ethereal mist. This, the kind of poetry his school paper advisor invariably struck out of his articles with a thick blue felt pen.

Bill, set on interviewing Mr. Sortwell about his life in show business, had so far heard about his decision to move 'down to Carolina' as he puts it, buy the Palmetto Grande and the Sky-Vue Drive-In sitting north out of town near the airfield. With exhibition all he knew, he continued a professional career here begun as a young man ushering at a famous house called The Stanley, with marbled columns and chandeliers and a sense of grandeur, in his boyhood home of Jersey City. One of the true palaces where they book what he terms 'roadshow' pictures like *The Ten Commandments* and *Lawrence of Arabia*, also serving as a vaudeville house and performance venue, the theater held almost three-thousand.

"About the size of your Township Auditorium down in Columbia—a big room."

"Sounds magnificent."

"Like everything, eh. It's going downhill."

"The Stanley — or New Jersey?"

"Both, kid."

With the Palmetto Grande's trade self-evident — major studio pictures on double bills — the drive-in, Sortwell explained, was where he ran B-pictures, a fact Bill knew well from frequent attendance with his mother and the variety of suitors who passed through her life in the years since the death of Mr. Wimmel.

Two years back, Sortwell's Sky-Vue Drive-In bookings had precipitated scandal: he tried to get an 'adults only' night going, on Sundays of all times, with cinematic fare to match. Met with odious disapproval by the community at large, the idea had not taken flight. This being an interview for a student paper, however, the young reporter held no call nor license to ask about that salacious story, though he burned to do so.

Now that he had written for the paper, Bill — they had called him Goochie-Goo because of his baby face; looking like seventeen going on thirteen, still, and a loner, any nickname at all would have to do — became certain this trade, journalism, his sacred calling. Collecting facts, arranging them in order of relevance along a spine one defined for the story.

Imagining being grown, living down in Columbia rather than sleepy old Tillman Falls. Reporting on the doings at the State House — jostling with TV reporters, filing stories shouted into the phone. Bill remembered James Stewart in *Call Northside 777*, an old movie about a crusading, heroic journalist trying to keep an innocent man from being convicted of murder. A noble enterprise. It felt like service; it felt powerful, writing up the news.

He asked Sortwell about the Stewart reporter movie. Being a buff, the hepcat theater owner could recite chapter and verse about where and when he'd seen it, in a house he was managing. "Not exactly a permit to print money, the issues picture. Except maybe for Stanley Kramer. He's got what you call a niche."

Bill jotted down in shorthand the phrases *issues picture* and *nitch*, terms unfamiliar to him, along with *print money* and *S Kramer film director*.

"I love James Stewart."

"Me too, kid."

Sortwell, a pompadour, horn-rim glasses, fussy, exacting, impatient. Always wrinkling his nose and blinking his eyes rodent-like, another way in which Bill knew he shouldn't describe the theater owner in his article. "Stewart's the movie star of the age rather than Wayne, honestly. *Liberty Valance* proved it beyond a doubt."

"But wasn't John Wayne the star in that picture?" Bill despised the cinema icon, all that manly cowboy nonsense. "Despite being the villain?"

"It ain't about Wayne being bad—he's more than a face, even if it is usually the same face. It's about how good Stewart plays against all that. The dignity of his character. That's all. It's art, kid. It ain't a competition— other than at the Oscars, I guess." He busted out laughing, glancing around at his desk covered in mail and paperwork, and the gray, hexagonal film cans sitting lined along the floor, prints of last week's movies waiting for shipment. Wiping his eyes: "Art, with a little business on the side. Yeah. That's show-biz."

Bill, giddy at another solid and pithy quote. He had read from a college textbook on how to interview. Gold, he was getting from this Norrie Sortwell. Interview gold.

Sortwell explained how he also came down south for 'health reasons,' the milder winters and so on. A problem with arthritis, he said, running in his family. "You Southerners, you're good folks—everybody waving, and so on. A little backward, sometimes. Maybe a little too much chewing tobacco during those John Wayne pictures, ya know? You ever clean an auditorium, pick up all those used cups? Yeah. Right."

A wonderful tidbit of insider detail. Now for some boilerplate human interest specifics. "Are you married?"

"Hah, no. Forget it. Never married." Mr. Sortwell took a deep breath. Removed his horn-rims. "Are you?"

Married—what a stupid question. Bill, hair slicked back and old-fashioned the way almost nobody still wore it except old men who had fought in World War II twenty years before, pulled at his shirt collar buttoned all the way up. "I'm a little young."

Sortwell made odd, invasive eye contact. "You're not a day over sixteen —are you?"

Bill looked down at his reporter's notebook, its pages covered in scrawl. "Well, I've been sixteen all year—since the spring, anyway. But I'll graduate early and go on to college. So I might as well be seventeen, or even eighteen. To tell the truth."

"You might as well be." Leaning forward, a dazzling smile. "Am I right?"

"I—couldn't say."

He slapped his thighs and said, "Well—when you get out of school, don't go marrying the first Mary Sue from down the block. She might not be right for you. That's the read I'm getting."

"But, how—how could you know such a thing?"

"Just a feeling."

The callow, budding reporter, aiming to edit the school paper in his senior year, flushed with embarrassment. Sortwell seemed to know about Gaston's secret self. As though able to see the confused desires in Bill Bundrick's heart, twisting like forbidden snakes. And possibly judging him for it.

Or else — no. Bill couldn't conceive of it. Which would be worse — confirmation, or condemnation?

Bill shouldn't be thinking about any of this confounding jive. They beat men's asses for doing what he had envisioned. Mr. Sortwell was a Mason and a Rotarian and a respectable businessman. Maybe he's trying to let Bill know that what's in his heart is not only wrong, but illegal. That's what the smiling and eye contact mean.

To put off any further repartee Bill scribbles like mad for a long minute while listening to Mr. Sortwell breathing with a gentle rhythm — in, out, again.

"Getting it all down?"

"All the details." While trying not to think, oh my god, he knows. He *knows*. "This was an — illuminating interview. I hope you enjoy my article. When it's published."

"You'll bring me a copy?"

"Oh for sure. And I'll — " Bill struggled to remember the standard line. "I'll telephone if I have any followup questions."

"You do that — m-kay?"

He said the 'm' sound a long time. Wriggled his eyebrows, pupils big behind the thick eyeglasses. Sortwell's handshake at the office door lingered, warm and damp; the man pressed his index finger into the flesh of Bill's wrist as thought taking a quick pulse.

Outside Bill felt sick to his stomach, but in a good way. Liberated, yet also caught in a snare. Whatever was going on between the lines there, it didn't feel right. Sortwell had to be forty years old. Older, even.

Bill couldn't wait to get done with high school and out of Edgewater County. Forever, if possible. Atlanta. Atlanta held promise, or so he'd heard. A big city with morning and afternoon papers, opportunity. Lots of folks of all types — like Bill, even. Or so he hoped.

For now he climbed on his bike and went pedaling across the town green toward Congress Street, where he'd cut through and head back to the high school, where he and the other newspaper staff held special dispensation to use the electric Smith-Corona Super Sterlings in the typing classroom to produce their copy. Bill, a furious typist, a WPM of seventy, the fastest in class; at the conclusion of the previous semester, he had been awarded a basket of fruit and candies from the typing instructor.

Once there, the rest of the school quiet and empty but for the janitor waxing the main hallway outside the front offices, Bill put on his journalist's hat and forgot about the weird sense of exposure in Sortwell's office, with its framed pictures of cowboy stars from decades ago hanging on the walls, most of them, he explained, left over from the old owner. Bill had meant to ask Sortwell what his favorite movies were. A foolish omission, a missed piece of human interest material.

He couldn't go back. Not now.

Or, could he?

What would Sortwell think?

Bill, later that night at home, thinking about heading downtown and seeing a movie.

He put it off until the next day, when he lingered on the sidewalk for close to fifteen minutes, debating going inside. Finally he forced himself to act, flung open the unlocked door nearest the box office.

Bill jumped out of his skin, startled to see Mr. Sortwell lurking in the dim lobby, leaning against the candy counter with burly, folded arms, his hair slicked back, a smoke dangling from his full, smiling lips. He'd been watching Bill dithering and pacing the whole time, the man's presence hidden by the glare on the glass doors. That rascal.

"I'm here to follow up," he announced in a voice that trembled, on questions from yesterday.

"Well. That's fine, Bill. Fine as wine. Come on in."

And if Sortwell noticed how the young scribe hadn't bothered to bring his reporter's notebook, Gooch hoped his new friend would take no offense, or think him an unserious journalist. Sortwell locked the outside doors and ushered Bill Wimmel into the theater office to continue the interview.

THE EPISTLE OF BUDDY SYKES

Dear Dad (else *To Whom it May Concern*):

I'm sitting on the post awaiting my discharge after having had one more strong-arm session selling me on another tour, and I keep trying to tell them I have grown up in the house of a salesman, meaning that their platitudes and other techniques have little effect on me. Ten thousand in cash and another stripe for a six-year reenlistment might sound good while standing in the showroom, if you know what I mean, but wait till you get her on the road and you will find a lemon underneath your behind. Sorry, Uncle Sam, but it's true.

My answer was no, that graduate school and work in the civilian nuclear sector was my personal decision, and this was accepted by my superiors, albeit with reluctance. I must be terribly careful about how I put my feelings. Because of the knowledge that accompanies my leave of service to the country, as a security liability my activities may be monitored well after my term of enlistment concludes.

In fact, I could be imprisoned for writing this very letter, for what I aim to put into print. This work is not so much to get guilt off my chest, though perhaps in some ways it is. Mostly, it is offered as protection and testimony for later, in case there are consequences and ramifications to my family over my health from activities while on active duty in Vietnam and Cambodia, which remains classified and may yet stay that way.

In fact, I doubt that many of the details of my mission will be put into writing to be available to non-security clearance personnel or civilians at all, ever. Officially there are no nuclear materials deployed in Southeast Asia, and certainly not in the theater of combat in Vietnam. My experience and records stand in direct opposition to this official policy in line with international treaties, however, in that such materiel was deployed from bases outside Vietnam, principally in Thailand and also out of Guam.

The facts: My unit, the 5015 Ordnance Company (Special Ammo); my MOS, designation 55G20 (Nuclear Weapons Maintenance Specialist). My job, servicing small-scale nuclear warheads and weapons, including shells and a backpack weapon. The backpack weapon, a secret device little known even within the military itself, is portable by one soldier, but requires two to deploy and three to detonate, a fail-safe measure, one of several.

Based out of Udorn in Northern Thailand and later Guam and at sea about a vessel whose name I will redact for now to preserve anonymity for fellow members of my unit, we are typically housed and work in relative secrecy alongside other services like the air corps. We are prohibited from discussing our work with personnel outside our unit, nor with fellow unit members except in the course of the technical work.

As it turns out we are also prohibited, or

perhaps better termed 'strongly discouraged,' from airing doubts about US foreign policy or mission particulars, or even military history. An overheard debate between myself and a fellow NWMS, in which I corrected the idea of the Communists coming to power not as a direct response of Chiang Kai-Shek's military blunders and refusal to accept FDR's offer of control over the former French Indochina countries of Vietnam, Laos and Cambodia, but for the more simple reason that the Communists fielded, and may still be fielding, superior forces to the Western powers. In any case, statements to this effect on my part had me standing tall before the unit commander, as well for which I was sent to the base psychiatrist for an evaluation.

I'm fortunate that I was returned to my unit at all. My psychiatrist, a Captain whose name I will also redact, agreed with me that I was as sane as anyone on the post, and that to him the report was an overreaction on the part of my CO due to the sensitive nature of my speciality, of which the psychiatrist himself, thanks to both classification of information and a layering of bureaucracy only Kafka himself could have dreamed up, only had the vaguest notion. I would think my commitment to confidentiality regarding my work throughout my service indicates a certain degree of patriotism, though perhaps once I am finished there will be no recovering such notions, at least among my military brethren above a certain rank.

My MOS meant that I was charged with ensuring a number of eventualities: that when called upon to do so, nuclear weapons under my care and service will detonate; also that the weapon will not detonate unless called upon; and under any circumstances, and going without saying, to never, ever experience rapid disassembly of the weapon. It's an orderly sounding process, but is in fact how we in ordnance term it when one of our firecrackers goes off in an unintended and unannounced capacity. Imagine the consequences of such an occurrence under my watch. Unthinkable.

This long preamble is intended to set the stage for what I understand and accept will perceived as a damning indictment contained in these pages, of not only this country's commitment to abiding by international convention and law, all the way down to the safety of the personnel handling nuclear materials—surgical gloves, cotton smocks and masks are not sufficient protection. While it is true that film-badge monitors are always worn, with Geiger counter checks performed at the end of each shift and would indicate unsafe exposure, it is my opinion that more data and research on the effects of radiation on the human body under these conditions is necessary to know with certitude what constitutes a dangerous level of exposure.

All due respect to the chain of command and to the government scientists working on the U. S. nuclear program, but the idea that radiation "can't get past paper" is at best laughable, and at worst perhaps criminal. The tritium gas contained within the warheads of thermonuclear devices would bring instant death to the wearers of paper face masks such as our standard issue gear and protocols call for. Joseph Heller, writing in one of his literary satires, would be hard-pressed to top this level of absurdity.

❁🆖⊘

CPL. BURTON SYKES, HIS HANDS CRAMPING, STOPPED TYPING — AS IF HE hadn't caused enough trouble back home with his diminutive 'war bride,' as his father kept calling Tinky, and with a tone like marrying her represented the exact wrong move to have made while overseas. Exactly wrong. That his hands also cramped from working on papers for his master's degree and preparing to interview for the Sugeree Station weren't enough sign that Burnham Sykes's son knew 'his ass from a hole in the ground'—knew what love was and what it felt like when it welled up inside him at the sight of

Nguyen-Thanh Thi Trinh—he'd like to know what would be. A golden chariot out of heaven's gate? Please.

Despite having little English, Tinky endeared herself to the returning veteran's father and mother well enough. The language issue would be first on the list for improvement, because standard English would be spoken in the house and all in good time.

Plus, the war was ending, or so it sounded like. All will move on to live their lives, the outcome Burton wanted for his wife more than anything. After the experience of seeing her country torn apart, and mainly torn apart by the activities of the United States military, Buddy Sykes swore upon his love of country and love of life that he would make hers an existence of comfort that defined his nation and homeland. That made prosecuting such wars worth doing, if that made any sense.

Burton prayed every day his life wouldn't end with cancer from handling those nukes. When the typhoon smashed into Guam, and the igloos, the rounded, earthen ammunition bunkers holding the nuclear shells had flooded, his unit had been ordered to put five and six weapons at a time to be dried out in the shop, when normal protocols called for one weapon-in, one-out. So much additional exposure—terrifying.

And not only for the NWMSs: the base at large lay at grave risk of cont-amination. Giant curtains hid the work of the secretive army unit handling the nukes, stationed there on the Navy-controlled island and patrolled by sour-face Marines who resented the Classified Clarences, as the unit of twenty or so GIs were called to their faces and otherwise. Curtains not lined with lead, mind you, only offering visual opacity to the eyes of restricted personnel.

But his orders came through, and the marriage protocols had been followed and the immigration of his wife would be approved. When his tour of duty drew to a close, Burton, who had to leave her behind, waited for his predawn transport on a C-130 to Hawaii in the middle of the night, standing in the ready room full of its pictures of the top brass going on up to the Commander-in-Chief. Buddy had to resist the urge to draw thick black Hitler mustaches on the lot of them. He felt conflicted about this job he had been tasked with performing, nor the ultimate aim of deploying secret weapons of mass destruction.

His confusion over the invasion and war redoubled upon meeting Tinky, seeing her plight, falling head-over. Buddy had heard General Westmore-land speak about how 'those people, the Orientals,' simply don't feel loss and pain and grief and love the way 'we' do, but Burton's romance with the small Vietnamese woman, separated there in Thailand from her birth family and forced into prostitution by a countryman Burton beat toothless and bloody outside the hooch after she begged him for help to escape, proved otherwise. Her gratitude, turning to love. Before, Lt. Sykes had been a virgin. Had done nothing but study facts and theories. Here was love, two bodies conjoined as one. He got it.

And back home, he'd do right by more than his immediate family by turning what he learned in the military into a positive effect and running that nuclear station. As much exposure as he already suffered, considerable, what better engineer to come home from war otherwise unscathed and keep the nuclear fires tended and controlled?

Whatever his fate, and he believed he'd live long enough to have children with Tinky and see them grow up, Burton Sykes felt his destiny manifesting. He felt moved to do good in the world. It wouldn't bring back Ronnie Ed Pettus or any of the other casualties of the war, or reunite Tinky with her family who were all dead, but maybe he could make a safe future for the people of his hometown. His contribution.

That, and this letter, which he knew he needed to finish there in the office he'd set up in the front bedroom of his parents' house on Whaley Way, where they would live until he finished his degree. The letter was important. A chain of evidence.

In case one day he got sick and the government, in an attempt to deny that Buddy had served in his unique capacity in Vietnam, tried to slither out of paying for his treatment.

He hadn't even gotten yet to spraying the dioxin in the jungle to prepare their fire bases; how they breathed it into their bodies and absorbed it into their skin. If he got cancer one day, it'd be the Agent Orange. That exposure worried him much more than the radiation, which he considered merely part of his job.

RABBIT, RUNELLE AND ROY EARL'S MAMA

Ain't been nothing but darkness and hell. For months.

Shit—it was that way already, before your son Ronnie Ed returned as cargo on a manifest.

Claudia, a hellion. A child herself, still wild-ass as they came. No wondering at all how she ended up pregnant.

All of them young'uns acted out, now—unbridled, wild horses. What you see on the TV, and with your own eyes: running around painted up, half-naked, pie-eyed on reefer and worse. And the music—the biggest mess of noise you ever heard. Could have imagined. You could understand R&B and could live with it, but straight up rock & roll wasn't nothing but trash. Getting worse all the time. What little you heard. Screaming and moaning and wailing guitars; like instruments being sawed apart instead of played. You go looking at the latest records and hear it. Howling like the devil.

You think to yourself: Lord, don't let that mess come to Edgewater County. You wasn't having no free love festivals on your back lawn. Or the town green, but plenty of others besides you were set on keeping order to the daily goings-on in Tillman Falls, SC.

If it wasn't for the grandchild in her belly, you'd have told Claudia to wait with her own people for Ronnie Ed to come back. Hell, you all but did.

And what did she say but, "I'd go from this damn place, if I had somewheres. He didn't leave me with nothing. And I ain't got nothing waiting back home."

Lord, but she sounded like them hillbilly coal miner girls from when you were a boy, half their teeth missing from coming up way back in the West Virginia hollers. In her case she still had her teeth, and only come from as far away as Pumpkintown, which made her a mountain girl, at least by South Carolina standards. Hicks were where you found them. Look at all them who leave money on your bar every night.

THAT'S THE BULLCORN YOU FEED YOURSELF TO FEEL BETTER. YOU DON'T bother with saying it to Runelle, or the girl who at receiving the telegram from the army messenger had cried till she puked, doing the same at Ronnie Ed's internment in Forest Knoll. And worse, the first word out of Claudia's sorry-ass mouth after everyone left later was to whine about being stuck with you two, now, and no father or other man coming to rescue her.

You wanted to give her space; knew women held grief and questions you sure as shit don't, and can't, answer. Not even for yourself.

One thing you knew? You didn't need hearing the next words out of her trashy mouth: "I need to find me another man. I ain't got nothing, now. And nobody to help raise this baby."

"Hush up." You cuss her into silence, her lips poked out. "My grandbaby ain't even come out you yet, and you going to look for another daddy? I'll be damned."

"You c'ain't tell me what to do, old man."

Watch me, you said, taking a good stiff drink to calm down and keep from hollering any more.

And going outside, away from her and from Runelle back in her sewing room, crying and laying on the daybed. You had seen boys die every which way a body could, boys you cared about, and now yours done died one of those many awful ways, thus needing a closed-casket service.

All you said to the Army messenger on the porch was to ask where the body was located; he told y'all when it would arrive at the train station, and how all the details would get handled through further telegrams, or, you were entitled to call a number on a card if any concerns or questions. Saluted, and left. An officer, with a driver—they sent an officer to make you feel better about losing your flesh and blood to the war overseas. Like that was supposed to temper a father's grief over losing his only son.

"YOU JUST SIT OUT HERE ON THIS DAMN PORCH," YOUR WIFE HOLLERED at you the other night, "like you waiting for the news to get better. Well —it ain't."

"Ain't that what we supposed to do? Wait for this mess to get better?"

"I'll be damned if I know."

"Well—this is what I'm trying. And if don't work, I'm-a gonna try something else."

Runelle, going from sad to spitting mad, knocks the cigarette out of your hand with a big spray of orange sparks. When she's mad, you know they's nothing for it. Don't know who she ought to be mad at, though. They didn't draft Ronnie Ed's cracker ass from straight out of the bassinet.

Nope. Your boy? He signed up.

Hurt you to think it. But your son, already running with a hard crowd even before he'd become a soldier. Worse'n the kind that drank at the bar, that much for sure. Running with Jezmund Rembert.

You wanted to keep Ronnie Ed away from all the homegrown vice and crime, much of which flowed through your own place of business, but maybe, you wondered, if you hadn't kept him far away from that, but rather from you. He had a durn chip on his shoulder about you, and The Dixiana, and his lot in life, it seemed. Smart as hell, but flunking tests and messing around. Ronnie Ed had always been that way. A fussy baby. Ill-tempered.

Only time you boohooed in front of anyone was standing with Burnie outside Karlaney funeral home. You said, "I hoped going into the service would straighten him out. Show him what it meant to be a man. And it took him before he even finished growing up."

And damn if that rascal Burnie hadn't coughed, sudden, crying like a little girl and blowing snot out of his nose. And you had, too. Standing with your backs to each other, hands on your hips and heads down pacing back and forth, that'd been all y'all had to say to each other about losing Ronnie Ed.

Your boy being dead was one problem, but: That little mountain trash what spread her legs for him, that held immediacy. That had teeth. She who got you into this cock-up now with a baby in the house.

Cock-up. Hell of a way to put it. You swore that if you heard one more damn complaint out of her mouth. You wished to hell she never come down out of them upcountry Carolina mountains. Them pellagra-ridden hillbillies, bad—worse?—than the backwoods West Virginia trash you grew up around.

That you came from, 'from' being the key word. You wasn't nothing like them. Or her.

So: you were gonna.

Gonna what?

Nothing—not a goddurn thing. Not while your grandbaby was inside her.

◦ⓜ⊘

AT THE COOKOUT AFTER RONNIE ED'S FUNERAL, WITH FULL MILITARY honors there in the town cemetery and a gun salute that'd made you wince with each pop, you wandered round under the pine trees, drinking a cold one and asking:

Wasn't you and that boy fishing?

Up on the bluff at the river?

Only yesterday?

Wasn't you standing there looking out at the god-awful flat plain when she told you she was carrying him?

And that she wanted to go home?

No—if you wanted, she said, you could go with her. If you were of a mind. How that's where she was going, and if you wished to continue journeying alongside her? Welcome aboard, Sergeant Pettus.

Otherwise?

The otherwise part—losing her—made your stomach drop. You wasn't doing the damnable farm work for yourself. It was for all of you. All three, now. And so you moved back.

God help you, though—you hadn't the wildest notion this is where it'd lead. To your boy being gone. And not even twenty years-old.

Mercy. Mercy.

Or had you known, the day he went over with Travis Latham and signed up? You always held had the feeling you wasn't supposed to come back from Europe like you done—without a scratch. And you were anxious it would happen for him that way, instead. At least if the powwow you worked done its job. Never a sure bet, messing with such forces. Entreaties and bargains, sometimes fulfilled, but often not for the longest time.

Oh, mercy, but you couldn't let these feelings of failure pervade your other workings. No more than you've already done.

◦ⓜ⊘

THE LATEST FIGHT HAD TO DO WITH THE GIRL AND RONNIE ED'S hardtop Mustang, the one old man Hampton was still taking you for payments, a car which in all the grief and turmoil of the new baby, she run bone-dry out of gas down River Ridge Road.

Sitting on your sacred porch listening to the whippoorwills you seen her emerging out of the dark of the long driveway from the highway, a ghostly child-creature in a dress and with her straight unkempt hair down, and you blinked a few times to make sure you wasn't imagining things, which happened from time to time. One night out here on the porch you could've sworn a river-bird the size of a man cruised low through the tree canopy, leaving an awful stink in its wake. You'd had a few snorts, though. Chalked it up. Growing up in the mountains taught you how interesting creatures often lurked back in tucked away hollows far from the developments of man. Nothing you went around saying.

Claudia come into the yard with her arms held straight down, going boo-hoo-hoo and red-faced and shouting about you letting her run out of gas. And being stuck out here in these damn woods. And how she hated you both, and hated being all fat, still, despite the birth two months ago, and her feet were so huge and red, still, and they ain't never going down, never never never. And it was all your fault, you and that old hag sitting hunched over holding that baby—her baby—and damn if she wasn't taking that child and going.

"Ain't nowhere for you to go. You said so yourself."

"I got people back home."

"Not to hear you tell it."

She cussed you. It was true.

The baby? You and your wife worshipped him as your own. Roy Earl, tiny and round and so precious, now, in a way the little upstate trollop would not understand, not at her age and with an ignorant, white-trash background.

Runelle got Claudia calmed down while you took Jasper Glasscock, who had got his driver's license not long before, down the road to fetch gas and then to drive Ronnie Ed's car back home behind you. Jasper, thrilled to be needed in such a fashion, but his sister Letty, a fussbudget if you ever met one, had a fit. Said her brother better not drive too fast. That Ronnie Ed always roared like a madman up and down nearby roads, and while Letty chagrined to say this, sad but true.

You told her not to worry. How you and his mama more than felt the same way. "He was hardheaded, though. Wouldn't listen."

"Boys can be that way," Letty said.

"He was so stubborn I figured he wasn't gonna let himself get so much as a blister over there. To tell the truth."

And how you'd made them both feel uncomfortable you hurried with Jasper to the filling station where you filled up a gas can for Ronnie Ed's car, while trying not to think about how he would never drive it again — hell, or see it again, or you, or Edgewater County. Nor his baby, the one you browbeat Claudia into naming Roy Earl in the fine tradition of the Pettus men you've known and loved and now continued by your pea-picking, apple of the eye of a grandbaby.

Oh, the scenes now brewing, like thunderheads towering over a hazy summer horizon. You didn't know how this would break.

You need to consult a lawyer. Wouldn't have to go far. On most afternoons the elbows of attorneys — and cops, judges, councilmen and crooks alike — polished the gleaming bar top of The Dixiana, shot pool, played pinball. You stopped short of warning the girl about a legal remedy, which would go your way; nor of the dark arts at your behest, if you wished to risk the retributive cost of a working to remove her from your life, and that of the baby. That, the darkest notion. Keeping the child; losing the mother. You can feel your wife thinking the same. It passes between your eyes, and in small gestures.

This young'un's got no idea who she's dealing with, but few townsfolk do. Not even Burnie, bless his heart, who thinks all their successes and escapes from difficulties with the blue-room trade are all thanks to his street smarts. Sure thing, old pal.

⊙☷⊘

IT GETS WORSE. WORSE AS ANYONE COULD IMAGINE.

One night Claudia, who had gone to see about getting on at Lucinda's, an interview you set up, came home with her ass up on her shoulders anew. You and Runelle reasoned that if the girl got her own money, maybe she'd find contentment and settle down and y'all can think about building on an addition so there'll be more room. Screaming at you both about how she wasn't gonna waitress across the street from that juke-joint so they could keep her under observation and pinned down. It deteriorated from there.

You having been drinking, in this case to calm yourself and get a decent night's sleep here on Sunday when the bar's closed except for the games in the upstairs, makes matters worse. This makes it well-nigh-on im-pissable, as Burnie says, to hold thy tongue.

Thy wicked, wicked tongue, as Claudia says to you, screeching and stomping back and forth to where you want to snatch the baby and the girl up by her hair, and Runelle does too, but she goes at it in a more gracious fashion, cooing straight to the infant:

"Here, come to Mee-maw, Roy-Roy. Let grandmama hold you. Come on, now."

No, Claudia yells, making him cry and for the dogs in the backyard to bark up a storm.

Your blood—it boils. Folks always say that, but this time you swear it's the way you feel inside. "Quit your hollering in my grandbaby's little ears."

"I done decided, I'm going. Tonight. I got the car gassed up. And I'm taking this baby back to my home, where at least I still got a cousin or two who might help me. And so, y'all can't keep me."

Your rage, it's never felt so raw. Your voice shrieks and shreds your throat as your loom over and clasp her by arms tiny and frail, hold her against the wall and have to make yourself stop when she hollers out in pain.

"Y'all are demons from hell, you old sinners," rubbing her forearms and starting to boohoo. "You run a pure-T den of iniquity in this town of your'n. Oh yeah—and I'm gonna take my baby away from that sin," yelling as though the devil possessed her rather than you and Runelle: *Not another minute of this! Now! Now!*"

"Oh, Lord." Your wife praying means this is bad, because neither she nor you ever done much of that in the open. "Lord help us."

She's right to turn to God. Even before the horrors at the end, twice during the war you and your comrades had executed German troops rather than turn them in as POWs, if under orders, you always try to remember. You have been initiated in blood—perhaps its why your powwow has often proven so effective. God only knows what you're capable of, under the right —or wrong—circumstances. Murder? Now your turn to pray for serenity.

◌◍◎

BEFORE YOU KNOW IT, YOU COME RIGHT UP ON HER. FLASHING YOUR lights. Honking your horn.

And causing the wreck.

Claudia peeled out in Ronnie Ed's Mustang after y'all stood yelling one last round on the porch. Runelle, ordering you to go, go; crying, don't let her take my sweet Roy Earl.

What was you supposed to do?

The girl wasn't speeding too bad, you guessed, because you came up on her quick. And when she saw you in her mirror she hit the brakes at first, causing you to lock up yours and slide. Next she punched it, and the car fishtailed on the wet road so the right tires went onto a shoulder soft and wet. She jerked that wheel hard, and the Mustang spun a different way—into the ditch, the steep ravine down into a stand of hardwoods a mile from Pike's Bait & Pawn. So much rain y'all had had. She should never have jerked that wheel.

You almost pissed yourself as the taillight flipped over and off the road; thought you were dreaming: Ronnie Ed's car now upside down, headlamps shining all cockeyed. Brake lights, glowing demon-red.

You scrambled down the wet and grassy ravine, slick and muddy and no wonder she spun out, and the first thing you hear's the ticking of the engine and no, not that, please God no not an explosion—you have come so close so many times from that already, Lord, and you know it is so—and the second is your grandbaby's crying, his normal I-want cry.

Down in the car you find a scene out of hell, but remain stoic. You've seen shit no one who loved you would believe. They all had their version and vision of reality, and you had one given to you overseas—you seen heads blowed off and bodies tore up and friends of yours with their guts hanging out, guts and nuts half gone, saying goodbye to you in a mist of red breath. And you, staying out of the way every damn time shells or bullets or bombs ripped through, finishing the war with but a sprained ankle, and when you look down and see Claudia with her head twisted back and wide, wet eyes gaping at eternity, you don't feel nothing except thinking how to reach and grab that squalling grandbaby.

The blood, pounding in your temples as you brace your lower body against the car and hang down inside to grab at the baby's leg, sticking out of the car seat y'all bought at the Sears in Columbia; a new safety bit they got going so's little ones can stay secure inside the metal petroleum bombs in which everybody trundles around. You lift and push her broken neck forward, heave to shove her small body out of the way and feel more than hear a rush of air out of dead lungs. Yes, you have seen it all and worse, but your gorge, still rising.

At last Roy Earl Pettus, upside down and crying, but in one piece. You can't get to him, though—her body is pinned. You need to wrench the door open wide enough to get leverage, and room, to work.

You holler and feel a hot rush of power, grab hold of the door frame that's bent inward and yank, but stuck solid. You ain't quitting, though. Your arm burning like fire, you heave and pull back with all a body ever had.

It works—the metal loses all mass and rips like paper from the hinges, the bulky Ford driver's side door now feather-light as you toss it aside to retrieve your grandbaby.

You draw him out and carry the car seat back up to the road, falling down and heaving for breath on the slick, bumpy macadam of the county road:

If I die now, Lord, I thank thee for giving me the strength to save this child.

Rolling onto your knees beside the car seat, you next ask forgiveness— for Claudia. For what you have wrought. For what you and your wife both have done with your wishes and hopes. You both ran her down so much— had run her off, trying to get him back.

And you literally killed her.

What version will you tell—to the police? To Runelle?

Oh, how you feel gut-shot until the baby hollers, and you comfort him standing on the shoulder of a country highway in the rainy dark by making a hex of healing and calm, three tiny crosses of your side-turned thumb over his squalling face, and a prayer of appreciation for his survival.

AFTER AN UNGODLY NUMBER OF HOURS PASS YOU'RE SITTING ON THE front porch with a hot towel around your shoulders, shivering and smoking cigarette after cigarette. Calming down. It started raining harder while you stood on the roadside with the ambulance and the wrecker and Sheriff Truluck. Gonna catch cold.

The story you told: y'all had a fight, the girl got wound up the way young'uns were these days; worried about the baby, you argued with Runelle before going after the mother of your grandchild. How you waited a few minutes.

"So you wasn't chasing her."

"Naw, beau. I come up, and—she was already off the road," trailing off and looking the Sheriff, a boy you know and who knows you well, dead in the eye. "Seen the taillights in the ditch."

"If this don't beat all. I swear to goodness." Truluck, removing his hat, had gone dew-eyed. "Y'all been through so much."

"My stomach dropped into my dick. All I can tell you."

The Sheriff of Edgewater County spat and cussed. "What a mess. Thank god the baby come out all right. I sure am sorry, Mr. Rabbit."

"He was hanging there, upside down."

"Bless his heart."

"I pulled the door off."

"Dang—by yourself?"

You can only shrug, and it hurts your shoulder to do so. "Stranger things."

"Reckon so. When a man's scared? He's capable of anything."

You go *mm-hm* and drive yourself over to the hospital to be with your wife and grandson, where the medics are checking the boy over to make sure he hasn't suffered any hidden fractures. That little, they can't tell you how much it hurts or if it did at all, not when one cries all the time, anyway. Thankfully, as two different people already tell you, Roy Earl shouldn't recall a durn thing about the awful night on the road.

The hope of this coming to pass gives you a hard point on which to pray —with your son and daughter-in-law dead, now your main task comes in hoping this baby never remembers the horrors of his mama's death, in a wrecked Mustang before his sweet, innocent little eyes. That, and raising him to manhood. A second chance.

As with all your other traumas, by the time 1970 rolls around you turn the page and move on with survival. It's the only way you know how to get by—forgive and forget, in this case your own sins and transgressions.

CAUGHMAN HOWARD SHULL

High achievement in law school now a *fait accompli*, C. Howard Shull stalked the campus of Southeastern University, his mind racing with facts and fantasies and the future, which would be his over which to lord like a master.

All the professors agreed—Howdy's intellect, razor-sharp. Not that anyone called him by his ridiculous childhood name. The moniker of a wooden puppet on the flickering cathode-ray screens by which all so entranced, never more than after the introduction of color. COLOR, the banner read hanging from that coarse gangster Sykes's appliance storefront downtown.

But facts, difficult to corral, in particular the notion of conjuring them from before their future arrival. Facts had to bloom like daisies in the otherwise green front yards of Whaley Way back home in Tillman Falls. Counseling young Jasper Glasscock, struggling through his first semester as an undergrad, the two of you sipping vending-machine coffee out of paper cups in the brand-new Law Center near the equally brand-new basketball arena Collegiate Coliseum, you advised that facts contained between the paperboard covers of volumes situated along library shelves could be set to use, but only through diligence and memorization strategies such as he'd learned from a mail-order course.

But the linearity of reading to retention, Shull cautioned the freshman, depended upon the vellum leaves containing the marks symbolizing the truth, and the receiving set of eyeballs. Jasper left the pep-talk looking less than enlightened, seemed out of place amidst the hustling law students burdened by bound texts big enough to choke an elephant.

Brushing off the rube from back home and his petty problems 'learning to study'—please—Howdy made his way to the Campus Club South, a former fire station a block behind the State House on Main Street. A beer, perhaps two, a night. His way of relaxing before evening studies.

Exposed beams, brick, a warm feeling inside the building, a sense of permanence, as though it'd always been a comfortable bar. While the Old Market to the east, Columbia's first suburban commercial corridor, had sprouted a number of watering holes catering to the growing legion of the collegian young, this old firehouse-turned-tavern had become the *de facto* hippie hangout closest to campus; its proximity to the law school also made it attractive to the chino-wearing button down set in addition to ethereal young women in gauzy tops and natural hair, and hirsute men smelling of exotic tobaccos.

Howard Shull, considering a career as a prosecutor, judge, State Senator, Governor, and Attorney General of the United States of America—and who knew from there—would handle those recalcitrant dopers. And far from shy about saying so, there in public and among them who'd disagree. This day ended up like many others, in a debate about the recent student marches and classroom walkouts, over the arrest of an activist for burning a Confederate flag on the State House grounds, and about the drugs, the drugs, the drugs.

The two hippies who argued with Howdy did so only up until a point, after which they backed down in sudden generosity and offered to buy a round.

Howdy, perceiving their magnanimous attitude a welcome turn of events, accepted the drink they procured and toasted to the university atmosphere, at which all intellects and points of view could be aired without fear of reprisal or consequences, and viva the good old USA for this fine state of being and discourse. An exultation and handshakes all around, longhairs and buzz-cuts alike.

Only later, after having two more drinks courtesy of the freaks, Howdy —floating on a crystalline alcohol buzz back to his car in the law school parking lot—became entranced by the wondrous, almost complete lack of twilight in the otherwise darkening night sky. Fireworks went off every direction he turned his head, silent color-bursts where should be only the faint scrim of lavender following the sunset.

Strolling and laughing along sidewalks transformed into rainbow carpets of undulating snake bodies pooling and curling around his ankles and legs, his wonder changed to fear to a status of consuming regret and disappointment at having lost the twilight.

His quest to recover the vision of violet heaven along the horizon he'd glimpsed would dominate the rest of Howdy's days, a journey on foot that began at a nightclub and ended thirty-seven miles away in Edgewater County late the next day.

After being picked up by a sheriff's deputy and taken to the hospital, only much, much later did Howdy Shull at last return to his family home on Whaley Way, where his mother and sister, no doubt concerned, awaited to receive and care for him. And where facts inside books awaiting wrangling.

RABBIT, BOB DYLAN, GEORGE WALLACE AND THE MAN IN BLACK

The tour bus farting diesel down Common Street has that look, fancy as all get out, you've seen outside the bigger shows over at the Township Auditorium. With Johnny Cash about to play the new basketball arena over in Columbia, you get a tingle along your spine, wonder what the heck this could be.

Your tingle turns out correct—damn if it isn't the man in black himself. Coming to see you-all. *Well: I'll be dog.* That's what you say, and so too everyone else when you tell them the story.

⦿ⓝ⊘

THE NIGHT THE STARS ARRIVE HAPPENS THE SAME DAY YOU INFORM Burnie, the Mayor and the rest how you'll be bumfuzzled before that strutting rooster George Wallace would use The Dixiana as a backdrop for his upcoming Edgewater County stump speech. That if there's to be music—country music like regular folks enjoyed hearing—the candidate could provide it himself outside on the green.

Old Man Glasscock's kid Jasper says he'll be honored to sing a few songs, if Governor Wallace were to have him. Reminds you how a bunch of country stars in Nashville have come out for Wallace.

"I always thought you and Burnie said what was good for Nashville was good for The Dixiana."

"That was a coon's age ago," you explained to the idealistic young man, a guitar slung across his belly every time you see him. "I don't want politics mixed up in this music. Bad enough my own wife listens to all that folkie mess."

"But Governor Wallace—he's gonna make sure we all don't get run over and forgot."

"Shit." You spat near Jasper's penny loafers and said you didn't care how they done it in Nashville or anywhere else but you ain't using the honkytonk as part of no political campaign. Everyone had got so hardhearted and obstinate about events that you couldn't get across, though. Nobody around this two-bit town thinks music is sacred the way you always have, and you's just against George Wallace. It ain't entirely untrue. Man like that will divide this country worse than it already is.

"All them politicos is the same. Talk one game, play another. You'll find out when you get older."

"I hope there's a South Carolina left for me to grow old in. One I'll recognize."

All you can do is laugh. These young'uns. No clue about the true dangers in the world, only repeating what some nimrod cooked up and spread around like verbal manure. A man's got to come to the truth on his own, though. You can't force it down nobody's throat. Jasper's young. He's got time.

❂◓⊘

YOU WONDER AT FIRST IF THIS BUS PULLING UP NOW AIN'T PART OF Wallace's entourage, in fact, but the rally on the town green, as close as you'd let them get to the honkytonk and no closer, ain't happening until tomorrow. If there's TV cameras, you hope they're pointed away from the neon sign.

A man in a cowboy hat and sport coat comes shambling out of the bus. You wait, smoking in the shadows by the bench.

"Say, pard. This your honkytonk?"

"Depends on how much I owe the man asking."

He laughs. "Nah—we heard about this place."

"Our reputation precedes us. From who?"

"Hawg Hickens. Said if we were rolling down to Columbia, we ought to stop and check it out."

Lighting a fresh smoke, offering one to the stranger: "Who's we?"

"Me and the folks here in the bus."

"Not much swinging in there tonight but the jukebox." Slow at The Dixiana these weeknights.

"Don't think they'll mind."

"Well—y'all come on in the house, I reckon."

When Johnny Cash and June Carter climb down off the bus with a beak-nosed longhair, you realize your old hole-in-the-wall joint must have more going for it than you thought.

Introductions, handshakes, questions all around. "Mighty pleasant to meet you," Johnny Cash says in that voice of his. "What do they call you?"

"Besides boss, it don't much matter. More names than I can count. But Rennie—hell. Folks call me Rabbit, to tell truth."

"Those other names they call you? That comes with success," he gravels with a wink up at the glowing neon sign. "Now let's see this stage of yours we heard so much about from Hawg."

It's a quiet and cool vibe as they amble into your honkytonk, take it all in; Faron Young on the jukebox, 'Live Fast, Love Hard, Die Young.' A few shitkickers at the bar; the smell of chicken frying, but few orders tonight other than takeout.

The longhair's reticent and tough to read as he checks out the 8x10s tacked up everywhere. The wrestlers like Gorgeous George catch his eye, in whose publicity shot he takes particular interest.

Meanwhile, the Man in Black stands in front of the small stage with arms akimbo, the few rednecks in the bar all gawking in silence.

The country music and television star says without turning, "If you don't mind, Mr. Rabbit, it might do me some good to play a room this size. Maybe we'll sing a couple of tunes?"

To this you say, well, nobody else on the bill tonight, and so they do. Johnny Cash, the one and only, is brought a guitar and sings a few numbers, his hippie friend sitting in a chair with his legs crossed, watching with June.

Now that you have your wits about you again, you hustle into the office to make a couple of calls—young Jasper Glasscock, the music obsessive; and home to your wife. But the phone rings. And rings.

Last to Burnie, and all Henny says is he's out "doing his thing," using the words of the young people. They're gonna miss out, is all you can tell her.

❂ ▣ ✎

Jasper arrives in time for a brief word with the superstars of music, but for the most part he stands tongue-tied and breathless—a young man, callow and impressed by masters of culture and music like these folks.

As they go to board the bus, you ask the man in the blazer and cowboy hat about the longhair.

He laughs at you and says, don't tell me you don't know who Bob Dylan is.

"No kidding—well. He don't look like he did on them records of his my wife's got at home."

"Listen—nobody's signing any LPs."

You snort. "I ain't asking, pardner."

Next thing, signed glossies of Johnny, June and Bob Dylan get handed to the man by a young woman who leans out of the bus doorway, and he grunts in mild embarrassment. "Well—I suppose these'll make up for it."

"Appreciate it. We'll find a place of honor to tack 'em up in yonder."

This Nashville manager type laughs at you. "You folks have seen it all here, haven't you?"

"Reckon we have now, anyway."

This'll be a good one, this story. You know it's a tale you'll tell and tell, or so you already figure. You won't hear nobody bigger than this sing from your stage, that much for sure.

Never cared much for Bob Dylan, though. You worried about him being a little commie. All them folk singers seem that way. You suspect you'll recall Dylan as but another audience member watching Johnny Cash sing, and clapping along with the few folks inside who got to see the miracle occur in person.

When Jasper later points out how Dylan went country and now sings on records with Johnny Cash, you reply, "That sounds better—rock & roll's bringing this country down. Everybody should've stuck with hillbilly music." And while you're not the only soul who feels this way, you might as well be.

Hell. Long as you're allowed to play what you want in your own place, anyone else can keep pouring piss into their ears all night, every night. From now until doomsday—until the twelfth of Never, for all you care.

JASPER GLASSCOCK AND
COY WANDO

A shaft of blazing sunlight beamed through the smoky gloom and fell across the stained and picked felt of the pool table on which Jasper Glasscock lined up what looked like a sure shot. Awash in the smell of broasting chicken for the dinner rush later, Jasper thought he'd take Coy Wando for a sawbuck, drink another'n. Maybe write a set of lyrics. Call it a poem.

He dropped the thirteen, tumbling orange over white into the corner cup. Nudged his cue indicating the side pocket, lined up the eleven.

Coy cussed him bloody. "You ain't gonna make the cut on that."

"Watch if I don't." He made it, but missed on a bank shot to drop the eight to wrap up the rack.

Coy started chalking up and going heh-heh-heh in that snaky, greasy way of his. Five solid balls on the table, three of them clustered, said to Jasper he still had that ten bucks in the bag. And if not, double or nothing on another rack. Coy dropped the blue two and the red five, but cussed as the one, yellow and bright, sat tucked behind the shiny black depths of Jasper's eight.

Fulfilling as this gamesmanship might appear, Jasper needed to head back to work, though. Serving papers. Later, looking into a thing. If you'd told his teenage self he'd be twenty-five but still drinking and shooting pool in the middle of the day at the honkytonk, Jasper, why, he'd've told you to kiss his foot. He'd be writing songs in Nashville. Surely. Nope.

Bad enough Letty had made him major in criminal justice, pushing him to think about law school. Pushing pushing pushing. He wished she'd keep to baking and being his big sister, which in her mind gave her many rights Jasper did not believe carried over to other such sibling-type relationships. For all he knew.

Duwayne Driggers, the daytime bartender, nodded at Jasper and ducked out from behind the bar and out the loading dock door, probably to go do himself a J, since Rabbit wasn't here today, not as rare now that his grandbaby was old enough to take fishing. In the early years the honkytonk held hootenannies out back and where once, as he had heard tell, deliveries of dry goods were unloaded, in the days of the Dixie-Anna grocer. Young enough to have only-just missed the days of the hoots, and hearing Mama Runelle sing onstage too, a veritable legend around town, made Jasper rue being born too late. You could keep the 1970s—malaise, indeed, as our peanut farming president would put it. All in for Jimmy Carter, though. Boy had already proposed decriminalizing grass. Sign me up.

Jasper would love to join Duwayne out back. But after putting on a tie and dealing with folks at the courthouse and lawyers and insurance claims adjusters, even tailing a wayward spouse like he'd be up to later, he swore he'd give up smoking dope. Since coming back home from school—for good, it seemed—he'd done PI work for Blanding MacDougal, which allowed the fat sum-bitch to sit behind his desk more and get fatter, far as he could see. In any case, time to forget youthful collegiate experimentation and grow up, as his sister kept saying whenever Jasper brought up childhood avocations, like picking on the guitar and writing country songs.

Look where dope had gotten Howdy Shull. A wreck. He'd been into more, though, than burning a stick of Mexican ditch weed. Town mythology held that Howdy conducted massive LSD parties as some kind of guru on the Southeastern campus back, including one that got out of control for its host. All this happened not long after the protest riots and the coffee house sit-ins that peaked in May. The sixties, in other words, finally arrived in sleepy old South Carolina. At least it only took until 1970.

In any case, Howard Shull, a first year law student, allegedly ingested an extra-crispy dose of a substance unknown, suffered himself a helluva good time from which he never came back from 'the other side,' as he would mumble in explanation out of the side of his mouth when Jasper would see him wandering around downtown, or along the shaded residential blocks of Whaley Way, sometimes as far as the river highway. Poor Howdy's mother, back to feeding him his meals, no more law school.

A drooling idiot, Howdy almost made the propaganda about drugs seem credible. He now spent his days the hair corkscrewed like he never looked into a mirror, always with his nose in a book Jasper doubted the acid casualty understood. Howdy, always drinking a twenty-ounce soda, one of the new bottles, much better than those heavy glass ones. But to Jasper, soda didn't offer the same pop when served out of plastic. Nothing like capping one of those little Cokes on a hot day and tipping it back.

Duwayne craned his skinny neck out of the back door at the end of the bar, having himself a hushed conversation. With the restaurant side under control—meaning quiet as church here at mid-day—and no drinking customers but Jasper and Coy, the bartender eased out and the heavy door thumped behind him.

Coy, with a second wind, talked shit and tried to sneak the one from behind the eight, but all he managed was to line up a winning shot for Jasper.

"That's better. Appreciate it, Coy." Sipped his Natural Light; chalked his cue. "Reckon I'll put this to bed, now."

"Well, shit. You best get on with it."

Coy, redneck as the days were getting long, talked like he come wandering out of a holler in Arkansas, which according to him was pretty much his background, so there you go. Had moved around a good bit throughout the sixties—all the way to California before the Army got him, but he had lucked out by knowing how to type and ended up in Germany for his service filing invoices and documents in the stockroom of the PX. Got caught running a racket, did two years in the stockade besides his tour.

"Like everything we got going ain't some kind of racket," he said in finishing off the story the first time Jasper heard it. Quite a character.

Sure enough, Coy suggested a chance at double or nothing.

"Maybe. You ain't going back to work today?"

Coy, an Adam's apple as big as his nose and a face scaly with eczema, worked part time at a machine shop near Hampton Motors, close to where they'd started clearing pine trees for the long-promised bypass to skirt traffic around downtown Tillman Falls. The old Pisgette Forest Highway had been a dogleg route people coming down I-26 could use to work their way east toward Myrtle Beach without going through Columbia. Makes the trip quicker, less congestion for residents at all times.

"Mr. Hampton give me the rest of the week off."

"Must be nice."

"Ain't like it's vacation pay. Not enough work right now."

"Oh—sorry."

Coy, short and dangerous, squinted down his nose. "You ain't done nothing to be sorry for. Save that sentiment for the day you really need it."

Merchants like Lucinda and Rabbit and Burnie Sykes had all put up a fuss over the bypass, saying it would take traffic away from downtown and hurt business, but councilmen like Hiram Hampton and Congressman Mauldin Saugus, the first black House representative from South Carolina since Reconstruction, and who had gotten the federal money for the project, held more sway. The four-lane bypass would encourage industry to locate here. Loading docks could ship goods east and west to the two different interstate highways within a half hour of each other. Subdivisions. Schools. Couldn't get past needing highways. Reasoned arguments, as Jasper reckoned.

But despite shooting pool with him, he didn't much like Coy Wando. Didn't cotton to how he talked about women—all he seemed to care about was running down to Columbia to the XXX drive-in on Two Notch Road. What had times come to?

Jasper, spending so much of his life as a boy with good country folks like Runelle and Rabbit, held sensibilities that came offended with the way the world had gotten. He felt the urge to write about these feelings, to look for creative fulfillment through poetry or perhaps one day writing a novel, a literary note 'Pure and Easy' as The Who sang. Jasper had seen Townshend and crew play in the Omni on the 1975 tour. Eighteen months later, his ears still rang.

Nothing would ever top the Atlanta Pop Festival back in '70, though, the Southern Woodstock Jasper attended during the summer of his first year at Southeastern University, right as Howdy was getting his brain fried. The Allman Brothers, Hendrix—helluva wild scene. Jasper loved music—all kinds—and the energy he felt in the crowd from the amplified guitars had been one of the most extraordinary sensations he'd ever experienced. Music —WABA playing country songs, Mama Runelle sitting on her porch warbling folk songs, and later, yeah, the power of rock stars from Jasper's record player, singing their hearts out. It got to him. Gave him goosepimples, a good solid song did. An impassioned reading. Pithy and cutting poetry for lyrics. High art. Music.

Jasper would rather play and sing, write poems or even books, or anything but serve papers and sneak around following people.

Law school. Letty was right, and that's what he was working toward. But otherwise, thinking of getting into bail bonds for a while instead of this PI mess. Seeing the sordid side of life these days more than he wished.

SPEAKING OF 'SORDID' AND OF ROCK & ROLL, LAST NIGHT THE DIXIANA had been at its rowdiest. If its rafters were ears, they'd still be ringing from them outlaw fellas from the upstate who tore up the stage, and their fans did the same to each other—a big ass brawl, one spilling out onto the back porch, with deputies called to break it up. The band, a bunch of bad-asses looking to follow in Marshall Tucker's footsteps, got pissed at the commotion and played louder.

During the day, serving up barbecue and burgers and dogs on the restaurant side, you'd never know the mess going on at night. Especially upstairs. Such was never discussed in the light of morning, not by anybody. No one with good sense, anyway.

As for the music, The Dixiana had been an important stop on that road for quite a few names. Hell, the Allmans played here, back working the Florida-Georgia-South Carolina chitlin circuit before they blew up, and when Burnie had talked Rabbit into having younger bands and rock music; same with the Marshall Tucker boys from over in Spartanburg. And you had a few living legends pass through like Jasper once met, but everybody's heard that story. Hard to believe, but yeah: he was there. "Shake the hand that shook the hand" of Johnny Cash and Bob Dylan, as he would tell skeptical first-time listeners. "It's all true."

The headshot and promo photos framed and hung proved the historicity of the joint, though Jasper had been shocked to learn how so many of the oldest pictures were bought in bulk by Burnie at Colony Records, on a trip to New York City he and his bride Henny had taken in 1953 to celebrate their tenth anniversary—the same year, Rabbit explained, him and his pal cooked up this crazy idea to open the honkytonk.

Jesus, the stories Rabbit and Burnie could tell.

And, Lord, but Jasper loved this old barn. But he had to get moving on something besides a beer-buzz and another rack.

"I c'ain't shoot no more. I'll take more of your money another time."

"Suit yourself. Pussy not to give a man a chance at getting his money back. But I ain't gonna hold it against you." Coy handed Jasper a ten-dollar bill damp like a used snot rag.

"Damn boy. That's raw."

"Can't help how my butt sweats into this cloth wallet. This humidity y'all got here about to ruin me."

"You one nasty old hillbilly, Coy."

"Ain't never claimed to be anything else."

Duwayne came back in, counting money he slipped into the register. Jasper went to get a beer for the road while Coy wandered over to the front window, watching as a pickup with a load of whooping high schoolers roared around from Common Street to head north out of town.

"Look at them titties bouncing." Coy, smoking and working his Adam's apple. "God-a-mighty."

After reassessing the one-more question, Jasper asked Duwayne for another round. "What you got working back yonder?"

Duwayne capped an icy bottle, slid it over. He'd been a few years ahead in school, a football player with a big helmet of curly brown hair and a mustache and a chain around his neck; a lover of women. He checked himself in the big Budweiser mirror behind the bar more than the ladies in the powder room. "None-ya. Taking a breather."

"Looked profitable."

"So did taking Wando's money," Duwayne said loud enough for Coy to hear.

Coy, a Marlboro tucked into the corner of his thin-lipped mouth, flipped him off and kept gazing out the front door after the kids in the truck.

"Rabbit's gonna skin you alive for selling out the back to underage."

Duwayne snorted. "Them's seniors. Boy that paid's eighteen. Girls was under, but they don't matter."

"Oh. The girls matter."

Duwayne laughed and slapped five with Jasper. "For a few things, yeah. Believe me, old Rabbit'll care more about moving a case of beer than who it was to. Especially a bunch of shavetails cutting school to run up to the high bluffs to drink and screw."

"The bluffs near Parsons Hollow?" *Holler*, as he pronounced it. Coy, intrigued. "Sounds like a lotta trouble just to party."

Duwayne wiped down the bar top with a rag that stunk of sour sugar. "You couldn't get to them granite bluffs as easy before they cut the new power line road. Now it ain't nothing to wander up yonder."

"Well-sir, one day soon I'll have to go check that out." Coy counted out more of his damp money while Duwayne rang up the tab. The bartender left the limp bills out to dry.

Belching light beer, Jasper ambled back to the poor table. He ought to work instead of drinking another day-brew, but fuck it. And if it wasn't tailing and process serving for MacDougal, Jasper didn't know what else he ought to be doing. Or what he could sing or writing about, either. Lying in a ditch trying to get pictures of unfaithful redneck spouses parking outside houses they weren't supposed to be. He figured there might be poetry in all that somewhere.

It'd come to him. You couldn't make money writing anyway, though, and Letty, she pushed him to be level-headed about a career and a future. His sister, more right than wrong; a grudging admission. In the couple of years since he bailed on law school, started smoking dope and seen the light about his politics and worldview, this transformation and lack of ambition had not suited her one bit. Letty had liked him better as a Dixiecrat than a liberal, for starters.

"You read much, Coy?"

Wando snapped his pool cue into the rack on the wall. "You mean like the Bible?"

"More like novels. Poetry. That shit."

"I take a gander at the paper. Scan the obituaries. Why?"

Jasper, racking his cue next to Coy's. "Thinking about writing a book one day."

"About what?"

"Before? It seemed like whatever come along. But nothing would stick."

"And now?"

"More I think about it? Maybe this old barn."

Wando snorted and shoved a greasy Allstate Auto Parts ball cap onto his pointed head, jug ears sticking out like red signal flags. "Ain't nothing worth saying about this dump."

"If only these pictures could talk. Then we'd have ourselves a story."

"Tell you what," Coy said. "I'm-a give you a story to write, boy. Already have. You'll find out. And when I'm ready to declare my truth, I'm-a say to them I want you, Jasper Glasscock, to write it up. Deal?"

Jasper started to answer 'I reckon', but for the life of him hadn't a clue what narrative he could shape around a redneck machine-shop employee, nor the identity of 'them' to which he referred. But Coy, in a hurry, left with no further elucidation other than the jangling of the bells in his wake.

Duwayne sneered at the wet money on the bar. "That nasty motherfucker's crazy. Hate to see his ass come through the door."

"I don't know what the hell he thinks he's done that's worth writing a book about. I'd call that delusional."

"Wando's a bullshit artist. Unless you ain't figured that out yet."

"Sometimes I'm a little slow on the uptake. I reckon."

DuWayne cleaned under a grungy thumbnail with the same toothpick he stuck back into the corner of his mouth. "It's going around."

A woman smelling of a fresh perm from the beauty parlor came bustling in to order broasted chicken and burger baskets, a whole mess of them for a Wednesday night church function. While she waited, she enjoyed herself a cold one, went to buy a pack of smokes and drop a few coins in the jukebox. Soon Waylon Jennings mused aloud whether Hank Williams really done it this way. And Jasper wondered right along with him.

MANNY THEODORE AND HIS
COUSIN LATRICIA

His cousin visiting the Desire projects from up in Baton Rouge, Latricia, with booty and boobies all week long, she walk into his room right as Manny changing out his basketball shorts. Buck naked but for jersey, which ain't long. Ain't long enough, anyway.

Shut the door behind her. Standing, smiling.

Manny holler, "Go on, now."

"I thought this was the bathroom."

"Well, it ain't." Manny heart like it beating up inside his head. She so pretty and all. She like a grownup.

Latricia go, "Manny, move them hands."

"Nuh-uh."

"Let me see it."

"No. Go on, now." But that thing moved Manny hands out the way all on its own.

"Oh, mercy—your granddaddy must-a made sure on you, son."

"What that mean?" Manny can't catch his breath. Now his heart beat down in his dick, too, and it stand up and he can't hide it but he try. "About my granddaddy."

She smile, looking all up under her eyelids like a movie star on a magazine cover. "It mean you got a nice one, son."

Manny, shaking like he cold, shrug and say, it all good.

She says, "Don't tell grandmama nothing about this. And don't you holler out, neither."

Manny stomach drop into his feet. "*What you gonna do.*"

"Look here. Let me see something."

That tube now harder than concrete. A burning inside. He try to hide his excitement. "Don't—don't touch it!"

"Hush." A finger to her lips, whispering. She push against his chest. "Lay down, son, and I teach you a trick."

"What kind-a trick."

"You ain't know what it for, yet?"

Manny not understand why it stand up, but he hear at George Washington Carver Middle School that you mess around with it inside a girl, but it don't make no sense to Manny. He tell her what he think you do, but all that do is make her laugh so hard she slap her knee.

"You a trip. Now lay still." She thumped against it real soft. "Lord—you got a brick."

Manny's head go all funny. He can't find no words.

"See the grease leaking out?"

"Uh-huh?"

"That the stuff. Start of it, anyway." She rub it all around—now the tip real slick.

His breath—he try to speak, but it gone.

"Watch what happen now." She start tickling.

Oh, gracious—Manny almost float off the bed. Fore he know it his first jism bubble up, a thick glob, and the burning move through and out of him in a way he couldn't describe to no one if they asked. Manny can't help but holler.

"*What going on in yonder?*" His grandmama, calling from the living room.

"We just rasslin', Gramma Theodore," Latricia yell. She laugh and stick out her tongue at Manny. "That all we doing."

"*You best not hurt my littlest grandbaby.*"

Their mutual granny turn the afternoon stories back up. Manny hear her blowing her nose. She do it all the time. She say these projects all got mold growing inside from Hurricane Betsy, which Manny don't remember cause it from before he was born, the same storm that blowed down all the trees used to be near the buildings. A long time done passed for mold to still be around. Desire ain't no good place. Manny gonna get out one day, get on one of the trains along them tracks that run down one side of the projects. Go and see what else exist besides this place.

For now, Manny lay and feel at peace. He don't understand nothing. He love his cousin, though. That much he know.

But she ain't love him. All she do is wipe her hand off on his sheets. "You promise not to tell nobody, and I tickle it one more time for you while I'm here."

"We cousins."

"Aw, ain't nothing but a game." She lean down and plant a kiss, making that mess twitch like it about to go again. "You gonna make all the girls happy."

After that day and the next, y'all, Manny love women in a different way. His cousin, she change him. Now? He pulling at that thing like there ain't no tomorrow.

BURNHAM SYKES

Hell of a note having to meet with them snakes and vipers down at Pike's, and before dinner. Sunday morning, always the time for that crew to settle accounts, some damn tradition like antichurch.

No—it was like actual church. Only a different brand of tithing.

And not unlike them hypocrite Baptists—one thing you never do is acknowledge another Baptist in line at the liquor store, or out at Mama Beaudock's, and not a chance around the gaming tables upstairs at The Dixiana—Rembert's coffers, Burnie Sykes suspects, sit right full of lucre.

Burnie's coffers? Not so much. Not with the bite Rembert the Lessor be taking.

Asshole had heard that Burnie called him that. It'd gotten back to him. Good. That'd been the idea. That pipsqueak, looking poured into that suit of his and strutting around the way Runelle complained about Ralph Stanley, like a preening, midget rooster in love with every mirror he runs across. But the acting boss now, and not yet forty. It didn't seem time yet to pass the mantle.

On another anxious note, the letter of his son's he finally read had chilled him to the bone.

Buddy'd told him some hellacious stories about Vietnam, but luckily for him, as he always said, he didn't have any primary experience, not being the man carrying around The Bomb in case Nixon took a notion to use it, and end that mess like Burnie knew he could have, if he'd wanted.

The epistle his boy had wrote, though, and which he said only to read in case he got sick one day (but of course Burnie read it anyway) laid out a helluva story of having some big ball-busting ordnance at hand, but not using it. Why Nixon let them boys die, fifty-thousand of them, when we could have fried their yellow asses but-good was beyond Burnie.

His son Buddy seemed more worried about handling them nuclear shells and what might happen to him from it. Burnie said p'shaw. They wouldn't let American boys handle materiel that didn't have the proper safety checks. In the Air Corps they had done it that way, anyway. Burnie was sure his son's hifalutin top-secret unit and commanders stayed safe as kittens. Too much at stake. If they went to the trouble of doing all that human reliability testing that Buddy had gone through, they wouldn't just expose them fellas to radiation. Every swinging dick among them would-a been sick as dogs from moment one.

Burnie, cussing and pissed, had burned the letter, but only after assuring his son he'd put it in the safe deposit box where it would sit unread. If any misfortune befell his only child, them young'uns of Buddy's didn't need to read no anti-government mess like that. It might change how they felt about their daddy.

◌◍⊘

GOING INTO PIKE'S, NODDING AND TRUDGING PAST THE MAN HIMSELF working some poor bum out of his money over a grease-spattered Harley with a rebuilt engine, Burnie knew he had trouble. He owed too much to too many people, the appliance business was getting sucked up by Circuit City over in Dentsville, and times under Carter wasn't what they used to be. Gas alone was about killing everything. He had swore he wouldn't ever pay over thirty-five cents a gallon, and look at him now. For a business called Pike's Bait & Pawn, the whole property smelled like the gasoline from the pumps and the oil lubed back in the garage bay.

But the price of gas wasn't the problem — Rabbit, having had enough of running the blue trade at the honkytonk.

He'd get away with pulling the plug, too. The Hillbilly, as Burnie had always thought of his erstwhile business partner, wasn't into Burnie Sykes the way he'd been in the past. Not after twenty-two years, all the money they had run through there. For a time, the upstairs at The Dixiana felt like the local hall of congress. Nothing happened in Edgewater County, legal and otherwise, that didn't have a thread running through those rooms of men who gathered in relative secret. Many debts paid, and currently, Reynolds Pettus occupied a far more stable, and safe, position than he'd ever known in his life.

One agreement left between them, though, a sole proviso Burnie amended to the separation ritual Rabbit invoked: should he renovate The Dixiana in the future, to leave untouched the sacred mural painted alongside so petitioners on Redtails game days could continue to pay tribute and seek its blessed betting energy.

The Hillbilly grumbled about that part. Negotiated a detail, that the mural would never get repainted or retouched; would fade away into obscurity, seen and pondered by the next generation, or however long it lasted before turning to powder. Same way he treated the round hexes affixed above the stage and front door, on his house in the woods, too. Burnie knew it was old country magic, but you didn't talk about such matters aloud. Lips pressed together and guts tightened even at the semi-mentioning of the mural's power and mystery.

This agreement, however, had been between Rabbit and the lodge elders, which included Burnie. But whatever debts held only between them, the old friends, were long dissolved. The Dixiana property deed, as it always had, held Pettus's name. And now a guest for certain at what he'd always thought of as his own god-durn honkytonk.

A customer? Christ-Jesus. What had it all come to?

Being into Rembert now represented only part of the shitty Sykes financial picture. He'd come to terms with selling the lake house on Jensen's Pond. Owed money all over town. And yet, pulled a sign and drive off Hampton's dealership asphalt last week in the very Olds 88 in which he'd rolled over to Pike's, driving and smoking and scheming about how much more cash he could raise to settle last season's Redtails gaming losses and get straight for an autumn full of those beloved football Saturday afternoons. His season tickets had come only last week. The dues were in arrears for the Redtail Century Club, however. Polite phone calls, along with a letter suggesting his premiere parking spot in the stadium's shadow might be in jeopardy, lit a fire under his ass to get squared away. He did well betting with his guy in Atlanta on the Braves all summer long. He had that going for him.

It was never enough.

And never would be.

He didn't let himself think about that. Not with food on the table, booze in the gut.

No one but him knew how bad it looked on paper. How little liquidity. How down the stocks. Henny, bless her, she didn't understand money or much of anything else. They had not made love since the change came over her. Burnie had been paying for it more often than ever. That didn't help the bottom line.

Thank god the mortgage on Whaley Way, the first, anyway, was paid up. Asian as they might look, he had grandbabies to care about—their future.

Business would come back. There'd be some new doodad men like Burnie Sykes could sell in his stores. It was competing on price that was killing him. People burned up their expensive petrol all day long to go to Columbia to pay less for a washer or cabinet TV or Hi-Fi gear.

So he always ran the side deals with Rembert on the poker machines and the games at The Dixiana, but now they had moved over to Pike's, where Thurmond's expansion into the pawn trade had, at the behest of the lodge members, included a build-out for meeting rooms. From the outside, the back area appeared as a standard metal prefab warehouse, but inside? Finished like a proper gentleman's club, including small bedrooms with sinks and other built-ins.

Whispers on the wind already blowing in from being the Hillbilly's best friend and hearing the warnings and subtext he'd been dropping, Rabbit stood up one Saturday night and called for everyone's attention to announce his 'privilege of refusal', a term Burnie had given him which said, if you ever need out of the upstairs deal once the debts are square, you may invoke the clause. And so he did, using certain terms with which no one of initiated stature could credibly resist or argue over without risking grave censure.

Instead, them tough old birds all went misty-eyed. The air in The Dixiana's VIP lounge went dead and cold. Just like that, powerful hombres afraid of nothing and no one stubbed out cigarettes, doffed hats, bit the inside of their cheeks, cleared their throats and cussed in that quiet, futile manner folks did when the inevitable end of an era had come calling.

The lodge to which Reynolds Pettus belonged without being a true signatory—a fellow traveler—gave dispensation to Burnie to negotiate this opt-out for his friend long ago, and instigated only on his part because of Runelle's feelings about the blue rooms and the trade within. And so, the time drew nigh, and at last she came to him on her own and declared, I am pressuring my husband and now you to extricate my family and its business from the doings of men like Jezmund Rembert.

Imagine saying no to her. He couldn't. Burnie did what the songbird wanted.

And her reason? "Roy Earl's getting too big, now. He's going to realize soon about the business his granddaddy allows upstairs at that honkytonk. Maybe it's too late already."

His heart, touched. "Moving it off reservation ain't gonna be favorable to my wallet, girl."

"Too damn bad."

Wasn't no arguing with Runelle Pettus any further. Burnie would make do.

He had told Rabbit about this conversation, to which he said, yep; she'd been on him about the Roy Earl problem, too. He didn't want to hide his work from his boy. Didn't want The Dixiana seen in Roy Earl's eyes as anything but a place of music, some of Rabbit's hoodoo horseshit about being true to original intentions. All of which, Burnie figured, was also Rabbit's way of saying, now I done paid you back many times over. And that's that.

He remembered standing on the street corner that first night they switched on the neon sign, waiting for the sun to go down far enough; how the green and orange letters glowed against the cool purple of the twilit sky, casting its big-city light on downtown and feeling like all futures were shining, new and possible. The curved corner of the building, the upstairs with the faux-balconies and wrought iron making it look like New Orleans on that corner, where before an ordinary boring old mercantile—what a joint they created, known as much for the pulled pork and chicken as the honkytonk aspect.

Burnie always cajoled Rabbit in whatever direction he needed—it was how Burnie worked people. Not that he didn't love them. But he saw the world different from most—that you had to work to gain control of folks's thoughts and actions around you to get what you deserved and wanted. He burned with love and sympathy for Reynolds, his best friend, in particular over Ronnie Ed—Burnie's boy had come back, and his friend's hadn't. But Buddy, he hadn't been infantry. But he still wasn't above using his friend, either. Thinking it all through gave him snakes in the gut.

❋

Mercy, but Burnie felt for Rabbit and Runelle, having to raise their baby's baby while grieving too, grief for both of them. Not so much for that little piece of hillbilly trash Claudia Ballahack that Ronald Edward knocked up before shipping out. But then, he knew Reynolds wept over that young woman for all his own reasons. Runelle, too.

Not that any of them talked about what happened, especially not ten—eleven—years later. For what? That-which-must-not-be-uttered-aloud was an Edgewater County way of life. Maybe it's like that everywhere. But Burnie Sykes only understood about here and now.

He had to help his old buddy with that special grandbaby, though, and if part of it was getting The Dixiana cleaned up, which needed to happen now and then anyway when the sheriff's office turned over, Burnie held a moral obligation to do so.

And as for his debts, Rembert could strut and peck at the ground and talk his talk, but Burnie was an elder of the town, now, the way Josiah Rembert had been. Rembert's boy would listen, would take no for an answer, and would learn his place in the pecking order of things. Oldest guy in the room always called the shots. It was a rule. Used it a thousand times on Rabbit. Used it to get his way. Employed many mind tricks on people—Henny, Rabbit, Runelle, customers. The great unspoken lesson—how to make them do what you want.

Wasn't magic, though. It came from wheeling and dealing to sell folks on big-ticket items, which took talking. And tricking. The numbers did most of the work. The rest went on charm.

And tenacity, like Reverend Duson Mire and them damn street preachers standing every Friday night hollering outside The Dixiana, as though the sound of their shrill voices talking the God's gospel would ever change the real world on which Burnie stood. Get real, he would shout back at them, while Rabbit stood stoic and smoking, occasionally making his subtle crossing gesture with his thumb, the one he thinks nobody ever notices. The dumb hillbilly and his cracker superstitions, like those round hexes painted everywhere. Rabbit was a hoot. No question.

◦ ▣ ◦

HE CARRIED HIS WHOLE FAMILY IN THE SUBURBAN HE'D BOUGHT TO FERRY them all—Buddy, Tinky, Thim and new baby Button, sitting in the back silent and looking at her stack of Little Golden Books they toted around to keep her busy, keep her from making noise and getting impatient and bored. Bumping down the long dirt driveway through the crepe myrtles he helped Reynolds plant, Burnie mused that boredom appeared to be his littlest grandbaby's biggest issue over hunger, thirst, fatigue, sorrow or grief. Strange little girl.

Thim always seemed so outgoing and smart, and nobody much worried about her—she was five going on thirty-five, to hear her talk. Button, though? Never said anything, which didn't seem right.

They had her checked for being retarded, deaf, all of it. "She just quiet baby," her mother Tinky insisted, forever peeved about Henny and Burnie sticking their beaks into her maternal business. Wasn't anyone else to do it —Buddy, off working at the plant ten, twelve hours a day. Pursuing his trade.

Buddy made good money, for which his father was thankful. He didn't have to worry about his boy and the girls. But Henny, such a need to have cash in the bank—she remembered going hungry back in the Depression as did Burnham Sykes, thank you very much—kept him in a state of urgency. Not to mention having cars moving through the used lot, and tenants paying their goddurn godforsaken rent. One day he would gentrify Mayfield Acres. Get the trash out of there, and turn that trailer park into a real subdivision. The way Columbia kept creeping north, he'd find a developer to buy the property and do it themselves.

No work. Only cashing checks.

That was retirement. Burnie, a young man, still. Far as it went.

Hell, he proved his vigor out at Mamie Beaudock's every time he could afford it. Ask anyone. He felt certain his high-hard-one enjoyed a well-deserved rep among the Beaudock girls.

Shit. Not even getting laid sounded all that good anymore. Hated to own up to the sentiment. But there it was. A drink or three with his elbows on Rabbit's bar took care of what ailed him. Maybe he'd stay away from the joint, though. Make some new routines, like he did for a spell years ago over that business with Runelle. All a misunderstanding.

Inside at Pike's, Burnie went through the pawn shop and into the PRIVATE door beside the office, hanging out in the refreshment room on the couches and waiting for Rembert and the others to work out the details. Pike needed to put in two taps for kegs, one blonde and one ale, that much for sure. These pine-panel walls, tables and chairs didn't hold enough sparkle and personality as the good old Dixiana. But where else could? Heavy drinking would dull the pain.

◎ ▥ ⊘

BURNIE TALKED OVER MOVING THE GAMES AND OTHER TRADE OUT OF THE Dixiana with young J. W. in the honkytonk that next Sunday morning,

Rabbit in the office snoring on the couch while Rembert played that Kristofferson record, a tradition at these little sabbath day settle-ups.

Having been up all night on a couple of rails of cocaine Burnie did every so often when the games ran late, him and Rembert sat down along the sticky bar from the last night's rowdy crowd, both nursing headaches, smoking and drinking fountain Cokes.

"Here's the prob," Burnie said, ginning up to explain himself. "The man wants it gone, and Rennie done paid me up long ago. He's square."

Rembert, musing, not arguing. A thug and a gangster, but fair-minded and a follower of codes. Held respect for Rabbit he didn't for Burnie, that much obvious. So in that light Jez said, well, inside these walls what Pettus says goes.

"Gonna miss the atmosphere. A town tradition just died."

"Nothing lasts."

"Nothing? We'll see about that."

At that moment Rabbit Pettus snored from the office, like a wounded, otherworldly beast. Burnie and Jezmund could but laugh. "Poor Mama Runelle," he said.

Burnie's laugh dried up. "Yes-sir. You should hear her tell about his bad dreams."

"What—like a little kid?"

Burnie told Rembert to hush up. "From the war. His unit come onto one of them death camps."

The Edgewater gangster scion's eyelids fluttered. "God-dog, beau. You're shitting me."

Burnie said Nuh-uh. "If I told you what he told me, your hair would turn white."

"Poor old Mr. Rabbit." Chewed his lip. "What happened?"

After Burnie swore him to secrecy, he shared the horrors his friend had with him, about the ghostly prisoners, and the troops executing lots of German soldiers in retribution.

"My service wasn't nothing like that. I was fucking whores and dropping ordnance on Jap ships, a cakewalk compared to Europe. Bless his heart."

For the first time he'd ever seen, the hardness disappeared from the tough guy's eyes. His face looked soft and doughy. These kids ain't been through nothing, as Rabbit and Burnie would often say of Rembert's generation, even with Vietnam. His daddy had gotten him out of the draft, the way men of influence did for their sons.

The hardness returned, and he made a bunch of threats and high-talk about stories staying straight and the numbers working out for everyone under any new rubrics. Rembert, a crazy short temper at some point bound to blow back on him. Had beat hell out of people over little stuff like back-talking, or delivering unwelcome news.

Or so the stories went. Burnie, one of the people telling the tales and thinking of J. W.'s daddy, himself a mean, scary son of a snake, one like a hard, bitter apple off his daddy's black-hearted tree, if he could mix a metaphor to two for emphasis.

Burnie, glancing around at the dusty stage, the dance floor, the tables with all the chairs piled on top, all of it alien in the white light of early morning. The Patsy Cline oil painting he commissioned for the bar. For Runelle in particular. But for the good-old Dixiana, too, and the spirit of real country music. A shadow of its former self these days. Not much happening.

"Oh hell, Burnie—I know what this is really about."

"Do tell."

"The ELMS squeezing your balls. And his."

"Nothing new under the sun there."

"Ain't no thing. We can run our games anywhere there's a locked door. Made it convenient being located here on the green. Didn't it?"

"Ain't the ELMS. It's because of the grandbaby."

"That fat little shit?"

Burnie tried to explain. None of it came out right.

Rembert eyed him with mild disgust. "You soft-hearted geezers. Whatever."

"You know how grandmamas are. They spoil them."

"Don't remind me." Jez sipped a weak Bloody Mary he mixed for himself, made a face. "Wish Etna was here. Get the grill going and fry a pile of eggs and links."

"I can wake up Rabbit. He's got bacon. No sausage."

Belching, he waved away the suggestion. "Let me see about this last game."

Pausing at the door to the upstairs, the criminal, hard as shoe leather, sniffled at the sentiment he'd let slip out. "Damn. Feels historic today. Don't it?"

Burnie reckoned it did.

But Pike's made sense. More—and he hated saying it—than running a club out of the back part of his own appliance store, though it had more room in what used to be the jam-packed warehouse.

He wandered out to drink in the morning air, clear his pounding head. He sat with his legs hanging off the concrete 'back porch,' the scene of so many Friday night jamborees. Those were the days. Mercy, but a long time ago. So much had changed.

Lord, but he suffered murderous debt. Hoped for a quick sell on the lake house. Them girls of his—the little ones—will be disappointed as hell. Maybe he could mortgage the—mortgage the—shit.

Hell. Forget it. Another time. Burnie had run poker games for twenty years or longer, but his debt to Josiah Rembert, and now his ass-wipe son, would never be paid all the way. Not like Rabbit made Burnie whole—this was an honorarium, 'protection' money, after a fashion. Like in some gangster movie. Redneck gangsters. Nothing new under the sun.

He supposed, all things considered, that he ought to be glad to have protection.

Rembert ambled out onto the loading dock from the days of the mercantile and said well-look-here. "Mr. Burnie? Here's the news. I don't need you to run this trade for me. I got other guys. You fellas—Rabbit, The Dixiana, the old-timers—you're all right. Laid the stones in the path. But it's time to forge new agreements, new blood. Just like you had with Pettus."

Knew it was coming. Nothing to be done. "You know how long this has been my game?"

Rembert didn't have any reaction but to laugh. "Come up with me and watch these guys play out. One more time. If it's all over—is it?"

Burnie, hesitating and working his lips like a crappie caught out of the river. Until he drew a finger across his throat. "I got to do what Rabbit wants. It's his place."

Rembert, nodding. I can respect that, his face said. "Good run here. Hope he can keep it going."

"Don't see why he won't."

"Old buzzard. You're like Heckle and Jeckle, the two of you."

"Two wisecracking old birds? I reckon so."

"Birds I'd like to take a shot at, sometimes."

"You and everyone else."

The easy banter said that all was simpatico. And Burnie Sykes could walk away from the encounter to get on with his life. Do good, instead of all this underground crap. Wore on you after a certain amount of time. He could see it all worried his best friend ever since the day it'd begun, all the way back at the beginning. Time to let go. The magic of all that cash flowing through hands had lost its allure.

No, it hadn't. It was about to stop flowing. That's the part Burnie would miss.

AT THE PETTUS COOKOUT BURNIE WENT OVER TO ROY EARL, SITTING BY himself at a picnic table with his back to your little squirt Button, looking at her book with not a care or sound or emotion to offer the world. Rembert's crack about Burnie's little godson being fat had been rolling around in his head. A boy needed to be slim and slender and out running around. Runelle fed him too much candy and sweets, but it wasn't his place to say anything.

"Roy Earl, I have a proposition for you."

His eyes got big. "Yes sir?"

"What do you think about baseball?"

He chewed and thought about it. "I reckon it's all right."

"Now, I don't mean sitting in the air conditioning, watching the World Series on that nice color Zenith we set y'all up with a couple Christmases ago." Rabbit said how concerned they were with the time Roy Earl spent in front of that TV instead of out playing like boys should. "I'm talking about the team Sykes Electronics sponsors."

Roy Earl started bouncing his knee. Put down his burger dripping with ketchup and mustard, slurped his Co-cola and belched. "Nuh-uh. I don't want to."

"Now, son, don't say that. You ought to give it a try."

"But I don't like — baseball."

"It's my team. Uncle Burnie will watch out for you. Like he always does."

Something about all that made Roy Earl's face turn red. "I don't need no one to watch out for me."

"Well — good. *Good*, boy. That's what I want to hear. Stand up for yourself."

"I don't want to play baseball."

Burnie sighed. If only this little shit-ass knew the trouble and personal expense he was putting himself through for him. "All right. Sleep on it tonight. And hit the ball around. You and Thimmy and little Button-Button. Y'all go and play — but after your lunch settles."

Watching the boy wobble away, Burnie nodded and decided he would talk to Sherm Wrightson. Maybe the boy'd be comfortable coached from outside the family, playing on Gray-Peele and competing against Uncle Burnie's team. Would make Roy Earl feel more independent. Toughen him up, throwing in with a bunch of turds who don't give a rip about him — almost like going into the service. Not that the Pettuses would let him do that. They'd rather him turn out a swish than send another one to die overseas.

Satisfied, Burnie stood over with the grownups talking about Carter and the oil sheiks and the whole mess that it was, and inflation, and gas, and money, and it all damn near made him want to puke. No—money worries give him the urge to drink his fill.

Only beers for now, at the cookout. A taste of stronger measures later. No way did he want Henny, his grandchildren or anyone else to see him tippling-drunk during the day. That's what vagrants and wastrels did with themselves, not town fathers like Burnham Sykes.

ROY EARL PETTUS

The cookout before you move over to Columbia to go to Southeastern, as you keep telling yourself, will be the last time you put up with this ceremony, ritual, and down-home Southern-family foolishness. As soon as you can get away you're going drinking with Devin and Dobbs to celebrate being finished with Edgewater County, and your matriculation to the illustrious state college at the heart of the capitol city. You've been celebrating all summer, in fact.

Your Pa-paw's playing scratchy old blues 78s through the outdoor speaker, the wires for which you helped run after he showed you how to use the trenching tool. He's had a few beers, singing along with Elmore James and Big Mama Thornton and tapping the foot of his work boot. He told you about when pickers would come on Sundays for these cookouts, and they'd have themselves a regular hootenanny. Made it all seem like a thousand years ago. Now? Only recordings left from those days, all those players gone one way or another.

Records? Those are fine with you, long as we're talking Led Zeppelin instead of that country crap.

And this rural family shit, it's for the birds.

You have outgrown it all.

Damn them.

A MAGIC HOUR SCENE, THIS COOKOUT, LIKE ALL THE FAMILY AND FRIENDS gathered at the airport at the end of *American Graffiti* to see Richard Dreyfuss off for college 'back East,' an exotic notion to your small town South Carolina brain. To you, an 'old' movie fifteen years later, in 1987. You couldn't have been but four when it played the Palmetto Grande, watching it between your loving grandparents, your view blocked each time they passed the popcorn.

Still, you remembered the plane taking off and Dreyfuss looking down at the ethereal dream girl in the white car—how she glimmered, a photographic technique appearing like magic to a child's eyes.

More memorable, the little yearbook faces of the actors popping up one by one with the text you could not read, only scrutinize the murmurs and gasps of the audience. Only knew that your grandfather exclaimed, Well, I'll be shit, and it wasn't like him to cuss. And how your granny, Mama Runelle, whispered in grief, "Poor Toad. Poor, poor boy."

The sniffles and looks between them outside on the sidewalk—grim. You had never seen your folks this raw.

You asked later, and when your grandmother wasn't around your Pa-paw explained in his gentle way that the pictures before the crawl of *American Graffiti* told how two of the boys were killed later on, after the end—in the movie's future, as he struggled to explain. One of them, he said clearing his throat, went missing in the Vietnam war. Choked up talking about a fake person missing in a war. Confusing.

Now, you realize they were in the grip of anxiety over the day they'd have to tell you what happened to your daddy and mother, which didn't occur for another year or two.

You don't understand why you must go through this cookout nonsense —your are mostly grown now. By your age, Pa-paw had been in the army for two years, overseas in Panama first and later heading off to land on D-Day in the third wave. But they couldn't stand for you to drive to Columbia by yourself, still.

As for the rest gathered to fete you, other than Uncle Burnie you don't much care for the Sykes family, except sexy little Thim. You've watched her blossom from a gangly adolescent dork with braces into a gorgeous, gamine teenage girl sporting elegant Asian features, jet black hair, a body like a master sculptor's view of the ideal female form, skin flawless and creamy. She made you want to explode in your shorts, watching her and her horrid creature of a sister fix their burgers from the condiment table. You keep pressing and flipping meat on the grill. That's your job, and your granddaddy has high expectations.

"Got to know how to keep the customers happy," he always says, and Rabbit Pettus's barbecue, chicken and hot dogs at The Dixiana being known far and wide must mean he's right.

You suppose he's justified in making you grill-man at these gatherings, even your own darn send-off to college down in Columbia—the man sweats over roasting meat all week long. Lunch trade keeps the honkytonk going, he often says. "Shitkickers drink the beer and there's good money there, but that lunch pop makes our nut. You make it however you can, Roy."

Sounded obscene.

You didn't know why he was so full of life lessons about running that crappy honkytonk. You would not have shit to do with all that—like, as soon as you and Devin and Dobbs piled into your truck and moved the stuff over to the dorm-suite you'd all got in together, you are done. No one could compel you to have forced family fun.

That made your Mee-maw so happy, you having your friends instead of strangers with whom to live while away at college. She had threatened to make you drive back and forth as a commuting student. She said, I just don't know if you're ready, son.

You always wanted to say, who cares what you know; I ain't even your son, you crusty old crone.

How you would sit and gaze at your mother's high school senior portrait, along with the one of your Daddy in his uniform; the familiar, grainy, fading snapshots of what looked like the same cookout, only twenty years earlier and with all the men sporting mid-60s Carolina crew cuts. One shot of your father, leaning back onto the polished hood of his Mustang and laughing, his bare feet kicked up, always so peculiar and poignant—a surfeit of sparkling life on display, a life begetting your own, yet one you'd never know with intimacy. The hollow silence of his frozen exuberance haunts you.

One day when you were fifteen, the stains on his dirty soles in the image jumped out at you. Edgewater County river clay. You glanced to your own fat, unshod feet crossed underneath you to discover a similar reddish cast, stubby toes, wide but with narrow heels. You had to try on for an hour to find the right pair of sneakers thanks to such triangular feet.

A gushing rush of shock—your father's feet were your own.

You threw down the photo album, suffered an extended crying jag unlike any since the time you faked a nuclear meltdown to get out of playing Dixie Youth baseball. Nobody had been in the house, thank god. You would not have found words to explain this reaction to a picture you'd gazed upon hundreds of times in the past.

Maybe you hadn't a mother and father at all; Mee-maw and Pa-paw

found you under a cabbage leaf. Felt that way most of the time. Like they—
or you—were from another freaking planet, man. Old people. You don't
know how to act around actual folks your age. Adults, they'd always said
how mature you seemed. Trudy Pirkle, for one. For all the good her attention did. A doubled-edged sword.

❂ ▩ ⊘

EARLIER IN THE DAY AMIDST THEM BOTH HOVERING AND FRETTING, THE
stress of preparing to move caused you to blurt how you disliked being
doted over by your grandmother, how much you despised Edgewater
County and detested The Dixiana, and couldn't wait to see it close or else
get run out of business by a new owner offering class and decent music.

All this vitriol came hateful of tone, and in response? Your granddaddy
had sputtered and pounded the table and said he'd be damned if you'd ever
own the place, not bad-talking it the way you done, and you replied the hell
you would want it, anyway. Half the time at night it wasn't nothing but a
biker bar, now, with the music onstage more rock than country. Rabbit said
his hearing was gone from the racket, but oh-well: no rest for the owner, not
when there's beer awaiting sale.

Mama Runelle, cussing and making you feel kicked in the gut. Dabbing
at her eyes. "Sometimes you act like you don't love us no more."

"That ain't what I said. It ain't got nothing to do with 'y'all'."

Your granddaddy's face looks carved out of stone. He's hurt. "I should-a
known you's gonna turn out like this."

"Why you say that, Pa-paw?"

"Because your Daddy, rest his soul, had him a mean streak, too—always
talking down to us. Like we ain't nothing but country folk who ain't got
good sense. You ain't got the first clue what it's took to keep that barn
running, that honkytonk you hate so much. And keep a roof over all three of
our heads. Worst, though, you made your grandmother cry, Roy Earl. That
don't seem wrong to you?"

Humiliated and put in your place. The tears begin to well. It cannot
happen. Your crying problem, a persistent issue akin to another adolescent's
bed-wetting, drove your granddaddy to distraction, and required discipline
and concealment to manage.

His jowls shaking: "It's like there's a cloud in the room whenever we're
all together. So, I'm-a gonna be honest with you. Unlike your grandmother,
who your smart-ass hears in yonder blowing her nose into a wadded up
Kleenex, I think you going down to Southeastern, and living in Columbia,

and taking care of yourself, and cleaning, and living—seeing how it feels to live—will be good."

Cracking voice: "I know what it's like to live. You had me working since I was twelve. Swabbing out your durn toilets."

"Yes-sir. You've worked like the lowest man—the shit-scrubber. That means you're always gonna strive to do better than that. See?"

You did, suddenly. In a way you hadn't—before, it'd all been punishment —but now you could perceive the wisdom. You read *The Lords of Discipline* in your senior year study hall and felt thankful you weren't shipping off to 'Carolina Military Institute.' You can see in an instant that you're seasoned; you've survived your grandfather's boot camp. Or at least, you understand a version of this.

A strange sensation of forward-leaning deja vu seems to show you will turn all this over in your mind many times, a golden ratio of repeating considerations of the past, until it either all makes sense or becomes so small as to be unseeable with normal vision or insight. Dizzy, you feel stoned like on that good pot Dobbs bought during the week at Myrtle Beach, when you drank until you puked, smoked dope, sniffed a line of supposed cocaine doing little for you except make your sinuses burn and itch. Tried to talk to girls, here and there, but got nowhere fast. Embarrassed yourself a few times. Glad your memories were fuzzy.

A hug offered to your grandmother, who weeps and says she knows you didn't mean to hurt their feelings.

"I'm just stressed about going off to school. That's all." A lie.

"A boy's got to become a man in the way he thinks he ought to, and what his grandparents think don't matter too much," Pa-paw says to you in a further speech about bygones and not worrying, a long and loving oration you appreciate, that clears the fog in the room of your earlier spiteful remarks. He wishes you could look at his old Dixiana different. But you don't; and so it ain't that way. And that's that.

"Now tell her you're sorry, and that you didn't mean none of it."

"Yes, sir." With great sincerity.

She seems to forgive you when you tell her—for what seems like the first time, or else ever of your own accord, you realize—how much you love her, your voice trembling and trying to hold it together. "You're my mother, Mee-maw. You and Pa-paw's the only parents I've ever known. I'll never hurt y'all again. I promise."

That makes her cry harder, which makes you cry, and your Pa-paw to say, 'Shit' and amble onto his porch to sit and smoke. Your grandparents, their generation, they keep all that emotion inside. They show feelings but don't talk about them, describe the consequences in the manner you have.

It's like your grandmother explained about Pa-paw's unwillingness to discuss his wartime experiences. "He can't talk about that, son. It hurts too much. The only time he talks about those days is in his dreams, and when he does, he starts to hollering. So don't ask him no more." You hadn't, not for years.

The gray cloudy energy among you all now dispelled, Mama Runelle went back to fussing with the suitcase and cartons of toiletries and food you'd be taking with you to school.

◌◧⊘

"LET'S GET MOVING, MEAT-BOY," DEVIN WHISPERS IN YOUR EAR, startling you into dropping the spatula on the greasy black grill. "I want meat in my mouth."

Hot as hell—who wants to cook out in August? Your granddaddy, that's who. "So I read on the bathroom wall about you. Relax—I got to finish this grillwork first."

Devin, musing. "Told Uncle Rabbit I wanted him to roast a whole pig to pick on today, but he said, no sir, too much trouble. 'I'll just get my grand-baby to boy-scout us up some mystery meat burgers instead'."

"And here we are."

A cloud of beer wafts on Devin's breath. Earlier he stashed a cooler of Coors in your truck, but you turned one down—you didn't want Mee-maw smelling it on you. With a bloodhound of a nose she seemed capable of detecting scents at a hundred yards, never failing to report on any specific suspicions.

After getting high with Dobbs one day after school you also shared a Winston Light, which another kid told y'all was a good way to cover up the dope-smell. Nobody will give you grief over smoking a cigarette. Except your conscience—you swore up and down you'd never start (and didn't, not exactly), but that one day you puffed on one and she could smell it on you from across the room.

But you have an out: She asked if you'd been down at The Dixiana.

You say no, you hadn't. The truth.

"Then why, young man, do you stink like one of your Pa-paw's dirty ashtrays?"

High and self-conscious, you had stammered about standing with Devin Rucker while he had smoked.

"Just like his mama—lord, but that Eileen sucks on them things like there's no tomorrow. Don't tell me you going down that road too, son. Ask your granddaddy—once you start, you won't never be able to put them down."

You knew she was right, so the next time you got high you gnawed on a mouthful of bubble gum, two sugary chunks of grape Bubble Yum®, before going home.

That old lady ain't right about much, but smoking, you can get on board with her attitude. You cannot stand the stench from riding in the truck with Pa-paw, or being inside that god-awful shithole of a honkytonk. Mercy, but once you move onto campus, you hope Devin and Dobbs won't start puffing any more than they already do. Drinking, that you can handle. Within reason. Eff the cigs, though.

And eff this hot grill, too, which you announce is closed. You've seared all the flesh, more than anyone could eat, and which you and your buddies would take with you on your drive over the next morning, a Monday filled by getting settled alongside your best buds, on a new adventure—a rung up the ladder to adult freedom. Applause rings out from the gathered adults and family members, the Sykes girls, the cousins from your grandmother's side and your granddaddy's folks, too, as your Uncle Burnie makes a toast about the future and hope and youth. You don't feel as though you knew any of them as intimates.

But truthfully, inside you know you only lack what Devin has attained with his characteristic confidence and ease: female companionship with his girl Libby Meade. Libby, a gorgeous flower who moved to Tillman Falls in ninth grade, and which he'd plucked before you ever got a semblance of a chance, and who'd be living right across the street in her own dorm. Your friend had it all.

You try to figure out how he manages it—you'd been conducting such analysis since middle school. Devin. A cool cat. A wild man. Too much like the drunk rednecks at the honkytonk. But Devin, also deep. Not afraid of anything. At fourteen, he'd pulled a drowned man out of a pool at the country club.

Hell, in that circle jerk? That time? He'd been able to shoot off like, not only the farthest, but with the most ease, and when you, with your self consciousness and embarrassment, hadn't finished at all. Devin knew tricks and secrets you didn't—he was the leader of your little ersatz scout troop, then as now.

Nothing the same once Libby came along, though. Then she'd become his best friend instead of you. You supposed it happened that way with couples. Best friends with benefits. Sounded sweet as honey wine.

You just didn't have your Libby. Not yet.

God, but you'd love to give it to Devin's little sister Chelsea. Yowza. Long legs and freckles, blue eyes. Too young—you were going to college. Plenty of tail—Redtails tail—down in the big town. Like, starting tonight.

You sit eating with your misty-eyed grandparents watching you gnaw your burger, the last one cooked, and feeling on display at the various faces smiling your way.

The summer, ending as it began: a cookout, the one three months ago to celebrate graduation, followed by the crazy trip to Myrtle Beach with the boys for first-week; and here now the going-away gathering, which felt the same as every other backyard cookout amidst the tall skinny pines, with the hilly river-land sloping down from the property into the dense woods toward the Glade in which you went and sat by yourself earlier in the morning, when you told your Mee-maw you wanted to go for one final stroll before you finished packing.

In the Glade, you sat. Not to read or meditate like some hippy guru with a long beard. To be still for a few moments and remember, for what you thought the last time, all the ills and unpleasant identity nonsense you've made a pact with yourself to leave behind. For keeps. By driving your truck down the freeway to college tomorrow, all of thirty miles away, your world will start turning right. A first step, at least. And taking one is all it requires to get somewhere.

❁ ⊞ ⊘

AFTER THE COOKOUT YOU AND DEVIN PICK UP DOBBS FROM HIS CRUMMY house and sad situation, mom still a wreck after his Dad left, and his sister gone off to California and now only the two of them. Soon only one— Dobbs, leaving his mom for the dorm-suite.

You drive your granddaddy's blue two-tone Ford pickup—your truck, as you ought to think of it now—while Devin futzes around, not in the cooler of beer that you hid from prying eyes under a tarp, but in his backpack. Dobbs, crammed in the middle, complaining that you smell like the grill from the cookout, which embarrasses you. Eighteen, a college man, and still getting picked on. When would it end?

Devin produces with a flourish a liter of high octane vodka, good stuff like you'd never serve at a craphouse like The Dixiana. "Look at this blue ribbon ethanol here, bro."

"Damn—Smirnoff Silver?"

"Only the best."

Dobbs, riding bitch in the middle: "Colorless, almost odorless. Good call."

Devin cracked the seal and to your amazement gurgled the bottle, bubbling it once, twice, three times. A madman—straight liquor after drinking beer for several hours?

"Shit, beau."

"What?" He hands the bottle to Dobbs, who sips and coughs.

"You're both gonna puke."

"Bullshit." Devin, his words strangulated and eyes watering, issues an order. "Get me one of those brews."

At a stop sign, you reach through the back sliding window and grab an icy cold Coors. You had employed your Uncle Burnie's trick for icing down beer—put it in the cooler first thing in the morning, pack it down with ice, and then sprinkle rock salt on top—and indeed, the golden can felt so cold it hurt your hand.

"Here." Devin trades you the vodka for the Coors, cracking it open and guzzling. "Phew. Needed that chaser."

"I'll pass." Last time you drank vodka with Devin, you'd gotten sick as a dog. "I'll just drive you madmen around."

"A gentleman and a scholar. But don't be a pussy. Here, at least one nip."

"Nah, man."

"'Nah, man.'" Devin, mocking.

Always such a smart ass.

Driving the back roads in the western part of the county you nurse a beer while Devin and Dobbs get drunker and louder, shouting bullshit at each other and throwing trash out of the truck, which pisses you off, but you don't say anything.

Finally, you've had enough. More than half the Smirnoff, guzzled. Ridiculous—they would suffer hangovers tomorrow for the move, the most important morning of your lives.

Devin, belligerent: "Take us to the boat landing. I wanna watch the sunset and see if there's any pussy around."

"Skeeters this time of year down there." Dobbs, wrinkling his nose and belching. "But yeah—pussy, too. Right on. I'll be sure to tell Libby."

Devin cackles and winks. "Sounds like a real swell plan."

Now all the way out in the Pisgette National Forest, you cut a U-turn in the road and head back toward town and the river beyond, avoiding the bypass where patrolmen often lurk behind bridge abutments.

AT THE BOAT LANDING YOU FIND A FEW OTHER PICKUPS AND MUSCLE CARS with high school kids partying, local yokels as Devin calls them with provincial disdain, as though the three of you aren't local as sin.

Devin, drunker than shit. Gurgling the vodka, staggering over to the carload of jocks. Expansive, drunk and gregarious, he forges fast friendship with them, sharing the 'Russian potato water,' as he keeps shouting about the vodka.

Dobbs, too, sits potted like a houseplant and gazing at the jocks. One of them, Rutledge Newborn, a rich kid and pretty boy; the homecoming king type, if not the actual one, last year if memory served. You have seen him naked, Newborn and other jocks when you suffered through phys-ed. Him and every other muscled jock had looked like they were in their twenties to you, with dorks like elephant trunks flopping around.

"I'd like to suck his cock." Dobbs, as though nudged by your passing thought of wet jock penises, if for his own reasons. "Yes, I would."

Thanks to a semi-cranked stereo, AC/DC 'For Those About to Rock,' you're the only one to hear. An aside. "Well, I ain't gonna go ask for you."

Dobbs blinks into lucidity. "I was bullshitting." Panicking. "Wait—what *did* I just say?"

"A joke. Whatever."

Slurring and folding his arms. "You know when I'm messing around. I mean, really."

"I do. And it's okay."

"Those fucking jocks are gonna finish the rest of the vodka. Devin's a little shit."

You tell him, it's okay. You've all had enough. It's true.

The inevitable occurs: Devin, foolish, takes a slug of Jack Daniels another dude has been passing around. You can see it sticking in his craw, and he starts coughing.

"Here we go."

Devin staggers over to the river's edge and becomes ill. Violent. Heaving. Heaving. Heaving. At last he falls back into a fugue state of dribbling and moaning, his eyes crossed, hands, face and clothing splotchy with river mud. A circle of teens, girls and guys, guffawing and having a time over the spectacle.

The jocks take pity and assist you and Dobbs in dragging him up the bank into the back of your truck, where you slide your buddy between the various boxes you've already packed and lashed down with moldy cargo straps older than any of you.

Dobbs, tender, crawls up and slides a pile of greasy rags under the side of Devin's slack face, which makes him awaken and blurt, "Smells sharp like your mama's pussy—haw haw haw," and everyone laughs along with him, two of the jocks slapping five.

"Well, that sounds like him. He'll be fine." You thank Newborn and the others.

"You dorks are all right," he says, punching you hard in the bicep and leading his fellows back down to their own party.

With Devin now slobbering, incoherent and finally still in the truck bed, by the time you get to Pine Haven, the nice subdivision in Chilton where the Ruckers live, you're worried your friend will die.

Dobbs leans out the beer window to check. "He's breathing. But, turn around. Take us to my house instead."

"You sure? What about your mom?"

Dobbs, scrunching his mouth and calculating a scheme. "She'll be asleep. Here's what. I'll call and tell his folks he's drunk again, and got sick."

"Duh."

Snaps his fingers, a loose gesture lacking the 'snap' part. "I know—I'll say it was those meathead jocks who gave us the liquor—they tricked us and said it was white wine. And so—and so—he'll sleep it off in my bed." He nods over at you as though answering a question, albeit one you haven't verbalized. "It's a queen-size. Plenty of room. But, I won't tell anyone we were with you."

"You won't? I can't get into trouble tonight. Tomorrow's too important."

"Tell me something I don't know." A flash of clarity. "Damn. We're fucked up. This was stupid."

You drop them off at Dobbs's, both leading Devin down the cracked sidewalk in the old mill village with puke all down his shirt. He mumbles a soliloquy about Libby, nonsense and drama about how he's no good for her, better off without him, he's a bad penny, he's like the Death card in a Tarot deck, stuff you don't even understand. You've heard this talk before. It's creepy in the moment, but also because he never seems to remember a shred of it.

Dobbs says to lay him down on the lush grass on the side where the leaky hosepipe coil hangs dripping, where he'll rinse him off best he can. Your other best friend, barely capable of standing himself, now.

You should help, but know what? Time to bail. It all seems like high school foolishness, and you are college men. A drinking bacchanalia to come, of this you're sure, but sufficient for now. Let's at least get out of Edgewater County.

You tell Dobbs a version, but fading into stumbling incoherence like Devin, he can only babble and fuss over Devin, now sitting up and shaking his head from being hit with cold hosepipe water. He'll be aces in the morning.

Time to split the scene, man. You have fish in need of frying—finishing packing the pickup, avoiding your grandparents, and so on. A new life awaits in the off-world colonies. No time to waste. On the drive home you chew three pieces of gum, air out the truck, pray she won't detect any forbidden scents.

◎⊞⊘

LATER THAT NIGHT DEVIN'S MOTHER, EILEEN RUCKER AND AN OFFICER of the ELMS, calls Mama Runelle and cusses her to the moon. Says Dobbs reported how they 'rode around' with you all evening, leaving Devin so inebriated that he nearly died, had to be taken to the hospital.

Your grandmother, pale and angry, rushes into your room as you're packing the last odds and ends to report what's been said. "Your Pa-paw's gonna have a thrombo over this, son."

You explain that after the cookout you picked up Dobbs, and they wanted to go to the boat landing to talk to girls but with only jocks partying there? You left your friends with those guys you didn't know too good, those football jocks.

"Sorry to hear about him. Devin's a hard drinker. I hope he can still move in tomorrow."

"Well, those boys got him into some-kind-of-trouble this time, I tell you. I told his mother that you came home sober as a judge."

You shrug. "I wouldn't lie."

"I know, sweetheart." Her eyes well up. "I can't believe it's here, for you to be going off to college. Oh, me—if them dumb-asses still had the mill going, all you fellas could get good jobs and wouldn't need to go away to school. You could stay here with us. Build a little house over yonder across the drive. If you asked him, your Pa-paw would do it for you in a heartbeat."

You tell her that sounds like a great idea but too bad, Gray-Peele's kaput.

She takes a moment to press an envelope in your hand—cash she produces out of a pocket of the baggy sweater she wears around the house, even in the summertime. A wad of wrinkled money, some of the bills looking faded.

"Pa-paw's already got my checking account set up."

"I know, darling. But take this and put it somewhere safe. That's your extra. Always have a little squirreled away for later. Slip this in the pocket inside your suitcase. Forget it's there. And one day when you need it, you'll have some folding money waiting."

❋ ❋ ❋

ONE AFTERNOON A FEW WEEKS AFTER MOVING IN TOGETHER, YOU HEARD a ruckus coming from Devin's bedroom, one of four narrow single-student cubbyholes upstairs with a shared bathroom, living room and kitchen below, a 'suite' as the dorm catalog called the aging, paint-peeling apartment house built in the 1940s.

You rushed out and flung open his door only to interrupt Devin and Libby amid vigorous and joyful intercourse, which made him furious and her suspicious and embarrassed.

She shouted, "How many times are you gonna do this to us, you creep?"

Yep. It happened before, back during the crazy Sun-fun Week. That time, you stumbled drunk and high into that cheap room at the Pirate's Bay Inn there on Ocean Boulevard, fumbling through the door right as they both cried out in orgasm, Libby's tanned legs wrapped around Devin's midsection, her toes curling. In the dorm incident, she had been on top grinding away, her buttocks pale and lined like the little girl in the suntan lotion ad. Both times it appeared their bodies and spirits were communing into one. A sacred and beautiful act. That your presence had now profaned twice.

Your main takeaway? Having enjoyed a taste with Trudy, you had to grow up, get older fast. Show her you weren't sixteen anymore. Have that connection again. You'd never gotten over her.

How you craved Libby and Devin's relationship. Not the climax. Not to give a woman pleasure or experience it yourself—no. The ineffable linkage they shared, too. During the sex you observed true communion between their spirits, literal and energetic—your friends had been glowing, a ball of light in the beach hotel and in the dorm room. You swear you saw it. But really, you saw it in their everyday interactions as well. Best friends, too.

Yeah. The right girl. The right time. You stated the intention every morning, a routine like shaving.

❋ ❋ ❋

AFTER SLOGGING THROUGH MIDTERMS YOUR FIRST SEMESTER, YOU'VE settled into a groove—you have this college nonsense well in hand.

Now, though, you recall words of wisdom from Uncle Burnie, back at the going-away cookout for you and your buddies: focus on your studies, and if you need more pocket change than your skinflint granddaddy parcels out, only then should you get yourself a 'piddly-ass' part-time gig like in high school.

To make sure his advice stuck, he even put some folding green in your hand—walked his talk. Burnie: not a blood uncle, but good as one. Better than most, for all you know.

Not that your grandparents don't take care of you. They do. The 'skin-flint' dig? That's part of the banter between the lifelong friends, Burnie and your granddaddy. You can cite chapter and verse. The only fathers you knew.

Working for Pa-paw, now, that'd been hard. Not mopping up after rednecks, or helping behind the bar—putting up with him riding you like a mean boss instead of your loving granddaddy. Not to mention working the bar. Sure. You, a kid, popping the caps off longnecks and serving them right up. Who would come into Rabbit's place and tell him he couldn't have his grandson helping out with the family business? Nobody in their right mind. Sheriff Truluck would sit his fat ass at the booth over by the back door to the secret poker rooms upstairs and watch you pour beer, which was all The Dixiana served in those days, not even mini-bottles yet—South Carolina's liquor laws remained draconian well into the 1970s. And yet, you, underage and pulling a tap for the Sheriff. That's Edgewater County—it makes its own rules.

"Look here, Roy Earl," he'd say. "Not so much head, now." And put a dollar bill in your hand, his heavy, golden lodge ring cold against your fingers.

And, oh, the first time the sardonic Mr. Sortwell issued you a proper paycheck. All the folding money your granddaddy had given you for mopping up the bathrooms and sweeping off the floors and the sidewalk and taking the trash out, that never seemed like wages. You were his grandson— you had to do it. That's what Mama Runelle always said when you complained to her about having to work at The Dixiana, and so the check held a different connotation. Here now were actual verified, validated, consecrated Social Security wages.

"They got ya, kid," Mr. Sortwell said as he passed over the paycheck and shaking his head.

"Who?"

"Government's always gonna take their slice now, boy. You'll see."

You kept a Xerox of that first pitiful little check for one training shift—$16.26 after deductions.

Sixteen by then, still stupidly halfway in love with Chesnee two freaking years later while watching her date a series of absolute goons. But taxation or not, working for real wages assuaged your loneliness. Enduring much of the same toil as at The Dixiana, sure, including sweeping and trash detail and serving, but more legit. Employment at the Palmetto Grande had been as transporting for you as the movies themselves, the pictures that swept you into their fanciful storylines and exotic milieus.

With all this mind and in need of cash, you strategize about inquiring at one of the multiplexes—a paycheck, along with free screenings. The pitch? Thanks to Mr. Sortwell, and your folks for dragging to one movie after another, you know the theatrical exhibition business cold. That's what you'll say in your interview.

DRIVING OUT TO THE MULTIPLEX AT THE OLD MALL NORTHWEST OF THE city, you wonder if you didn't love movies because of the effect *American Graffiti* had on its audience at that indelible screening from your late toddlerhood. All during the film everyone had been laughing so much—you too, though you couldn't understand what was funny, not at four.

But the energy turned so melancholy as the audience shuffled out of the theater to the happy peppy Beach Boys song. Anytime you hear that xylophone intro, it still gives you chicken-skin like nobody's business.

Movies had to end.

The boys had died.

Death was the last cookout.

Bummer.

Flickers on a wall—powerful. Conjurers of emotion.

No wonder you had gone to work for Mr. Sortwell at the Palmetto Grande. You hung out at the theater so much, he finally said that I might as well pay you. Those were 80s movies, though. Not as rich and important as the ones you saw as a little kid. They were getting sillier, now.

As modern pictures also seemed to Mr. Sortwell, at least once *Star Wars* happened. Norrie Sortwell, the kind of film fan who had pictures of cowboy stars framed in his office. But he wasn't having any of that argument that George Lucas's epic saga is only a Western set in space, an idea you read in some movie magazine.

"All little kid crap, that space stuff. Flash Gordon? You kiddin' me? Gimme a good film noir. A tragic romance. Or yeah, a decent oater. Men on horseback, taming the wild country."

You had had to ask what he meant by film noir. He told you about it, suggested a few. Cool old black and white movies about betrayal and murder and mystery, perhaps best seen now, he said, on late night TV.

At this memory you experience only a mild twinge at the intention to seek employment at one of the shoebox corporate mall theaters killing the old houses like the Grande, that dingy, curtained two-hundred seater so close to your heart. Man had to make ends meet, though. God knew you understood that. Had been taught as much by your granddaddy, and by Burnie, both owning businesses and understanding about the capitalistic ways and means of the world.

◌ ▨ ⊘

YOU PULL THE FARTING, HUMILIATING ANCIENT PICKUP YOU 'INHERITED' into the half-empty daytime parking lot. The marquee of eight movie titles looms back by the entrance and positioned on a slight rise to be seen from the expressway. You recall your quaint days of standing on a rickety wooden ladder and clomping heavy, translucent letters the color and opacity of grape-flavored cough drops onto the rails of the Grande's by-comparison minuscule marquee, but only after the last showing of the outgoing feature had begun.

Sortwell considering the timing of this sacred ritual a matter of mystical juju or karma. "Not a second before the last run's underway," he insisted, "do you change those titles. And I don't mean the trailers—only after the last patron's seated and the feature underway. No sooner."

"What might happen?"

"Bad luck. You'll have a flop weekend. Or worse, like your old lady leaving you for the first dude with a bigger schlong. Mark my words."

The mall interior smacks you in the face with smooth jazz muzak and a sickening fragrance from the *Taper & Tealight* candle vendor. You present yourself to a pale, slender box office cashier, striking eyes but way too skinny, a papery, unhealthy countenance perhaps from being trapped within a box inside a mall all day. With a nod of her head she sends you upstairs through a nondescript door that says Employees Only, which gooses your adrenaline.

As you ascend the stairwell you anticipate the clatter of projectors, but hear only a faint swishing sound. At the top you squint down the endless, long booth necessary to serve so many screens and find eight state-of-the-art platter systems running far quieter than the old 50s-era projector Mr. Sortwell still uses at the Grande. These projectors, which you read about in the NATO magazines your old boss keeps around his office, allow for one large reel to spool out for the length of the program. The old system, actually a pair of projectors side by side, required a manual changeover between film reels.

Seeing it before you eyes, you get the necessity of the platters: with eight houses running, a multiplex would require a swarm of projectionists changing over reels at the cigarette burn-marks, like you sometimes did at the Grande. This way, a single worker could manage the running of all auditoriums. Genius. If you could only automate the rest of it, you wouldn't need a projectionist at all. Now that would save on payroll.

At the top of the dim stairwell you wait as instructed, your hands resting on the cold metal rail, the faint babble of the movie unspooling in the first auditorium tickling at your ears. Standing on tiptoes you can see through the tiny window that it's *John Carpenter's 'They Live'*, which you have seen and liked. The scene of Rowdy Roddy and Keith David fighting for so long seems incongruous and over the top, though, and you noticed it so much it must have a deeper meaning than only as an action sequence. Maybe if you're hired here, you will make a second look at *John Carpenter's They Live* the first of the many free movies you'll screen.

A door opens and light leeches into the projection booth. A silhouette, Hank Halvorsin, manager of the multiplex and in his early 30s, whispers a greeting, grabs you and leads you down a narrow hallway running parallel to the booth. Officious and hurried and quiet, he sits you down in his office, where you find you're surrounded by framed one-sheets of the biggest hits of the last few years. Posters—your new boss loves them, too. A kindred spirit.

Looking over the application, Halvorsin expresses a modicum of duly-impressed. Prefacing his speech with a disclaimer—*working in 'exhibition' as you have, you must know this already, but here goes anyway*—he expounds upon the overall guest experience:

"It's the movies themselves, sure. But more: it's about how much the guest enjoys the ancillary aspects of their time screening the films. How they dig the fresh and delicious popcorn, and gazing upon the 'coming soon' posters, and watching the trailers and thinking, 'maybe we'll take in that one next week,' or, heck; even how convenient we make it for a quick lavatory break so's they don't miss any good parts. *How fizzy their soda pop.* See my point?"

You declare with confidence that you well understand the concept of customer service.

"Terrific. But the crux of the gist of the thing about working in this biz," leaning in, "is that we as movie-lovers ourselves've gotta train our attention to stay one level removed from the experience of viewing the movies. Vigilantly so. As ushers, we are not here for our own entertainment: we exist to serve the guests. To manage lines, tear tickets, clean up, and maintain order, sure; but on an essential level it is all in service of providing a satisfying entertainment experience for the paying customer, without whom show business doesn't exist. Serve their experience, without *sharing* their experience. You see? We are seeing the movies from one level back. Levels. Layers. The cogs behind the curtain—or in front, in the case of the usher. We're like the postpartum version of the grips and other crew who facilitate the production of the movies."

"Um—sure. I get it."

"Tremendous. Part of being a professional in this business is understanding your place in the firmament. Once the blue blazer goes on, you-are-a-representative of the corporation," tapping out the rhythm on his desk. "Not here to 'watch movies'," making air quotes. "We're professionals plying our trade."

You are so onboard with all this. Sortwell had outlined the same rubric to you, sure. But more because you've watched your grandfather run The Dixiana, day after night after day. Because you yourself worked at jobs ever since you were twelve—if not for Granddaddy, then Uncle Burnie, then Norrie Sortwell, all true and straight hardworking guys, definitely not shirkers or hustlers, types you've gotten to know well from growing up around a tavern. "Fact is that I came up in a service industry family."

Intrigued, Halvorsin probes this assertion. After a brief flutter of eyelids you fib that your granddad owns a restaurant in the upstate, a simple country diner.

You can't put a finger on why you're always so embarrassed about your family owning The Dixiana, but you have been and are now and probably shall be—oh, my granddaddy was a honkytonk man. Maybe one day you yourself'll write a short story about it all.

"Home-style fare?"

"One of those meat-and-three places. Fried chicken. Twice-baked mac and cheese. Warm rolls under the heat lamp. Sweet tea by the barrel." You're thinking about the Redtail Roost, the restaurant near campus you visit almost every day—out of your nearby dining choices, it's the one serving what best recalls the comfort of your grandmother's home cooking. "Peach cobbler. Big trays of it, all sweet and gooey."

Halvorsin moans. "You're starving me over here. So you worked the restaurant?"

A shrug—it's what you had to do. "It's the family business."

"Handle money for your granddad?"

Holding out your hands—*of course*.

"At the theater as well?"

"Sure."

"Concessions? Cashier?"

"Yes sir, I did a little of everything."

"Another small, family business, that independent theater."

Nodding. "That's life in Mayberry."

"Ah, Main Street USA. Backbone of the country. That's a helluva background to have at your age. Impressive." Satisfied, he offers you an usher position, which you accept with eagerness.

"Terrific—just terrific." He stands and extends a cool, mushy flipper. "Before you leave today, Roy, we'll shuffle some papers. Get you fitted for your blazer. Saturday night ushering shift to get your feet wet sound all right?"

It does.

You hold his eye, tell him words to the effect that the investment in you will result in profit on any number of levels. Mr. Halvorsin beams and says, call me Hank.

Exhilarating. It's about as grownup as you've ever felt, shaking that hand a second time and driving yourself back to your pad on campus. Forget Main Street USA; for all you care, Reagan could order carpet bombing of Tillman Falls. This, the big town; this, the multiplex.

"THANK YOU ENJOY THE SHOW. THANK YOU ENJOY THE SHOW. THANK YOU ENJOY the show..."

Tearing tickets on a busy moviegoing night: a lesson in robotic repetitive speaking while ripping colorful pieces of paper in half. No big deal, except for the scale—like eight Palmetto Grandes but with staggered showtimes and end-times, waves and trickles, ebb and flow of humanity, the lobby bustling, the lobby at a slow simmer. And after the last show of a cycle begins, hundreds of butts in seats and eyeballs glued to screens shimmering with drama and fantasy, all quiet and time to restock, clean, take breaks. You dig the organized chaos of it all.

At first you're thrilled to be a player in top-shelf theatrical exhibition, but like any crap job—and you've had a few—this feels like work: feet hurting at the end of the shift, skin covered in popcorn grease and soda-pop syrup, grouchy and demanding 'guests' who're always right and to whom you must cater, and pernicious earworms in the form of the cacophonous sound effects symphony of distinctive musical flourishes from the row of arcade games aligned across the far wall—*Galaga*, *Robotron 2084*, *Track & Field*, *Stargate* and others into which you'll have no trouble dropping quarters while on break.

While doing so on that first break a veteran usher at the cinemas, Rip Shorley, makes all friendly-like. Tall and angular with a sharp nose and slit eyes like a 50s cartoon character, Rip leans on the *Donkey Kong* machine, an old one that still asks 'How High Can You Get' instead of 'How High Can You Try,' a line which the authorities made the game maker change because of the obvious drug reference, all of which you know but allow him to explain to you, anyway.

Rip further explains that everyone refers to the cinemas as 'the Enemas,' and that this here's a party crew, bro, and provides info to help sort the 'hot numbers' from the 'freezer queens'; gives you the rundown on all the chicks on the roster present and not, and how by the time he finishes, bro, you're gonna be surprised which is which.

As for your new pal, they call him either 'The Ripper' or 'Rip *Snort*-ley,' nicknames he has embraced. But more than mere introduction: it is to Rip you must pay heed, show obeisance, the whole hierarchical territory-marking. What a bore. Like watching dicks being measured among the redneck gangsters back home at the bar.

"I'm lead usher of the floor staff." He said it with an involuntary quaver in his voice, self-awe and respect. "Yeah. That's the dynamic. That's what you're working with."

"I don't—not trying to—compete." Terrified. Reminds you too much of the bullies back home. Looming. Reducing you to a stammering idiot the way girls do, also to using a sports analogy, the lowest form of literary allusion. "I—I'm a team player. And all."

"Awesome. That's real copacetic." In demeanor he's now chummy, a new best friend with searching, persistent gazes and a conspiratorial tone that gives you the creeps. "Cause that's what we gotta have around here. Ya dig?"

"I think so."

A while later in the supply room, with its humming ice makers and hanging brooms and rolling mop buckets, you're ordered to fill spray bottles with blue-green industrial strength cleaning fluid for use by the *concessioneers*, as Mr. Halvorsin designates the popcorn crew.

Rip, his footsteps masked by the noisy ice machines, startles you out of your loafers. "Whoa."

"Jumpy, dude. My bad, my bad." His eyes, icy blue and boring into yours. "A question: You down?"

"Like, how?"

"Well, you're into partying. Right?"

"Like—in what way?"

"Like how is that, after the shift? The cool kids hang around out back. Drink a few beers. Get into trouble. You know the drill."

"Oh. Sure."

"You drink beer?"

You nod. "Here and there."

"So—you down, then?"

Even though you don't feel excited about drinking in the parking lot— with guys like Rip, anyway—you're eager to make friends, to be one of the gang—to be liked—so you say, okie-dokie.

As you watch him go be-bopping back onto the lobby floor, at the last second grabbing two heavy black trash bags from the big industrial roll by the door—a reason for having gone into the supply room—you understand Rip carries himself with that quality you often saw growing up around a smelly old tavern: the smooth-talking grifter, of which y'all saw more after Pa-paw put in the pool tables and poker machines.

The snake on the make.

The hustler.

Around Rip, your antennae? They wiggle. Pa-paw tells you that's called intuition, and you better pay attention to it.

As such, you avoid the dumpster after-party. Instead, you clock out and skedaddle down the auxiliary stairwell and through the lower-lobby side door where patrons exit from houses 5 through 8. You drive home to campus feeling shit-faced tired instead of drunk, which seems the wiser condition.

In the living room you kick off your black loafers and toss your blue coat, emblazoned with the Consolidated Cinema Corporation crest like a prep school blazer, onto the coffee table, knocking over beer cans. At the stairwell you stand listening for the tell-tale sounds of lovemaking from Devin's room upstairs, but on this night? Only silence.

Then, with more reverence, you pick up the blazer and place it in the coat closet on a heavy wooden hanger as your grandmother has taught you. You brush lint from the royal blue sleeves and feel solid about your position. Rip *Snort*-ley can hang fire—you'll party in your own space, time and manner.

◎⊞⊘

YOU PILE UP A FEW SHIFTS, GET SEASONED USHERING THE HOUSES.

Besides the tearing of tickets and checking on theaters (while endeavoring to remain one level removed from the experience of enjoying the entertainment products on display; check), the floor staff must hustle between screenings to clean auditoriums—a methodical shoving, row-by-row, of hinged sliding seats back into an upright position; the sweeping, the hauling of dripping trash bags bulging with food waste; a pair of sharp THWAP-PING sound effects as fresh can liners are installed and the heavy plastic receptacles tacky with syrup get repositioned; last, the entrance doors propped open to receive the next audience.

The big dumpster often overflows with slick black bags stuffed with rubbish like holiday turkeys. It gets emptied twice a week, could often use a third. Your mind reels at the number of wax-coated paper drink cups this one entertainment complex sends to the landfill, much less all the moviehouses everywhere. And if wading in people's cast-off food cartons ain't bad enough, you know from experience about finding the occasional dirty diaper, cup of tobacco spit or used rubber makes cleaning the auditoriums an exercise in revulsion and growing misanthropy.

After finishing with the aftermath of a packed matinee of the latest Stallone actioner, you mosey into tiny Number 8 at the end of the long dogleg of the lobby where you earlier sneaked out; where pictures nearing their sell-by date unspool to near-empty houses.

Here you discover an interesting situation: Rip's made himself a neat stack of drink cups, one he stashes in a seat instead of chucking into the greasy trash-carts. You've noticed that when Rip cleans a house, the quote-unquote senior usher seems to take an unhealthy interest in examining certain cups and popcorn buckets.

About this activity, you think in a Spock-like voice, you stand understandably curious. Finding the courage to inquire: "What's the deal with the cups?"

A finger to his lips. "Cleaning the auditorium, shavetail."

A nosy Nelly, you press gently about the stack o'cups—they could almost pass for new.

Rip sizes you up, cranes his neck toward the booth portals. "Look—finish this house, meet me at the dumpster in five."

You stand frowning, your hands out.

Hushed, serious. "Relax, I'll spill. But out there."

He snatches the cups, conceals them in a sleeve of his doffed blue blazer and scurries out the emergency exit as though cradling a sleeping baby—but only after flaring a final glance of willful determination back into the still and shadowy projection booth. Your wiggle has become a tingle, and in the worst way possible.

OUT BACK YOU DRAG TWO LEAKING GARBAGE BAGS IN THE DESERTED service lane behind the mall where Rip, leaning on a concrete bollard once bright yellow but faded dull and scarred by multiple encounters with the trash truck, smokes and waits for you.

"So what's your name again?"

You remind him, 'Roy.'

"Roy. Roy-boy. I like it."

You're finally broken the habit of saying 'Roy-Earl' as they call you back home. Hell no. The moment you drove out of Edgewater County and down to Columbia to move into the dorm, the hick-sounding 'Earl' tumor you'd been saddled with had gone into remission, and Roy into an identity of his own. Or so you're aiming.

"Roy—right. Rip and Roy. So. You down, or what? You didn't show last week to party."

"Sure. I'm down. But—"

"Maybe I'm asking this time in a different way."

In this moment you believe it's still about the partying—like, if you get high on any serious drugs, maybe? Standing next to the grimy dumpster, however, which reeks of rancid sweet syrup and toxic yellow popcorn seasoning, the thought of drinking beer or snorting coke out here seems remarkably unappealing; what folks like your granddaddy's longtime bartender Duwayne Driggers did whenever the old man wasn't around. Trudy told you Duwayne had been coked up the night he burned his arm dumping the grill traps from the kitchen into the grease barrel out back, which was a big to-do a few years ago.

How you despised that skinny beak-faced redneck Duwayne. The last time you stopped by The Dixiana you saw them working together, perceived from the nuances of their interactions he and Trudy have become lovers—glances, gestures, intimacies. Don't ask how, but you knew—wiggling and tingling, again. It made you sick. Duwayne's forty, worked at the bar for fifteen years. Way too old for Trudy. Her phantom scent lingering in your mind, that night you cried yourself to sleep hating every tear, hating her, hating yourself and the world.

"Ripper, I'm missing a key detail here."

"I gotta know if you're down... or not."

Like a melodramatic beat from one of the movies themselves you want to scream *Dammit, man, out with it!* "In what sense?"

"Look, Benj," a pleasant enough usher and fellow country boy and sounding as yokel as most of your neighbors back home, "says he thinks you're all right. And I do, too. So: we'll let ya in. Mainly because we always need another mule, a set of eyes we can freakin' trust. Ya dig?"

You nod, perplexed. But as he next outlines what he calls 'the cup scam,' you reel with semi-concealed shock: Rip explains how sorting used soda cups and popcorn buckets deemed clean enough are later resold.

That's right—soiled product containers. After a cursory rinsing and drying of said vessels, a concession-stand conspirator managed reintegration back into the inventory.

Gagging at the thought, you ask to what end this horrid perfidy.

"Are you like, six years old? What do you think?"

Breathless, you can hardly speak: "You—take money out of the register?"

Pitying your innocence, Rip explains like a patient parent how later, *yes,* there's an equivalent removal of cash from the drawers to match the number of second-sold cups put back into circulation. The inventory's correct, the money's not off enough for anyone to notice—it's always rubbery, he says. He tells you all this standing only a foot away, breath sharp with nicotine, sour onions and vinegar from the dripping sub sandwich you saw him eating on break, a fetid reek intermingling with the dumpster stench.

A massive and depraved conspiracy.

Heart racing, you think through the years to all the movie soda and popcorn you've consumed. Acids within, roiling. A splash of briny bile gurgles in the throat. "That's—wow. Really?"

"I know what you're thinking: How-much. A busy frame or two?" He grins, shakes his head at the good fortune. "We clear a couple hundred beans, brah. Each *Batman* this summer? Biggest weekend ever. We drank Crown Royal that night instead of Old Milwaukee."

Stalling, you feel protective of Hank, the company's reputation, the guests themselves. "Man, that's—sweet. But I'm new. I shouldn't. I won't."

Sucking his teeth, he misperceives the stalling. "Incentive. I get it, I get it."

"That's not what I—oh."

In a grand and sweeping gesture, Rip produces a money clip appears out of his black polyester pants pocket and snaps off a wrinkled sawbuck.

"Here, hard-bargain Roy: your cut for that stack earlier, which Benj is processing even as we speak. In advance—ya dig? So's you know we're legit."

You eye the money like the crumpled bill Sport threw into the window of Travis Bickle's cab. Dragging your vision back to Rip's creepy squint, you're halfway shitting yourself with fear. But then, you've known tough guys your whole life. Seen bar fights break out. Ducked for cover under a table and watched scuffed boots knocking against each other, and not in the romantic sense.

Eff this a-hole. You tell him to forget it. "Guess I'm not 'down.'"

Rip, a flicker of doubt crossing his disappointed, hard-case glare. Shoves the bill into your palm. Squeezes with force.

"If nothing else," about six inches from your face, "this is for you to freakin' make sure this conversation stays between us. If you want to keep enjoying working here. Pal."

A quiet standoff. You don't appreciate this, especially from some dick-weed ex-jock, the kind of asshole who used to shove you against the lockers back home like Cecil Waugh.

You push away his hand. You allow the money to flutter to the ground like the first leaf of autumn.

He can't believe this crap. Curses your name.

You heave your trash bags into the dumpster, a feat of strength made possible by adrenaline. "I won't play ball. But I'm no rat."

Chewing the side of his thumb and avoiding your eyes, however, makes him seem more shit-scared than threatening. "Better not be."

For the rest of the shift all you can see are unsuspecting patrons munching and drinking and enjoying their movies, never knowing how unsanitary their cups might be, and no way to warn anyone.

Outrage builds—the theater feels sacred to you; your church. The cup scam, a rank and offensive desecration and breach of public trust. And now you've been made guilty by association—an unwitting accomplice; your pledged silence equalling complicity.

But you're scared.

Admit it: you're intimidated by the Rips of the world.

But no more.

Growing up at your granddaddy's place, though, you saw what happened to thieves: the had their asses whipped behind the honkytonk, and not by other thieves—often by the big boss himself. And around here that's Hank Halvorsin, not a slit-eyed creep named the Ripper. This is what you fear the most—Hank's judgment.

◌ ℝ ⊘

THE NEXT WEEKEND YOU ARRIVE HOURS EARLY FOR A STANDARD EVENING usher shift, planning to kick back and catch a screening before you have to clock in. Free movies, man. It's the principal fringe benefit of working at the Enemas, one you've yet to fully exploit.

Your own personal multiplex, eight features at hand.

At will.

Can you dig it?

Except you haven't been hanging around on your days off watching movies. You don't feel comfortable. Not with the theft, unsanitary and otherwise.

On your watch.

Ouch.

Before you even get past the enormous fake potted ferns framing the mall entrance, though, it's like a bucket of cold water's dumped on you: Lottie, the pale cashier in her early twenties in whom you have fostered warmth and mutual attraction, says that Mr. Halvorsin left a message to send you upstairs.

"Whatever it is, I didn't do it."

Her eyes like saucers: "Don't tell me. Tell him."

You float up to his office, the actor's eyes in the framed one-sheets following you like the glares of a hostile tribunal of elders.

"Roy." Your manager, smiling and pleasant, bids you to sit. "Take a load off."

"Mr. Hal—Hank."

"That's right. Hank." His smile unnerves you. "So listen: I've had a very troubling conversation with Evan," one of the union projectionists along with Phil, two older guys who operate in a separate orbit from the rest of the staff, "about certain puzzling observations."

"'Puzzling observations'."

"Houston? We have an echo on the com."

Ruing your choice of words, you stumble onward. "I'm—puzzled, too. By the puzzling. The puzzling bit."

Dryly. "What Evan saw?"

You tell him you don't got a clue, repeat the phrase with better grammar. "Haven't a clue, sir."

"I see. Outstanding. But riddle me this, Roy Pettus: rather than throwing drink-cups into the waste receptacle, why instead would an usher *stack them in a seat*?"

You will your face to stay poker-calm. To not blush. To own up to knowledge regarding the cup scam might indicate complicity. Accomplice after the fact. Hell, during the fact: the scheme happened every time you worked this week.

And you've said nothing to the boss yet.

You scramble. "To compress the cups? To make more room in the —receptacle?"

Thrown off by the inherent logic. "That how you'd do it? Stack the cups?"

"Stacking hadn't occurred to me, no. Huh." You run with it as though catching a hail-mary pass: "Maybe there's some wisdom here. Last Saturday night, I must've filled up two whole bags with cups alone. Seriously. I bet I could've gotten them all into one bag, however, if I'd stacked. Otherwise, I'm drawing a blank. On why."

Holding the moment. "No other reason? That comes to your mind?"

You hold out your hands, penitent. "Not one in particular. No."

"My intelligence—the intelligence I have—suggests another purpose. To this stacking business. A darker reason."

"If I knew what you wanted me to say besides the truth, I would tell you."

Hank hangs his head. "Remarkable. I'm so disappointed. When we hired you, it was because you seemed more mature than many applicants your age."

"I'm not sure what you're getting at, sir. I like my job."

Kinder, gentler. "Listen—I know what's going on. I'm trying to find out who's involved. All right?"

In a rush, you release a breath held too long. "I'm not. Swear to you, Mr. Halv—"

"Wait—*in on what*?"

"Your observations. The puzzling evidence."

"Evidence of—?"

"If you know... then you know."

Leans forward like a frazzled police captain warning Dirty Harry to dial back the gunplay. "Pettus, for god's sake. The health department could shut us down. Cost us all our jobs. This is serious."

So he knows the particulars. "Sir, I think the cup-stacking is disgusting. And I didn't, and wouldn't, want any part of it." A deep breath. "Said so to Rip. When he approached me about it. That's the truth."

"Rip." Sighing. "But you didn't come to me?"

Ashamed, you own up to cowardice in response to feeling bullied. "I'm still the new guy. He threatened me."

"Who else besides Mr. Shorley? I've already got him dead to rights, so —"

"I can't say. He's the only who said anything."

"Last question: You lying to me? About being involved?"

Emphatic. "I work for my money. I'm no thief."

"You protecting anyone? A girl you like?"

"I wish. I haven't made many friends yet."

"But you've been here for weeks, now."

"Just over a month." The Thanksgiving movies all set to open, including the latest *Star Trek* sequel. "And I enjoy it here. By the way."

"You're doing a fine job. You're a self-starter, which is hard to find in an employee. Have I told you that?"

Your smile is genuine. "I'm not sure you have."

"All right. While I had to pry it out of you, I appreciate your honesty. For the moment, please keep this conversation between us. Now: go and clock in."

"Sir, I don't come on until six. Thought I'd screen a feature before work."

"Stupendous. You do that. And listen. I'm proud of you. You did the right thing: you reaffirmed my trust in your integrity. I think."

"It's how I was raised."

"I know why you were hesitant. You're worried about being an outcast. Hey, I was a dork, too. Hard to believe now," though with his weak chin and blotchy skin and thick glasses, not so different. "Anybody who'd get you into this kind of trouble, and for a few bucks, isn't much of a friend."

Unlike your interview, he offers no handshake this time. Which worries you. Maybe a word like 'trust' is lip service.

You can dig it — he doesn't know-know you yet. Or, now he does. You showed him the real you by turning Rip down straightaway.

As you walk down the upstairs cinderblock hallway lined with waist-high plastic bags of popcorn stockpiled for the weekend you hear Hank echoing on the box office intercom. Telling Lottie to send Rip to his office as soon as he arrives for his evening shift.

Instead of watching a movie you ease out to go sit at a fast-food table for two hours to be certain to avoid facing Rip *Snort*-ley, but it's more out of guilt than fear. Why you feel you betrayed him, you can't say. Except that you've become like an adult instead of a fellow kid. A strange feeling, like betraying your tribe or class.

During a shift that next week, somebody slashes two of your truck tires. You figure it's Rip but never know for sure, and suffer no further consequences, other than finding that life at the Enemas grows boring fast. To keep from telling your grandparents about all the drama with the revenge incident, you spring for a pair of Goodyear re-caps using your own wages, and wonder about finding a new job in the spring.

◌▥⊘

A MONTH LATER YOU'RE ALREADY PROMOTED TO BOX OFFICE ALONGSIDE Lottie. It's a serious and responsible gig, but skipping the *concessioneer* stage produces no additional compatriots other than your fellow cashier, a flirt who keeps tickling your ankle with cool, bare toes slipped out of her black, cloth maryjanes. Zing!

Not only this fast promotion, but at a recent staff meeting Hank Halvorsin made noise about a slot in the spring for Assistant Manager in the works… to the right candidate. While locking eyes with you.

You were flattered. More cash, sure, but a ton of hours. What about school work?

What would Uncle Burnie say? You'll be home for the holidays in a week. You'll ask his wise counsel.

That same evening, however, you mull over the future by heading down to the commercial strip next to the sprawl of Southeastern where you discover a hand-lettered *NOW HIRING* sign in the window of supercool, hiply iconic coffee shop called Maxine's. You say to yourself, self? Maybe the feature film exhibition trade feels like being stuck in your own past. That it's time to leave movies behind. Try something new.

Heck, you could walk down the hill from your dorm to this job, which you admit is hospitality service, yeah yeah, but nothing like working fast food, or your granddaddy's rancid old honkytonk. A classy joint, Maxine's. A legacy business here in the campus ghetto. Nobody to slash your tires here. The well at the theaters, poisoned.

You go in. Smell the pastries and fresh-roasted beans. Feel at home. Apply.

◉ ▣ ⊘

OVER THE HOLIDAY BREAK AND IN THE SACRED PECAN ORCHARD, OF ALL places, Trudy drives a final stake through your heart.

She had come alone for Christmas Eve dinner at the Pettus house, a tradition for the key Dixiana employees. You had already tried to kiss her the previous night, in the stockroom at the bar where it all started, but she had cussed and pushed you away and seemed shocked. It's now two years since she took your virginity. Nothing but frost ever since. And wouldn't make eye contact at the table.

Begging her to come outside the traditional family holiday dinner that also includes Runelle's cousins and grand-nieces from eastern Beauchamp County, you stroll through the narrow footpath leading to the dark and secluded pecan orchard. Out of sight, you reach over and hold her hand, which she also rejects.

"Quit it, now."

"At first last night? I thought you wanted to kiss. I wouldn't have tried, otherwise."

"I did. Sorta-kinda. But not in front of —"

"And why won't you hold my hand? I'm in college, now."

"Cause your Pa-Paw, and Mama Runelle too, would skin us both alive."

You cuss, your voice breaking. Don't cry, Pettus.

She goes to hug you, but you push her away. "But, don't you understand I love you?"

Trudy says, no, sugar. That what happened between y'all was not only two years ago but wrong and weird, and not love.

"Plus, I don't wanna lose my job."

She might as well have taken a shit on you. "At the god-durned Dixiana? That's more important?"

"Was always my dream to work at the Dix. I love music so much, but c'ain't hold a tune worth a poop, wouldn't you know. I just want to be in it. Around it. Somehow."

All your sorrow evaporates. You are as steel inside, cold and sharp. "Nice speech. Question: Those as big as your dreams get, bar-maid?"

"Fuck you, son," she says, glaring. "Go on, now."

"Seriously. You're doing me a favor."

But your voice breaks enough to shatter the illusion and illuminate your heartbreak; that her repudiation of your feelings gut-punches you anew.

You don't care about her being a redneck, a Pirkle. She took you inside her, called you baby, let you come without a rubber, all when you were sixteen; and damn if it hadn't been magic. A gauzy but vivid, magical, damp dream of heavenly union; of tension and release.

Love.

Rejection.

Forever paired. Frustration, thy name is you.

◈⬛⊘

AT A HOLIDAY PARTY DURING CHRISTMAS WEEK WITH OTHER MULTIPLEX employees, Lottie corners you and stands so close while chatting and flirting that your attraction becomes present and clear, her cheeks flushing as she innocently bumps her hip into your swelling genitals five or six times, lips pressed together like she's concealing a sweet and naughty secret.

Before the night is over you're no longer thinking about Trudy, not while making out in the parking lot of an apartment complex with your cute co-worker. Slurping, groping; tropical heat, foggy windows. Your heart and loins, they soar.

A pale mouse compared to Trudy but demure and who smells sweet, Lottie plays with you through your jeans and you're so hard grease leaks out, and the next day she will become your second lay, at her house in a nearby neighborhood while her mother is out exchanging holiday gifts.

It's hot and feral; in her girlhood single bed she defies her demeanor through enthusiasm bordering on sexual abandon. To keep from finishing too fat, you think about the time you played baseball in front of people wearing a pink shirt and missing an easy grounder.

Afterwards you shower together, where she fellates you until ready to do it again under the hot water, and Lottie seems to come hard, holding onto your neck and moaning your name into your ear against the tiles.

Whoa. This is a dream come true. Lottie. She's the one.

You'll date for two weeks into the spring term, but she turns out to be a needy flake with three other lovers, it all falls apart and it sucks, a fling that adds up only to added sexual experience, helpful but confusing all the same. This breakup provides further motivation for walking away from the theater job—Maxine, an old character full of pep and leadership qualities, has made an offer.

After this depressing episode you find yourself later that spring in Edgewater County trying to score with a freaking high school girl, Devin's sister of all possible choices, which you will cultivate over many months and phone calls until it blows up in your face over getting fucked up on beer and acid, like some druggie, and missing your first real date with her.

You? Your own worst enemy. And damn if that's it for you and women for a period long enough to be worthy of academic study. Gun shy. Again: it's your own damn fault.

Once you become a sweaty, hardworking barista at Maxine's—'The Greasy Barista,' the title of a short story you draft that first season working the café and one of several attempts at fiction you will never complete—coffee becomes your life more than anything from your childhood, be it work experiences; favorite movies; or women who broke your heart, like the mother you would never know. Much strange energy anytime you have brought up the car accident that killed her. Your grandparents often seem filled with secrets, and it drives you nuts.

Worst of it as time goes on? A sense that your childhood tormentors are all proven right, at least when it comes to romance:

What a freckle-red; a reecie-cup; a chubby chump.

So be it. Forget companionship, intimacy, finding the dream girl. You will attain success in other venues.

CREEDENCE AND DEVIN

November 11, 1989

Dear Diary:

Well, I tell you. If me and Roy Earl Pettus will ever be 'anything' (hint HINT), and it looks like we will not, we are off on the wrong foot. That much I know.

He went and forgot our date, or so he says!

After making plans together!

That he was too drunk to get me the night of the Deadhead concert!

Oh my sweet Jesus, have you ever heard anything like that? Because I have not. Knowing he lives with my brother, though, helps it make sense.

Devin and his drinking. It will be the end of him one day. I will never get like him. Maybe buzzed.

The beer I drank of Daddy's while I waited in the bushes for my dream-date, who never came (hello!), made me feel real good. For about five minutes. Till I had to pee.

Seriously, though. It was quite relaxing. A lot

of my nervousness went away. Whoosh. Just like that. Mama has made me a nervous kitty cat, I think.

I had this moment one day this past summer, where it was real hot and I got dizzy and then came into the cold house and sat down and my head felt whirly-gig, and I stepped out of myself for a minute. And I could see all around, including myself on the couch. Could see Mama in the other room, worrying about this and that. Hollering at Daddy about how he better do what she says, and look at all this mess, and then she had her duties with the ELMS, as she always ends up saying, and which includes hovering all over me.

It's gonna rain, I heard myself say. And later, it did. I could've swore I was dreaming. But I wasn't. I went back into my body.

At supper I told her, Mama, it feels like you watch my every move. Which she does. She said p'shaw. Of course. No wonder I had to sneak out to see that concert (UM that I did not see, thanks for nothing R. E. Pettus!!!). No wonder I feel like I don't do anything right. You don't even let me help in the kitchen.

"You"? Who am I talking to? I meant Mama.

I tell you. I started this diary because I thought it would help me sort out my feelings, and figure out what I wanted out of life, as well as get in typing practice on the big humming IBM that Mama has in her cubbyhole to type up ELMS stuff. As I wrote before, the night of the concert, I went and gave myself to Dusty, finally, since no college boy like Roy Pettus gave a rip enough to come and get me. Dusty felt like a king, but I didn't get much of anything except stinging and blood. He took me home. I cried. That's what I got.

But I think you are supposed to cry, at least the first time. All Mama told me was that sex is a chore you got to put up with whether you want to or not. I guess I kind of get what she means, now that Dusty has done it with me. Twice.

I know, diary. I didn't write in you about that second one. It wasn't any longer than the first time, but felt better.

Already he says he wishes he could slide it in without the condom, just to see how good that feels. I want to, but I know Dusty. He won't be able to hold back, no better than the first time I touched it, when you would have thought his peterpiper was a little red stick of dynamite. Ka-pow. He acted like he would pass out that day in the woods. I thought I had done something wrong. Like a dummy, I asked him if he was alright. He just blinked at me and was like, duh.

Why am I writing all this again? I need to get moving around. I feel stale. I been sitting in this house all afternoon, doodling and sketching and now typing.

Next year I will get serious about going to college. Me saying I wanted to go to Savannah to SCAD went over like a lead balloon. Like I wanted to go school on the moon.

That's what I keep saying about Mama. She's right there all the time, a big-old 16 ton weight that looks like it's gonna fall on me.

I had a dream a few times back when I was little. I would be at the county or the state fair, or at Myrtle Beach at the Pavilion, anyplace I guess having roller coasters and Merry-go-rounds and rides like the big pirate ship that rocks back and forth. That was the thing in the dream. Like the pirate ship swinging back and forth was getting closer to me. And over the top of me. And then falling, falling down on me big and heavy. And I can't breathe, and I feel people screaming.

And I wake up, and ha-ha, maybe it's one of the cats on my stomach, or maybe it's nothing. But the feeling is the same. I don't want to feel like I'm under a big hairy cat-butt. Smothering. Dying.

When I get older, I ain't even having pets. I'm sick of Mama making me feed the cats. I hate chores.

I hate Mama.

I hate Chilton and Tillman Falls and South Carolina.

I hate the Grateful Dead, who I could not go see, and Roy Earl Pettus for leaving me behind.

I hate Devin.

Or the little shit-ass, as Mama would put it. Maybe I need to write to him instead to me. Nobody will ever read this, anyway.

(Or they BETTER NOT, I mean! GRRR!!).

Creedence yanked the second of two pages out of the typewriter carriage. She read and fixed errors with White-Out; took a marker and drew a blood-red skull and crossbones beneath the last line. She almost hoped her mother would read the diary, and see the truth about her daughter. Maybe that's why she started typing instead of writing it. Eileen would get curious and snoop.

Creedence rued becoming like her mother. Mama made adulthood sound like a passel of chores with little payoff, to hear her tell it.

Creedence couldn't see why folks act like they do, but she thought, that sounds like little-kid reasoning—people do what they do because they have responsibilities. Look at her father. Always working. Never home. He has three insurance offices in three towns; he goes fishing, and hangs out at Pike's Bait & Pawn every chance he could. Was this what being married and grownup was all about? Mercy—she hoped not.

Creedence, thinking about Devin and seeing red. Calling him at his dorm room to bless him out one more time about getting her date all drunk. Maybe she shouldn't be mad at Roy Earl Pettus. Devin did it to him.

Her stomach felt pinched and heavy. She almost wanted to go and drink another one of her Daddy's beers out of his fridge in the garage which had so many, he wouldn't notice if she did. But wasn't that what pissed Mama off? Drinking alcohol?

Beer was different. Devin drank the hard stuff. He had poured liquor down Roy Earl's throat and told him, screw her, she don't drink like men do. Leave her ass behind.

The phone rang and rang. With four guys living there, you'd have thought one would pick up.

It didn't matter—she heard Dusty's grandmother's Olds pulling into the cul-de-sac, confirmed by skipping to the window and looking through the sheers. She guessed that was okay. Better than being alone.

Maybe she would let him do it again—with the rubber—and they could try with her on top? Or something? She didn't feel like anything, his thing slipping in and out so fast. Dusty—he wasn't doing it right. Yet.

Two more years, and she would not have to think about Dusty or Roy or Devin or her mama ever. Again. If she didn't want to.

Heck freaking yeah. Goodbye, Edgewater County! Nice knowing you. Savannah, here I come.

BUTTON SYKES, JEREMY AND HEATHER

After the misbegotten trip back home from Foothills State during fall break, Button swore she'd never return to Edgewater County.

Yeah. That bad.

The twist for her was coming home to make peace with her family by showing off an attempt at a boyfriend—i.e., the brutal denial phase, as she thought of her experimentation with activities hetero in orientation.

To stop fantasizing about Heather Ponderview. Months now. She sleeps across the room from Button, but she cannot have her.

Blargh. Forget about it.

The couple: Button, nineteen, on her second college after a partial year at Southeastern; her beau Jeremy Chimiento, a mature New Jerseyian of twenty-two, both displaying dreadlocks and clothing that made them look as though they'd wandered out of a Grateful Dead concert parking lot.

Which they had, in a sense, albeit with one of the successor bands carrying the torch of the hedonistic, improv-minded music and dope scene: Phish, whom Heather and Jeremy both insisted Button see when they came to play near Foothills State, and becoming transcendently high for the first time in her life, too. A show of such energy, with young musicians, offered a connection that felt more contemporaneous and present, especially with the Dead now dead.

As frenetic progressive rock filled the small, smoky arena in the mountains and a sensation of floating crept into her consciousness—add in a touch of anxiety and heart palpitation, sure—she realized Jeremy's pungent, resin-sticky nugs made the dirtweed they sling in Edgewater County seem like rabbit tobacco. Transportation ensued, especially when the lead guitarist began a sort of recitativo, a storytelling interlude within a long song describing how the band, the audience, indeed, the whole building, were merging and transforming into an enormous ball of cosmic muck orbiting the center of the galaxy and pulsating with the vibration of love, light and life. She understood every word.

In that moment of high-mindedness she 'got' Phish—the quirk, the vibe; their musical style, difficult to pigeonhole and define, an approach that signaled playfulness leaning at times toward arch parody in the vein of Zappa. The act also featured such eclectic elements as a secret language of onstage cues to which longtime fans would respond, confusing newcomers and making the whole trip clubby and cool. Phish exuded misfit power. Button had come home. Had gone hippy in, like, five minutes, all skirts and hair-wraps and tie-dyes and dope.

Her initiation began two years earlier while seeing the Grateful Dead, and only months before Jerry Garcia died. The forbidden drive to Charlotte —no way his little girl would commune with 'those people,' she had been warned—had cost Button her literal freedom. In the aftermath her father, furious, committed her to a behavioral rehab center under a diagnosis of Oppositional Defiant Disorder. This ridiculous and embarrassing story she kept from most new friends she made—oh yeah, they put me in the nuthouse for sneaking off to a concert.

She'd show them, though: in the wake of Garcia's death, the eclectic scene outside Phish concerts would serve to shock and annoy and worry her parents.

In Button's hand-me-down, knock-engined Ford Explorer they crossed the concrete bridge over the Sugeree, a structure that in her absence had been christened the Lance Cpl. Lawrence Lautenschlager Memorial Bridge, named for a county cop shot and killed during a nearby roadside stop a few years back, the perpetrator never caught. The wide Sugeree ran low as it bubbled its way beneath the bridge, the water deep green and mounds of smooth river boulders dried by the sun. A little farther upriver toward the ridge were the 'falls,' exposed, clay-coated rocks through which flowed a bare trickle, and only after steady rains. The river's course, shifted decades ago through damming and mighty mankind's ingenuity and determination.

She didn't consider such attempted control of natural forces a good thing. Many arguments with her dad. No wonder he had her put away. Didn't like what she had to say—that civilization itself might represent civilization's biggest problem.

Button noticed, too, the sandy, low bluff way down the channel of the river and remembered the times of her life spent thereupon with her grandfather and his best friend, fishing on a humid summer morning. Uncle Rabbit said little Button made a fine replacement for Roy Earl, who had gone off to college.

Sense memories: Catching bream, but feeling bad about sticking them with the hook; eating sandwiches of baloney on white bread with yellow mustard; mosquitoes, minnows and tadpoles in puddles. Salty, oily Wise brand potato chips. A transistor radio tuned to WABA playing twangy country music that, uncool or not, she associated with innocence and fun. Swatting flies and drinking Co-colas and listening to the old men's banter, not understanding much of what they said except, perhaps, when they started bickering. She could always tell when her Granddaddy and his friend Rabbit were really mad instead of normal bantering. Like all friends, disagreements happened. The tone of their voices with one another could turn cutting, and their statements cryptic.

Making their way onto the business part of Highway 1 into Chilton, the commercial area and bedroom community near the freeway interchange, they drove by Mr. Hampton's car dealership and the filling stations, the fast food and grocery stores; under construction, a plaza being prepared for an anchor and smaller shops. Barf.

What hadn't changed were the great plumes of the Nuclear Station forever dancing along the horizon, the plant at which her father earned his living.

"So—you didn't bring any weed, right?"

"Like you asked."

"Good."

"Really that uptight around here?"

"Cops suck everywhere. Don't they?"

All she knew was Edgewater County, which featured a fat, red-faced young Sheriff already sporting a nose full of spidery red veins; oh, how her grandfather cussed Whardell Truluck, who didn't 'play ball' as readily as his father, the former sheriff, did over certain mysterious activities and goings-on. Her granddad called Truluck's cops 'greedy lapdogs,' all on the take, and not trustworthy. A warmth in her belly made her wonder if the cop they named the bridge after hadn't run afoul of one of granddad's more sketch-ball associates.

Button continued, "But I'm only worried about my dad. He'll cut my butt if he detects herb."

"Sure he'd know what it was?" Glancing out at the passing countryside. "Being from the sticks like this?"

"*Buddy Sykes served in Viet-nam,*" in low, mocking mimicry. "The mo-fo knows the smell of pot."

"Word. I burn incense when I'm home. Been blazing upstairs since ninth grade. Crack a window and the reverse pressure differential from the HVAC system pushes the smoke and smell right out into the backyard garden area." A budding journalist prone to detailed explication, now in pity of his oblivious parents: "*They don't have the first fucking clue. It's truly remarkable.*"

"Don't be too sure about that."

"Please." Jeremy, thoughtful, tugged at a scraggly beard coming in patchy on his boyish face. "Vietnam, huh? I'd love to interview your dad."

"For what?"

"Magazine writing. I have that next semester."

"You're about to meet him. Just ask. He did a bunch of like, classified junk. He doesn't like to talk about it."

"We'll see about that. Not sure if I brought a notebook, though."

Jeremy, on the five-year plan, had 'two to four' semesters remaining to complete his Mass Comm degree. He'd said to Button he 'thrived' when taking only six credit hours a term instead of a full load, and becoming degreed would occur when spring rains came and the blooms of his ambition greeted the rising sun heralding the professional phase of his life.

Well. She hoped he wouldn't tell her father this news, and certainly not in that way. Her dad would deem such an attitude 'laziness' and suspect Jeremy of being high. Based on appearance alone, he'll already think her boyfriend a vagabond derelict. Perfect.

❁ ✖ ✎

THE UNINCORPORATED AREA BETWEEN CHILTON AND TILLMAN FALLS called Easton sprang up: An old gas station-slash-general store that appeared open in spite of its dilapidated appearance. A wooden shack with a hand-painted sign on the front reading SMALL ENGINE REPAIR. Scrawny cats and mangy dogs wandering around. Men standing under trees in clusters, or else plopped down in lawn chairs. Fast food wrappers, beer cans and empty forties littering the roadside.

The homes visible from the highway ranged from tarpaper shacks to a few of the old two-thirty-five HUD houses, brick and sturdy but tiny and aging, to clapboard affairs and rusting mobile homes surrounded by junked vehicles. Unpaved driveways snaked away into mysterious stands of trees. No fewer than three liquor stores within a single half-mile stretch. A Dollar General; a Dollar Federal; a Family Dollar, all within a mile. Several tenth-rate used car and mobile home lots. The county trash dump. Only a single new Mexican grocer signaled a change in demographics. Easton, traditionally the 'black side' of town, now growing more cosmopolitan, Button thought.

"Downmarket neighborhood through here, boy." *Click*—Jeremy, hitting the door locks.

What a pussy. "C'mon. It's a poor county."

Button, remembering how self conscious she'd been about her South Carolina vocal inflections. How the closer the two had gotten to the flat-lands, as Jeremy called this part of the state along the fall line, the more she tried to sound ordinary—not Southern, only American. "There's few job opportunities around anymore, other than the truck factory in the next county and the nuclear plant. Ya know?"

"There's work for those who wish it." Jeremy came from money, with attitudes often belying his hippy exterior. "Some people don't want to live any better than they do. Or just too stupid to do anything about their circumstances."

"The mills closed. Where folks used to work."

Not listening to her in the least: "In fact? If you ask the universe, see, and put out the right frequencies and vibrations, prosperity will flow back to you. But only to the pure of spirit, and intention," he said with a dreamlike cadence. "Or so my wacky mom claims. She's a yoga nut, meditates, all that new-age BS. Crunchy-granola girl—that's what my dad calls her. But you know, I do think there's something to it. Are these poor dumb bastards merely accepting of their fate? Or what?"

"My grandfather owns a trailer park, and the residents look none too happy about being stuck there. All I can tell you."

"They could leave. What—is it a prison?"

"No."

"Well."

"Easier said than done. When you're poor."

Her boyfriend shrugged and frowned at a stooped black man walking along in dirty work clothes and swinging a battered lunch box in time with his stride. As they passed, the laborer saluted with a tired flick of his left hand.

Jeremy twisted his neck to gawk. "That brother tried to flag us down. Should we go back?"

She laughed. "That's the way folks are around here. He was only saying 'hi'."

"They wave—*at strangers*? That's preposterous."

Jeremy, not a Southerner, hadn't encountered a collegial nature and practice of basic small town social interaction Button took for granted. They might talk smack behind one's back, but she knew enemies who still offered a wave when passing out on the country roads or through the middle of town. Cordiality, formality—the way of the South.

Button noticed that Jeremy, to whom she'd been introduced by her roommate Heather, suddenly seemed baked—he'd eaten two chocolate-chip cookies laced with the last of the Mendocino County butter he'd cooked from part of his stash, a green, fatty palliative he'd made after scoring a decent amount of the Emerald Triangle's finest. As a consequence of such high quality, the ganja treats, delicious on their own merits as mere snacks, were also potent as all get-out. Button herself only ate one, and despite concerns about him having brought bud, now realized she was also ripped.

This amazing weed came from Heather Ponderview's peeps, stalwart road outlaws with crazy-brave courage who trucked two vacuum-sealed pounds of dank all the way from NC to NC, Northern California to North Carolina, a high-wire act. Every time she pulled out the bulging Ziplock freezer back stuffed with reeking blue-ribbon cultivated and manicured cannabis flower, Button's roommate had had to re-tell the hero's journey of the kind bud, as though her friends had scaled a holy mountain, an act worthy of veneration through oral history lessons delivered to unwashed aspirants yet to pass through such a trying veil of initiation.

Jeremy may have grumbled at her rules, but only a moron would believe she was unreasonable in being paranoid about smoking up in the car: at the beginning of the term they had gotten popped for simple possession while puffing and walking across the darkened campus following a late movie in the student union, *Trainspotting*, ripping good cinema. Choose life, indeed.

The worst of that debacle came, however, in having to call Thim, in grad school at the time at UGA, to drive from Athens up to Pinebelt and bail out her sister on misdemeanor drug charges. Not a pretty scene. Thim's disapproval of Button's life and personality mirrored that of their parents, and in earlier times would have reported this childish stupidity. But in young adulthood her sister now also wanted to coddle and protect their mother, disappointed as the matriarch had already become with her second-born child. Keeping quiet the news of black-sheep-daughter's drug arrest made the most sense at the time to the older and more sagacious sibling.

Thim got no argument from the parolee who endured a speech echoing flavors and notes cadged from many overhead dressings-down by their father. Tree? Meet apple. They could keep one another, Button's overwrought sister and parents. The closer they had gotten to her childhood home, the more a cold knot of anticipation welled inside. Maybe a second cookie before they arrive, Button suggested. To take off the edge as the holiday dinner progressed.

◎◙⊘

TRUTH: THIM DETESTED HER LITTLE SISTER. THE FEELING, RECIPROCAL.

Button called her sister's brand of boutique-clothed on-campus power trippers 'little sorostitutes.' Despite her ostensibly highbrow ambition and study of political science, to her Thim seemed shallow as a rain puddle. At the last Thanksgiving, after enduring Thim and her right-wing bullshit, which of course her father ate up and believed and supported, Button had swiped her sister's car keys out of her purse and shoved them into the trashcan full of discarded holiday food.

Mean? Yeah. But not as much as dosing her with LSD, which Button desperately wanted to try.

Ever since getting turned onto acid and finally feeling a meaningful part of a greater whole in the universe, she had become quasi-obsessed with coming back to Tillman Falls and dosing the entire water supply, rationale being that a good trip would fix the constipation problem around here. The revelation had come during a profound experience with Heather and her artsy friends one night while chanting, watching trippy movies, playing with a Ouija board in rooms lit only by colorful taper candles. Some real mystical shit. No idea where to procure acid in vat-sized quantities, though. How much would it take?

In coming down the next morning, she had thought, man, that's a little twisted. Dosing your whole town. *Let them turn on in their own space and time, little sister.*

The voice made her feel high again, and all of it seemed freaking profound. Who was that, she asked the air.

Twisting a segment of his wispy chin-beard, Jeremy cringed at a bloated carcass on the side of the road. "Aw—a dead deer."

"We need to get rid of all these fucking cars." Button, lighting a clove cigarette. "We need walking communities. We need solar and wind. We need to put billions into fusion research instead of occupying some piece of desert ten thousand miles away so we can suck up the last of the black gold like some, some energy vampire." She turned to him. "We *need* a fucking revolution."

Jeremy sighed, skeptical. He dug into a snack-size bag of Funyons and crunched through his next, brief words. He had a bored, rich boy prep-school cadence to his voice. "Fat chance. We need a technological solution. We need a venture capitalist and a scientific team of visionaries to come up with a solution that's not controlled by the government."

"Or a corporation."

"Hrm," he crunched. "Of course it'd have to be a corporation. But who owns it? You don't get the venture capitalist without the ownership part. The profit part. A necessary evil. Money's not all bad. Depends on what you want it for."

At this she felt the enormity of the charade. Had not enjoyed sex in the least. In her defense Jeremy himself hadn't seemed that interested in screwing, so no great drama there. Jeremy, short, and his penis, small and well suited to Button's narrow channel which didn't much want a penis inside it, at least not a real one throbbing and stabbing and going *sput-sput*. He had at least inquired about her reciprocal pleasure, citing a rigid body language during the act that featured clenched fists and forearms drawn up next to her breasts.

"Money? Money's not the answer. The shit is coming down, Jeremy, and not just in our lifetime but, like, next fucking week if we're not careful. Money won't buy us out of inevitable collapse." She tapped the steering wheel in time with her next words. "Not our kids, not our grandkids. We—us—*must act now*."

"Now-now? Can it wait until after Thanksgiving dinner?"

She smacked him on the arm, hard. "The future's here. We are it. We are on our own."

Jeremy crunched his snack-food. "Some of us'll be okay."

She asked what made him so fucking sure.

"Americans will do fine. It's the third world that'll suffer."

"They already do," remembering how this country had dropped fire, phosphorous and dioxin on her mother's homeland, denuded the jungles and forests with chemicals. Which were coming back in a karmic sense on her family.

Yep: This trip home to see her father and mother and grandparents and sister, mainly because of the news of her father's lymphoma. Her cheerful dad on the phone saying, no worries, it'll be fine; a little chemo, and this is one they can nip right in the bud, it's from all the defoliant we sprayed around in 'Nam.

Button, a possessor of extreme empathy, welled up with fear and sorrow for her father. Buddy Sykes—friendly, helpful, cheery to the outside world; at home, taciturn, serious, uncompromising. He'd come back from Vietnam with the love of his life found in one of the little villages that popped up near American fire bases, with his spirit intact and a personal discipline he felt duty-bound to pass on to his children.

But now this bullshit disease. Cancer. The word itself held so much power. The vibration of fear.

Thinking: *You sure it's 'only' that pesky Agent Orange, Daddy? Sure it's not the Sugeree Station?*

No one in Edgewater County talked about cancer. You didn't dare think about it. Not if you wanted to keep believing that nuclear energy came with a price that didn't include a devil's bargain. One hell of a way to boil water, as Einstein remarked about plans to build atomic power plants. Button, a budding no-nukes activist.

They passed the welcome signs to Tillman Falls, with the badges and symbols of Rotary Club and VFW and Masons and ELMS and other civic organizations emblazoned upon the decorative brick and iron work. "Almost there."

"Do we go through town?"

Button said yeah. That he was about to see a real sleepy old Southern burg.

They bounced over the railroad tracks, and the road became four lanes. Next the grand old columned homes and enormous elms and oaks appeared, and the football stadium and high school; and merging onto Common Street, soon came the cemetery and The Dixiana and into downtown itself, a side-trip that takes all of two minutes.

As a town custodian watered and tended the landscaping, the rhomboid-shaped park and its monuments glistened in the yellow autumn sunlight. "Now this is how I imagined it, complete with erect phallic symbol jutting out of the town park," Jeremy said. "Somebody tell Norman Rockwell to lube up his paintbrushes."

"More like Bogdanovich." On her film studies professor's recommendation Button had watched a letterboxed VHS of *The Last Picture Show*, as melancholy an evocation of a dying American spirit as any movie or book she'd encountered. She now saw Tillman Falls also in black and white, with tumbleweeds blowing through, and tall, eternal Uncle Rabbit a dead ringer for Ben Johnson's Sam the Lion character. "Not much happens here anymore."

By the time they looped around the green so he could get a gander at the old courthouse, legacy oak trees and fountain, she'd become lost in memories and pot cookie effects. As she turned by The Dixiana to finally head to her house, she nearly crapped her worn and patched dungarees when a cop siren blipped beside the honkytonk and its ugly Confederate flag mural.

"Damn," Jeremy said. "Not the heat."

"I wasn't speeding."

"Here's hoping they know your family—this is your town, isn't it?"

"Well—yeah. Sorta."

She signaled and pulled over next to Forest Knoll cemetery. Button hoped he hadn't lied to her about leaving the stash behind. Her boyfriend had turned white as fresh-milled Adluh flour.

THE COP, ROLLING OUT OF HIS CRUISER THE WAY THEY DO.

Jeremy's voice, high and thin. "Hope this asshole doesn't have a K-9."

"*Why?*"

"Fuck. Fuck. Fuck. Be cool."

"You be cool. I'm the one who can't get busted. *Not here,*" with rising panic.

"We both look freaking baked."

"*Please shut up.*"

Her lips felt heavy. Her mouth, crackling and dry. She peered into the rearview mirror at the cop, and shit a brick: a mean bastard named Timmy Truesdale. A couple of year older than her in school, he hadn't only been a bully—for a season or two he'd suffered unrequited, mad love for her.

Wait—maybe this was their lucky break.

"License'n registration please," Timmy said in his slow rural patois, all running together in a rote, practiced, unemotional rush. "You like to blowed my doors off back there in town, ma'am."

"I don't think I was speeding. Oh—hey, Timmy. What's up, bro?"

"Ain't the speed limit that's up. I can tell you that much, Ms. Sykes. Didn't recognize you at first with that crazy hair of your'n."

Truesdale peered in with palpable disgust at Jeremy's dirty, bare feet propped on the dash, dreadlocks bundled into a flamboyant pile on top of his head. "That wooly-booger your boyfriend? Or did you pick up a bum?"

"Afternoon, sir." Jeremy, with forced cheer, flopped his hand in a tiny wave, displaying his school ID against his forehead as though playing Indian poker with the cop. "I'm like, not homeless. Foothills State senior. Well—second-year. Call it postgrad."

Truesdale scrutinized her license. "Tell you what—you Sykes girls grow up awful fast. Can't believe you're nineteen years old."

Her ears, hot with irritation. "Time marches on."

"You and that other one—?" The cop all-but licked his lips. "Two of the sweetest, cutest little honeys who ever walked the green. Thim, especially. What's that hoochie-mama up to these days?"

Button, patience razor-thin, tried to use her locality to some advantage and slipped into a legit Tillman Falls drawl. "Well, shoot," giving the officer a little wink. "I'm sure she'd love to hear from ya. Maybe you can write up one of those warning-thingies. And I'll tell her you asked after her."

"Oh—some kinda bribe?"

"Dude. I'm only three blocks from home. And we weren't speeding."

"Here's the news: You don't tell me what you were doing. I already seen it, girl. And I can smell it, too." Slapping her license against the door frame: "Glad it was me who pulled you over. Since I know your family. And all."

"Yes sir, Timmy. I really appreciate this."

"You appreciate what?"

She flailed. "That—it's you. Who pulled us over."

His pursed lips held no portent of goodwill. "Look here—you keep calling me Timmy, girl. I done knowed you a long time, now. We good friends, yo. But hang on here for one little second." He ambled to his cruiser speaking into the shoulder-mounted microphone.

Gripping the steering wheel, she watched in the rearview as Truesdale talked on his radio, shook his head, tapped her license on the roof of his prowler.

He came back. Asked her to step out, if she would.

Shit. When they tell you to exit the vehicle, as she'd learned, that's that. Nothing for it but to comply.

And sure enough, as Timmy Truesdale grilled her with questions about possible 'contraband'—weapons and such—another Edgewater County cruiser appeared behind his, blipping its siren. And carrying the K-9 officer Jeremy had feared.

❂🅗⊘

AFTER SITTING CUFFED IN TRUESDALE'S PATROL CAR FOR AN HOUR watching him and the other cop tear apart her Explorer looking for additional contraband, the miscreants were bailed out thanks to a back-room deal cut between her grandfather and the sheriff and the judge, Harold Hartsook.

Hartsook, in his eighties with a spindly black mole dangling below one eye and a jiggling pink chin wattling as he pontificated with disdain, remarked to her and Jeremy in his chambers about how disappointed he felt on a personal level with how she'd turned out; but thankful how, as a friend of her grandfather's, he got this opportunity to prevent her from further progress down the path of judicial censure by instilling not the harsh punishment she truly deserved, but instead? A measure of Christian charity.

The speech failed to impress her, though she and Jeremy, still high as shit, both had the sense to pledge with faux-sincerity an intention to attend NA meetings arranged through a school counselor back at Foothills State.

In the hallway of the courthouse, her grandfather had pressed bills into the hands of both judge and sheriff, all of them speaking in low tones and shaking their heads.

This, the only true price anyone had to pay, a payoff and a redneck judge's lecture, but better than spending the night in the lockup downtown, no record, it all went away, poof. Jeremy had had only a little herb anyway, a single tiny bud pressed flat in the corner of a baggie the K9 still sniffed out from way down in a backpack. Familial connections and good fortune had borne them from difficulty, however, and only hours later they sat free to enjoy holiday dinner, all normal except for a pall of unease over the bust.

Worst of all? Thim. In a private moment on the back screened porched she grabbed Button by the throat, threatened to murder her if she didn't cease and desist the antisocial behavior.

"You got off twice, now. I can't have a fucking sister in prison. Not where I'm going in life. Understood?"

"Sure," she croaked. "If it means that much to you. I'll just kill myself."

"Oh, honey. Stop teasing me and try cleaning up this pathetic, retro hippie act instead."

After dessert her father took her aside and confided to the final family member to be told about beginning his treatment for the cancer, and the possibility he might not recover. Now the bust seemed so childish, Button suffering deep and abiding guilt for adding to her family's present distress.

Wait—her boyfriend caused the drama. Good. A reason she would use to break up with him, as soon as they returned to cap off the fall semester.

For the moment, though, she and Jeremy got super-stoned off the rest of the cookies the cops hadn't seized—idiots.

In the backyard on the swing set, shielded from view by vines and over-grown wisteria, he started to make out with her, and she allowed him to bone her in her SUV like high schoolers. Other than mild discomfort and disgust at her stretched and slimy hole that later discharged involuntary juices between her pale thighs, she felt little other than a falseness to the whole enterprise: Her body, responding to Jeremy's narrow, angular penis in only the most primal of manners, with her mind and soul remaining as unmoved as the flesh.

Heather.

Heather awaited.

Nothing else would do.

⬤⬤⬤

BUTTON'S DAD GETTING SICK WAS A PROBLEM, BUT THIM, DONE WITH HER masters thesis, had returned to live and work in nearby Columbia, where a job awaited with a senior state legislator.

Good—Thim would be the sister on whom Button's folks counted, and by whom they weren't horrified; Thim, seeming to everyone from the time of her adolescence to be so grown already, and the student councils and debate club at the private school their daddy had paid for after Thim had tested so highly, the little shit. Thim, the kind of high school girl who gives the speech at graduation and gets chided around the table later while celebrating at Red Lobster with the family for using too many 'big words.' Thim, perfectly capable of dealing with the daddy cancer problem, and with mother's behavior which gets weirder by the year, not to mention both her grandparents who were still alive but aging fast.

Sorry, but Button would follow her own track. The holiday visit to Tillman Falls, a sojourn. Like Jeremy, too.

At dinner that Monday night back at Foothills State, she broke the news.

Pouting and stunned, he acted like he couldn't believe it. Accused her of being a dyke. "You're the only chick who hasn't come with me," he shouted, jumping up to shove his uneaten dining hall meal, tray and utensils and drink cup as well, into the trashcan. Every head turned. "You bitch."

Mortification.

For both, however: A waggish member of a frat called out after a retreating Jeremy, *"Maybe she needs a real man, because you're a limp-dick fruitcake, hippie boy."*

Heather Ponderview, OTOH (as Button would type it on the rec.music.phish Usenet newsgroup on which she'd started posting for half the day instead of studying or working on her school assignments, like screenplay pages due the next week in Brenda LaRose's writing class), said as though reading Button's mind, and further implanting the notion that Button in fact loved Heather and not Jeremy or anyone else alive:

"You go girl—Jeremy, a side trip. Wasn't he? I knew it was a no-go."

"My heart. It wasn't in it."

"I could tell. Now that you're unencumbered, let's think about going to Phish in Boston for new year's eve—I'll pay to fly us up there—and look into these rumored dates for next summer. Make our plans. We're gonna do the whole tour, sister. You and me."

On the road with Phish and Heather Ponderview? What felt like the blossoming of true love, her fondest wish in life, seemed poised to come true.

◌▥⊘

THE DALLIANCE THEY SHARED, A DREAM COME TRUE, HAPPENED DURING and after a party in the upper-class student dorm, McKendrick Hall, when everyone was tripping or doing X. The making out began there and culminated back in Heather's bed, a session which turned into full-on, feral fingering and tonguing. With the sheets freaking soaked, they giggled and went over to sleep nestled together in Button's dry bed.

The first day of Button's new life.

But not a word about any of it—Heather, hurrying to get ready for class and looking embarrassed. Forced smiles. Pounding headaches. Saying, wow, what a party.

Shit.

And with X or Molly involved, as Button would learn to call MDMA in the Phish lot, Heather could always say, it was only the drugs, sweetheart. It wasn't love.

Which she had, finally, walking across campus one day when she tried to hold Heather's alabaster hand worthy of a sculptor. "Oh, sweetie—no. It's not like that."

"I'm so confused."

A sweet smile. "Your bestie. That's all I can be. It's enough. Trust me."

Button, crushed but hiding it. Feeling humiliated in the middle of a campus walkway in broad daylight. "It was a party. I can dig it."

"That's right—nothing to take seriously. But fun," she whispered, a naughty aside. "I was sore from those fingers of yours. In the best way. Promise."

"Yeah. Fun."

◌▥⊘

THE SCENE WOULD BE ALL-BUT REPEATED ONE NIGHT ON TOUR THE NEXT year, in summer 1998 while bunking in a posh hotel room. They were spent and filthy after camping at The Gorge, a scenic Washington state music venue overlooking the Columbia River, the most spectacular and heady natural environment to see a concert, and time for hotel comfort.

The desk manager eyed Button and Heather with suspicion. They had been tripping on and off for two weeks and looked like a pair of crunchy little dirt surfers, if closer to the trust-fund variety than true vagabond wastrels — Heather's credit card, a platinum-grade edition, quelled most all concerns.

Button, spun and exhausted, soaked in the hotel tub for an hour; Heather had come in, once, to offer Button a packed bowl, and to urinate. Making small talk like a married couple, the sharp stream of Heather's urine splattered the fine porcelain of the top-tier Marriott property, a Renaissance in the heart of San Francisco to which they'd retreated after the brutal drive down the coast. Rested and ready, they'd be better prepped to shake their bones anew at the following gig, Shoreline, heading next to Ventura, LA and Arizona.

Heather and Button had both been handing out Greenpeace literature all tour, and had almost talked to the guys at the Waterwheel Foundation table into letting them volunteer there, too, but those guys — friends of the band, insiders — heard this at every show from every crunchy spun-out phan wanting to get closer to the band, be an insider themselves. Get their ego trip on. It's why dudes liked to yell out at quiet moments, like when the band came out and did *a capella* or acoustic stuff, which in the pre-arena stardom era they'd perform without mics, a more innocent time in the band's history Button ached at having missed, before Garcia died and the Deadheads had blown Phish up into arena-sized rooms.

High, clean and sleepy, she emerged from the steam of the spotless, chrome-accented hotel bathroom stretching and cracking her back. The only room available had been a king, so they'd planned to sleep together anyway — proximity not a factor. Best friends, they had camped huddled in a small tent against rainstorms. But never any funny business.

The lights down low, Heather switched on AMC running a B&W medical drama.

"Is that Brando?"

"Yeah. It's soldiers in a rehab place. After some war."

Button had checked the channel guide to see it was Stanley Kramer's *The Men*, indeed, a drama about war veterans with spinal cord injuries.

"Marlon Brando's film debut? I always thought it was *A Streetcar Named Desire*."

Heather, drowsy and sweet. "I never heard of it."

"One wonders how much else we haven't heard."

Heather gave a shrug. Gestured for Button to join her.

"Let me get a T-shirt."

"Un-kay."

Button slid into the fine sheets, reclined against fluffy pillows. "Nicer than the Range Rover, or a tent."

"I'm so tired."

"Me, too."

In a hypnagogic state, Button snuggled closer. Let the pad of her right sole, thick from dancing barefoot all tour, rest on top of the arch of Heather's own curled and tucked girl-foot. Rested her head in the crook of Heather's shoulder. Said, *mmm*.

Heather, snaking her arm around and squeezing. "I love you," she said. "My angel-girl."

"Me too," she gasped. Warmth bloomed between them. "More than you know."

Heather, sighing; Button, sweating. But both dropping off to sleep, with nothing further along any romantic lines.

The next day, not as much affection—Heather, always a grouch monster in the morning. They had a ton of chores to accomplish before heading down the peninsula to Mountain View; and, what time do the lots open, and wondering if they could get away with driving all night after the show to Ventura, find a sweet spot to camp on the beach ahead of the crowd of wooks following the band. The previous year's stop along the California coast had produced a real 'heater' of a concert, fiery and epic; 1998 would only produce a fatter trip—Heather, predicting magic, but only through their efforts to get underway again.

"Ventura even more awesome than the Gorge?"

"That was only a river. Now we're talking the ocean."

Downstairs, they waited for the valet to bring up Heather's Range Rover, its grill and windshield covered with insect splatter. Button huddled next to Heather against a crisp Bay Area morning breeze. Put her arm around her best pal.

"Thanks. For the hotel. And everything."

"The Foundation pays for it. It's like, a write-off. Or some straight-world nonsense. It doesn't matter. My dad says I can go to town, anytime. Within reason. And you're like my sister, sissy." She hugged Button tight. "So it's all good."

But this had been the last time they'd felt so close, after which Heather began to drift away, staying on with her old friends living in Southern California, where she explained how her rich family also owned property, and buying Button a plane ticket back to South Carolina as a consolation prize.

A sad period persisted until the next tour, when being on the road again made it feel as though Heather Ponderview, a ghost to Button by then, still strode alongside her. Those last shows seen with her bestie, though? Big jams. Four-song second sets. Fucking killer Phish. Button convinced herself she could remember every note.

RABBIT, RUNELLE AND BILL
WIMMEL

Sunday afternoons are a quiet time for you and your war bride along the river ridge, a perfect time for Gooch to do his little interview for the special spread about The Dixiana next week in the *Advocate*. Rather not face up to it. Seems like it went by in five years, not fifty.

But wait—the more time put between you and the war, and that'd be sixty years now, was fine by you.

Before the reporter got here, y'all celebrate the milestone that The Dixiana opened this week in 1953 with her working out in the garden and you sitting on the porch drinking a beer—it's okay now that Roy Earl's grown—and looking at the Sunday paper, the *Parade* insert and the funnies, or else staring down the long driveway of crepe myrtles bigger than you ever imagined you'd see them. Wondering if your grandson would come one of these Sundays. He didn't live but thirty minutes away, but he acted like it was having to go to the moon and back, which was so much trouble nobody had done it anymore after having done it, which wasn't like humans.

But you're too needy and hard on him. He ain't doing anything but what you done—running his trade, or rather, his several businesses since he's started with them milkshake stands of his. The boy's opening one in the mall, he says, and you can believe he'll make bank at that place—the nice new mall in Columbia. If you said it a hundred times since he bought the coffee shop, thank god he got on the right track. You paid for him to get an English degree, cussing the whole time it ought to be more useful. That he ought to study business, because look, it's in the boy's blood.

Never came to you for any money. You got all that cash sitting there, waiting for him one day. You didn't force it on him. By the time he told y'all he was gonna go into business for himself instead of get a job somewhere — you knew all about it — dang if the boy hadn't worked out every blessed detail, had put the capital together himself, and seemed so puffed up and proud you didn't say a peep about your mad money. What you call your Sunday stash — what you'd skim and toss in after Saturday night. Look at it now. Money in the mattress. How you were raised.

"What are your specific memories about the origins of The Dixiana?"

"From fifty years ago? Not much, boy, I tell ya."

"You and Burnie used to raise a lot of sand back then, didn't you?"

"Says who — Burnie? Shit. He's got a good imagination, that one."

Runelle snorts. "Doesn't he, though."

"Which is my way of saying if it weren't for Burnie, and how he conjured all this up, there wouldn't be a Dixiana to write about. That's about as specific a memory as I can offer. Oh, I mean, we went to the Opry in Nashville and looked at honkytonks there, and knew what we liked and what we wanted. Knew you could keep a successful place going so long as you took the music part of it seriously. Or that was my contribution. What I kept insisting on." You spark up a cigarette, cough through it. Probably gonna die of lung cancer soon, but no need to say it in the god-durn newspaper. "Burnie, though? Smart as a whip about the business side. Couldn't've done none of this without him."

Gooch, scribbling in his reporter's notebook, the two of you with your legs crossed behind the green sun shade on the porch, Runelle down on her knees with a gardening spade and digging out a cussed choke-weed tuber the size of an eggplant, damn evil things. "You know he wouldn't sit for an interview, though?"

"He's not usually too modest."

"Said it didn't matter what happened fifty years ago. That you were the one who deserved all the credit."

"I've put in some sweat equity, yes sir. But in my mind, it'll always be a partnership deal. Me and him. I don't care what anybody says."

Gooch, a sharp cookie, had a twinkle in his eye. "You've given me good material today. So much I didn't know. Hey — somebody should do a book about the honkytonk. Shake my tree if you ever want to write a memoir. Folks love country music as much as ever."

"Writing an article like your'n's probably pushing it, Gooch. History? Better to stay in the moment. Keep it all right-now. That's what we're up to at The Dixiana. The people who run it. Trudy. Fridge. Mama Runelle over there."

"What about you?"

"I'll accept any credit that's due me. But to tell the truth? It all seemed to happen whatever I did or thought—I've been along for the ride, beau."

"That's your worldview—that it's all happening regardless of our efforts?"

"Wouldn't go that far."

"How far would you go, then?"

Damn reporters. "Old Rabbit might've rested a finger on the steering wheel, here and there. Call it a nudge."

As he scribbles your poetry you shoot a furtive wink in the direction of the faded, round hex displayed near the front door of your home. The painted mandala is a protection power-symbol imbued with divine energy you channeled into it decades ago and maintained through daily discipline, ritual and unerring faith—not only in the unconditional love-light bestowed upon you by the Lord above, but also in yourself, which in most ways are one and the same.

Understanding this has taken you far in life. Would that more folks did. It'd make it all easier for them, knowing how much responsibility they truly held over the course of their lives.

PART THREE

Return Echo

Is this the human sacrifice part of the show?

— TREY ANASTASIO TO PHISH AUDIENCE, HAMPTON
COLISEUM, NOVEMBER 22, 1997

Never's just the echo of forever.

— KRIS KRISTOFFERSON

ROY AND THE FESTIVAL
COMMITTEE

Twenty years pass like the whisper of a wink—or no time at all. Eternity time. That's what you're on now.

The first couple of winters homesteading in the mountains were rough. You're a South Carolina boy, a flatlander. And these ancient hills ain't no Sedge Island snowbird paradise.

A few many seasons have passed since your granddaddy died, and that by-comparison brief but memorable interlude in your life in Edgewater County one last time before settling here, which you did after Uncle Burnie died a peaceful death in his sleep, a smile on his face.

Settled here, in the mountains.

A prophecy fulfilled.

A wish come to manifestation—you have peace and serenity in your heart, a low hum below the threshold of true hearing. An assurance beyond emotion.

All that matters now? When the sun comes up. When it goes down. When the seasons change. When to harvest the fruit. When to plant the next year's crop.

The totality of your lives.

Time turns elastic on the other side of the membrane; the age of Aquarius. Cosmic events and positioning and such have their influences, but that's over your head. And matters not to you—a farmer, and a father-figure, if not always by blood.

Yours isn't a refugee camp; it's a family.

A tribe.

A community.

And as for time, if it moves at all, it does with stolid, silent purpose. Your life now unfolds at a higher vibration, in a new reality. Whatever else happens or has happened in the broader world, here it's sunny and temperate, and in the winters, there's still so much light y'all stay warm in the gathering house, temple and huts tucked away across what you call Ponderview Mountain.

The enclave.

The colony.

Your entire universe.

You thumb through the small book that Button gave you, the worn, blessed pocket-size copy of the Tao that has never left your side. You still open it daily to a random chapter. Read. You've done it so many times now, the book's barely holding together. With a strip of tape you'd put on a while back, before you'd even come here to the mountains, its spine has stayed strong.

Today's reading, near the end. Chapter 80. You know the words by heart, which is good, because as you squint at the text, it is rubbery and slippery, out of focus—aging eyes.

> *If a country is governed wisely,*
> *its inhabitants will be content.*
> *They enjoy the labor of their hands*
> *and don't waste time inventing*
> *labor-saving machines.*
>
> *Since they dearly love their homes,*
> *they aren't interested in travel.*
> *There may be a few wagons and boats,*
> *but these don't go anywhere.*
> *There may be an arsenal of weapons,*
> *but nobody ever uses them.*
>
> *People enjoy their food,*
> *take pleasure in being with their families,*
> *spend weekends working in their gardens,*
> *delight in the doings of the neighborhood.*

And even though the next country is so close
that people can hear its roosters crowing and its dogs barking,
they are content to die of old age
without ever having gone to see it.

HERE ON THE MOUNTAIN YOU WANDER IN THE WOODS ON YOUR BAD LEG, which despite the years and unusual stresses on it living in a place like the hidden hollow, continues to hold up well. You stroll and meditate not unlike the endless afternoons in the pecan orchard, or down in the Glade.

Another lifetime ago.

Nothing is the same.

Nothing.

Anywhere.

Not even the sun shines like before—more pale now than yellow. Weird, white skies. You have grown used to it, as you have the total lack of air traffic.

Having entered this new age means that the greater world—the planet outside your reality bubble here in the secluded green mountains—spins wobbly on its precessional axis. Great earthquakes and upheavals have occurred; coastlines, you suspect, have changed. History as you knew it before ended and has begun again, you reckon. Other than the few other small enclaves nearby with which you barter and trade, you've had no contact with anyone for ages. And may not again, whether they come, or whether your tribe survives into the future.

The end of history as you have shared and known it has come and gone.

And you soldier on.

Your reality is that you persevere.

Few came here who didn't come with you, or else showed up not long after you put out the word you were looking for a few good folks—evolved souls—to accompany you on this journey, back when you were considering setting up what you called an artist's colony in the mountains.

And the rain falls; the plants here, lush and giving, as you give to the earth that sustains the colony. Some years there's scarcity, but in others a veritable bounty. A balance to such matters, at least with a long enough view.

But whosoever knoweth what the rain contains? All those nuke plants, and so many leftovers of the ruinous industrial age the world over, all still degrade the environment. All you know is that, here? The children you've sired, some in their late teens, seem normal.

No; more than normal. Extraordinary in their abilities. Remarkable. Magical, almost. Another story, for another time.

Chipping away at it. That's what you do here in the camp compound, revolving around the gathering house that was the Ponderview estate where Button, your beloved fried, breathed her last. A magical place infused with her spirit, that pyramid.

The core of the group lived out a few bad years inside, emerged when a protracted period of raw weather seemed all at once to break, and now these old mountains sit in their dignified and ancient grace, often more warm than cold. The small fields you tend all flower fertile, your animals graze content, you have created a place of peace and plenty.

The colony.

The enclave.

The pyramid.

Perhaps generations will live here, be born and die; some may choose to venture out again. And carry with them the knowledge you've gleaned and nurtured and kept.

If y'all live long enough as a species.

In the water from the sky comes nourishment, but also heaviness, density and acid, not the kind Button would have taken at a Phish show, or you, for that matter, at a Dead concert like that one you attended with Devin fifty years ago. Alternate realities had attracted you both back then, worlds within the greater world that'd drawn you and encouraged you and your friends and fellow travelers to do what you're doing right-now, which is co-creating the reality of the moment, and your overall lives, which you live here in the turquoise smoky mountains where you said goodbye to her.

Your collective—farmers, poets, singers and herbologists, family and friends, strangers before but now no more—manages the ebb and flow of the plants and the wind and the sun and the snow and the flowing water, and abundance is in evidence. Manifestations of wonder occur with a frequency that's routine without being rote. You give and share freely, and bask in love here in a green crook of the old mountains. Where the trees scrub the radiation leaking from Fukushima and the other failed reactors the world over. Radiation—the true dark angel of it all.

The equalizer.

The great culler.

The Event before the pole shift that mattered most; and made the jobs of the depopulation engineers even more easy. You spell it out, day by day, page by page, in a personal recounting and inventory you've been prompted, destined, compelled to write. For whom, you know not.

The kids? Who have no knowledge of the old world, except perhaps the albums and books you, your grandfather, Button, Heather and Heather's father all collected? If any eyeballs remain to read the tales, your words will await them. That's what keeps you writing.

Outside you rinse your hands and feet in cold mountain water, dry them and enter the gathering house, a true homestead built into the side of the hill in the before-time and expanded in the time since. You and Dobbs hang out the rest of the morning to smoke and read, write and talk about interesting occurrences. You look for meanings, patterns and signs the way Button taught you those many years ago. They'd led you here, reading the signs and perceiving the wonders. All roads you'd treaded upon, from the early days, led to this place, this sacred moment.

You're no less keen to read old books than you were in the time before, the ones you'd loved as a kid and many more you continue to discover for the first time. Besides the record collection, you still have your books, plus the immense library in the blue temple.

Y'all need those books now, folks, don't you? Mercy. No phones or TV or laptops here. But you severed the other cultural media wires even before the collapse. It'd been the hardest part of settling here in the hollow—not the farming and herbing and composting and working on the pipes from the spring, but detoxing from the wi-fi and the shimmering screens. At least it was by choice at the time, not by necessity. Good practice for what lay ahead.

"What's the news today?" you ask your oldest friend there in the compound, nosing through the stack of wax he's got lined up. Big band stuff. And a few hillbilly records, too. Bluegrass. Fiddlin' John Carson. Some of Rabbit's most beloved 78s. Banjo-picking Buell Kazee. "Somewhere my Pa-paw is smiling."

Dobbs, flipping through an art book, peers down his angular nose at paintings, masterpieces with meaning defined not through their worth on the market, or within the perceived context in the broader culture, but in the eyes of the beholder. Or so he would put it. "We venerate the predecessors with daily duty and willing willfulness. And play his records."

"What you know good this fine day?"

Shrugging. "Sun come up. Sun gonna go down."

And so your conversations go. You sit reading for a time; time no longer matters. You've a surfeit.

You have forever.

A CURVE-BALL, RARE: HEATHER, STRUGGLING WITH A BAD SET OF KNEES from gardening and with twigs in her wide mane of gray dreadlocks, crab-walks into the gathering house. "Hey—now here's a surprise. There's someone here."

"Besides all of us?"

"*No*," beaming that wry Heather grin. "Or rather, yes—a traveler down by the gate near the old highway."

Dobbs, stroking his chin. "Had to know we were back in here."

Agreement. "No one would scale the rockfall otherwise."

The mountain road had long crumbled away, and leaving by the old vehicular routes involved a treacherous traverse down to Hot Springs and the French Broad River. Better to hop on the A-T, only miles away along other well-tended trails.

No visitors in ages. But, no worries. You have firearms, still, and will use them bastards to protect not what you possess, but your people from unnecessary suffering. Well, they aren't 'your' people, but you attracted them here and possess voluminous response-ability when it comes to their wellbeing. How you roll.

Dobbs, who has mastered remote viewing, asks for silence and closes his eyes, which dart behind the lids as though dreaming. He grunts with psychic effort and breaks out in visible sweat.

Releasing a pent-up breath: "It's true. A scraggly old road-rat. Skinny as a rail."

"How's his aura?"

"Bluish-lavender." Dobbs comes out of his trance, shakes it off. "He's tired and hungry, but there's more to his anticipation."

"Can you see his face?"

Trembling, Dobbs shakes his head 'no.' But his eyes, wide—whom did he see?

All-right you say, crackling knuckles and deep-breathing and pretending nonchalance despite your racing heart. "Let's meet and greet. Let's get some monkeys in the trees, some cover," meaning a couple of the teens, armed with deer rifles and scopes. Hard world, still. Remnants of the vile ways of civilization.

To Heather: "From whence hath this traveler come? Doth he have a name?"

Before she can answer, Dobbs, whom by some mad miracle you note now seems able to stand: "Oh—I already know."

The fist to the head again, his other hand held aloft as though he's become Edgar Cayce, the Sleeping Prophet. "At first he said he was a pastor, then a pusher; partly truth, and partly fiction. He has a beard and gray hair. A twinkle in his eye. A guitar strapped across his back. And a song in his heart."

You share a look with Heather. Now it's your turn to feel the tingle of your own skin dimpling and your hairs all standing end-wise. "But who is he, really?"

Heather smiles and holds out her arms, filthy with peat from the gardens: "Does it matter?"

It does—because you feel scared. And when you become frightened in a dream, it makes you freaking sit up straight among twisted, damp sheets and think, fudge: it all seemed real, so real. But I'm still here in Edgewater County. Check.

◌◍◎

WHAT IN THE EVER-LOVING, MUDDER-PUDGING KIND OF LUCID DREAM IS that to endure? Way too realistic. You've cut back on the weed and the vaping. Restless nights; vivid dreams you can almost control from within.

The other night, in fact, you enjoyed an amazing nocturnal journey far more stylized than your 'golden age' homesteading vision, its details finely rendered and experienced only minutes before, now a fading haze beyond your ability to remember, describe or imagine. This other dream you can recall—you called it Springs in your Feet, an ability to STEP OVER fences, buildings, a wall.

And indeed, you awakened within this dream, realized your power and leapt in the air from a powerful squat, traversed the sky in an arc, a golden shimmering cloudscape receiving you, pillowy and unreal as you hurtled over a mountain and began to come down... at free-fall... with no parachute. Screaming.

Awakening. The heaven of super-powers followed by the hell of remembering the limitations shown in the light of day. Well, shucks. Defying gravity had been so liberating.

Cannabis detox is causing these vivid dreams. Maybe you'll fire up the vape again. That's what you think about this latest adventure, in which you were pretty sure Jesus had arrived intending to check in with you-all.

◌◍◎

INSTEAD OF BLAZING UP FIRST THING IN THE MORNING, A MUCH CRAZIER idea lands with your first sip of home-brew:

Burn the money.

The money your Pa-paw had saved up in the hole in the floor.

Oh, not all of it—but some. Every day, at the break of dawn, a chorus of crickets and songbirds greeting the act.

A ritual. Button taught you how money, as a carrier of what she might have termed 'legacy energy,' held an irredeemable falseness often misperceived as value by those ensnared in a system of commerce that represented a modern form of chattel slavery.

It may seem perverse—you have too much cheddar, at least the digital kind. And here, you getting a charge from making a flaming sacrament out of old fives, tens and twenties? Like your version of secret-shame, a titillating porno-fetish addiction. Dusty old money, the maturest of which, you discover, disappears inside the rusty trash barrel with a POOF of yellow smoke.

That's the excuse you're using—the age of the currency. Some of these bills have been stashed for decades. Worn, thin, prone to rips and tears and stains. Sure, the bank would swap out such bills, report to the IRS, whole shebang.

Forget it. They ain't taking their piece.

You have decided to burn this cash, though, in the old charred trash barrel out behind the shed, a little ceremony to greet the day before you meditate. Right—instead of burning incense or white sage like Button suggested? You? You'll burn your inheritance money.

❋❋❋

THIS CONTINUES FOR ABOUT A WEEK, UNTIL YOU PUT ON THE BRAKES AND suffer the worst panic attack you've faced since discovering the truth about Creedence and your assistant GM last year:

Wanted on a variety of felony fraud charges, Rodney Cowan, the trusted financial advisor to you and quite a few other fat-cat investors, was last seen boarding a flight to Mexico City. Wearing a disguise.

A thief. Millions, gone.

Yeah. Seriously.

You ain't busted. But your portfolio has been fudged, and royally.

You spend the rest of the day on the phone and online, gazing in slack-jawed shock as your holdings have now become diminished in value by a magnitude or so, and only just-shy of exponentially disastrous. Your net-worth dingus is shrunk, as though your wealth climbed out of a winter pond during a polar-plunge challenge.

No getting around it. You have limitations, suddenly.

The lawyers, two of whom took a serious haircut on this deal—Adger and Hagood turned you on to Cowan, both expressing weary chagrin in a video chat that afternoon while also sunny optimism, and who now have smears of fragrant Cowan blood under their noses as part of the legal war paint—suggest the possibility of various insurances and safeguards and remuneration-remedies for which petition and litigation would likely return 'some' losses. But to a degree, they cautioned, and only after a protracted enough-already interim of time.

You said, finally, "You know what? I won't starve. Keep me posted. For now, I'm getting on with my life." All agreed such an attitude seemed best; what more to do in the face of undeniable catastrophe? If only money were real, you hear Button's voice saying, you might have a problem.

Still—that's it for the money-burning. What were you thinking? You never had such an effed-up idea in your stupid life, even while being stoned all day.

Oh, wait. That's when the dumb notion had come to you. During a sesh. D'oh.

❋ ▦ ⊘

WHILE DRIVING AROUND THE COUNTY IN YOUR GRANDDADDY'S F-150 cranking tunes, some early Bowie, *The Man Who Sold the World*, you work on forgetting those money troubles by paying an overdue stop by Hillsborough, the plantation house still owned by heirs of the Beauchamp family that include your resident Southern literary novelist from the EC, Cortland Beauchamp. It's been on your list for weeks, this visit. Time to make a check-mark.

Why? Well, you finally trudged through *The Diary of Anna Dixon* your wife gave you for Christmas. Pretty good novel, the first you've read through to the end in years. Real exciting scenes set around the burning of Columbia. Tearjerker ending. A modern patina of punishment for several recalcitrant Southern characters. Probably selling a million copies on that kinda soap.

Driving in through the stone and iron gate, you admire columns of roughhewn granite carved by a one-legged soldier who, as local legend claims, spent months and perhaps years here recuperating following the Civil War. The house, and all of Tillman Falls, had avoided being burned and sacked by Sherman's departing regiments from the ruined and smoldering town of Columbia, decimated in an act of cruel and destructive vengeance, or else properly karmic retribution for having been the seat and hotbed of the rebellion that'd resulted in so much American blood spilled over keeping human beings in chains. Back in February you read articles in the *Columbia Record* about the hundred-fiftieth anniversary of Sherman's March. War. It sucks. Shit gets broken. That's your takeaway.

The sagging upper porch, the vine-choked columns; a sense of decay and disorder to Hillsborough. Not what you expected. A disappointment. This ought to be a showplace. Gothic, though. You'll give it that.

A man you assume to be Cort Beauchamp comes out onto the front porch, but after a brief explanation and introduction, you find that it's Arthur Beauchamp instead, a cousin that from his unsophisticated and drawling countenance—he reminds you of Earl, the mountain man who pulled your ass out of the ditch that time—pegs him as the Mervin to your Roy.

Cort lives elsewhere, Arthur reports, barely coming to his childhood home anymore, "For 'personal' reasons."

"I wanted to tell Mr. Beauchamp how much I enjoyed his latest book. And that we're next thing to neighbors."

You explain who you are and where you live, which prompts a hand over heartfelt offering of condolences on your grandparents' passing late last year. That Arthur Beauchamp's ass, in younger days anyway, often polished the padded, swiveling red vinyl barstools of The Dixiana. How his time of raising the wrist at a place like your granddaddy's beloved honkytonk were long past him now, however.

"You retired, Mr. Beauchamp?"

"Yes sir, from the Sugeree Station."

"What'd you do?"

"Electrician."

"You work for Buddy Sykes?"

He gives you a look like *of-course*. "Good man. Kept that plant running on a dime. Heard his daughter died recently. That's a helluva note."

All you can do is nod and shrug. "Cancer got them both."

"Terrible disease. Sure is manifesting in people an awful lot these days."

It sounded so much the way Button might say it that your short-hairs rise to attention. "More than medicine can keep up with."

"That's for damn certain. Doctors—nothing but white-coated, would-be village shamans believing their own bullshit." He offers you an iced tea, says he'll tell his cousin of your visit and sentiments. "You gonna run the honky-tonk now? Or close it down?"

"I have the sense it'll continue."

"Good to hear."

"Tell me something—what's retirement like?"

"Love it. Keep myself busy down on the backland, mostly."

"The backland?"

"Got a place down the hill. That track round the side goes on a good ways." He squints at Hillsborough, the sagging smile of its upstairs porches, the vines, the clutter, the decay. "Nobody lives in there, now."

"In the woods near the river?"

"Yep." Seems to read your mind. "Want to have a look?"

"Is it interesting?"

"You're free to tell me if it ain't."

○🅱⊘

MIND? BLOWN BY ALL THE 'SYNC', AS BUTTON WOULD CATEGORIZE WHAT most others call spooky coincidences. Dream about a backwoods commune; stumble upon the makings of one about ten minutes from where you sit pooping every morning.

Arthur Beauchamp calls this part of the land 'the compound,' down a dirt track leading away from a large metal gate like on a cattle ranch. He has to stop, get out and unlock it for you to pull your truck through, after which he repeats the procedure behind your tailgate and hops back in. Security conscious. Right on. You'd build a proper gate with a garage-door clicker setup, but whatever.

Quiet and still, this is the backland all right, not unlike what leads down to the river from your property to the south, but denser and darker. Older growth trees, the afternoon sun slanting through—it gives you a sense of the cathedral of the forest, as it's called.

An impressive and pervasive sensation of solitude.

Of peace.

You park in front of what seems a single-story structure, nondescript facing with faux white-pine planking and top of the line shingling and a chimney and a set of solar panels and dense hedging all around. The house feels low, nestled into the land. Tons of windows. Solid.

He leads you on an inlaid stone path down the side, through a short dirt walkway that separates the house from a tiered, stacked garden area lush already with spring plants growing in planters and along trellises.

Around back, you're surprised to find another level jutting out from the down-sloping angle of the land. Deceptive—more square footage than at first appearance. Nice.

Gloomy and damp, though. A little spooky. Out here y'all aren't far from Macon Crossroads and Parsons Hollow, backwoods so-called towns where it'd always been said there was dug-in dogfighting and cockfighting culture, a ring run for ages by Edgewater County organized crime types like good-old Jezmund Rembert, including a famous case from about ten years ago where folks got busted, somebody was killed, a whole sordid business that made the news. Growing up you heard stories, but had never been concerned by the goings-on in the sticks to the north of Tillman Falls. You were a river-rat, not a hillbilly.

It chills you to the bone, though, thinking about the Remberts setting up dogfights there in the honkytonk. That your granddaddy and Uncle Burnie probably wagered on. For all you know.

"So—what's the intention here? Seclusion?"

He searches for the words. "I reckon you could say that."

"Almost like you'd have to know this place is back here."

"Yep. That deadfall the road was cut through—it could be filled in right easy."

"Thinking a few moves ahead. I can dig it. Feels safe. Tucked away."

"That's the idea-r."

You are led farther down a steep grade of rich, earthy ground he says will be fixed with a stairwell he's been putting together in the workshop.

Stunning—now that you've climbed down you're looking at the front of a lovely mountain-cabin half dug into the side of the hill, what Arthur explains is an earthen-berm style of construction, in which part of the structure is formed by cutting a wedge out of the slope. He remarks at length about the energy savings in the summer, when the ground's natural cooling keeps the house temperate.

"And in the winter, them big windows let in so much light that on a mild day? You don't half need to burn the wood stove but first thing."

"Winters in South Carolina, they're usually weak, anyway."

"There ya go. This past one? Right toasty in yonder."

He points out where he'd cut off the tops of the trees in a swath down the hill to allow the rising sun to provide what he called passive solar energy to heat the house; how the walls have cores constructed out of tires filled with sand, though from the finely finished exterior, one would never know such materials had been used; and many other 'green' amenities and off-the-grid homesteading innovations.

"Long story short: what'd it cost?"

"Built this for less than ten thousand, including renting the backhoe for a day. Hell—Hill Hampton, Junior paid *me* to take the old tires off their car lot. Another ten on this and that. It goes on."

God-damn—twenty thou? "Extraordinary."

"Anything can be done."

"If you can pay for it."

Arthur gets a grin, devilish. "If you know what it is you wanna do. And how to envision yourself doing it. The cost otherwise? You figure that part out."

"Which is what, in your case?"

"What I wanna do?" Takes a minute with it. Smiles hard into a cool breeze coming off the river another hundred yards down through the forest. "Survive."

"Survive what?"

"Whatever's coming."

"Not 'the shit'?"

He asks do-what; you clarify that you mean the collapse of civilization as you've all been living it.

As he chuckles without mirth Arthur Beauchamp's chin-wattle jiggles. His pitted eyes and a large liver spot on his left cheek make him look aged and wearied. "S'good way to put it. Short and sweet. Here's all I know: they done propped up this dance party for a long time, now. Can't nobody go on dancing forever. Sooner or later it's gonna crumble, the music will stop, and they won't be no chairs left for nobody playing the game. And when it does, it'll happen fast."

"Like, an hour or two before people lose their dang fool minds and strip the IGA faster than you can drop your drawers and kiss your lily-white, drunken Edgewater County Scots-Irish ass goodbye."

"Oh, my—the grocery stores, the Wallyworld. Gas Chief's got a pretty good selection of potted meat and beer-skis. But I ain't in need, because I'll be ready."

Admiration blooms in your belly. "You're stocked up in there."

"Root cellar, too. There's a shipping container buried down below. Kind of a panic room, if you ever heard that term. Back near the main house is about a half-acre of mature fruit trees, with another half planted and growing. Somebody could hold on for a good while. All things being equal."

The road down here had included a power line, to which you point. "And when this goes?"

"Well—come over here."

He shows you an under-construction hydroelectric project he has going across a babbling brook curving around and through the deeper woods. "This here's a branch from Twenty-Five Miles creek back over that-away," karate-chopping in the general direction. "This, solar and wood's gonna provide the juice we need to get by. That big-old creek never dries up, though. Not all the way."

"Why, it's Beauchamp Water and Power."

"A theme in my life, you might say." He leads you back to the house. "Last big expenditure is a few more panels. I'm waiting another season on them. According to the politicians—and I wouldn't put no stock in them and what they say—next year's supposed to bring reductions in the costs that'll let a solar buyer get twice as much generating capacity for half the money. Might be too good to be true."

"Even so, you could settle in today. If 'the shit' started. You're ready enough."

"Just about there. You?"

"I'm seething with envy. I have resources, but I've done no long-range planning. At all."

He nods. "Don't fret. Jealousy ain't never fixed nothing. Besides, you ain't alone."

"That ain't comforting."

"But you know—certain levels of 'shit' coming down? Not sure I want to survive it. Nuclear war. All this is more about civil unrest. Collapse of supply lines. And so on."

No doubt. But barring ELE-style catastrophes like a comet striking the eastern seaboard or the Yellowstone caldera blowing or all the plants like the Sugeree Station melting down, Arthur Beauchamp could live here in the woods, untroubled, until he died. His, an example.

"I better get to work. If I'm gonna be ready."

"Same here. Find your way back out okay?"

"Absolutely. A question, though—what made you bring me back here? A stranger?"

"I hesitated. Got a little healthy paranoia, as any sane person should these days. I ain't up to nothing untoward, of course—ain't like we're growing weed, heh heh. But, I've bought a good bit of survival supplies online. You wonder if they don't watch people like me. To make sure we can't get too far off the grid."

"I hear you. Nowhere to hide these days, is there?"

"Suppose there ain't. Anyway, my gut said to show this Pettus character the backland. So I did."

"And he thanks you for it." You give him a little namaste bow like Button taught. "I'll call with any questions, coach."

"You do that, my friend."

Driving out the mile through the woods before you again see the back of Hillsborough, you're gripped with the idea of what this guy has done. Ten thousand dollars? Even with the Cowan fiasco, what a joke. You can write a hundred checks of that size. Nothing left at the end of such a mad spree but the equity in the marsh mansion and Pettus land, but still. Formidable resources. Cowan's perfidy but a speed-bump.

You got this.

That's it. After this festival's over you're gonna take Creedence back to the mountains, this time to Heather's; and you will write the first of those checks to buy the secluded land the Ponderview heir owns near Cat Pen and Max Patch.

As for Arthur Beauchamp, all this was fated to happen, this remarkable spark to your imagination, a direction regarding the next steps in your life, and what you can do with the remainders of your once-beaucoup fortune. An enclave in the woods? Money or not, if you wish it the dream can become reality.

⊛⊞⊘

YOU'VE ALREADY HAD ENOUGH OF THESE CURSED RABBIT FESTIVAL planning meetings, but here at the end there's drama not only over an over-booked sanitation company's ability to deliver the requisite number of portable lavatories, but one of the food vendor licenses, of all crisis points.

As though the controversy of you MAKING YOUR PRESENCE KNOWN a month before the event with the announcement you wished to rebrand the damn thing the Rabbit & Runelle Pettus *and* Button Sykes Memorial Bluegrass Festival hadn't caused enough trouble. The train had left the station, they all said. Promotion well underway, ad buys made in regional media, press releases and so on. Ha, you replied. It's your family legacy on the line, along with a chunk of your change. And so, you will do as thou wilt.

REBRAND, you had thundered.

Grumbling and resistance around the table in the elegant, wood-paneled ELMS executive conference room, but perhaps having heard about the razor-sharp cut of your blade the committee members think better of challenging your element of primacy over them. Not after informing them about who's deciding what.

On their own turf, no less.

Ha.

In truth the ELMS contingent, with its experience putting on street festivals, were mostly helpful and supportive and, dare you say it: motherly to you. Your season of loss, well known around a town suffering its own losses, one after another, from Rabbit Pettus to Howdy Shull to the more recent iterations. Tongues still wagged, tragic, about what could have become of poor Bill Wimmel, who suffered from dementia and had driven off one day and never returned, leaving Dobbs Vandegrift terribly broken and guilt-ridden, certain it all his fault for not getting Gooch into the elder-care facility alongside Dobbs's mother. A fruitless law enforcement search; a terrible end to an iconic townsman. And your precious Button Sykes, Edgewater oddball, gone at such a young age—not even forty. Chilling to those of you already on the other side of that milestone, in your case pushing fifty. You can only imagine how such news feels to the elder ELMS's at the table, most of whom but for Becky L are well into their dotage.

Becky—poor woman. Seems broken. Manny did a real number on her head, so much she's leaving Tillman Falls. The search is on for a replacement to run the Fine Arts Center. Dang. But you get it. Heartache changes everything.

After confirming another last-minute change—you requested booking a regional Phish cover band called Gnarly Armor to the talent roster—you bring up a personal bugaboo. "I'm less concerned about the port-a-poopies than assurances about keeping a lid on the VIP laminates."

Feebee Elmendorf, the PR and event planner on the committee, grits her teeth and says VIPs are fine; badges, under control. "We've issued under forty so far."

"Total? May I see the list?"

"Certainly."

You sniff and peruse, slide the sheet of paper back to her with one digit. "Stinkin' badges better be kept secure. I didn't spend all that renovation coin in The Dixiana only to see it receive censure from the fire marshall on the day of the festival because we've caved and given out credentials to every entitled nitwit who's come begging a favor. Based on the requests run by me, most of them didn't give a crap about Pa-paw when he was alive. Sorry; not-sorry."

The honkytonk, freshly re-furbed, will serve as the musician's green room, with the bar area open to a select echelon of festival attendees, a standard determined to restrict access to certain elements who'll be expecting special treatment, namely Jezmund Rembert and his crew of redneck thugs. You can't say that in an open meeting, though. Reasons abounded. "Besides, we have celebrities who will require an extra layer of privacy."

Becky LaFreniere, despite her role as a short-timer, remains your literal right-hand man on the committee. She pats your arm, her words all correct, but trickling out featuring little of her old spark. "I'm keeping my eye on it. Don't worry. The tented area will be set up with a view of the main stage, anyway. That's where most VIP guests will congregate, I would think."

"Terrific. Now. Somebody explain this vendor license hoo-hah," glaring down the table at the cops, who are the ones who've raised the objection to a falafel cart.

The Department of Homeland Security rep, a humorless bureaucrat named Special Agent Rufus Bindernagel, reports that a particular vendor's name has popped up on a list; rather, an addendum to a watch list. That this individual, a local merchant, has a number of relatives living back in the Middle East also appearing on official watch lists, and that on the intel from no fewer than two authoritative acronym agencies and as a representative of the federal government charged with advising y'all on matters of festival security and the general welfare and wellbeing of the community at large, it's his recommendation that the jubouri license be flagged. "If it was my town festival, anyway. That's uh. What I'd do. And that's what the government suggests you do." Throws up his hands. "I dunno. Having to explain it in this day and age seems, like, weird."

Bindernagel relates all this with a series of distracted sighs. Seeming prone to fancies and whims, he speaks while scratches a long nose, a prominent Adam's apple bobbing in time with a series of resigned shrugs, shifty eyes darting out a window perhaps in lament of a sunny day he's missing while stuck in a low-stakes meeting like this. In a cadence bored beyond petrified wood, he reiterates how all data points to a DHS official advisement for the festival to reject that one particular vendor app.

Bag of bones Ruth DeKalb, with whom Becky seems to have a rather chilly relationship of late, speaks up: "It's not our 'town festival', sir. It's a onetime event taking the place of our spring festival."

Bindernagel's all like, "Whatever. A public gathering is a public gathering."

Musing over this behavior, your conclusion? Dude seems stoned, way too chill, to perform as an effective federal agent. Probably has a pocket vape out in the car like yours, inherited from Button and which you sucked on like a baby bottle before the meeting. You must get impossibly high to persevere through these meetings, a state of being that mitigates your

CONSTANT IRRITATION at having to put up with bureaucratic foolishness of any nature.

But the Fed's words carry weight, inspiring agreement from Sheriff Oakley, with whom you continue to have issues over the Howdy shooting incident. Other nervous chitter-chatter bubbles up.

"I think better safe than sorry," Becky says.

Feebee agrees. "Can't be too careful. Should a demonstrably preventable occurrence occur, we'll all have to answer for it."

Your response comes so quiet and small that the other end of the table, the one with the cops, all lean in and frown. "Me? I didn't want to have outside food vending in the first damn place. I had this whole a 'taste of Tillman Falls' in mind. Dixiana chicken. Manny's on the Green barbecue. Congress Street burgers. Hermie's Hot Dogs."

Becky's smile is thin and forced. "No need to revisit. This is a vendor who counts on the SpringFlowerFest this event is replacing, however, and so we felt an obligation—"

"So: the falafel guy's a legacy licensee?"

"As of two festivals ago."

Oh, for heaven's sake. "Whoop-tee-do. Strike the license. He'll get over it."

The cops all relax. You wink at Bindernagel, who sits birdlike and blinking. Weirdo.

Feebee, relieved: "Striking the license."

Pleased. You are in control.

But you experience guilt-pangs about feeling so proud about this state of being. Button—she'd be disappointed. You're supposed to allow all to unfold, the Taoist woo-woo bit; not your constant scheming, cajoling and manipulative strategizing, navigating everybody's ship using your own sextant and nobody else's stars. Hard habit to break.

"Next order of business," you shout, usurping Feebee's chairperson role and making her visibly irritated. "Who will deliver my toilets that morning if our vendor 'craps out' on us, ha ha ha? With all the beer we'll sell that day, people will need containment of the resultant waste stream," sounding like you know the deal. Fake it until you make it. "I want concrete answers on the piss-pots. And I don't mean five minutes ago." Bossman. Like riding a bike.

❁

ADJOURNMENT IS THE MOTION. RELIEF.

Other than the tidbit of conflict over the terrorist falafel vendor, who turns out to be the guy who runs the Gas Chief, the festival is planned, booked, squared away; all-but ready to occur. All this means is that you and many others have been busy beavers, and to be frank you've had it with untangling the gordian knot of details.

Furthermore, you haven't had a chance yet to grieve for Button.

And when you let yourself realize this?

It hurts.

Bad.

The staying-busy bit they advise when you lose folks? Over the last month or two, you've taken that to heart.

And plenty to occupy your mind. Between tweaking the almost complete rehab and build-out of The Dixiana; getting the sign taken down and trucked, carefully, over to the shop where two young hipster beard-o metal-working-types continue rehabbing it from the inside out; dealing with many legal and probate issues relating to your grandparents' estate, which isn't a complicated affair to settle; and planning this misbegotten, godforsaken music festival? You ain't found much time to grieve for your friend, nor anyone else.

You've focused in a principal sense on grieving for your marriage, anyway, which is on the road to dissolution. As it should be, you reckon. If that's what she wants.

Hell, you don't know — maybe you can still save the marriage.

But that's not what she thinks is right. Or isn't sure. An ocean of unsure.

One of Button's many lessons is to not go against the flow of the energy, and if two souls aren't flowing together, there's little way for their co-created lives to harmonize fully. So none of it sounded like that good a deal to force into reality, this post-affair marriage between two people who don't have that much in common. Sure, you said when Creedence called to say she had had the formal separation papers drawn up. Makes the most sense.

Still the matter of the mansion on the marsh, but who gives a rip. Hell, you'll sell and triple your investment without breaking a sweat, monies you need to rebuild the portfolio.

Lose your life partner; make money in real estate. Sweet trade-off — not.

Amidst a bubbling of hubbub, everyone folds up their tents. Despite no one wanting to leave more than you, however, attention is called to your end of the table one last time by the rapping of Pettus knuckles:

"Since this is the last meeting of the full committee, I need to make a few statements. Wait — no. A restatement of purpose. So here goes. It's like this — the music, the beer, which I'm not the biggest fan of, we're only trying to do what The Dixiana's always done, but bigger and grander and out in the street under that big, open Carolina sky of blue we're hoping to see on the big day. A community event intended as an exclamation point on the life of a man, and now a woman—two women—who made an indelible effect on the town. Who served us all in their different ways with a deep and abiding love, and honor, and dignity. And who tried to do the right thing—by me, and by all of you. Best they could; within the limitations and obligations they suffered, oh, woe unto them. Joke.

"But for real: I know they're watching down on us now, and I'm betting they feel right squared away about the whole deal, as do I. So, I just wanted to thank you all one last time. It's true gratitude I feel for all the energy taken out of your lives to help me plan this here hot-potato sacred task I got handed. But if you all didn't understand, none of you would even be here."

Nods and appreciation from the LEO end of the table, even sour-apple sad-sack Bindernagel, a subtle, flashed peace sign.

Various chests move to speak, but your hand shoots out like a Nazi salute to forestall their remarks: "And further to this," you add with glee and sparkle, "I'll have you all know this favor's not a one-way street. We're gonna leave the town better than we found it. Know why? Because I've arranged—on my own dime—to get the sidewalks pressure-washed, have paint touchup on benches, lampposts, waste containers and the bollards out front of the courthouse, along with a few other cosmetic changes I'm working with the city manager on implementing. But not merely for that one day; rather, a contribution for the ongoing good and pleasure of all. My gift to the town. God knows how long any of us will be here, so I had to make a difference while I could."

"I'm choked up." Feebee Elmendorf, PR maven and disciplined meeting facilitator, thanks you right back and moving again to adjourn. "That's the most beautiful speech I've ever heard in a municipal event planning committee meeting like this."

You ain't done. No, ma'am. "And further-furthermore, as long as I got my Free Speech Zone, I will say that DHS and you other badge-holders can check all the backpacks and purses you want, and prohibit whatever you want, keep an eye on folks, tell us how we think the festival ought to be run, and so on." On the spot where Button had put her EZ-Up for several months would be a small platform with a microphone, a mini-amp and a sign-up sheet, on which speakers may reserve fifteen-minute blocks during which to expound their views to anyone who'll listen. American as apple pie and bong hits. "As long as I have a protected space in the form of Button's Free Speech Zone," you feel moved to reiterate, deep-voiced and peering out at the faces from under your brow, "you can get me to agree to just about anything."

There'd been much grousing about this free-speech element—the codified notion caused consternation to some authorities and citizens nowadays—but you had already designed the layout of the festival with Darren Woczinski, the logistics manager and sound reinforcement provider, to situate the soapbox so orators might have a fighting chance at their message being heard. Now, the hearing-part never matters as much as having the right itself to speak. You get it. But all other freedoms, perceived or otherwise, flow from this right, as you inform a hostile and fidgety festival committee. And you will welcome all speech, except hate speech and anyone shouting 'fire' or 'bomb' or 'gun' when none of those items are present.

Becky manages to angle in and cut you off: "Thank you, Roy. Another issue, already settled. But your gratitude is noted and welcomed."

Feebee Elmendorf, a busy woman with other duties back in Columbia, fixes you with the smiling slit-eyes of a liver-feasting cannibal demon. "We're all gratified to be here," she purrs, calm and still like Dr. Lechter. "But we've covered the agenda. That's all I'm gonna say. Any other speeches or concerns? Please send a group email. If you must."

"Can do, Feebs." You brandish your phone. "Already got a draft saved."

◉ ▥ ⊘

THE POST-MEETING CHATTING AND BACKSLAPPING WINDS DOWN ON THE sidewalk in front of the granite columns of the ELMS lodge, imposing and formidable. You tell Bindernagel how you 'appreciate his service to the country,' and for him to keep 'em straight down at the Federal Building in Soda City.

Outside you linger with Becky, who in most ways looks lovely as ever, but the last few months have left her frayed around the edges—gray roots, three to four smile lines where before had been one. Neither acts nor sounds like she's been sleeping much. A lethargy lurking beneath the otherwise blue-chip pro exterior.

You lean in to give her a hug, think better of it. Best not to touch anyone anymore for any reason, even friends.

A handshake instead. "Well-sir, we've been chipping away at this thing, and now it's all in place. It's gonna be a peaceful, inclusive crowd. Why anyone's worried about security issues, I dunno."

A sad smile. "We can't rest on laurels yet, but we're getting there."

Her forced cheeriness makes you depressed. Much remains unspoken between you—many times did she appear at the old house to commune with Manny.

"You must be busy."

"With festival stuff? Totally."

"No. Your other matters."

"I—don't know what you mean. Oh. My leaving the FAC?"

"There you go."

"No big whoop. We look for new challenges from time to time. Ten years to get the arts center on its feet? Long enough."

"I hear you're moving."

"New York."

"Dang. That's pretty exciting. What-cha got lined up?"

A slender finger to her lips, a gesture that makes you notice the hollows lurking under her eyes, shadows beneath a patina of cover-up. "Don't want to jinx anything. But—an arts-related position, of course."

"Fantastic. Living the dream. I love it."

You observe as the sedan carrying the DHS rep and the Sheriff pulls away from the curb without using its signal. "I appreciate Homeland Security's investment in the proceedings, but seriously: WTF on all the gates and wristbands and bag checks and nonsense. Nobody around here, not even the known criminal element, has the stones to show their ass at my Pa-paw's music festival."

"Just dotting I's and crossing T's." One of Becky L's favorite sayings. "In this world of ours, you can't take any possible occurrence for granted."

Ruth DeKalb, a shriveled, puckered old matron who sat all-but silently through the various festival meetings, appears in the ornate, heavy wooden double doorway. "But if the 'known criminal element' were to patronize this festival, then perhaps you'll know why we stood opposed to your father's desire to stage—"

"My grandfather. Not father. And as I said, my dear, I'm not expecting the criminal element."

Both women tense up at your term of endearment.

"Other than the criminals I see every day on this green, and in the court-house, that is. Maybe in this very building itself. For all I know."

"What are you implying?"

"C'mon." Now you feel unleashed. All is set and you no longer need them politically, these ELMS. Rather than giving into the adrenaline squirting into your belly, which is shrinking for the last month since you've taken up jogging along Button's concrete river walk, you stand outside your emotional response. Watching the watcher. Still, you can't help a little healthy rhetorical cruelty. You are still smarting from having to get permission to do anything, not from these distaff gangsters nor anyone else. "Life is far too short to stand in the blazing white sun explaining how the world works to one whom, at her advanced age, ought to already know."

DeKalb, the mother of a former governor, sputters and mutters about selling beer in the streets, trash and loud music. "The neighborhood up behind that Dixiana of your *grandfather's* had enough of the loud racket from the back porch decades ago, and we did something about it. So all this 'partying' in the street feels like a step back. But as you seem comfortable saying to my face, I'm old, Mr. Pettus. And out of touch with what most folks want from life."

"Let's just remember our place and our purpose, the equivalent of a memorial service for my granddaddy, my grandmama, and now also to honor a proud daughter of these hills, Button Sykes. Apologies if I present as blunt. The patience you've all shown me and my family is considerable, appreciated, et cetera. I hope I can live up to your trust by playing impresario to a clean and safe community event. Long story long."

That shuts the old crone up. Your vibration, purring. Honey, rather than vinegar.

Poor Creedence. How you used to yell at her. This feels new, lately. The meditation, more faithful since Button's death. The exercise. A feeling of clarity, presence and wakefulness. Of wanting to simplify, downsize, get rid of all this material crap, give the money away, do something meaningful with your life, after only having chased success to the point of mass deception — diabetics came to you for smoothies without sugar. And you had dosed them, anyway. The karmic implications, difficult to comprehend without getting a knot in the gut.

But forget all that; water, meet underside of bridge. Will she give you a chance to make it up?

Maybe if you can get this effing festival staged. And pay attention to her.

A truck pulling up to green across from The Dixiana catches your eye. It's a flatbed with an object on the back under a tarp and secured by straps. "Madam DeKalb, Ms. LaFreniere, would y'all care to join me in welcoming back an iconic part of Tillman Falls to its proper place hanging high above the green?"

Becky, a glimmer of her former sparkling enthusiasm: "Oh, the sign —!"

"At last."

"I'm sure it's duly impressive, Mr. Pettus. But owing to my bad hip, I'll see it when it's in place." DeKalb wobbles over and extends a frail, arthritic hand in perpetual gnarled discomfort, lips thick with red goo and exuding a floral old-lady smell. "And I, too, hope for a fine music festival with no problems or issues. And despite my salty talk, I do have faith in you. I apologize for being snappish. Indeed — I'm old, and in pain, and if I'm brusque —"

"No prob. I invented brusque. It's all good. Bygones," all of which only seems to confuse her, your sub-literate, pop culture-informed vernacular. "It's chill — partner."

The delivery truck, joined by an extended cab pickup hauling gear and a group of dudes in work boots, discharges a crew who hop out along the curb and don reflective vests, leather work gloves, and tool-belts jangling like the spurs of approaching cowboys; like the arrival of *The Wild Bunch*.

Exuding courtesy but conscious of your soft, pink rich-boy's palms against the coarse callouses of their workingmen's hands, you greet the workers with genuine good cheer. "You fellas look like you could erect some mean signage."

"You bet, soon as you 'sign' off on the work," the supervising beard-o says, offering you a clipboard and a ballpoint pen, cackling and making you laugh, too. "We had a marvelous time with her. A beauty. A piece of art."

"I just got a chubby. Let's see it, dude."

Bubbling with excitement and bustling from all directions many others gather round, including Manny and Neecie who come out of the restaurant across the way, as do Trudy and Etna Dixmont, inside rehanging all the 8x10 country music glamor shots, the Patsy Cline painting, the Hawg Hickens memorial, leaving wall space blank for the portraits of your grandparents you've had commissioned; and folks like Dobbs at the paper and Jasper at his law office leaning out of windows, and Cecil's salon and piercing crew and customers all emerging to see:

Two workmen, the youngest, scrambling onto the flatbed, untying the straps and heaving off the heavy gray tarp, and here, here she is: The Dixiana's neon sign, beautiful and new again. Exactly the same. But new. Endlessly renewed, like the inside of the bar itself.

A cheer goes up — not for an old neon sign, not for you, but for themselves, and the possibility of eternal return; and you have done nothing for yourself here, only for them, within and without your granddaddy's honkytonk. You have no skin in this game. You give with no expectation of recompense, energetic and otherwise, other than seeing their relief and pleasure.

And for which you feel satisfaction, a welling of contentment, which continues throughout the wellwishing and congratulations you receive for the rest of the afternoon, the thanks offered for all you're doing to raise the vibration and profile of the community. Making your grandparents proud, as more than one person puts it, often with a tissue dabbing at watery eyes.

All you need do before the festival now, at least in an energetic sense, is push hard on the final detail work inside to maximize the coolness of the experience of having a Dixiana VIP area and green room where stakeholders and talent will convene; where the musicians can relax and prepare themselves to play outside in front of your grandfather's eyes, God's and everybody else's, too.

At long last. You are a caged man counting down the days until freedom. Single digits, baby. Single digits.

◉ ⬛ ⊘

AS THE SIGN IS LIFTED BY A SMALL CRANE AND MEN ON SCAFFOLDING wait to receive it, the Mayor ambles over from the municipal complex behind the courthouse.

"Now that the rest of your score's getting settled, what you think about the water tower? No pressure, or nothing."

The naming rights—lord help you. Mayor Hampton's been pressing you to consider having The Dixiana logo painted on the old water tower near the freeway, where everyone who passes through Edgewater County would see the commemoration of your grandfather's legacy; the county would license the water tower metal to you in perpetuity. And passersby, all hoped, would wonder what 'Dixiana' meant enough to pull off, explore the town and leave money behind in the fine manner of commerce as it is practiced the world over.

Old-fashioned, however, a water tower promotional logo, especially compared to how you've advised Trudy, which is become proficient at social media. It's how she'll best promote the new Dixiana going forward, you told her. It's the modern age.

But you remember the Dr. Grabow's Pre-Smoked Pipes advert you saw a few months back, think about the idea of years passing and nobody remembering you or your family, who you were and what you did. The Spotted Banana Brand being rolled out across the country, it would become increasingly recognized, but few would ever care who you were. Not since you cashed out. They remember Ray Kroc and not the McDonald brothers, and in your case that would end up being fruitshake owner-manager Colin Kwoth as chairman of the new corporate sub-entity known as Spotted Banana Legacy Partners.

You want nothing to do with any of it. Maybe cashing the checks, reinvesting the stock dividends. Maybe that much. For the present moment, anyway, with your fortune suffering a rebuilding season or three.

No—this legacy, here in Edgewater County, would constitute your truest and most personal stamp on the world. The Dixiana. The water tower. Sure.

However: "Let me get through the festival." Winking, playing the game. "Let's see if it pays for itself first. I ain't made outta money, after all. We'll have people negotiate it out for us. Like grownups. Like gentleman. My lawyer don't have enough to do," nudging an elbow toward Jasper Glasscock, who's come over from his law office two blocks away with Burnie Sykes following behind, a slower gait. Burnie, staying with the Glasscocks since Button passed. His mind, going. You and Letty and Jasper will have to figure out what to do with him. Your gut says no to institutionalization. Not with your other resources, like, for one, your plentiful time. Soon as the festival's over, the honkytonk back open, and a few other loose ends, and you'll be there for Burnie full time. Least you can do.

"Ain't none of us made of money, boy. Not like in the old days. We grew up well off, I got to admit it. And sometimes you wonder if the old days, well —they ain't never coming back."

"Wouldn't count on it."

"Well, dang. What're we all supposed to do? All the small businesses comprising the literal economic backbone of this once-great country of ours? Dry up and blow away?"

"Beats me."

You and Jasper, wiping an ever-loving tear out of his sentimental old drunk's eye, watch as the workers hang and bolt and connect your granddaddy's sign back into place.

You feel like all is coming together as you'd envisioned, your reality now the general unfolding reality of the town, which was your goal when you first came back here last year. Button taught you well—it occurs to you she co-created all this too, in fact. But they all did, right alongside you.

A wave of positivity—that's how you greet the day. The torpor and depression of the winter following Button's death has receded with the warmth of another growth season. A game with yourself—you feel better. Keep saying it, and one day it will become true.

You've even reached out to Mervin and his wife Carla, mending filial fences. A lunch at the Congress Street Grille, baskets with those burgers served on thick white bread and fries and slaw, and at the end a misty-eyed hug between you and the cousin who'd assaulted you over not being given something that wasn't his. Especially since you offered to help them with their housing situation. Again, after the festival, when your life will be obligation free.

Even the neon sign glows with possibility. The last of the connections made and a switch thrown. All the neon tubes working, its vibrant color glowing faint under the unrelenting, all-revealing illumination of the mighty star around which you spin.

"Gonna look real pretty later after nightfall. Won't it, Jasper."

Jasper can hardly speak. "I don't think I ever seen it looking so good."

Burnie, sitting on the bench out front.

The bench—another big idea. A granite memorial bench, with a little plaque. Your Pa-paw's bench. Add it to the list.

You go ask your 'uncle' his opinion of the sign. His words come muffled from inside a wadded-up handkerchief he's got stuffed into his nose, honking like a goose, hiding what you know to be tears of grief and loss. How else could he feel? Last man standing.

You leave him be and drape an arm around Jasper, who clasps you in a hot bear hug with breath tinged by the sharp smell of whiskey and Listerine, waxing philosophic upon the reemergence of the sign Burnie and Pa-paw commissioned almost sixty-five years ago.

"You've done a wonderful thing, son. Not just for me, Burnie, Trudy, or any one of us. All of us. You're giving us continuity. There's precious little of that in life anymore, don't you know. The world's people are connected better than ever, yet our bond as human beings sometimes feels like it's falling apart, bit by bit. We have communities, but virtual, inside our computers. The Dixiana is part of something real. Something that lasts. God bless you, Roy Earl Pettus."

You got it; you're down with the sentimentality. You're awash in it, every day you live in your grandparents' house, which you hope won't be much longer. Your fondest wishes, in fact, involve sentiment, and love. They involve—

Oops; your phone, buzzing. A text.

From Creedence.

Creedence!

Your heart pounds now whenever you get a message from her. Praying it's sweet and flirty instead of dry and officious about the separation, or the coffee shop, or money.

You finger-swipe to reveal:

CALL ME!! WE HAVE A KITTY EMERGENCY! :(

Oh, by the seven sisters, by the sword of Damocles; not a cat crisis.

Wait—*she's messaging about a cat crisis*. This feels so normal. As such, you break into a happy grin and call her back, like, five seconds ago, dude.

⊛⊠⊘

Damn if you mustn't be courting conflict in your karmic conundrum. As though Creedence's aggrieved report when you call doesn't get you enough into panic mode, now you face assault at the gas pumps by a merchant, a member of your own social class, who appears to have gone mad.

⊛⊠⊘

First, the crisis: Sissy, the tortie-girl, of all the cats the one you most adore, has developed symptoms of a possibly fatal illness, and your ex—not 'your wife'; see, you're starting to transition—didn't know what to do but call. That you would want to know. Maybe have input over the cat's treatment and disposition.

"I'm on my way," is all you suggested. "I wanna be in on this."

"I hoped you would, baby. She—Sissy—misses you. Isn't that so, Miss Sissy," reassuring the cat and holding the phone so you can hear the cat's purring.

She called you baby. Creedence, not the cat. Hot damn. This sick feline feels like the best news since flush toilets came in.

Now, two months ago? You'd have said, let prettyboy Phil Webhannet take you and the cat to the vet. That was before you got wise and cut his ass off, both monetarily and otherwise. A dressing down; an interrogation about his and your wife's relationship that had horrified the young cop.

Webhannet, pleading for you to not think anything untoward had occurred, because it hadn't. His proximity to her, a professional service. That you, Mr. Pettus, had hired him to do.

"About that—I don't need you to do it anymore. In fact, you can make a big show now of not doing it. If you don't mind."

The cop sounded relieved. Not even money was worth being in the middle of two wackos and their unresolved marital woes.

Maybe the Creedence train is finally back on its tracks. Who knows.

But when you stop to fill up the truck at the Gas Chief, you find your wave of positivity crash against a craggy promontory: when you get out, whistling a happy tune and thinking maybe you should grab a quick shower and shave and nose-hair plucking before hitting the road to the island, the proprietor, the Iraqi man named Jubouri, comes charging from behind the counter and outside to the pump island.

Thing is: You only know his name because of its presence on the rejected festival vendor app.

This is the falafel dude, dude.

The watch-list guy.

Somehow he's already heard.

"*You*—you are the one to keep me out? Who says I cannot sell?"

You stop pumping, supplicate with open palms. "Mr. Jabouti. It's not me."

"My name is Jubouri!" Unhinged, eyes spinning around. Grasping and groping for words. Furious. "What was it for? Eh?"

"The application? I'm not—"

"No, the war on my country—what was it for? Saddam, Saddam, yadda yadda. If not for someone like me to come here, and to make money and pay taxes and share a piece of the pie, then what? This is what I am asking you. To make the money, yes? But you? You say no. Say no to my family. My daughter Aisha, she is ill with cancer, the cancer of the blood."

You don't know what to say.

The first thought coming to mind? One of Button's pamphlets describing the possibility of juvenile and adult cancers developing from the United States military's use of depleted uranium shells in countries like Iraq. You can't cop to that, though, not on top of the festival rejection. Talk about digging a hole.

You finish pumping at the odd amount of $33.18, put the handle back in its greasy cradle and wrench closed the gas cap on the truck. "Your daughter. How is she? How bad is it?"

His anger, like a crackling field of static in the air with enough charge to power a roomful of Tesla coils. "What was it for? To make my child sick? She is dying—my dear Aisha, she is dying. Music festival man. Honkytonk man. And I cannot get paid. I cannot pay for what she needs even if it were to save her, but it is stopgap, from what I've been reading on the internet, her disease. Death, my child is facing. It is probably from living here, with the water and the Sugeree Station. So I see opportunity to sell to all these people you gather on the downtown, on the beloved town green. Yes? It is an opportunity, one I've already been granted, and now taken away? You are the one to say no."

The reference to the nuclear plant makes your skin stipple and your antennae wiggle. "It isn't me. It's not my decision. It's government bullshit."

He spits on the concrete. "No more gas. You buy from Gulf. You buy from Cheep-O's. You buy from anyone but me. No more. No more."

"But your daughter. Is there anything—I can—do? We can get you in the festival. It's my show. I didn't know."

It's too late—he's gone in a huff, bursting back through the automatic doors and shouting at the woman behind the counter, his wife. A dying daughter, and he's going off on her, and you, over this vendor license shit.

Last straw. That's what the app turndown is for him—the camel's back, broken. It isn't the money. It's the injustice.

You understand how it feels.

Don't you.

No. Not really; perhaps not at all.

With your presence needed down on the island, and keen to switch off the truck for the Mercedes, you'll see about funneling some festival profit to the Jubouri family. You'll stop burning that cash-stash of granddaddy's, sitting in a little home safe you bought, and throw a wad on the table—literally—like you've been wanting to do at those stupid meetings over many issues. Here, here, take a couple of thousand; whatever you claim you might make on the falafel trade that day.

You do not care about money; you could not care less.

Almost done with festival stuff, though. Almost done with it all.

Moving on.

Except that here, a step backward: a trip to Sedge, to interact again with Chelsea Colette Rucker.

A curse?

A blessing?

Like any budding Taoist worth his Tao, you know the master judges the action of the moment as neither good nor bad, only what-is. Every day after you meditate you're sure to read the little Mitchell translation that Button used to carry around. If nothing else it helps keep her alive, which after two months isn't so hard. Still feels like she's right here with you, a thousand-petal lotus blossom engaged for eternity in the divine act of blooming—of becoming. So long as you live and carry her in your heart, anyway. And maybe beyond.

But, who you think you is, Roy E. Pettus, to speculate upon that which lies beyond the veil of death? Nobody. That's who.

TRUDY AND SAMSON

Whining and moaning, her man gave in at last to Trudy's fretting: "I'll go. I'll go tomorrow. The doc in the box said he'll give me a podiatrist referral."

"You can't put it off no more."

"I won't—it hurts, sugar. I mean worser."

"A lot?"

"A lot."

With a heavy rain thumping down on the tin roof and a stink in the living room like farts and feet, Mickey—Samson, the once-mighty biker king of Edgewater County, an engine mechanic like few others, who at one time had actual stories and legends going around about his feats of strength, like a semi-outlaw folk hero—wailed all afternoon now over a hurt big toe, waxing and waning with pain and infection for months. Pitiful. Had put on weight. Trudy'd been trying to get him to drink less beer, if for no other reason than the god-awful gas.

"I'm-a go lay down." He spent most of his time on the couch in the narrow, low-ceiling'd living room of the old house. "Help me in yonder."

"Let's be careful getting you up."

As he rocked himself back and forth to get some momentum going, he ripped a ripe one. He'd long quit apologizing. She held her breath long as she could.

Luckily for Trudy, her job was on hold while they fixed up The Dixiana.

Roy Earl, bless him, had kept her on salary. All so sweet between them, now. Like a changed man.

And Trudy, hungry to repeat their performance at the motel. But Roy, saying, no, honey. We can't. Him saying no this time. It was fine. He earned it.

The rest of the old Dixiana crew was more or less retiring or moving on. Fridge decided to go line-manage at Manny T's, to replace Bernice Theodore's brother Ahmad who moved back to New Orleans. Etna Dixmont took ill over the winter and it sounded like her age was catching up to her. Roy helped others get jobs at the Congress Street Grille, or at Applebee's. Only Newbie Harrell, it seemed, had not landed on his feet. Trudy saw him and some big fat kid at the Gas Chief one day, two squirrelly little fuckers if she had ever seen fuckers, and one animal Trudy recognized from working in the bar trade was fuckers. Newbie lost all his chubbiness. Had that red-eyed shadow-cheeked look of a tweaker. Sad.

She suffered her own travails. Mickey's bad foot, for one. His feet carried so much weight now, three-fifty easy. Maybe more. Always a big boy, but gracious.

Between her and his cane, she shuffled him into the bedroom where he slept. Only that morning she did his sheets, nice and fresh.

"Why don't you stay with me for a while," his sad voice gurgled. "I don't know how much longer I'm gonna be around, girl."

"Don't you say that, Samson." She never called him that, his biker nickname. Lots of people did, not that any of the old crew came around. Not since he quit hanging out at the honkytonk; not since quite a few of them had passed on. Maybe he wasn't wrong. She tried not to think it might be best. It wasn't nothing but an infected toe. If he quit drinking and lost weight, he could live and get better. "You shouldn't never say that aloud. It's bad luck."

"I done had me a vision," he whimpered, covering his watering eyes with a shamed forearm. "I'm scared."

"Here." She took off her jeans, keeping on her long-sleeved hot pink Dixiana Darling T-shirt and slithered into bed with him, snuggled up next to that mountain of man, her husband. He didn't smell good, but seemed so grateful, sighing with a peace and quietude she hadn't felt from him in maybe ever. She tried not to mind his B-O, which smelled of almonds. She hoped it wasn't the toe stinking like that. Almonds would be bad.

STEPHEN FREAKING KING COULDN'T'VE WROTE IT NO AWFULLER.

Seriously.

That's what kept running through Trudy's head as her husband's still-sweating but inert bulk lay collapsed across her lower body, trapping her in the well of the fetid, soft mattress that supported him through the long nights and days of the toe ordeal.

Wasn't his foot what got him, though: the apnea. His durn snoring had killed him, finally. And now, he was about to kill her, too.

Her legs, tingling, going to sleep. Her knees were about-near bent back and starting to hurt. "Mickey!" she hollered. "Wake up, sugar!"

Nothing.

But not dead, only comatose—she could feel his pulse beating. Heard a light wheeze.

Still, something bad had happened. She'd awakened from hearing him shout OH and feeling a massive convulsion and his collapse across her. Trudy figured he sprang upright and went to roll off the bed where she usually wasn't, her bony ass having dozed off.

The rain had stopped. In the quiet she shouted HELP HELP HELP, but it was stupid. Not another house for a quarter-mile in either direction.

Her whole body went hot with panic; her legs, sweating underneath his clammy, cool gut. Drool ran out of his mouth and nose, head drooping off the bed and mucus oozing onto the floor covered in awful old carpet and socks and underwear and trash. She needed to clean up. That's what run through her mind. Clean house before the ambulance gets here. Get that stink out of the air. Open windows.

But most of all, she needed to call. She broke out in sweat and hollered again.

Wait, that was it—the slickness of her sweat.

She pushed and wrenched her hips; movement. She tried to be careful and not roll him off the end of the bed—he could break his neck.

She reached back and pulled herself using the headboard, which started to crack under her effort, a cheap-ass particle board bedroom suite they bought not long after getting hitched.

"God, please—don't do this to me. And poor Mickey. We don't deserve this," she wept.

After a moment of recrimination, she cussed herself and got busy wiggling.

Traction, finally, and leverage. She slid out from under the husband and onto the hard, messy floor amid the socks and underwear. She'd soon find

out not only that her husband had a gangrenous toe, but worse, had suffered
what was explained to her as a massive brain-stem stroke.

◉ ⚇ ⊘

THE AWFUL NEWS CAME FROM A RESIDENT AT EDGEWATER MEMORIAL
Hospital, this following the horrendous drama involving the EMTs who'd
come to the house, a kid who seemed so young he still had red streaks of
acne. The attendants could barely get Mickey onto the stretcher.

The doctor asked, "I understand there's a living will?"

"There is."

"Good. I'll say that his prognosis isn't wonderful." The young doctor,
struggling to find the right words and tone in his nasal yankee accent,
blinked behind round glasses and kept pulling his lips as though the words
tasted bitter. "Mr. Samuelson's stable on the ventilator, for now. But with
test results like these—a really problematic EEG, and slim chance of
recovery—you may need to make a decision."

Trudy, feeling outside herself, his words echoing in the waiting area.
Like a character in a scene on one of the soaps. Dialogue. "Let me think all
this over. I got to give him a chance."

"I wish I could tell you more. Give you more hope, rather."

"It's okay. I ain't one of those types who think y'all can wave a magic
wand and fix everything."

Nodding. "And with an event of this magnitude? The prognosis is what
it is. Again, I'm sorry."

Now, Trudy, alone and bereft in an otherwise empty hospital waiting
room, with nothing for it but to wait and see when her husband passed
away. Didn't matter if she pulled the plug, it could still be hours, days
or weeks.

First, she turned to the only person she could think of, mainly because it
was easier than calling Mickey's brother, a history way unresolved
compared to others: she dialed up Roy Earl, the smartest and richest human
being she knew, to ask him how he would handle this medical dilemma.

It rang until his VM picked up. Her voice and nerves broke while
leaving the message. She started sucking wind and sounding like someone
having a meltdown.

Poor Roy, after all he'd been through, now having to deal with her mess.
She could tell he was serious about not wanting to go on with her any more.
That the reconciliation had been a one-nighter. Still, she wept into his voice-
mail, and couldn't help but ringing off by saying *I love you, sugar.*

MANNY, BECKY L, NEECIE, LILLYANNE AND A FIREARM

Manny amble round the rest-runt dining room soaking a new reed, a Rico Jazz Select instead of his preferred brand, LaVoz. Rico more expensive and not as good in Manny opinion, but he let the boy at the music store in Columbia talk him into a box. He still got a couple good LaVoz's he keep for the parade and the show on the day of the festival. Brand loyalty with reeds, it based on mouthpieces more than anything. LaVoz sound like shit on one mouthpiece, like a dream on the other, able to play soft on the low end and thick and rich in the midrange. Ain't gonna take no chances with switching reeds on show day, though. Messing with these Ricos to stay busy. Keep his mind occupied.

Now that Manny personal life settle down, and he get that old boy Fridge back in yonder stead of Ahmad and his recalcitrant black ass, and there ain't no bunch of money sitting there hanging over his head—temptation, like they talked about in the Bible, yo—Manny feeling okay about shit. Missing Becky L hard on some days, but trying to do da right thing, here. Life good at Manny T's. Neecie a hard-ass and bitchy, and they ain't fuck now in a long time and for a long time, he bet, but that the price. He got to suffer some for all he done. For his disloyalty.

Used to think you could get off for doing shit—that when nobody watching, it don't matter. But it do. Roy Pettus say it one night when they hanging out. He go, "Character is what you are in the dark, when no one is looking," and damn if Manny got a chill down his spine. After digging on

Roy Pettus wisdom, Manny, his worm turn about Becky L. Cutting the ties got easier.

Still.

What they worked out between them two, the women, it driving him crazy. Then Becky L up and announce she leaving the Fine Arts Center and moving on from Edgewater County. Manny read about it in the durn *Advocate*. He say, damn.

Lillyanne come busting through the front door, bright-ass light filling up Manny eyes and flashing on the bells of his horns in their stands on the small stage of his joint.

"Yo, hold up," cause she don't even see him over across the dining room. She going right for the kitchen.

"Daddy—something awful's happened." She come over boohooing and going off about one of her friends, Clarissa or Alyssa or some shit like that, now having leukemia.

"Which one, now?"

"The girl from Iraq, the sweet one, so sweet." And his babygirl collapse on Manny and go boo-hoo-hoo.

His daughter, she been put through a lot with Manny and his dick shenanigans, but she ain't know much death yet. It like when Mr. Rabbit die last year, she real upset about that for days. Talk it about all. She ain't even lost no grandmama yet. She lost the city of her childhood, but she too little to remember much about New Orleans and the storm. Manny wish he didn't. They look at that Spike Lee documentary one night, and start watching that *Treme* thing on another, and it like, pick up right after the durn hurricane with all these cats and they problems, and Manny go, why I want to watch this shit? I lived through it.

No more.

No more living problems. Only solutions. Praying for them.

You finally got round to praying, he can hear his granny's voice saying. *Well, well.*

No more dick wiggling with no women from across the green, for one solution. But other behavior too. Being present. As a husband, and father. And town father, as Roy Pettus always talk about. Him and his merchant association, his eye on revitalizing the town, which in sync with Manny all the way back to when Roy Pettus first come here to deal with his mess. He all big talk about it for a while, but lately he ain't no more. Keep saying, after the festival, we'll figure something out. Maybe.

"What can we do about it, your sick homegirl?"

"*Nothing*," Lillyanne shouts. "That's the problem."

"She need a fundraiser, or —"

"*I don't know.*"

She dash off through the kitchen doors, *bang-bang* like Manny can't half stand. Ain't heard her shriek like that since she was a squirt.

He ain't know what to tell her. People get sick and die. Look at old Button Sykes out yonder in the cemetery. Manny head turned sideways by that one. She went from being the hippie on the green to like, dead in three months — girl was there, and gone.

Roy Pettus tore up about that shit, too. Manny, he the only one who seen him after she die. He get lit up on brown liquor out at the house, cussing up a storm and fighting with himself and with God, it sounded like. It was scary as shit. Ended up shirtless and barefoot, rolling in the dirt. Sitting on the front steps. Running out of gas, finally, and passing out. Manny help him into bed. Put Roy Pettus so he don't puke in his throat and choke.

Roy Pettus, he better the next morning. All calm like a placid lake, he say.

Manny miss living in the woods with that old boy. His sojourn getting down with Becky L and sucking weed outta Roy E. Pettus's volcano machine, and the money in Mr. Rabbit's floor — it all starting to seem like a crazy dream.

◌ ⊞ ⊘

THE FRONT DOOR BY THE HOSTESS STAND OPENS AND LIGHT FLOOD IN for the second time; a tall silhouette in a sharp ladies' business suit and stalker heels fills the doorway.

And of course it turn out her. It Becky L.

This untenable, but thrilling. Somehow, Manny making shit pop up just by thinking about it. He got to be more careful what his ass think.

And when she come over with 'that look,' like she about to crumble into little bits of broken Becky everywhere, and says, "I don't know if you know, but I've been excommunicated from the ELMS. I once held the thought the three of us might continue here in town," her voice breaking on the edge of shrill, "but that was another of my delusions."

Now Manny sense real trouble brewing. Had to break wide open one last time, eh?

All too easy before. Manny know you don't love hard like him and Becky L done and walk away without nobody getting hurt.

Ain't like that at all, though. She get a nice speech going instead.

"But leaving the FAC and the ELMS and my lifelong home? No choice.

I have to, it seems. I thought Bernice and I could put this hot mess to bed, with us able to continue as friends. Colleagues. As—as—downtowners."

"What Roy Pettus call all us?" Manny go warm and gooey inside. Damn, he love this girl. She trying so hard to be good. "What his word?"

"Stakeholders, I suspect you mean."

Manny think, 'town fathers' more like it, but yeah, he guess Roy Pettus put it that non-genderfied way to Becky L.

All nonchalant, Manny take his new reed and slip it onto the mouthpiece, tighten down the ligature. Slide it onto the cork, fix it into place. Play a run of notes, all light and airy. Good reed.

But he don't know what to say with his regular voice. "Right on, right on. I hears you on all that. It a hot mess, all right."

"All so stupid. My therapist says we were both caught in a reverse narcissism vortex. We used each other for our own psychological ends, without any thought as to a lasting relationship. If it were possible. Appropriate. Any aspect of it. We were both ill, Manny. Sick with hubris."

"Well now, hold on—what'n no hoodoo about it." He start whispering. "Baby, what we did wa'n't sick. That some sick sweetness maybe, yo. Don't take that part away, now."

"Don't. Stop."

"My ass speaking da truth." All he can do not to reach over and pull her close. "Girl—you know it true."

"Please. I've worked all this out in my mind. Do you know how difficult it's been?"

Course Manny know. She kept on texting him like a thousand times after they was broke up. And come for booty call half a dozen times. At least. Wa'n't like he didn't do his part and cool off. Yo. "I know, I know, baby."

"Don't call me baby."

"'Don't'—that your favorite word, ain't it? This 'friendship' you got working on," playing a flourish of an arpeggio. He take off the tenor and set it on the stand. "It ain't based on mutual respect. All this order-giving."

"You're lucky you're getting off the hook."

"How that? You ain't got no clue the shit I been through."

"Because you were playing with my heart, not just my body. Because you told me 'I love you.' It's almost too much to ask to forgive. And go on. But I'm standing here. Like you didn't break the fuck out of my god-damn, fucking... god-damn fucking... *huh-huh*-heart."

Da-yum. A breakdown, more like it. She letting the waterworks go now.

Manny see the shadow of Fridge's head poking out the kitchen door; he wave him off, hope the new man understand that mean keep the babygirl back, too.

Manny go to Becky L. She done plop down at one of the tables, stems crossed in her slacks and them sexy stiletto heels and crying.

She go to reach in the purse.

That little gun she carry.

Oh, shit.

Manny, taken back in an instant to that club in DC he play, a kid jamming away with these older cats getting down and suddenly, dudes be popping caps in the park cross the way, running and hollering and a bullet, it come PLINK through that glass. Later, he look and see a hole in the wall not a foot from Manny head, and coulda gone right through him. He like to change his drawers then, yo.

Becky L, though, ain't pulling out nothing but a tissue. Honking her red nose in it. Putting it back.

Da-yum, boy. Chill. The fuck. Out.

Manny get down on one knee in front of her. Put his hand on her face, cupping all gentle-like. Like he used to do. "Hey."

And right then Neecie come busting in from the street, and Lillyanne from the kitchen. At the same durn time. Yep.

◎⊞⊘

MANNY PUT ON THE BIGGEST GRIN HE EVER PRODUCE. "Y'ALL COME ON over here, ladies. We was wondering where you was."

Neecie, blazing daggers. "Were you, now? How lovely."

"Oh, mama—was it her? The arts center lady? OH MY GOD—!" The babygirl bust out crying and rush through the kitchen door again today. This like a bad play, a comedy of errors.

"I was just trying to help Ms. LaFreniere through a rough patch, yo."

"Bernice." Becky L, collecting herself, cheeks scarlet, nose red, eyes running. "This is my fault. I came here to tell Manny how sorry I was we wouldn't be going on as colleagues. And that I wanted to apologize again. How it turned into me blubbering, well—that's my own cross to bear. Hasn't the first thing to do with your family."

"Girlfriend, you better hope it don't. And as for Manny over there, he on triple secret probation. Ain't no more apologies, no more visits in the restaurant when I ain't around. You in violation."

Manny, for a minute there, could see all this going another way—Neecie or Becky L throwing down on each other over his fine ass. That kinda thrilling.

How he make all this up to the babygirl, he ain't a clue. He got it—he lie and tell her Becky L want him to give her money for the arts center, and when he say no, she start crying. He fix it up with Neecie, and she tell her the same shit. That how you get a durn story straight.

And as for Manny, his story about as straight as he could hope to get it, all things reconsidered. He miss Becky L, the way she feel next to him. But if it all work out, and his nuts ain't cut off, and everybody still friends… he reckon he live with it. He couldn't have imagined it working out so good like this. But then, he couldn't imagine taking that cash from the Pettus house and starting over, with or without his sweet ladyfriend, either.

Actually, he *could* see this shit the way it was. His woman. His babygirl. His joint; his horn.

He needed to practice and get limber, get this reed broke in. He about to be playing in front of more muh-fuhs than in a long-ass time; since Jazzfest, twenty years ago. That feel good. That feel right. He thankful to Roy Pettus for all he done for the town, and for taking care of Manny. That a good man, right there. Manny, if he had any sense, would know he not fit to lick any one of their shoes, these people he got on his side. Manny had been using at Jazzfest, though. And being on the big stage wasn't nothing but a smeary blur. Manny OD not long after. Go in the hospital. Meet Neecie. High point; low point; high point.

Becky L nervous and cowed before Neecie. "May I have a final word with your husband?"

"What for?"

"Afterwards, I'll be gone forever. That's the bargain. Out of your lives, I mean."

"You mean leaving town."

"That's what I'm saying. Soon as I wrap up Rabbit Festival business next week, I'm history. In fact, I already have an offer on my family home from the county—the archives will be relocated there."

Neecie, an air of graciousness. "We all know you leaving is for the best. And the archives deal—yeah. Who you think help make it happen? Huh?" A big, sassy wink, and she go sashaying into the kitchen. Taking her time. Boss-lady.

Alone again, Becky smile tight and hard at Manny.

"Dog, girl—what you clearing on that deal?"

Her face go bright pink. "You fucker. You men are pieces of living, stinking shit."

"Naw, c'mon. It take two to—seriously. How much?"

"What does it matter? You're not having to give up your life over 'getting some'."

"That part I ain't understand. Who say you got to give up your life?"

"No one." She go digging into her purse. "I do."

Manny heart about stop—now out come the gun.

Pointed at him.

"Oh, shit, shit, Becky L, don't—"

But she laugh and put the barrel up to her own forehead. She holler HERE WE GO and pull the trigger.

But it go *click*. Ain't no shot.

But Manny, he piss himself in his white jeans anyway. Bust out crying like a pussy, fall down on his knees, head against the bandstand.

"Go on, now… god-dog, girl. God-dog."

"Got you, didn't I?" She gather herself, put away the gun and walk away with head held high. At the door she call out, "A good one. Thanks, Manny. I 'love' you."

Manny pissed, now. He go, he go—shit.

Aw, fuck it. What he go and do is change his pants. In his gym bag he think he got the black 501 button-fly that hold his package just right, and the black classic logo *Star Wars* shirt to match, too. Manny look fine for all the ladies during the buffet. Nobody know how stupid he look now. How weak. A secret, kept close. Ain't no thang.

CREEDENCE, ROY AND SISSY

A gentleman and a prince, her husband, rushing down to the island to attend to her during this Sissy crisis. Heartfelt, his pledge on the phone in response to her text.

Much more of a gentleman than Phil Webhannet turned out, that much Creedence knew. Tried to pass off a crazy story about Roy paying the junior-rank police officer to hang around her. That it wasn't the attraction she thought it was, so she should stop all her hinting and flirting, which to be honest she guessed had been taken up a notch after the new year. What an insult, lying to her face. Not that she was supposed to be getting into some stupid relationship, anyway.

Next, though? Parading his off-island girlfriend that he'd had all along, this perky little church girl from Beaufort, bringing her into the coffee shop on their way to the beach on the first warm Saturday, Phil's day off, a cherubic little small-town girl with curly black hair and a nice shape. The nerve.

Creedence had been cold to the young woman, whom he'd introduced with what seemed innocent good cheer. But yeah, the Phil story about Roy, crazy and brazen and offensive, sad and childish as well. Best of luck to them both.

But anyway, seeing the foolishness in her mild flirtation with the cop for what it was—euphoric recall to the wildly dysfunctional and destructive relationship with Estes—resulted in feeling, like, literal growth and maturity and all. Russ, her sponsor, so proud. Finally letting her give him a lingering hug and wet smooch on the cheek.

◎⊞⊘

WHICH SHE ALSO GAVE ROY WHEN HE GOT THERE LOOKING GREEN around the gills; a hug he didn't want to end. Besides a ton of traffic on the interstate—in the middle of a weekday for some stupid god-durned reason, as he complained—he said this-and-that drama tugged at him from back home. Said right as he merged onto the island connector, Trudy Pirkle called about her husband having a heart attack or some such malady, and the poor dear was facing the decision to pull the plug.

The horrible thought made Creedence gasp, like when they decided Devin was dead. "They're dropping like flies back home."

"Yeah. So many I can't stand it."

"I know it."

His eyes, watering. "What does Dr. Kip say about our little tortie girl. How is she?"

"I thought we could both go to the vet together. To find out the test results."

She described the cat's condition, which over the weekend seemed to deteriorate from clumsiness to outright imbalance, foaming at the mouth, loss of appetite. "It was awful. I felt so bad for her. He said it might be a stroke. Or a brain tumor. Or, in the best case? Vestibular disease, which might turn out quite treatable."

"Poor Miss Sissy!" Seeming to mean it, like really troubled. "When will we know?"

"Couple hours."

"I don't believe it's possible for the news to be anything but vestibular disease," Roy affirmed with conviction. "It's treatable. End of story."

"I hope you're right."

"Hoping is for suckers. Creating reality is where it's at. You'll see."

◎⊞⊘

ROY, GRINNING; COULDN'T HAVE BEEN BETTER NEWS, SPECULATION though it was.

Dr. Kip, curly salt & pepper hair, goatee'd and muscular in a Hawaiian shirt—the aging hipster as DVM—came into the tight exam room to report to Creedence and her hubby, who stood with his hand on the small of her back while the vet flipped through the cat's chart and Sissy mewled from inside a plastic carrier on the stainless steel exam table. "No way is this a tumor. Symptoms? They'd have manifested much more gradually. But this is sudden."

"Doc, you're that sure? With no further tests?"

"Not a hundred percent, not without an MRI. But we can't scan here—you'll go into Savannah or up to Charleston if we wanna take that route."

"Money is no object." Roy made a sweeping hand gesture over the cat carrier, a wizard casting a spell. "Just putting that out there."

"Understood. But look: Me? This cat? Mine? If it were?"

Creedence watched Roy leaning over Sissy's carrier. His eyes boring into Dr. Kip's, who stared right back.

"This is it—I take it home tonight, watch behavior through tomorrow. We send a bag of fluids with you to keep our girl hydrated. Doses of anti-nausea medication."

"And—?"

"Observe. Watch the appetite. If my hunch is right—that it's vestibular—she'll recover as suddenly as it came on her."

"You're sure? Observe and report? That's it?"

"Yeah. No. I'm satisfied with this diagnosis. Cautious but hopeful, optimistic—all the best words. Aren't I? Aren't I, sweet girl?" Sticking a finger through the wire of the carrier door. "Let's get you better without all those pesky tests and scary stuff."

"And if you're wrong?"

The vet stood back up to his full height. Clasped Roy by the hand. "We'll burn that bridge after we cross it."

"Check."

Good bedside manner. She felt secure as she could with Dr. Kip, handsome healer of the animals. Hiding the panic that wanted to bubble up like acid reflux: "I'm comfortable with it. If y'all are. I just—want her to eat. I need to see her eat again," last couple of words a breathy, fraught whisper.

"It's fluids that'll get her through. The body can go a long time without eating."

"It's true. Read it in one of Pa-paw's men's adventure magazines when I was a lad." Roy, bless his heart—right after he said all that, his tummy growled loud as heck. Everyone laughed. "See? I'm living proof. Skipped lunch for a stupid meeting."

"A meeting?"

"Planning the festival honoring my grandfather."

The vet asked what kind of festival; Roy told him 'roots music.'

He said well-dang, what a wonderful tribute to your forebear. Dr. Kip went bustling and whistling out the door to assemble the fluids, needles and nausea meds.

◌▨⊘

AFTER GETTING THE PETTUSES SQUARED AWAY ON THE PROCEDURE, A snap because Creedence had done it with her beloved Miss Pickles who suffered kidney failure over several tear-stained months back when they still lived in Charleston, Creedence and Roy went to pay the deductible on her pet health insurance policy. Roy almost broke his neck rushing over to the cashier and saying, go go go and sit with little Sissy in the car; I will pay, I will handle everything; I want my girls comfortable and untroubled. Besides, at that moment a lady in tennis whites dragged in a slobbering, woofing brute of a mastiff that scared both Miss Sissy and her cautious, hopeful mama.

Creedence, complete and relieved at having Roy to take care of the paying part. But more than that. Much more. A warmth in her torso, like a ruby glowing orb in her lower regions that she could almost see when she closed her eyes, sitting there in Roy's Mercedes with the cat who would not stand up straight, like the title of a Lilian Jackson Braun mystery. A red crystalline light, streaming out from her groin and little bolts of lightning like roots reaching into the ground all around her, and when he flung open the car door and piled in she felt startled out of a waking dream.

"How's our girl? Huh? Huh?"

"Better now."

They locked wet eyes. "Already?"

"I think so. Now that you're here."

Another look of incipient tears—of gratitude. "Let's go home, then. Get her back on her paws."

As he pulled onto the cross-island highway, she relaxed enough to notice the condition of the car. Filthy. Trash inside, speckled and splattered with Edgewater County mud.

"Yuck. When's the last time you had her washed?"

Roy turned pink. "Aw, don't remind me. Nobody I trust upstate. I'll get it knocked out while I'm here." He's got a lodge buddy who owns a chain of carwashes, and they have some deal worked out between them.

Driving back over the great curve of the connector in Roy's Mercedes, the marshland laid out on both sides and the shimmering ribbon of the intra-coastal waterway, all of it glowing orange from the sunset and the cat howling with displeasure at its confinement, Roy complained about Tillman Falls business stuff. Telling her once the festival was over? He wanted to divest all interest back home and split for good; there's no reason to stay; all their people, gone.

"What's there for us?"

"Zilch."

"I came back long enough to play my part."

"It's all anyone can do."

"I know this: I'm glad the cat has fluids, and I feel like being together with you tonight is right. This is what seems like home."

Whatever happened with them as a couple, she felt relief. She didn't want Edgewater County back in her life. "It's good to be here now. And yeah. With you."

It had occurred to her she could want Roy E. Pettus again. She reckoned trying to fall in love anew with her husband didn't count as a hookup. Not yet, anyway.

Not until she got him home, and back into her bed again.

Their bed.

Together.

To light the lamp, so to speak.

She'd be sure to journal about this decision, maybe write to Devin, for old time's sake. For now, she'd live out the moment instead of trying to describe it. Anybody interested is free to use their imagination about the reconciliation that occurred; suffice to say, it felt more meaningful than any sex Chelsea Colette Rucker—no; Pettus—had ever enjoyed. The connection, it seemed real. Careful and awkward at first, followed by feral fast collapse into mutual tears and apologies. Pledges. Whispers. Love.

Afterward he snoozed, and she withdrew from his damp embrace to pad into the kitchen.

He woke up. "No—don't go."

"Take your nap. Then we'll have more fun."

"I love you, angel."

Giving him her squeeze-y-est eyes. "I know."

In the kitchen, and only after a deliberation she struggled to keep from tipping over into more epic dithering, she embraced a decision:

Chelsea Colette "Creedence" Pettus—that's right—tore up the separation papers left sitting on the breakfast table in a folder; shredded them with hands that shook as though she could use a bracer; ripped and torn until the legal documents became confetti tumbling into the wastebasket slid back under the kitchen sink.

Shutting the cabinet door, a stab of fear. Under scrutiny, she suspected impulsiveness. Her biggest problem.

Nah. An echo of the old junk. She'd come far in only six months.

Outside on the deck in her short robe where a cold morning moon shone down, she watched in its light her breath billowing and forming a halo around the satellite that quickly dissipated.

Imagining the moon as a radio to God, she prayed all their old difficulties would also disperse like the dissolute, wispy mist drifting spectral among the reeds of the marsh. Bowed before the lunar light, letting her robe fall away and standing naked and cold before the marsh, her freckled skin stippling and shaking. Needing to warm up inside afterward with tea, not wine.

Only the sound of a car rolling through and pausing at the four-way stop at the end of the block broke the still of the morning. A rattling muffler, the muted thumping of subwoofers—it reminded her of Estes Patel's rickety old Tercel. Probably a wealthy teen from the neighborhood, all of whom drove fast around the nearby curve. Living it up in their affluent adolescence on the island.

She felt silly and exposed. Pulled on the robe over freckled, shivering skin.

At last the car rolled on, its muted bass fading into the night.

No worries, not with the rock star gone on tour and Roy home, at least for the moment, to stand beside her. Now the affair, and its brutal aftermath, were certifiably over. Not that they would ever speak of the events of the last year again. Not if she could help it.

If only the quiver in her gut didn't make her pine for a drink—you know, to fully relax and enjoy the sex. That's all.

Was she kidding? No.

Instead of drinking? She'd text Russ. See if he had five minutes for her, not that she had any doubt. No good sponsor ignores that kind of call. Thank goodness for meetings; thank god for Russ.

CHRISTY BEAUDOCK AND NEWBIE HARRELL

Christy has cooked up quite a grand ritual, yes he has, and it accomplishes so much and feels so right that by the time he finishes explaining all the ins and outs, Newbie's head sits spinning like a figure skater, or so he says.

"Dude, you're about to creep me out with all this magic shit. You might be messing around with some bad stuff, *bruh*."

Christy, dismissive. Besides the book he took from Button's trashcan, he had done plenty of internet searching to find out how magic worked. How to summon helpers. A working, it's called.

They go out to Big Rock with that stolen book, the one written in her own hand; a grimoire, as it is called, but Christy, he isn't sure how to say the word.

In any case, he understands now how the hooked crosses represent a sigil he can charge up and use. A powerful symbol with multiple and hidden meanings, one threading its way through Christy's life and demanding that he use it. He had studied how you could take someone else's symbols and invert them for your own purposes.

Much power available on what they call the left-handed path. And Christy, why, he had always been left-handed. It all made sense. After watching a YouTube video about past life regressions, Christy, now certain he had once been a warrior-wizard like Gandalf.

Christy tricked Newbie into coming into the woods, suggesting they go there to hunt for high schoolers to sell pills, Adderol and some Xanax he had stashed from some deal. Newbie, forever trading drugs with scum-bag creeps.

If there's money to be had, I reckon we ought to think about doing it. That's how Newbie rolls. Like Christy's Daddy. Made it all easier, what needs to happen.

❂ ▣ ⊘

WALKING OUT THROUGH THE HEAVY PINE FOREST NEAR JENSEN'S POND, all quiet, the woods deserted, birds calling and chirping the only sounds, Christy, he clears his mind. Big Rock, like its name suggests, is a mossy, craggy boulder twelve feet high and jutting out of a rise in the woods like an Indian mound. It's a rock like you usually see closer to the river over in the mill village part of the county, but way out here, it's stuck off by itself and hard to get to, which is why folks party back in here. Secluded and creepy, the jagged edge of the rock looks like an owl's head. People have cabins and houses on the other side of the pond, but not way over here. No wonder. Spooky in these old woods. Cold and dark, even though it's warm today.

Better not be anybody partying here today. Not with what Christy's got in mind. The ritual he prepared, if he goes through with it, will render him powerful. It came to him in dreams. Stealing and flying the Piper Meridian would only be the start of the energy about to flow to, and through, him.

If he completes the ceremony. If the serrated steak knife concealed in the narrow pocket of his cargo pants where a comb or a pen fits, is sharp enough to achieve what Christy plans. Now that spring's arrived, it's time to soak the ground of a sacred circle — a blood sacrifice. To both attract and appease mighty forces.

A bargain.

"Ain't never been in no plane before." Newbie's pace, flagging. He keeps stoping and picking bits of bark, or stooping to yank up early weeds. Bored, he didn't want to come today, not even to sling pills. "Dunno if I wanna do that part."

"You're nuts. After we buzz the festival and scare the crap out of them all, we're gonna want to get away fast, beau. That's why it all makes so much sense, all fits together so good. Ain't nothing faster than a plane."

Fretting. "I don't care what all's supposed to happen. You ain't never flown no durn plane."

"Hell I ain't." Christy, he huffs and puffs and cites a made-up number of hours logged on his simulator. On planes like the Piper Meridian

"It ain't the same."

"It is if I say it is."

"Bullcrud."

"Is too."

"Nuh uh."

"Kiss my ass, Newbie."

"Shut up, Christy."

Holding his rage at bay and smelling sulfur like somebody struck a match, every muscle in his face jumping and quivering, he shoves Newbie against a pine tree trunk. Christy, he explains that, having worked the simulator so long, he's certain he can fly that bitch.

Ain't no reason to believe he can't—on that simulator game Christy had run across every durn crisis you could. He had set it that way, finally, to try to challenge himself. Had downloaded a hack to make it harder, more perilous. Between the flight simulation and the magic book and the internet searching about occult rituals and accumulating power and calling out in ritual fashion to the dark spirits who await to fulfill our desires and destinies —carrying out a blood ritual, ultimately—Christy wanted to say, Newbie, shut up. You ain't gonna have to worry about flying in no plane.

Flying somewhere, maybe. Not in a plane.

Once it was done out here at Big rock, maybe Newbie's soul would continue to aid and assist Christy.

He couldn't explain all that to Newbie, though, who wasn't too bright. Christy didn't have enough of the good words. Not like Roy E. Pettus. And not like his precious Button, who Roy had kidnapped and taken away for his own. And celebrating by putting on a big party there in the middle of town, like a monarch telling everyone what to do. That's Roy E. Pettus, yes, oh yes—Newbie had been right all along about him being a bastard.

But Christy, preparing to make sure Pettus understood who was power-ful, and who was not. Flying all around His festival in His own plane, dipping the wings and sticking up his middle finger at Him, Roy E. Pettus.

Flying to where, then? Christy, he hopes he can go high and fast enough to escape.

The vision floods back. Hurtling along the tree tops. An ice cube. A blue pyramid, and with it, a feeling of salvation.

But not flying over it, whether the cube or the pyramid.

Flying into it.

Flying into a building.

Now that would get people's attention.

Christy had been little when them rag-head fellas pulled that mess. But wisdom, there. Nothing had been the same after terrorists flew planes into buildings. Maybe flying his own plane into Roy Pettus's own honkytonk, right down his Button-stealing throat, would change the bossman's life, all-right. The asshole had earned it, since his heart was so wicked.

Now that sounded like an act worthy of ascension. Christy—not only an indigo child but a particularly adept initiate having been led to, but also chosen, the powerful left-hand path—would be transformed into a living god.

☉🝍⊘

IN THE END NEWBIE, HE STRUGGLES WITH CHRISTY, BUT IT AIN'T NO kinda fight. Christy, he must outweigh his buddy by a hundred pounds. More.

Their brief scuffle obscured Christy's upside down pentagram, his magic circle, that he'd made in the peaty underfloor of the forest, having bidden Newbie to help him clear off the thick carpet of pine needles and beer cans and fast food wrappers and old rubbers and cigarette packs and blunt butts, the fresher straw orange on top but underneath faded to a pale yellow.

And below that?

Dark, moist earth.

That would soak up Newbie's blood.

The rock, with the old hooked cross sigil barely visible, stood vibrating with a greasy cold iron sloshing in Christy's guts. Spray painted long ago, the symbol seemed to glow.

Christy, with Newbie unconscious in the middle and the pentagram redrawn with the toe of a sneaker, kneels before the sigil, filling it with power by thinking hard about it. The veins in his temples pulse, a squirming in the center of his forehead like a worm. He visualizes the flying and the ice cube and the pyramid and the screaming of the crowd and the bossman, his face, terrified, running away from Christy, who sees himself as a hundred—no, a thousand—feet tall.

Pulling up short, though. When the time comes. The knife in his pocket, sharp, but the human neck, thick with cords. Looking at Newbie's pale throat—no.

This was crazy.

Christy. Not a monster, hacking at a neck. He needed a razor blade, clean and neat. Dang-durn-it.

Plus: Newbie, his partner.

Blood. Needing the blood to make the magic and get the power.

No. Christy, reading about other fluids. And besides—not another body. Jensen's Pond, not deep enough. Newbie would float and be seen.

Gently lifting his friend, Christy, he removes Newbie from the circle. In putting him down over against a thick oak tree, he moans *Christopher, whut-up bruh*.

"Rest here, buddy. I ain't gonna cut your throat with no steak knife. I don't want you to suffer."

"Do what?"

"I'm-a kill you later, that's all."

Groggy, his head lolls back. "Man, you're fucked up."

Christy, taking off his clothes and thinking about Button Sykes. When ready he goes into the circle, kneeling. He plays with his dong until he coming up in three fitful spurts, all the while charging the sigil of the crosses and seeing the bossman's terrified face fleeing and screaming and dying under a pile of flaming rubble like one of the 9/11 towers collapsing on his head. Christy knows the image well. The teacher showed it over and over to the students in class the day they taught about the attack.

Hearing his partner groaning again, Christy wipes the spunk off his hand onto his thigh, goes to get dressed.

What to do with Newbie now?

What more did Christy need with him?

The ceremony over, the circle needed closing.

But—so much trouble to come back. A trip to the drugstore for a razor. Rigmarole with Newbie's body—a do-over of all that again?! No way.

Or abandon altogether. Fly the plane without killing Newbie. Christy, confident—he didn't need any magic. Squirt water on his friend's face instead of killing, wake him up. Tell him their fight was only a dream.

A sound from behind Christy—not Newbie, because he stood looking at his friend, who seemed still and quiet. Too quiet.

A rustling, a rush of warm air against Christy's neck. A stink.

Christy, he turns around, his stomach filled with the opposite of the comfort he takes from the whiskey that stills his troubled waters; for what sits on top of the owl-rock also looks like a big owl, one crossed with a man and with arms and hunched shoulders, muscular legs bent in a squat and eyes like saucers, as though the rednecks have been fucking the chickens, which have been fucking the owls and producing mutant creatures out of an unholy, triune union of DNA.

Christy's throat closes and he cannot scream, no. It is a dream now, he reckons, and the bird-man looks at him, cranes its neck side to side, a horrifying unnatural movement in a creature of this size. Grunts. Stinks. Moves faster.

And it lunges, wings fifteen feet in diameter flapping and creating a sudden storm of dust and leaves from the forest floor.

Christy, finding his voice and dropping with a shriek, rolling, a rush of wind like swamp gas full of rot and evil across his shaking, terrified body.

All falls silent. Christy rolls over, opens his eyes. He is not in his bed, it is still the forest by Jensen's pond, and Newbie Harrell is nowhere to be found —only his ball cap remains.

Christy, knowing he has done this conjuring of the demon and a-loosed it upon Edgewater County, thinks to make a symbolic gesture of bowing before the rock, burying Newbie's hat, saying a proper dying prayer for his friend, and heading off to drive Newbie's truck back, and thank god he already took the keys.

In the rush to haul butt out of the woods, though, Christy, he forgets to close that sacred circle. It occurs to him later, but dang, no way he's going into those woods at night. Never. What's done is done.

It's probably all bullcorn, anyway. Newbie left on his own, and Christy imagined the rest about the forest. That's possible. But he can still fly a plane. This he knows; this is what the magic's for. Either way, ain't coming back here again.

He will miss Newbie, but puts out of his mind that a monster swept his friend away, because the thought might make all that went down seem brutal and cray-cray. Couldn't be a fantasy, an alternate scenario to take the place of Christy having gone through with it all. Nope.

❊ ⬛ ⦸

After another week of simulation practice and planning, the morning of the festival arrives and Christy's got good luck going because he has an idea to do a burn-out of his old junk, leaving it all behind. Wealth and plenty awaited him following his grand act today, his magical working. He starts a pile of rags burning on the bed in his Daddy's old room, and when he turns back at the highway, the fire in the trailer has sparked right up and other residents are coming out and hollering and pointing.

Before the smoke started pouring out of the trailer he cranked Newbie's truck, grinding the gears and not driving near as good as he was gonna fly. Having to take a back road because of all the mess going on in downtown Tillman Falls, the policemen around setting up orange cones and fences, Christy tries to muster confidence.

But at the airfield, a curveball: he discovers a plane on the runway with its motor already going and a shrimpy little old man for a pilot, one who's easily dealt with. This aircraft, a Cessna, simpler to pilot than Roy Pettus's Piper Meridian.

Which doesn't seem to be here, anyway. It's been awhile since Christy came and gazed through the fence at the sleek aircraft. Gone. The bossman had flown it away, like Button. Son of a bitch.

But the magic, working. Manifesting in front of Christy's eyes. A better solution. A Cessna, fueled and ready to taxi.

Easy peasy.

Christy, seeing the ropes attached to the tail and realizing what the plane's for—the banner, he can't read it, but he figures it has to do with the festival, and reckons on towing it anyway. He'll adjust for the drag, right? Because, won't that be sweet? To crash the banner plane into Roy Pettus's big fat music festival, if not The Dixiana itself? Right?!? It's on.

ROY EARL PETTUS AND THE WHOLE DAMNED TOWN

No good sleep all night before the fest. Not with the death threat over the Reverend Nixon's town name-change referendum next week casting a pall over the final festival preparations. You had stood around the desk in Dobbs's office examining the email, which suggested retributive mayhem over injustices perpetuated by a variety of colorfully described actors and agents of same. Alt-right tripe. Probably some meth-mouth teen in a mobile home trolling for online kicks.

But you can't ignore it, not these days, so powwows over security issues consumed all of yesterday. Worries and busyness inform your restless half-dreams, flopping around in what passes for slumber. It ends early anyway when the alarm blares like a klaxon at four in the *ayeem*.

Festival time.

It recalls your days in Columbia's Old Market district, the morning of the annual St. Patrick's Day street party, when for only one day you sold cheap draught beer out of wagons instead of coffee and smoothies. Once the fruitshake success took on a life of its own, however, you'd simply closed both businesses during the fest. More trouble than it was worth; you had more important action items than fleecing hard-target, captive-audience inebriated marks for a few thousand bonus-bucks. Your sights by then, bigger than one neighborhood, one fat payday.

Action item number one: send a text to your gal on the island, who'll be up getting the cats squared away before heading into the coffee shop. Yeah —Creedence, she's missing most of the Rabbit festival to work the coffee shop. The woman's dedicated to her work. Maybe too much. But as much as y'all got along on the last visit, which was considerable, healing and wonderful—even Sissy the cat recovered, regaining her balance and appetite—no way would you hector her about her decision to get the business up and running.

She's thinking like an owner, now. Because she is.

Fudge it—instead of texting, you decide to call. Every time you do so, your heart pounds in anticipation that her voice will have gone cold again rather than inviting. That she will reverse and say, no, I want out again. You constantly dither and worry over this fear.

But unfounded: *"Hi,"* cheerful and bright. "I was just thinking about you."

Sigh of relief. "Break of day. Not used to it."

"Speak for yourself. I got to bed early, though."

"Since the festival ends at sunset, we'll get you into bed early tonight, too."

"Will we, now."

"Mark it down."

Says she had a premonition about your call. Or maybe a dream, she wasn't sure. And that it's time to talk about the future for real.

Gulp. Your guts hit the floor. Here comes the bad news.

"I wanted to wait a year. Get a year in, like the book says about life-stuff like relationship decisions. But after talking it over with Russ—my sponsor? Well. It doesn't matter what some third party thinks about the state of our marriage. Does it?"

"Not on your life. No third parties. At all."

"No."

You note a micro-hesitation. You're hanging on every passing instant of digital information coming out of the earpiece. "Go on."

"I miss you. The sweet part of you."

"Aw, god. I miss you too. I miss you so much. I've been wanting to say that."

A speed bump: "I can't put up with the other you."

"The other—me?"

"Captain America."

"Pardon?"

"The superhero in the room. The big boss man. The savior. The judge," the last appellation coming on a down beat, a grim finality. "We have to go forward as equals."

You think you can be what she needs—you've made so much progress.

Button taught you well. You've been meditating. You have equilibrium. Perspective. The urgency you suffered—the burning urgency to make the money, which is what made you an overbearing, distant asshole—has dissipated like smoke in wind. And not only because you still have plenty of cheddar. Ron Nawalinski bought the Piper himself, paid up last week. Working with a new financial guy to rebuild the losses, conceal the capital gain, lay down a fresh cornerstone on the rebuilt financial pyramid you'll need to keep ROLLING INTO THE ROOM as the bossman.

And then…?

Buy some land. The mountains.

"Equals is good for me, my love."

A tiny mm-hm betrays a touch of skepticism; how can you blame her? "I need to say 'sorry' about something."

"Oh—not recent unpleasantness."

"No; god, no. It's that I should have been there for Button's funeral."

"You didn't know her."

"No. But you did—you loved her."

"*Ack*," you blurt, your throat closing up. "We were best buds. I thought she would be a different partner going forward. But all too brief."

"Poor Button. Poor Roy."

"She seemed to think her illness was okay. Like a puzzle-piece falling into place. This odd serenity she projected. It was—weird. Or 'just right', to hear her tell it."

"It's like my mama pretending all the way through her cancer that nothing was wrong. Like it was all part of the game for her, concealing it from us."

"Button said the disease was her play this 'go-round,' as she put it. And that many lives led up to it. All that new-age junk."

"Like reincarnation? Was she Buddhist?"

"Not sure how to answer that. She was Button. She contained multitudes. Like the breakout side character in the sitcom of my life—but only for one season, I guess."

"That's the most poetic thing I've heard you say in a long time."

"Could be the poet in me is waking up. That only took thirty years."

"Be better than the bossman. That much I know."

"Check. Bygones. Et cetera."

You hesitate, decide not to tell Creedence about all the true weirdness to which you'd referred with Button—her remarkable specialness. The feeling of her being inside your head; her talk about magic and telepathy and philosophy. You haven't felt that since she died, the sense of her words echoing in your mind. Since you left her there on Heather Ponderview's mountain, Button's voice has gone silent.

You will have to grieve for the girl soon. After the festival. After tomorrow, you affirm to no one. To the wind.

"Can't wait to see you later."

"Same here. I feel so different, now."

"I can tell."

"You're gonna be proud of me."

"I already am. Look at the CBSI numbers for Q1. Yowza."

"Roy—I don't mean the numbers."

"I know." Trying to find the words. "I want us to go back to—how it was before."

"But honey, we can't."

"We can try."

"No—did you hear anything I said earlier? We can try to make it better, not the same. Because it needed to be. Is that okay to say?"

You affirm that it is, and was, and is. That you believe growth has occurred on both sides. And that it's time to re-harmonize, to test the waters of your newly mutual vibration. And that it's the moment for you to go put on this music festival in memory of your grandparents.

You tell her you love her; 'me too' is the reply, and the connection is broken.

A tinge of panic. It's not perfect. It isn't even 'back.' Perhaps you need to think all this reconciliation stuff through. It's not like in stories, the romances with the HEA—happily ever after. Is it?

Yeah.

No.

Maybe.

Standing on the front porch in the predawn darkness, hitting the vapor pen and doing some stretching and yoga poses, you ruminate on the fact that you could use a good conversation with Button. Best you can do for now? Meditation, breakfast and a quick shower; wake and bake.

The festival. Time to get it on. Still way too early for all this activity, but you fire up the F-150, spin some loud rock & roll, and make your way downtown—what choice do you have now but to see it through? The hours will pass as if in a dream, and it will be tomorrow, and all the buildup will be over.

LOCKDOWN.

That's the only word shrill and melodramatic enough for the tone of what's become of the town green — nay, the entire Historic District — now fenced-off, cordoned and controlled, regulated and managed by yellow-shirt security, cops, dogs and metal detectors. And now you see why you had to write such a big-assed check. You've gone through the line-items with a microscope. You get it. You know how these events go.

When Feebee Elmendorf called to give you the quote on the rain, hazard and other insurances required by the town council and the DHS, you intoned, *Leave them to me*. You negotiated the rain insurance with the agent, a skill gained during your time on the Downtown Business Alliance down in soda city. And gave concessions to the insurance firm, and were given concessions unto you, and with your business acuity and experience — or bullshitting ability, a finely-honed instrument — all had been resolved to your satisfaction, and in a manner equitable.

But the more you considered the concept, you thought insurance loomed as a ridiculous aspect of capitalism at its worst, in its protection of money for growth's sake and for money's sake and with little of the energy going for any meaningful act of human existence other than amassing corporate prof-its. But one day you need a mechanism like insurance — the homeowners covering a tree blown onto the roof, or full collision after you rear-end some dude who's sitting at a green light texting, maybe because you were distracted answering your own text. Breaking your hip. Getting cancer. Having any surgery at all; staying in the hospital a day. A hundred-grand, boys; call it a million. Nobody can pay these bills. Nobody. Need your ass bailed out. Need your policy and premiums paid. Need your in-surance, beau.

How empty this day feels, you think, as you wait in the line of idling cars at the gate to the lot behind city hall and the courthouse complex, where the principals, talent and VIPs may park. Neither of your grandparents lived to see it, Button's gone to hippie heaven, and Creedence, well, you've little reassurance yet it'll work out, only that she seems cautious but willing to give marriage another shot.

In any case, if anyone had told you that this time last year you'd be running a music festival in Edgewater County after a cosmic level of sea-change and death and possible divorce and all that's happened, and was to happen, you'd have said:

Get.

The fudge.

Out.

But here you are.

"I need to see your wristband," the kid at the VIP parking gate says, holding up a flashlight in his safety-orange reflective vest as you turn down The Who.

"They didn't give me one—I'm the dude."

"Gotta have a wristband to park here."

"It's my festival, son."

"But I'm supposed to—"

"Now look," you breathe fire at him, beginning to seethe. A warmness spreads across your back and flows into your abdomen. Time to die, son.

But you don't unleash. You feel only patience and kindness—he's doing his job. You told them you wanted this event to run like clockwork, and here, a manifestation of your orders.

"Buddy, you're doing a heckuva job. But see those two gorgeous festival officials? They'll vouch." You wave with passion and zeal to catch the eye of Becky L or Feebee, both striding across the courthouse plaza with clipboards and phones jammed next to ears, wearing comfortable shoes and workout clothing to suit the active day ahead. "Run my street cred by those bonded officers of the event, if you dare."

"Yes, sir."

He does so, and you're waved in. After parking you take the time to express your appreciation to the kid, a skinny, dorky high school or college doofus—you can't fudging tell anymore; they all seem so young—and he seems surprised and gratified by your firm handshake, direct eye contact.

"They—told me how important this was," he says. "To not let it get out of control."

"Who told you that? Those gals?"

"The cops."

"Oh—I see. But they aren't in charge of jack-squat here today. I am." A hooked thumb into your proud chest. "And I say, manage the flow, but don't try to control it too much. Holding on too hard, you can break it. Understand?"

He doesn't but nods 'yes,' curt, and trots back to the gate to address the next vehicle, a black SUV likely carrying more authorities.

It gets real, now; the festival is on.

You grab a small backpack with snacks, your sun-hat and glasses and sunscreen, wince as your gall-darn shoulder hurts like it does, oh, every day now, and go skipping across the grounds to watch your granddaddy's music festival unfold—as you also hope he watches from his heavenly perch on-high.

EXCEPT IT'S NOT ONLY BLUEGRASS MUSIC — YOU FEATURE THREE STAGES, three genres: bluegrass/Americana, classic country and classic rock, which also includes an r&b component in the form of Manny T's house band kicking off the day. A reasonable mix suitable for the spirit of the event.

First idea you'd said at the initial planning meeting? Got to have a rock stage. Your granddaddy would approve. He was a fan of Bob Dylan as well as hillbilly music, as you kept insisting to your fellow organizers. Next came the Phish cover band you forced onto the bill. Only last night you emailed a brief paragraph to the band to read onstage about the importance and significance of Phish to its fans like the late A. Button Sykes.

Feebee, younger than the rest on the committee by a generation, needed no convincing — in fact, she'd said a hip-hop stage would make for an inclusive and potentially profitable, promotable aspect of the festival, especially considering the demographics of the area.

Had not gone over at all. Landed like a lead zeppelin. Thud. The cops, including Oakley, who had locked eyes with you and given a little headshake, and the ELMS and pretty much everyone all went like, hip-hop? Rap music? Forget it.

You hadn't argued the case. Besides, all you could imagine was that little fuckstick Estes Patel's band Meatbody getting booked. And having to pay him. Like you had while he was porking your old lady.

Stop.

Breathe.

Conscious breathing.

Let it go.

What's done.

Is done; is done. Faulkner was wrong about the past. That's what you keep saying.

"You all right?" Becky L, taking you by the elbow and gesturing into the command center, a conference room at the bank y'all used a few times for committee meetings that conflicted with day-to-day lodge activities in the ELMS building. "All 'squared away', as you would say?"

"Nerves."

"Comments? Remarks? Concerns?"

"Be glad when this is over. Won't you?"

"Oh, no, Roy! Events like this, they're part of the lifeblood of the community. I hope we — they — you — present this festival every year. It's the biggest thing to come to Tillman Falls since — since — I don't know when."

Her voice dropped to a hush. "We have celebs. Actual celebs, in the press tent."

With press releases issued far and wide regarding the Rabbit & Runelle Pettus and Button Sykes Music Festival, trumpeting the rebirth of the Tillman Falls downtown as an arts and music destination, sure enough, Becky L's right: you have a press line going with celebs working the four different TV-reporter stand-ups, a rep of each Columbia station waiting their turn with the stars. "It's a glorious moment in the history of the town. And we have you to thank for it. So, thank you."

The happiest you've seen her in a long time, Becky L, but you also keep catching her furtively wiping away sneaky little tears. Poor girl. Got her heart broken.

Hey: If it didn't work out with Creedence, you could—wait.

You stop yourself from thinking this about Becky. You don't want to queer the energetic deal with your wife. Thoughts are energy; thoughts are powerful. The wise thinker wields them with a judicious discernment.

For the last month your productivity has been of the highest quality, especially for a lazy piece of Scots-Irish Edgewater County mill trash like you: you tried dealing with Button (yes; that's the only way you could let yourself think about the fact that she's dead and you need to grieve, an item to be checked off), you got The Dixiana interior gutting and build-out complete, got the sign rehabbed and made your little side-deal with the Mayor about the water tower. One more fat check out of your dwindling stash of cash, your once staggering, mindblowing fortune growing endlessly and without effort and of its own volition, now in need of fertilization, tending and toil.

The final expense, however, a gesture you figured that'd leave your family's mark on the town in a way anyone passing through would see and be forced to acknowledge; the forever-branding opportunity. Paid out over time, the cost didn't seem too dear, not against the spiritual benefits as you perceive them: Your grandfather didn't enjoy a blessed resting place, so now the whole of the city would suffice to serve as a headstone; and his will read:

New Falls City, SC:
Home of the World-Famous
'DIXIANA'

◐🅽⊘

LAST NIGHT'S OPEN MIC IN THE SPARKLING AND UPDATED DIXIANA, A strange combination of a thousand little updates yet to the casual eye the same in most details, and at which some of Becky L's celebs and today's talent had played a pre-show show, you all enjoyed a banquet catered by Manny's kitchen now run by Fridge, and a joyous affair, indeed.

No moment more special than sitting with Trudy, close together in your Pa-paw's old booth, your energy and elbows mingling.

In the wake of her husband's death from his brain-stem stroke, she quit smoking and gave up drinking, but for a few cold beers like the one you shared, sipping and passing the longneck back and forth with intimacy while toe-tapping and singing along to Jasper's indelible Edgewater County anthem 'Mama's Pussy.'

At the end you all cheer, and he presented a new ditty he felt good about. "This one's called 'Hopelessly Helping,' and I hope you all enjoy it," a mournful, classic country heartbreak number that goes:

> *There's grit in them-old greens*
> *You asked me to clean*
> *And the salt I took for sugar*
> *Tastes sharp in your cake*
>
> *I've tried hard to learn*
> *But you wouldn't budge*
> *Said, "Just let me cook,"*
> *And I pray not to judge*
>
> *But now brunch's served burnt*
> *Thanks to me flaking out*
> *I was hopelessly helping*
> *And flailing about*
>
> *This kitchen's a tough scene*
> *Tell ya what, missy-lou:*
> *How about you keep cookin'*
> *And I'll keep it all clean…*
>
> *I'm hopeless, but helping*
> *It's all you can ask*
> *It's hopeless, my helping*
> *It's the vote I can cast…*

After chuckling through Jasper's tale of kitchen-related relationship woe alongside local swells and other gathered luminaries, you dare to peer deep into Trudy's grateful eyes and experience not only a welling of love but long-sought forgiveness—at last—for breaking your tiny babyboy heart; you understand now it had been the best decision. And you will carry forward the satisfaction of the union you shared in the past, both recent and otherwise. You will treasure your tender nights with her, in doing so continuing to heal yourself of the residual energy from that ancient history.

"We gotta talk soon." You have an idea to lay on her. "Not tonight, though. Not until after."

"Okay, sugar." Her voice, trembling. "Whenever you're ready."

Manny, shaking his head and toasting how everything y'all discussed in the time that he lived in the old house could come true, about how to turn Tillman Falls around and make it a tourist destination, the real way to make money, one of the last. Why? Because people coming to a specific place with particular experiences in mind, Manny said to you re: his life and work back in N'awlins, are more apt to lay down a little scratch.

"Look here at this honkytonk, at that stage. We got to keep it filled with hot licks, and hicks from the sticks and the city alike leaving behind a little taste." Inelegant, but inspiring nonetheless.

Of course you paid top dollar for an updated, modern digital lighting and sound rig. "You approve of the improvements, Mr. T?"

"This some classy-ass shit, here."

Whatever you feel about money, and it ain't much, you know the rest of them must continue trudging along capitalism's rocky shores following your departure from Edgewater County, which won't be long in coming. You want to leave your loved ones with the best chance to thrive.

But after this festival's done, you will divest energetically in this place. You say this aloud a few times a day in order to put the words and the vibration into the air. As well as invoking your intention, you also acted:

The houses on River Ridge, a pledge to sign the whole tract over to a perplexed Mervin and Carla Mae, while leaving yourself at least a year of wiggle and margin to get fully out of the county. Let them remain as the caretakers of what you termed "a legacy for the Pettus family name here in Edgewater County, for you and for the boys, Dale and DJ," all for the price of the yearly property taxes and upkeep.

Carla Mae, tearful; Mervin, dumbfounded and rightfully mistrustful. Not everyone understood your transformation. "I don't get it. This some kinda trick?"

"No. Everything I do and say is on the level, Merv. I have no agenda but love in my heart. All I ask is a little patience."

In that same spirit, you would sign over the deed to The Dixiana to Trudy and Jasper's new company, but only if they both agree to the shared ownership plan you've designed, and that stipulates how the decor, basic business plan and contents of the jukebox be preserved in perp, as they say. They would run this place, now, until... you didn't know when. Neither of them have heirs, either. But, who the honkytonk went to after them, if anybody? Not your problem.

The thought lifts your spirits like a hot-air balloon tethered by a slender strand of gossamer silk in a vibrant field of flowers, constrained—barely— from floating languid and free into the sky above blue and clear as a clean glass hot out of an industrial washer, one recently serviced and sanitized.

◉▦◎

FEEBEE ELMENDORF'S PR ONSLAUGHT SEEMS EFFECTIVE:
Lines of county residents and attendees have formed along the highway for the parade scheduled to roll from Pike's Bait & Pawn, with floats designed to promote local businesses, at least those willing to sponsor the festival: Cecil's body art empire, the Gentlemen's Affair consignment shop, Hampton Motors, Pike himself leading the way with Chesnee waving like a beauty queen from her perch in the three-wheeler, followed by the Marching War Eagles from the high school playing your request, a brass-band arrangement of the Grateful Dead's seminal disco-era classic deep cut 'Shakedown Street.' It hadn't been a problem. For better or worse, the band director, Wade Leaphart, clings as you do to like a pop-culture life raft of rock-era albums and damp teenage memories. He's even sporting a tie-dye. Festive.

At the rear comes the official Manny's on the Green float, with Manny T and his combo ripping through R&B covers from the back of a flatbed, the last but far from least: it'll park right inside the gate, with the sound of Manny's saxophone bright and bracing as it cuts through the cool April air, the musicians all wired with radio gear you rented so they can march off the float and onto the main stage to kick off the festival proper without missing a note.

After a consultation, Manny decided on "Good Lovin'" for the parade tune, followed by "How Sweet It Is" once parked at the gate. This festival, you declared, was all about love, and community, and a sense of music and fun and being alive. What better songs? This act on your part seemed more than anything else you'd done, Free Speech Zone aside, to make it Button's event as well as your grand-folks's.

Walking through the town center now transformed into the festival grounds, with a Trabant ride and a mini-Ferris wheel, a bounce-castle and the smell of food vendors including the spicy scent of falafel frying in Mr. Jubouri's stand, whom you went back and finessed at a secret meeting in the ELMS building, a closed-door executive session of principals during which you wielded a modicum of dark sorcery to get your way, you feel that Roy E. Pettus glow of success. Everything you touch, baby. Gold.

A golden age, upon us all.

Soon, the sound of sweet music from multiple stages filling the air. It all worked out. You arrived back home in Tillman Falls for real; for one last instance of honoring those who walked the path before you. Least you can do. And then? Free of obligation.

◉ ▣ ⊘

AS A TOUR BUS GETS DIRECTED INTO ITS PARKING SPOT INSIDE THE secure staging area and VIP backstage tents to the rear of the courthouse lot, damn but you wish they could be there to see this, your grandparents; how you managed to book Gillian Welch and David Rawlings, two of the most accomplished and authentic practitioners of American roots music, for the festival headliners.

The limo already parked, you're informed, has delivered the Button Sykes VIP guests, including the second appearance in town of superstar Maddy Durango, this time with her equally famous sister Vangie, as well as Tillman Falls's own contribution to Hollywood: an actor and the son of Ruth DeKalb, Ray-Ray DeKalb. He gotten superrich off providing a number of key voices behind the longest running animated show in the history of TV, and from whom you'll hear the sort of respectful standup an eighty-five million dollar actor—dude voices a smart-alecky talking dog every kid in America can imitate on command; that's the show business earning value of one creative throat vibration, mad cash, crazy money—can deliver between sets on the main stage. A prince and a scholar for doing the gig, as Becky told you, and arranged by DeKalb's grande-dame mother. Sick money. You can't hold a candle. Color you impressed by the booking and the vibe the cat puts off. Not a care in the world.

Catty, you nevertheless flutter your eyelashes and do your own mincing version of Droopy Dog: "I thought Queen DeKalb of the Highlands didn't give a rip. Thought this showbiz stuff was so low and distasteful."

"Ruth loves the town, too, and wants it to succeed." Becky, scribbling on her clipboard and calling into a walkie talkie for additional recycling bins behind the VIP tent area. "But she's also holding on to traditions and decorum the way she sees fit. As our forebears did, and do."

Musing like Button Sykes. "Don't they? Hold on? Especially when all they should want is to let go? Of desire?"

"How's that?" Becky, intent on listening to her walkie talkie, but giving you an engaged side-eye. "They hold onto desire when they should let go? *What's that supposed to mean?*"

Oops. "A paradox. That's all."

"I'm sorry—*a what?*"

You give her a gentle chuck in the upper arm. "Nothing. Now let's go stage ourselves a music festival."

⊙▣⊘

Long story short: the fest is fine. Until it isn't.

⊙▣⊘

By noon, you're sick of yakking with folks. But it doesn't stop. Endless. You can't hide in The Dixiana; you can't hide anywhere. They are all making you feel like it's about you, when nothing could further from the truth. It's for them. Not you.

At different points you get onstage and make little speeches. Receive more condolences on your grandfather and grandmother than you can shake a stick at. Keep ducking into the VIP tent to look for Karen Black, whom Maddy told you had planned to fly from LA in their Gulfstream—now that's mad money, honey—but had begged off at the last moment. Maddy reported that your iconic screen girlfriend had been feeling unwell, the notion giving you a cold knot in the gut.

Crazy, your luck. Just happens that Karen Black—the fantasy woman of your childhood dreams—gets invited to your festival, but can't make it. Upon learning of Button's death and suffering from cancer herself, Black, Maddy said, felt moved to appear and participate in this public memorial for a young woman she hadn't seen in nearly two decades, and rued her decision to remain on the west coast.

Wait—was all this Button, working her magic from behind, and beyond, the scenes? If so, it hadn't quite delivered Karen Black. A tall order.

Who cares—look at how well it's all working out. Are you living inside your own happy dream? Did you actually drown yourself that evening down on the island, or the F-150 tumbled over on the mountainside that time and crushed you in the cab, or maybe the landing lights at the airstrip never came on, with this time of good cheer and celebration a mere pleasant-valley bardo of imagined wishes arriving in the manner you had hoped—well, except for Button?

Is this all your dying dream, this year back in Edgewater County?

Did the landing lights never come on?

Are you still flying?

◉⑭⊘

BUT AS THE DAY GOES ON, THE DRAUGHT BEER FLOWS AND THE trashcans fill and a couple of busses of college kids disembark and start drinking hard. Two alpha males get belligerent about wanting access to The Dixiana to buy shots, and this after causing trouble inside Manny's on the Green over the cost of the specialty cocktails.

Outside? Throngs. A huge success.

Meanwhile, you stagger around the carnival-like atmosphere aghast at every cigarette butt on the ground, gazing baleful into thousands of glazed peepers, the older patrons jostled by the younger crowd brought in by the rock bands, who're so loud that the Americana stage often gets bled into, which makes you bitch out Darren Woczinski's sound guys, pointing and gesturing and hollering to be heard.

But not yelling out of anger, as you also try to explain, wishing to employ the black blade metaphor so as to further explicate that you aren't angry; but they react to you that way anyway, the soundman large, curly-headed and petulant.

Your point? When I'm mad for real? You'll know it, pardner. No question. And this ain't it. Not yet.

"We'll dial it back a bit." The sound guy, making no move to twiddle his knobs and sliders. "Soon as this Phish act wraps up. Which can't be too soon —I fucking hate jambands."

The blade thrums. You breathe in, deep, conscious and present. Stand apart from your emotions. "Pretty please," you say, not caring if it's loud enough for him to hear. "My grandfather didn't even like this music. We only added this stage to sell tickets. For the money."

"Brother, I can't understand a word you're—"

You head out into the roiling, jostling crowd

... in time to see what appears to be a scuffle over near the Free Speech

Zone, at which you stride with curiosity changing to concern bordering on FEAR and a flat-out run, shoving your way through the throngs lining the streets around the town green, and hearing its buzzing engine you feel glad that the goddamn banner plane's finally shown up, which you notice isn't in the air circling but arcing in at a crazy angle from out of the west, from out of the sun, toward the festival grounds.

With only one other problem now, other than being late: they're flying the wrong direction, and the banner is illegible. Your message, about how much the namesakes of this festival mean to you and to Edgewater County, obscured and useless; your money, wasted.

Yeah. Best you can tell through the red veil lowering over your simmering vision, the banner's twisted or backwards; and upon your leg quivers black retribution, yea, to those lost souls contributing to this cluster-fuck of an unacceptable, unforeseen occurrence.

◉▣⊘

ROOSEVELT NIXON, YOUR OLD BUDDY, STANDS AT THE FREE SPEECH microphone in between acts to promote his message of reconciliation and progress. You remain in full support of the name-changing business littering yards throughout the county yet again with political signs, many of which read VOTE NO on a red field meant to evoke a stop sign, while YES TO NEW FALLS CITY screamed from opposing, green-background placards featuring a bright starburst in one corner like a sunrise on the new morning such a name change portends for all citizens. The vote looms in another week. Thank goodness. Tempers are short, nerves frayed. Edgewater County feels one argument away from a mass shooting over this name-change bit.

You don't much give a crap about what they want to call this township, but if it rids the green of that ridiculous Ben Tillman statue, not even a full-sized effigy of the crusty old racist liquor-dealing backwoods cracker of a Governor and a Senator—a legacy South Carolinian, sure, but as ignominious and unworthy a human being as had ever been memorialized in stone—you can be counted in the 'Yes' column.

Nixon's voice, booming out about the municipal name change campaign, when in the middle of the crowd, a knot of undersized fedoras you have managed to not notice begin catcalling, led by that louche thug Rembert.

Mother-fudging gangster. And with a goddamn set of All Access VIP credentials slung around the open collar of his black silk shirt alongside the tacky gold chain and graying thatch of chest hair. You not only want to puke at his shit-eating grin, you wish to behead the lot of them, along with whomever he fleeced or threatened to get his forbidden backstage pass.

Control, slipping away.

You must ACT.

Your grab Edgewater County's most powerful agent of the underground economy by his shoulders, and as you scuffle and scream epithets you feel hands fall upon you while the lizard blows spit in your face; Roosevelt calls for order from his microphone.

Rembert rages venomous at you, even more than toward the Reverend-turned-politician pushing for change. "You fucking ass. Your hillbilly grand-daddy, he could've had this whole county in his hand. He did for a little while, fifty years ago. But he give it up. And now because you got some scratch, and can wave your wallet around so's they'll rent this green to you today, you think you're in charge?"

"I'm not in charge of anything, dipshit."

"I can believe it. Your money don't mean you're in charge of shit around here, fatboy. And you ain't got no right to support this crazy-ass snowflake bullshit. You don't give a shit about Edgewater County."

"How can you say that?"

"Cause if you did? You'd have stayed like me."

Before you can retort, Roosevelt Nixon appears at your side. "Mr. Rembert, if you don't agree with my politics, you may sign the sheet and have your say. But I won't be interrupted. That stage is open to your voice as well. Feel free to stand before God and mankind to disagree. But allow me to speak my truth."

"I'll do more than disagree with your ass, boy," the fumes from Rembert's breath like rubbing alcohol. "Watch if I don't."

"Please," gesturing to the microphone as a trio of female voices harmo-nized from the Americana stage. "Lay your rhetorical worst upon me."

In the crowd you note a shiny head bobbing closer like the dorsal fin of a shark cutting through a choppy sea—Cecil Waugh. The briefest of eye contact between you speaks enormous volumes:

I need you, buddy.

Just in time: Rembert's rhetoric goes live—a pistol, a shiny nickel-plated .38, brandished in his hand. Right as Cecil Waugh appears.

Shouting. Shoving A Doc Marten connects with Rembert's forearm. Shots.

Screams. Everybody scrambles.

Everyone's worst nightmare—a mass shooting.

You hurtle through panicked festival goers to get to the low, wooden

Free Speech riser made of pallets and plywood. Grabbing for the black iron microphone stand, cold and smooth as a prison bar, you drag yourself up as a phalanx of police descend into the anarchic mad convulsion of the crowd. With Rosie's body lying prone and bleeding on the ground, guns are drawn on Rembert who holds up his hands, defiant, until he steps toward the cops; he's killed in a fusillade of gunfire—you see fire, literal flames, spurting from the barrels.

And right as you're about to wail, "Enough! Enough! Enough!" in the mic, the banner plane's engines ROAR as if right in your face, and a gale of a sudden gust lifts the soles of your sport-sandals from the wood of the platform; and holding onto the microphone stand it rises with you, and for a second you hang in the air as though a glimpse of eternal serenity before your eyes, stillness, the holy instant, perfection, levitation; before slamming back down onto your bad shoulder.

The wood of the stage seeming to fold in upon you and itself, a sharp searing pain rips down your leg; and you shriek into the red madness of what has to be a nightmare you're having the night before the festival; waiting to wake up; thinking, if only this were one of Button's lucid dreams, you could stop all this chaos and control it; asking what the hell's going on; what the hell has happened; and why isn't anyone responding to your screams for help. Why aren't you waking up at home in bed. Why.

BUTTON SYKES

G osh, how much she'd understood!

Gosh: how little she'd understood.

Oh, by the standards of most folks occupying the realm of physicality, her knowledge had been considerable, she now could see; yeah yeah, yep yep.

But, oh—so much more.

The etheric plain. The real action. Real as real is, anyway.

Kinda cool. Liberating.

Nah, not kinda. Totes cool and liberating.

Dude.

But a tug. The pull of the flesh.

People still need me. They need my help.

What is me, though? Sometimes when she would successfully detach from emotion, she would inquire, *If I am detached from Me, watchful and nonjudgemental, who is the watcher?*

Jerry. He had shown her the way.

Wait—that Jerry?

Yeah. Jerry freaking Garcia.

Oneness, in which her journey to wholly integrated element of such— that it was ever anything else!—manifested as a familiar image, an icon. It's one of the mechanisms of transition from physicality to Oneness, as she intuitively understood.

They sat together in a hazy space, a basement apartment decorated like a college dorm room—a coffee table littered with ashtrays and bongs, book-shelves made from boards and cinder blocks, magazines and books. Guitars. Records. Smoke wafting.

"Nice digs, huh?"

"Reminds me of Foothills State."

Garcia cackled and sparked up one of his beloved jazz cigarettes. White speckles dotted the front of his black T-shirt, dandruff that when Button looked close twinkled like tiny stars. Scratching at his beard with the nub of his missing finger, he seemed young, so young. Not papa bear Jerry from the 1980s and 90s, but the young and beatifically reluctant spiritual guru, the way people regarded him back in the psychedelic heyday. Captain Trips. Sweet.

"Ah-ha—this must be one of my lucid dreams."

"You sure about that?" His laughter, bubbly and self-effacing, but also dismissive of her notion. "I don't think I'm dreaming, so why the fuck should you be?"

"I dunno. Just seems like a dream."

"A dream we dreamed, one afternoon long ago? That type-deal?"

"Uh—yeah. Sure."

"Well, there you go."

"You were telling us that all along?"

"Well, Lesh wrote that one, but: you were telling yourselves."

Wait—a dream, yet not. He's not there. Nor is she.

Yet they are.

Okay. It was understandable this way. More understandable. To one who'd recently departed the 3D world below.

As above, so below.

She understood this idea differently, now. Before, it had been about an ability to discern the vastness of the cosmos while at the same time moving downward into an appreciation of the life of the smallest particle, and envisioning with clarity how the same energy moved both star and starfish, albeit at scale. Leveling up? No. Scaling up the energy.

Understood so much, now. She did, she did.

Said so to Garcia, who laughed again, but this time with immense pleasure.

"Just surprised to see you."

"It's whoever you believed in—I'm the Buddha to some Chinese guy from up in the mountains. Or Jesus to a typical Edgewater County-ian, such as yourself. Get it?"

"I think so."

"You know how transitional Oneness is gonna manifest for your pal Roy?"

"Oh, tell me."

"A character from some movie—let's see." Garcia consults an enormous, bundled computer printout. Licks a thumb, flips through sheet after sheet saying, let me see here, let me see here. "Oh, it's called *There Will Be Blood*."

Button, chagrined. "Not Oscar® winning English actor Daniel Day Lewis. That character is a monster." Unlike her earthly speech, her words flowed so with ease. "And a movie character's not even a real person."

"No freaking shit. But—is Buddha? Or Jesus?"

Another glow of understanding. "Ah."

"Now you're onto something, kid."

"Life is but a dream."

"Merrily, merrily." He winked. "Maybe hoax is a better term."

She wanted to feel fear, but it wouldn't come. She feigned it instead: "Wait, I'm frightened. What are you? Where am I—?"

"C'mon. No, you aren't."

Questions were a fraud, too. She already knew. The play on earth, one of light and dark, duality; a play ongoing for time immemorial. But here a different, alternate performance, one she thought should 'play out', a script like she'd once tried to write; like she'd scripted for herself before incarnating this time.

The scripts—back in college.

Heather.

Heather.

Heather. Who had so eased Button's transition.

A fondest wish, realized.

She beamed light and love not to Jerry but back down to Heather Ponderview, whom she couldn't see, but knew now knelt weeping over Button's body lying still on the bed in the blue pyramid, where only seconds before her final breath had pulled itself in, pushed itself out; life, beginning with the first intake of air out of the womb and ending with a final exhalation; one long breath. Button, dying with peaking on a mushrooms Heather prepared to ease the transition, a trip to put that chocolate she'd eaten at her fabled Colorado Phish shows to shame; a Technicolor® rainbow carpet she'd ridden here to Oneness. Button, held in the arms of Heather Ponderview one final time and breathing that last rush of graceful, magical air into her lover's tearful mouth; an opening that became a tunnel like snakeskin, mottled and molting and peeling away. Like the aya ceremony.

Passing through the veil.

Fulfillment.
Arrival.
At this moment.
Which is every moment.
Endlessly looping; endlessly renewed.
Forever.

◦🔲⊘

HOLD UP ON THE FOREVER THING.

Jerry, a scene shift, appearing to her now in a comfortable, warm room of soft pulsating purple walls made out of light, featuring two sets of opposing doors, one in each of the prime directions, all old, wooden and ornate in their incongruity with the amorphous celestial walls surrounding their frame; the stations of the cross; the place whence the four winds come; the four elements, the four agreements. She turned in a slow circle as in her banishing ceremony, but no matter which direction, Jerry, always in her field of view.

"I came to see you play, this one time? It cost me so much."

"We all paid a price for the energetic exchange."

"Who are you? Who is 'we'?"

He only smiled and lit another cigarette rolled from a stick of the finest cannabis. Coughed; glanced with self-conscious disdain at the smoldering vegetable matter that gave off no smell, unlike in 3D reality. Said, "Eh," and flicked ashes flaming like tiny comets, an Oort cloud circling his glowing face a few times before dissipating into animated starbursts.

Jerry explained again how he wasn't God, but he also wasn't Jerry either, not the human one who would appreciate the sentiment, only light coalescing into a non-tactile plasma-like form intended to ease her transition. That she had to choose one of the doors but could wait, long as she didn't mind entrapment in this transitive, liminal state to endure the challenges inherent in putting off a well-earned final ascendance from the karma chamber.

"I completed my earthly transit? Really?"

"I mean—I can double-check." He again consulted the enormous computer printout, his whole let-me-see mantra again. "Yep, right here. The numbers don't lie. You've completed the spiritual growth cycle, little sister. How's that feel? Huh?"

"Like, tons of work went into it. For like, I dunno. Ten-thousand freaking years."

"So, why this perverse notion of going back? To eat more from the table," how Jerry put it, "when you don't have to? That's gilding the lily. You got far enough this time. Ate of the fruits and whatnot. You figured out all the secrets. Well—most. Enough."

"Did I, now."

"Yep."

"Really?"

"Far as you know."

"Dude—!"

"Farther than most. Jeez. Enough. This game takes a long time. And you've been at it. As have I. I mean—really. Our souls were needed; they were called. And we answered the call. But the work, our part, it's been played."

"That's terrific news. I think."

But wait—how much farther could one go in the earthly realm of materialistic dimensionality? Her magic hadn't manifested as anything near the scale of priests moving two-hundred-ton blocks of limestone into place for a pyramid foundation. Instead of pervasive understanding, she sensed a fresh element of mystery remaining not unlike that of the living creature contemplating the gauzy veil of death. Well, dang.

How much farther?

How much more to learn and experience? To manifest?

Well now, such a notion made it hard to decide which way to go. Beam of light; or another go at physicalized incarnation, slate wiped clean. Another learning-turn at the game. Or, come back as a cat, or a moth, or a butterfly. And simply exist as living energy without all the existential angst and striving for metaphysical meaning.

Or, a purple humpback whale, bathed in Fukushima radiation.

Now there, a pesky, earthly thought needling at her. Like the one of Roy still needing help through one final trial.

Her sacred pledge. Unfinished.

"Getting anywhere?" Jerry asked.

"Maybe." Wait—a tingling, as if still in her body! The old intuition. "Definitely maybe."

The game, afoot—should she hang out on a lower astral plane? Keep an eye on her charges below, make sure her Grandpa Burnie and Roy Earl, among others, were comforted and kept safe from unforeseen occurrences? Not so much a compulsion to incarnate again, more like a return echo of her prior service, but on the astral plane?

"Do what you like. But, hey, not me," he said, shaking his head. "Levels and layers to the whole shebang. Be where you'll be; incarnate again; dick around here. Think it over. No worries. But to mess around on the astral plain, that's dicey. You don't wanna get stuck."

"Stuck?"

"It happens. Look at your Agatha of Aberdeen."

If she'd had arms, there'd have been some major horripilation. "That you said her name, it's a synchronicity. That's who I have to keep from hurting Roy and the others. *This time, it's personal.*"

"Ooooh. Are you kidding? Everyone has to watch out for themselves. To a certain extent. So it's all personal."

"My charge was one of service. And it includes this experiment."

"Braver than me, kid. All I got to say. Sheesh."

Button, expressing concern about the chatter, and too much time passing.

The deceased guitarist, smoking and grumbling under his breath. He played a most glorious run of sixteenth notes on a lyre that'd appeared, shimmering, in his angelic hands, notes she both heard and saw as iridescent, sparkling energy bubbles. "God, listen to you. Time, again? Get over it. Here on the way to your ascendance as a fifth dimensional entity, time is a fucking different animal, man. Take a look 'down'."

Button, concentrating, viewing the physically incarnated blue globe, which appeared quite different from how earthly eyes decode the energies, even from space. Levels, and layers. But the 3D surface as she remembered it, still visible. But scarred and changed. Coastlines altered. The blue of the water, not as clear. Fiery patches. A giant glowing hole where Yellowstone used to be. Little reverse-meteors, streaking upward—she didn't have to ask. Those were souls dis-incarnating.

"Whoa—*the Yellowstone caldera blew.*"

"That was the big reset this go-round. Shit happens. Et cetera."

"How long? *How long have I been too late to help my friends?*"

"A thousand years passed while we've been dicking around here. If you must persist in thinking of 'time' the way you used to."

"But—"

"Oops, there's another century right there." He cackled with glee. "And yet, not really. It's totally fucked up, man. Well, I mean it's perfect. Fucked up in a good, perfect way, that you can never see from down there. It's a fat trip. That's all I'm trying to get across."

"But time's arrow—"

"Remember the yugas? Those are cycles, dude, but all coexisting in simultaneity. Ain't linear."

"Mindfuck."

"Right on." He waved it all away, the hand with its nubby middle finger. "You'll relax into getting it. Here, 'passed' is relative. Wrong way to think about it. No back and forth. No past. No future. Decide to visit your buddies whenever you feel like it. Pick it up from where you left off. It's as easy as one-two-three. Not accounting for the extraordinary energetic expenditure and risk of purgatorial entrapment involved in doing so. Just sayin'."

"No big whoop," Button said, glowing. "I feel up to the challenge."

Jerry, impatient. "Fine. I don't have all of eternity for this. Do you have the faintest idea how often the aging Deadhead population now sends up another one? If I could make money on this deal—well. So, like, what's the call?"

Her halting way of thinking. Coming back with a vengeance. "I'm not sure. How to take. All this. I guess. I'm happy. Completed. Digging the Oneness. But—*ack. Blargh.*"

"You kids, man. I tell ya. Nobody can make a decision anymore."

"Affluenza. A symptom." A delaying tactic. "What's behind the doors?"

"The guardian angels you've been invoking. The last step is that you get to meet them... before you become one yourself."

"Wow—that sounds sick."

His voice took on a low hum, almost sexy, like a wolf laying a line on a hottie at a bar; very un-Jerry. "Want a peek, little lady?"

Reassurance that her intuitive sense was intact, she shook her head. "I know who they are already. And who you are."

A little dejected. "I know you know."

"And I know that you know."

"No time for Abbott and Costello, now."

"Guess not. Sorry."

The being played a run of notes on the lyre, hit a few clams. Fiddled with the tuning. Looked less like Garcia than a Jerry Halloween mask.

Sighed, lowered the instrument. "No way to sugarcoat it: Some of us cycle through forever. The souls of the damned. But look, you've transcended that. You've earned your retirement, in twentieth century capitalistic terms. My little tricks here to throw you off? Embarrassed that I tried with you, Button. Nope. Too smart for this wicked demiurge."

She understood her choice. Which wasn't one at all. "Whatever you are, I'm not sure my work. Is done. Back there."

"So you keep saying, and like I'm telling you: kid, there're other choices you can make. Infinite paths."

"Right on, but I feel. Compelled. To hang around. Back there. If it's. Ya know. Permitted. For only a little 'while'." Now referring to the dimensions of time sounded sillier than heck, stupid and facile before she'd even said it.

"Do as thou wilt. But man, you shouldn't get involved in anybody's trip. Remember: you don't want to foster attachment, not hanging around those bags of wet, ropy gristle any longer than necessary. Why do you think I keep my distance?"

"And if I dig? Hanging with the meat-bags?"

"Depends on what you do with the fetish." Garcia, playing again with aplomb and sing-speaking familiar words. "Oh, what I want to know? Are-you-kind?"

"Very much so."

"Noted. Your mind's made up. I know this because your mind is my mind. So go ahead. You don't need anyone's permission but your—our—own. You won your imaginary ten-thousand year battle already. But if you want to screw around with Agatha of Aberdeen, don't let me stop you. Not that I could."

"What about influencing somebody still alive, too?"

"She's been messing around with IRL folks for centuries—why not you, in your little benevolent way?"

Truth. She understood, now. "Why not, indeed?"

He knew. "It's the other kid you're worried about."

"Yeah." Christy Beaudock. Button, seeing him wielding the yoke of a small plane, struggling for control. Screaming about a dream, a dream, it's the dream. But not even this knowledge could replace the warm glow of assurance with that of bodily fear. Not here. Not as part of Oneness. Nothing but a shimmering blue field of ultimate love here now, a vision, a reality, an eternity.

That she was willing to give up. To help Roy. And all of them. She had to try.

Now she could see all that had happened and all to come, mainly because it was all happening right-now, and for once she couldn't let what she understood as Christy's black magic prevail. This infection came from Agatha of Aberdeen, and with it the danger that the two acting in concert, the wicked spirit and the misguided person together, tended to end Roy Earl Pettus's physicalized trip way too soon—an aberration in the tapestry, the way Button saw it, anyway.

However it would work out—and she didn't know for certain, only that she wished to change the results she'd already seen, of the plane crashing into The Dixiana and the gun battle between Rembert's men and the police that kills so many bystanders, along with Roy himself—perhaps her energy's proximity to him throughout the event would keep him infused with the cosmic Oneness of it all, giving him the life-force and good luck in continuing his journey to where Button had arrived.

It's like, decided, man. She had to make the attempt. To help Roy complete his life scripts, which were underway, she could understand, amidst all the loss and pain and what he'd term rigmarole he'd endured, with only a sick spiritual conspiracy standing in the way of his complete actualization as a leader of humankind.

"It's an aberration I go back to forestall. No, prevent."

"Aberration, my eye. All possibilities are possible, man, no matter what you do. You're just an old softie, that's what you are." Jerry's laughter more sad that mirthful. But his eyes, twinkling, held admiration. "Whatever, man."

"Do I—need to clear this with anybody else?"

A peal of faraway thunder.

Jerry hunched his shoulders, dropped his voice. "Better to ask forgiveness than permission. Besides, it's your funeral. Nah, nah—kidding. You already did that. But look." He became dead serious. "Don't go too far. There aren't rules. But there are lines. Your reality bubble, it's taken out of the equation now for your friend. Mostly. So don't bring it too much— whoa. You make too much magic in front of them, it'll only confuse the issues. You wanna end up another Agatha of Aberdeen? Messing with everyone's heads? Or worse?"

"Discipline. I get it."

"Seriously. Otherwise? You'll only scare them like that loon does. So: tread on cat's paws."

"She's a wounded, wicked spirit."

"Nasty, ain't she? Energetic bodies disconnected from the oversoul. They're pure-T troublemakers. Know why?"

"Why?"

"Because they can't let go."

"I get it. And, I hear you."

"Okay, then. Enough said."

She got it so much, in fact, that Button, ascendant almost as much as a soul could hope for, now not only struggled—toyed, a better word—with going back for another actual round, she suspected she might not have a choice. Fated—they had agreements on this side. Her and Roy. That part wasn't clear. Only that she needed to watch over him for a bit. A personal case.

Button drifted over toward one door. "One last temptation? Like a movie trailer?"

"Oh, why not. Go for it."

She cracked open the door she would have chosen.

Wow. Knowledge flooded in. The totality of the lifetimes, over countless millennia. The repeating personalities with whom she'd concocted life-scripts on this side, only to play out there. It'd taken many trips for her spirit to have gotten as far in the game as she had. Always powerful, though, in whatever form her incarnations took—her aya visions, a freaking documentary.

And not always powerful in a benevolent way—one vision of standing on the platform in a high headdress, attending to a king, and being attended by others to whom she showed no love, no loyalty, no empathy; a young, albeit powerful soul. No, not as court jester, rather the magician. Presiding over the sacrifices. Blood, soaking the ground; bloody red light suffusing all of that vision. Mercy, she thought. I have been a bad soul at times, but Jerry, hearing this thought, said, but don't forget 'good and bad' are but polarities of the same energy.

And now that she'd seen all these past lives, the 'prize,' if it could be thought of in such a base and crude way, here in a dimension in which simply 'being' was prize enough, loomed self-evident. Spirits and souls choose to incarnate into the world where pain is possible, and love has to exist not solely as itself in eternal glowing loving perfection, but rather in opposition to forces to provide contrast: not written on the light-beams of Oneness the spirits occupy when not incarnate, but as lower forms of themselves—sometimes lost, often malevolent but all Separate, and whether they realize it, aching with relentless desire for the same end: to return to Oneness.

At-one-ment.

But the worst of the callow souls, not understanding this. Feeding on the pain of others. A different dope addiction.

Button had carried enough of her earthly self into this realm, enough of the ephemera, to remember the old Talking Heads song called 'Heaven.' And got it, now. Big time.

I get it, she beamed again into the Oneness of which she'd always been a full partner. Her birthright. All of us.

I know you get it, Oneness beamed back, not sounding like Jerry Garcia, or anyone else human. *Now make up your mind if you're to complete the transition, like, for reals, yo. Or go help your buddy out. It's fine either way.*

I'm certain, Button beamed. More nudging, from this side. Till the cycle of events is complete per Roy's adjusted script.

Fine; oneness did not contemplate individuality, thought it useless, the stuff it goes to the third dimension to examine, experience, and then slough off like the skin of slithering creatures, traversing meatspace bedeviled by half-souls and elementals and other lesser aspects of Oneness that so challenge the higher souls occupying form as the most sentient of the creatures. But go for it, Oneness thinks. Nudge and cajole, if you wish. It isn't your part to play in that realm anymore, not unless you want another go, but 'want' isn't a factor, not along the razor's edges of light and motion and ultimate being here in a glowing, endless field of eternal perfection.

❁ ❖ ⊘

AND BUTTON KNOWS THIS BECAUSE ONENESS KNOWS THIS AND ALL ELSE, and has always known, and she sees all that has occurred and all which will occur, and because of this chooses neither to dance away on the light nor to incarnate again, but instead to dwell in the lower aether for as long as her energy safely allows, and to nudge enough to assist Roy and others whom Button feels need help in the physical realm to complete the work their journey of discovery includes and entails.

Oneness grants this desire because there's no Oneness to deny it, and Button is delighted to have her glimpses best she can reckon of what happens amidst the baser and harder elements, which includes many of her favorite souls making their vibrations on stages of wood and steel with joy and abandon; and Button feels the pull of the realm and has flashes of her vibration-worship at the music concerts; we want you to be happy, words that come to her as much as 'words' can come anymore, and only again if she chooses to rejoin, which at this time isn't clear, and it all depends on elements that have already occurred and that will likely occur, absent a massive co-creating of reality here in a physical state among the beings that somehow changes that which is foretold and has happened, both at once.

Again, but even that could turn malleable and changeable, because of all possibilities this current version is the one occurring based on the mutual reality generated by Oneness, and Button knows now that the variations and realms and universes are endless, but she stays invested in this timeline and nudges, nudges to her heart's content, hangs around the area where she'd occupied space and time and made her own throat vibrations to all who'd listen about some lessons now confirmed and being confirmed and coming to confirmation, all a million times over during what they call a 'second' there on the lower-vibrating plane of physicality, and seeing and knowing the small airplane backing out of its berth and taxiing away from the man running and calling, she understood all her angels and her Walfredos and future selves; and they were all the same self.

But the airplane, and the one called Christy, his vibration, so mixed up and wrong as hers had felt right while in her body; a call to her on Earth she ignored, and now time to check her response-ability here on the other side to a spirit crying out in pain.

But thanks to the state of Gaia in humankind's hands, her body in this timeline had gone sour before she could finish helping Roy or Christy or her granddad, and this portended not-good, nuh-uh, for all the souls incarnating in a time of such spiritual and vibrational dichotomy; but in the era of change and ascension underway—the Age of Aquarius, as the phrase comes to her in clumps of data and logic unfiltered by the light of knowledge and eternity pulling her back from all this low-aether nonsense—there is the possibility of redemption. And transformation of all that is.

Names for things—how much of the illusory time wasted on assigning abstractions to that which is, and must be, and always will be nameless and formless.

There, but not.

She already knows and has lived a thousand times over the events to come, in their wink of an eye an endless looping occasional digression, and it's this tangent her nudges allow and create; she wishes and desires, a no-no, to see Roy stay and complete his tasks in this incarnation. She sees how it will go, sees his own desires, sees how they play into so many other lives, including a few about which she cares deeply, including precious beloved Heather, who will remain incarnate for a long long time yet there in the earthly realm, and will need multiple partners to help her live and carry out the dream they'd both shared, at least at one time, a silly and untenable concept that only slows Button down:

It takes almost all her energy to nudge Christy's aircraft and cause him to lose control as it hurtles downward to buzz the town and the festival; Button, knowing Christy intended to flip Roy off out the small sliding window of the metal can with wings slicing crude through the heavy ocean of aether through which it all occurred, graceless and profane, before a fiery, spectacular, unforgettable mind-altering crash at top speed headlong into The Dixiana, an event that'd happened time and again and here again, but would be slightly different, and despite her agreement with Roy from eons ago (or perhaps only a second) to help him finish his incarnation here, it's apart from the familiar timeline that sees the town square named for him and so many other threads affected and continuing on in a reality much less bright than one that includes Roy E. Pettus remaining incarnate, and so her nudge makes happen what needs to happen.

A micron or two of pressure is placed against both the fuselage of the plane and Roy's body on the Free Speech stage is spared; Roy, who had bravely rushed over to help his friend Roosevelt Nixon, who'd been speaking from the platform with compassion but receiving only anger from the men shouting at him. Dude-bro deserved a break this time.

Right—in most iterations of this theatrical play, Roy is done and over, his karma earning only death while watching his grandfather's honkytonk burn, ironically one of his own fondest wishes; but instead her nudges turn the banner plane's sharp angle of descent, screaming from the engines and from Christy, who cannot believe what he's seeing is real; and believes he is either dreaming or playing his game—and is, of course, the game of his incarnation—but his physical shell and his soul remain far from ascended; and to this he says, after the crash he will reboot his game, but he's not thinking about this in the right way, he believes only that in the physical realm he will wake up and perform this resetting action, yo. And she feels for the kid. Misguided. Abused. Who wouldn't?

His dream isn't to be, and his soul, young and unwieldy, doesn't get to choose, will go by force because this is the way of Oneness for all eternity and for always; and contrasts with Button's rather advanced placement in the old ascending soul game; and knowing all this and seeing it happen, she feels secure in knowing that if Roy has more time this time, his own soul will complete its own ascension; and perhaps in the future which she already knows but which is changeable, maybe-sorta-kinda, he will vibrate into the forever dimension where she will wait, and perhaps he will be far enough along to be able to choose, and the same for Heather, and maybe the three of them will stay together again along the light-beams, blade-running and existing in the purity and perfection of love that is eternity, and is right-now, and is every outcome and every possible time and place and dimension all wrapped in glowing white-purple light, light that informs and illuminates every soul, would they only deign to see it shining above them, their highest chakra; but all this beside the point, especially when you are Oneness, and you see that what you have done comes at enormous energetic cost to this aspect of your spirit, which will swim amidst this aether for some number of epochs, now, in order to recharge enough to return to the upper realm. As Oneness.

Instead?

Purgatory.

To wait for her friends.

And welcome them into Oneness herself.

Button's big idea.

Meanwhile, on the earthly plane in Edgewater County, vibrations and auras and souls all rush about crying amidst the fire-elements and the smoke and the injuries and the few deaths, souls convulsing in fear, in confusion, in agony and in darkness, but this duality, Button understanding and conveying to Roy best she can while he lies trembling and fearful and praying for salvation, is why we incarnate; it's because you don't know how good existing in pure love truly feels until you have suffered, first; until you have felt. Felt anything at all. Even pain.

In the afterworld, feelings are different; for one, they don't exist, not the way people think of them in meatspace. Made existence as pure energy easier, if a touch more colorless than an existence of contrast and high drama. Feelings—they're why we show up in bodies. An experiment in emotion; to find out what feelings feel like. So it goes.

JASPER GLASSCOCK

Other than the banner plane being MIA for a spell, nothing festival-related had been troubled by any hitches, not far as Jasper knew. Way to knock the cherry off the deal on a damn near perfect day so far, pilot for hire. Roy Earl, pissed and tired as a whipped mule, said that when he got hold of him, that drunken pilot's ass was grass.

Here, deep into his kickoff set on the 'Rabbit Pettus' Stage—sponsored and presented by The Dixiana, LLC, a new parent company for the honky-tonk and related promotional activities that Jasper had set up in Roy Earl's name, and which 'leased' the Dixiana™ trademark from the estate of Reynolds Pettus, an estate almost, but not quite, through the probate process; the will, straightforward as you could want—Jasper reveled in a crowd, respectable, for so early in the performance schedule.

It'd been a dream come true hanging out earlier in the 'green' tent with the talent, set up in front of the honkytonk and granting access inside to the VIPs. Jasper, maybe for the first time in his life, walked around with the straight spine of a working, professional musician. Seasoned players, men and women, schmoozed and tuned guitars, treated him like a peer, all laughing and singing and marveling at the weather and the reconstructed Dixiana; still itself, yet fresh and real.

Gillian and David arrived; Jasper's hands shook as he introduced himself, so he kept them jammed into his pockets.

"Mr. Rabbit Pettus sure admired y'all. Always said he wished he could book ya onto the Dixiana stage."

"Well-sir," Gillian Welch said with an impish twinkle, "we would've been right honored to play here. Hope we can make up for it later today."

"There's one song he'd've asked for."

"Anything for Mr. Pettus."

Jasper requested 'Red Clay Halo,' a favorite, and Gillian smiled. "Already on the set list."

Jasper went to hug her; they bumped guitars. "Oops."

David Rawlings swung the body of his Martin away from Jasper's own fine instrument. "Watch it now, pardner."

"Lemme ask you something, David."

"Shoot."

"The house is on fire—do you save Gillian first, or that Martin?"

Big laugh. "Dunno, Mr. Glasscock. Tough call."

High-larity.

Afterwards, Jasper had to blow off the juice of having joked with Gillian Welch about burning up in a fire by strolling the festival grounds, which on any ordinary Saturday would be plain old Tillman Falls with a few folks milling around, some antiquing groups. Preachers preaching. Button, her tent on the corner.

But more than her tent was missing. A shock.

At least the urgency she'd shown about preparing end-of-life documents made sense. Getting her mother into the home. And so on.

Burnham, though? She had arranged little for him. "Roy'll take care of Granddad."

"You sure?"

"Yes."

"Did you ask him?"

"Verbally?"

Jasper held out his hands: *how else?*

"I have. A feeling. That he will. Agree to. Having power of attorney."

But for all the loss of the last few months—including the man himself— Rabbit Pettus's dream of music in the streets, now for real. Happening. Jasper, grinning nonstop. Getting a warm glow in his chest. Someday had arrived.

⊙▣⊘

EARLIER IN THE DAY, HIS ACCESS LAMINATE RESTING ON THE CREST OF the belly on which he would prop his guitar, Jasper took a brisk stroll out of the gates, waving to the ticket-takers and yellow-shirt security. He ambled toward the police command post set up down the block on the plaza in front of the old courthouse. Lots of plainclothes cops standing around he didn't recognize—Styrofoam cups in their hands, danishes, pleasant enough demeanor. Sheriff Oakley, him he knew well, and Timmy Truesdale and the other locals, yeah. But the rest, no.

Feds. DHS, he guessed.

With all their toys: A tank-like vehicle built to withstand roadside bombs called an MRAP, Mine Resistant Ambush Protected, painted black. Next to that, on a trailer and covered by a tarp, a mystery object. Rounded on top. An odd shape.

Jasper, peeking underneath. Looked like a big loudspeaker.

Plainclothes dude appeared out of nowhere, inches from Jasper's ear. "Excuse me, sir—step away from there. Please."

Jasper brandished his laminate. "Keep your drawers on. I'm talent."

"Talent's not authorized back here."

"Okay, Agent Smith."

"Bindernagel."

"What the hell's this thing, anyway?"

"That's classified."

Jasper snorted—who did this pencil-dick think he was? "If you don't tell me, I'm just gonna go ask somebody who will."

"Nobody here above my head, sir. Respectfully."

Jasper explained he was more than talent, he was Jasper Glasscock. A town father. An attorney; a lodge brother; a member of the broader fraternity of jurisprudence. He pointed down the street to his office above the CashAdvance on the corner of Congress and Beaumont, made one of the secret signs shared among the sons of widows. "I'm sure I can keep a secret."

Bindernagel responded with the counter-sign, but kept firm his stonewalling. "I'll still have to ask you to step away from this security apparatus, else you'll be remanded to federal custody. And I'll take your little laminate myself, slip it on, and strut around the festival. *Then I'll be talent.* Won't I."

Jasper, feeling intimidated as heck. "I just want to make sure nobody'll vaporize me while I'm onstage."

A polite but firm gesture with an outstretched hand: *away from the gear.*

Ambling over to the table with the danishes and coffee, of which Jasper availed himself despite having had a pot and a half already, along with a few slugs of whiskey to take off the edge, he rubbed elbows with Sheriff Oakley as the cop stood gnawing on an everything bagel.

"What you boys expecting here today? A freakin' riot?"

"I'm not expecting anything but music, and a few unruly drunks. Can't speak for anyone else."

"Looks like the Feds are loaded for bear." He cocked a thumb at the mystery machine. "What's under the tarp? A *Star Trek* photon torpedo launcher?"

"That?" He chuckled. "LRAD sonic cannon. Nonlethal crowd control. That's playground-level junk compared to some of what they have. But it works."

Jasper, sucking his teeth. "Under what circumstances would they need to deploy that at an afternoon music festival?"

"Any gathering of more than a small group of citizens has the potential to escalate beyond certain parameters of public safety and behavior. That's the mindset now; that's the protocol. Groups larger than a few people, the apparatus exists to manage them. Or so the conventional wisdom in law enforcement goes." Lecturing, dry and clipped, in his no-nonsense cop cadence. "But one vendor had some relative on a DHS watch list, if memory serves. That fact alone triggers a more flexible and comprehensive response mindset protocol and deployment."

What gobbledygook. "They're going overboard with all this gear."

"One can never be too careful. Not under modern conditions."

"I don't know what's become of us."

"We're more safety conscious. Not an unwise position to take. But look." He dropped his voice. "You and I know the truth—ninety-nine percent of the time, it's all for display. This formidable potential for a quick and varied response is a deterrent. DHS wouldn't issue orders to fire that sonic cannon into a crowd of ordinary citizens listening to music on a Saturday afternoon in a thousand years. Not unless some real trouble had already broken out. Which won't happen on my watch."

"Nor mine. Gotta go tune up."

"Break a leg—that's what they say in show business. Yes?"

"You got it, Sheriff. God bless."

"Same to you."

Creeped out, Jasper did the hot-foot-hurry back to the super exclusive VIP green room to complain about this shit to Roy Earl. Whose dollars, both tax-collected and voluntarily paid, went to cover all this over-militarized, hysterical chickenshit weaponry. Pettus better not receive some BS invoice from the Feds after all this was over. Jasper already started preparing briefs and motions in his mind, just in case.

NO CHANCE. MUSIC LOVERS BEGAN ARRIVING, AND THE STREETS FILLED up. The smell of frying food permeated the green as though the County Fair had come in the spring instead of fall, and the daylight shone bright; it'd been one of those mornings where you needed a jacket at first, but underneath the bracing chill dwelled the promise of a day nurturing and warm. The American South in springtime—not much to compare. Not that Jasper ever lived anywhere else. He had to reckon that this place, with its buds and blossoms and birds chirping, represented the best of all possible worlds. Or at least the worlds at hand.

The sun at last rose from behind the municipal building and illuminated the colorful banner-wraps of the vendors and the sponsors of the three stages. Bright blue recycling cans throughout. Stolid teal chemical shitters lined along Congress Street like troops at attention. White beer wagons with tall red flags that read BEER WAGON. A music festival.

Last, The Dixiana, festooned with balloons and streamers and three sepia-toned, stylized, oversized portraits Roy had had printed as part of his deal with the beer company:

Reynolds 'Rabbit' Pettus
'Mama' Runelle Kittery Pettus, and
Allyson 'Button' Sykes.

Jasper surmised that the quote marks meant Roy must not have known 'Button' wasn't a nickname.

Speaking of Roy, Jasper watched from the Americana stage as the event impresario made his way around the festival grounds, shaking hands and pounding backs and working his way through an ungodly number of small-talkers and well-wishers. The next mayor of Tillman Falls—that's what Jasper would push and organize his life around. He'd be Roy Earl Pettus's Karl Rove or Lee Atwater.

Yep: It was time to get back into politics—George Wallace standing on this green, that'd been a long time ago. Jasper, a different person. Roy, a real leader. He wanted to help Rabbit's boy succeed, and for the whole county to prosper. A late-life mission.

As he got closer, Jasper caught Roy's eye, gestured to his wrist. The grounds were far from full, but Manny's parade-ending set had been done for twenty minutes and it was time to fire up the stages.

A playlist Roy had given Jasper had been running over the PA, a cool mix of mellow Grateful Dead and other jamband tunes, acoustic stuff, hill-billy music, and an odd duck, a George Harrison single called 'Crackerbox Palace'—catchy, but out of left field with the other music. Next was Blue Öyster Cult, of all things, 'Fire of Unknown Origin.' And enough of Roy's weird playlist. Time to make real music.

Honored as heck, Jasper Glasscock had been asked to both open and close the festival by leading a singalong at the climax with all the main stage talent, the big goodbye to Rabbit and Runelle, and Button, too. That was hours off. Many songs to go before saying fare-thee-well.

He stepped on the pedal that allowed him to speak into Darren the sound guy's headset rather than blast it out over the PA. A big, burly teddy bear who'd become one of Jasper's biggest fans, the front-of-house tech waved in acknowledgement.

"Darren, how about pot down Roy's playlist. Let's make some current magic out here."

"Was fixin' about to roust you, bubba. Time to play."

"Then let's do it." Jasper switched back to the PA and called "Hey-ho, it's festival time," into the mic, his amplified voice echoing around the green. His backing band tuned and vamped, warming up for the set. Scattered applause; a young girl's voice chimed '*Woo-hoo*!'

"All right, boys—let's lay down some hot licks for these folks. And for Mama Runelle watching down over us. If we don't get this right, she'll never forgive me."

◉▣⊘

TOOK A COUPLE OF NUMBERS, BUT A DECENT CROWD FORMED IN FRONT of the stage. Better, though, was seeing the long lines of festival-goers now streaming through the gates, and vendors doing business and the side-stages could be heard cranking up. Too loud, all of it; bleeding all day. Jasper, his hearing a little buzzy the last few years, would have to deal. But a successful festival already, and barely a note played.

"Turn up my guitar in the monitors, Darren." He cussed himself when he realized he said it to the crowd instead of hitting the direct pedal. Either way, Darren Woczinski heard. "And look, let's get Roy Pettus up here. You out there, Roy? I know you are."

Jasper craned his neck back at the drummer and the others, called a tune. "And while we wait on him, let's play a marching anthem. How about some good old Rolling Stones. The Rolling Stones," he repeated, reverent, before counting off 'Shine a Light,' which made sense when he got to the *come on up now, come on up now* lines.

Roy Earl, red-faced and flustered, clambered up the steps helped by the yellow-shirt guarding the stage right as they wrapped up the tune, a real gospel-style coda with Jasper and his impromptu, revolving sidemen made up of the young kids from down in Columbia who strutted their chops during the open-mics. The keyboardist, a girl with black-dyed hair and fingernails who played in some punk band, laid way back into the end of the song, real Hammond B-3 goodness out of a vintage Leslie speaker. Sweet.

"That gave me chicken-skin," Roy said into a wireless mic one of Darren's stagehands handed him on the steps to the stage. "Sounds great, Jasper. And thank you, Edgewater County, for showing up today."

Big cheer. He forced a smile and nodded.

Roy stumbled through a few further statements thanking various actors. Mentioned all the sponsors. A standard set of emcee remarks. Jasper could see that Roy was worried and distracted, though.

Next he expressed gratitude to Jasper. Made a speech about Rabbit, and Runelle, and the historicity surrounding The Dixiana and traditional country music; about Button, too, whom most of them didn't know, and wondered about, Jasper was sure, but Roy didn't do that good a job of articulating Button's contribution. He stumbled and stammered; said that how she acted was more behind the scenes of it all? That if you pay attention to her, she's still there, and all, but she's not, and never was? And somehow out of that she wasn't not there, but instead endlessly renewed, in a state of endless return?

Because the way of return was... the way?

The audience, shuffling its feet, had fallen silent. Roy's face turned redder. "It's some woo-woo she was trying to teach me. And so, I tried to sneak it in on y'all disguised as innocuous presenter remarks. Joke. But that's dishonest, right? And I still have too much to learn to start teaching anyone. She got me started, though, Button Sykes. Bless her heart. And I mean that in the best sense—the true sense, not Southern snark."

That made everyone laugh, a big hearty swelling sound of relief that Roy's arcane discourse ended with a joke to which most could relate. Jasper hoped he got done soon.

"Boo," a lone male voice called out. Jasper squinted against the mid-day sun.

Jez Rembert, a paper cup of beer in his hand and laminate around his neck, sneered up at Roy. "Music," the redneck gangster demanded. "That's what we paid for today, you blowhard."

"Don't look like you paid for nothing, VIP laminate boy." A huge laugh for the bossman.

"Hypocrite." Jez yelled this with humor, yet smiling. "Dixiana boy."

A shadow crossed Roy's face. He started to speak, instead covered the mic with his hand and caused feedback. Jasper said no no; don't hold the mic like that.

"You dumbass," Rembert catcalled. "Naw, I'm just funnin' ya, beau."

Now Jasper saw the real problem with Roy: "Damn it all—the banner plane's facing the wrong way." The plane, late had finally appeared, but with the letters all backwards and twisted. Unreadable. "Sorry for cursing, y'all."

"Well, I'll be dog. Them boneheads." Jasper cupped his hands. "Turn around and fly clockwise, you dope!"

"All right. Somebody get this mic away from me. Let's hear some tunes here on my Pa-paw's stage." A roar of relief.

Roy, through clenched teeth, whispered about having toked on some reefer earlier with one of the younger bands out by their van, potent stuff, and how his mind may have since left his body. He felt detached from himself.

"And you didn't come get me?"

"Raincheck. Sorry. Bygones."

Roy disappeared into the crowd, his eyes trying to follow the banner plane flying its crazy pattern overhead. Jasper hadn't been kidding—he would hit up one of his bandmates, who all carried those little vape-pens. Hi-tech. All but legal. What a world.

Later, though, Jasper was glad he hadn't smoked dope. Might've made what was to come seem too real. Realer than real. Because real was about to get bad enough.

THE SHARP CRACKING OF GUNSHOTS RIGHT AT THE END OF THE MAIN stage set, unmistakable. How anyone had gotten a weapon past security, the first thought flashing through Jasper's mind.

The second? John Lennon.

The crowd, screaming and convulsing and running; cops everywhere, including in full riot gear, rushing toward the Free Speech Zone from where the gunfire had come.

Jasper scrambled back onto his Americana stage as the Prairie Willows, a female old-time acoustic trio of beautiful virtuoso musicians fighting for aural traction over the plodding din from the rock stage, stopped in the middle of a hot-stringed breakdown.

Furious, he grabbed the mic from the mandolin player. "Enough with this bullshit," Jasper called out, but his words came strangled. Pain in his arm, flaring. His chest, tight as a springboard—chest and neck both. "We need to keep singing, girls," he ordered. "This is about the music today. Somebody sing, damn it—!"

But the voice came further garbled. Jasper found himself sitting down, heavy, onto the stage, his teeth biting into his tongue and tasting hot salt as more shots went off and the confused musicians scattered clutching their precious and delicate instruments. Knocking over his mic and a guitar stand —the Martin—he fell backward to see the banner plane looping around. It had been doing crazy eights in the air for an hour.

Funny thing was, as Jasper's vision grayed and tunneled and the cacophony of the terrified crowd became echo-y and far away, he enjoyed the most bizarre hallucination: the plane swooped down toward the festival, a dive-bombing, but at the last minute a ghostly figure appeared in front of its propeller:

Button Sykes.

A hundred feet tall.

Moving. Beyond graceful. Her arms, sweeping in an arc, as though doing tai-chi. And the plane tilted away, with its banner whipsawing down low through the mass of fleeing festivalgoers like the swipe of an angry drag-on's tail. Right at the Button Sykes Free Speech Stage.

Another hallucination: Roy Earl Pettus, levitating with a sword in his hand in the wake of the banner, grasping a blade blacker than onyx, yet glowing like light managing to escape from an insurmountable gravity well of power. A dark light of doom, and death. Roy, rising into the air; falling; a crash, out of Jasper's field of vision.

A call, an enormous trumpet; a rippling shriek; and the crowd all stag-gered with their hands on their ears, screaming and weeping and injuring themselves.

A mind movie.

Damn-dest thing.

More to come.

Jasper, jumping up and running in a mad rush now, running, running, running along with the panicked throng; and thinking there's no way he can keep this up, not with his heart, his joints, his age.

But light on his feet he crossed the river, and raced across endless fields of flowers and wheat and corn, Whitman's 'quintillions' green,' and Jasper wasn't alone. All the people escaping from the ruined festival were lined up now as spectators, beckoning and cheering his race.

"C'mon!" they all screamed, and it's a science fiction movie now, a glass tunnel crystalline with starlight and time slowing down, way down, way the hell down, and Jasper becomes like the Silver Surfer; but when he looks down, he sees that his cosmic surfboard is a 1976 white Travis Bean TB-1000s, and purple sparks fly from its pickups and lightning bolts crackle from the strings vibrating with notes as though the herald of angels.

Jasper, forever arriving but still not getting there, felt as good and relaxed and joyful and alive as that time when he took LSD in the early 1970s, same grade that caused Howdy Shull to lose his mind, come to think of it; and it was like Howdy was one of them cheering him to get where he was going, this place of cool blue violet placidity with a glow off in the distance, all of it close by, yet faraway.

And Jasper suffered not a care in the world. No anxiety, no pain, no stress.

For the first time.

In his life.

Yeah.

Jasper, thinking, this little nap is the bee's knees. Sleep off that round of bracers that led to this alcohol delirium, keep his throat warm for the singa-long later this evening at sundown. He guessed they would wrap up the festival with 'Will the Circle Be Unbroken,' which is how these things ought to end. Smoke cannabis flower with the young kids. Right on.

But the festival's over, apparently. He must be home in bed asleep, because it feels way too much like he's dreaming. A peaceful nap. Not a bad way to spend an afternoon.

❂ ❖ ❂

HALFWAY DOWN THE TUNNEL JASPER REALIZED HE WAS DEAD, BUT DAMN if he didn't hear Letty boohooing back behind him somewhere and he said, well; and turned to come on back. The cheering crowd went AW, dropping their arms and standing stock-still like doll-eyed mannequins watching while he hurtled back downward into his painful body.

Except 'back' wasn't right away. A whole day passed, they told him. Woke up to find the pearly gates included a bed and a room over in Columbia at the heart hospital, a view of downtown with the State House and tall buildings.

First person Jasper saw upon awakening: Yep. An angel—Dr. Patel.

"Oh, Mr. Glasscock. My goodness, you are again with us. I must inform your sister."

"Wait—I'm still here?"

"Are you kidding? You will be here another few days. You went away from us, but we got you back."

"You did?"

"Oh, yes. I unplugged you. Well—not from the machines, oh no. Ha ha. I mean, your artery. You have a pacemaker installed in your chest. We were heading this way, as you know. Add in the stress, and *voilà*. A cardiac event."

He reached across with hand o'er heart, as though about to say the Pledge of Allegiance, and found a knot of bandage on his chest. "Well-sir. If that's what it takes. What was the stress from?"

"Don't you remember?"

He shook his head. His neck was sore. So too the chest and ribs.

A sad smile. "Mr. Glasscock, did you know my son is also a musician? In a band? They are very successful. Going on the tour, and with the records and all of it."

Left-field Lucy over here. "No'm. I didn't. Why?"

"Because, silly. I had no idea about you, and your music." She mimed strumming a guitar. "The festival with all the bands and the turmoil. You were performing when it all happened."

Jasper—the Rabbit festival. Playing it. Sure. He remembered.

No, he didn't. All that had been part of the dream. Hadn't it?

Oh, no. The festival.

Shit—he had no clear memory. Maybe walking around before it started. Noise, a bunch of people, Roy. But he didn't remember singing on the town green like Rabbit always wanted to see. What a rip-off heaven suddenly seemed.

"Dang it all. So, was it as bad as in my dream?"

Dr. Patel, scribbling a note on the whiteboard, checking her wristwatch and clattering into a computer terminal, didn't bother making eye contact, not busy as she was doing data entry: "Oh, my. We have so much unpleasant news to catch you up on. Much indeed. But in the meantime?"

She stopped typing, rolled her chair over to nudge Jasper and point up.

The TV mounted high on the wall, tuned to CNN, displayed on its screen the refinished neon DIXIANA sign in the foreground, the glass government offices way in the background, and a blurry, fast streak as what appeared to be an aircraft plowed into the third floor of the Edgewater County Municipal Building.

They showed the crash again, slowed down; and again; and again.

HOMEGROWN TERRORISM IN SOUTH CAROLINA read the custom graphic in the corner of the screen; "We'll be back after these messages with more emerging details about this fascinating case of Southern-fried small town terror," said the newsreader with a cheerful countenance and grin. Looking at the unreal TV and its impossible news made Jasper fall sleepy again.

When next he awoke the set was turned off and night had fallen over Columbia, Dr. Patel was gone, and his sister Letty, who looked like she had aged ten years, loomed over him with a weeping smile. He noted how her love and concern seemed etched into every line on her strained, elderly face. Jasper felt thankful. She had been a good mother to him. He needed to start listening to her advice more often.

ROY AND KAREN BLACK

The chaos rages, and the screaming and hollering and sirens all ring in your ears.

You feel hot-cold as the Free Speech bandstand wreckage—splintered plywood, boards, and folding chairs—gets pulled off you, and you lie in pain, half-blind with dust and sweat as they get you onto a backboard and with a neck brace; they keep messing around with your hurt leg.

The first responders must wrench the black microphone stand from your iron grip, which you had grabbed to use like a broadsword against Jez Rembert.

Once you get toted out of the pile of wreckage by the EMTs and shoved into an ambulance, you realize you don't know how much time's passed. Gave you an injection. Woozy.

At this point you feel half-ready to puke, and the stretcher, it's facing inward and you twist your head best you can in the neck brace, cringing at the cacophony of sirens and general hysteria instead of music from your granddaddy's festival stages, and all you can think is that, damn if you didn't end up screwing the pooch on this project. That all your meticulousness and preparation failed you. You are zero steps ahead this time.

Chump.

Loser.

Might as well die.

The EMTs shut the door, closing out the noise. A shadow, and a voice, comes close. Another person in the ambulance with you.

"You just relax and enjoy the ride," she whispers, husky and familiar. An alabaster hand rests on your chest. You feel light—that's right—flowing from her into you. "Hush."

You have gone over. You were alone; now you are dead. She is a ghost; you are a ghost.

Warmth floods in replacing the panic and fear, with no sense of gray-black death filling you anymore; or maybe it *is* the grim reaper but it's a positive development, like Button insisted before you took her to Heather Ponderview's for the last time. You're happy but cheated, though—you've skipped the life flashing before your eyes part; you bypassed the tunnel of magic to arrive fully formed at land's end, in heaven; and here, greeted by your spirit guide and personal angel to welcome you into the state of blissful eternity, finally free of all the nonsense like what has now happened in the streets of Edgewater County.

Her glorious eyes; her face so young and perfect, still. It's had reconstruction and stretching and whatnot, no doubt. But no less her.

Her.

The woman leans over, shushes and reassures. "You relax. They'll take care of you. You did your best."

"No. Not with this result."

"Twaddle. You had to delegate too much on this one."

A Virgo, you admit to wanting to shove everyone out of the way to handle matters yourself. "Don't remind me."

"If only you knew all that came to play in this moment in co-created time together. If only."

"Karen? Is this—really real? Is is—you?"

"They will help you." And her smile fills you with more light. It sits in your belly like a chocolate peanut butter-cup the size of a softball, unbranded, gourmet, small batch artisanal dessert treat, afternoon snack, what have you. "We're about to leave. You will be fine. It's over. You're already better."

"How can you know?"

"By not-knowing. That's how."

And with that you realize you aren't dead, rather stoned as a bat and having a walk along the river trail with Button, because that sounds like too much one of her sermons out of the little Tao book.

You begin to lose consciousness again—this time forever, right?—but it's okay. You have solace. You have completion. Your ascension is upon you, and the universe has sent you a synchronicity and sign all your threads and dramas and loves are now complete, including the one you could truly never have, the woman of your dreams, whom you could hold only so long as her image flickered on Norrie Sortwell's shimmery screen; also that still photo of the actress pretending to cry, a frame from the movie you liked the least but that featured her so well and with such poignance, a magazine cut-out that stayed tacked on your bulletin board all through high school and college and the first coffee shop office until it became thin and finally crumbled apart the day you signed the papers on buying the smoothie stand, and you tried and failed to relocate the image to your new office for good luck, but watching her face crumble into dust in your trembling hands, the goddess you loved but disliked in that waitress role; and for a specific and personal reason, in the same way her existence had felt so real and personal to you at such an impressionable, important and formative age: you despised the country music on the soundtrack of *Five Easy Pieces*. Otherwise? Top-tier Karen Black. Way, way up there.

Please tell me that you love me, she says in that one, *and I'll do anything you ask*.

Oh, baby. If you only got the chance.

But comfort you take in finally hearing country music twanging and jangling from the stage of which your grandfather dreamed and hoped to see his whole adult life spent creating jobs and allowing music to happen and bellies to be filled and folks made happy, all that's expected from a town father, or mother; and that the last image you will ever see, real but fading now into reddish, moist occluding mist of your coming death—your forever moment, the takeaway, the culmination, the redemption—is the face of Hollywood character actor Karen Black, smiling down upon you, holding your hand.

Luckiest man alive. Every dream coming true. How you roll.

As in: If this is the tunnel, you are satisfied to switch on the headlamps and truck on through. Happy motoring. And so on.

After which, as a fading, final coherent thought, you realize it shouldn't be Karen Black at all, rather Creedence, your wife, your beloved, your person, here for you. For real. You require no abstract representation to stand in for the love you experience with your spouse. You are no longer a child needing a symbolic sexual surrogate glowing upon the silver screen. All this business, like a movie, is only in your imagination, anyway.

Or else: it's as real as it needs to be. Like magic, in other words. If you believe in it, it will happen. Try it and see.

All the secrets coming fast, now. If only you could live long enough to use this knowledge, this key to the wonder and joy of life, this understanding of reality-creation to which Button led you. If only.

An attendant cracked open the door letting in light, the smell of smoke, the sound of sirens and police radios and shouting, still, over bullhorns. It's like being awakened on the first day of school by your grandmother —unwelcome.

"What the freaking fudge."

"We're heading out in a sec, pal."

"Where's Ms. Black?"

"Who's that?"

"The woman who was here."

"The other EMT? That's Darlene. Girl'll rock your world."

"No. Karen Black."

"Darlene. Should-a seen her doing CPR earlier on this one old fella. Brought him back, she did."

"Tremendous."

But, no Karen Black? Fine. Besides, at the tail end of your conversation a flash-frame flickered across her features, a trick of the light that made the movie star look more like a grinning, shining angel you once knew named Button Sykes.

He answered a quick call, rang off. "Cool, we got the all-clear, but big traffic jam ahead. At least now we're able to go get that leg fixed up, squared away, stitched and straight." Gentle and comforting. A pro. "Sound like a plan, Mr. Pettus?"

A welling of emotion. The young man's words float across your ears like the finest Mozart melody. Through a fog of painkillers you draw in enough breath to ask: "Already got your route figured out? Lot of street closings today. For the festival."

"Covered. Always gotta have a plan. Maybe a backup; maybe two or three."

"My boy. My son."

"But for now? Plan A," he says. "Let's roll."

Your throat again wells with gratitude—this EMT talks your talk. "No time to waste. I gotta get started straightening out this god-damn mess I dreamed up."

GOOCH WIMMEL

Gooch, stuck in an odd, midday traffic jam on the bypass, rolled down his window and flagged a passing redneck kid on a bicycle.

"What the hell's all this ruckus?"

"That music hootenanny they put on's all fucked up—they had a shooting, a riot and a plane crash into a building."

"A music festival? Sounds like a helluva party."

"You must be drunk, mister. Somebody done got killed." *Kilt.* "Ain't no party no more."

Noticing a pall of greasy black smoke in the distance, Gooch's reporter instincts flared with delicious urgency. "*Wait*—did you say a plane crash?"

The boy said yup, that he heard it had to be one of those ISIS monsters. "That's what a cop said. Anyway, I gotta get home." Looking for all the world like Bill did at twelve, the boy pedaled away on the shoulder past the line of vehicles. "They said for everybody to clear the streets," he called back after him.

Gooch, after this lengthy peregrination back home he decided, on a whim, to take today, had gone to all the trouble and travel only to find himself blocked out of his own stupid hometown. First responders everywhere. News trucks—three of them, their dishes pointed heavenward. Another pulling up, all the way from Charlotte, the biggest of the network affiliates.

He'd have to get in touch with his man at the paper—the name escaped him, tip of the tongue, a longtime friend Gooch could see clear as a bell and who had a bad leg or walked funny or some such malady—to see if he could help report the breaking story.

Terrorism? In Tillman Falls, SC? Hate to think the neocons had been right.

Or wrong, depending on how one looked at it. The GWOT, failing big time if attacks on American soil were gonna be the gall-darn result.

Damn! Above-the-fold story, international, in fact. Gooch had to get in on this action. A duty. A calling.

No, wait: Considering the likely source—his own malfunctioning noggin—an assumption came to him: Bill Wimmel must be dreaming all this activity. All part of his delusion. The smoke over the trees; the people running every which way, and the blonde from WKNO doing her standup by a firetruck with its red-yellow rollers going around. The teenager on the bicycle not real, merely a symbol like out of a movie, a play, an hourlong drama or a novel. A representation of youthful ignorance and inexperience; a younger Gooch. No voice worth hearing regarding interpretations of current reality.

Fiddlesticks.

Now he remembered imagining seeing a plane towing one of those banners come swooping down into the middle of town a mile away. Mercy. Everyone else in the traffic jam acted like they saw it too, jumping out of their cars and hollering and pointing, but hell, they're part of this illusion, too. That's what Gooch concluded. The participants in his hallucinations, they're an aspect of the game. They just don't know it.

He had been in Asheville for weeks, now, staying at an ashram with women and men a third his age, tending to herbs and feeling much better. Enough to get his bearings and memories to decide, I reckon I should go back and finish settling my affairs.

As for his stay there, it had thrilled the members of the commune to welcome a gay writer full of Southern charm and stories and raconteur-ship to beat the band. That's what Bill Wimmel's known for—a sharp wit and recall of facts and figures, the ability to boil it down into succinct cogency, making his reporting easy to digest as a perfectly light, buttered breakfast biscuit served with a smear of fig preserves and coffee along with, yea, the crisp morning paper; the window onto the world through which many perceived their greater reality. The news.

Oh, well. Traffic not moving anywhere; his hallucination, roiling along. He'd sit in his car on the side of the bypass, wait for this spell of his, along with its vehicular congestion, to pass.

Wait: Whatever this story represented besides a figment of his fractured and fraying imagination—say, a scene from his big Tillman Falls novel that he'd been pecking away on for so long, now—it made little sense to sit by the road in anticipation of further events requiring his journalistic presence.

Not to mention the gasoline stashed in the trunk.

Oh, right—Gooch, goaded by Howdy Shull into buying several cans and filling them up; Howdy, whom he had picked up hitchhiking earlier, but who now seemed to have disappeared. Gas, Howdy suggested, to the burn the town to the ground, for once. For keeps.

But Gooch, his memory—! He couldn't put his finger on what the arson would accomplish or avenge. Or where Howdy went, either. There, and gone. *Poof.* No way Bill would torch Tillman Falls alone. He had been able to get the sloshing, full cans into the trunk, but barely.

Forget it, Caughman Howard Shull. Gooch, no firebug. An upstanding citizen.

After watching an ambulance hurtle along the open southbound lanes, Bill shoved his thousand-pound petroleum bomb into gear, executed a three-point turn out of the traffic to roar bouncing across the grassy median and back down the highway out of town. He drove toward Columbia, like the first time he'd left home so many decades ago.

And from there? Who knew where the man behind the wheel would land. Maybe a postcard would come their way, one addressed to the former journalism intern Gooch so loved and lusted for, whose name kept wanting to slip off his lips, but wouldn't quite materialize. Something with a D.

In time, however, he intended to head back to the ashram of youth and herbs and mountains, where it occurred to him he should finish his book before getting on with all his pernicious forgetting.

He had time. He had been better. The forgetting, maybe it was running its course.

Yes: He would get his faculties back; that which had been forgotten would return, and it would stay this time. Sounded like a laudable wish for an old man, one still hale, hearty and capable as the mysterious, nameless one driving an unknown highway and thinking these thoughts. Didn't it? You bet.

CHRISTY

Three airfield guys, all kinda old, come hustling out of the building to chase after the banner plane, but way too late to catch Christy. They might have hesitated when they saw what he did to the pilot, yanking him out of the running plan and, bending the man's head straight back with one hard shove from the heel of his huge hand.

Too bad. Christy knows the man was only doing his cool flying job. But the plane sitting there ready? It had been all too perfect.

One airfield dude, the youngest but still somebody's grandfather, had made a good show of running to grab for the banner, got hold for a second, but fell hard onto his face and yanked across the rough tarmac. Ouch.

As though that man could have stopped Christy from lifting off! Nope, too much speed. Too much intention. Too much magic.

The moment his whole life led toward, now here—the horizon and pine trees, falling below the nose. He angled up, felt a rush he could only assume was akin to what people called ecstasy.

But the drag from the banner. Christy, he wasn't as prepared to account for it as he thought. Wonky steering. *Grrrr*.

◌◌◌

APART FROM HAVING HIS MIND BLOWN BY BEING IN AN ACTUAL PLANE IN the ever-loving air, manageable and not unfamiliar except in the unfamiliar sensation of airborne movement leading to a wave of dizziness and nausea; Christy, needing to get sick. All over himself.

For killing that other pilot. And for the others.

And Christy, afterward? He felt more alone than ever, except at first when he done his Daddy on the couch that night. Alone-alone. With throw-up all over himself.

Well, alone in the plane except for the lady in the passenger seat.

Oh, right—Christy, when he saw her beside him? He knew he was dreaming. No one else had been in the Cessna when he took off. And now this old-fashioned looking hag in a fancy, frilly dress who smells like burnt matches, crying oily, black tears down her cheeks? Oh-kay.

Christy, if he *were* living in a dream? It would be wishing to die in the arms of Button Sykes and not struggling to control this aircraft, maintain airspeed and not stall out while side-eyeing this stupid woman, like she's out of a dumb old history book. Or Christy's mind. Or from wherever she'd come.

And in dreaming this, Christy wrenches the yoke and pilots the Cessna like he always knew he could, looping around for a long time before pushing the nose down toward the festival and its main stage, and that, he's decided, shall be what he flies into rather than The Dixiana.

But the dreaming-dreams bit gets mighty hairy when Button Sykes herself appears before Christy—no, really. Bigger than life, like King Kong or Godzilla. But she beckons toward him not like a monster but with love, and his heart swells as he pushes the yoke straight down; but it's as though she doesn't want him, rejects him with a sweep of her mighty arm and the plane veers off to the left, the left-side path and now begins the nightmare for real—the ice cube, the glass building sitting upon the hill behind the town and THE DREAM THE DREAM THE DREAM, as Christy shrieks all the way to the point of impact, hurtling into Button's smiling face superimposed over the front of the municipal government building.

Button, chanting, *Christopher, let go. Let go, let go of the anger and the fear and join me here.*

But Christy, he cannot comply and finds himself tumbling downward into oblivion, screaming and angry and fearful, the fuselage of the plane crumpling around his body in its horrifying descent through the shattering glass and steel girders of the building; and this continues for eternity. This crashing into nothingness lasts until forever rolling into one moment, and an unpleasant one at that.

Once this moment ends, however—and they all do—his journey and dream continue on a different path, best described in another venue where words no longer act as abstractions, and ultimate understanding is available to anyone with consciousness, including two unloved losers like Christy Beaudock and his Daddy, who sits on a smelly couch and greets Christy arriving home from school in another trailer, in another place, another time.

"We got to talk, son," Christy's Daddy says. "Come sit down over here."

CREEDENCE, RUSS, ESTES AND PHIL

As if she hadn't displayed enough garbage judgment already tonight —impulsive decision-making, the mark of an addict—Creedence now allowed Estes, who'd shown up in the middle of the night ringing the video doorbell and pleading into its tiny camera, to come shuffling and yo-ing into the foyer.

With Roy's recovery from his injuries proceeding from afar—his busted leg would heal, and she had seen more of him on TV than in person, yakking about the terrorism and the kid who'd been stalking his friend and tried robbing The Dixiana, who later went round the bend and stole a plane to crash into a music festival.

The cable news channels made specials around it, gave the event its own theme song and graphics, and The Dixiana was now about as famous as a honkytonk ever became—Creedence had been struggling through a confusion patch. Grappling with urges. Uncertainty. Compulsion.

Attraction.

Russ. Her sponsor.

She knows. It's bad.

Meanwhile, they talked on the phone, her and Roy. Continuing to work from his sickbed on all his passing-on of Dixiana business. Missing his weirdo friend Button. And how the town would heal from the shit-show his festival had wrought, because flowers of commerce would now sprout from all the publicity—Music City, South Carolina would be an actual reality, or so he and Manny now plan.

But at what cost? People died. The Reverend got shot, but survived, thank goodness. Creedence, saying see, y'all? Fuck haunted, shitty Edgewater County. She didn't care how many tourists came through and spent money.

But, oh; such loneliness. And so, chatting with Russ—on the phone, on Facebook, and texting. So much texting.

Until a dinner, here at the house; sitting together, watching the sunset over the marsh. Giving in; a chaste hug at the door on his way out turning into unbridled passion. Spectacular. Twice, three times.

Creedence, spun. Best ever.

Oh, no.

Russ, crouched on the edge of the bed, his legs shaking with fatigue. But not happy. Coming out of the sex-trance, doing the math, taking an inventory, and saying, fuck, fuck, fuck. And not referring to the great sex.

"We made ourselves a red-alert shit sandwich tonight."

"Russ—that was incredible."

"Yeah, well. No doubt." His vibration, turning icy. Clearing his throat: "But I'm here to tell you one thing now."

Her heart, racing. "Yes?"

"This idiotic mistake did not happen. Is that understood?"

And the enormity hit home; not only the decision, but how she felt about Russ; the kind of gentleman he really was, to put it so cold after making love with her three times, when she was pretty sure he had time to think about it and bail, at least between number two and three; like no one ever, patient, vigorous and huge; but a typical guy. Spelling out how it was all gonna go. Jesus.

"Dude—I don't disagree. No prob."

"I gotta split."

"Yeah. I'm sorry."

Yeah, his chilly eyes said. *This crap is your fault.*

Her anger flared. She felt violated. Adrenaline squirted, amplified next by the stupid doorbell bonging in the middle of the night.

Russ almost shit himself, thought it must be Roy. She knew better—the whole reason she'd had the video doorbell installed had been because of other late-night visits like this, knocks and ringing she'd ignored. Estes.

She bade Russ to stay quiet. Checked the cam feed on her phone and saw her ex-lover. And chanted her own version of fuck, fuck, fuck.

SMELLING OF WEED AND WINE, ESTES'S EYES SPUN AROUND AS HE STOOD in the foyer, grinning and wanting to hug her. Reason? He had news, immediate-like, which he had to deliver while she cinched her robe tight and kept freckled forearms folded crossways upon a tense, quivering torso.

"So: it's gonna happen."

She asked what.

"The big-time. Everything'll be different."

"Getting me out of bed was a raw deal no matter what you're excited about. You're wasted."

"*No*," Estes all but shouted. He shook his hair and plugs as though still onstage. Stuck out his tongue. "It's-all-happening, woman."

"All that's happening is I'll be a sleepy-headed wreck tomorrow at work."

"Work. Hah," waving the notion away and dancing a little hip-hop style jig on the tiles in need of a good sweeping—his dance moves kicked up tufts of kitty-cat hair. "Nobody's ever gonna have to *work again*, yo."

"What the hell are you talking about?" Yawning. "And besides. I told you to leave me alone. If Roy were here—"

"Fuck his ass."

"Estes. Stop it."

"No, you stop it. Cause I'm gonna take you over the top, baby."

Chilled to the bone. Nobody was taking her anywhere. "I told you: it's never happening again."

"Wait, what? I'm talking about Meatbody. *We're gonna make it.*"

"Do tell, Mick Jagger."

Estes, breathless, ranted about their contract for a thirty-date package tour, third-billed behind a DJ called Digital Ozmosis and a rapper named Husk. All had been signed to an indie label of rising repute out of Greensboro.

"I know it don't sound like anything hot. It ain't LA, or Athens or whatever. But it's the break we been waiting for."

"I'm so happy for you."

His high energy flagged. Stomped his foot. "Don't you get it?"

Creedence, explaining that, at this tender hour? He'd have to spell it out.

"I'm gonna be rich. Like your husband."

"Just like that." She channeled Roy. "Check."

Puppy-dog eyes, if a touch red: "And so, we can be together."

Creedence, stunned into frozen silence. Finally: "Not money again. No."

"Yeah. That's what I'm talking about." Sudden, he lunged and pushed his body into hers, pulling at her robe and pressing her against the wall of the foyer. "Don't forget how good it was."

Creedence screamed and shoved back, knocking Estes toward the table with its clear decanter full of small seashells. The jar teetered and fell, shattering like a bomb as Estes lost his balance and followed it to the tiles, equally hard.

He rolled over, nursing his elbow. "Oh shit, oh my god—shit is broke, yo."

Russ had appeared, muscular, tattooed and nude but for a small white hand-towel pressed into his still-swollen private parts. "What the holy hell is this?"

Estes, in shock. "Who the—*that's not the bossman.* You fucking cheating-ass cunt."

Russ stabbed a thick finger. "Now listen here, little man, I've already called the heat. This is an assault. This is home invasion."

Estes rolled onto his side, covering his face. "Who the fuck is this? Who the fuck is this naked granddad standing behind my freaking woman, man?"

"*Your* woman?" Russ glared at Creedence. "What the Christ is this garbage situation?"

Her nerves jangled and blood pumping, she went to help up an angry Estes. "Every time I have to deal with this one, something gets broken. So if it's his elbow along with your heart this time, that's on you, buddy. And this is Russ, my AA sponsor. And we both made a stupid mistake tonight."

Her old lover, blinking back tears, scissored his legs and tried to kick at her. "I'll say you did. I'm trying to tell you I love you and want to pay for your shit, and you're in there fucking this bald geezer, plus start hitting me again? You're always hitting and kicking."

"Get out of here," Russ said. "And I'm not far behind. This is all more pathetic than I probably even realize."

"Russ—it's too much to explain."

"Hey, don't bother. You think I'm a stranger to this? I'm a drunk, sister. I've been mixed up in more stupid clusterfucks than I can remember. And you know what this is? An echo of a hundred other fuck-ups. So screw this sick scene." He sighed. "But—I'm sorry."

She held his gaze. "Two to tango."

Estes wept, clutching his elbow and struggling to his knees. Sucking wind and gesturing: "I'll see you next Tuesday, you selfish bitch." *Boo-hoo-hoo* he cried, toiling to wrench open the front door, screaming in fresh pain from the hurt elbow he nursed. "I'm-a sue your ass for this."

"Oh, mercy." Creedence, looking at a half-hour's worth of sweeping ahead. "Thank god Roy wa'n't here. S'all I know." Shot a look at Russ. "Oh —I'm so freaking mixed up."

But he'd already gone back into the bedroom.

She went to the front door, saw Estes stumbling along the curved driveway.

Calling after him. "Did you walk?"

"I got dropped off." He pulled his hoodie up over his head, slouching away. "Was gonna get you to give me a ride home tomorrow morning."

No more rides of any kind. But she couldn't shout it out in public. So instead she said only, "Sorry, but I keep making mistakes. All I can tell you."

"Fuck off." He took out his phone. "I'll Uber."

She jumped as a set of blue rollers popped on from half a block away behind the thick hedges. Tires screeched, and an amplified voice boomed as the cops roared to the end of the driveway. Estes, frozen in the floodlights.

"*Stop and drop—Sedge Island Police.*" Phil Webhannet's voice. He had lied to Roy about leaving the island. Had no plans. Not with his girlfriend living nearby.

Estes, startled, thrust his dark phone at the light. He called out, "Aw, yo, hey, no way, bro—!"

The shots didn't carry a return echo, or sound loud as a cannon like in the movies. Three quick cracks.

"You little son of a bitch," Phil the cop said through the PA, his voice breaking. "Get down on the ground."

And Creedence screamed anew, because Phil, after she had confessed one time about how her illness had led her to an affair with a boy like Estes, had looked so disgusted and heartsick at the thought of her, whom she knew he loved, having had sex not only with her husband but a boy, a brown boy in a band like Meatbody, a youth who had not served his country, and who she knew conservative Phil would see as a taker and not a good citizen and who offered nothing to the community, and it all ran through her head as she charged screaming down the driveway to find that selfsame boy twitching and bleeding on the concrete.

Phil Webhannet, his eyes bugging and hands shaking, still shouted for the wounded rock singer to keep his hands where they could be seen, keep those god-damn hands where I can see them, he shrieked, the policeman's voice high and shredding with an abject, mechanical rage.

Because of her.

And yet, all she could think? Oh—what would Roy say. How angry will he be this time? How disappointed?

Phil's automated cop response only dried up when he saw Russ standing behind Creedence on the driveway clutching the small towel in front of his dick, still otherwise nude.

The policeman, blinking in disbelief. "Mrs. Creedence?"

"Oh, Phil. This is bad."

Estes, still conscious. "Yo, this is some fascist bullshit here. My mom's a freaking doctor, dude. And I'm fucking bleeding all over Mr. Pettus's driveway. He's gonna know it's mine." The wounded musician wept. "He'll know everything. Again."

"Wild scene, man," Russ said as Phil, in shock, staggered back toward his cruiser and called for an ambulance while Estes, bleeding from both legs and a shoulder, crawled over into the front yard, where he collapsed face down onto the dewy, manicured lawn. "What a night."

"It's just how addicts roll," Creedence said. "Isn't that how you'd put it?"

"Unfortunately, yes. Better believe it. So what's the price of liberty," Russ asked, flat, as the sound of sirens and neighbors rushing over from their mansions on the Carolina sea island marsh echoed in the humid, opaque low-country night.

"Eternal vigilance," she whispered, shooing her latest lover inside to put on clothes; to make himself scarce before anyone discovered what she's pulled this time.

ROY

The high, ugly heat of Edgewater County summer breaks at last, but flies, gnats and mosquitos still swarm, and heavy humidity lingers into September along River Ridge Road like a wet woolen blanket. A year since you flew home and got stuck here.

Phew.

It's now that scene you've conjured in your mind so many times where you're on the way out of town conquering-hero style, with the folks all standing on the green and along the sidewalks, cheering, waving you onward; ticker tape, marching bands, floats, speeches, quivering chins and men biting the inside of their cheeks to keep from weeping…

Or else laughing with relief.

You'll take either reaction.

You sit detached from both extremes.

Done.

But it's not like all that; it's only an ordinary late-summer day. Quiet. Still. Perfect and calm out here in the country, ain't it? A dance of energy and life around the edges of the flowers and leaves. Reality.

All the strife, from the spectacular world-famous mess on the town green, or the whole media circus over your wife's lover being shot by the cop you were paying to keep an eye on her, a fact that had not gotten out mainly because no charges had been filed against Phil Webhannet, because indeed, from the dash cam footage it looked like Estes lunged at the dude with an object in his hand. But only a phone.

And Webhannet? A terrible marksman. You aren't sure you were getting the best bang for your security buck all those months.

And yeah, the same street-execution had almost happened to you once, and you felt only sympathy for Estes and his family, who were suing Sedge Island for physical and mental distress. A sad, litigious mess, as was the aftermath of the Rabbit Festival, though who should be sued for what had yet to be made clear by any single legal filing or motion.

Creedence, suffering a brief relapse, but sober again. Thank god her sponsor had been so near that night, had been there for her. Why she now drives all the way onto the mainland for her meetings, and has a new sponsor, you haven't the first clue.

If only your spider sense didn't tingle about her and Russ. And how you suffer reminders of the difficulty ahead once you get back together, which has been put off by circumstances and recoveries and busyness. An unspoken separation, lingering.

For now? A getaway planned. Solo.

These many months of busted-leg recovery, as well facilitating the repairs of downtown damage and dealing with the festival insurance situation, have left you in need of solitude. Add in rigmarole helping Creedence and Sharolyn cross I's and dot T's with their Carolina Beanery expansion plan—Savannah and Charleston to start, and who knows where from there—and you are spent. But at last, the truck is packed with gear, and you're on your way to the mountains to camp on Heather Ponderview's 'back land.' You've walked your own family land enough all year long, baby steps at first after the cast came off. Change of scenery-style.

But to this home you must return. For now, it's only a visit to the secluded hollow in the hills. For now. If only Button awaited alongside Heather.

And yet she rides beside you, anyway; a sense of her. A presence. Objects may be closer than they appear.

◌ ▩ ⊘

Months after all the attention from the media, life has settled into a new normal here in the EC. For a time, Tillman Falls—too bad the name change hadn't kicked in yet; missed branding opportunity—and The Dixiana became a household name, not to mention the fallout from the Estes Patel shooting, in which you had told authorities and press alike how he held a grudge; had been let go from the CBSI last year for poor performance, had stalked and pestered ever since, made bad decisions in life to end up creeping around Marshside in the middle of the night.

And while you hadn't wished him dead or even wounded, you hoped now a lesson learned about choices and decisions. You're not in favor of executions upon suspicion, you pointed out, but early to bed and early to rise, and don't be shuffling around in somebody's neighb at some raw hour on a street where folks have assets and property values to protect. Sorry; not sorry. The kid will be fine.

Hell—he's not even a kid. A man of thirty. And with a new mission—he's started a blog tracking and editorializing about police brutality. Good luck with that.

But still, this shooting, with its clear footage involving a potential suspect lunging with an object and without a death, barely made it out of the regional news cycle, notable but forgotten in the wake of Trump's ascension to the GOP nomination, which continues to dominate All Media Worldwide.

But, back in the spring? Press, press and more press, including inquiries from agents regarding book deals and personal appearances relating to the historic honkytonk, all of which you put onto Jasper Glasscock, who also spent the summer recovering and rehabbing, but now seems spry and ready to thrive as co-owner of The Dixiana.

But, yeah—anytime you get nut-cases crashing planes into government buildings, it's top-shelf, A-list, numero uno on the news cycle. Showing it over and over, Christy's wild flight captured on surveillance and cell phone cameras alike; that mad whipsawing of the banner, snapping into the crowd, striking and lifting you into the air with the mic stand in your grip, again and again until the chaotic and frightening visions burned into eyeballs and consciousnesses, like afterimages seared into retinas by looking at the sun too long. Don't ya know.

As for the publicity, you've refused any further interviews about the domestic terrorism event that occurred on the occasion of your grandfather's memorial music festival. Anyone can imagine how you feel about how it all worked out; but you're thankful, you'll remind anybody listening, that despite the injuries, the gunshot wound to Roosevelt Nixon, Jezmund Rembert's death by cop fusillade—a downright regular occurrence there on the New Falls City green anymore—all else survived. Everyone but Christy, the little SOB.

For whom you nevertheless suffer empathy and heartbreak, a sweet-seeming kid you realize you must have somehow failed. You let him get mixed up with the wrong crowd. Had killed and dumped Newbie Harrell, too, his remains found by a hiker on the Palmetto Trail way up in the foothills, the mutilated and decomposed body at the bottom of a steep ravine near the north end of the county. What a sad life that kid suffered. Both of them. Instead of yelling at Beaudock that night over breaking in, you should have given him a job. Set him straight. Your loss. And his.

Your intuition about people, so honed and acute from all your years in food service and working with the public, failed you with Christy. Perhaps if you had taken him flying, none of this would've happened.

But you didn't, and it did. And here we are.

Kidding yourself. They now think Beaudock killed his own father, too. Dude was a murderer, no better than that sick fuck Coy Wando. They could relax in hell together comparing notes on how best to slaughter and dispose of Edgewater County rednecks.

The horror. Can you imagine such a perfidy as patricide? Or killing at all? Not I, said he.

Oh, you'd kill, all right, but only for a good reason—say, the chance to shake your father's hand, if only one time. Or receive a kiss on your cheek from your mother, proud to see what a fine man you've become. A fantasy. No one left alive to impress. None but thee; a tough customer.

❋ ❋ ❋

THE HUG AND KISS FROM TRUDY OUTSIDE THE DIXIANA YESTERDAY, lingering in the moment and in your mind. She's thankful you've made it possible for her to own this most famous of famous honkytonks, now.

That's right—for the price of one dollar, you have 'sold' this building and the business to Trudy Pirkle and Jasper Glasscock, who continuing to renovate from the inside out, except in her case from the outside in: fencing not unlike that from the day of the festival isolates The Dixiana from the rest of the town, allowing for pressure washers and painters to work their magic on the old facade, making the rest of it match the beauty of the already restored sign and the interior.

One day soon there'll exist a fresh mural. Trudy will work on it with the ELMS. You suggested a painting of the heyday of the post-war town, when the honkytonk was new and the streets sat lined with busy shops and happy American consumers.

Manny's on the committee as well. Awesome-sauce that your pal and Neecie have worked out their issues. Good on them. As for the Theodores, you not only know how difficult it is running a small business, but also putting a marriage back together.

Becky L, she's put the LaFreniere property on Whaley Way, one of the grandest and oldest, up for sale at a cool million, shepherded a new Fine Arts director you have not bothered to meet, and packed her own bags for parts unknown.

So much, in fact, you haven't quite pulled that off. Insert multiple smiley-face emoji and valentine hearts, but, to be honest? Enormous work and distance remains between you and Creedence, and the jury remains out. Hell of a note after a whole year, but there it is. Not a satisfying way to wrap up this episode. Real life is messy. Sorry.

Sitting on the new granite bench beside Trudy, however, and feeling the engraving behind your back—it reads Pa-paw's full name and says **HE SERVED HIS FAMILY AND HIS COUNTRY WITH INTEGRITY**—you worry little about the future, or anything else. Worrying is like wishing for terrible events to befall the worrier.

"I can tell you're stoked."

"It's what I was born to do, sugar."

"If it wasn't before, The Dixiana's place in history is assured, now."

"I'll take good care of her legacy, hon. Don't you worry."

And the kiss and hug, lingering, by the fencing wrapping the block along the green and down Common Street.

Damn if you still didn't want her again, one more time.

No. Not with your other agenda at hand. Besides, mixing business with friendship and love, it's a sticky wicket. That's why Creedence ramping up the Carolina Beanery Sedge Island empire will no doubt cause friction at home. It's doing so well, though, that she can't say no, nor can you. It seems like her baby, she says. Her new child.

You can't blame her; you know how good success feels.

◦◦◦

THE F-150's PACKED WITH YOUR GEAR, A CAMPER SHELL YOU BOUGHT used for a sweet price. The back window features a wicked-looking eagle and flag decal you thought about removing, but said, nah. Your story, it couldn't have happened anywhere but the good-old land of freedom whence your pudgy redneck ass came, right?

You cruise across the green by l'il pigeon poop-covered Pitchfork Ben, keep your eyes straight forward, away from Button's corner. A little salute. You ain't saying goodbye to Button Sykes, though. No way no how. Not after all she taught you. She's with you every step, still teaching. For all you know.

The song on the Sirius radio classic country channel you're digging changes over from Waylon Jennings to Merle Haggard, 'I Had a Beautiful Time,' and every last little tidbit of your year here feels like synchronicity in action.

Because it was.

You hit the freeway, checking out the water tower, a work-in-progress. You admire the outlining job done on the DIXIANA logo, enjoy the notion that your fees for naming rights will help realize Manny's dream of transforming this place, whatever you want to call it, into Music City, SC:

Once finished, the water tower logo, proud, hip and lovingly updated into a perfect painted replica of the iconic sign, will be visible now for miles; a better icon for Edgewater County than Thurmond Pike's yellow Bait & Pawn billboards, though they are unlikely to disappear anytime soon—his business is up, like everyone's in the area.

From all the worldwide news coverage of the music festival disaster—a moment when almost everyone alive for a time stopped what they were doing and focused their attention on your little corner of the universe—the symbol of your childhood and your whole life now stands known as representative of South Carolina and of America, familiar to all humans with eyeballs stuck to a TV set or computer screen for those few days after the incident. The coverage went on and on and on, from every conceivable angle and with discussion, analysis and debate from a formidable array of talking-head security and terrorism experts. During this news cycle, the image of the aircraft slamming into the glass facing of the municipal building played again and again so that anyone watching would never forget it.

Wall-to-wall coverage, like a billion dollars in free advertising for town and its Dixiana, continued unabated until it could be determined that Christopher Beaudock's airplane ride had not been an act of Islamic terrorism, even if terrorism it was, after which the word 'terror' was no longer uttered in connection with the event. Going forward it is said that young Mr. Beaudock had been a 'troubled youth' from a broken home; a family history of prostitution and drugs; and as collateral damage, the authorities finally put the brakes on all the sex trade out at Mama Beaudock's. End of an era. Penicillin prescriptions have likely plummeted in local pharmacies.

Meanwhile, poor Mr. jubouri got hauled in and sweated down for two days in a dark, dank room. His daughter's doing better, however. Gone into remission. It was a wish you had, that his pain would be assuaged.

But yeah—famous.

Dang.

And here all this time you thought your legacy would be fruitshakes.

This, the right decision, for the honkytonk to live on. But as for giving it all to Trudy, you hadn't wanted to run that bar any more than you did a coffee shop, or a fruitshake company; you have cashed out on a spiritual plane.

You are ready, now, to be; and to allow everything else to be as it is. This, the true journey and path of your sojourn here in the physicalized realm that your pal Button set you upon; Button Sykes, the best friend you ever had, as you now understand in a manner beyond feeling.

Beyond conscious thought.

Her example, masterful.

Now, you are ready to camp; now, you are ready to live.

◌🆖⊘

HOOKING ONTO THE FREEWAY NORTH, THE WATER TOWER GROWS EVER smaller in the passenger side mirror, until the optical illusion of its curvature reduces the structure to a speck.

There—and gone.

But stuff's bugging you. Unfinished business. You fire up the device and the bluetooth.

Back at the house you left only moments ago, your eldest surviving forebear, Burnie, answers on the first bounce. "What'd you forget, dumb-shit?"

"Listen, Uncle Burnie—my Pa-paw. Did he tell you about his time overseas?"

"In the war?"

"When else?"

"Shit yes, he did. You don't stay best friends for seventy years and not tell each other everything."

"I can only imagine."

"What you wanna know?"

How to answer this? "All of it."

"That's a lot. So let me see. Wait—you mean Panama, or Germany?"

"Both. I reckon."

Musing. "We couldn't have been more different, the two of us. That coal mining hillbilly and the city-slicker whose Daddy ran a variety of trades there in the bustling county seat. Those differences extended to being in the service, too. Our MOS's, now, what were they?"

"It's not that important."

"Yes, it is. Ah—mine was Flight Engineer, that's 737. And hi, Light Truck Driver. Maybe 345? It's the kind-a thing you don't never forget, your MOS. But you don't need to know everybody else's to makes sense of it all. Too many numbers to remember."

"Too much to know. Nobody can keep up anymore with all the numbers."

"Oh, great God, no. He shipped out before I did, left me here to woo Runelle out from under him, but it didn't take. Hah. That was my first mistake, not following through with your grandmother like I should've when I had the chance. So anyway, he went to Panama, and later landed on Omaha Beach with jerries shooting at him; meanwhile I had plenty to distract me flying over the Pacific. Let me tell you, I first got to Port Moresby in early '43, and those girls, those native girls? Ay-yi-yi, my boy. I didn't think much about Mama Runelle anymore. Not once I got there. One of the first things I did, though, was scratch out a letter to your granddad. To tell him how I was doing, and to wish him well, because the last thing he'd said was, if you're going, guess I got to go too. That's the way teammates think, and of course we'd played football together, so that's how that stuff works."

"Y'all were true partners."

"Damn straight we were. To the end."

"Wait—I thought you said he shipped out first. Why didn't you go together?"

He's quiet. "I thought I done explained about your grandmother, son."

He wanted his buddy gone. Check. "You rascal."

"Lord, Runelle was a looker. And a voice like from on high."

"Can't blame you a bit."

"When old Rabbit got punted down to Panama, thought I had a chance. But I didn't. Some things you don't never get over, Roy. Your grandmother's mine. Hope it's okay to say that to you."

As the miles pile up and the foothills near, your Uncle Burnie continues telling you the story of his time overseas, and all he knows about your grandfather's time fighting the Germans in Europe. So many details; so much emotion, trauma, pain and horror. What all had happened; how awful it was. It's a lot to take in; good you have a couple of hours to kill before you get to the mountains.

◦◙◦

Nearing the state line, however, the connection begins to crackle, a bad spot.

"I should go. Losing the signal."

"Hang on, boy." Muffled: "Do what? Thim wants to speak."

Oh, right—Thim Sykes is often at the house with you, ostensibly to help care for Burnie, but also because, in her professional parlance, she's between projects after having resigned from the Governor's campaign for the Senate. Now? Into soul-searching after losing Button.

All good, all cool. No fooling around. You only have so many loved ones left, including her; enjoy her company while you can. That's what you've learned.

Too much enjoying, in fact. A crackling of the old attraction from adolescence; but something new. She has changed—you're even getting high together. No kidding. A little twitchy and wide-eyed, still with a kind of shock she won't own up to feeling over losing her sister, she shows up in ragged jeans and Phish T-shirts you recognize. You found her in the yard one day sitting in her car listening to Trey Anastasio's guitar wailing and throbbing, one of his modern, sad ballads of loss and love.

But the temptation remains, all the adolescent fantasies and affection for Thim from afar, and now, all these years later, seeing her daily of late. Bringing you food. Sitting on the front porch, barefoot, high and sighing. Sneaky little affectionate smiles.

Asking about Creedence, on Thim's first visit or two. But not since. Hugs, when she departs. Changing to cheek kisses.

And a wet flat-out smooch, earlier, when you left. An eye-lock, imploring and fearful. "Be careful," she said. "Call me later."

Testing yourself, maybe, having this sexy as heck, clearly damaged friend hanging around tousled, vulnerable, lonely and confused.

One night after about six bags of vapor, you asked, "You really ditched it all, eh? Even your—boyfriend, or whatever?"

"No," she blurted, sitting up straight. "I didn't have one. I—no serious relationships. Too busy."

"I was that way, once."

Her spirit, glowing. A full-on smile of appreciation. Or more.

Either way, Thim's presence is a comfort. Platonic is fine for now. You're a married man, still, maybe working it out with your partner.

◦◙◦

MEANWHILE DOWN ON THE ISLAND, CREED, ALONG WITH SHAROLYN, IS gonna FREAKING OWN artisanal coffee in the Southeastern United States by 2025. They're now brimming with ideas to launch their own brand name, which is fine, you don't have any ego needs to satisfy from them carrying the CBSI torch—Honey Red Roasters, they're thinking of calling it, after a sweet medium-roast El Salvadoran bean processed to render notes of strawberry and brown sugar. For now it's the two new locations for the Carolina Beanery. Wise—the brand enjoys a certain cachet that'll will be easy to exploit. Then, they'll grow their own with the proceeds, and all-good on their vision and ambition.

Yeah—you hope and need your wife to succeed, what with the Pettus portfolio still long in recovering the losses from Cowan's perfidies. Especially since you dropped so much of the cash left on various projects and the payment to the Ponderview Foundation for the land to which you hurtle.

Oh, please—compared to most humans alive, you have enough to live like a king until you die. King of the woods, maybe. But the truth is, you lost most of your fortune, blew or gave away the rest. Ain't that America, beau.

Having made it across the state line and up the first steep grade into the lower Appalachian Mountains, the truck engine whines on the incline as Thim gets on the horn.

"So look," sounding brittle, more like the old Thim, "there's some creeper in the yard."

"A dude?"

"Yeah. He's asking for you, or Creedence—but he called her 'Colette' at first."

"Dang. That's old-school. A local."

"He's a scraggily sketch-ball with a beard like he's been in a cave for ten years. Also, his boots are dusty."

"Probably some loser looking for a handout."

"Doubtless. Should I call the police?"

"Wait." Not a hair on your body remains at rest; all stand erect, and a bloom of Knowing like a Button Sykes-style thousand-petal lotus flower opens within the green-glowing heart chakra. "Ask the stranger his name."

Only silence—the connection, dropped. "Thim? You there, gorgeous?"

A garbled response. Breaking up.

"Fudge." You signal to merge into the North Carolina Welcome Center. In no rush. All the time in the world. "Hold on. I'm pulling over."

Signal locking back into place and wavelengths reconnecting, Thim's dear, trilling voice calls from your bluetooth speaker, as though it's inside your head. "Roy? Are you okay? Roy?"

"I'm here. It's chill."

"You shouldn't talk and drive. I'm already worrying about you on the road as it is."

"You are?"

"I am."

"C'mon, I'm a big boy."

"I know. I'm sorry. It's stupid, but—be careful. Please."

Now parked by the dog-walking area of the rest stop, you contemplate the first modest swells of the mountains ahead, as well as the demure and loving tone in Button's sister's voice. You kept thinking how she would make a helluva partner if you were to stay in Edgewater County, or wherever two powerful personalities like yours might end up. Who knew a crush you had at fifteen would become a potential companion so far in the future, and under such ungodly complicated emotional and practical circumstances. Be careful what you wish for, eh?

"Check. No prob. You can count on the Royster. Now—*who is in the yard?*"

Lowering her voice. "Honey—I mean, Roy Earl? Grandad talked to him. The dude says his name is Devin, and that he's your wife's brother. No —seems too old for that to be true. What should I do?"

No question: "Invite that fella inside; ask him to wait."

"Really? How long?"

"Back before you know it—it'll be like I never left."

"Aw. I like the sound of that."

"Me, too. Sit tight." Already in gear and punching the gas, you think ahead to the next exit. There, you'll pull a U-turn and go into warp drive back to Edgewater County, which awaits along with the beloved friends, family and pets who have made a life there alongside yours. No greater honor has come than co-creating this place together, one so friendly to you, and many others alike. A dream come true; every hope an eventual reality— every worry and fear, too, or so it has started to seem. "Tell my old friend this: unlike him, I never strayed too far from home."

THE END.

**CHELSEA COLETTE 'CREEDENCE' RUCKER
DOBBS VANDEGRIFT
The Reverend ROOSEVELT NIXON
DEVIN RUCKER
and
ROY EARL PETTUS**

will all return in

Mansion of High Ghosts

A 

Prequel

Coming in late 2020 from

THE
EDGEWATER
COUNTY SERIES

CHARACTER GUIDE

**POV Characters
(with supporting players)**

ROY EARL PETTUS

Despite tremendous financial success, a lovely wife, and a wide-open future ahead for him, Roy suffers a midlife crisis of confidence and inwardly flails for purchase…but it's for good reason: When we meet him he's discovered his dream girl, Creedence, has been unfaithful. Not simply sexually—the letters he's read indicate more than a fling, rather a full-on love affair. At the same moment he gets news his grandfather has fallen ill, perhaps critically so. He flies home to Edgewater County, where he'll end up staying for some time and through quite a number of story lines, all of which revolve around his grandfather's honkytonk, The Dixiana, that Roy will find is now his to run. It's not a welcome inheritance — he blames The Dixiana for most of his childhood ills.

- **REYNOLDS ELDER 'RABBIT' PETTUS (also POV in** *Dixiana* **and** *Dixiana Darling*) — 89, "father"/grandfather to Roy Earl, his presence hovers over the rest of the story, culminating as it does in a town music in his honor festival; 'Pa-Paw' to Roy
- **RUNELLE KITTERY PETTUS (POV in** *Dixiana Darling*) —

88, "mother"/grandmother to Roy Earl, the Darling of The Dixiana, 'Mee-maw' to Roy. She calls her husband '**Rennie**'.

- **MERVIN PETTUS** — a cousin, 40s, who attacks Roy over a dispute regarding Rabbit's estate (wife **CARLA MAE**, kids **DALE** and **DJ**). Grandson of Rabbit's brother Rutledge Pettus
- **RONALD EDWARD 'RONNIE ED' PETTUS** — Roy Earl's father, long dead before the events of DIXIANA, a haunting presence: his father, like his grandfather in WW2, he served in war, Ronnie-Ed ends up giving his life in said service.
- **CLAUDIA BALLAHACK PETTUS** — Roy Earl's mother, also deceased, a young waitress struggling along after the death of her equally young husband in Vietnam. Claudia, killed in what Roy Earl will find out was a car accident that also almost took his infant life.

ALLYSON BUTTON SYKES

Dreadlocked granddaughter of Burnham Sykes, this iconoclastic second principal character has already retreated to Tillman Falls well before the arrival of Roy E. Pettus, a family friend, obviously, owing to her grandfather's close friendship with Roy Earl. In her mid 30s and considering herself a failed writer, Button cares for her mother Tinky, left bereaved by the cancer-death of Button's father, as well as her grandfather. A new age devotee of the jam-band Phish, when we meet her Button has decided on a new mission in life: to protest the new nuclear reactors being built. Her plan of outreach? A good old fashioned American pamphleteering campaign on the town green. A lifelong outcast—a mix of ruddy Irish and Vietnamese, an odd physical combination—she is the story's heart, soul, and conscience.

- **BURNHAM 'BURNIE' SYKES (POV in *Dixiana Darling*)** — 90, Rabbit Pettus's best friend for 75 years, a very important character to the overall arc of the story, and to Button and Roy personally. In the old days, Burnie's business success made much of everyone's reality possible
- **HENRIETTA 'HENNY' SYKES** — Burnie's wife, dead for a number of years prior to present day narrative
- **THANH THI TRINH 'TINKY' SYKES** — Vietnamese mother to Button and Thim, a nervous type, has panic, is medicated and near irrational, but as Button says, "she always was."
- **THIM SYKES** — Button's older sister, and nothing like her

boho younger sibling. An aide to Governor Sandra Three-Rivers, who has her eye on the U. S. Senate. Thim leaves the care of her mother and grandfather to Button.

- **BURTON 'BUDDY' SYKES (POV in *Dixiana Darling*)** — father to Button, dead already prior to events of novel. The Vietnam vet who'd gone off to war with Ronnie Pettus, the one who'd returned sporting an Asian wife. He'd been a part of a unit that carried around the "backpack nuke" that could be used on short notice should President Nixon have wished to ramp up the firepower. Buddy died of cancer, possibly from his service in Vietnam, but also possibly due to his long career as an engineer at the Sugeree River Station.

CHELSEA COLETTE 'CREEDENCE' RUCKER-PETTUS

Roy's wife Creedence, 40ish (childhood initials CCR, nicknamed by her beloved late father for the 60s rock band Creedence Clearwater Revival) is in crisis as well: in love with another man but not out of love with Roy Earl, alcoholic, confused, stuck. She writes her journal in the form of endless letters to her brother Devin, missing and unheard from for 10 years—an inveterate drunk, likely long dead. Once the affair is discovered by Roy, however, reality comes crashing down, and so does her alcoholism.

- **DEVIN RUCKER** — vanished older brother to Creedence, and to whom she writes epistolary-style letters that provide exposition along with raw inner monologue
- **LIBBY MEADE** — Devin's college love, referred to in flashback only
- **EILEEN RUCKER** — mother, deceased, referred to on occasion, a former esteemed member of the Edgewater Ladies Munificence Society (ELMS)
- **DWIGHT RUCKER** — father, deceased, a town father who appears in flashback

BILL 'GOOCH' WIMMEL

Gooch Wimmel, the publisher and editor of the *Edgewater Advocate*, a once thrice-weekly paper now reduced to a weekly, is an aging, closeted gay who is lonely and unhappy about his waning influence in the town. He'd been a reporter and editor in big city newspapers for years, but found that as he aged, he longed for a more quiet and peaceful life. Working the crime beat in Atlanta left him cynical and burned out at a young age, and now in his late 60s, he suffers from severe memory issues and dementia; he keeps forgetting that he's already retired, and only helping out at the paper. Another man's the publisher now, and Gooch is supposed to be following his dream to write a great novel.

CHRISTOPHER 'CHRISTY' BEAUDOCK

Christy Beaudock has a heart filled with pain and hatred. A fat, unattractive kid with a girlie name, bullied, unhappy, and hopeless. At 15, he's now a physical giant, if emotionally stunted. Special Ed classes. But there's a secret: Christy's much smarter than that. His quiet demeanor has been mistaken for mental deficiency. His father, a meth-head, and his grandmother, the madam of Edgewater County. Quite a troubled background, living in his trailer park and playing his flight simulator game, an obsession. When he decides he's had enough of his Daddy, then he has a new problem: what to do with the body.

- **CHRISTY'S DADDY** — Identified only in this manner, what happens with him sets this storyline in suspenseful motion.
- **MAMIE 'MAMA' BEAUDOCK** — The legacy madam of Edgewater County, she runs a brothel that's been around as long as The Dixiana. Mama Beaudock's is out near the bump in the road called Red Mound. Why she's still allowed to be in business —who doesn't know about Mama B's?—is something of a mystery.

JASPER ALVIN GLASSCOCK

A small-town, small-time attorney, Jasper mainly handles poor clients from "across the tracks," which in the case of Tillman Falls and Edgewater County means across the Sugeree River in recently-annexed Easton. Jasper, when we meet him, is in much worse spiritual and financial dire straits than Roy Earl: at 60, his practice is unfulfilling and barely pays the bills, he's moved back home with his sister Letty. A musician, he only wants to play guitar and sing, but how can an old Southern lawyer make a living doing that? In his younger years, Jasper had been a bail bondsman and PI, as well as a published author: he interviewed homegrown serial killer Coy Wando from death row about all the other heinous crimes the murderer committed. After Jasper finished that book, he swore he'd never want to write another.

- **LETTY GLASSCOCK (also POV in *Dixiana Darling*)** — Older sister to Jasper; they have a very close relationship, one that will be clarified by novel's end to reveal that she's actually Jasper's mother. The truth had been hidden from him because of family shame over her becoming pregnant at 14.
- **OLD MAN GLASSCOCK** — Letty and Jasper's widowed father, a farmer with a sordid family secret Jasper has never known

MANFRED 'MANNY' THEODORE

Manny Theodore, 50, an ex-pat New Orleans resident driven out by Hurricane Katrina, as well as his wife's desire to return to her roots in order to care for an aging set of parents. His wife Neecie thinks that, among its many possible meanings and causes, Katrina was a sign that they needed to get out. After moving to SC, money they received from an insurance payout was used to purchase Lucinda's, the dying lunch counter on the town green in Tillman Falls, which they remodel and re-christen as Manny's On The Green, a restaurant and music club that mainly features Manny himself on saxophone, as well as the occasional touring act and open blues jam night. Manny, when we meet him, is in deep trouble: he's been foolishly unfaithful with Rebecca LaFreniere, a town stakeholder and member of the venerable Edgewater Ladies' Munificence Society—as is Manny's wife Neecie.

- **LILLYANNE THEODORE, 13, daughter** — Lillyanne, a lovely, intelligent young woman who disapproves of her father's behavior
- **BERNICE 'NEECIE' (DUCKETT) THEODORE, 42, wife** — She handles the discovery of her husband's infidelity, a recurrence, with an unusual approach
- **AHMAD DUCKETT, 40, brother-in-law** — brother of Neecie, Ahmad is a troubled ex-addict from New Orleans that Manny's giving a second chance. They butt heads frequently, eventually become unwilling roommates mixed up in the discovery of a large amount of money

TRUDY (PIRKLE) SAMUELSON

Rabbit's longtime bartender and manger of The Dixiana, 51, a one time lover of Roy's, when she was twenty and he was only sixteen! A heartbreaking experience for him, she has watched through Rabbit's eyes as Roy became a millionaire. Married to an aging, sickly biker, Trudy is terribly conflicted and unhappy. The Dixiana is all she has. When Roy fires her in retribution for her rejection thirty years before, their reunion turns toxic.

- **MICKEY 'SAMSON' SAMUELSON** — Trudy's husband of twenty years, and nearly that much older than her. A former motorcycle mechanic and member of the Pagan Knights biker club, Samson has a bad toe and bad knees and a big alcohol problem.

NON-POV CHARACTERS
Note: listed in order of relevance to the plot

- **HEATHER PONDERVIEW** — wealthy heir to the Ponderview Trucking Company fortune, owner of a magnificent estate in the Smoky Mountains of western NC. Button's one time lover and Phish fanatic on tour, Button still pines for her. She will prove crucial to Roy's development and to Button's redemption. Crucial flashback scenes with Heather take place in San Diego, at Foothills State, on Phish tour.
- **CAUGHMAN HOWARD 'HOWDY' SHULL** — The town crazy, 60s, walking the streets with his two liter bottle of ginger ale and babbling about ancient history, secrets, esoteric knowledge, and generally being that afflicted soul that every small town seems to have. It's sad a bad acid trip did him in. He will make new friends in Christy and Newbie, with disastrous consequences for Howdy and his sister.
- **REBECCA LaFRENIERE** — 40s, a legacy matron of Tillman Falls society; old money, the town green is named LaFreniere Square. She's having an affair with Manny Theodore. She's secretary of the ELMS, runs the Palmetto Grande Arts Center, located in the old town movie theater. She left Edgewater County to become a New York theater actress, failed, returned to her home.
- **DOBBS VANDEGRIFT** — paraplegic reporter/writer/ad salesman for the *Edgewater Advocate* and close childhood friend of

Roy Earl's. He was in a car accident with Creedence's brother Devin in college, leaving him in the wheelchair.

- The **REV. ROOSEVELT NIXON, PhD** — a contemporary of Roy Earl, he's running for Town Council now that the formerly unincorporated and traditionally black area called Easton has been annexed into Tillman Falls. Nixon has a a mega-church, a significant force in the community, and his Sunday sermons are broadcast on WABA. He has a large family, including son and presumptive heir to the Nixon pulpit should the Rev. win election to public office. He's been agitating for more political clout from "across the river" ever since the town annexed Easton into the city limits, a move designed to capitalize on a huge project going into the impoverished county, a regional distribution center for a discount retail giant. A key plank of his platform is controversial —to remove the reference to Pitchfork Ben Tillman, Nixon wants to change the name of the town itself. A high school friend of Roy Earl's, Nixon is also an Egyptology scholar with four sons: **Denmark Vesey, Eusebius, Syncellus,** and **Hammurabi.**
- **NEWTON 'NEWBIE' HARRELL** — a former custodian at The Dixiana, Roy's first act as new owner is to fire him. Newbie becomes fast friends with Christy Beaudock, who will get him mixed up in the disposal of the body of Christy's Daddy.
- **ESTES PATEL** — Assistant GM of the Carolina Beanery Sedge Island, 30, Creedence's younger lover and lead singer of rap-metal band Megalith
- **PHIL WEBHANNET** — a Sedge Island cop and Army veteran of Afghanistan whom Roy will pay to keep an eye on Creedence, which makes her think the guy has a crush on her
- **RICO** — an enormous white dog, a Great Pyrenees, for whom Roy will take responsibility
- **JOUQUOYA MOULTON** — a pharmacist who will become Button's friend and lover
- **JEZMUND 'JEZ' REMBERT** — Edgewater County's chief crime kingpin, the Southern mafioso if there ever were one: his hands are filthy, into drugs, prostitution, gambling. His father and Rabbit Pettus were once partners in the underground economy. Rembert will be furious about Roy's decision regarding the mural on the side of The Dixiana, and the threat of violence from this quarter is possible throughout the story.
- **THURMOND PIKE** — He owns Pike's Bait, Pawn, and

Motorbike, whose billboards covered in dollar signs can be seen for miles on the interstate. More importantly, he has a series of 'back rooms' where organized crime figures gamble and politic among themselves, a power center to rival that of the ELMS on the legitimate side. Pike rides a motorcycle in and out of scenes but doesn't have much of a role to play in moving the story forward, but what's disturbing is that he's married now to a trophy wife, one who happens to be another unrequited childhood crush of Roy's. He's like the "tricycle man" character from Altman's *Nashville*.

- **AGATHA OF ABERDEEN** — a pyromaniac of a spirit who stalks the town and may be the cause of a number of historical fires. Grief-stricken over the death of her handsome British captain, Agatha, who had traveled from Scotland during the Revolutionary War to be with her love, she self-immolated in the middle of then-McBreeley's Crossing, forever after haunting Edgewater County
- **TRAVIS 'LUCKY' LATHAM (POV in *Dixiana Darling*)** — friend to Ronnie Ed Pettus and Buddy Sykes, the third friend who went off to Vietnam, who like Buddy returned safe and sound
- **CHESNEE CAMPOBELLO** — wife of Thurmond Pike, at thirteen she broke Roy's heart: there's no way her father, a recovering alcoholic, would allow her to date the grandson of the man who owned The Dixiana.
- **SHAROLYN MONTINE** — Roy's GM at the Carolina Beanery Sedge Island, with whom Creedence will bond as a co-worker and receive both wisdom and understanding
- **CECIL WAUGH** — The owner of Head Trauma, a tattoo, piercing and hair salon that took the place of the old barber and beauty shop on the town green. A former football player like Roosevelt, Cecil and his brother Harlem bullied and tormented Roy Earl. Adult Roy wants to recruit Cecil (and others, like Manny, Becky L, etc) to become part of a new merchant's association to challenge the old order represented by the ELMS, especially after he finds out how much Cecil has changed.
- **GAREN OAKLEY** — Sheriff of Edgewater County, Oakley is a tough as nails Marine and veteran of Desert Storm, an African-American authority figure, but no less corrupt than some old redneck like Whardell Truluck, the man he replaced.

- **TIMMY TRUESDALE** — a police Lieutenant to whom Roy will be 'assigned' for special attention after bribing Oakley
- **YAZID OMAR JUBOURI** — An Iraqi refugee family who have made their way to Tillman Falls, SC, based on Yazid's friendship with an American contractor from the area, and who have managed to become the proprietors of a convenience store called the Gas Chief. Christy Beaudock is obsessed for a time with his daughter Aisha, and a controversy over a vendor license for the Rabbit festival will cause tension. (**Fatima,** wife, **Aisha,** daughter)
- **MADELINE 'MADDY' DURANGO** — Maddy, along with her child-star twin sister **Vangie**, are one-time America's Sweethearts: Twin actress/singer/entertainers/activists. Maddy is friends with Button Sykes, who as a student worked on a movie shoot on the campus of Button's college, a remake of Disney's *The Computer Wore Tennis Shoes,* a reboot that also starred Karen Black, for whom Button worked as a PA
- **COY WANDO** — Edgewater County's most notorious murderer, a killer of children in the late 70s who Jasper Glasscock interviewed on death row and wrote about. Wando claimed to have killed 'hundreds' and provided gruesome detail about these other murders, including his involvement in the Tragedy of '77, the mysterious drownings of six high school seniors in the river the week before graduation
- **COLIN KWOTH** — Roy's handsome, outdoorsy business partner in the fruitshake empire, and a potential rival for Creedence's sexual attention while on vacation together
- **GOV. SANDRA 'SANDY' THREE-RIVERS** — two term governor of the state and Thim Sykes's boss, she'll give some key advice to Button: cut off those dreads!
- **EVERLYNNE SHULL-SCHLOSSER, PhD** — Howdy Shull's older sister. A confrontation between her and Christy Beaudock will turn deadly.
- **ARTHUR BEAUCHAMP** — Roy goes looking for the writer Cort Beauchamp and finds his brother instead, who reveals an unknown corner of Edgewater County: a survivalist compound.
- **PASTOR DUSON MIRE** — a corpulent Baptist preacher, part of a group who once used to street-preach on Friday nights outside The Dixiana.
- **JOSIAH 'J. W.' REMBERT** — Father to Jez, Josiah will have

to do prison time for a shooting he commits during a civil rights protest outside the Congress Street Grille

- **RON NAWALINSKI** — one of Roy's buddies from down on Sedge Island at 'the hanger' where the hobby pilots hang out. He has two key roles to play in the story: he recommends a hike, and gives Roy and Button a ride
- **HODGES 'THE COLONEL' RINGHOLDER** — A Vietnam POW war hero and former jet pilot, he's a mentor to Roy down on Sedge Island at the hanger where the other retired and hobby pilots gather for bull sessions
- **CAL LUCHOK** — another hanger buddy of Roy's
- **RUSS WETHERELL** — AA sponsor to Creedence, a wise figure for whom she struggles with attraction, a big no-no in recovery
- **KIP EPPERTON, DVM** — a Sedge Island veterinarian who dispenses advice to Roy while caring for Creedence's kitties
- **SISSY** — one of Creedence's cats on Sedge Island for which Roy holds great fondness
- **COLE BREEDLOVE** — a deacon in Pastor Mire's church, he'll reinstate the oldschool street preaching outside The Dixiana, but against Button and her free-speech tent on the town green
- **NORRIE SORTWELL** — the former owner of the Palmetto Grande movie theater and influential figure from Roy's childhood, to others as well
- **PORTER BUCKNAM** — a former *Columbia Record* writer and editor, Gooch's successor and new publisher of the *Edgewater Advocate*, with Dobbs Vandegrift taking over as EIC
- **SHIGEHARU 'SHIGGY' HAMASAKI** — another of Roy's business partners, while on a golf retreat together Shiggy will procure salacious entertainment
- **SAMMY MACKLIN** — another of Roy's business partners, and partner in crime with Shiggy
- **HANK HALVORSIN** — another movie theater manager, this one to Roy when he worked at the multiplex while in college
- **RIP SHORLEY** — a dishonest usher at the multiplex where Roy works in college
- **MAGGIE PASSANANT** — a petsitter on Sedge Island whom Roy will retain to deal with the cats
- **FRANKIE 'FRIDGE' WASHINGTON** — longtime head line cook at The Dixiana

- **ETNA DIXMONT** — one of the kitchen workers at The Dixiana
- **Dr. KADAMBARI PATEL** — cardiologist to Jasper Glasscock and mother of Estes Patel
- **RUSTY NEDDICK** — a contractor skeptical of Roy's desire to rebuild The Dixiana exactly as it is now, only with materials to insure that it will last 'a thousand years'
- **KALLEN SWYGERT** — a stereo salesman who hooks up Roy with a turntable, amp, and speakers costing forty grand
- **Dr. DAHLONEGA** — a d0c-in-the-box whose misdiagnosis of Button's throat condition reveals nothing about Button's true medical condition
- **RODNEY COWAN**—Roy's financial adviser, assuring him that money will always grow, and his money in particular. He ain't wrong. Money is never an issue for Roy Pettus, so much so that it's both fraught with meaning and yet meaningless.
- **FELICITY BELINDA 'FEEBEE' ELMENDORF** — a colleague of Roy's from his time as the president of the Downtown Business Alliance in Columbia
- **RUTH DeKALB** — éminence grise of the ELMS, mother to a former governor and a Hollywood voice actor
- **MIRIAM VANDEGRIFT** — Dobbs's mother, in the local nursing home where Bill Wimmel will consider placing himself
- **ALICE FAITH WESTMORELAND** — member of the ELMS, more Edgewater County royalty
- **RUFUS BINDERNAGEL** — the DHS rep to the Rabbit Music Festival, he expresses a number of security concerns, in particular the vendor license application from Yazid Jubouri, whose family back in Iraq has ties to terrorism
- **JEREMY CHIMIENTO** — Button's college attempt at heterosexuality, he'll get arrested with her on a visit to Tillman Falls
- **DR. ABUTO OLABODE** — Maddy Durango's private physician, who helps Button Sykes get through a rough patch
- **HERBIE BERTRAM** — a fellow Boy Scout who introduces Roy to smoking weed
- **CARLOTTA MALDONADO** — Edgewater County Memorial hospital counselor, she wrote a twice-monthly self help column for the paper and helps Gooch

- **JENKINS** — a security agent who assists Button with the recovery of her personal items from Sancho
- **CHAMBLEE** — with Jenkins, he accompanies Button to the New York apartment of Maddy Durango
- **CASSI** — a barista whose tattoos—FORGIVE and FORGET—spur Roy toward action regarding his marital problems
- **KUMARI KANDAM** — a hippy kid living in the Heather Ponderview house in San Diego
- **CRUNCHY CAL** — a hippy kid living in the Heather Ponderview house in San Diego
- **JUDGE HAROLD HARTSOOK** — a back room deal with Button's granddad will pull her and Jeremy's asses out of their hometown pot bust
- **JUDGE SHULL** — Howdy's father and an old-line Edgewater County power broker
- **OTILYA DUCKETT** — an Edgewater County civil rights pioneer
- **EVAN TYGH** — the Roy of Independence, VA, he pulls the F-150 out of a ditch on the side of a mountain where Roy has gone for a retreat
- **LATRICIA THEODORE** — a naughty cousin of Manny's who introduces him to sexuality
- **ENOCH ROYAL** — a teenaged street preacher who taunts Button at her free speech tent on the town green
- **CORT BEAUCHAMP** — Edgewater County's novelist of note, his book *The Diary of Anna Dixon* plays a role in Creedence and Roy's relationship
- **ANNA DIXON** — protagonist of Cort Beauchamp's novel-within-the-novel *The Diary of Anna Dixon*
- **DURHAM DOVER** — second protagonist of Cort Beauchamp's *The Diary of Anna Dixon*
- **TUCKER** — a big box employee who assists Roy with a TV purchase
- **RODRIGO** — a big box employee who assists Roy with a TV purchase
- **MR. KARLANEY** — a funeral director who assists Roy
- **PATROLMAN HERTFORD** — a highway patrolman who almost shoots Roy during Rico's crisis over failing to stop for his blue lights

- **CALLIOPE GILDERBLOOM** — an august elder of the ELMS who presides over a tribunal of one of its members
- **SKEEBALL** — a Dixiana kitchen employee
- **DICKIE GIUFRIDDA** — a member of Roy's childhood baseball team
- **HARLEM WAUGH** — Cecil's twin brother, tormentor of young Roy
- **SHERM WRIGHTSON** — Roy's little league coach
- **TIMMY LATHAM** — son of Lucky Latham, and a positive baseball team member to young Roy
- **MARLON KETCHAM** — a little league player who taunts Roy
- **STONEY MARCHANT** — another little league doofus, the only player more inept than Roy
- **KAITLYN** — a barista at the Carolina Beanery Sedge Island
- **BRENDA LaROSE** — college writing mentor to Button
- **MARGARET TUGGLE** — Roy's middle school yearbook editor and crush
- **GREG RINKER** — handsome jock and rival for Margaret's attention
- **GLORIA GRAYMONT** — Roy's high school newspaper advisor
- **KITTY BERWICK** — Roy's 1st Grade teacher
- **MRS. GARFINKLE** — Roy's yearbook advisor
- **COACH PEMBROKE** — Roy's physical science teacher
- **MR. HALSEY** — Roy's childhood barber
- **MR. BATES** — Christy's high school science teacher
- **MRS. DUNWOODY** — Letty Glasscock's fifth grade teacher and fellow survivor of the Sunbury School fire
- **LOTTIE** — a cashier at Roy's college multiplex job, a brief romantic relationship
- **BENJ** — an usher at Roy's college multiplex job
- **LENZA SPINNOZI** — stylist at Cecil Waugh's salon 'Head Trauma'
- **SCOTT 'SANCHO' McKENDRICK** — the head of Button's Phish tour 'phamily'
- **SHARAQUE** — Creedence interacts with this doorman at the Sandflea rock club
- **SEDGE ISLAND CABBIE** — returns money Creedence left in the taxi
- **RAY DeKALB** — Tillman Falls native and now Hollywood

voice actor, a celeb who attends the festival at the (presumed) behest of his mother Ruth DeKalb.

- **Mr. DeKALB** — a presumptive forebear of the DeKalbs, Ruth and Ray, the builder of the ill-fated Sunbury School
- **AVALON** — a hippy chick Spotted Banana manager
- **SHELBY FORDHAM** — Roy childhood crush
- **NATASHA PROTHRO** — Roy childhood crush
- **BEV LeSAGE** — Roy childhood crush and dance partner
- **LaVISTA TUCKER** — friend of Sharolyn who bakes cakes and cookies for the CBSI
- **DAVIS MACON** — a 1960s peer of Josiah Rembert, known as a dogfighter
- **IDAHLIA** — kitchen worker at Manny's on the Green
- **OLD NEECIE** — kitchen worker at Manny's on the Green
- **SEAN PAUL** — a former coffee shop manager of Roy's to whom he sold the original Carolina Beanery
- **MAULDIN SAUGUS** — US Representative from the district that includes Edgewater County
- **MOUSAM 'SAMMY' BEANHOPPER** — longtime member of Tillman Falls Town Council, the first African-American member and a legacy figure
- **DUWAYNE DRIGGERS** — an oldschool Dixiana bartender, drug dealer, and friend of Coy Wando
- **Lt. WETHERELL** — an officer under whom Rabbit served in WW2, possibly Russ Wetherell's father or grandfather
- **Pvt. MAHONEY** — a corpsman serving with Lucky Latham
- **MARTY HARRELL** — Newbie Harrell's grandfather, a gas jockey at Pike's
- **CORDELIA KARLANEY** — curator of the Edgewater County archives
- **UNCLE WALLY KITTERY** — Runelle's uncle
- **CHESTER** — a Dixiana bartender from Roy's youth
- **DR. WISE** — town GP
- **Lance Cpl. LAWRENCE LAUTENSCHLAGER** — the Sugeree River Memorial Bridge is named for this fallen highway patrolman

HISTORICAL OR LIVING FIGURES
WHO APPEAR IN THE TEXT

- **KAREN BLACK** — Roy Earl has had a crush on her since adolescence. Along with a few other celebrities, she will be in Tillman Falls for the Rabbit Festival at the end of the third book.
- **GILLIAN WELCH** — The musician plays the Rabbit Music Festival in Book Three
- **DAVID RAWLINGS** — The musician plays the Rabbit Music Festival in Book Three
- **PAGE McCONNELL** — Keyboardist for the band Phish with whom Button and Heather interact, albeit indirectly
- **GEORGE W. BUSH** — After making a photo-op stop at a nearby US Army base, the President drops in on Trudy and Rabbit for The Dixiana's famous Broasted Chicken Basket
- **JOHNNY CASH** — in 1969, on his way to a State Fair appearance, the country music icon stopped in and did a few tunes at The Dixiana, along with his wife and a friend
- **JUNE CARTER CASH** — accompanying Johnny Cash
- **BOB DYLAN** — accompanying Johnny Cash
- **GEORGE WALLACE** — the presidential candidate makes a speech outside The Dixiana
- **JERRY GARICA** — a pre-stardom Garcia and a friend attend a bluegrass jam at The Dixiana in 1962, where they get in trouble with Mr. Rabbit over recording
- **SANDY ROTHMAN** — Garcia's friend and fellow bluegrass traveler

ABOUT THE AUTHOR

James D. McCallister is the author of novels, a short story collection and numerous other shorter pieces of fiction and creative nonfiction. A lifelong South Carolinian, he lives in West Columbia with his wife and beloved brood of cats, muses all.

CONTACT JAMES D McCALLISTER:
www.jamesdmccallister.com
editor@mindharvestpress.com

RETURN TO

James D. McCallister's "EDGEWATER COUNTY, SC"

in

King's Highway

Fellow Traveler

Let the Glory Pass Away

The Year They Canceled Christmas

Dogs of Parsons Hollow

Dixiana

Down in Dixiana

and

RECONSTRUCTION OF THE FABLES (2020)

MANSION OF HIGH GHOSTS:

A DIXIANA Prequel (2021)

THE NIGHT I PRAYED TO ELVIS: Stories (2021)

MIRIAM MULLINS: A DIXIANA Sequel (2022)

MHP

Mind Harvest Press

COLUMBIA, SC

www.jamesdmccallister.com